ROCK HARD

—— The Power Station Boxed Set ——

T. GEPHART

For the Power Station readers
who needed more after Lexi.

Without your enthusiasm this series
might never have been written.

HIGH STRUNG

I FELT BEADS OF SWEAT STARTING TO FORM ON THE BACK OF MY NECK as my fingers drummed restlessly on the arms of the chair. I needed this job in the worst way and I didn't think I could cope with another rejection. Despite being ridiculously overqualified for the position, I would do anything to get out of the hospitality industry. Sure, it was something I was good at, having parents that owned a small Irish pub meant I grew up in a bar, and being able to pull a perfect draft was a skill that provided no trouble landing a job back in the industry. However, I was getting really sick of being called "sweetheart" and if one more jerk grabbed my ass while I served him his beer, I was seriously going to lose it.

This had not been my dream when I moved to New York five years ago—making minimum wage and living in a shitty, cubby-hole apartment I was sure violated every safety code known to man. Still, it beat living on the streets, which is where I would find myself if I didn't start earning more than I was now. Of course, I hadn't always been so desperate. I couldn't believe my luck when I had landed an entry-level associate's role at a small brokerage firm straight out of college. I had stepped off the greyhound bus like a cliché in an '80's hair band video, leaving my nervous, conservative parents and six siblings back in Boston. I should have known it was too good to be true. Three years later, just as I was about to make the progression to junior broker, the company—like so many others—went bankrupt and closed its door. I found myself out of work and out of luck.

There weren't many opportunities for a commerce major during a global financial crisis. Any jobs there had been were snapped up by seasoned veterans, which is why I'd had no choice but to take a job at Garro's, a sports bar on the Lower East Side. My previous bar knowledge had made it a safe and familiar choice even if the money wasn't great. At least it was only a short commute from my Brooklyn apartment and it meant I had at least one hot meal a day.

I looked nervously at my watch. Two o'clock. Shit. I still had another thirty minutes to wait before my appointment, and my bravado had already started to wane. Desperation was a horrible thing, because I knew either way this whole experience was going to suck. If I got the job, I was going to hate it, as it would no doubt be mind-numbingly dull, and if I didn't, I should pack up my shit and reserve my park bench in Central Park. I was out of options and out of time. I took a deep breath as I tried to harness the nervous energy buzzing through my body. Rock stars. This is what it had come to.

The job I was so desperately vying for was personal assistant to Lexi Reed, the head of Reed Public Relations. She held the account for a massive local rock band, Power Station. I was not a fan. Of the band I mean. The five-piece New York natives were gritty and raw with their sound featuring torturous guitar riffs with an unrelenting rhythm section. It was in-your-face loud. Obnoxious. Sure they were blessed with good looks. Okay, each one of them was insanely handsome but that still didn't mean I would throw myself shamelessly at any of them and lose my self-respect. I never understood the allure of a rock band or why women with so much going for them would lower themselves to being groupies.

Ms. Reed, on the other hand was, by all accounts, a fierce businesswoman. An import from the land Down Under, she had a reputation for being a hard-ass with an amazing sense of style, and a respected determination that led to her playing with the big dogs in the industry. Despite me loathing the assistant position I was hoping to land, I did have an amazing amount of respect for her. She not only held Power Station's PR account, which was huge, but she was also successfully building her own company by bringing in lots of new business. Smart move. The growth projections in the industry were huge if she could land the right clients - a statistic I was hoping to wow her with when I finally got into the interview. It wasn't my style to go in unprepared and my late night research had been fruitful.

"Ms. Murphy?" A slender and attractive blonde with a strong English accent approached me.

"Yes. Ashlyn." I stood up and offered her my hand hoping it wasn't too clammy.

"Ashlyn, I'm Sydney. I'm Ms. Reed's current assistant." Her bright blue eyes sparkled as she accepted my hand graciously. "Lexi is just finishing up with another interview and then you are up next. Is there anything I can get you while you wait?"

"No, I'm fine, thank you." I was relieved the wait was almost over.

Sydney nodded and disappeared back through the doorway from which she had emerged, her cute bob haircut bouncing with each step.

I sank back down into my seat, rubbing my palms nervously against the fabric of my skirt. I hated job interviews. They were the intellectual version of a beauty pageant. Here are my qualifications. Smile. Judge me. Smile. I hope I'm good enough. It was enough to make me want to vomit. My stomach churned in solidarity with my train of thought.

The previous candidate stepped out from Ms. Reed's office and into the reception area, signaling the end of her appointed interview. She used her sly glance and cocky grin, I assumed, to unnerve me further. So that's how we're going to play? I'm one of seven children, honey. I am the master of the mental psyche-out.

I stood, in preparation for my turn, when I felt a shadow cast over me blocking out the midday sun. It was just my luck to finally get an interview with a halfway decent job and some crazy-ass Armageddon took over New York. I slowly turned—might as well get a good view of whatever fate was about to befall me—and I almost smacked directly into Alex Stone.

crickets

Alex Stone was the lead guitarist of the band, Power Station, and while I had not been a fan of the band, I was definitely an appreciator of this fine specimen in front of me. Standing six four, with an amazingly toned body, ice-blue eyes, and magnificent blond hair, he had been engineered to be a sex symbol. Rivaling Michelangelo's David, he was chiseled to perfection. The fact I didn't care for his music did not detract from my fascination. In fact he could probably give up his music career, stand in the Met Museum and allow us mortals to glare longingly at him all day. What? Living art is a legitimate gig.

"Hello," Alex purred, dazzling me with his amazing devilish grin. "Are you waiting to see Lexi?"

Of course I knew Lexi Reed was not only the band's publicist but also married to the guitarist, aka the guy in front of me, but man, Lexi was like Barbie. The bitch had everything.

I blinked, allowing my eyes to float down his sexy muscular chest and noticed he had a Baby Bjorn carrier with a sleeping infant inside strapped across it, hindering my view. I think my ovaries just exploded. It was too much. Because when Alex wasn't sending the panty-wearing population into overdrive by being a rock god, he was a new dad to his baby daughter, Grace. I mean, seriously, how could a woman not swoon over that deadly combination?

"Um," I mumbled like a moron, all my years of education flashing before my eyes, unable to make my mouth function. He was talking to me?

"I'm just going to need a moment of her time, mind if I step in ahead of you?" His smooth voice curled around every word, making love to it.

I nodded wordlessly, feeling compelled to continue the moronic theme I had running. It was better than throwing myself at his feet and worshiping him, a very real danger the longer he stood there. He was more than just good-looking, he was obscenely attractive, and I had this unbelievable urge to lick him, slowly, like a cat.

Taking my wide-eyed, enthusiastic nod as a yes and seeing he wasn't going to get anything more intelligible out of me, Alex strode into Lexi Reed's office. I watched as his ridiculously hot body disappeared through the doorway, my eyes straining to catch the last glimpse of his incredibly toned ass before it slipped from view.

"He's married and a douchebag," an uninvited voice said, pulling me from my happy place.

"Huh?" I twisted around, ready to disembowel the owner of said voice for ruining my Alex Stone fantasy.

"He," the owner of the voice pointed to the door Alex had just walked through, "Is. A. Douchebag." He enunciated slowly before continuing, "Alex. Is. Also. Mar-ried." He paused before each syllable for effect.

Standing in front of me, marring my memory of Alex, was the owner of the voice – an annoying man. Shorter than Alex, at what I assumed to be roughly six foot, he eyed me with more interest than I was comfortable with. He had a mess of dark hair, smoldering dark brown eyes, and was covered in tattoos, the evidence poking out from the sleeves of his T-shirt. Next to the word badass in the dictionary, I'm sure there was a picture of this guy. Dressed in torn, dark blue jeans, and a Misfits T-shirt, he was the epitome of a rock star, without the finesse Alex possessed. Despite his unkempt look he was strangely sexy, although his smug smile made me want to add ripping out his tongue to the disembowel-ment I already had planned.

"I heard what you said," I snapped. "There is nothing wrong with my hearing. I just don't know why you cared to volunteer that information." Despite his good looks, I think if either of those two men was a douchebag it would be the one who was still talking to me.

"Oh cool, you talk." He laughed. "I just wasn't sure if you were just a star-struck fan or you had a disability. I was trying to be polite." He moved closer, stretching out his hand. "I'm Dan. Dan

Evans."

"I'm not a star-struck anything. And I don't have a disability. I don't know what you are talking about." I purposely rejected his handshake and instead adjusted my jacket, annoyed he had assumed I was just another one of *those* girls. Who was this guy anyway? Judging by his appearance, I guessed him to be another member of the band, possibly the drummer? He probably needed to compensate about not getting enough attention being holed up behind a drum kit.

"Look, it's fine, babe. We're used to it. Girls get crazy over us all the time. You don't need to be embarrassed." He pulled back his hand and shrugged, seemingly unfazed by my lack of civility.

"I'm not embarrassed. And I'm not your babe. Whatever you think you saw, you were mistaken. I don't get crazy." I was slightly embarrassed, but more irritated I'd been caught staring... *and* called on it.

"Sure. Okay. You don't want to admit it, that's fine but I know what I saw, and you were throwing so much heat in Stone's direction I'm surprised the paint didn't peel off the wall." He pulled out a stick of gum and popped it into his mouth, thoroughly enjoying the fact I was irate. Clearly not a gentleman.

"Oh my god. I was not throwing heat. Are you insane?" I hissed, my embarrassment manifested into full-blown anger as I tried my best to save face. No matter how gorgeous this man in front of me was, I was not going to let him get the better of me.

"You can keep denying it all you like, babe. Makes no differ-ence to me. I just thought I'd be charitable and point out it's a waste of your time." He chewed on his gum, smirking. "You have a better chance of the Cleveland Indians winning a World Series than Stone sleeping around. Now me on the other hand, I don't have those kinds of restrictions."

My face flushed with anger, as I officially wanted to kill him. Yet stupidly, I couldn't deny how attractive he was as he smugly stood in front of me, his broad chest filling the material of the tee that did little to hide the toned flesh that lay beneath. What the hell was wrong with me? He was rude, arrogant and probably teeming with every STD known to man, and he'd called me babe...

twice. I was not going there.

"Did you take some kind of class to learn how to be so offensive or is this a natural ability?" I leaned forward, refusing to allow him the pleasure of knowing he was getting under my skin.

"How did I offend you? I have been nothing but polite. I haven't even looked at your tits." Dan stared at me bewildered, actually confused.

"Wow. My *tits* and the rest of me thank you for your lack of interest." I gave him my best death stare, disappointed I didn't have some mutant ability that would render him incapacitated. I blamed my pre-teen fixation with comic books for giving me such unrealistic expectations.

"Don't mention it. They are a little on the small side, it makes things easier." He shrugged, talking about my breast size like it was no big deal. The edges of his mouth curved as his eyes dipped down to gaze at my aforementioned *tits,* which were thankfully contained by my conservative business shirt.

"Really? You're not even going to hide the fact you are now staring at my breasts?"

"Well now we are talking about them, I kinda can't help myself." He grinned, not even having the decency to be remorseful. "You know, now that I've looked at them, they don't seem so bad. You should maybe pop a button or two though, work with what you got."

"Dan!" Ms. Reed fired from the now opened doorway startling me from my seething rage. Alex Stone, aka sex god, was standing beside her, looking somewhat amused.

"Don't harass my candidates." Lexi turned to Alex, gently touching his arm. "Can you please remove him from my office? I'll call you later." She tenderly kissed the top of baby Grace's head and whispered a soft goodbye.

Alex nodded as he walked over to us. "My apologies for Dan, he has no impulse control." Alex gave me a blinding smile, grabbing Dan firmly around the arm. "Let's go."

"Don't apologize for me, numbnuts. We're just talking." Dan protested against Alex's grasp.

Lexi rolled her eyes at the commotion before addressing me.

"Ashlyn, if you are ready I can see you now."

"Your name is Ashlyn? Unusual. It's pretty." Dan's eyes lit up with excitement at finally learning my name. Not that he'd asked, clearly he was too preoccupied with being an ass to worry about regular pleasantries.

"My life is a little more complete knowing you approve. Thanks for that. Have a wonderful day." I gave a forced smile as I pushed past him and strode purposely toward the open door of Lexi's office.

I needed to get my head in the game and flirty Dan was not aiding my cause. Instead I focused forward as I followed Lexi into her large and neatly maintained office, mentally evacuating thoughts of the tattooed, scruffy rock star I left in the foyer.

"I'm sorry about him. Dan really is a unique human being." Lexi gestured to the large plush chair opposite her desk. "Please, take a seat."

Lexi Reed was stunning; a petite brunette with feminine curves, she owned the fitted, bright green shift dress she was wearing. Finishing her look with an impressive black pair of heels and a fancy twisted up-do, her appearance had me feeling slightly underdressed in my Target-purchased jacket and skirt combo.

"He is harmless. Obnoxious, but harmless." I settled into the chair not willing to admit Dan Evans had unnerved me. After all, if I was going to be Lexi's assistant I was going to need to be able to handle the likes of Dan.

"Well, that is reassuring." Lexi smiled as she settled into her leather office chair. "So, Ashlyn. Tell me why someone has a commerce degree from University of Massachusetts, and who previously worked on Wall Street, wants to be an administrative assistant?"

I took a deep breath as I tried to determine the best way to rationalize my position. Damn. This was going to be a hard sell.

"Dan, do you go out of your way to piss off my wife?" Stone chuckled as we walked back to the car.

"Dude, come on. You know she loves it, her day isn't complete until she has gotten her daily dose of Dan."

Lexi and I were cool; she knew the score as far as I was concerned. Granted our friendship had started with me trying to crawl into her panties; she's a solid ten. Who wouldn't try for that? But I totally respected she was now off the market and happily married to Stone. I never understood what the attraction was. Sure the man wasn't ugly but he got *way* more than his share of pussy. At some point when Lexi crossed our path, the two of them had started fucking and somehow managed to keep it from the rest of the band. I was absolutely appalled. If you're banging a girl like that, then it's your civic duty to share details with your brothers. Fuck, photos would have been better. Instead they kept that shit on the down low leaving us oblivious and not contributing any new material for my spank bank. Of course they eventually got it together enough to be a couple and did the whole walking down the aisle thing, and as much as I think marriage is for suckers, those two pretty much belong together. Not that I'm getting soft, 'cause Dan Evans does not get soft, but after the amount of shit those two have gone through, to see them happy with a kid was kind of fucking awesome. Oh and the kid, Grace, pretty much owned me. That little girl had me wrapped around her finger so tightly I'd move the world to please her. Between her and Noah, James and Han's little dude, I was happily playing Uncle to some of the coolest kids on the block. Not to mention the gaggle of nieces and nephews my sisters had given me. Being Uncle Dan was a pretty sweet gig.

"So what was up with the stare down with the redhead? Wasn't the whole reason you begged to come with us was so you could put the moves on Sydney, despite her telling you there was no chance?" Alex hit the keyless entry on his brand new, fully loaded Escalade. The bastard had caved and bought a family car, leaving his bitchin' Maserati parked in his garage whenever he had Grace in tow. I guess it could have been worse; at least the Escalade was still pimp. If he'd bought a Dodge Caravan then I'd have had to take him outside, kick his ass, and check his man card. I don't give a fuck he's got a kid, Power Station does not do minivans.

"Oh, Syd wants me. She's just being English." I watched as my former fellow skirt-hound loaded his daughter into the car seat. Man, times had changed. Back in the day the only time we were utilizing the back seat was to get lucky, now it was being used for its intended purpose. It was just all kinds of wrong.

"What do you mean she's being English? How is that even a thing?" Alex handed Grace her fluffy pink unicorn as he covered her with a baby blanket. I hoped my balls weren't going to suddenly shrivel up surrounded by all this pink.

"Really, Stone? Aren't you supposed to be smart? We totally told her country to go fuck themselves, don't tell me the fact we're American isn't the reason she is blowing me off." I jumped into the passenger seat, no longer caring about why Sydney wasn't interested, as I tried to shake off the memory of the redhead who made my junk get tingly. Despite trying to keep her body under wraps in that lame-ass corporate get-up, there was no denying she was hot. She was rocking some killer curves. Granted she spoke way too much—I liked my girls with a different kind of mouth action—but other than that, I would totally be down with her playing naughty secretary.

"Dan, I seriously doubt the Declaration of Independence has anything to do with her disinterest in you." He slid into the driver's seat and hit the ignition.

"Don't kid yourself, Stone. Those bastards are still pissed. Anyway, her loss."

Sydney had been fun. Lexi had hooked up the date with her friend-assistant so I wouldn't have to brave a family wedding, stag. I knew she wasn't a hundred per cent cool with it, thinking I would be a total ass-wipe and try and hump her friend's leg or something, but I promised I'd keep my dick in my pants. Family celebrations when you are a thirty-three-year-old single dude were down right dangerous. Sure they accused me of acting like a teenager, but getting older didn't mean I had to change. It's who I was. They didn't care I was livin' large and didn't want to be saddled down with one girl. It was like talking to a fucking wall. So going solo into the lion's den with as many meddling aunts as I have would have been catastrophic. Fuck! They would have sent out the bat signal in the hopes of finding me a wife. Luckily with Syd on my arm, radiating professionalism and that cute English accent, they'd been appeased enough to stay off my ass. We both actually had a really good time, which was unexpected bonus. So when I took her home and she paused before stepping out of the car, I knew I had an in. She gave me this speech about it being one time and shit, and neither of us wanted anything more so what the hell. It had been good, real good, and I was all up for perhaps working her into a constant rotation but she hadn't been down with it. Giving me some bogus line about me being a bad investment. I didn't get it. Was I supposed to be showing her my investment portfolio? My 401K? I would have thought the only thing she would have been interested in was my ability to make her toes curl—which I did, no less than three times—not whether or not I had a retirement plan.

"Please tell me the redhead wasn't your attempt to make Sydney jealous? Lexi will have your balls if you're messing with her applicant pool." Stone continued to run his mouth as we pulled into Manhattan traffic. We weren't going anywhere, anytime soon. NYC in the afternoon was solid gridlock.

"Oh no, she was just some random groupie I was having fun with. Way too uptight but I thought I'd give her something to tell her friends about. You know me, always thinking about the fans." I omitted telling him she'd obviously had a thing for him. Despite the bastard being married and a walking advert for Babies-R-Us with all his diaper bags and shit, broads were still throwing themselves at him. I really needed to work on either him or James letting me borrow a kid for a few hours. Girls just seemed to eat that up

"She didn't look like a groupie. What she looked was a lot pissed off." He raised his eyebrow and gave me his usual cocky grin.

"Listen, brother, not to be an ass, but you're out of the game now so you don't know how it works. Trust me, I got this. Fifty bucks says as soon as she's done with her interview she is going to find the nearest bathroom and rub it out." I stretched out my legs hoping to ease some of the tightness in my crotch. Imagining Ashlyn scratching that itch had me thinking I was going to have to do the same. That tight little body, those fiery green eyes, those cute little freckles on the bridge of her nose. That's putting aside the fact I have a thing for redheads. It looked natural too; wonder if she had any hair down there? Yeah, a stroke was definitely on the cards.

Stone popped me in the arm, crashing through my triple-x fantasy just as it was starting to get good. "Dude, my daughter is in the car."

"She can't talk yet, so she has no idea what I'm saying." I turned around and checked on Grace who was oblivious to anything I was talking about. Her tired little eyes were fighting the rock of the Escalade that was bound to send her to sleep. Her lips curled into a precious little smile as her eyelids finally gave up the fight. "But if some piece of shit ever speaks to her that way, you need to call me and we're putting that asshole in the ground."

"Don't even go there, I'm already contemplating buying a gun." Stone gave me a sideways glance and I knew he wasn't kidding

"Fuck the gun, she looks like her mother. You're going to need a motherfucking arsenal, brother."

TOO DEPRESSED TO GO BACK TO THE APARTMENT I WOULD PROBABLY be evicted from in the next few days, I took a bus to Megan's loft. Although we had only met about a year and a half ago, we had become incredibly tight in a remarkably short time. She was my best friend. We had both started working at Garro's around the same time, with me working behind the bar and Megan as a waitress. Her warm smile and easy personality were a welcome change from the cold world of the brokerage firm I had come from. The sports bar was meant to be a temporary job for both of us until we gained more meaningful employment.

Megan Winters had studied psychology at Georgetown and after completing her psych degree she had decided to take a year off before going into practice. She was a five-foot-four powerhouse with long blonde hair, bright turquoise eyes, and an obscene IQ. Her dad was a highly respected cardiothoracic surgeon and her mother a pediatrician, so it had been assumed she'd follow in their footsteps and go into the medical field. Megs had said that going into psychology was as rebellious as she dared to be. Her parents were both lovely people who, despite their high-geared careers, were supportive of their daughter slumming it for a year. In fact, they had encouraged her, as they considered it to be character building, and were proud they had raised a daughter who, despite her privileged life, wasn't afraid to get her hands dirty. My hiatus from the business sector hadn't been by choice. The forced redundancy and a slow economy sealed my fate. Eventually Megs's time at the bar came to an end and she was now a clinical psychologist at Mount Sinai while I, unfortunately, was still fending off drunkards and popping caps off pilsners.

"How did it go, Ash?" She welcomed me with a hug as I walked through her doorway. Her Greenwich Village pad, flooded by the midday sun, was as warm as her beautiful smile. Her surrounds reinforced she had money. It wasn't flaunted, but it stirred my desire to have nice things too.

"Terrible," I mumbled returning her hug. "Not only did I probably not get the job but I made a complete ass of myself in front of Power Station's drummer." I had officially hit a new low.

"You got to meet Troy Harris?" Megs's eyes opened wide with excitement. I must be the only person in the five boroughs who wasn't a fan. "Ash, he's all kinds of hot. Those hazel eyes, the Mohawk, that body. Wow, just wow."

"Hazel eyes? Mohawk? No, I met Dan Evans. Dark messy hair, dark brown eyes, bad attitude. Isn't he the drummer?" I collapsed onto her sofa not needing an invitation. The beautiful plush cushion that wrapped around me allowed my muscles to ease. Mismatched thought waves continued to turn in my head despite the meeting being over. While I really didn't want to relive my meeting with Dan, I needed to somehow expunge him from my mind and figured a debrief with Megs was the best way to do it.

"Ashlyn, seriously? Dan Evans is the bass player. I saw him at a nightclub once; he's really cute. Troy Harris is the drummer." The iPad that was never far from her grasp was commandeered for my education and thrust into my hands. The band was the background wallpaper. There he was, his smug sexy smile, taunting me from behind the glass.

"Well hopefully if there is a god, I will never see Dan again, so it doesn't matter which instrument he plays." I handed the iPad back to Megs and let my head fall back against the cushion of the sofa, closing my eyes in an effort to ward off the headache threatening to take up residence in my frontal lobe.

"Why? What happened?" The couch cushion beside me compressed as Megs obviously joined me on the two-seater.

"He caught me gawking at Alex Stone like I wanted to eat him." I cringed, squeezing my eyes tightly, stupidly believing that would shut out the embarrassment of my earlier activities.

"Alex Stone was there, too?" Megs's voice rose in excitement, taking my arm and shaking it vigorously.

"Yes, and he is every bit as impressive up close. I'm pretty sure my tongue was polishing the floor." I opened my eyes to Megs's beaming face.

"I just want you to know I hate you right now. It's not fair you got to meet Alex and Dan and you aren't even a fan." Megs folded her arms across her chest and pouted. "So...were they nice?"

"Trust me, I would have rather it had been you. No matter how cute Dan is, he is also an obnoxious pig." I can't believe I just called Dan Evans cute. Why couldn't I focus on the fact he was offensive rather than the fact he was attractive? When was the last time I had eaten? Maybe my blood sugar was low.

"Aw, you think Dan is cute?" Megs smiled, unfortunately not willing to let the tiny word that had unconsciously slipped from my mouth, go. "Wow. Your libido is still intact. I was sure it had taken a flight to Boca. When was the last time you went on a date?"

"There is nothing wrong with my libido. I'm just choosey about who I date. I don't see the point wasting time with someone who obviously doesn't have the potential for my long-term goal. I told you, I have criteria."

Sure, there had been guys that had caught my attention and I had dated sporadically in college, but I hadn't met anyone I'd really wanted to hold on to. I could count the number of guys I had slept with on one hand and still have a finger or two spare. It's not that I was saving myself or I had an aversion to sex, I just had found it a little underwhelming, usually having to take things into my own hands—literally—to climax.

"Ash, you know you are allowed to date just for fun right? You don't have to see every guy for his *long-term potential*. Maybe just go out and let your hair down. Screw your criteria."

"No. I refuse to be a woman who settles. I worked my ass off to get into a decent college, and even though things are tough right now, I'll eventually make it back onto Wall Street. I want to find a guy who's going be a good husband with a decent earning capacity. I'm not trying to sound conceited, but my parents have both been slaving away at that bar their whole lives. They'll be working till the day they die. I'm the first one of my family to go to college. I love them, but I don't want that life for me. If my future husband and I are smart, we can build up a sizeable nest egg and let our money work for us. I need someone who is disciplined and like-minded in order to do that."

"What about being in love, Ashlyn? It can't just be about money and security. Don't you want a guy who will give you butterflies? Someone who is more than just a financial partner but who will also love you back?" Megs was ever the romantic. Her ideas of love were twirled around a wonderful fantasy, tied with a fancy red bow, and while my heart craved it, it was luxury I would admire from a distance.

I winced, realizing how contrived it all sounded. "Well of course I have to like the guy, it's not like I'm going to marry someone I don't like. I'm not that shallow." *Is that how I came across?* Shallow? Conceited? Vocalized, the clinical plan for my future sounded so much worse than it was. I envied the freedom Megs had, to live without the fear of being broke. With that freedom, love stood a chance. How did the conversation turn from the interview from hell to my dating life?

"Okay. Here is what is going to happen." Megs's eyes gleamed with excitement. "The interview is done and we have no way of controlling the outcome. Right?"

"Sadly, you're right." I nodded. There was really nothing I could do. While I had answered Lexi Reed's questions competently, I could tell she wasn't convinced. She saw through my bullshit and knew it was a Hail-Mary move, an effort to reenter the corporate world in the hopes of getting something more suitable in the future.

"So why don't you take a night off from your grand plan and get crazy with me?"

"Um, no. My plans for this evening include being online, job hunting, while drowning my sorrow in three-cheese pie from Carmine's Pizzeria." The promise of cheesy goodness was guaranteed to make my night suck slightly less than my day had.

"Ashlyn, you can take one night off from being responsible. One night, come out with me. Get drunk. Act like a regular twenty-seven-year-old. Who knows, maybe find some totally inappropriate guy and make out with him on the dance floor." Megs lifted herself off the sofa; the conversation was far from over.

"Megs, you know that isn't me. Besides, I can't afford it and I have nothing to wear."

"So borrow something of mine. I have a whole closet full of clothes; pick anything you like. And it's my treat so you can't use money as an excuse."

"What do you think one night is going to achieve?" I couldn't see the point in her expedition, other than delaying the inevitable mind-numbing search through pages of dead-end employment opportunities. And possibly sparing myself an increase of calories that was probably going to land straight on my ass.

"Nothing. That's the whole point. Sometimes you don't need to achieve anything. You can just do it for fun. So come on. Be reckless, we can even pick up some pie on the way out. Angelo's is just as good as Carmine's." Megs wiggled her eyebrows enthusiastically.

I wanted to argue, to tell her no, but in all honestly, it was easier just to give in. One night wasn't going to change anything and if it meant appeasing Megs and making her happy, then I could put off my pity party for twenty-four hours and hit it hard tomorrow. Besides I knew she wasn't going to let up until I agreed. She would probably blow up my phone until I eventually gave in, so I was probably just saving us both the time in between.

"Fine. I'll go," I conceded, raising my hands in defeat. "Tonight better not suck."

After a quick trip home to Brooklyn, I packed an overnight bag, ignored the final notice bills stuffed in my mailbox, and made my way back to the city. I had decided that while I was happy to raid Megs's wardrobe for our evening adventure, I wanted to get a few personal items to equip me to crash on Megs's sofa, rather than to try and navigate my way home later in the dark.

I had settled on a simple, fitted, little black dress that was way shorter than I was comfortable wearing, teamed with a pair of my own chunky black wedges. It was by far the most conservative outfit Megs had decreed acceptable, nixing most of my earlier choices. I made my peace with the fact I was going to be flashing a little more flesh than usual, applied some makeup, and left my long hair untethered to tumble down my back.

"You look great. Stop tugging at your hem," Megs whispered as we stepped out of the cab and onto the sidewalk.

I couldn't help it; the dress barely covered my ass and it had been a challenge not to flash anything as I navigated out of the cab.

"It's so short." I couldn't resist giving the dress one last tug as we made our way to the long line that stretched out in front of the doorway of *Panic*, the ironic name of the club Megs had taken us to.

"We are going to be out here forever. This line is so long." The girl in front of us complained. Her male counterpart simply shrugged and pushed his hands into his pockets. She was right; it was going to be a long wait.

"Let's see if there isn't a quicker way." I smiled, pulling Megs out of line and approached the giant who was guarding the entrance.

"You ladies on the list?" The large bouncer looked us over, his security number swinging from the chain around his thick neck.

"Sure," I smiled hoping we could wing it and get into the club sooner. While I wasn't thrilled about coming out in the first place, getting inside was going to be a hell of a lot more fun than standing outside on the street. Especially given the cheery disposition of our fellow waitees. Losing my nerve and hailing a cab was also another possibility the longer we stood outside.

"I'm Ash and this is Megs. We should be listed there somewhere," I bluffed, wondering if we got caught out whether he was going to make us go to the end of the line.

He consulted his clipboard before raising his eyebrow in question. "Ashley Brookes?"

"Yep. That's me and this is my plus one," I lied, silently hoping karma wasn't going to bite me on the ass and the real Ashley Brookes didn't arrive in the next five seconds.

"Says here your guest is supposed to be your husband, Keith Brookes."

"He's not feeling well tonight, so I decided to drag out my best friend instead. You know how men can be when they get the sniffles. I left him tucked up in bed." I smiled sweetly wondering where this new bravado had come from. I guess I had committed so it was best just to see it all the way through.

"Well okay then, show Mack your IDs on the way in. Have a nice night." He pointed to the other bouncer, sporting the number thirty-four, whose job it seemed was solely checking IDs. I guess there was a pecking order even with security guards.

Mack grunted as we held up our IDs for inspection, barely taking the time to check if they were authentic before waving us over to the line that required no payment of cover charge. Score.

"That was amazing, Ash. I can't believe we bypassed the line." Megs's face beamed with excitement as we walked into the belly of the club and were hit by a wall of flashing lights and deafening noise.

"So now what?" I screamed over the loud music pumping through the space. The wild strobes that were sweeping through the room seemed to have no sequence or rhythm.

"Drinks. Lots and lots of drinks. You, my friend, are going to have a good time tonight. Forget your grand plan, forget the interview, and forget everything else. For one night, you need to just *BE*," Megs screamed back, her voice barely audible over the thumping bass.

"Is that some new-aged therapy shit?" I laughed as we waded through the crowd toward the bar, feeling more comfortable taking my chances with the friendly bottles of alcohol rather than the dance floor.

"You don't need a therapist, Ash, you need to relax. Stop putting so much pressure on yourself." Megs put her arm around my shoulders and hugged me. She was right. One night wasn't going to kill me.

"I'm trying." I shrugged, wondering when was the last time I had honestly loosened the reins. While most kids had been partying through high school I had been studying my ass off for my SATs. When I hit college, I continued to keep my head down, not willing to throw away the opportunity to achieve my dreams for some keg beer and Sorority parties. Besides, when I wasn't studying I was helping out my parents, hiding out in the kitchen until I hit twenty-one, and then behind the bar.

"Well, try harder. We've been in this place for fifteen minutes and we haven't had our first drink yet." Megs squeezed her body close to mine. Her gorgeous face had started to bead with a thin sheen of perspiration.

"Okay, okay." We made our way to the bar in order to rectify the no-drink situation. Knowing how obnoxious it was when some jackass waved or hollered in your face, I waited until the bartender made his way over to our side of the bar before attempting to place our order.

"What can I get you?" The bartender leaned into us, grinning appreciatively at Megs's barely there dress. Out of the two of us she was the one who usually got the attention. She was not only extremely intelligent but she was also classically beautiful. Her blonde hair and blue-green eyes complemented her delicate features. Add to that her pint-sized figure, she was most men's dream girl. If she wasn't my best friend I would have had to hate her.

"I'll have a Long Island Iced Tea." Megs smiled, thankfully not ordering anything that required a cocktail umbrella and embarrassing us.

"And I'll have a Dirty Martini, but can you make it fifty-fifty

Noilly Prat and Tanquary 10, lots of brine with three olives." I leaned over the bar in an effort to make myself heard.

"She'll have a Dirty Martini, make it how you want to make it." Megs waved me off. "You're not working tonight, remember? Let the man do his job. After a few of those suckers you aren't going to care how they are made."

"It's no problem, sweetheart. You're paying for it so I'll make it anyway you like." He smiled. I wasn't sure who *sweetheart* was directed at but either way I was happy to see he was making my drink as per my prescription.

"Thank you." I watched as he grabbed the liquor bottles off the shelves and started mixing the drinks. There was something poetic about watching the liquid spill from the measure pourer and into a Boston glass.

I tried not to stare as he shook my Martini, giving me a wink as he poured it into the chilled glass resting on the bar. He then turned his attention to building Megs's Long Island in the high ball in front of us, garnishing it with a lemon spiral. I had to hand it to him, he took pride in his craft.

"Keep them coming." Megs handed over her black Amex that he happily exchanged for a bar token.

"Megs, you don't really want to do that. Remember, I grew up in a bar." The delicious icy gin-vermouth sensation complemented by the saltiness of the brine exploded across my tongue as I took a sip.

"Yeah, I actually do. Last time you were drunk was New Years Eve when we were doing shots of Jose Cuervo in my apartment. I think you're due." Megs grinned, reminding me of the impromptu party we'd had after finishing our shift at Garro's. Having not being able to participate in the revelry until after the bar had closed, we'd made our way to her apartment and did shots of silver tequila until we both passed out. New Year's Day did not treat us kindly.

"Fine, it's your money." I took another sip from my glass.

Megs held her glass up with a mischievous grin. "I propose a toast. To great friends and great futures, and to wherever either of those takes us."

"And to the questionable decisions we're undoubtedly about to make," I added before clinking my glass against hers.

Megs shimmied with excitement, her grin splitting wildly across her face. "Now you're talking."

4

Dan

"I'M TELLING YOU, I THINK WE SHOULD HAVE SOME INPUT INTO WHO Lexi is hiring." I threw back the Jack and Coke the waitress delivered, wanting to get my buzz sooner than later.

This wasn't our usual hang out but I was in need of a change, bored with the same faces I'd been seeing at the other Manhattan clubs. The strobes flashed with an irregular cadence while the big-ass screens designed for our privacy shook under the thump of the bass. The gen pop part of the club was separated from us by a bunch of drapes and out-of-work linebackers.

I'd dragged Jase and Troy along for the ride with neither of them giving me much resistance. It's not like either of them had plans, and with Jase having recently broken up with his off-on, long-distance girl, Erin, I decided it was time to go on the prowl, and for me and my brothers to enjoy being single in the greatest city on earth.

"Why the fuck do you care who she hires? This isn't the whole Sydney thing again, is it?" Troy stood and grabbed the two beers off her tray and handed one to Jason.

"Thanks, Beth. Give us twenty and then bring another round." He slid a fifty onto her tray giving her the all clear to leave. She gave him a pretty smile before she turned to walk away. He didn't even look at her ass as he sat back down on the couch. Troy had always been so fucking smooth; why he wasn't banging a different broad every night still perplexed me.

"No, it's got nothing to with her." I put my tumbler onto the table in front of us. "Fuck, you boys gossip more than a bunch of old ladies. Who even told you about her and me?" Syd and I had only happened one time but everyone seemed to know about it. I assumed she must have talked; after all, it had probably been a while since anyone had made her come like I had. I wore the scratches she tore into my back for a fucking week. Who knew she was that wild in the sack.

"You did, numbnuts." Jason laughed, bumping my shoulder with his fist.

"Okay, so maybe I did. Who remembers?" I couldn't recall spilling but honestly it was months ago, it's probably for the best, I didn't like hiding shit from my brothers. "Anyway, it's got nothing to do with Sydney. Shit wouldn't have worked out with us. She's *English*."

"You make it sound like she has an extra head or something." Troy laughed as he nursed his beer. He and Jase hated clubs, preferring shit-hole bars with pool tables, dartboards, and draft beer. He didn't bitch about it though, which was cool, proving what a team player he was by tagging along.

"Not you, too. I explained it to Stone this morning." I failed to understand why this concept was so fucking hard. Didn't we all study this shit in school? No wonder there is an outcry over the state of the education system.

"Is this the Declaration of Independence thing or the zee versus zed thing?" Troy piped in giving me faith the bastard had been paying attention.

"It's the Declaration thing but seriously, who even says zed?" I shrugged.

"You do realize the language we speak is *English* so *they* are probably right," Jason added smugly, the fucker probably thinking that because he had a college degree he knew better.

"Screw zed. As far as I'm concerned, that fancy piece of paper our forefathers signed means *I* get to say zee." How this was even up for discussion was beyond me, Ben Franklin would be turning in his grave with this completely unpatriotic banter.

Troy placed his longneck on the table, stretching his hands behind his head. "I'm sure that's exactly what old Thomas Jefferson was thinking when he dipped his quill in ink."

"I assure you, Tom J would have definitely been a zee man." I'd have put my nuts on it.

"How did we get from talking about Lexi's new assistant to Thomas Jefferson?" Jason grinned as he took another swig of his beer.

"Who knows, but I now could totally go a Philly Cheese Steak." Troy laughed, scooping his beer back off the table and taking a mouthful.

Jason leaned back into the couch. "So, Dan…enlighten us as to why you are so passionate about this cause."

"I was just thinking, seeing as whoever it is will be working with us, we should probably get a say. Technically we're like the boss, aren't we?" I scratched my head wondering why I hadn't thought of it before.

Troy's face lit up with a big shit-eating grin. "Wow, can you please call Lexi and tell her we're the boss, that shit would make my week." Bastard knew there was no way I'd call Lexi and poke the bear. I'd rather keep my balls attached, thanks.

"Whatever, nutsack." I gave him a friendly punch in the arm. "I was there this morning while Lexi was interviewing and I saw some potential." I couldn't help but think of the smokin' redhead I'd caught staring at Stone's ass.

"So who's the girl?" Jason chimed in, guessing correctly it had been a skirt that had got me interested.

"Here's the thing, she was totally into me. She didn't say she was but I could tell. You know when you can just tell?" I figured maybe if we did a recap I could work out what got her panties in a twist. All I had done was point out Alex was off the market, why she got all ate up was still a fucking mystery.

"So she shot you down, huh?" Troy cupped my neck, giving me a shake.

I shrugged him off not wanting his fucking sympathy. "She said I offended her."

"Go figure." Jason laughed, the wiseass not adding anything helpful to the conversation.

"I was just being myself but she got all defensive." I pushed my hands through my hair, honestly confused as to why she had been so pissed.

"Was this before or after you opened your mouth?" Jason chimed in.

"Shut up, asshole. I was just introducing myself 'cause she seemed like a fan, but then we started talking about her tits," I tried to explain, replaying the conversation in my head, unable to stop my grin at the thought of Ashlyn.

"Only you can go from *hello* to *tits* in zero point three seconds." Troy chuckled like a fucking schoolgirl, getting all up in my grill. It's not like *they* didn't think about tits all the time. I was just more honest about it. Girls should be thanking me.

"I'm choosing to ignore you right now 'cause you're shitting on my parade." I pushed my palm into Troy's face and shoved him out of the way. "She had some bullshit business shirt and jacket on, but hiding underneath there were these amazing perky tits. Now, you guys know I generally like porn-star big but seriously, all I could think about was licking them. I'm getting hard just thinking about it."

"So did *tits* have a name? Or did you scream out your own when you jerked off." Troy knew full well that an image like that would have sent even the strongest man to go have a stroke. I don't know why anyone fights the urge to masturbate; it's in our nature.

"Yeah, her name is Ashlyn." Just saying her name sent a shiver down the length of my cock, and I may or may not have screamed it out when I jacked off into my hand earlier. Granted it would sound even hotter if I was calling it out while I was balls deep inside her, but that was a whole other story.

"I need to get her out of my head or I'm going to need to jerk off again." I shifted in my seat as my pants started to get tight around my crotch, just thinking about her was giving me a wicked hard-on. "I'm going to go check out the talent. There are a couple of girls over in the corner who look keen."

"Maybe give them a few minutes before you talk about their tits." Troy snorted as he grabbed his beer off the table and took a swig.

I flipped him off as I walked over to the two gorgeous brunettes who were giggling nervously in the corner. While they might have been working the shy vibe, I was willing to bet there were a few Trojans tucked away in their tiny purses.

"Hi, are you Dan Evans?" The shorter one bit her cherry-red lip seductively, flicking her long hair over her shoulder.

"Sure am, sweetheart, and what would your name be?" I moved in closer, tilting my head to the side as I took them both in. They looked so similar they could be sisters, dark brown hair with large brown eyes. They looked like they'd had been poured into the tight, tiny dresses they were wearing, not that I was complaining. Both of them were sporting rather impressive racks.

"I'm Lili and this my friend Skyla." She nodded to the cutie on her right. "I thought it was you but was too nervous to come over. Is that the rest of the band?"

"You don't have to be shy, I don't bite. Well, not unless you want me to." I couldn't help but smile. It wouldn't be the first time a girl liked it rough and I would be happy to play it either way. "James and Alex aren't here but those two losers over there are Jason and Troy."

"Wow, we've never met famous people before." Skyla stepped toward me, her pouty red mouth looked primed for a monu-mental blowjob.

"We're just regular folks, babe." I brushed some hair away from Skyla's face as Lili slid up beside me. "You wanna come over and say hello?"

"Yes," they chimed out enthusiastically in stereo. I was definitely getting lucky tonight and these two lovely ladies seemed more than willing to get onboard. Even if I struck out with one, I had the other ready to go. Like a boy scout, I was prepared.

I wrapped my arms around both of their waists, letting my hands drop down to skirt the top of their asses, and pulled them in close to my side. While I was happy to do intros, I wasn't planning on sharing. The other two would have to find their own tail tonight.

We walked over to where the douchebags were sitting; Troy was busy running his mouth about some bullshit while Jason deep-throated a beer.

"Ladies, meet Troy and Jason. While I can confirm I've had all my shots, I make no promises on these two."

"Ladies," Troy tipped his chin hello, standing up to offer them the couch, no doubt hoping to get lucky with whichever one I struck out with.

"Hi, girls," offered Jason, sizing them up as he drained the last of his beer. Both of them were sadly mistaken if they thought they were going to get in on this action.

The girls both giggled nervously and introduced themselves, hugging each of the boys before returning to my side - as it should be. I pulled them onto the couch that Troy had vacated. My ass had barely made contact with the chair when Lili forgot all about her shyness and slid her hand up my thigh, her long red nails squeezing as they neared my balls. My grin widened as I leaned back into the couch spreading my arms across the back of the chair and inviting more. If this fine piece of ass wanted to jerk me off with an audience, I wasn't about to stop her.

"Hey, I saw him first," protested Skyla as she grabbed my chin and whipped my head around to face her. "I'm a *big* fan," she breathed into my mouth. "I know you probably hear that all the time but I want the opportunity to show you."

"Relax, ladies, there is plenty of me to go around and it would be very rude of me to not show my appreciation for such huge fans." I tilted her chin and brought her lips closer to me. My cock jerked assuring me, in case there was any doubt that we were on the same page.

"You think you can handle us both?" Lili's lips hit the skin on my neck as her hand moved from my thigh to my crotch, making me slightly nervous as she squeezed the denim separating her fingers from my cock. "'Cause there is no way I'm going to let Skyla have all the fun without me."

If I wasn't hard before, that situation had well and truly rectified itself as my dick struggled not to be choked out by my jeans. "Babe, no one is missing out tonight." I moved from Skyla's mouth to Lili's, proving I wasn't about to let anyone feel like the consolation prize.

As the girls moved around me, taking turns with my mouth, I shot a glance over to Troy who rolled his eyes and shook his head. "Dude, do what you want, but if it hits the papers tomorrow, it's going to be a shit storm I want no part of. Keep it clean or find a room."

Jason nodded, siding with Captain Fucking Lame. "Take it to the bathroom at least, brother."

I didn't bother to answer, instead flipping them off as I continued the tongue action I had going on. Assholes were just jealous I had scored both of the hot girls while they were left with their dicks in their hands. Besides, if I wasn't seeing Ashlyn anytime soon, I needed something to tide me over. Jerking off wasn't exactly what my dick was after.

"Wanna grab another beer?" Jason pointed to the vacant couch on the other side of the VIP section, "I'll meet you over there."

"Yeah, I'm going to take a lap first. I'm getting bored." Troy shrugged as both of them walked off in different directions.

"Did we make your friends mad?" Skyla blinked as she ran her hands underneath my shirt, her nails against my skin making me shiver.

"They're just jealous, babe, pay them no mind." I wasn't about to have the fun police cockblock me, it had been a while since I'd last had a threesome.

"Good," Lili licked her lips, "because Skyla and I are about to blow your mind."

THE ROWS OF LIQUOR BOTTLES CAUGHT THE LIGHT, SHINING DOWN ON us like twinkling stars. It contrasted nicely with the dark red walls of the club. We had managed to secure two unoccupied bar stools and perched ourselves at the bar. This meant two things: the drinks were readily refreshed and replenished, and we didn't realize how much we'd drunk until we stood up.

"I need to pee." Megs giggled, pulling gently on my arm. "We need to find the bathroom."

"Okay." I giggled back like she had delivered the world's greatest punch line. "There's bound to be one around here somewhere."

"If you head upstairs, the one up there is bound to have a shorter line," Kirk, the bartender we'd become rather fond of, helpfully offered.

"Thanks, Kirk. We love you." Megs blew him kisses as I pulled her from the stool.

"You need to walk, Megs. I can't carry you," I protested, trying to right her back onto her own two feet.

"I feel like I'm wearing stilts. How high are these stupid heels?" Megs lifted her foot in amusement, inadvertently flashing her crotch to the group of guys in front of us. Thankfully she was wearing underwear, though that didn't stop the whistles of encouragement from our makeshift audience.

"Just walk slowly," I encouraged, our swaying bodies making little progress as we moved to the edge of the stairs.

"But I'm going to pee my pants." Megs laughed as we slowly navigated one stair at time. The click-clack of our heels against the wooden steps could still be heard above the music. At this rate there was going to be a puddle on the floor before we'd even made it halfway. "Take your shoes off until we get to the bathroom."

"Ew. I'm not walking in bare feet. It's a club, Ash, lord knows what's down there." Megs scrunched her face in disgust.

"Well then, walk faster or your pee is going to be added to the list of unidentifiable things *down there.*"

While our ascent up the stairs was painfully slow, we did make it to the top without any incidents, be it falls or further indecent exposure. The sacrifice of footwear was also avoided, Megs unwilling to let herself be defeated by a pair of Loubutins, despite their height.

"Salvation." Megs pushed opened the door of the bathroom, sending us almost spilling onto the tile floor, the shiny, white-tiled floor and chromed surfaces, pristine, and thankfully, vacant. "Kirk was right, there is no line. Remind me to give him a big tip." She hurried into the stall.

I shuffled into the stall beside her, using the walls to steady myself before allowing myself to feel the sweet relief.

"Ash, I heard this story of this girl who was drinking all night and didn't pee and then died the next day. Lucky we made it to the bathroom," she shouted despite there being only a few inches of wall separating us.

"That's just some bullshit urban legend, Megs. You have to stop reading Internet spam," I shouted back, having trouble regulating my voice. I blamed the booze or perhaps the onsets of deafness, probably escalated by prolonged exposure to DJ madness from downstairs.

"Hey, if you get this job with Lexi Reed you need to introduce me to the band." Megs giggled through the wall as she hit the flush. "I want to make out with Troy Harris."

"I thought we weren't talking about it." I tried to stand and pull up my panties, the seemingly easy task almost beyond me. "And you aren't just going to make out with someone you don't know, even if he is famous."

"Why not?" We both exited at the same time, Megs pulling at the fitted, glittery scrap of material she was passing off as a dress. Her effort to cover more of her breasts almost exposed her ass. "We can be bad girls. Why can't *I* kiss some random guy? Even if I sleep with him, who cares? Everyone is so judgmental. I say, it's my vagina, if I see fit to give it away then it should be no one's business."

"Megs, when you are throwing out the word *vagina*, I would say you have had too much to drink." I laughed and adjusted her glittery scrap so while she was showing a little more cleavage, the rest of the club wouldn't get a free *up-skirt* on our way out of the bathroom.

"Vagina, vagina, vagina," Megs gleefully sang as we washed our hands, her inhibitions long gone.

"You have issues, you know that?" I threw paper towels in Megs's direction, which she tried to deflect with uncoordinated karate-style moves.

"I wonder if there is a bar up here? I am not liking the idea of going down any stairs right now." I pushed open the door and we exited the bathroom, returning to the light and sound of the club. Had it gotten louder? Or had our bathroom visit just given us a reprieve?

"Surely there's a bar up here, the VIP section is down that hall. You should use your super powers to sneak us in there. I bet they have free snacks, those slices from Angelo's were hours ago."

"Yes. We should go to the VIP section." I raised my hands in agreement forgetting that it inadvertently raised my already too-short dress higher. "You're a genius."

"I'm a doctor, all that schooling has to count for something." Megs held onto my arm as we pushed through the throng of people assembled near the VIP area.

"Everyone who doesn't belong here, move along." Two security guards attempted to clear the area.

A large ornate chandelier peeked out from the top of the massive erected barriers, its shimmering gleam taunting us from the other side.

"Someone good must be in there," Megs complained. "Security is tight."

Pulling Megs with me, we squeezed back through the throng of people and circled to the opposite side of the club. "Let's go around to the other side, if we go over to the balcony, we can probably see through the screens."

On this side of the club there was a small balcony, which jutted out like an old school theater. The gilded railing and large velvet curtains fringed what I could only assume was the designated resting area, a chaise lounge and a couple of plush armchairs sat vacant in this forgotten corner.

"Can you see anything?" Megs happily fell onto the chaise, her toned, bare legs stretched out in front of her. "I'm just going to lay here, maybe take a nap."

"Oh you have got to be kidding me," I huffed, able to catch a glimpse through the thin gap between the barrier screens.

"What?" Megs sat up suddenly her quest for a nap forgotten.

I pointed wildly, wondering if the universe was somehow conspiring against me. "Dan Fucking Evans is right over there." Of all the gin joints in all the cities, he had walked into mine. Okay, we weren't in a gin joint and he hadn't walked in, but still, what were the chances?

"Are you sure? We've had a lot of drink. It could be some random who looks like him." Megs jumped off the chaise and moved to my side, squinting her eyes in an attempt to see.

"No, that's him. I'd know that smug grin anywhere. Seriously, twice in one day. Look at him, smirking his ass off with a couple of girls draped over him." My fever rose as I watched him through the gap. I despised him and yet, he looked downright edible in tight black jeans and a vintage Ramones tee. Clearly I was drunker than I thought.

"Wow, he's actually better looking in real life." Megs pushed me out of the way, able to see more clearly from my vantage point. "I know we are staring but I can't stop looking at him. I think his tattoos are hypnotizing me."

"I should go tell him what an ass he was," I stated, fuelled with a good dose of liquid courage and a case of I-no-longer-care-what-anyone-thinks.

"Ash, this is probably not a good idea." Megs swayed unsteadily on her feet, having as much trouble standing as she was trying to convince me of my bad idea.

"Didn't you say you wanted to meet him? Well, let's go over there." I turned and made for the VIP area, unsure exactly what I would say to him once I got there. Ass. How dare he? This was my night of irresponsibility. I didn't want him here.

"Is there anything I can say that is going to stop you?" Megs grabbed onto my arm, trying her best to keep up with my accelerated pace and not trip over her own feet.

"No, probably not." I smiled, knowing my mind was made up.

"Okay, fine. Let's go over there but don't get us thrown out, all right?"

I dragged a stumbling Megs by the hand as I wandered to the VIP area, trying not to make my forced grin look like something out of horror movie.

The large security guard put his arms out to hinder us moving forward. "Sorry, ladies, this area is reserved."

"But my friend is in there, I just need to tell him something." I sounded surprisingly calm despite my quickened heartbeat. I gave him another smile, not sure if I was going for seductive or meek. The twitching of my lips probably made me look more like a stroke victim than a femme fatale.

"Who is your friend?" I could tell he was skeptical, and had probably been fielding women all night.

"It's Dan Evans, he's just over there. If you let me through, I'll just talk to him and then we'll be on our way." I placed my hands on my hips, hoping the fact I was wearing very little clothes would work in my favor. If I'd been less inebriated I would have been horrified by my brazen attempt, but in my current altered state I was resisting the urge to give myself a high-five.

"Listen, babe. You aren't the first lady here tonight to tell me he's your *friend*. Either way, unless a VIP escorts you in, I can't let you through. It's nothing personal, I just have a job to do." While he wasn't rude, he wasn't sympathetic to my plight either, shooting down any further conversation. I narrowed my eyes, silently cursing his personal integrity.

"But I really do know him," I protested, wondering if my earlier conversation with Dan constituted *knowing* him. I'd met him; that had to count. Semantics.

"I'm sure you do but rules are still rules."

"Well your rules suck." I stuck out my tongue defiantly. Seriously, who was I and where was Ashlyn Murphy?

"Hey, Barney." A tattooed, guy with a Mohawk, and the most amazing hazel eyes tried to squeeze past. His large frame inadvertently brushed up against us. "Hi, ladies."

"Oh shit, that's Troy Harris. He's so hot. Did I say that out loud?" Megs panted as she smacked her hand across her mouth.

His lips spread into an amused grin. "Yes I am, and yeah you did." It made him look sweet actually, all tough guy exterior paired off with a really nice smile. I was either drunker than I thought or I had never noticed.

"So you are the drummer? Huh, I had totally thought that dickwad was." I pointed to where Dan was sitting, his duo of *skank sca*rves still draped around his neck. "My apologies to you. You are so much *nicer* than he is. He is a total jerk. You even said hello without being an ass."

Troy's face looked animated as he laughed. "I'll take that as a compliment. I assume you are talking from experience?"

"I met him this morning. He told me I had small tits. Look at them." I glanced at the swells of my breasts that peeked out above the tight black fabric. "They look adequate, don't they? Who even says that to a girl?" Did I just ask Troy Harris to inspect my breasts? The words coming out of my mouth were fuzzily entwined with my internal thoughts, so I couldn't be sure which was which. Not with any certainty anyway.

"Sure they look...um really nice." His grin widened as he briefly looked down, confirming I had in fact verbalized the request.

"Troy Harris. Hi, I'm a fan." Megs grabbed his hand and started shaking it wildly, his arm bouncing up and down as Megs continued to shake. "I just want to say that I told Ashlyn you were the drummer when she thought Dan Evans was the drummer. Tell him, Ashlyn. I totally said Troy Harris is the drummer."

"You don't have to say my whole name, you can just call me Troy." He smiled carefully using his other hand to free the one currently caught in Megs's death grip. He surely had to think we were insane; he was just too polite to say so, further proving what a nice guy he was. Not like Dan. Dan was un-nice. Huh? That's not a word. My eyes crossed as I tried to find the adjective I needed, *sexy* was what kept flashing repeatedly, unwelcome in my mind.

"Wait, did you say your name is Ashlyn?" Troy studied me curiously, must be my freaky crossed eyes that had him interested. I really am such a catch.

"Yes, I'm Ashlyn." I stood up a little straighter, pushing back my shoulders proudly. Seriously, who the hell was I right now?

"Oh this is perfect." He clapped his hands together as the smile hit his eyes. "You met Dan this morning when you had an interview with Lexi, right?"

"Yes, I had an interview this morning and Dan was there with Alex. Not that I even looked at Alex. I mean I looked at him but not in *that* way. I mean he's *married* with a *baby*. I was most definitely not throwing off heat of *any* kind." Abort! Abort! My mind shouted and my mouth refused to obey. It's as if the words spewed from my mouth like inmates in a jailbreak. Sound the alarm. It was anyone's guess what I would be saying next.

"Ashlyn, are you drunk?" His eyebrow rose as his smile widened, clearly enjoying this, whatever *this* was.

"I would say if we are talking probabilities, the chances are pretty high." I stepped closer in an attempt to whisper in his ear but ended up smacking my forehead against his cheek. "Are you going to get us thrown out?"

"This just keeps getting better and better." He threw his head back in a full-throated laugh. "Hell no, you ain't getting kicked out. I think you lovely ladies need to come back and be my guest. Barney, I'll take responsibility for these two."

He offered me his arm that, thankfully, I latched onto. Megs, bypassing formalities, hugged his chest, her grin threatening to split her face apart.

"Your call, man. Just get them to drink some water. Lay off the booze for a few, yeah?" Barney offered as he stepped aside, shaking his head.

"You cool, ladies?" Troy asked as he looked from his arm that I was holding like a life preserver, to Megs who was snaked around his waist like a human boa constrictor. Neither seemed to faze him.

"Hell yes, Troy Harris, we want to come back. I'm Megan Winters by the way but you can call me Meg or Megs or just call me Megan." Megs nodded, her head bouncing so violently it seemed she had lost all muscle control in her neck.

"I'll make you a deal, you just call *me* Troy and I'll call *you* Megs." He chuckled at Megs as his bright hazel eyes moved to me. "Ashlyn, you want to come back and hang?"

I tried to harness what control I still had over my mouth to smile, but as it had been spewing crazy talk, who knew if it actually had the ability to curl upward to form anything close resembling to a grin. I was going to enjoy this. "Lead the way." I smirked.

THINGS WERE JUST GETTING INTERESTING WHEN SKYLA AND LILI excused themselves to hit the bathroom. We'd been making out and playing touchy-feely for a while and both of them seemed eager for us to make tracks and head back to their place. They shared an apartment in the Chelsea area so I guessed sharing bodily fluids wasn't going to be a big deal. Who was I to argue? I wondered if they would let me film it? They seemed up for just about anything, so it couldn't hurt to suggest.

I pulled out my phone and scrolled through messages, nothing really interested me but it sure beat sitting on the couch by myself looking like a douche. How long does it take to go to the bathroom? Women take too fucking long. What do they do in there? I've been in a few ladies rooms and it's not like they have anything interesting going on in there. It's just toilets and sinks. I wondered if they were getting started without me? 'Cause straight up, that would *not* be fucking cool.

Out of the corner of my eye, I saw Troy saunter in with two babes wrapped around him. Well, fuck me. Looks like the big guy finally got some sack and was taking my lead. I immediately snapped my head around to get a better look; no harm in admiring the view. After all, I'd just given him *that* pleasure not half an hour ago.

Was that? I felt the blood drain straight from my head and into my cock as they got closer, confirming that the smoking babe holding onto Troy's arm was the same feisty redhead from this morning.

"Ashyln?" I rose to my feet like a marine called to attention. Holy shit, she was hot. She looked so different, her long wild hair probably covering more of her pale skin than the dress she was wearing, not that I was complaining.

"Hello, Dan." She breathed into my face as she leaned into me, swaying slightly on her feet.

She said my name with such distaste and venom, her breath smelling of gin and the possibility of bad decisions. I'm not sure why, but I fucking loved it. The outfit she was wearing made me instantly hard.

"I seemed to have stumbled onto some fans." Troy grinned, his arm still wrapped around the other girl. "I think they might be *friends* of yours."

I swallowed hard as my eyes raked up and down Ashlyn's body, my balls begging me to hurry up and get with the program. "Nice...very, very nice."

"Um, Dan?" Skyla appeared at my side like some wicked magic trick, looking all pissy.

"Yeah?" I responded not wanting to be distracted from my current view, completely forgetting I had already made plans to leave.

"We're ready to go," Lili snapped, tapping her foot impatiently.

Ashlyn continued to eyeball me, ignoring Skyla and Lili.

I waved them off. "Yeah, I think I'm going to hang for a while longer." Strangely no longer interested. "You girls go on without me, have a good time."

"Are you *fucking* kidding me?" Skyla or maybe it was Lili shot in my direction. "You are just going to ditch us?" Okay, that time, it was definitely Lili.

Ashlyn leaned closer and whispered into my ear, "Your pussy party seems angry." She paused before adding, "Tell me, Dan, are there any women who *aren't* pissed at you?"

"You think that getting girls is a problem for me?" I laughed. No really, the fact she thought I ever needed to spend a night alone when I didn't want to was seriously amusing.

"Listen, girls." I twisted back to face my *pussy party*. Pretty cool name actually, I should think about getting shirts printed. Like an unofficial Dan fan club or something. "This isn't going to happen tonight. Thanks for the hand job but I'm no longer feeling it." I shrugged deciding that should be enough of an explanation.

"You are such an ass," shouted Skyla, or was it Lili? I'd be lying if I said cared.

"I have to agree, he *is* an ass," Ashlyn slurred as she backhanded me across the chest. "Ass," she repeated.

"Come on, Skyla, let's go. No way is he getting laid tonight." Well that one was obviously Lili. She frowned at me before pulling her friend toward the doorway.

"Well done, you're all class, Dan," Jase said, chuckling. "I'm Jason, don't judge me by my association with this numbnuts." He bumped me out of the way and offered Ashlyn his hand, like he was negotiating a used car deal.

"Hi, Jason." Ashlyn grabbed his hand enthusiastically and pulled him in a little closer. Her body crashed against Jase's arm, the dickhead smiled smugly as it made contact. "I'm Ashlyn and this is my friend Megs. She's a big fan."

Ashlyn motioned roughly to the direction of the short, sexy blonde who had walked in with her and Troy. I must be losing my edge 'cause I hadn't even noticed the rocking curves she was working.

"Hi, Jason Irwin, I'm Megs. I'm a big fan." The blonde nodded, talking so fast she sounded like she might be high. Come to think of it, they both were acting really strange. "He plays keyboard, Ash." Megs cupped her hand and attempted to whisper but it was actually louder than her regular volume. This was so fucking weird. "I'm so excited to meet you, Jason Irwin." She waved, not letting go of Troy. While she might be a fan, obviously she had a favorite.

"She has a tendency for saying our full names. I think it's easier if we just go with it." Troy grinned like a douchebag, giving Megs a squeeze. He clearly wasn't hating the attention. Not that I blamed him, the blonde who had the death grip on him was all kinds of hot. Troy glanced up at me, biting back his shit-eating grin. "Ashlyn apparently thought *you* were the drummer, Megs was kind enough to set her straight."

"I sure did, Troy Harris." The blonde bobble head chimed in.

"Are you girls loaded?" I asked, looking between them. They had to be. Their eyes were glassy and they could barely stand straight.

"My alcohol level is not relevant here." Ash strutted back over to me and I could feel the heat roll off her body as it stood inches from mine, her lips in my face were driving me insane. "What is relevant is that *you*, are a pig."

"Is this shit for real?" I wanted to laugh, I didn't care she was paying me out. She was drunk, and her pouty lips fumbling with words was fucking hot.

"It's pretty awesome if you ask me," Jase added from the peanut gallery.

"No one asked for your opinion," I shot back, not even attempting to take my eyes off Ash. I couldn't look away, hell, what I wanted to do was throw her over my shoulder and take her home. Let her work out some of that aggression.

"You were rude to me this morning." Ashlyn pushed her finger into my chest. "I need to set you straight."

"Babe, you were practically hyperventilating when you met me. You don't have to deny it now." I couldn't help myself as I pushed a little further. My dick screamed in agony straining against the fly of my jeans.

"I am not a fan." She breathed into my face. "I worked my ass off and graduated from college with honors. I was working fifteen-hour days and handling accounts worth hundreds of thousands of dollars. I wouldn't just hyperventilate over someone like *you*."

"What do you mean someone like me?"

"Someone like you. You play in a band. How is that even a real job? Did you even graduate?"

Well fuck me, she thought because I played in a band it somehow made me stupid? I didn't need to go to College. I'm doing what I love and making bank doing it. I've come across people who judge us 'cause we have tattoos and don't dress a certain way, but I couldn't give two fucks. I'd rather hang myself than have to wear a suit and tie all day and punch some fucking clock. I didn't care what anyone thought. I was living my dream and if anyone had a problem with my lifestyle, then it was just that – *their* problem. "Do you get lonely up in your ivory tower, sweetheart?" I tilted my head back and laughed.

Ash smacked me across the chest with her hand. "Why are you laughing at me?" It was just enough to sting.

"Jesus, woman. Why the fuck are you hitting me?" I laughed harder, seeing how aggravated she was that I hadn't been offended by her attitude. She was so fucking adorable.

"Don't laugh at me." She huffed, planting her hands on her hips, giving me a better look at that fine body of hers. If she was trying to turn me off, she was failing.

"Babe, you can think whatever *you* want about me and *I* get to laugh at whatever I want, that's how it works."

"I hate you."

I leaned in and whispered, "No, you don't. You're just mad 'cause I make your panties wet."

"You disgust me!" She pushed against my chest.

"And yet, you still want to sleep with me, don't you?"

"What? No. Are you insane? I don't want to sleep with you. Not *every* woman wants to sleep with you."

"Maybe that's true, but you do."

"You...you...ugh!" She opened her mouth and shut it, wordless.

"It's okay, sweetheart, don't fight it. I promise it will be good for you."

She slammed her lips onto mine, her tongue invading my mouth. It was hot and I could taste a hint of whatever she'd just been drinking as she swirled her tongue around mine. I pulled her head closer, ignoring our audience, as I fisted her crazy red hair.

Her tits pushed up against me and I heard her moan as I pulled up her leg, hitting that sweet spot with the throbbing hard-on that was begging to climb out of my jeans. I didn't care she said she hated me, or that I disgusted her, her body was telling me she wanted me, wanted this and I wasn't about to deny her.

She leaned into me, her hands getting crazy as they moved down my back and squeezed my ass, pushing her hips harder into me. I could feel her grind against the friction of my jeans, using it to work herself up, the action making us both crazy. It felt so good, her mouth hungry for every little inch of tongue I gave her. I could only imagine how amazing those lips would feel wrapped around my cock. I needed to get inside of her before I blew my load in my pants. I couldn't remember a time I had been this worked up over a girl. It was like someone had flicked a switch in her and all that anal control shit just exploded into a big ball of want. Oh yeah, I said anal and I would be happy to work that out with her too, but right now, I need to get my dick suited up and buried into her pussy.

She pulled away in a rush, her face flushed and her lips puffy from making out. Her chest heaved up and down as she pushed her hair out of the way. She backed away steadily and gave me a fucking drop-dead gorgeous smile, her tongue tracing her perfect cock-sucking lips.

"There, I've made a questionable decision. Megs, I would say our night is done."

Smart! Seems like that fancy degree was worth something, despite getting hot and bothered. She was telling her girl to wrap it up so we could go get busy. I had to respect the fact she didn't want to fuck me right here in the club, it was a little skanky. I mean, I would have done it if she'd asked but I was looking forward to taking her home and fucking her properly, having her come so fucking hard around my cock she forgot her own name. Yeah, we needed to eject from this club ASAP.

Megs's bugged eyed expression matched that of Troy and Jase. "Uh Ash, you just made out with Dan Evans."

"Wrong, he just made out with me." She smirked and turned away from me. "Troy, Jason. Have a good night."

What the actual fuck? Is she leaving? No, she can't be leaving. Coming up for a breath I understand, but calling curtains is a whole other matter. One minute we're getting hot and heavy, going at it like a porno, and the next minute she is saying good-bye? Who does that? I've got the worst case of blue balls and she was just going to walk away?

"Wait, you are just going to leave me like this?" I pointed to the bulge in my pants thinking she must be kidding. Maybe this was like foreplay for her, we could get aggressive and then fuck hard.

"Kind of ironic, isn't it? Think of it as character building. Write a song about it. Either way, I am not sleeping with you. Megs, let's go."

Shit, she was serious. She stalked over to a bewildered Troy and unwrapped her friend from his body. Megs was not able to offer much more than a wave as Ashlyn pulled her out to the main area of the club.

"What the fuck was that?" I stared dumbfounded at Troy and Jase.

"I believe you just got owned, my friend." Troy patted me on the shoulder like some poor little puppy. "Looks like it's just you and your hand tonight."

Jase gave me a friendly punch in the arm. "I like her. I'm going to see if Lexi will give me her number. Maybe I'll ask her out, she seems like a fun time."

"Don't even play me right now, asshole." I ran my hands through my hair, five different shades of worked up.

"Oh come on, Dan, you've got to admit that was funny. You did the same thing to those other two girls not five minutes before." Troy crossed his arms in front of his chest. He was a big bastard too; all that cymbal crashing and drum bashing made him solid so I wasn't going to argue with him even if I didn't agree.

"She was totally hot for me, her leaving was to prove a point." I flagged over a waitress, needing a drink to calm me down. I should just tell her to bring the whole bottle.

Beth brought over our standard order and I snagged the tumbler of Jack and Coke I knew would barely make a dent. Troy grabbed his bottle of beer. "Well I guess she did that, didn't she?"

"Whatever man, that was fucking bullshit. Bullshit. Who gets a guy all fucking hard and then walks? Not even an offer of a blowjob or anything. It's not like I wouldn't have reciprocated." I swallowed the drink and slammed down the glass.

Jase tipped his bottle of beer and took a swig. "Don't be looking at me, dude, I'm not blowing you."

"Nice one, asswipe. Like I'd want to have my dick sucked by you." I've got nothing against dudes sucking other dude's cocks; I just don't subscribe to it for myself.

"You baited her dude, what were you expecting?" Troy took a seat on the couch and pointed at me to do the same.

Like I was going to chase after her like a loser. Dan Evans did not chase after a girl no matter what she looked like, even if she gave amazing head. Okay, if she gave amazing head, that would be grounds to break my rule but it was too late now. She had too big of a lead and I had no idea of her head-giving talents so therefore, by my own rules, I could not pursue.

"Just let it go, man. You've both had your fun, now move on." Jase sunk his ass into the chair beside me.

He was right. I should let it go. She was beautiful, there was no denying that, but she had a chip on her shoulder a mile fucking wide. A girl like that meant work, and she obviously thought she was too good for me, her and her fucked-up idea of who I am was too much trouble.

I clenched my fist, my body still all jazzed up from her little stunt. I should just go find a random girl and forget it even happened. Forget her and her delicious fucking mouth. Damn it, now I was thinking about her again.

"Dan." Troy snapped his fingers in front of my face, snapping me back to attention. "I can see your cogs turning, let it go."

I nodded, pretending to agree with him and he rolled his eyes, giving me *that* look. The look that told me, we both knew I wasn't letting it go. I don't know why but that girl had gotten under my skin and come hell or high water I was going to need to figure out why.

7

Ashlyn

With the dawning of the new day also came panic. Panic induced by the foggy memories that slowly bubble to the surface, panic about the half-remembered words that float in your subconscious that you hoped never spilled from your lips, and panic from the body aches echoing through your muscles which point to an *active* night.

I was home in my Brooklyn apartment which gave me pause, as I had remembered deciding to spend the night at Megs's, but after leaving *Panic*—the club not the state of mind which was burning through my body today—I had very little recollection of what had transpired. Perhaps, I just caught a cab and came home? Maybe Megs had found someone she wanted to share her vagina with; she'd been pretty intent on it earlier. That would have definitely prompted me to hightail it back across the bridge. Or maybe the need to play show-and-tell had been mine. Megs's borrowed dress from the previous night was strewn carelessly on the floor beside me but I was still wearing my bra and panties. That had to be a good sign, didn't it? The bile in my stomach churned as I slowly turned my head to survey the other side of my bed, praying with everything I had it would be empty. Rumpled sheets and a pillow were my only bedfellows. I slowly breathed out a sigh of relief. Whatever I did last night could be forgiven, as long as I didn't continue those mistakes in the morning. I could chalk it up to an unfortunate evening resulting from questionable judgment and move on.

"Good morning," a husky voice greeted me, my previously forgiven sins now flashing before my eyes. "I was hoping you would wake up soon."

Standing before me was Dan Evans, still wet from a shower with one of *my* towels wrapped around his hips, barely affording his modesty. Seriously, I had bigger towels; did he choose the tiniest one? Ashlyn, you are worried that he chose the tiniest towel? Seriously? Dan Freaking Evans is in your bedroom, has been in your shower, and...is. In. Your. Bedroom. *What the hell?* But damn, he looked good. All the exposed ink covered skin glistened as he moved closer to my bed. It made the colors in his tattoos more vibrant, life-like. His chest flexed as he lifted his arm to dry off his hair, thankfully with another towel and not the one wrapped precariously around his lower body. He was lean but incredibly toned, his body resembling a poster you might find in a biology lab. Each muscle clear and defined, it would be so easy to take a marker and start labeling - starting with those lower abdominal muscles no one knows the name of and what most women simply call the V.

"FUCK!" My horror overrode my libido as I realized what must have transpired.

"Now, you're talking," remarked a grinning Dan as he sat down on the bed, the mattress compressing under the weight of his body. "You know, for someone so uptight, you sure have a dirty mouth when you're drunk."

I raked my hands through my messy morning hair in frustration trying to remember how he got here, surely Dan didn't just teleport into my bedroom. Half-naked. Wet. "How? What? Where? I said goodbye to you. I remember saying goodbye to you."

"Yeah, that. That was not cool." He tossed the towel he was using for his hair onto the floor casually as the smile teased at the edges of his mouth. "Why did you kiss me and then run away?"

"Because..." The reason no longer made sense in my own head. "Because I thought I should loosen the reins a little, make out with some random guy. Megs was on my case about being normal, and you made me angry. I wanted you to stop talking."

"Way to make me shut up. You showed me." Dan's fingers slid up my arm pushing my hair out of the way. I hated to admit that him touching me didn't feel so terrible. It actually felt nice. Gah! No. I was not willing to allow myself to make the same mistake twice. I shrugged off his hand, determined to fight off any further advances. At some point I needed to get my head in the game, now would be a good time for that. I sat up, hoping my vertical positioning would prompt my smarts to kick in. Unfortunately becoming vertical also highlighted that I was in my underwear. The sheet slipped down to my waist and revealed my bra. Dan's eyes dipped down and gave me an appreciative smile before I was able to scramble and pull up the sheet to cover myself. Not that it mattered at this point; he'd seen it *all* last night no doubt. Regardless, the free show was not going to continue today.

"I know I left. Megs and I walked out of the front of the club. I know we did." I scanned my memory for an anchor - nothing.

"Yeah, you did. That's where I found you two, at the front of the club, on the floor. I don't get why girls wear such high heels. I'm all for being sexy but the ones your friend was wearing were bordering on stilts. Anyway, she twisted her ankle walking out. Fell straight onto her ass. I'm pretty sure it's just a sprain but she flat out refused to go to the ER, babbling about looking like an idiot with her folks." He shrugged, not knowing the context of Megs's refusal. Even in her inebriated state, Megs knew the minute she stepped into an ER someone would have recognized her last name and possibly connected it to her parents.

"So I called Troy and Jase and they came out the front to helped me get the two of you home. We got Megs situated with some ice and ibuprofen, incidentally repeatedly saying our last names got old, real quick." He rolled his eyes before continuing, "And then we headed out of the city to your place."

"So what? You followed me up to my apartment and took advantage of me?" I cringed knowing how low my judgment had slipped; I'd let a stranger into my apartment and let him do who knows what to me. "You are such a creep."

"Me? Oh sweetheart, last night was all you. You were all over me in the Suburban on the way home. Practically jerking me off in the back seat. I was just going to get you into your apartment and leave but you begged me to stay. Told me how much of a good girl you'd been your whole life and that you wanted to be bad." His grin widened. "It's the good girls you need to watch out for."

"No, this isn't happening. That sounds nothing like me. I don't jerk off random guys in cars and I don't have one-night stands, especially not with musicians. Hell, I've never even been to a concert." I shook my head, wishing I could go back in time, tell myself to stop drinking, tell myself not to go the VIP section, tell myself to stay home and order pizza instead.

"Whoa. Hold up a minute. You've never been to a concert? Like ever?" Dan recoiled in horror.

"No, never. That however is not relevant, what is relevant is that even when I have been drunk in the past, I have never just gone home with a guy. Someone must have slipped something into my drink. I surely must have been drugged."

That had to be the explanation. Of course, drugs. Let's go with that, except that our drinks hadn't been left unattended at any stage and there had been no opportunity for drugging to take place. Ugh! Back to square one.

"Wow, Ashlyn, You're a virgin. I'm sorry, babe. I had no idea." His voice softened as he looked on me with pity-filled eyes. His ill-directed compassion made me angrier.

"I'm not a fucking virgin, you idiot. I've had sex before."

"I was talking about a concert virgin. I kind of feel sorry for you." He eased back onto the bed unconcerned or oblivious to the telepathic mind bullets I was shooting him with.

"I just told you I think I might have been drugged and you are more concerned with the fact I've never been to a concert before. What is wrong with you?" I narrowed my eyes, wondering if this was an angle or he was just genuinely simple minded.

"Nothing is wrong with me, what is wrong with *you*? You've never been to a concert, had a one-night stand, or jerked off a guy in a car. What the hell did you *do* in college?"

"I studied, asshole. What you are *supposed* to do in college. Be a viable member of society, get a degree, try and gain a future so I wouldn't be a drain on welfare. Of course you wouldn't know about that, would you?" I spat back indignantly.

It wasn't the first time I had been questioned about my lack of college-experience. I wasn't a prude and I wasn't boring, I was a realist. I wasn't gifted with an obscene IQ and while I was far from stupid, I had to work my ass off for every single "A" I got. I literally couldn't afford to fail, knowing even if I passed every class I would still be crucified by student debt well into my thirties. Adding another semester or two because I wanted to party or make out with imbeciles who wouldn't even respect me enough to call me in the morning was not an option. I had to stay the course, knowing my pay-off would come later in life when I would be rewarded with a six-figure salary, making the sacrifice worthwhile.

"Did you have any fun? Like any at all? Your life sounds like it was a major snore." Dan yawned, punctuating his stance. His arm grazed mine as he moved. My bed wasn't huge, and his large body took up much of the space as he sat beside me.

"I had plenty of fun. I didn't have to degrade myself to do it either. Aren't you a little sick of being a crotch hound? Is that what you want on your headstone? Here lies Dan Evans, spent his life in between the legs of women."

Dan stretched his arms and folded them at the back of his neck, the colorful canvas of his breathtakingly chiseled torso flexing with his movements. He noticed my eyes dip and gave me a satisfied smile.

"I'd die happy that's for sure." He raised an eyebrow and smiled, his pleasure evident. "Can you preorder headstones? I'm thinking that would be a good one, and I don't want to forget and then someone write something lame."

"Are you ever serious? Even for like a minute?" Something told me he wasn't joking and somewhere in his mind he was leaving a mental note to commission said headstone. How this man had gotten so far in life was bewildering to me. I refused to believe that his good looks had paved his way to an easier life, that shit would just not be fair.

"Why? So I can conform to whatever fucked-up idea you have in your head? There are plenty of people who like me just the way I am. I see no point changing."

Dan grinned, edging closer to me with a complete disregard for my personal space. He invaded my safe bubble of insulation, dipping his chin so his face was inches from mine. I could feel his breath tickle my skin as he studied me with his dark brown eyes. Their warmth gave me tingles in places, *places* I'd love to see him peering up at me from. My breathing deepened as I felt my nipples harden against the fabric of my bra. What? I wasn't sure if I was angrier at my erotic thoughts or my traitorous body.

"You are making my head hurt." I pulled my knees up to my chest, affording me the slight physical distance I required to think straight, 'cause if I looked at his eyes any longer I was probably going to kiss him. I hated the lack of control I apparently seemed to exercise when I was around him. Why could I not remember? "I can't believe I slept with you. Please tell me we at least used protection?"

"You don't remember last night? Not even a little bit?" His voice sounded skeptical, almost incredulous before he barked out a laugh. "Now who is being offensive?"

"Now is not the time for me to pad your ego. No, I told you. I don't remember last night. I'm sorry if that ruins your reputation but you have at least one dissatisfied customer."

I couldn't admit that while I couldn't remember, I wasn't halfway near as pissed as I was pretending to be. It was bad enough those feelings were waging a war inside my head, battling between high fiving my drunken self for bedding one of the hottest guys I've ever seen, and the disgust I allowed myself to slip into the cliché of being another notch in his belt. Stupid girl. He's never going to respect you. How could I have given it up so easily?

"Oh you are so wrong." He leaned closer ignoring my knee barrier. "I have never left a woman dissatisfied."

I swallowed. All that skin, and he had to be naked underneath that towel. Somewhere, digging deep, I found a small pocket of bravado.

"There is a first time for everything. Don't take it too hard, I'm sure there will be someone just around the corner to scream your name and be thankful. Sorry, but you won't be finding gratitude here."

"You really have no idea, do you?" He narrowed his eyes, as if weighing my words for the first time this morning. Perhaps I should use more simplistic language, he did seem to confuse easily.

"No. I don't, so let's say goodbye and move on. Last night was an oversight. A hiccup. I can move on knowing that men like you are definitely not for me. So for that, I owe you a thank you. Now if you can kindly put on some clothes and vacate my apartment I'd appreciate it."

I turned my back to him, pulling the bed sheets around me. While he might have seen it all last night, he wasn't going to get another peepshow this morning. Besides, facing away from him was definitely the smartest decision I'd had so far. The longer I looked at him, the greater the chance I would be saying something stupid, like offering to towel off the remnants of moisture that clung to the curve of his neck...with my tongue.

"You know I didn't see it initially but you really are an evil bitch and surprisingly that kind of turns me on more." I could hear the smirk in his voice as his finger traced the line of my bare shoulder.

I felt I had no choice as I opened my mouth, and lied. "And you are still the insensitive pig I pegged you for. So now we have established this was purely one sided, please leave and allow me the courtesy of wallowing in my shame privately."

"Fine, babe, I'll leave but we both know you'll be calling me." I felt him move off the bed and heard the thud of his wet towel hitting the floor. All I had to do was turn and I would see what I had obviously been too drunk to remember. I wanted to, desperately, but refused to give him the satisfaction. *Don't turn around. Do NOT turn around!*

"I've taken the liberty of programming my number into your

cell." After some rustling, I caught the telltale sound of a zipper being pulled up. "I was disappointed there wasn't even one dirty selfie on there."

I whipped my body around, too consumed by anger to worry about what I might be seeing. Thankfully while he was still naked from the waist up he was wearing jeans. "You went through my phone?"

"You didn't have a password on it." His satisfied grin danced across his smug, sexy face.

"You can't just invade my privacy like that. Who do you think you are?" I was barely able to spit out the words through my seething rage.

"Relax, babe, it's just a phone. It's not like I went through your underwear drawer." His playfully raised eyebrow did little to convince me he hadn't.

It took every ounce of self-control I owned not to launch myself off the bed and punch him right in the throat. Maybe I was wrong and he was just baiting me, he seemed to gain an inappropriate amount of joy from our exchanges. Let's not overreact just yet.

"Dan. Did you go through my underwear drawer?"

He bit back a grin, unashamedly admitting his perversion. "Okay, maybe a little, but you fell asleep so fast I got bored. Nice stuff by the way. I dig that little red thong you have tucked away."

"Get out," I shouted, grabbing a pillow and tossing it at his head wishing I had a more solid projectile within reach. I didn't even recognize the demonic voice that sprouted from my throat, it was like it was coming out of someone else.

"Okay, Okay. I'm going." He winced in the wake of my small but efficient explosion, snaring his shirt and boots from the floor before stepping to the threshold of my bedroom doorway. "See ya, babe." He waved casually pulling the shirt over his head and walking out of my line of sight, not even offering a sorry. Of course he didn't, he wasn't *sorry*. In his mind, he'd done nothing wrong. I guessed as far as he was concerned, riffling through someone's panty drawer after you had just been *inside of them* was hardly a violation. From that perspective, his stupid and idiotic logic was actually somewhat rational.

As soon as the door slammed shut I grabbed my phone from my nightstand, and scrolled through my contacts. Sure enough, DAN EVANS was now listed with an attached profile photo. It wasn't a typical smiling profile however, oh no. It was of his naked torso, a display of colorful flesh that started from the bottom of his neck and stopped just before it became X-rated. It was the ultimate tease pic: no face, just sculptured, masculine skin. It was raw and unfiltered, just like him. I couldn't stop staring at it; it was possibly the most erotic image I'd even seen. My finger lingered over the glass as I enlarged the image to fill the screen, prompting an unfamiliar tug in my core. I hated him, there is no way I would be calling him and yet I couldn't bring myself to delete it. He was trouble. He was everything I had spent my life trying to avoid – reckless, dangerous and a guaranteed broken heart. He wasn't what I needed and yet I couldn't stop wanting him, even though I needed to. A part of me wished I could recall the details of the night and I wondered if it had been good; the fact he was still here in the morning had to mean it, or *I* wasn't totally bad. Damn him! I wasn't going to allow myself to be dragged down that path. I needed distance, a very cold shower and the biggest cup of coffee I could find, and then I would do whatever it took to exorcise Dan Evans from my body and my mind.

Dan

"**She threw your ass out, huh?**" **Troy's smug fucking face** beamed at me as he slid into the booth and sat opposite. "I tried to tell you last night it was a bad idea dude, and here you are sitting at a Starbucks looking like a douche."

I didn't have much choice when I left Ashlyn's apartment, shit had definitely not gone to plan. I was hoping after working over that tight little body of hers with a session of morning sex, we hit up an IHOP and maybe head back to her piece-of-shit apartment and have a go at round two. Fuck knows I had been packing the biggest set of blue balls all night while I slept beside her, the only hands around my cock being my own. Each time she moaned in her sleep I had to fight the urge not to jack off. 'Cause that would be creepy, right? Does it count as creepy if I jacked off and she didn't know? Fuck there were too many rules for this shit. This broad was messing with my head.

Knowing I was probably going to end up loaded last night, I hadn't driven to the club. Troy, Jase and I had requested our regular driver, TJ, to chauffeur.

TJ had been our wheelman for years. Nothing fazed him; he had seen it all, especially in the early days. Back then, all the boys partook in the spoils, even James after Hannah dumped his ass. Of course, it lasted about five seconds before he went crawling back to her like a pussy and handed her his balls. They had been together forever but got into a few fights early in the piece, the label putting pressure on James to be the single front man to earn us more pussy points with the fans. Had to hand it to her, she wasn't with him for the fame or the money and she would have kept walking if he hadn't fucking begged her for another chance. James wasn't into the lifestyle; he just wanted to sing with his band and have a regular girl to come home to. We all knew they'd end up doing the walk down the aisle.

Alex Stone was another fucking story. That good-looking mother-fucker had girls creaming their pants with his iceman routine. He didn't even try. He was the one I least expected to take a knee. Enter Lexi-Knockout-Reed, a feisty brunette from the Land Down Under. Done deal. And then there were three...Jase, Troy and me.

"Don't even start with me, asswhipe. If I'd known you were going to be such a whiny bitch I would have called a cab." I took another swallow of whatever it was the blonde behind the counter had recommended. Even coffee wasn't simple these days, though I had to admit, whatever it was in the cup was surprisingly delicious.

Troy shook his head. "I'm not a whiny bitch, and you know I'll come pick your ass up from wherever you call me from. You would do the same for me. I get that. What I don't get is why you have such a hard-on for this girl, when she clearly can't stand you."

Girls were a dime a dozen, especially for us. I'd never really chased anyone. Sure I'd throw a line out there and see if I'd get a nibble but I was more a numbers man, and if a girl wasn't feeling me then I wasn't about to waste time trying to convince her. To be honest, I didn't have a solid answer for him, not one that made any sense.

"You don't know that."

Troy eased back into his padded chair, the grin on his face hinted he wouldn't be letting this shit go. "Then how come you're sitting here with me instead of doing your usual morning-after pancake routine with her? I'm actually surprised she didn't come to her senses earlier, I was half expecting to get a call an hour after we dropped the two of you off."

"She pretty much collapsed once we walked in the door. We made out for about ten minutes, and I had barely got my hands on her tits when she passed out."

As much as I hated to admit it, nothing went down last night. Ashlyn had been talking a good game up until I got her front door unlocked, telling me how she'd wanted to just have one night of fun and then it was like the alcohol finally hit her. Honestly, I had been ready to see her up to her apartment and call it a night, and not because I wasn't interested. I knew she was loaded and not making rational decisions, but I wasn't about to take advantage of a girl, even if she was begging. The touching the tits happened before she passed out. Then it was either carry her to her to her room or lay her down on the tired looking couch in her living room.

Troy eyeballed me hard. "Please tell me I'm not going to have to take you outside and beat your ass for being a scumbag." I had no doubt he would take me outside and we'd have to go a few rounds if that kind of shit had gone down. None of us would ever cross that line.

"Look at me, brother. I am many things but not *that,* and I would never put my hands on a woman without her okay. No fucking way, not ever. I didn't even jerk off. I just helped her out of her dress and put her to bed."

Someone should give me a medal 'cause I can tell you it wasn't easy being next to someone that hot and not want to at least have a stroke.

"But you still spent the night? Why?"

"I don't know. I just wanted to stay. She lives in a shithole dude. Seriously, how that place isn't condemned is beyond me and she looked, I don't know, vulnerable, and I didn't want to leave. So I stayed and held her for a while. It was kind of nice."

I shrugged, not really caring it made me sound like a complete pussy. Honestly, if it had been someone else, I would've probably just made something up, but it was Troy and he knew me better than anyone. We had been friends since we were kids and had been in bands together long before Power Station formed. It wasn't until we heard James and Alex were looking to form something solid, that we actually thought we'd play a genuine gig. We'd seen those two kids in the neighborhood and one day we heard them jamming in James's old man's garage. Troy knocked on the door and asked if they wanted a rhythm section, and that's how it started. Being in a band, making money doing what you love is a dream come true, and there isn't a day when I'm not thankful. But to do it with your best friend by your side, that's the motherfuckin' ultimate.

"Am I hearing right? The great Dan Evans spent the night cuddling?" Troy laughed not even trying to hide how much he was enjoying the situation.

"Whatever, asshole. I seem to remember you going home alone, and whether or not I got laid, I still went to bed with the hottest girl in the club."

I could have gone home with the two girls who had been getting hot and heavy with me earlier that night. Now I couldn't even remember their names but truthfully, after seeing Ashlyn, those two broads didn't even stand a chance.

Troy smiled, not the least bit pissed off. "I went home alone because I needed to help *you* get the *hottest girl in the club* and her crazy-ass friend, home. By the way, one of them left their purse in the Suburban. TJ found it in the backseat this morning when he took the car to the Wash and Vac."

"Well, whose was it?" I took another sip of my coffee.

"I don't know, I didn't go through it, dude. Girls have all kinds of weird shit in there, and I prefer to live in ignorance."

"Truth, right?" The man had a point. Some women were like Mary Fucking Poppins with their purses; god knows what you are going to find. A man had no business going in there; some things are best not seen.

"We'll make Jase go through it, the man was in the Army. He's trained for that shit."

"I don't think they covered purse recon in basic training, Dan."
Troy laughed,

"You know he was in IT, right? He wasn't actually on the front
line dodging bullets. Not to take anything away from the man,
'cause straight up I am fucking thankful for his service and
sacrifice, but unless you count hostile computer viruses our man
wasn't in any danger."

The Army is still the Army. I don't care if you are sitting at a
desk or on the front line. Those bastards are tough, and I'd rather
have an IT guy who used to wear camo by my side when shit went
pear-shaped, than a juiced-up security guy whose biggest claim to
fame was being a mall cop.

"You wanna go through the purse?"

"Nope."

"That's what I thought. Jase it is then." I rested my case.

"So getting back to your wild night of spooning. What happened this morning? I assumed even though she isn't your biggest
fan, she still would have been impressed you didn't try anything
last night." Troy continued, not willing to let it go. I swear sometimes he was worse than my ma.

"Yeah, well maybe I didn't tell her that part." I'm not sure why I
didn't, I know I should have told her, but I guess it pissed me off a
little that she had just assumed.

"What? Why the hell not? You'd rather her think you are some
asshole who takes advantage of women? No wonder you aren't
getting laid." Troy chuckled. The bastard actually chuckled.

"Firstly, I can get laid any time I want. You seem to have forgotten, I scored two fine broads last night that would have more
that scratched that itch. Secondly, Ashlyn had zero recollection of
what went down. When she woke up, she just assumed we'd done
the deed. She was too busy telling me she isn't that *kind of girl* to
give me a proper chance to explain. Then she found out I went
through her underwear drawer and she threw me out."

I would have told her, eventually. Not to say that I wasn't
hoping to rectify the no-sex thing in the morning but she
completely lost her shit and told me to leave before I had a

chance.

"You went through her underwear drawer? Jesus, Dan. Do you have any impulse control?"

"Oh not you, too. I was fucking bored, okay? I just looked, it's not like I sniffed it or did anything freaky with it." It was just a look, the way everyone was acting you would have thought I put it on and paraded down fucking 42nd Street. What is the big deal? It's not like she was *in* it at the time. Then, maybe you could call me a pervert.

"Well thank fuck for that. You want to wear ladies panties, knock yourself out but maybe in future get your own Victoria's Secrets."

"You are such a tool." I'd go commando before I'd pull on a pair of panties.

"Tool or not, I need to head back to the city, so if you're done crying into your caramel macchiato, let's make tracks." Troy tilted his head to my now empty cup.

"Is that what I'm drinking?" I angled the cup so I was able to read the writing on the sleeve. "It was actually pretty good." Kudos to the counter chick for her recommendation but I had to agree, it was time to eject. The small coffee shop was starting to fill with too much morning cheer for my liking. We both stood to leave. "Yeah, let's get out of here. I'm starving and there is fuck all in here to eat. No way I was chowing down on a fucking muffin." I needed food.

"What's wrong with muffins?" Troy scoffed. Poor fucker had no clue.

"It's like a poor man's cupcake. No frosting. So fucking dry. I'm putting something cake like in my mouth then I want it to be sweet and fucking tasty. Not some lame-ass muffin that has all the promise of goodness and then leaves you unsatisfied. It's like a girl who stuffs her bra to make her tits look bigger and then you get her home and boom, no big tits. I hate false advertising man, makes me angry."

I slid out of the booth and tossed my empty cup in the trash. Troy followed suit stretching out his back after standing and joined me as we strolled toward the door.

"Does it always come back to tits with you? No wonder you are sitting here with me instead of your girl. I've known you a long time, brother, but some of the shit that comes out of your mouth surprises even me."

"Tits are important, I don't know why you are fighting me on this. Cupcakes too, I love those little fuckers."

"You are so fucking weird, dude."

"Let's go, asswipe."

It was like a standoff. It eyed me from the other side of the room, taunting me. My hands fisted in agitation as I sat in the armchair across from it, watching it, wondering why something so small was giving me such a headache. I'm from the Bronx for Christ's sake, it's not like I had led a sheltered life. I've never backed away from a confrontation, not ever. And we have played some shitty dive bars in our time, especially when we first started out. Hell, some of those places we'd been lucky to walk out in one piece, and yet if someone were itching for a fight I would look them dead in the fucking eye and ask them if we had business. Now, I was getting my ass kicked by a six-inch, glittery purse that sat on my fucking coffee table. What's worse is that I'd rather take my chances with a drunk Giants fan from Jersey than crack that fucker open.

"FUCK!"

I moved to the edge of the chair wondering where the hell I'd left my balls. It was a purse, for fuck's sake, not a fucking bomb. I looked over at the half-eaten box of cupcakes sitting beside it, the lid still cracked open, reminding me I had smashed four of those bad boys on the way to my apartment. And despite Troy being an argumentative bastard and not being on the same page with my cupcake love, I let the big guy snare a couple of them too. I was a giving kind of guy. I looked away from the box, deciding I was probably already way too hyped on sugar to eat anymore, which is probably why I was jittery as fuck.

I ran my hands through my hair, frustrated, knowing I was just going to have to man up. Jase had already shot down my idea that he do it when I called him on the car ride over, laughing his ass off telling me to stop being a pussy and do it myself. What's the worst that could be in there? A tampon? It's not like I hadn't seen one of those before. Jase was right. I was being a pussy.

"Okay then, let's do this." I cracked my knuckles as I reached over and snagged it off the coffee table. I had half expected for it to shock me or something. For it to have some magical powers that meant if anyone with a dick opened it they'd get Tasered or some shit. Nothing. No sparks. No jolt of electricity passing through my body. Nada. Well thank fuck for that.

Slowly, I popped open the clasp. It looked innocent enough so I might as well dive in there and see if there was an ID or something. It had to be either Ashlyn's or Megs's and I hadn't paid enough attention to which of them had been holding this thing when they had gotten into the car. Both of them had fished out their apartment keys before we left the Suburban with Ash, who'd also pulled her phone out so she could text Megs she was home when we pulled up to her building. So that didn't yield any clues either.

I shook the contents onto the coffee table and out rolled a lipstick, a few dollar bills, and a condom. Nice, this was like CSI...piecing together a profile based on random shit.

I tossed the dollar bills to the side and I moved on to the condom. It was standard, nothing exciting. *Ribbed for her pleasure.* That shit always made me laugh. What kind of numbnuts needs a special condom to get off his woman? Straight up, if he is relying on the latex *for her pleasure* he is not doing it right. When I'm with a girl, I make her come at least once before I even stick my dick inside her. I get her nice and lubed up, soft and ready for me, so when I finally get my cock in her, she is so wound up she has no choice but to come again. I don't get the amount of girls I do solely 'cause I'm a good-looking guy. Women know when they are with me, I take care of them. I might not call them back later but while I'm fucking them, no one else exists. I was getting hard just thinking about it. Seriously, I was going to need to go jerk off soon or my dick was going to fall off. It had been hard so many times in the last twenty-four hours. I was surprised I still had the ability to fucking walk.

Next up, lipstick. I slid open the lid and rolled up the stick. Red. Like let-me-fuck-your-mouth red. I knew this color. I had washed it from my neck early this morning in Ashlyn's shower. This was hers. I'd bet my balls on it. I rolled the stick back down, imagining the color on her lips like it had been last night. That sweet, fucking mouth that talked way too much trash. Yeah, I wanted that mouth. I wanted to own every inch of those beautiful full lips, watch them stretch around the head of my cock while those sweet green eyes looked up at me.

"Get it together, asshole." I laughed out loud as I shoved the lipstick back into the purse, and had a quick look to see if there was anything else in there. Sure enough, there was a small zip sewed into the lining, and I'd figured I'd come this far, I might as well continue, right? I pulled the zipper across, the pocket it opened barely big enough for me to slide a finger or two inside. I pulled out a driver's license and an ATM card. If there were any doubts as to who the owner of the purse was before, I could put them to bed. Ashlyn's passive face looked up at me from the plastic, Boston-issued ID. She was about to turn twenty-eight, her birthday was in less than a week, and either she had never gotten around to changing her address to New York or she didn't plan on sticking around for very long. I tapped the card against my fingers hoping she wasn't planning on leaving soon. No one ever looked good with a DMV issued photo, but fuck me if she didn't look drop-dead gorgeous. She wasn't fancied up with makeup and her hair was pulled away from her face. She didn't need all that stuff to make her look good. She was beautiful without it.

"Fuck!" I closed my eyes and leaned back into my armchair. What was it about this girl that was turning my brain into a pretzel? It wasn't just the way she looked, though that sure as shit didn't hurt, but it was more than that. For the first time, I think I was actually *interested* in someone. I needed to see her again and now I had my opportunity. I would play it smart; for this girl, I was going need more than just my usual tricks.

9

Ashlyn

"MEGS!" I YELLED INTO THE PHONE WITHOUT GIVING HER THE opportunity to say hello. I needed to debrief and I needed it now. I sat on the edge of my bed, still reeling from the events of the morning.

"Ash?" Megs groaned into the phone. "My ankle is killing me. What happened last night and why aren't you here?" Her recollection was obviously just as unreliable as mine. Note to self - keep better track of how many cocktails consumed and don't go wandering around a club looking for trouble.

"So much happened last night. You fell as we were leaving *Panic*. I think we should probably go get it X-rayed. What do you remember?" I sighed knowing it was up to me to piece the riddle together.

"Did we meet Power Station last night?"

"Well I guess you could call it meeting them."

I would say what happened last night went a little beyond just an introduction, considering I woke up with one of the band members in my bed.

"The details are foggy. I think I remember hugging Troy Harris? Did you make out with Dan Evans?"

I let out a long, slow breath. Megs was my best friend. Not only did I tell her everything but I also needed a sounding board. I needed her to help me make sense of this in my head, how I could have done something so out of character. "I think I did more than just make out with him."

"Ashlyn. You better start talking and fill me in with details."

"Let me get dressed and I will come to you. There is way too much to discuss over the phone. Do you need me to get you anything on my way over?"

"You don't happen to have any Percocet do you?"

"No, Megs. While I'm sure the apartment downstairs is probably a meth lab, I don't actually live in a drug store."

"Okay, then just get me the biggest coffee you can find and maybe a muffin. And hurry, I need details."

"I'll be there soon. Chill."

We said our goodbyes and ended the call. Tossing the phone onto my bed, I moved into my tiny bathroom. The fuzzy, faded bathmat was still damp from when Dan had taken his shower. He had been naked in this very spot. I tried to ignore my excitement as I stripped off my clothes. Shit. I looked around my bathroom in a moment of dread. He had seen this. A bra hanging from the towel rack, my messy vanity that was crammed with cosmetics and skin care. My wicker laundry hamper filled with dirty socks and polo shirts from the bar. The chipped paint, ugly pea-green tub with it's discolored shower curtain. The rust-covered faucet that spewed brown water for a few seconds when you ran the water for the first time in the morning. He had seen all of this. Mortified. That was probably the only apt description of what I was feeling. How he hadn't run a mile the minute he stepped inside was beyond me. I shook my head, solidifying my silent resolve to never see him again as I turned on the faucet and stepped inside the tub.

The old pipes groaned in protest through the thin plaster wall as I turned up the water to maximum capacity. It was the only way to achieve any kind of water pressure and even then it wasn't great. Still, today I had bigger problems than my ancient bathroom.

I showered and then dressed quickly, throwing on a pair of

jeans and an old T-shirt before pulling on a pair of Vans. I just needed to grab my purse, my phone, and get out of here.

Now, where did I put my clutch from last night? It had my ID and my ATM card in there and while there was probably less than a hundred dollars in my savings account, the least I could do was spring for coffee this morning given Megs had paid for our night out yesterday. Hmm. Where did I leave it? I searched in the regular spots, the bedroom, and the kitchen counter - the places I would usually toss it when I walked in the apartment. Though given last night was not usual, it could be anywhere.

I ate up valuable time tearing from room to room, trying to locate the small, sequined culprit, but came up empty. I had my keys and my phone, so where was my clutch? I slumped onto my bed, willing it to reappear but sadly my *willing* did nothing but intensify the headache I was already fighting.

Giving up any hope of finding it, at least in the immediate future, I grabbed a random twenty-dollar bill I had found in my change jar and a handful of coins, and decided I would look harder when I got home. It had to be here somewhere.

"Hey." Megs greeted me at the door, hobbling while trying to balance a bag of frozen peas on her ankle. "I was getting concerned and was going to send out a search party."

"Sorry, Megs. I couldn't find my purse from last night. It had my ATM card in there. I still don't know where it is." I handed her the prized coffee before opening the paper bag that housed her muffin.

"Where did you leave it?" Megs asked, balancing her precious muffin and coffee as she hopped back to the sofa where she allowed herself to fall into the large, plush cushions. Once settled, she lifted the lid from her cup to lick the whip off the top of her coffee.

"If I knew where I left it, it wouldn't be lost." I strolled out of the hallway and joined her on the sofa, pulling my cup of coffee out of the cardboard carrier and taking a sip.

Megs blew over the surface of her cup before taking a big gulp. "Okay, well you obviously got into your apartment so you must have had it on the way home...wait. How did we get home?"

"The Power Station Express," I deadpanned.

"They drove us home?" Megs's eyes widened.

"Yeah, well according to Dan, so not sure how reliable my information is." I bristled, annoyed I was at the mercy of his version of events.

"You better start telling me everything you know, Ashlyn Marie, or you are going to be wearing this coffee." Megs held up her paper cup up to verify she wasn't kidding.

"Okay, okay." I took a long breath and settled in, this story was going to take a while.

I started explaining how Dan had found us at the club's entrance, and how Megs's Louboutins were responsible for her rather undignified spill. Deciding to play hero, when clearly no one had asked him to, Dan had stepped in and with the help of Jason and Troy, bundled both of us into their car to drive us home. In reality, it could be seen as kidnap, who just takes two girls and puts them into a car? My theory was solid except obviously I hadn't been resistant to the idea and according to him, had my hands all over him on the ride home. A vague recollection of giggling in the back seat flashed into my mind as I recounted the story.

"Let me touch you." I moved my hands down his chest as I pushed my lips against his mouth, his hand threading through my hair as our kiss deepened.

"Fuck," he groaned as I flattened my palm against the front of his jeans, he was hard. The denim between us was so tight it left little to the imagination.

"I'm such a good girl, such a good, good girl," I moaned into his mouth, sliding my hand into the front of his pants. He hissed as my fingertips made contact with his skin.

"Yeah, you're really good." He gently eased my hand away from his erection, his sexy smile making me want him more. "But unless you want me to come in your hand you are going to need to stop

that, not that I have a problem with it, 'cause I don't, but I think we should probably get your friend home first."

"I want you, Dan. I want to have sex with you," I whispered into his ear, trying to be seductive but for some reason the word sex sounded so funny coming out of my mouth, it made me laugh.

Dan teased my lower lip down with his thumb. "Ashlyn, you're so drunk you have no idea what you're saying right now, babe."

It's strange, it was as if I was someone else, like I could say or do anything I wanted. I was braver, bolder, and his hand on my lips just turned me on more. I captured his thumb with my teeth, drew it into my mouth and sucked it hard. His jaw tightened. "Babe, seriously. I'm not even kidding. I'm so primed right now I'm going to blow my load in my jeans like a thirteen-year-old boy. I need you to really think about what we are doing, I'm not smart enough to be thinking for the both of us."

"It's killing me," Megs whined from the row of seats behind, reminding us she was still with us. "It's okay, Troy Harris, you can chop it off, I'll be brave."

"Megs, we're not going to chop off your foot." Troy chuckled, his voice surprisingly calm. "It looks like just a sprain. I still think we should swing by the ER and get it looked at."

"Noooooooo," Megs begged, sounding less like the twenty-nine-year-old professional she was and more like she just caught underage drinking. "They'll tell my dad. I'll be a laughing stock. We can't go to the hospital. Just get me home."

"Okay, Megs, we'll get you home." Troy tried to comfort Megs and he was being so incredibly sweet with her. "If you twist around, I can elevate your foot for you. Hopefully it will help with the swelling."

As I leaned up against Dan's chest, a sense of ease flowed through me. Strangely, it was as if I didn't have to worry about Megs. She was in good hands. Whatever my thoughts had been about these guys, I was wrong. They weren't bad guys.

"Oh thank you, Troy Harris," Megs crooned, her discomfort eased by Troy's hands on her feet.

"Megs, just Troy. Seriously, just Troy." Despite it being the fiftieth time Troy had told Megs, there was no annoyance in his voice.

"I like saying your name though...it's sexy, like you, Troy Harris," Megs said sweetly.

"So you keep saying." He chuckled.

"I have to hand it to you, Dan, I was convinced tonight was going to blow but it has been rather amusing." Jason's voice floated from the front seat. I had forgotten he was with us, obviously sitting next to the mysterious driver who had barely spoken.

"Whatever, douchebag." Dan flipped him off which for some inane reason made me laugh.

"That's such a funny word." I smiled as my hands once again slithered southward.

"You girls are so wasted." Dan smirked as he gently stroked my arm.

I tilted my head to look at him saying the words I'd been dying to say all night. "Take me to bed, Dan. Stay with me tonight."

"Oh shit." I rubbed my hands across my face, Dan hadn't seduced me. I had seduced him. A fractured memory was providing more insight as to how Dan ended up in my apartment last night.

"What? What *oh shit*? Tell me I didn't make an even bigger ass of myself than it sounded like." Megs paled. While I had wanted to spare her the details, I figured it was better to be honest and tell her exactly what I remembered. Her muffin and her coffee forgotten as she carefully placed them on the side table. Obviously, the caffeine hit and nourishment was going to have to wait.

"I threw myself at him, Megs. He confronted me with it this morning and I denied it. I flat out refused to hear him out, but I remember being in the car, I remember having my hands all over him and asking him to spend the night." Sipping my coffee, not willing to forgo my caffeine injection.

"So you slept with him?" Megs's eyes widened.

"I guess I did because he was still there this morning, but I honestly can't remember." My fingers squeezed at the bridge of my nose. "Who forgets they had sex? Is that even possible to have sex and have no recollection of it at all?" I mean, surely I should have remembered something? It's not like I had sex a lot, surely it would have stood out in my brain as something noteworthy.

"There's a few times I'd rather forget but sadly they are still with me," Megs commiserated. "So you guys dropped me off and then you went to back to your place. Do you remember anything about getting home?"

I closed my eyes, trying to force the fragmented night to somehow piece itself together in temporal lobe.

"Babe, you sure this is where you live?" Dan glanced out of the tinted window of the Suburban, studying the derelict building I had directed the driver to.

"Yes, this is me. I have to grab my keys, the security light is out again and I can never find the keyhole in the dark." I fumbled in my clutch for my keys, pulling out my phone instead. "I have to text Megs, she likes to know I get home safe. Unless I stay at her house, then she automatically knows I'm okay." I hoped the sentence made sense to Dan, the words didn't sound right as they spilled from my mouth but there wasn't a lot I could do to steer them into anything more coherent.

Dan opened the door as I finally fished out my keys. I held them up victoriously, jingling them in my fingers as I placed my clutch on the seat beside me and unhooked my seatbelt.

Dan stepped out of the car and walked around to my side of the car. "Let me walk you up, okay?"

"You aren't staying? You said you would stay." I pouted as I stepped onto the sidewalk, doing my best puppy dog impression and trying to not drop my keys or my phone.

Dan pulled me into a hug, his breath tickling my ear. "Babe, I don't think that's a good idea. I'm really trying not to be a piece of shit here and I have to tell you, my dick wants to kick my ass right now."

"But I want you." I wrapped my arms around his neck, ignoring the idling car waiting for his return. "Maybe I should have words with your dick, we both seem to want the same things."

"Fuck, Ashlyn." He released himself from my embrace. "Look, give me one minute."

He moved over to the car and spoke to Troy through the window. I couldn't hear what was being said but it felt like victory. I had convinced him to stay. He was going to have sex with me. It was going to be good sex too, I bet. He looked like he was built for it and I couldn't tell you the last time I actually came. Well not when a guy was present anyway. Dan Evans was going to make me orgasm.

"Okay, babe, lead the way." He put his arm around me and *walked me up the stairs of my apartment building.*

While I was no closer to finding out how *good* the sex had been, I was fairly sure I knew where my clutch was. Probably sitting on the backseat of the Suburban, where I had stupidly left it after grabbing my keys. I scrubbed my face with my hands. I was going to have to call him. I wasn't sure if it was excitement or dread bubbling in the pit of my stomach.

"I have to call him," I vocalized, clueing Megs into my internal thoughts.

"Well I was hoping if you'd slept with him, at the very least you were going to see each other again."

"I hadn't planned on it but I guess I don't have much choice. Unless I get him to UPS my clutch to me." I laughed, knowing how ridiculous that sounded. We were adults, sure it might be awkward, but we could move past it so that he could give me my misplaced item and I could try to salvage some self-respect.

I placed my half-empty cup on the coffee table in front of me and pulled my phone from my pocket. I scrolled down my contact list, angling my screen away from Megs so she wasn't able to see the sensual shot Dan had gifted me with this morning. My finger hovered over his name, not quite able to make that final step.

"Just call him already." Megs gently shoved my shoulder.

"Don't rush me. I'm calling." I pressed call before I had the opportunity to chicken out. My heart was beating so fast, I was positive he was going to be able to hear it.

"Yo. Talk to me." Dan's voice burst from the speaker. His New York accent seemed more pronounced on the phone.

"Dan? Is that you?" I knew it was him, so I'm not sure why I asked for confirmation. No doubt my subconscious was buying me some precious time so I could work out what I was going to say.

"Ashlyn." He said my name and all I could think about was him standing in my room, wearing only a towel. "Miss me already? I knew you'd call."

His arrogance grated on me. Had this been his plan the whole time? Knowing I would have no choice but to call? No, while Dan was cocky I didn't think he would be *that* premeditated. Still, I decided to play it safe. "Yeah well, this isn't really a social call, so don't get too excited. I need my clutch, I left it in your car."

"You left your clutch in the car? Is that some kind of riddle?" The confusion in his voice was adorable. "Isn't that where a clutch belongs?"

"Not a clutch for gears. An evening bag, a clutch." I bit back my smile as I explained, Megs watching me closely.

"Your purse?"

"Yes, my purse. I think I left it in the Suburban. Can you have your driver look for me?"

"Yeah, you left it. Troy had it with him when he came and picked me up this morning."

"Well if you had it this morning, why didn't you bring it to me?" I was slightly annoyed I had been worried about it the whole morning and Dan had known the whole time.

"'Cause you were moody and I was hungry."

"Okay, so why didn't you bring it to me after you had breakfast?" I tried to remain calm despite his bogus reasoning. Five minutes. It would have taken five minutes to make the exchange and then he could have gone on to stuff his face with whatever he chose to.

"Oh we didn't eat in Brooklyn, we drove back to Manhattan. I wanted cupcakes."

I pulled the phone away from my ear and stared at it. I shook my head at Megs as I tried to follow the conversation. He wanted cupcakes? Is he for real? Or is he just pushing to see how far the dopey routine will go before I blew.

"So why didn't you call me then?"

"Um, to ask if you wanted cupcakes?"

"No! To tell me you had my purse!"

"I didn't have your number."

"How do you not have my number? You went through my

phone and programed in yours."

What was it about this guy that seemed to push my buttons so hard? There was no middle ground with him. The embarrassment I had felt when I started this conversation had long been forgotten. In its place was a simmering rage that at any point could explode into something more substantial.

"I just looked at your photos, I didn't go through your contact list. Besides, stealing your number is kind of an invasion of privacy."

"Are you kidding me? You went through the photos on my phone and my underwear drawer but you drew the line at my *number*?"

Megs stared opened mouthed as she sat beside me. I possibly had forgotten to mention the fact Dan had been sniffing around in my panty drawer, my brain misfiring as the memories of the evening were coming back to me in slow bursts.

"Well...yeah. I'm not a stalker, babe."

What in the hell? His logic made no sense. None at all. Not even a little. Was he just trying to infuriate me?

"Just give me my freaking purse back," I spat out through my clenched jaw.

"Geez no need to get mad about it. It's not like I was going to keep it. I figured you'd call eventually."

He seemed so unaffected. This wasn't an act; he really just had a basic and simplistic view of things. How he had managed to get through life unscathed astounded me. Perhaps I should be impressed but it only served to remind me of the injustice in life, how not everyone had to work hard for their rewards.

"Okay, so I've called. Can I have it back please?"

"Sure, especially seeing as you said please." I sensed his smile through the phone. "I'll pick you up for lunch in an hour? That good?"

"What? No! We're not having lunch."

Did he just ask me on a date? While we were in the middle of a heated discussion? This man had zero boundaries, either that or an incredible self-assurance with no fear of failure.

"We can do dinner if you prefer, I just figured you'd want your shit back sooner."

"No, no dinner either. I just want my stuff. I'm not going out with you."

"But you have to meet me somewhere so I can give it back to you, right? I don't see the problem," he reasoned, unable to see why I was refusing his offer.

I took a deep breath while Megs tapped my arm, silently encouraging me to go. I was glad I was only going to have to recount the one side of the conversation she hadn't heard, though I'm guessing she was catching the vibe all by herself without my input. I needed to be honest. Something about him fried my brain. I didn't trust myself around him.

"The problem is that when I'm around you, I obviously exercise poor judgment. So I think it's best if you just drop off the bag and we go our separate ways. No dates."

"Lunch isn't a date." Dan laughed.

"Are you holding my clutch for ransom?" I half shouted into the phone, still a little hung over and too tired to deal with his circular logic. He just didn't get it.

"Why are you being so bitchy? I'm trying to be a good guy here. I have to see you anyway to give you your purse so let me buy you some lunch."

"If I'm bitchy, why would you want to buy me lunch?"

"Even bitches have to eat, don't they?" He laughed, clearly enjoying himself.

"Calling me a bitch is not endearing yourself." I narrowed my eyes, unsure of whether or not I was glad he couldn't see me right now.

"You're a bitch, I'm an asshole. Can we move on to lunch already?"

"Ugh. Fine. Buy me lunch."

"So where do you want to go?"

"Just meet me at Applebee's on West 42nd."

"You want to go to Applebee's?"

"Yes! Just meet me there in half an hour, okay? And bring my purse."

"Okay, see you then."

I ended the call and pushed my hands into my face. "He is so impossible," I groaned, annoyed he had somehow talked me into going on a date with him.

"Ash, unless you are in high school, Applebee's isn't a date." Megs laughed, pulling me into a hug. "Applebee's?" she repeated as she pulled a funny face.

"I tried to think of a place I was least likely to want to get naked around him. I clearly can't be trusted."

"Sweetie, you've already slept with him. A meal isn't going to kill you. Go have fun and then come back and tell me all of the details." Megs playfully pushed my shoulder. Of course, she was right. I could sit across a table and eat and not feel the need to sleep with him again. If anything, this would be the closure I needed. I would ask him calmly exactly what had happened last night and then say a final goodbye. I looked down at my phone's darkened screen, sitting in my lap. That goodbye would definitely be bittersweet.

"CAN I GET YOU SOMETHING TO DRINK WHILE YOU WAIT ON YOUR guest?" the pretty blonde waitress asked as I drummed my fingers across the table. She had to be barely twenty-one but her smile told me that if I were into it, she would be happy to show me a different kind of menu.

"No, I'm fine for now, thanks." I smiled back, not wanting to cash in on what she was offering. This was so unlike me. Ordinarily I would have taken her number and found out exactly what was hiding underneath that little black polo she was wearing.

"Okay, well let me know if you change your mind." Her hand floated down and trailed along the top of my knuckles.

So this is why Stone got so much pussy? Girls liked it when you pretended not to be interested. Well, fuck me. Wasn't that just the revelation of the century? Son of a bitch could have clued me onto this earlier though.

I gave her a smile, figuring I had to give her something, and that seemed to satisfy her. She sauntered off leaving me to sit in the booth by myself like a douche. I hadn't even bothered to check out her ass as she walked away. I must be off my game.

I had arrived at Ashlyn's choice of restaurant right on time but she still hadn't showed. I asked for a booth toward the back and let the waitress know I was expecting a guest, although why she picked this venue was a mystery. I can't remember the last time I was in one of these places. Still the location was unimportant, she had agreed to meet me and I had that tiny, sparkly purse to thank.

"Hey, sorry I'm late." Ashlyn rushed in, her face a little flushed. "I walked from Megs's apartment." She collapsed into the bench seat opposite me. "It took a little longer than I thought."

"It's okay, babe, I haven't been waiting long." I watched as she nervously picked up the menu in front of her, a few strands of unruly red hair fell across her face, the rest of her curls were pulled back away from her face and secured by a hair tie. She looked completely different, no business gear or short dress and come-fuck-me heels. Just a pair of jeans, some faded bar T-shirt, a pair of Vans kicks, and no makeup. My dick punched out in my jeans in appreciation. She was stunning.

"Here," I slid the purse across the table, feeling kind of stupid staring at her while she sat uncomfortably studying her menu. "I went through it but just to see whose it was. I wasn't doing anything shady."

She glanced up, her big green eyes looked at me and then dropped to the purse on the table. "Thank you. There wasn't much in there for you to see."

She looked awkward, nervous almost. It had seemed like such a good idea at the time, getting another opportunity to see her but now I felt like a giant dick making her sit here when she didn't want to be.

"Look, Ashlyn," I couldn't believe I was about to fucking say what I was about to, both hating myself but knowing it was the right thing to do, "you don't have to stay, you have your purse. You can take off if you want."

Those big green eyes nailed me as she disregarded her menu. "Dan, I'm sorry. This is just really—"

"Weird?" I finished for her. She wasn't hard to read; I felt the vibe the minute she walked in.

Strangely, I hated she felt that way and what I hated even more was that she was feeling it because of me. Maybe touching all that girl stuff from her purse did something to my balls 'cause seeing her like this was giving me feelings and shit. Next I'm gonna need a fucking box of Tampax and start blubbering while watching *The Notebook*. It's not like I hadn't cared about girls' feelings in the past, they just seemed less important than my own. Yeah, I know I'm an asshole, but I just didn't feeling like being one right now, even if the rest of my body didn't agree.

"Yeah, weird. I've never had a one-night stand before so yeah sitting across from you pretending you haven't seen me naked is...well it's awkward." She smiled and damn if that didn't make me want to reach across the table and kiss those sweet lips.

"Ashlyn, listen...about last night." My dick punched out in protest, warning me to keep my big fucking mouth shut. "I don't think you really know what went down." Her eyes widened, as she waited for me to finish. "We didn't sleep together last night. I mean we slept together, but we didn't fuck." I managed to say the word fuck just as the blonde waitress returned to take our drinks order.

"Uh...can I get you guys some drinks to start off with, maybe some appetizers?" She fumbled through her regular, obviously rehearsed speech. Thank fuck she didn't ask if we wanted to hear the specials.

"You want a soda or something?" I asked Ashlyn who continued to stare silently. I wasn't able to get a read on whether it was a surprise we-hadn't-slept-together or you're-an-asshole-I-want-to-hurt-you look. I'm going to be honest, both of them kinda blew.

She nodded, responding, "Coke."

"Make that two."

The waitress quickly left after it became obvious we were in the middle of something.

"Then we didn't do *it*?" Ashlyn leaned closer across the table. "But I remember, telling you I wanted to, in the car. You tried to talk me out of it but I..." She didn't need to finish the sentence. I remember that car ride; hardest thing I ever had to do was ask her to cool it. I wanted her so bad but I knew it was just the booze talking.

"Yeah, you said that and I have to admit, you weren't making it easy for me. We made out but that's it. You were drunk and you passed out. Nothing happened." I looked her in eye, I don't know why, but it was important to me that she knew it was the truth.

"You could have...there are guys that would have..." I hadn't seen this side of her; she'd always come across so confidently, so feisty. I wasn't sure if she was embarrassed or the realization of what could have gone down hit her.

"What? Done it anyway? Fuck, Ashlyn, no. I know you don't think very highly of me and that's fine, but if I'm going to be with a girl then she has to be able to say she wants it and she is going to damn well remember what it felt like after we're done."

"But if we didn't have sex, why did you stay?" Her green eyes sparkled with genuine curiosity.

"'Cause you asked me to." It didn't make a lot of sense to me, either. I'm not a cuddler. The whole big spoon, little spoon thing bewilders me and yet, last night, it just felt right.

"But I've been nothing but horrible to you. I don't understand." She stared me down, owning the fact she'd been bitchy.

I couldn't help laugh, all that feisty bullshit made my balls get tight. If her intention had been to turn me off, she had failed. "Yeah, you haven't been my biggest fan but you're honest and I can respect that, and the shit you said didn't really bother me."

"How? How can it not bother you? I mean honestly, doesn't it hurt when people say mean things about you?"

"Hell, no. Look at me. I am doing what I love and getting paid bank to do it. People think I'm not the smartest guy in the world but who the fuck cares? People slave away every fucking day killing themselves lining someone else's pocket with green, hating their jobs and hating their lives. I've got none of that. This is exactly what I wanted to be doing. This is exactly who I want to be. I get to travel the world and play gigs with my four best friends who happen to be some of the coolest people I know, even though sometimes they act like a bunch of douchebags."

Admittedly, I did care what *some* people thought. That group—the people I cared about—was very small however. Everyone else could take their best shot and it would slide right off me. Hell I'd be in a nuthouse if I bought into my own press. Half of the shit printed was genuine lies but I didn't care enough to set them straight.

"I just don't understand how you can be so cool about it." Ashlyn shook her head, for some reason she was having difficulty accepting my reasoning. Maybe I wasn't explaining myself clearly enough. No one had ever bothered to ask me before so it's not like I had a speech prepared.

"Easy, I'm not trying to live up to anyone's ideals, babe. I've got my own gauge. I'm fine with it."

The waitress came back with our sodas and seeing as Ashlyn had made the choice to stay, we decided to order. I was freaking starving so went with a cheeseburger and fries while she opted for a standard BLT. At least she didn't order a salad. Girls that didn't eat were always super cranky and I think Ashlyn had enough attitude without adding being mad because she was hungry to the equation.

"Wow, Dan, I feel like I owe you an apology." Ashlyn watched as the waitress left the table. I kind of wished I hadn't have left the venue up to her. The place was starting to fill with families and tourists and even though we were seated toward the back, it was getting noisy.

"For what?" We'd already placed our order so if she was having second thoughts about being here, she should have said something earlier.

She leaned in so I could hear her better over the kid that was crying two booths over 'cause he had to eat his Mac 'n' Cheese before his mom would let him have dessert. "I judged you. Assumed the stereotype was right."

"Ha, well for the most part it kind of is. James is the sensitive one - girls eat that I'm-going-to-love-you-forever bullshit. Alex is the cool one - he has the iceman routine down and it drives girls fucking crazy. Troy is like a big teddy bear – big-ass dude, but hilarious and has a really good heart so naturally he has no problem with the ladies either. Jason is the smart one – serious, but one of the most loyal dudes I know. Girls get wet knowing that he is technically an IT nerd and if the earth tilts off its axis and the band was to end tomorrow, he could go right into a job that pulls six-figures. And that just leaves me."

"The bad boy. The life of the party, sleeps around and the one ladies want to try and tame," she concluded, thinking she had me all worked out.

"Bad boy makes me sound like a jerk-off." I rolled my eyes, fucking bad boy? Made me think of eighteen-year-old punks from fucking Beverly Hills driving around in their old man's Porsches. I think not. "Let's think of something else instead."

"But that's why girls want to sleep with you - the challenge." Ashlyn smiled, no fucking doubt pleased she had hit a nerve.

"I don't know, Ash. I never really asked any of them." I rubbed the back of my neck thinking this was dangerous territory. Wasn't it fucking bad to be talking about other women with the chick you hoped to get lucky with? I'm sure Stone told me something, not that I'd ever admit he was right, but when it came to ladies, the asshole knew his stuff. "It's not like I give them a survey to fill out after."

"Might be an interesting marketing exercise."

She obviously wasn't letting it go, and it was making me confused. Were we supposed to be talking about it or not? I wish I had a phone-a-friend option 'cause I could use a lifeline right now. It was a hell of a lot easier just to get them in bed; conversation was a fucking minefield.

"Nah, I don't want to know."

"C'mon, Dan, you're not that shallow. You are sitting in an Apple-bee's with a girl who you haven't slept with, having a normal conversation. I think maybe there's more to you than that."

"Well, maybe that's how I am and you are just seeing me differently." I needed to change the direction of this conversation quickly. "I'm the same guy you met when you were staring at Stone's ass. This place is kind of lame though. I should've vetoed the decision and made you meet me at Hooters."

"I was not staring at Alex's ass."

The red that crept up her cheeks told me different and damn if that didn't make me jealous of that bastard.

Our server approached the table, balancing a plate in each hand. He was a pimply kid who probably had more hair on his chin than he did on his balls. Shady little shit's smile widened as he placed the plate in front of Ashlyn, making her visibly relax and sit up straighter in her chair. He looked over at me, the smug smile disappearing as I eyeballed him. He put the plate down, and wouldn't you know the kid must have been a genius 'cause he wisely kicked up the speed and took off. I wasn't about to let the Stone issue go, hell no was she getting out of it that easy.

"Ashlyn, come on. I thought we were being honest here."

She took a sip of her Coke before answering, "Fine, I'll admit it. Can we move on? Don't you dare tell him, I'll deny it and then say the reason we haven't had sex is because you couldn't get it up. Incidentally, I wouldn't have minded Hooters, I like their chicken wings."

I couldn't help myself, bursting into laughter. Wow, she was good. I backed her into a corner and she came out swinging. Fuck if that didn't just make me want her more. "No one would believe you, sweetheart. My cock has never had a problem getting it up. But don't worry your secret crush is safe with me. Oh and Ashlyn, I'd marry a plate of Hooters wings if that shit were legal."

"See, even *bad boys* want a commitment." She stole a French fry from my plate and popped it into her smirking mouth.

I could see this *bad boy* bullshit was going to give me grief. "You know, if Troy hears you calling me that he's going to be paying me out for weeks."

"It's funny, I know I met him last night but I don't remember a whole lot about him." Ashlyn turned her attention back to her own plate, picking up half her sandwich.

"Yeah, you did. He found you and your friend Megs trying to sneak into the VIP section. Maybe if you play your cards right, you might get to meet him again." I picked up my burger and took a bite. While our meeting might have started off weird, we had slipped into something else and it felt really good. I wasn't going to let this chick walk away, that's for sure.

"Why? You see us hanging out again after this? Isn't that kind of bad for your image, spending time with a girl you're not sleeping with." Ashlyn took another bite of her sandwich.

"Well maybe you should sleep with me and we can save my reputation," I suggested. Mighty fine suggestion too if you ask me, I wanted her under me so badly my balls hurt.

"No, Dan. As tempting as that offer is, I'm going to have to decline." She shot me down without even considering it. Time to work a new angle.

"Your loss then." I shrugged before adding, "Maybe you can be my exception?"

"Your exception? What do you mean?" She stopped eating and gave me her full attention. I liked it, her eyes on me, listening to what I was saying. Not just because she wanted to end up underneath me but because she honestly wanted to hear what I had to say. It had never really mattered before, having a girl's attention for reasons other than my dick. Now that I had it, I wasn't in a hurry to give it up.

"I mean, this has been surprisingly kind of nice. I don't usually just hang with girls and as long as you don't spread any bullshit rumors about me being sap or having a limp dick maybe we should do this again." I gave her a smile, knowing it would probably set her off again.

"Spread rumors about you?" She huffed from across the table. "If anyone is spreading rumors it will be you about me."

"Yeah well, we can only improve your reputation with that rumor. Who the fuck has never been to a concert in their lives? I'm still in fucking shock." I coughed trying to suppress a laugh. I was enjoying pushing her buttons a little too much for my own good.

"I believe there were other things on that list too: a one-night stand and jerking off a guy in a car," she threw back, fighting a grin.

"Well I hate to break it to you, but the jerking off thing…you did it last night. You were pretty good for a rookie." I leaned back, my cock suddenly needing more room in my pants. The memories of last night were going to be in rotation in my spank bank for weeks.

"Oh my god. If you were a gentleman you would kindly forget that happened and not tell me any more details." Ashlyn grabbed her paper napkin and tossed it rather poorly at me.

I deflected her friendly fire with very little effort. "That's your mistake, babe, I'm no gentlemen."

AFTER SPENDING A REALLY PLEASANT FEW HOURS WITH DAN, I, OF course, had to return to Megs's apartment and give her a very detailed debrief. I was surprised she hadn't asked me to put together a PowerPoint presentation. She made me repeat everything over and over, laughing over how funny he was and obviously how sweet he had been with me the night before, while I had displayed questionable judgment and even more questionable sobriety. I agreed with her in that perhaps my initial summary of Dan Evans being a disgusting—albeit delectable —manwhore was somewhat skewed. I still believed him to be a manwhore, and he was definitely still delectable, but something had shifted and I really liked being around him. I begrudgingly made my way back to Brooklyn.

I had my usual Saturday night shift at Garro's, the shift hardly anyone wanted to work because it was usually date night despite the guarantee of earning big tips. Granted those tips were well and truly earned and I usually had to spend most of the latter part of the evening swatting away hands from my ass. Why did men get so grabby after sinking a few beers?

It had been loud and hectic at the bar. College ball had dominated the big screens with Syracuse defeating West Virginia just before the end of the final quarter. Football games always packed the venue and it generally meant my eight-hour shift seemed infinitely longer. A fight had broken out around half time when some out-of-towner wanted to start trouble with a local, but Kenny, one of the large bouncers, soon saw those two work out their issues with some choice words and a stern look. Still, game nights meant a larger crowd so when I finally dragged my ass home at three a.m. I was dead on my feet.

I peeled off my standard Garro-issued polo and stepped out of my black pants, tossing them into my neglected laundry hamper, its contents now spilling onto the floor. I was going to have to lug it down to a laundromat tomorrow, which was really just later today. I turned on the faucet, needing to wash the smell of beer and sweat out of my hair and skin and waited the obligatory few minutes until the water ran clear. I closed my eyes knowing that one day I'd be able to take a shower without this ridiculous ritual.

My stomach growled. The only food I had consumed since lunch had been a grilled cheese sandwich that Reuben the cook had whipped up in the fifteen-minute break I had taken. I was pretty sure there wasn't any food in the apartment, so growling or not, my stomach would have to wait until daylight hours.

After a quick shower, I continued to ignore my protesting stomach and crawled into bed. I closed my eyes and tried to sleep. Not happening. I tossed and turned, crawling over to the opposite side of the bed. I could still faintly smell Dan's scent on my pillow. I brought it closer to me, inhaling the rectangular feather bag like a drug addict taking a hit. Insanity. Perhaps the poison from the lead paint peeling from the walls had finally seeped into my brain? That had to be the only explanation as to why I was up at three thirty in the morning sniffing a pillow.

I punched it. The pillow. Because *that* made all kinds of sense. I groaned in frustration, annoyed that I wanted Dan laying beside me and knowing it wasn't going to happen. It couldn't happen. We were too different. I had no place in his world, how could it even work? The minute he slept with me I would turn into one of *those*. Another story to tell, another fun time. But still...I wondered if it would be worth it. I had seen another side of him today, a sweet man underneath his ever-present bravado. Was it an act?

"Ugh!" I punched the pillow again. Sadly it didn't make me feel any better than it did the first time I'd punched it, my misguided emotions still twisting through my head. I took a deep breath and reached for the phone that sat idly on my nightstand. The dark screen illuminated with a swipe of my finger. Without thinking I scrolled to his name and pressed on his photo, that erotic image teasing me from behind the glass. I could look at it for hours. Torture. Obviously that was the solution, because clearly punching a pillow hadn't worked. I brought the phone closer, the screen inches from my face, the temptation to touch it too great as I ran my finger down the image, imagining what its reality would feel like.

I continued in my silent indulgence, committing every line of his torso to memory. The sweeps of color in his tattoos burned into my brain. The light in the image shifted momentarily as I ran my finger along the glass, his name highlighted across the screen. Shit! I watched the phone dial of its own accord. My finger must have inadvertently hit call while I was stroking the image. I fumbled with the phone managing to quickly hit end before he had a chance to answer. I breathed a sign of relief silently thanking the gods the call hadn't connected.

The relief and thanks had been premature however, as my phone once again illuminated with that taunting image. Fuck. Dan was calling me.

"Hey," I answered, trying to sound casual but ended up sounding like an airhead.

"Ashyln?" Dan's voice flowed from the speaker. "Did you just call me and hang up?"

He sounded good, his voice husky from sleep. My call had obviously woken him.

"Oh. Yeah. It's my bedtime routine. I pick a random number to prank. Must be your lucky night."

"Yeah, I'll say." A low chuckle filled my ear and vibrated through my body. "Are you just going to bed now?"

"Yeah, I just got home. Sorry. Honestly. I didn't mean to wake you." I pulled the phone closer, hearing the distinct sound of sheets rustling. I liked that we were both in bed, together, even though we really weren't.

"Babe, you can call me anytime. I hope you weren't terrorizing some other band in a club, 'cause I kind of thought that was *our* thing." The smile in his voice was unmistakable.

"I was working, Dan, and we don't really have a *thing*."

"So you get drunk and hassle other guys?"

"No, of course not."

"See. Just reserved for me. *Our* thing."

I sighed, surprisingly he was so easy to talk to. "Whatever, Dan, it's too late to argue with you."

"So where do you work that gets you home at this hour? Have you been holding out on me and you are really a stripper?"

"Dan, there are lots of jobs that have night shift. Most of them don't involve removing my clothes. I could be a nurse, or a gas station attendant." I pretended to sound annoyed.

"I prefer stripper." He laughed, indulging his fantasy a little longer.

"I work in a bar, Dan, serving assholes beer and nachos. Sorry, there is no pole involved."

"Why you working in a bar? Is this like Good Will Hunting where Matt Damon was working as a janitor but was a genius at night?"

"Sadly, I'm neither a genius nor doing this by choice. It's the only job I could get. Not a lot of brokerage firms were hiring commerce majors who had less than four years of experience."

"Wow, Ash, I'm sorry. That kind of sucks."

"Yeah, well it is what it is. No point bitching about, so I guess I'll just pour beers until I find something else."

"But you went for the interview with Lexi, she's bound to hire you. Why wouldn't she?"

"I don't think so. I'm not really assistant material so I don't blame her if she doesn't. I only wanted the job as a way out and I think she knows I probably won't stick around. Anyway, let's change the subject. It feels weird talking about it with you."

"It's okay, babe, you like weird with me."

"Don't flatter yourself, Dan, I never said anything about liking you."

Dan laughed, the ease in his voice warm. "So if you were slaving away all night serving assholes why didn't you collapse into bed the minute you got home?"

"I'm in bed, I just couldn't sleep."

"Hmm, so what are you wearing?"

"Dan."

"I'm sorry, babe, you want me to talk dirty while you touch your-self?"

"Um, no."

"I'll touch myself too, just so you don't feel like a pervert."

"I'm still going to decline. We're not having phone sex."

"Suit yourself, but I'm just putting it out there that I would be okay with it."

"Yeah well, I wouldn't so don't hold your breath."

My stomach picked the exact moment that neither of us were talking to break the silence with a very loud and aggressive rumble. Reminding me that in addition to the arousal I was now feeling, I still hadn't dealt with the other primal need, hunger.

"Holy shit. What was that?" His voice became more serious, obviously having heard the rumble through the phone.

"It was my stomach." I laughed, clutching it and silently willing it to shut up.

"It sounded like a fucking animal, you sure there isn't a rabid puma hiding under your bed?"

I felt my cheeks flush as I hid my face. "No, it's just me. I'm going to go now and be mortified by myself."

"Don't be mortified. It's no big deal, just eat something. I don't think that sound is normal."

"Okay. I'm going to hang up now. I'll talk to you later." I stupidly kept my face hidden even though he couldn't see me.

"Night, Ash. Eat something."

"Night, Dan."

I was equal parts horrified and elated as I placed the phone back on my nightstand. Well now I definitely wasn't going to be able to sleep. The sound of his voice was still ringing in my ear. The memory of his throaty laugh made parts of me tingle. Maybe I had been hasty in dismissing his suggestion of phone sex. Not that I had ever done it, no guy had ever asked. I'd touched myself before, lost in a fantasy while I brought myself to climax, but never with such premeditation. I chewed on my bottom lip as the frustration hummed through my body.

It had been a really long time since I'd had sex, at least seven months. Tim Reeves had been my last boyfriend, a law firm associate with a foot fetish. Of course I didn't know about the fetish until I had been dating him for a while and it seemed logical to move it to the next level. So one night after dinner and heavy make-out session in his Buick Regal, I told him to take me back to his apartment. He was smart, sexy, and had a promising career, and most of all, he seemed really into me. Problem was, he was more into my toes than the rest of me, spending a solid hour sucking and licking them before he even removed his clothes. When he finally got down to the actual sex part, he had worked himself up so much he barely got the condom on and was inside me, and it was over. I had initially chalked it up to first-time nerves so we persisted. Correction, I persisted. Six months of overpriced pedicures and bad sex. I didn't have even one orgasm that I hadn't manufactured myself. I had even tried ribbed condoms and lube. Nothing. No spark. And if the only way I was going to get satisfaction was from masturbation, I might as well cut out the middleman. It seemed like double handling, no pun intended. So I decided it was time for Tim to move on, and while he was disappointed, I let him paint my toes before I kissed him goodbye.

Dan was *nothing* like Tim. I was already wet thinking about his dark brown eyes and his sexy grin. I allowed my hand to move slowly down my stomach, settling at the waistband of my cotton pajama pants. I scrunched my eyes tight, feeling a little stupid doing this but needing something to help release some of my pent-up need. I slipped my hand a little farther down, my heartbeat kicking up as I toyed at the edge of my underwear. My nipples puckered underneath my cotton tank as I loosened the reins on my inhibitions. *Did you want me to talk dirty while you touch yourself?* Dan's words made me smile as I thought about what I was doing and how disappointed he would be if he knew he had missed it.

I was just about let my fingers slide into my underwear when I heard a thumping coming from my front door. What the hell? I sat up in bed and checked the time, four fifteen. This better be a pizza delivery boy with a prepaid order or someone trying to rob me because any other option was going to be met with grievous bodily harm. I kicked off my covers and jogged to my front door, greeted by a second round of thumping. I grabbed the baseball bat I kept in the hall closet for security and tentatively looked through the peephole.

"Dan!" I flicked open the lock and wrenched opened the door. "What the hell are you doing here at four in the morning? Have you completely lost your mind?" I stood in my doorway, the baseball bat still gripped in my hand. Honestly, I was still considering taking a swing.

"Oh easy there, slugger." Dan help up his hands in surrender, a white paper bag in this right hand. He looked just as amazing as he had earlier in the day, wearing a pair of faded blue jeans and leather jacket.

"What are you doing here?" I repeated, lowering the bat but not willing to relinquish it just yet.

"Well, you were hungry and I can always eat, so I went and snagged us a couple of hot dogs from Gray's Papaya. I figured we were both awake so..." He shook the bag in his hand. He came all this way because I was hungry? Who does that? Why was he being so nice to me when I'd been so bitchy towards him? Who was this man? What happened to the asshole I met a few days ago?

"Fine, come in." I stepped aside to allow him entry, resting the bat against the wall. "You can't just show up here at this hour, what if I had been sleeping?"

"Were you?" He didn't even try to hide the fact his eyes dipped down to my chest.

"No, not yet." I hoped to god he couldn't tell what I *had* been doing in the absence of sleep. Shit. Did I look guilty?

"So let's eat then." He strolled over to my couch and took a seat, ignoring the fact I hadn't followed him. "I'm going to start without you."

"Yes, we've already established you aren't a gentleman." I took a seat beside him and snatched the bag from his hands. "I'm starving."

"I told you to eat. I knew you wouldn't listen." He smiled, satisfied he had been right.

"It was time for bed, I wasn't going to go make something to eat." I pulled out a hot dog and took a bite. It was still hot and tasted like heaven.

"So you'd just ignore a bodily need?" He raised an eyebrow, taking back the bag and pulling out a hotdog for himself.

"No, just wait until a more decent hour," I explained in between chewing.

"That's such bullshit. If you needed to take a piss would you just wait that out too?" He shoved more hotdog into his mouth.

"God, you are disgusting. Tell me again how you charmed your way into my bed last night?" I rolled my eyes. He was so direct but despite me feigning annoyance it was actually quite refreshing.

"Sorry, let me rephrase. If you needed to *tinkle*... Better?" He smirked before continuing, "And I keep telling you, last night...all you."

"Tinkle? That was the best you could do?" I tried not to laugh. There was a strange innocence about him, he was kind of endearing.

"Says the woman who answered the door with a baseball bat. You either got lost on the way to Yankee Stadium or you were hoping to get a starring role in the next Pacino movie." He pointed to the bat still leaning up against the wall.

"Dan, just shut up and eat." I took another bite, wondering if there was another hotdog hiding in the paper bag.

"So...," he took a bite out of his hotdog, "you work a lot of nights?"

"As many as I can. Minimum wage blows and the tips are better at night." I placed the last bite into my mouth, savoring it.

"How do you get home?" Dan stopped chewing and looked at me seriously for the first time since I'd met him.

"I take the subway, sometimes a cab." I grabbed a napkin out of the now empty bag and wiped off my hands. Damn, no more hot dogs.

"Okay, how about this? You give me a call when you're working nights and I'll pick you up." He shoved the last of his dog into his mouth.

"What, you running a car service now? Don't you have important rock star shit to do? Thanks for the offer but I'm okay." I couldn't help but laugh. The thought of Dan waiting for me at the end of my shift and wondering how that would fit into his touring schedule, not to mention the scores of other women I had no doubt he attracted. I handed him a napkin.

"Ash, I'm serious. Don't take unnecessary risks. A friend of mine was hurt really badly not that long ago. Some asshole attacked her and she thought she was okay, too. I'm not saying that shit will happen, I'm just saying don't give it a chance to happen." He grabbed my arm, forcing me to look at him. "Call me. I will pick you up. I don't give a fuck what time it is, it will save you pranking me when you get home." His mouth curled slowly into a smile.

I knew what he was talking about. The *friend* in question had been Alex Stone's wife and their PR manager, Lexi Reed. It had made news when an ex-boyfriend had apparently stalked her and raped her in her Australian apartment. She had been beaten pretty badly, too, spending a lot of time in the hospital. I hadn't really given it much thought with celebrity news so far removed from my normal boring life. I guess you don't ever really see the human side to those stories, it was just more headlines. I was ashamed to admit, I had actually forgotten. Her violent attack had been relegated to old news that no longer seemed relevant. Not that she would ever forget, even if the world had.

I was genuinely concerned but didn't want to make him uncomfortable by talking about it. "I'm sorry, Dan. I hope your friend is okay." I knew it was probably a no-go zone.

"She is. You going to call?" He leveled me with a stare, he wasn't kidding.

"Fine, if it will make you happy." It didn't seem like he would be letting it go unless I agreed. I knew I probably wouldn't call but it was easier to appease him than to tell him that. Strangely, it was touching he cared so much.

"It will. Are you done?" He tossed his napkin into the paper bag before angling it towards me.

"Yeah, thanks for the dog. I was actually pretty hungry." I bunched up the napkin and threw it into the bag.

"I know, I think they heard the growl of the wildebeest in Queens." He bit back a grin, instantly lightening the mood.

"Ass. I'm going to get some sleep now. Thanks again." I stood up, ready to walk him to the front door.

"Yeah sleep sounds good." He lifted himself off the coach and stretched, moving toward my bedroom door.

"Where are you going?" I grabbed his arm stopping him from going any farther.

"I'm coming to bed," he explained, clearly puzzled as to why it was a discussion.

My eyes widened from hearing his plan. "You are not coming to bed with me." He couldn't come to bed with me, could he? No. He shouldn't. I shouldn't. We should definitely not do that.

"Why, I swear I won't touch you. Even if you beg me like you did last night." He honestly seemed perplexed as to why it was an issue, like it hadn't occurred to him what might actually happen if we were in bed together. Obviously I was the only one thinking about it, and here I was thinking he was the one with the dirty mind.

"Dan, you can't just show up here and climb into my bed." I tried to rationalize, my resolve waning. I wanted him in bed with me, I did. I just didn't want to have to admit it. Not to myself and least of all not to him.

"Listen, Ash, we can argue about it for the next hour but we are both tired and I proved to you last night I'm not a scumbag. Just sleep. I promise." He wrapped his arm around my waist and pulled me down the hallway. He wasn't going to let up and I knew he probably would stand there and argue until he finally wore me down. One thing I'd learned about Dan, when he felt strongly about something he didn't budge, and I knew the only way I was going to be getting any sleep tonight would be with him beside me.

"I'm bringing the bat," I warned, though I left it safely leaning up against the wall as I allowed him to drag me into my bedroom.

"Okay, slugger, whatever gets your rocks off, but if it's a homerun you're looking for I think I'm probably better equipped."

"Do those lines ever work?" I shook my head, not believing he actually said stuff like that. I released myself from his grasp and slid into bed.

"Ninety percent of the time. You'd be surprised actually." He toed off his boots and pulled off his jacket.

"Hold on a second. What are you doing?" I sat up, watching wide-eyed as he continued his strip show, peeling off his T-shirt before moving to his socks.

"Getting undressed, I can't sleep in my clothes." His hands moved to his belt before unbuttoning his jeans, letting them fall to the floor.

I heard my voice waver as I stared at him, all that sexy inked skin on display throwing off my game. "Don't even think about taking off the boxers."

"Relax. You talk too much." He slid into bed beside me, thankfully leaving his boxers on. I couldn't help but want to see what was underneath.

I turned onto my side, knowing there was no way I was going to be able to sleep if I kept looking at him. I felt the mattress compress as he nestled beside me. His arms wrapped around me and pulled me closer.

"Dan," I whispered. "Your hand is on my ass."

"Old habits." He chuckled as his mouth pressed up against my neck. He slowly moved his hand to my hip. "Shhh. Go to sleep."

I allowed him to hold me, feeling his warmth and his scent as my eyelids started to droop. Instinctively I moved closer against him so our bodies were pressed against each other. My thoughts floated back to what I had been doing before Dan had interrupted me. The need had not gone away. If anything, with this new development, it had intensified. I tried to ignore the throbbing between my legs by squeezing my eyes shut and trying to think about something else. Anything other than the hardening length that was poking me in the ass.

I turned, knowing it was not only a bad idea but that his erection would now be poking in an entirely different area. I shouldn't have turned. What I should have done was go to sleep. But I didn't and now it was too late.

"Ash?" Dan's hooded eyes opened slightly wider as I wrapped my arms around him.

"Shhh. Go to sleep." I pressed my mouth against his, my tongue teasing the seam of his lips.

"I can't, if you keep doing that." He moved his hands back down to my ass. "Ash, what are we doing here?"

"I just want to kiss you." My lips traveled down his neck, as my hands moved along his strong, corded arms. If my body had a game plan it hadn't bothered to share it with my brain. I was winging it and had no idea on how far I was willing to let this go.

I slowly kissed my way back up to Dan's lips, and he seized the opportunity intensifying the kiss. "Ashlyn." He moaned as his tongue swirled inside my mouth. He rolled onto his back and pulled me on top of him. We continued to kiss, as frenzied hands pushed and pulled as we rocked against each other. I felt his cock lengthen as he moved me up against it. Its hardness giving me the sweet friction I craved.

Dan's hands moved to the hem on my tank top, pushing it up my body to expose my skin.

"No." My hand flung down to his, stopping the cotton from revealing more. "No sex, just kissing."

"Can't I even have a look?" Dan's wicked smile teased at the corners of this mouth.

"No." I laughed as I moved my lips back to his mouth and kissed him again. He took over, pulling at my bottom lip and dominating my mouth.

It was amazing. It was better than amazing. I had never been kissed like that. It wasn't *nice* or *sweet*; it was passionate and intense and made me feel like nothing else mattered outside of what we were doing. As if the world could stop moving and I would no longer care. In fact, who needed the earth's revolutions?

The tumbling I had going on in my head was more than enough for me. Right now. At this moment. Nothing else mattered.

Dan groaned as he pushed his hardness against me, hitting me square between the legs. I gasped as he rubbed against me, the thin fabric of his boxers and my pajamas the only barrier between us. I felt something building, my body responding to his. I didn't want it to stop and I wasn't sure I should keep going. It felt so good. So very, very good. My nipples hardened under my tank top as he rubbed them against his broad chest. Our kiss deepened and he grabbed my ass underneath my shorts, guiding me as I grinded along his length. His fingers teased at the edges of my panties. His skin touching mine was electrifying. Caught somewhere between frustration and euphoria, I had never felt so alive. My heart was beating so fast and I knew I was going to come. The man was dry humping me and was about to achieve what other men hadn't while actually having sex. I arched my back and allowed the wave to take me.

"Ah." I involuntarily moaned as my body shook, the ripples of pleasure moving through me in a way I had never felt before. I should have been embarrassed, that he could do all that just by touching me, but I didn't care. I absorbed it, wanting to feel every last shudder.

"Mmmm." He groaned up against my neck. "I liked making you come." He was doing little to disguise his pride. "You know, I can make it better than that, really make it good for you."

"I'm sure you could." I smiled as the last echoes of pleasure moved through me, my body still entwined against him. He was still hard, the throbbing length pulsing against my clit. Without thinking, I reached for him, my hands floating down between my body and the tiny layer of cotton that encased his cock.

I lifted myself slightly off him, allowing my hand better access. I wanted to make him feel as good as he had made me feel. I wanted to touch him. My fingers breached the edges of his boxers, continuing until I wrapped them around his girth. He was big. Much bigger than I had felt before. Not only long but wide - my fingers could barely fold around him. Reading my intentions, he stretched out his body, raising his hips to meet me. He grinned.

"Just letting you know, you're sober this time so I'm not going to stop you."

"Good, because I really want to do this." My fingers slowly moved up and down his shaft, squeezing as I reached the top.

"Fuck that feels amazing." His eyes closed as I continued to move faster. "Mmmm," he hummed in appreciation, as my tightly wrapped hand traveled up and down his length.

I used his verbal cues to guide me, his groans more unrestrained the harder and faster I pumped him. I loved watching his face contort in pleasure, the desperation in his hips as he rocked them against my hand. He was close; I could feel the deep throbbing between my fingers.

"Ash, I'm going to come." I felt his cock jerk in my hands as his body shook. "FUCK." He moaned as his sticky, hot load spilled onto my fingers. I continued to pump, milking every last drop, watching as he splintered beside me.

"Some kiss." Dan laughed, I felt him soften in my hand. "Fuck that felt good."

"I'll be back." I smiled as I slid out of bed and padded to the bathroom.

I turned on the faucet and washed my hand, watching as his cum slid into the sink and down the drain. I didn't do this. Take men I barely knew to bed and jerk them off. Or use their bodies as an extra large sex toy. But it had felt so good. Uninhibited. Hot. I glared at my reflection. I didn't look any different, but my actions hadn't felt like they had been my own. I didn't regret them though and strangely didn't feel embarrassed. I quickly used the bathroom, cleaning myself up before rewashing my hands. I dried them off, carrying the towel out with me into the bedroom. Dan curiously watched me as I approached.

I tossed him the towel as I climbed into bed, watching him smirk as he wiped the remaining cum from his toned stomach.

"You know, I can clean you up too if you want." His fingers swirled around my hip.

"Thanks, but I've taken care of it." I snuggled onto my side, feeling more relaxed than I had in months.

I heard the thud of the towel dropping and he curled up

behind me, his hand pulling me closer to his body. "Let me know if you want another kiss," he whispered in my ear, a small chuckle traveling through his throat. I smiled in the dark, as his hands settled, resting just below my belly. He didn't go farther though and I knew he wouldn't, so I finally let my eyelids close and fell asleep.

WAKING UP IN A GIRL'S BED WAS NOT NEW TO ME. I'M NOT A COMPLETE asshole. Not going to lie, I prefer to leave after the fucking has taken place but I understand that's not cool so I usually suck it up and stay. This was different. It was the second time I had woken up in Ashlyn's bed, neither time, had there been any actual fucking. The first time, I really had no business being there, but I didn't feel like leaving and if no one was going to kick me out, then I'd just as soon stay in her bed. I hadn't really done that before, actually *slept* with a woman. I mean, what was the point? But after putting her drunk ass to bed there was nowhere else I wanted to be. Last night was different. She had pocket dialed me or some shit, and hung up before I had a chance to answer. I had been home, asleep. Probably the first time in a long time I hadn't gone out on a Saturday night. Not something I planned but when Troy asked if I wanted to hang out, I told him to come over and we'd just play some poker or something. We threw a few hands and drank a few beers and it was actually a good time. Just shooting the breeze, no fucking distractions, paparazzi, or groupies. We called it a night around midnight with Troy giving me some fucking weird-ass look like I'd fucked his sister when I'd said I was heading to bed. So that's where I was when I heard my cell. When I saw the missed call I was pissed. Not that Ashlyn had woken me, but because I didn't get a chance to talk to her. Did she need something? She hadn't even left me a voicemail. I didn't even think about it, I just called her back.

I could have spoken to her for hours, the subject of conversation meant nothing and everything at the same time. So after hearing her stomach making a noise like a dying fucking bear, I jumped in the car, grabbed some food and took the drive over the bridge. Gray's was open twenty-four/seven and who didn't like hot dogs. I didn't even think about it, I just did it. I didn't even consider the fact she might not want to see me or that she wouldn't let me in. To me it was simple. I wanted to bring her something to eat, so I did.

When she opened the door holding a baseball bat and wearing more fucking attitude than actual clothes, I wanted to laugh my ass off. There was no way I was just dropping off the food and leaving, and I wasn't even thinking with my dick. There was something about this girl and I couldn't get enough. She wasn't like the ones I usually met, she didn't give a shit about me being Dan Evans and she sure as hell wasn't shy about telling me. I don't know why I felt the way I did but I just didn't want to go.

The kiss had been something else. I ain't going lie, the minute we were in bed and her body moved up against me, I got hard. I couldn't help that though, I was in bed with a sexy woman; my dick was just doing what he had been trained to do. I wasn't going to do anything about it though. Fine, I touched her ass but that was a reflex, like breathing. I mean, how could I not touch it? It was so fucking perfect. The point is, even though I was packing a hard-on that could have drilled through metal and I had briefly touched her ass, I fully intended to just curl up beside her and go to sleep. I guess she had other plans. Plans I was happy to get on the same page with.

Kissing her was intense. Like being kicked in the balls intense. You can't think straight, you can't breath and all you can do is concentrate on what is happening right then. I could tell she was turned on. The little noises she made when I moved my tongue in and out of her mouth, the way her body moved up against me. It was killing me not to take off those fucking pajama pants and get inside of her but this wasn't about me. I wanted to get her off, to hear her pant and know it was because of what I had done to her. I had pulled her on top of me, positioned her so that my cock could hit her right where she needed it and made sure I didn't stop until her eyes rolled back and her legs shook. It was fucking beautiful and if I hadn't jerked off a few hours before, I would have spewed my load the minute her pussy came anywhere near my junk. The hand job had been unexpected. Who'd have thought I would get so fucking excited dry humping and getting jacked off by Ashlyn over actual sex? She had skills too, seemed like all that time pulling beers meant she was more than conditioned to handle me. I held out for as long as I could but when she looked at me with her hand wrapped tightly around my cock, it was game over.

I didn't want to wake her this morning but there was no way I was leaving without saying goodbye. She had this adorable dopey, sleep face and mumbled it was too early, while I explained I had to go but I would call her later. There was nothing I wanted to do more than to stay in the bed with her, having her tucked up tightly against me, but there was something I needed to do.

So without giving it too much thought, I jumped into my Benz and hightailed it back into the city. I didn't even stop for breakfast. I was focused on what I needed to do and I didn't want anyone talking me out of it, least of all not Ashlyn. Actually it was better if she didn't find out at all. It's not like it would make a difference; it was just useless information.

I hit the buzzer on the external door. There was no getting in unless you had a pass or were escorted in. Security was tight but I understood the why of it.

"Yeah," DarNell's voice boomed from the box fixed to the front outside wall.

"Yo, D. It's Dan. Let me up."

"A little early for you isn't it, sunshine? Your latest conquest turn into a pumpkin or she sober up and kick you out?"

"Yeah, something like that. Open up, will you. I'm starting to freeze my balls off."

The door hummed and then clicked, allowing me to open the gate and getting me into the building. Getting up to the Penthouse was another story. D would meet in the foyer, which was our usual drill unless he was in a mood and then he'd make me sweat it out. Lucky for me today he wasn't on his period and we can go about our business.

"Dan." Darnell gave me a once over, stepped out of the elevator and into the foyer.

"Hey D, we good to go up?" I stepped toward the big bastard and put out my hand. Six foot seven and as big as a linebacker from the NFL, he was pushing at least two hundred sixty pounds of pure muscle, with a big-ass bald head, and a stare that was as intimidating as fuck. I missed DarNell. Sure he used to ride my ass but he had been part of our security detail for years until last year, when he moved on to a private job. I understood things were different now and he had other responsibilities, but still, it was good to see him.

"Yeah, you're clear to go up but next time, maybe call ahead. You hear me?" And there was that stare that usually made the uninitiated piss their pants.

"I hear you. You need me to take a piss test or you relaxing the security measures?" I laughed as we walked side by side into the elevator, D inserting a key and hitting the access to the Penthouse.

"Keep your dick in your pants. I've seen enough of it to last me a lifetime, thanks buddy. As for security measures, you know why they are in place. Let's just get this over with. I'm imagining this is not a social call and pretty sure whatever is about to happen, while it might be highly amusing for me, is probably going to suck for you." His big-ass grin widened, showing his pearly white grill. He always was such a wise-ass.

"Yeah, no doubt," I agreed, knowing he was probably right, not that it was going to change my mind. It wasn't the first time I'd been torn a new asshole at the hands of Lexi Reed.

The elevator doors opened into the large entranceway of the

Stone Penthouse. This place was mint, huge by regular standards, but in Manhattan real estate terms, it was a fucking palace.

Alex was waiting at the door, wearing a stupid grin on his face like he usually did when he was around his hot fucking wife. "Dan, to what do we owe this unexpected pleasure?"

"Not here for you, asswipe, here for your Mrs." I gave him a friendly punch in the shoulder.

"Really?" Alex's shit-eating grin got wider as we walked inside the apartment. "Oh, I'm going to enjoy this."

"Yeah, yeah. You and D knock yourselves out with your merriment. Where's your wife?" I looked around the room noticing Lexi wasn't around. It was ten a.m. on a Sunday, so surely she wasn't too far.

"She's feeding Grace. You're going to have to wait." Alex pointed at the couch, clueing me in he wanted me to take a seat. I wasn't in the mood to sit and wait.

"I can talk while she's feeding Grace. I'll watch my mouth with the cussing. Where is she?"

"You'll wait, Dan." Alex leveled me with a stare. It seemed he and D had been spending too much time together; Stone had the don't-fuck-with-me look down pat. "Lexi's breastfeeding, there is not even a shadow of a chance you are getting anywhere near my wife. So sit your ass down and wait." He pushed me down on the couch. Touchy motherfucker. He had become so fucking territorial lately. Still, looking at what he had to come home to, I can't say I blamed him.

"So is that kind of hot?" It's not like I hadn't seen a woman pull out a tit and feed her kid before but I had to wonder if it was your own woman, if maybe that didn't turn you on. And don't think I hadn't noticed Lexi's tits had gotten bigger since being knocked up and having the baby. That shit right there was proof god was a dude.

"You did not just ask me that right now." Alex shook his head as he took a seat beside me. I couldn't believe the bastard was holding out on me.

"C'mon, dude. She can't hear us." I have to admit, I was kind of curious. "Tell it to me straight. Have you tasted it?"

"Tasted what?" Lexi walked in, her hand tapping little Grace's back who happened to be perched up on her shoulder.

"Nothing," Stone and I both answered in stereo. Good to know he was smart enough not to repeat it.

"Hey, Lex." I walked over to Lexi and kissed Grace's forehead. "How's my number one girl?" Man, that kid was something else. I think they must put some kind of crack in baby powder or something 'cause whenever I saw that little face, she could ask me for the pink slip of my car and I'd sign it over.

"She had a bad night. None of us got much sleep." Lexi continued to pat Grace's back as she took a seat in the armchair opposite us. "She's got a good set of lungs on her that's for sure."

"Well, looks like daddy's going to have to teach her guitar to back up those pipes." I couldn't help but grin as I sunk back into my seat. With her mother's looks and attitude and her father's talent, Grace Stone would be unstoppable. Of course she'd have her Uncle Dan's advice too so she wouldn't sell out and sing bullshit manufactured pop crap. She'd write her own stuff for sure.

"So, Dan." Lexi wasted no time cutting to the chase. Good to see not much has changed. "I didn't see any photos of you last night nor did I have any calls about your questionable behavior. Being that it was a Saturday night that can only mean two things. You were either in jail or you were laying in a ditch somewhere. Both are going to be a headache for me so you might as well come clean now."

"Geez, Lexi. I wasn't in jail or a ditch last night. I was home, I didn't go out." Really, this was just like old times. Lexi always assumed the worst, so it made me a little sentimental. At least I knew she cared.

"You were home? On a Saturday night? Are you feeling okay?" She stopped patting baby Grace and gave me a funny look.

"Yes, I'm feeling okay. I just didn't feel like going out. Troy came over we had a few beers and played a few hands of poker. That was my night."

Alex and Lexi looked at each other then back to me like I'd grown another head. Was it so hard to believe that I hadn't gone out? Sure I usually was at a club most nights during the week, especially on the weekends, but it's not like I had never spent the night at home. Shit. When *was* the last Saturday night I had spent at home?

"Look last night isn't important. I was home, that's all that matters. Why I'm here is I need a favor." I moved around in my seat, this crap was making me uncomfortable.

"What kind of favor? Dan, this better not be about Sydney. She's not interested," Lexi warned. Yeah I knew where Sydney stood on the dating issue, she'd made herself clear. Truth is, now, *I* was no longer interested.

"It's not about Sydney. I know she isn't interested. I'm fine with that. I've moved on."

"Well, good." Lexi looked relieved but unconvinced. "So what is it that you need?"

"I need you to hire Ashlyn Murphy as your assistant. Please."

"Ashlyn Murphy? The broker? Dan, while she's probably capable, she's not exactly suitable. She has no industry experience, she has never worked as a PA, and would probably hand in her resignation as soon as she got offered a job on Wall Street. I need someone qualified and reliable. I have three potentials and Ashlyn didn't even make my short list. Why are you asking?"

"I met her. I know she can do the job and she will stick around. In case you haven't noticed, there aren't a lot of jobs going on Wall Street right now."

"You've met her? You had an altercation with her in my reception area and from that one interaction you have surmised she is the correct person for the job? Is she threatening a harassment lawsuit? Did you promise her the job if she blew you or something?"

"Fuck, Lexi, why does it always have to be something shady? No, I did not ask her to blow me in exchange for a job and there is no lawsuit. Look, it's a long story but I got to know a little bit about her and I know she *needs* this job."

"Do you see *Goodwill* painted on the front of my door? I can appreciate she might need a job but so do lots of other people, people who are more qualified, Dan. I'm running a business not a fucking charity."

"God, you are being such a bitch right now. You know James took a fucking chance on *you*, didn't he? Why can't you give her the same chance?"

"Dan. You have taken it way too far this time." Stone was in my face before I even had time to register he had moved off the couch. For a tall bastard, he was pretty quick.

Grace let out a cry, the commotion upsetting her. Fuck. This was not going well.

"It's okay, sweetheart." Lexi cradled Grace in her arms trying to stop her from crying. Alex ignored me and walked over to where his girls were.

"I'm sorry, sweetie, daddy didn't mean to yell." He kissed the top of Grace's head and with the sound of his voice she started to calm down.

"Alex, calm down. I've got this." Lexi held up her hand to calm Alex who was shooting me dirty looks. He took Grace from Lexi's arms and continued to settle her.

Lexi lowered her voice, which made me edgy. "Okay, what the fuck is going on because this is not about some job. And Dan, don't you *ever* insinuate I got this job on anything other than merit. I had years in public relations and events. I worked my way up from a shitty assistant to running million dollar campaigns so I was *more* than qualified to handle the tour James hired me for. Me, running the band's PR now, having my own business, is because of all the hard work I put in over all that time. So watch your fucking mouth. I didn't get, nor have I ever had, a free ride."

"All right. You made your point." I shook off the murderous vibe that was currently being shot in my direction. "And I didn't mean it that way. Look, I know you are qualified and I know sometimes we don't see eye to eye but you do an amazing job and I'm glad it's you who's watching out for us and not someone else." I swallowed before continuing. "I know I'm a pain in your ass. I know you get sick of my shit. The girls, the pictures, and everything. I'm sorry if I have made your job difficult but I need you to do this and if you do it, I swear I'll never ask for anything ever again."

"Dan, you are starting to scare me now. Tell me what's going on. You better not be dying or I'll kill you myself."

"I'm not dying, but it's good to know that if I was, you'd end it for me early. Nice. Thanks for that." I couldn't help but smile. There was no doubt if I was ever in need of being put out of my misery, Lexi Reed would be the person I'd turn to. She was not only tough but she didn't flinch, not even a bit.

She returned the smile. "That's how you know I care. I wouldn't want you to suffer. That's the special kind of love I have for you."

"So you saw us argue. Ashlyn and me. At your office. Well later that night she ended up at the same club we were at. I was getting busy with a couple of girls when Troy found her trying to sneak into the VIP section."

"Classy, Dan. Two girls. Really?" Lexi asked, but she didn't sound surprised. It wasn't the first time. I chose to ignore her and continued.

"Anyway, she was pretty drunk and Troy found her poking around the VIP section and he thought it would be funny to bring her in because she was pissed at me. Apparently I had *offended* her." I rolled my eyes remembering that nothing I had said was offensive, if anything, she had been the one who had been rude.

"Cue my lack of surprise." Lexi smirked. I once again chose to ignore her. Seriously, did she want to hear this story or not?

"So yeah, she yelled at me for a while and then left." I didn't bother mentioning the bit about her making out with me before walking out, though no doubt Troy or Jase would flap their gums at some point and they'd both find out.

"So she piqued my interest. She is kind of a loud mouth like you, but not as aggressive. No offense." I held up my hands, not wanting to piss her off at this point.

"None taken. Go on." Thankfully Lexi didn't seem pissed.

"I found her and her friend at the front of the club. Her friend had twisted her ankle so we got them home safely," I explained, remembering finding Ashlyn trying to help Megs off the ground, her ankle already starting to blow up. I don't think I'll ever understand girls and their fucking shoes.

"Did you sleep with her, Dan?" Lexi looked me square in the eye.

"No, not like that. Honest, Lexi. I swear, I didn't do shit but spend the night at her place to make sure she was okay."

"But wasn't her *friend* the one who was hurt?" Lexi narrowed her eyes. I couldn't tell if she didn't believe me or was trying to slip me up. She always had a knack of making me confused and then I'd end up saying shit I didn't mean.

"Yes. What does it matter? I stayed." I pushed my hands through my hair. She was really enjoying raking me over the coals on this.

"So the next day we got talking and I got to really know her. No one will hire her even though she is super smart and amazing. She is working in a bar, Lexi. She spent all that time in college and now only works in a bar. She lives in a shithole apartment in the bad part of Brooklyn. Can you do this for me? Please?"

"Holy shit. You are really serious. You have feelings for this girl." Lexi's eyes widened.

"What? I just met her. I don't have feelings. I'm just trying to be a decent guy and I can tell she is doing it tough. So will you do it?" I didn't want to talk about the way I felt about Ashlyn, not with these two anyway. I didn't know what I felt. I knew I wanted to make her smile and try and make things easier for her. I knew I liked spending time around her and I hated she was working a job she hated, dealing with dickwads, and coming home late at night. I was just being a concerned citizen who was looking out for someone who was down on their luck. It didn't have to be about *feelings*.

"Dan, I can't just give her a job. While I think what you are doing is admirable and I love seeing this compassionate side to you, I can't afford to gamble on this. It's a big risk." I started to interrupt, wanting to argue if money was the issue, I would happily pay her salary when Lexi stopped me. "Wait. Let me finish. I'm still on maternity leave. I'm hardly in the office other than a few important meetings so I need someone who is not only going to be able to step in but step up. I need to hire someone who can do that, and while I don't think Ashlyn is suited to the role, I can tell she would be an asset to the right company." Lexi reached out and rubbed my arm. "Let me make a few calls. I think I might be able to find her something more suitable."

"Thanks, Lex." I nodded, the gratitude making me feel kind of emotional.

"Look, no promises. I'll get her in the door, a meeting with someone, but she is going to have to do the rest herself. It will be up to them if they hire her, I need you to understand that," Lexi continued, making it clear it wasn't a done deal.

"I got it. No promises." All she needed was a start. She would wow them. I had no doubt she had the goods to get a job if she was just put in the right place at the right time.

"Dan, if you really like her, make sure you play this straight, okay?" Lexi moved out of her chair, snagging her iPhone off the coffee table.

"Lexi, just make your calls. Not everyone has to end up with a SUV with a baby on board sticker on the back." I couldn't help myself; I knew that shit pissed her off.

"I do not have a baby on board sticker on my car," she spat out defensively.

"Let me do my thing. I know what I'm doing."

At least I thought I did, and if I didn't, I wasn't about to front to it now.

I WOKE UP ALONE AND THAT DISAPPOINTED ME. WHAT DISAPPOINTED me even more was I cared I was alone. Make sense? No, I didn't think so. In fact, none of it made sense. I had woken up alone more times than not, and I had never lived with a guy, so why I was feeling this way was a real mystery. The last few days had effectively scrambled my brain and I wasn't thinking clearly. How had I gone from disliking this crude, obnoxious rock star with questionable social skills to wanting to see him when I woke up? It was a slippery slope being with Dan, and I was free-falling.

Perhaps this is my version of rebellion, being with a man I knew I could have no future with. I knew whatever we were would be fleeting, a bump in my road. I could never assimilate into his world any more than he could to mine. He was a fantasy, a pot of gold at the end of the rainbow. You could run and run in an attempt to reach it but it never got any closer. But that didn't mean I didn't want to follow the rainbow a little longer, see my days through the magic of its colors. It would be okay as long as I kept my reality in check. I couldn't afford to lose sight of who either of us really were. Wow. This was all very deep. Too deep. Especially at this time of the morning.

Dan had woken me before he left, saying he had to *get some shit done.* I shouldn't have expected him to stay. It would have been weird. I had rubbed myself against him, climaxing before giving him a hand job. Sure, that wasn't awkward. What do you say to someone who you actually *haven't* had sex with? It was for the best. Him leaving, I mean. The no sex thing? The jury was still out. If Dan was able to give me the best orgasm I've ever had without actual penetration, I could only imagine what it be like if we actually *did* it. I really needed to stop. I was getting dizzy just thinking about it.

New plan. One that did not involve me moping around in my apartment analyzing all things Dan Evans. I scrounged through my kitchen cupboard and found a box of Cinnamon Toast Crunch. Things were looking up. So after devouring a bowl of cereal and my usual morning get-ready ritual, I headed out of my apartment to enjoy the sunshine. It was October, which meant that soon the warmth would be replaced by the icy chill. Just another thing I didn't want to think about it.

I don't know why I ended up at Columbus Circle. Today wasn't a day for making sense so I just went with it. It was liberating, not having a road map. Just walking around aimlessly like a tourist. I stopped for a coffee and sat on the grass. Everything I was doing was pointless and yet it felt great doing it.

I had just made it back to my neighborhood when my phone burst into life shaking me from my daydream. Nearby, pedestrians turned around at the commotion. I quickly grabbed it from my purse. The old George Michael song, "I Want Your Sex" spewed loudly from the speaker, the screen filled by Dan's photo. I can't believe he had changed my ringtone.

"Dan," I half-yelled into the phone, my finger swiping to accept the call as fast as I could. Really? I want your sex? Could he be any more obvious?

"Wow you answered fast." Dan chuckled. "Are you missing me, babe? That's so fucking sweet." I didn't have to see his face to know he was smiling. Smug. Confident. Sexy. I couldn't help but smile back. I almost jogged back to my apartment not wanting to be distracted by the outside noise.

"I'm not missing you, ass, I just didn't want the rest of the neighborhood to be subjected to my ringtone. Speaking of which, do you have any boundaries at all?" I tried my best to sound annoyed but as much as I tried, I was coming up short in the convincing department. I had become desensitized, his charm winning me over.

"What did I tell you about putting a password lock on your phone? Relax. It's just a ringtone. Besides, it's what we both know you're thinking when you see that pic." His low voice vibrated through the phone sending a shiver through my core. I would never admit it, but he was right.

"Could you be any more conceited?" I asked, glad he couldn't see how flustered he made me. I cleared my throat doing my best to sound like I had my shit together. "Does this call have a purpose, Dan, or do you just want to harass me?"

"I was thinking about you," he purred into the phone. He was too good at this. The seduction. The man needed a warning from the surgeon general.

I climbed up the stairs of my apartment building, juggling the phone while trying to open my front door.

"Okay, I really didn't need the update, but thanks." I tried to sound bored as I chewed on my bottom lip. Why did it excite me so much he had been thinking of me? This is what he'd reduced me to. Elated yet annoyed. I was my own contradiction. I collapsed onto my couch, no longer able to stay upright.

"Were you thinking about me?" His voice swirled around each word. I was going to need to sit down. Hell, I was already sitting down. Maybe I needed to stand up. Get the blood moving, hopefully enough to where my brain kicked into gear.

"No, I've had lots on my mind today, so sorry, you didn't feature," I deadpanned.

"You are such a liar." Dan laughed. "Was I doing dirty things? Whatever you are imagining isn't even close to how good it can be."

Yep, Standing up now. I think I could probably run a marathon at this point and it still wouldn't shake my train of thought.

"Well I guess I will happily live in ignorance, because you know *that* isn't going to happen." I wasn't really sure whose benefit I was saying it for.

"I think it will, but you keep living in denial."

"Look, last night..." I swallowed, my eyes closing slowly before I continued. "Just don't read too much into it. I had an itch and you helped me scratch it. That's all." Yep, that's right. That's all it was. At least that is what I needed to tell myself. I had a need, and he was able to appease it. Nothing more. Certainly nothing romantic. Dan was right. I was a bad liar.

"Is that what it was? Huh." A gentle chuckle vibrated through the phone. "I think you will find if you ask my dick, he would tell you different."

"Well then your dick is just as clueless as you are." I smiled into the phone like an idiot.

Dan let out a loud, throaty laugh. "It's been called a lot of things - huge, magnificent, amazing, outstanding, oh-my-god-don't-stop, but never clueless. If there is one part of me that knows what it's doing, it's *that* part."

"Okay, hanging up now." Before I said something stupid. Or *more* stupid, as the case may be.

"Wait. What are you doing later? I want to see you." His voice turned serious, not allowing me to end the call.

"Dan..." I blew a long breath into the phone. "Why?" Was I a game? The thrill of the chase? Was I just another name to add to his long list of conquests?

"'Cause I like you and despite you saying different, I think you like me, too."

His honesty startled me. Why couldn't he just say what I had expected him to say, that he wanted to sleep with me. That I could handle. The fact he liked me—whatever that meant—just complicated everything. He was supposed to say he wanted sex. I couldn't go down that road with him. A relationship? No, Dan probably wasn't even capable of that.

"Dan, we would never work. You know that I'm right. I want a lot of things, and dating a musician who can't keep it in his pants isn't on that list."

"That's cool, Ashlyn, 'cause I have a list, too. See my girlfriend has to have huge porno tits and be seriously good at blowjobs, so sadly, you don't really fit the bill either. Great news about that is, we don't have to worry about impressing each other or pretending we're each other's soul mates. We can just hang out."

I blinked. He hadn't missed a beat, throwing off my protest like water off a duck's back. He should have been offended. Hell, I should have been offended but his whole rebuttal was so comical and sincere it just made him more endearing. His way of making it okay for us. And damn him if at that moment, Dan Evans had weaseled himself into a tiny corner of my heart. He was going to be the death of me.

"You're crazy, you know that, right?" I giggled. "I'm going to give you a little hint, if you want a girl you probably shouldn't tell her where her deficiencies are."

"Just being honest, babe. Figured you've probably had enough douchebags lie to you to get you in bed. I'm never going to lie to you."

"So big tits and blowjobs, huh? She sounds like she is going to be such a catch." I smiled.

"Oh, hell yeah. The tits I *might* be able to overlook, as long as they are at least adequate, but the blowjobs, they are non-negotiable."

"This is all very informative, I'll let you know if I see anyone who meets the criteria." I continued with his ruse. He made it so easy.

"Aw, Ash, you are kind of making me hard."

"You are impossible, you know that?" I sighed, letting my head fall against the back of the couch.

"Yeah I know. Impossible to resist. So when can I see you?" he persisted. I repeated in my head my earlier sentiment. Death. Of. Me.

"I have to work tonight, Dan. Maybe some other time." I was more than just a little disappointed. I wanted to see him. I wanted that and so much more.

"Wait. You're working tonight? When were you going to tell me? I thought we agreed I would be taking you home." Something in his voice shifted, an edge I hadn't heard before.

"It's okay, Dan, I know you're just trying to be nice and it was a sweet thing to offer but I'm not going to hold you to it. I'll promise to be safe. I'll catch a cab."

"Babe, I'm not nice or sweet, and I offered 'cause I wanted to. Besides *you* already agreed to it so you can't take it back now. It's a done deal. So you can forget taking a cab. Tell me what time and where to pick you up." His tone darkened. Wow. He really wasn't playing around.

"Dan, this is really—" I didn't get a chance to say *unnecessary* before he interrupted me.

"I said where and when, babe." His voice softened, the edge was still there but I could hear he was trying to rein it in. "If you want to make something harder than it has to be, I've got something between my legs that would love the attention. If not, then tell me what I need to know."

I wasn't going to argue. Dan had a way of talking until he got his own way and I was having enough trouble keeping check of my own emotions. If he wanted to drive me home, then fine, he could drive me home. But that's where it would end. I would be sleeping alone tonight. As for his *something special between his legs*, he would be tending to that himself as well. I wasn't a doormat, no matter how well intentioned he might have been.

"Fine. Two a.m. Garro's. It's a sports bar in Lower East Side. Don't expect me to be friendly or give any part of you any attention."

"Yeah, I know. I'm not your type. Got it. See you then."

I ended the call more confused than when it had started. I had never met a man who pushed all of my buttons like he did, *all* of my buttons. He infuriated me and yet excited me. Gah! I was a hot mess and I didn't know if Dan Evans or I was to blame.

It was another busy night at the bar. My arms were getting a work out from the numerous pitchers of beer I was putting up on the bar. It was easy to forget my earlier annoyance, getting lost in the noise of the crowd. They commiserated, consoling each other after a Giants loss, the replay from the earlier game being piped through the big screens adding insult to injury. This only fueled the alcohol consumption.

"Another, sweetheart," Mack slurred, his crumpled fiver extending over the bar. Mack and his crew were regulars. Hard-core New Yorkers and sports fanatics, they had been coming to Garro's since the day it opened.

"Going to have to cut you off, Mack. Why don't you let me buy you and the boys a round of soda instead?" I smiled knowing while they were loud and rowdy they weren't the kind of guys to start trouble. Still, rules were rules and they were all on the other side of sober.

Mack swayed unsteadily on his feet. "My boys let me down tonight, Ash. A man needs to drown his sorrows."

"I know, but if I serve you another beer we are probably going to end up sharing a cell together and as exciting as that sounds, Rosie would probably have my hide." I shot him a quick wink.

Rosie was not only the love of his life, but a tough-as-nails housewife from Long Island. I wouldn't want to be on her wrong side or have to make the call that her husband had been hauled off on a public intoxication charge.

"You're lucky I'm not younger." Mack smiled, his light blue eyes twinkled hinting at the trouble I knew he must have caused in his youth.

"She's a handful, buddy. Lot's of trouble." Dan's smug face beamed as he took a seat at the bar. I did my best to ignore him, turning my attention to polishing wine glasses. I clearly needed the distraction, because these glasses were rarely used, no one ever drank wine. It had just turned midnight; I hadn't expected to see Dan for at least another hour.

"The best ones usually are." Mack nodded in agreement. "She your girl?"

"Nah, she's too smart for that. I'm just her ride for the night. My name's Dan." Dan stood and held out his hand. He looked good. Too good. His leather jacket was unzipped revealing a Black Flag T-shirt underneath, finishing his look with a pair of faded blue jeans.

"Mack." He clasped Dan's hand firmly. "Good to see someone is looking out for her." Mack turned to look at me, grinning approvingly.

"Doing what I can, but she isn't making it easy." Dan eased into his seat, doing little to hide the fact his response had been directed at me rather than Mack.

"Okay you two. I'm right here." I tossed the dishrag aside. They both now had my attention.

"Well if you aren't going to serve us any more beer, might be time for me and the fellas to call it a night." Mack shot me a wink. "Think I'm about done. Nice meeting you, Dan." He tipped his head to Dan before strolling off.

"Likewise, Mack." Dan nodded, watching Mack shuffle away. He waited until Mack was out of earshot before leaving across the bar. "You flirting with the customers to make me jealous?"

"Come on, Dan, Mack is like sixty." I rolled my eyes wondering if he was serious.

"Makes no difference to me. Do I need to lay him out?" I watched the smile spread across his face. He had such an amazing smile, why had I never noticed? I needed to concentrate on the fact I was still mad.

"You are such a tool. I'm still mad at you by the way. Don't think you can come in here and be all charming."

"I'd rather you be mad at me and know you're safe than the alternative." He didn't offer me an apology or explanation.

"I'm not the kind of girl who needs a man to tell her what to do." I planted my hands on my hips. If he was going to be standing here then he might as well know how I felt. I didn't need a hero.

"Look, Ash. I'm sorry I snapped at you but this is not something I'm going to back down from. I'm not trying to own you or order you around. If you want me to go wait in the car, I will, but you have no chance of me letting you go home alone tonight." His voice softened but was still resolute. His dark smoldering eyes didn't break contact with mine. There was something else I saw within those dark expressive pools. He wasn't trying to be possessive but protective.

"It was Lexi, right? Your friend." I felt myself relent. He was trying to be kind and while his execution wasn't great, his motives were sound. It was the *why* of the motives that still confused me.

"That's not my story to tell, Ash. Sorry." He reached across, his hand grazing my knuckles. The sincerity was not missed, nor was the sweetness in his tone. There was no way I could stay angry.

"Maybe I overreacted." I gave him a slight smile before warning him. "Don't start any fights with the patrons and you don't have to wait in the car."

"I won't start any fights if you stop flirting with other men." He gave me a cheeky sideways glance. It was our way of calling a truce.

"I don't know, Dan. That old-timer in the corner has been giving me the eye all night and I have to admit I'm kind of tempted." I fanned myself, biting my lip to suppress my smile.

"Just point him out to me, babe, and I'll set him straight."

THE BAR WAS DESERTED EXCEPT FOR A FEW OTHER STAFF MEMBERS and the security. The doors had been shut half an hour ago but they had let me wait inside as I was driving Ash home and it didn't hurt the bouncer was a fan of the band. I signed the back of his security shirt and handed him a guitar pick I had stashed away in one of my pockets, and he was grinning like a kid who'd just touched boobs for the first time.

Despite this being a bullshit job I knew that she hated, she refused to cut corners and she worked her ass off making sure the place was immaculate before she punched off the clock. I watched Ash move around the bar, the boring, shapeless uniform she was wearing trying to hide the smokin' body she had underneath. Fuck, she was beautiful. Not just in the I-wanted-to-get-her-under-me sense, but also in I-could-look-at-her-all-day. I watched as her perfect ass swayed toward the staff locker room, the thought of taking her to the shithole apartment she lived in made me want to break shit.

"I'm good to go." Ashlyn pulled on her coat, her purse in her hand.

"Let's roll then." I waved to the bouncer as I guided her out toward the door. Yeah, there was a lot on my mind right now. Sleeping alone was not one of them. I didn't even care if she didn't want sex, not that my throbbing dick would listen to reason, but I needed her tucked up beside me.

We walked outside, our feet hitting the sidewalk as the blast of the night air licked us in the face. It was October and the chill was starting to move in. She shivered as we made our way up the street to where I'd parked my ride.

I moved in close and pulled my arm around her waist. The feel of her body hitting me harder than any fucking breeze ever could. "Cold?"

"No." Her body shook in my arms as we rounded the corner, my car parked at the curb.

"So why are you shivering?" I moved my other hand around her waist, gently pushing her body against the hood of my car.

"I'm just tired." She sighed. I wasn't convinced and the thought I made her edgy made me all kinds of uncomfortable.

"You're not nervous around me, are you?" I tilted her chin toward me, hoping like hell I didn't, or worse, that she would lie about it.

"Don't flatter yourself, Dan. It's been a long day and I just need to get to bed." She yawned, relaxing in my arms.

I moved in closer, wanting to kiss her. "Well I'm all about getting you into bed."

"You know I'm not going to have sex with you, right?" She didn't pull back so I moved in closer. My body up against hers, there was no way she couldn't feel the hard-on I had going on.

"I know, but I still want to sleep with you. Come home with me, Ashlyn. I won't put the moves on, I swear." I took her face in my hands my thumb playing with her bottom lip. Even tired, sweaty, and smelling like stale beer, she was the sexiest girl I'd ever seen.

"You like torturing yourself, don't you?" She gave me a weary smile. "I haven't got anything to sleep in."

This was not a legitimate problem. In fact, if anything, I saw it as one hell of a positive. "So sleep naked, I won't mind."

"Nice try, but no."

"So I'll give you a T-shirt to sleep in. Come home with me."

I had never had to beg a girl to come home with me and I wasn't about to now. Still, if there was one I would get on my knees for, it would be the one standing right in front of me. Mind you, I could think of something else I'd rather get on my knees for and the begging would be coming from her, telling me not to stop.

"I'm wearing a T-shirt and a pair of your boxers and there is going to be no sex." She gave me a look that meant she wasn't kidding. I didn't care what look she was giving. It looked like victory to me.

"Yeah, yeah. Whatever you want. Can we go now?" I smirked, wondering how fast I could get from here to my apartment. Thank fuck it was at some bullshit hour in the morning and the traffic was light.

"Okay we can go." She nodded as I fought the urge to fist pump. Not only did it mean I got another night by her side but also that I had the home field advantage.

I hit the keyless entry and opened the car door. She slid into the passenger seat, her legs stretching out in front of her. I closed the door, trying not to imagine those legs around my hips. Ash was right about one thing - tonight was going to be torture.

"This isn't what I thought you'd drive." She smiled as I slipped into the driver's seat.

"Hey, pick on me all you want, babe, but leave my ride out of it." I hit the ignition and pulled out on the street.

"No, that's not what I meant." She giggled and man, if that sound didn't make me feel warm inside. "I mean, I thought you would drive something more pretentious, like a Porsche."

"I don't need to compensate. I like style and comfort."

I had always owned an American car and when we got our first big check I went and bought myself a sweet Corvette. I still had it, it was kicking around in my mom's garage but it just didn't feel right to me. The Mercedes SLK 55 AMG spoke to me. I drove up to the dealer and saw this baby parked on the lot. Looking all badass with the top down with all those sexy curves, I just knew this was the car I needed to be driving.

"You just continue to surprise me." Ashlyn nestled into the soft leather seat and I swear I heard her purr.

We drove the rest of the way in silence. It wasn't forced or awkward, just an easy ride with no need for dialogue. I saw her eyelids droop, fighting against her long blinks as we pulled into my undercover parking garage. I needed to get her out of this car and into my bed ASAP.

I flicked off my seat belt and ejected myself from the car. She sat unmoving until I popped open the passenger side door, the noise startling her awake.

"Shit. I must have drifted off." She blinked under the bright halogen lights.

"Let's get you into bed." I leaned inside the cabin, wrapping my arms around her and pulling her out.

"I can walk, Dan. You don't have to carry me," she protested, wriggling till her feet hit the floor.

"Okay, babe. Let's walk then." My hands found their way around her hips and guided her toward the elevator.

She mumbled something I didn't quite make out, leaning into me as we climbed up the belly of the building till we reached my floor. It was the top level, which only housed two apartments. Mine, with the other belonging to my brother, Troy. Having your best friend as your neighbor had been the coolest feature of this place so when the two penthouse apartments opened up, we didn't even think twice about signing on the dotted line.

We slid out of the elevator and made it to my front door, her hot little body molded to my side. I managed to open the door, while holding Ashlyn in my arms, kicking the door closed behind us the minute we'd stepped through it. Last thing I needed was for Troy to take an interest and poke his head outside his door.

"I need the bathroom. I can't sleep unless I wash this bar smell off me." Ashlyn stirred awake.

"Mmmm, you're going to need help washing your back." My dick punched out against my jeans in appreciation.

"No. By myself." Ashlyn struggled to keep her eyes open. "I mean it, Dan. I'm locking the bathroom door."

"Okay. Okay. I promise I won't look but leave the door

unlocked. If you fall and crack your head on the tub, I want to be able to get to you." She could barely stand straight; I'm not sure how the whole showering herself was going to work.

Still, I knew I had to pick my battles and this one wasn't one I had my heart set on winning. She was obviously trying to prove a point and I would let her do that. End result would be the same. Her. Me. In my bed. I half-carried her to my bedroom, stepping into the large en-suite and flicking on the overhead lights.

"Here are some towels." I placed them on the tub beside her. "You sure you don't want me to stick around?" I gave her one last chance to think it through.

"No, I'm good. I'll only be a few minutes." She yawned, leaning up against the bathroom sink. "Go!" She pointed to the door, slightly more awake than when we had walked in. Well at least now she wouldn't drown.

I begrudgingly walked out of the bathroom, closing the door behind me. I heard the spray of the water hitting the tiles of the bathroom stall as I made my way back into my bedroom. I laid out a pair of clean boxer shorts and my Ramones T-shirt on the chair in the sitting room between my bedroom and my closet. I figured she would work it out, having no other way to walk to get to the bed. I wasn't going to risk pissing her off by barging in on her.

I pulled off my clothes and shoes, leaving them in a pile in the corner. It had been a long-ass day for me, too, my sheets felt fucking amazing as I slid between them. My body relaxed between the layers of Egyptian cotton. No shit, as douchey as it sounded, you really *could* tell the difference between thread counts. I thought for sure the sales lady at Bed, Bath and Beyond was just flirting with me when she fed me that line.

No crashing sound came from the bathroom, so I assumed Ashlyn was doing okay. I closed my eyes and tried to not think about the fact she was naked and wet not more than ten feet away. Fuck. I squeezed the bridge of my nose. This was not going well for me. The water shut off and I rolled to my side, figuring it was probably better she didn't see the massive hard-on I was packing. I would keep my promise and not touch her but I couldn't stop biology from happening.

After what seemed to take forever, Ashlyn walked in, toweling off her hair. My Ramones shirt looked huge on her tiny little body. I rolled onto my back to watch her. Fucking mesmerized by her.

"Thanks for the clothes." She shot me a smile that hit me square in the balls.

"Don't mention it." No really, don't mention it 'cause the more I think about her skin touching my stuff the more I was likely to combust.

"They smell of you." She slid into the bed beside me, her hair still wet. Her leg brushed up against me and I tried to remember to fucking breathe.

"Is that a good thing? I promise they're clean."

"Yeah, it's a good thing. I like the way you smell." She moved her face close to me on the pillow. I was struggling not to kiss her.

A kiss should be okay though, 'cause I only promised no sex. Kissing was definitely allowed. I leaned and lightly touched her lips, my hand moving up her leg. The edge of the boxer shorts she was wearing hitting my fingertips as I moved up her thigh.

"I like that your pussy is currently sitting where my junk used to be. Please tell me you aren't wearing panties." I couldn't help grin. That thought alone almost made me come, hotter than imagining her in sexy lingerie.

"Dan." She smacked me across the chest. "You always have to take it that step too far."

"Ashlyn, I'm fucking dying here. I know you said no sex and I'm going to respect that, but you're fucking beautiful. As far as my balls are concerned, I'm not taking it far enough." I kissed her neck, slowly. I didn't want to scare her off but there was no way I could not touch her, even if it was just with my lips.

"You know, there are other things we can do other than sex." She gave me a slow smile.

My heart fucking stopped beating as I looked down at her, those gorgeous green eyes boring into me. "Yes, whatever it is, yes."

"You haven't even heard what it is yet." She giggled, scrunching up her nose. She had the tiniest freckles just below the bridge and fuck if that didn't make her more adorable. I wanted her in whatever way she would let me have her.

"I don't care. Whatever you are suggesting I'm down for." The realization of what I was saying hit me square in the nuts. I'd never wanted a woman enough to just have her any way she'd let me. Fuck, most of the time if the girl wasn't down for what I was suggesting, there would be ten others waiting in line to take her place. But with Ash it was different, and apparently now I was different.

"Dan, I meant just holding. Maybe some kissing." She turned in my arms, her back flush against my front. This was not what I had in mind.

My hands wandered down her body, moving across her hips before cupping her ass. It was so pert and perfect just like the rest of her. "Can I touch your ass when I hold you?" I nipped at her ear.

"Yes." She sighed or was it a moan? It was all kinds of fucking sexy and wrapped up in the same kind of need that I had going on. I don't know why she was fighting this. I wanted her and I know she wanted me.

"Babe, you have an itch tonight? 'Cause I'm more than happy to help you scratch it." I licked her neck, pulling her ass tight into my groin.

"Dan." I loved the way she said my name. She could ask me for anything right now and I'd probably agree. "Can I be honest with you?"

"Babe, my erection is poking you in the ass. Please, by all means be fucking honest." I tried not to laugh because it really *wasn't* funny. No girl had ever gotten under my skin like this one.

"I like you but this is moving way too fast. I'm not like those other girls, I don't just want to be a lay for you." She turned to face me, her eyes wide.

"Ashlyn, you could *never* just be a lay to me." My fingers tipped her chin toward me. "Or to any other guy for that matter. You're different." I was lost right now. The thought of her with someone else made me want to punch something.

"Are you just saying that because you want to sleep with me?" She wasn't convinced. I could hear the vulnerability in her voice. This was her, no bullshit, no attitude, just her. It twisted me in knots so tight my chest hurt.

I knew how to get a girl into bed. I knew how to make her feel good and come so hard she forgets where she is, but I had no idea how to convince a girl, *this* girl, that she meant more to me than that.

"No. I mean yes. I mean, I want to sleep with you but that's not the reason I'm saying it. Honestly, babe, I have no idea what I am doing here. I have no fucking clue but I know I would rather have no sex and sleep beside you all night than be screwing a whole bunch of random girls. I know it's not romantic but it's all I've really got."

"Dan, that was plenty romantic." She pressed her lips against my mouth, her sweetness fucking destroying me.

"Sooo does that mean we're going to have sex?" I bit back a grin, the throbbing between my legs unrelenting.

"No, not tonight. Just hold me." She flung her arms around my neck and nestled up against my chest.

I groaned as her thigh moved up my body, snaking around my leg. My balls were so tightly drawn up I'm surprised I wasn't gargling them.

"Okay, babe. But I'm probably going to have to go jerk off first." I squeezed her hip. "Unless, you want to do it?"

She smiled before closing her eyes. "You go handle it yourself this time. I need to sleep."

I choked back a laugh. The feel and smell of her on me meant it wouldn't take very long. I was so hard it hurt, and I wanted inside her in the worst way. Hell, at this point, I wouldn't even have to jerk off. Just thinking about her would probably be enough.

I woke up in a panic, like some really bad shit was going down. I couldn't work out if it was a dream or something else was going on, like some kind of alarm had sounded. I pushed myself up in bed, trying to work out what the fuck was going on and noticed Ashlyn was gone. I fumbled for my phone to check for a message. I had about ten unread texts but nothing from her, and it was six a.m. I kicked off the covers, my heart beating so hard in my chest I thought it would crash through my ribs. Where had she gone? Why was she not with me? The reasons *why* taking a backseat to finding her. I flung open my bedroom door and jogged out to the living room. The glow of the TV hit me as I entered the room. The sound had been muted. Ashlyn was sleeping soundly curled in an armchair, the remote control tucked up under her chin.

"Hey." I knelt down beside her, brushing the hair away from her face. It's like someone put my internal organs in a blender. I was so fucking relieved she hadn't left. "Ashlyn." I traced her chin with my fingers, wondering why she had left my bed.

"Hmm." She slowly opened an eye, mumbling something that made no sense.

"What are you doing out here?" I pulled the remote from her hand; the stupid buttons had made indentations on her face. I wanted to pitch it against a wall for trying to mess with the perfection.

"I woke up and I couldn't sleep." She yawned, stretching out in the chair. "I didn't want to wake you so I came out to watch TV."

"I don't care if you wake me." She didn't fight me as I lifted her into my arms and pulled her off the chair. "Just don't go leaving my bed in the middle of the night." As strange as it sounded, I hated the thought of her being out in the living room alone. It pissed me off, which made no fucking sense. Feelings are just plain weird. "I'm taking you back to bed."

The remote was still in my hand so I hit the power button and tossed it on the now vacant chair. Ashlyn's body was limp in my arms, allowing me to pull her closer to my body.

"Dan," she mumbled into my bare chest, the vibrations from her words kind of tickled as her head rested against me.

"Yeah?" I carried her from the living room back into my bedroom.

"I had an itch while you were sleeping." She had a dopey grin on her face as her sleepy eyelids closed.

My dick jumped in my boxer shorts, all of sudden very interested in the conversation we were having. Yeah, you and me both buddy.

"Fuck, babe, now I'm really pissed you didn't wake me."

"It's okay. I scratched *it* myself." She laughed to herself as I gently laid her on the bed. Well that sure as hell got my attention. The thought of her touching herself made me both hard and jealous. Jealous I had missed out on seeing it.

I slid into the bed beside her, pulling her body back onto mine. "That's kind of hot. Did you think of me?" Hoping like hell she did, 'cause if it were any other fucker I would be hunting him down and ripping off his balls. No shit. I would tear his sack right off.

"Oh yeah. I came hard, too." She mumbled against my chest as I hooked her leg up on my hip.

"Ashlyn." I swallowed, imagining her hot, wet pussy being teased by her fingertips, her body shaking with pleasure, as she got closer to climax. I'd only seen her come once and it killed me to know I missed it. Fuck, it killed me to know I wasn't the one who was making her come. The only consolation was that she'd had me in her head while she was doing it.

"Yeah." She opened one eye slightly, the slash of bright green searing me.

"If you won't wake me can you at least film it for me next time?"

"Maybe. You'll have to wait and find out."

"SO YOU GUYS ARE DATING?" MEGS HOBBLED OVER TO HER REFRIGERator. "I need more peas for this foot. The Physiotherapist said I'm so lucky I didn't tear anything. I can't believe I needed to take a sick day." She barely took a breath as she hopped back to the couch.

Megs rarely took a personal day and when she did, she was usually dying. Not literally, but really sick. So when I called her this morning and she told me she wasn't going to work, I thought it was the perfect time to spend the day with her. Monday was my usual day off and the only plans I had was more fruitless job searching on the Internet. Which was depressing. Plus, I needed to tell someone what the hell was going on.

"I guess we're dating. It's so weird, we didn't really talk about it. I swear I lose IQ points when I'm around that man. I can't think straight."

Only I would be stuck in a situation where I wasn't exactly sure whether or not we were actually dating. I mean, we hadn't agreed on anything and he hadn't exactly asked me out, he was just there. All the time. I had spent the last three nights with him. And I was seeing him again tonight. And despite him being a manwhore, he hadn't slept with me yet and was still interested. If I was compiling a case, the evidence surely pointed to the beginnings of a relationship.

"Just go with the flow, Ash, have some fun with him. No one said you have to marry him. I for one, think this is amazing news. Dan Evans. He really is hot." Megs piled the peas on her bandaged foot. Those shoes had a lot to answer for.

"Yeah, well don't go patting me on the back just yet. I'm probably just a phase for him or something. By next week he'll be interested in someone else. I'm not getting ahead of myself just yet."

By his own omission I wasn't his type - big tits and blowjobs. Big tits I didn't have and as he hadn't experienced my blowjobs, the jury was still out. I think I was okay. I hadn't exactly had a lot of practice, but of the guys I *had* blown, none had ever complained. I needed to keep perspective. Like working at the bar, it's for now not for always.

"So enjoy it while it lasts." Megs was constantly chasing that silver lining. She leaned forward to whisper despite us being the only two people in her apartment. "Is he...as good as they say?"

"I don't know." I shrugged. "I haven't slept with him yet but I've seen it and felt it and it's huge and I'm not sure how the hell it's going to fit."

By *it*, I meant his penis. I had taken a peek on the second night while I was giving him a hand job. Not that I'd seen it in its entirety, more like I surmised what it would be like from the sum of all parts. It was long and thick. It was definitely a two hander. Far from average. I could only imagine how spectacular it would be in the flesh. Flesh. An appropriate word based on what I was thinking.

"It will fit. I'm sure it will be fun working out the logistics." Megs laughed.

Sure, it was funny for her; she wasn't the one who would be attempting to insert *that* into her vagina. Although, I really wasn't sure I would be either. Now, there was this heavy expectation around the sex. What if it sucked for him? And I don't mean in the oral sex kind of suck, I mean just really average sex kind of suck. It was all too hard. No pun intended.

"I guess I'll find out. Eventually." Or at least I hoped. Maybe I didn't. Gah! I was impossible. Things were easier when he was just some sexy, cocky musician I'd never sleep with.

"Hey, you should invite him to your birthday party on the weekend." Megs sat up, prompting the bag of peas to spill off her foot. She was wearing her up-to-no-good face, the one that could only mean trouble. No doubt the trouble would be meant for me.

"Megs, I don't think that's such a good idea. I mean, I just met him," I said, trying to rationalize.

I need to gain control of the runaway train that was playing out in Megs's head. Oh I know I didn't know what she was thinking, unfortunately I did not possess mind-reading abilities, but I knew where this was heading. The trouble that I spoke of. Right here. Alive and well in Megan Winters.

"Not sure I want to subject him to something as personal as a birthday party. Besides it's hardly a party, just a couple of our friends getting together for drinks. Introductions to the friends is a pretty serious step. He will think I'm trying to show him off and it will make his ego bigger than it already is, or think I'm pushing the relationship issue." Solid argument. She could hardly argue with that logic.

As much as I wanted to celebrate my special day with Dan, it just didn't seem likely. Firstly, I'd known him for less than a week. It was too soon even if I was dating a regular guy—assuming what we were actually doing was dating—and secondly, it's Dan freaking Evans. The last thing he probably wanted to do was hang out with a bunch of my friends.

The other thing was the whole pressure of the occasion. I didn't want him to feel obligated to do anything. Best solution was to let it go. Just not mention it and if we were together next year...yeah like that would happen. Welcome to Delusionville, population one. Let's face it - we wouldn't have to *deal* with it next year.

"Well I still think you should ask him. So you've only known him a few days, big deal. He made you come without putting his cock in you, that alone deserves an invite." Megs was not buying my *solid* argument. While Megs liked to banter around idealism, I preferred realism. As in, I am really not going to embarrass myself by asking him and being turned down or worse, him saying yes and being bored. Nope. No chance. End of story. There would be no sexy Power Station bass player helping me ring in my special day.

"Nope." I folded my arms defiantly across my chest. "I'm not asking and neither are you. Besides, I assume that because they aren't touring right now means they are probably recording, so I'm sure he has better things to do."

"Fine. Kill joy." Megs pouted. "You know it wasn't just for your benefit you know. You could have invited that sexy best friend of his too so I had some entertainment. Has Troy Harris mentioned me?"

"I haven't seen Troy. Like I said. We haven't really done anything much other than be in bed together."

"Sounds like a fling to me. Minus the no sex part. In that department you are letting yourself down."

"You're impossible, you know that? This didn't start out as a fling. I'm not sure what it started out as, all I know is I'm now in it and still none the wiser as to what *it* actually is." Saying it out loud didn't actually clarify it either. Hell, was I going to have to ask Dan?

"So, you seeing him tonight?" Megs was fishing. Not that she really had to, I would happily volunteer everything I knew. Which we had already established wasn't a lot.

"Probably. He knows I have the night off. I told him I might see him around." I tried to sound casual but in fact I was an internal mess. I wanted to see him but that would mean I had seen him every night since I met him. I'm sure that wasn't smart. Better to leave it as a possibility. Maintain some control over this situation.

"Might see him around? What are you planning a date or a drive by?"

I had been at Megs's most of the day. Well, all of the day. The subject of Dan had featured heavily in the conversation, as had the consumption of Ben and Jerry's Half Baked. We had moved on to Chunky Monkey, and I was glad I was wearing my old jeans and Bruins jersey. That kind of indulgence was bound to end up on my ass. The ice cream I meant, though I'm sure if Dan had the chance he'd take a shot at my ass as well.

"You are supposed to be supportive. What happened to being on my side?" I took a spoonful and shoved it into my mouth.

"I'm supportive of you getting some. Stop playing it safe. Just turn up. Surprise him." Megs dug in with her spoon. We should probably stop before we finished another pint. *Should* was a word I seemed to be having a problem with these days.

"His apartment has a heap of security. I need like a retinal scan just to get in the door."

I was exaggerating. I had no idea what I needed to do to get in his building but I assumed I wouldn't be able to just walk in off the street.

"So surprise him at the door. Turn up." Megs stopped eating. She was serious. Like I could just turn up on his doorstep unannounced.

"What if he is doing something, or someone else?" Even though we hadn't explored the boundaries of what we were doing, I was hoping this wasn't a possibility. He had said things last night, things I hoped just weren't for my benefit. There was still I had a tiny bit of doubt. Okay, more than a tiny bit.

"Ash, he wouldn't."

"Do I know that?"

"Well, one way to find out. Go there and see for yourself." Megs pushed her spoon into the half-eaten pint, hopping to her feet. "Go, then report back." She yanked on my arm.

"I can't just go. I need to change or something." I glanced down at Jersey and jeans. I wasn't even wearing makeup.

"Ash, he won't care what you're wearing. Stop making excuses and go." She tugged on my arm again.

"I'm going, I'm going." I rolled my eyes, lifting myself from the couch. "Sit back down and elevate the foot. I can see myself out."

"'Bye. Call me," Megs called out from behind me. I knew she would start burning up the phone if she didn't hear within an hour.

"'Bye." I grabbed my purse and phone and headed out the door.

Megs was right. I needed answers or at the very least some kind of definition as to what we had going on.

I paced in the front of Dan's building; the wind tunneled through the high-rises and it was freezing. I needed a strategy. I had been partially right about the security. While no retinal scan was required, you did actually need to be a resident. Though the whole element of surprise would be gone if I called him and told him I was here. If he had anyone up there then she could easily be shoved out a back entry. Think Ashlyn, think. I paced. My Vans padded softly against the concrete. It came to me. Brilliance. Pizza.

I called a local pizza delivery and gave them Dan's address, paying for it on my sad and overused credit card. It's not like the pizza charge was going to make a huge difference in the big scheme of things, I was already skating on the poverty line. Besides, it would be worth it for my peace of mind.

I waited, hoping my brilliant plan would work. See, I'm sure I wasn't the only girl who had thought up the whole order-a-pizza-and-get-into-meet-the-band idea but my version had a twist. While ordering said pizza and making payment, I tipped them an extra ten bucks to deliver it with a message. I wanted credit for the pizza so when the delivery guy showed up he would tell Dan I had sent it as a gift. Which of course he would accept because, it's not like I was going to send him flowers. Then the second part of my plan would spring into action but this was largely dependent on the delivery driver. This was one time I was hoping for a bored stoner who didn't care about job integrity.

I waited. And waited. Finally after thirty agonizing minutes, a car with a pizza box mounted on the roof came into view. Thankfully no one had called the cops to report the redheaded loiterer who was talking to herself in the street.

I raced to the door just as the delivery guy was buzzing the intercom. I put my head down, pretending to fish for my keys in my purse.

"Yeah." Dan's unmistakable voice burst through the speaker.

"Hey dude, I have a pizza delivery for Dan Evans." The driver was not only bored but also clearly not interested. I hit the jackpot of slackers. Score.

"Um, I didn't order any pizza. Wait, what kind is it?" Dan's confused voice made me smile. He sounded adorable, knowing he didn't order pizza but still interested in the possibility of pizza.

I continued digging around in my purse, not that I needed to bother with my theatrical display. Delivery guy didn't even glance at me, let alone care I was there.

"It's peperoni with extra cheese but it's already been paid for. Some girl called Ashlee Murphy sent it to you." Delivery Dumbass read off his provided receipt. I wanted to choke him. How fucking hard is it you say Ashlyn? My parents had a lot to answer for - I'd never had my name on a lunch box growing up.

"Dude, do you mean Ashlyn?" I breathed a sigh of relief thankful Dan pieced it together.

"Dude, I didn't take the call, I'm just the driver. Do you want this pie or not?" Dumbass barked into the intercom. So much for service with a smile.

"Yeah, sure. Let me buzz you up. I'll code you into the elevator. Just hit P."

I pretended to insert my key as the lock popped open, walking through casually to the elevator. Dumbass followed close behind me, giving me a sideways glance as we both reached for the P on the button.

"You going to the Penthouse?" I raised my brow at him, pretending to act surprised.

"Yeah, I've got a delivery." He tapped his padded delivery bag like I was an idiot and couldn't see he was holding a pizza. Visual reinforcement was obviously important because the uniform he was wearing wouldn't be a big enough tip off.

"I didn't order pizza." I acted annoyed, giving him the stare down, holding the door open to stop the elevator's assent.

"Look, lady. It's for some guy called Dan." Dumbass was getting annoyed or impatient. I didn't care for either of his moods.

"Dan is my neighbor. He is also a shitty tipper and an asshole. He should know better than to let unauthorized people into this building. You could be a murderer or a thief. Give me your stinking pizza and I will deliver it myself to him, where I will give him a piece of my mind." I held the door open, unrelenting.

"Here." He tore open the Velcro flap and shoved the box in my hand. "I don't get paid enough for this shit." He stalked from the elevator and back out toward the door.

I smiled at myself, pleased with my ingenuity. I now had access and the pizza. It was a win-win. I let the metal doors close, my silent victory bubbling from the inside.

My heart pounded as I moved up the floors, I wasn't sure if it was from excitement or from nerves. Dan had asked me to come by later. Technically we hadn't discussed time, so this was later. He had also randomly shown up at my door so precedence had been set. Yes? Yes!

The elevator doors parted, opening out to the Penthouse floor, Dan's door only a few feet away.

I knocked loudly on the door, wondering if Dan had video surveillance. Pizza in hand. Feeling a little vulnerable.

A stunning brunette opened the door, her beautiful brown eyes shining brightly. My phone buzzed from inside the pocket of my jeans. I decided that what was in front of me deserved more attention. Her long legs clad in designer jeans, her ample boobs strained against her fitted cotton top.

"Hey, thanks!" She handed over a five-dollar bill and accepted the box from my hands.

I blinked, dumbfounded. Did I trip and hit my head on the way up here? My mind couldn't register what my eyes were seeing.

"Umm..." I looked at the money in my palm, which had taken the spot of the pizza box.

"Oh Sorry. That's just the tip. Dan said the pizza was paid for by some girl. Is that right?"

"Yeah." That's right, *some girl*. The very girl who is standing in front of you. What an ass. Not only was he with someone else but they were going to be enjoying the pizza I had paid for. I secretly hoped they both choked on it.

"Mommy," squealed a little boy as he ran to the door and hugged his mother's legs, aka the women standing in front of me; he must have been no older than three. What? I lost all muscle control of my face as my mouth dropped open and my eyes almost popped right out of my skull. There was no mistaking the resemblance, Dan's dark hair and eyes in a tiny little boy package. What the actual fuck? He had a fucking kid? I felt like I was going to throw up.

Unable to speak and quite impressed I still had the ability to move, I slowly turned to walk away. I should have known better. What was I thinking? He was a player. What did I expect? The kid had definitely thrown me; I couldn't believe that clown was responsible for another human being.

Blindly I rounded the corner, desperate to get back into the elevator and as far away from here as possible. Whatever we had been doing was over. Dan wasn't going to get the opportunity to explain, I believe it was all fairly self-explanatory. There was no way in hell I was going to stoop and make a scene, why should I bother? I was worth more than that. Granted, we hadn't spoken about being exclusive and technically we weren't even dating, but I would be no one man's alternative. My phone buzzed again from my pocket. Once again, bigger fish to fry.

I didn't see the body I collided with. My face mashed rather spectacularly into a warm and muscular chest. It was hard to breathe but he smelled good. Nice. Death by pectorals would be a cool way to die.

"Ashlyn?" Troy's throaty voice pulled me from destiny with suffocation. Great. The scenario would be so much more enjoyable with an audience. Not.

"Oh, hey." I casually righted myself, trying to keep my expression neutral. No doubt he had been covering for his bestie. Even though inside I felt like a bunch of explosives just had a party with a box of matches, I wasn't giving either of them the satisfaction. Yep, nothing to see here, folks. "I was just leaving."

"Leaving? Dan called and mentioned you and pizza." Troy looked confused. I wondered if woman and child in Dan's apartment would have the same level of confusion. Perhaps they needed a diagram. See here, people, this circle of crazy is you and *this* is Ashlyn, walking away. Dumbass. I wasn't sure if that insult was directed at Dan or myself. Either one was a viable option.

"Ashlyn. What the fuck?" Dan's unmistakable voice boomed from behind me. He actually had the nerve to sound surprised and irate. Seriously, the balls on this guy.

My mind conjured up which slow and painful death would be most satisfying. "I really underestimated you, Dan Evans. Well done. Worst judgment call of my life." I fought the urge to applaud. This for me was a new kind of low.

"Me?" He narrowed his eyes as they raked over my body. "I'm not the one who turned up to your apartment and disrespected you. Troy, so help me, if this is your fucking doing, I'm going to punch you right in the nuts."

"Dude, ease up. I get you're upset but it's not the end of the world. Now kick it down a notch or me and you are going to be having words." Troy glared at Dan.

"Troy had nothing to do with this. Your friend stayed loyal to the end." I had no idea why I was defending Troy; right now I couldn't stand the sight of either of them. A huge bonfire with all things Power Station sounded like a good idea, possibly followed by a Dan voodoo doll I would castrate. "And as far as disrespecting goes, you are in a class all onto yourself. Take a good look, Dan, 'cause I'm out of here."

"Fuck." Dan grabbed my arm and blew out a slow defeated breath. "Look, maybe we can work through this. I should have told you. It just didn't come up."

Was I hearing him correctly? Was this man actually that delusional? I didn't know whether to laugh or cry as I shook off his grasp. "Didn't come up? What is wrong with you? How can you be with me in any capacity and not have fucking told me, Dan? I shouldn't have to walk up here and find out like this. What if I hadn't been here today? Would you have ever come clean?"

"Of course, eventually. I didn't think it was going to be an issue. You know you are partly to blame here, too, Ash. You should have said something." He folded his arms in front of his chest looking disappointed. *He* was playing the victim card? No words. Okay maybe I had just a few left.

"Oh my god. You have the nerve to blame me? Excuse me while I call the men in the white coats, Dan, because you are even crazier than I thought."

"Hey guys, maybe lets move out of the hallway. I think you both need to calm down. Yeah?" Troy tried to play the diplomat. Delsuionville had another resident it seemed. Calming down was not on my agenda. Along with ever seeing or speaking to either of them again.

"I cannot believe you're asking me to calm down. Troy, I'm appalled." And disgusted and most of all hurt, I finished the sentence in my head.

"Ash, I know he sounds like a lunatic but Dan's just passionate. Honestly, let's sit this down and see if it's something you guys can work through. You came all the way down here. With a pizza." Troy smiled as he continued to mediate.

"Which was straight up one of the sexiest things any girl has ever done. Until you show up..." Dan waved his arms wildly in front of me, "like that."

"There is nothing to work out. I'm not sorry I showed up. At least now I know the truth. The only thing I *am* sorry is that I wasted any of my time on you." My voice sounded strangled, a mixture of anger and betrayal. I was trying to maintain control but my body was not co-operating.

Dan blinked as if seeing my hurt for the first time. His unexplained anger slightly receded. He had to know this was the end. There could be no coming back from here. He hissed out through his clenched jaw. "I hate the motherfucking Bruins!"

"What?" My brain went into free fall and I wondered if I had missed a part of the conversation somewhere. The part where that comment actually made sense.

"You," he paused running his hands impatiently through his hair, "are wearing a Bruins jersey." I glanced down the hockey jersey I was wearing. The same one my father had given me when I turned twenty-one. He had played hooky from the bar and taken me to a game. He rarely took time off but for each of our twenty-firsts he made the time. It was just the two of us. We had heckled the visiting side and eaten pretzels. He bought me a beer and told me that even though I was all grown up, I'd always be his little girl. It was one of the greatest gifts he'd ever given me. Every time I wore this jersey, it reminded me of my dad and how much he loved me.

"I hate them, Ash. I mean, at least you're not supporting a Canadian side but, Jesus Christ. The fucking Bruins?" Dan screwed up his face with such distaste.

"What?" I repeated, hearing what he had said but not understanding any of it. How did the Bruins have anything to do with the fact he had a child and possibly a girlfriend? Both of which he hadn't told me about. The fact we supported opposing teams was not an issue here, the fact he was a lying, cheating low life was.

"I said," he slowly repeated. "The Bruins—"

"I heard you, moron. How does that change the fact you have a son?" I planted my hands on my hips defiantly.

"What the hell?" Dan's eyes widened. "I don't have a kid!"

"Dan, I saw the girl in your apartment. That little boy looks just like you." I couldn't believe he was going to continue to deny it. There was nothing wrong with my eyesight, and I know what I saw.

"Ash, that's my sister Kim. The little boy is my nephew Sam. I guess he kind of looks like me, half the kid's luck if he does." He smirked before the smile slowly slid from his face. "Wait a second, you thought that he was *my* kid?"

"Well, what was I supposed to think?" His nephew. Well that would explain the resemblance. Still, it was an easy mix up. Dan wouldn't have been the first rock star to have a love child.

"I thought you were pissed at me 'cause I didn't welcome you with open arms wearing *that* jersey. Holy shit, you weren't even going to ask me? You were just going to walk?" The realization hit him. He moved closer, leaving little room between us. The tension was palpable.

"What about you? You can't get over the fact I'm a Bruins fan," I shot back. At least my reason, albeit misguided, was valid.

"Ash, that's a big fucking deal. You show up here on my turf, wearing the enemy's colors. What did you think was going to happen?" He stared down at my jersey with such disgust.

"Enemy's colors? You are seriously deranged."

"Children. Play nice." Troy stood between us, pushing our bodies apart. "Obviously there has been a misunderstanding here. Everyone needs to take a fucking breath and chill."

"Hey, Dan." The mysterious brunette who had now been identified as Dan's sister emerged into the hallway. "Looks like you're busy. We'll see you another time." Her eyes darted toward me. Great. She had heard everything. Not that there was any danger of her *not* hearing, neither of us had been using our inside voices. Could this get any worse?

"You don't have to go," Dan and I both echoed over each other, adding to the awkwardness. Apparently it could. Get worse, that is.

"It's getting late and I wanted to get Sam home before dark." She wrestled with the dark haired little boy in her arms.

"No wanna go home."

"Heya, buddy." Dan temporarily diffused the awkwardness, and gave his nephew his full attention. "Don't give your mama a hard time, okay? Your daddy is going to be getting home soon and will want to see you before you need to go to sleep. Don't forget what I taught you." He ruffled the little boy's hair.

"I wanna wock!" Sam proudly held his fist in the air.

"That's it, Sammy. You're making Uncle Dan so proud." The beaming smile was a dead giveaway.

"Stop being a bad influence." Kim rolled her eyes at Dan before turning to me. "Ashlyn, hopefully we'll see you again."

"Sure." I nodded politely. Not like I could say, *actually I'm hoping the earth beneath my feet will open up and swallow me whole so chances of us crossing paths are remote.* My silent prayer remained unanswered, Kim giving me an amused smile before ushering Sam into the waiting elevator.

And then there were three.

"We still need a Ref here or are you good?" Troy didn't even try to hide his amusement.

Dan and I stared at each other, neither one of us wanting to be the first one to cave.

"You are both nutjobs," Troy volunteered, trying to coax one of us out of the imposed game of verbal chicken we had going on.

"Dude, it's the fucking Bruins." Dan cracked first. Silently I celebrated. Victories were still victories no matter how small. Pretty sure I read that on a fortune cookie somewhere.

"She's from Boston, you moron. They don't have a lot of love for the Rangers over there. I can guarantee you that associating with her is not going to affect our chances of winning."

"I give up. I can't keep it a secret anymore." I couldn't help it; the situation was just too absurd.

"What?" Dan's eyes narrowed as he moved closer to me. "What secret?"

"The whole career thing on Wall Street was just a cover. I was really sent here by my city to infiltrate New York and send infor-mation back. I've been watching training camps and practices of all of your teams." I leaned in and whispered, "The end is near."

"I fucking knew it."

"Dan, she's joking." Troy shook his head, biting back his grin. "Ash, listen. He isn't the sharpest knife in the drawer but I assure you, he's no woman's baby daddy. And, Dan, there is no sporting espionage going on here. You are both acting like tools and on that note, I'm out!" Troy strolled past us and into Dan's apart-ment. He emerged a few moments later carrying the pizza box. "Neither of you deserve this, I'm taking this baby where she is appreciated." He shoved a slice into his mouth and walked into his apartment, shutting the door behind him.

"Well that was just fucking rude." Dan scratched his head. "So this is all kinds of messed up, huh?"

It was so hard not to smile at how adorable he was. "So you don't have any secret girlfriends or children?"

Might as well get it out there. I mean we were already knee-deep in craziness, what's an extra inch or two.

"Ash, I never have unprotected sex. Not ever. Unless I have some magic power that can get a chick pregnant through a rubber, there is no chance."

"You didn't answer about the girlfriend."

"I haven't had a girlfriend in three years and that's the truth. I don't really date. You know, being on the road, fans and stuff. Gets kinda hard to maintain a relationship." He rubbed the back of his neck and shrugged.

"Oh. Of course. Yep that makes sense." I swallowed.

Well, that answered *that* question. He doesn't date. My heart sank. I know this was the first time I was asking the question, I mean *seriously* asking the question, but I was still a little disappointed. He hadn't led me on and at no point did he tell me this was anything more than what it was. Which was nothing. I had to at least admire his honesty. Right? Why wasn't it making me feel any better?

"Ash, you wanna go inside? I don't think Troy is going to share so I'll order another pizza. We can hang out." Dan nudged my arm with a playful grin teasing the corners of his mouth. He had no idea how his honesty had punctured my heart. I had wanted to know and yet not been prepared for the truth, and upon hearing it, my heart retreated back behind its guarded wall.

"Sure." I pushed aside my feelings of rejection, plastering a fake smile across my face as I made my way to the door.

"Ash, can you take off the Jersey before we go in." Dan grabbed my arm stopping me from entering. "Please."

"Dan," I dug deep, finding the sweetest voice I had, "of course. That is no problem at all."

There were so many reasons for me to just turn around and head home. Or go back to Megs's and devour the pint of Clusterfluff she had tucked away in her icebox. Yet, I didn't. Instead, I found myself wanting to stay. Perhaps even make Dan suffer a little. Oh, I know it was juvenile but I shouldn't be the only one who felt the pain. No, I should share it. That would be the polite thing to do.

I peeled off my jersey reveling the cute, pale pink bra I had on underneath. After neatly folding my prized top and storing it in my purse, I found my real smile.

"Holy shit." Dan's eyes widened, unable to pull his gaze from my breasts. This really was just a little too easy.

I sauntered past Dan and into his apartment. Maybe now I knew where I stood, things would be easier. No more questions and I could stop second-guessing myself. Maybe I should just break the rules and have a one-night stand. If there were ever going to be time to do it, this would be it. Dan was sexy and interested in me. What could be the harm? I was willing to play the night out and see where it took me and if I ended up naked, underneath Dan Evans, rock star, I knew I wouldn't regret it. At least, I hoped I wouldn't.

I DIDN'T KNOW IF THIS WAS SOME BULLSHIT TEST OR SOMETHING, BUT there was no way I was *not* going to look at the pair of perky tits that Ash had on display. Who fucking knew that when I asked her to take off her top, she would actually do it? Of course, that hadn't been my plan when I'd asked. I just couldn't stand the thought of that fucking jersey being paraded around in my house. Shit, it took everything in me not to tear that monstrosity from her perfect, tiny body. It was like watching your enemy sleep with the girl you wanted and I was not going to let the fucking Bruins screw with me like that, not with her.

"Stop staring, Dan."

I couldn't pull my eyes away. She could dress herself up in a million cute little pink bras and it still would be like throwing gasoline on a fire. Fuck, it just made me want her more. Wondering what was underneath, feeling those perfect tits in my mouth, in my hand, surrounding my cock.

Ash snapped her fingers in front of my face, like that was going to be enough to hinder my view. "Dan. You're acting creepy."

"Ash, I'm not making apologies and I'm not looking away. You're fucking beautiful."

"So you're going to sit there and stare all night? I thought we were going to order pizza and *hang*?" She slid her hand down to her waist, popping her hip to the side, with a raised eyebrow. Daring me. Well, I didn't back away from a dare.

I grabbed her waist and pulled her up against my body, my lips going to work on her mouth. I wanted in her in every fucking way. My hard-on punched out against my jeans as her body rubbed against mine, the friction making me harder. She whimpered in surprise but she didn't fight me and just as well 'cause stopping was going to take an act of god.

I attacked her mouth, needing to kiss her more than I needed air. She let out a gentle moan as she rolled her hips against me. I didn't stand a chance. I was so far gone right now she could probably ask me to wear the fucking jersey myself and I would, if it meant I could be inside of her.

"Dan, slow down." She pulled her lips away, her mouth all puffy and swollen. "You aren't going to fuck me in your doorway."

"Ash, I'm not trying to be an asshole right now, but I told you I would be honest, so I am." I tipped her chin so she was looking at me in the eyes. "If we aren't going to get naked in the next five minutes and have sex then we're going to have to call this a night. My balls are so tight, I'm surprised they haven't crawled up inside me and become fucking ovaries. Now, if you want to cuddle, you're going to have to give me at least a solid hour in the bathroom to jerk off 'cause this," I rubbed my hard cock against her, "ain't going away by itself."

I watched her eyes roll back as I hit the sweet spot between her legs. Her hips tilted to meet each roll of mine.

"Dan," she panted, pulling away from me.

"Ashlyn, you need to tell me, babe. You need to tell me right now if you don't want this. I'm not playing tonight."

I stopped, giving her a minute to consider, my cock throbbing so hard I could feel its heartbeat in my ears.

"Yes." Her hands flew around my neck, dragging me back down to her.

"Yes, what?" My lips sucked against the soft skin of her neck. It was probably going to leave a mark but I couldn't make myself care. In fact, it excited me she would have a reminder, of me. Of this.

"Yes, I want this."

Conversation was obsolete. The green light was all I needed as I grabbed her ass and hauled her onto me. She wrapped her legs around me as I continued to grind against her and everything else just fell away. It was like my skin was burning and the only way I could stop the pain was by being inside her. It went beyond just a fuck; this wasn't about me getting my rocks off. This was some deep-seated need I had no explanation for.

I carried her through my apartment, my mouth locked on hers as my hands palmed her ass. This was not going to be a quickie on the floor, oh hell no. For whatever reason she was finally saying yes, and I was not going to give her an opportunity to regret it. Not even a little.

She moaned against my mouth as I threw her on my bed. Clawing at her body as I tried to rip off her fucking jeans. I wasn't trying to be rough but the time for easy had long past. She responded by yanking up my shirt, her fingernail grazing against my torso as she stripped it off. It was so fucking hot.

I lifted off her, pulling off her Vans before peeling away her jeans, tossing them onto the floor. Her hands latched onto the front of my pants, stroking me through the denim while I tried to rid myself of them. It was torture, sweet fucking torture.

"Let me get them off, babe." It killed me to pry her hands away from my crotch. No seriously, I died a little inside, but if I didn't get out of my jeans soon, I would probably be filling them with my load, and that was not an option.

"Get them off or get me off?" Her raised eyebrow and smirk almost did me in.

I kicked off my shoes, socks, and jeans like they were on fire, tearing off my boxers so that nothing was between us. Ash glanced up at me as I moved back onto the bed, her smile clueing me into that she liked what she saw. Her eyes widened when they moved down to my cock, I stroked it for her so she could get the full effect.

"That's never going to fit."

I suppressed a laugh seeing genuine panic cross those sweet green eyes. "It will fit just fine, babe, trust me." I moved my hands to her back and flicked off her bra. Fuck me if it didn't feel like I was unwrapping a present on Christmas morning.

"No seriously, Dan, that thing is huge. It's going to tear me in half."

I pulled the bra away letting her gorgeous tits spill onto her soft, warm skin. They looked even better than I'd imagined. Sure, they weren't huge but my hand fit around them perfectly, the pink tight nipples standing to attention under the roll of my thumb.

"I'll only give you what you can take, Ash, just relax." I lowered myself down onto the mattress, taking her with me.

"Let me make this good for you." My hand moved down her belly to the edge of her panties, deliberating whether or not tearing them off would be a good move. I toyed with the pink lace that matched her bra, not that I gave a shit. It would be so easy to make them disintegrate in my hand. Just one tug would be all it took.

Her own hands joined mine, skirting off her panties before I was able to give their removal any more thought. My fingers roamed in between her legs to feel her bare and wet pussy.

"Hmm, wet already." My fingers circled her core as my mouth lowered onto hers. "Let's see how much wetter I can make you."

I plunged a finger inside her, making her gasp at the invasion. It felt so tight and hot, better than I could have ever imagined. Her wide eyes softened as I slowly stroked her from the inside, my thumb getting busy across her clit. Her back arched, melting into me as I slid in another finger, stretching her as I fucked her with my hand.

"Dan," she moaned. Just hearing her saying my name was getting me off, my swollen cock begging for attention.

"That's it, baby. Let me feel you." I moved in and out of her slick, hot pussy, applying a little more pressure with each thrust. Her wetness coated my fingers in appreciation.

"Ah." She rocked her hips against me, her pussy tightening

around my hand.

"You going to come, babe? 'Cause I want to taste you before you do."

"Oh, Dan."

"Not yet, Ash." I shifted down the bed unable to stand it any longer. My fingers slid out of her soaking wet pussy so I could part her thighs. She was fucking beautiful.

"Dan." She grabbed at me with desperation but I wasn't about to be steered off course, my tongue traveling her belly until it reached the top of her pussy. I could smell the sex rolling off her. She wasn't going to last much longer.

My mouth covered her opening, my tongue darting inside and tasting her. Her thighs wrapped around my head in a vice-like grip as I continued to eat her out. I was merciless, plunging my tongue deeper and deeper into her while my thumb continued to circle her clit. I heard her muffled scream as she grabbed a pillow and bit into it. Her body shook as it got closer to its release. She was wound so fucking tight. I could feel the explosion building.

She was dripping—I felt it run down my mouth and onto the mattress —and bucking against me like a woman possessed. It had obviously been a while since a man had done this right, especially if those ribbed condoms were anything to go by. It made me fucking smile listening to the strangled noises she was making, hearing the girl who was usually so in control unraveling around my mouth. Her eyes were tightly shut as I watched her squirm. She was so close.

"Ash. Let go," I demanded, lifting my mouth away from her for only a second. I thrust my tongue inside her one last time, feeling her tighten around it, pulsing as she came hard. Her screams muted by the pillow that covered her face.

"That's it, babe, let it take you." My fingers replaced my mouth, as I gently continued to pump her, working every last inch of the orgasm through her body.

"Fuck, Dan." Ashlyn pulled the pillow from her face as she relaxed onto the bed. "I've never...it's never been like that." Her sleepy pre-orgasmic grin lit up her eyes.

"I'm not done yet, babe, that was just the preshow. If that

impressed you, just wait for the headliner." And fuck me if it didn't make me puff up my chest like a fucking superhero.

My fingers continued to play as she rolled onto her side. I had to momentarily let go as I moved up beside her, pressing my cock against the crease of her ass. The image was so fucking hot, I wanted to burn it into my brain. I reached across her, digging into the top drawer of my nightstand and pulling out a condom. My cock was so hard it hurt.

She turned, sitting up in bed, and watched as I tore open the packet and rolled the latex down my shaft, licking her lips as I stroked my dick a couple of times. I wanted to fuck that sweet little mouth of hers as well, but right now it was her pussy that I wanted.

"Dan—" I could hear the hesitation in her voice.

"Shhh." I moved my lips to her throat, kissing her skin. "Trust me, I'm not going to hurt you."

She nodded and relaxed back onto the bed, letting me take the lead. Her nipples were tight as my tongue flicked them, teasing the opening of her pussy with the head of my cock.

Ashlyn moaned as I alternated circling her entrance and her clit, and watched me as I stroked my shaft. I could feel her relax, tilting her hips up to me as I continued to tease her. I smiled, knowing that while it was driving me all kinds of crazy, she was riding that train along with me. Her tits bobbing up and down as she sucked in air.

"Dan," she moaned, her hand flying around my cock and pulling it closer toward her, "I want to feel you."

"Here I am, babe." I guided her hand up and down my shaft as I pushed the head of my cock into her.

"Fuck, you're tight." I breathed, feeling the walls of her pussy clamp around my dick. It took everything I had not to blow my load right there.

"Relax, Ash. You put the death grip on me, this is going to be over before either of us wants it to." My dick jerked in protest as I slid out of her. "Just going to give you a little more."

She nodded as I circled her clit with my thumb, watching me push in a little farther this time, her pussy stretching to accommodate me. God, she felt so good. I pulsed slowly, pushing in a little bit farther each time while I kept working her clit. The little noises she was making were driving me fucking insane.

"Oh!" Her mouth formed an "O" as I entered her a little more deeply, her hands bracing against my chest as I arched into her, finally getting most of my dick inside.

"That's it, babe, almost there." I slid in deeper. "You feel so fucking amazing." My hands moved to her hips to steady her as she bucked against me. She was so tight and wet, even with a condom I could feel everything. I imagined if there was fucking in heaven, this is what it would feel like. She stilled as I slide the last inch in, her pussy pulsing around my cock.

"Babe?" I stopped, wanting to be sure she was cool before I continued. Right now a squeeze of her pussy was probably going to set me off anyway, so the break served a dual purpose. She looked so beautiful, her red hair floating around her face like some kind of wild bush fire, her eyes wide.

"OH," Ashlyn moaned as she started to move again. "Holy shit, that feels so good." She rocked against me, grinding her pussy along my shaft.

It was all the reassurance I needed, as I started to pick up the pace. With my hands wrapped around her hips, I started really getting some momentum, sliding the whole length of my cock in and out of her hungry pussy. Her wetness coated me like a badge of honor as I hammered into her a little faster.

"That's it, babe, you got all of me now." I bowed my head down and sucked her neck, tasting the saltiness of sex and sweat. My heavy sack slapped against her ass as I pounded harder.

"Fuck!" I looked down at my cock sliding in and out of her, wanting it to last forever but I knew if I kept watching it was going to be over soon. Me fucking Ashlyn was hotter than any porno.

I slid my hands down her thighs and lifted her legs, resting them over my shoulders. She tilted her hips, her ass rising off the mattress as I got a deeper angle. So fucking tight.

"Dan. Oh. Yes. Yes," Ash moaned, her hands kneading her tits as my cock moved faster.

I could die right now, balls deep inside this girl and I would die with the biggest fucking grin on my face. I'd had a lot of sex over the years, been with a lot of different girls and fucked them every way imaginable, and nothing even came close to the way Ashlyn was making me feel. Fuck, I'd live inside her if I could.

I felt her clamp around my cock and her legs start to waver and I knew she was close. I wanted to make her come more than I wanted my next breath. "That's it, Ash, come for me." I lifted her hips and I drove in deep.

"YES," she screamed, her voice bouncing of the walls. "Yes. Yes." Her body shook as she came hard around me. Her pussy milking my cock sent me into oblivion. Not even Superman and his balls of fucking steel would have been able to fight the urge to come.

"Fuck." I groaned as I exploded into her, my load squirting so hard against the condom it almost hurt. I couldn't stop, riding out the rest of the orgasm while my dick continued to pulse inside her. I let her legs slide off my shoulders and lay either side of me. Her body was limp as I collapsed on top of her. I didn't want to move and hoped like hell I wasn't smothering her as I breathed heavily against her neck.

Ashlyn fisted a handful of my hair, forcing me to lift my head. "Dan." My brain rattled around in my skull as some of the blood that had been in my cock traveled back toward my head.

"Yeah?" I pushed her tangled hair away from her face. She was absolute perfection. I wasn't just thinking that on account having just blown my load either, she was just insanely beautiful in every way imaginable.

"I've never had sex like that. Come like that. I mean, I know it's no big deal for you, but I think you have pretty much ruined me for all other men." Her palm rested against my face.

The thought of her being with another dude made my blood run cold. Some other guy touching her, kissing her, being inside her? Hell, no. It made me want to kick someone's ass just on the possibility it could happen. I would do whatever I needed to do to make sure that shit didn't go down.

"I can assure you, that was a big fucking deal for me, too. And

I'm going to keep making you feel good for as long as you'll let me. So you don't need to worry about anyone else, you just bask in the afterglow." 'Cause if I had anything to do with it, she would be too busy screaming my name to worry about finding anyone else.

"Oh, Dan, you are such a romantic." Ashlyn laughed, running her nails up my back and fuck if it didn't make my cock twitch. Which conveniently, was still buried inside her.

"Give me a minute to lose the condom." I kissed her forehead and lifted off her, wanting to take care of business quickly so I could get back to bed. I wasn't usually a cuddler, preferring to get some sleep once the sex was done, what else was there? But having spent the last few nights with my arms wrapped around Ash, it's exactly how I wanted it to be while I waited for the sandman.

I kicked off the damp sheets and slid off the mattress, moving to my connecting bathroom and hitting the light on the way in. I pulled off the rubber, knotting the end and tossing it into the wastepaper basket beside my toilet. I gripped the sink, looking at myself in the mirror while I turned on the water to wash my hands.

"Staring at yourself now? I guess your fascination with me had to end eventually." Ash's sheet-wrapped body leaned against the doorframe.

"Just making sure I didn't break out in some crazy rash after sleeping with a Bruins fan. It's a legit concern." I cut off the water and turned around. Even with her lips puffy and her hair a mess she was still a knockout. It was the first time I'd ever felt I was out of my depth with a girl, and that feeling made me edgy.

"Ass!" Ashlyn punched me in the arm, her tiny fist barely making a dent. "If you're done priming yourself, I need to use the bathroom."

"So, use it." I smirked, not having anywhere better to be.

"Dan, I need to pee."

"Do you want me to put the seat down for you?"

"No, I need you to leave. I'm not going to pee in front of you."

"Babe, we just had sex and you're embarrassed to take a piss in front of me?"

"It's not the same thing and I'm not embarrassed. Bathroom stuff is private. I don't want an audience."

"Just go, what's the big deal? I don't have any issue taking a piss in front of you."

"Dan, I'd doubt you'd have an issue taking a piss in front of anyone. I, on the other hand, would rather keep some mystery about me. Thanks."

I didn't move, instead I settled up against the wall holding my arms across my chest and enjoying the show.

She stomped her foot impatiently. Seriously, it was too fucking adorable. "Dan, seriously. I need to go."

"Ash, you are way too uptight. Stop overthinking shit." I wrapped my hands around her arms and moved her to the front of the toilet. "Sit down and take a goddamn piss and don't care what anyone is going to think about it, least of all not me."

"I hate that you are making me do this right now." She lifted the sheet wrapped around her body, and sat on the toilet seat. "I can't even believe I'm doing this."

"Performance anxiety?"

"Stop it. Turn the water on or something. It's bad enough you're watching, I don't want you to hear it as well."

"Fine, fine." I turned the water back on, the free-flowing tap drowning out any other tinkling sound.

She obviously finished, grabbing some toilet paper and wiping before standing up and flushing. Honestly, the whole process was kind of fascinating. A lot more involved than just pulling it out and taking a leak.

"Better?" I stepped aside so she could wash her hands, I couldn't hide my shit-eating grin.

"Yes and I still hate you." Ash pushed me out of the way as the soapy water went down the drain, grabbing a hand towel and drying off. "We can never speak of this again."

"Nah, it was magic. The mystery is all gone and I still want to sleep with you. We're going to be friends for life."

I WOKE UP, TANGLED AROUND DAN'S ARMS AND LEGS, MY CELL impatiently ringing on the floor from the pocket of my jeans. It was morning but I had no idea what time it was, the light streaming through the gap in the curtain leading me to believe it wasn't as early as I first thought.

I reached down and retrieved my phone, fishing it out of the pocket and answering it before it went to voice mail.

"Hello." My voice sounded croaky and hoarse. I didn't have sexy morning voice, not even a little. Dan stirred beside me but didn't bother waking up. Ass. He just rolled over and went back to sleep.

"Ashlyn? It's Lexi Reed. Is now a good time?" Her bright voice burst through the phone. Her unmistakable twang, immediately identifying her as Australian. I totally loved her accent, not that I would ever tell her. That would just sound so condescending.

"Oh. Hey. Yes. It's me. Sorry. Just woke up." A jumble of disjointed words tried to form a sentence in my mouth. My brain not having the courtesy to connect the dots before it ejected them.

"Great. Ashlyn, I wanted to tell you how impressed I was with your interview. I think you presented well and you were obviously prepared..."

I knew a brush off when I heard one and this particular gem was the thank-you-but-no-thank-you where I was told my application had been unsuccessful. I was half expecting it, knowing my chances hadn't been great but hoping that maybe I had skated in. It was another disappoint-ment, you would think after twenty or thirty rejections I would be used to it. Sadly, it still stung.

"Thanks, Ms. Reed. I'm guessing I was unsuccessful." I thought it would be better just to get it over with. No point dragging it out. It wasn't her fault I was completely unsuitable for the position.

"Ashlyn, I'm sorry. Not this time." At least she had the decency to sound regretful. Some prospective employers had sounded down right chirpy while dashing my hopes and dreams. *Congratulations, you suck* doesn't sound any better with a smile in your voice.

"What I wanted to tell you is that though you weren't success-ful for my assistant's position, I have a contact who needs a financial analyst. Now I can't promise you a job but he would love to interview you if you are interested."

"Oh my god! Are you serious? Yes, yes. Of course I'm interested." It was like someone just plugged an IV of Red Bull into me and I was instantly awake.

"Great, I'll get my colleague, Matt Burns, to email you the details and I will pass on your resume to Simon Jennings. He'll be in touch so you can work out a time convenient for you to meet."

"Thank you so much, Ms. Reed. You have no idea how badly I need this job."

"I know, Ashlyn, and please call me Lexi. All I'm doing is getting someone with an impressive resume a job interview in an appropriate field. The rest is up to you."

"Thanks, Lexi. Goodbye."

"'Bye, Ashlyn, and good luck."

I ended the call and squealed. Unashamedly squealed like a little girl. This was my turning point. My lucky break. Things were finally going to start improving and who knew where it could lead.

"What the fuck, Ash?" Dan groggily turned to face me, his

dopey sleep face making him more adorable. "NSync getting back together? You know it will only work if Justin comes back, I don't like boy bands but that kid from Tennessee has talent."

"No, you moron." I swatted his arm. "How did you know I used to be an NSync fan?" Granted it had been a while, but I had loved their catchy tunes and stylized dance moves. So non-offensive and easy to listen to. Not bad to look at either.

"Lucky guess." Dan grinned folding his hands behind his head. "Can you pretend to listen to one of our albums, I don't even care if you like it. Just fucking lie to me."

"I'll listen to one of your albums if you get Alex to sign it for me. He's got such dreamy eyes."

"I thought it was his ass you were interested in, not his eyes."

"Ass, eyes. I'll take whatever's on offer. Has he mentioned me?"

"Don't even joke like that, Ashlyn. I can't tell if you are serious."

"I'm kidding, Dan. I'm not interested in Alex. Now stop being an ass and let me tell you my good news."

"What's your news? Can you pull down the sheet a little? I think we both will benefit from hearing your good news while you're naked. It's all in the telling."

"Be serious. I got an interview. A real interview for a job that I could actually be happy doing."

"Wow, Ash, that's awesome. Congratulations. I'm happy for you, babe."

"Thanks. I'm so excited. This is a big deal. I just needed someone to see my potential and take a chance. Can you believe Lexi Reed recommended me? Damn, I owe her huge for this."

"Yeah, she's good people when she isn't chewing us out. You must have really impressed her."

"Dan." I wrapped my arms around him and kissed him hard. Really kissed him. It was probably me getting caught up in the moment but it seemed like for the first time in a long time, things were actually going in my favor. Ordinarily I would have jumped on the phone and Megs and I would have screamed for a few minutes before deciding where we were going for a fancy celebratory dinner, but being in Dan's bed, having had one of the most amazing nights of my life, it just seemed right to share this with him.

"Well, good morning." His smile widened as he grabbed my ass. "I like seeing you happy, it makes me horny."

"You're always horny, but yes, I'm really happy."

"And I'm really horny. We should celebrate with lots of sex and then pancakes. Then maybe more sex."

"I'm not spending the day having sex with you. I've got important stuff to do, like get this interview locked down and research the company who is offering the position."

"You can do all of that *after* sex. I might be willing to let the pancakes slide, but feel this?" He grabbed my hand and placed it on his very hard erection. "This needs some special attention."

"Wow, that does need some attention." I slowly rubbed up and down the shaft of his cock before releasing it. "YOU should probably take care of that."

"See that's what I thought too, but I was talking with my cock earlier and he kinda has a hard-on for you. I tried to tell him it was a bad idea being you're moody and really anal, but fuck me if talking about your ass just didn't make him want you more."

I couldn't help but smile. Only Dan Evans could make being so crude so endearing. "You have problems, you know that? You and your cock."

"Babe, say what you want about me but you're going to hurt his feelings by saying shit like that out loud. He can't help himself. He sees a beautiful girl and he needs to show his appreciation. Think of it as a standing ovation."

"I'm not sure how I'm supposed to feel about that but I apologize to your penis if I hurt his feelings."

"It's okay, babe, he forgives you, but if you really want to make things right he says you should kiss him better."

"Creative way of angling for a blow job, Dan. I have to admit, I'm slightly impressed."

"Aw, Ash, I've impressed you. We all knew it was bound to happen sooner or later. You can try and resist all you want but in the end, my cock and I, we're just too damn charming."

Well damn him and his cock, because he was right, and I had been utterly charmed by the both of them.

So I caved. While my intention was to get up and head back to my apartment to prepare for my job interview, I ended up spending at least another hour in bed with Dan. In the end, it just wasn't his cock that was doing the convincing, his mouth and fingers had come into play as well and not even I was strong enough to resist him. He wasn't kidding about being amazing in bed. He actually had the goods to back up that big mouth of his.

I had never had sex like that. Not ever. Not even if you added up the sum total of my entire sexual experiences could you compare them to what one night with Dan was like. He was raw and primal but most of all, intense. He didn't poke and prod aimlessly hoping to get me off. No, every action was calculated and deliberate for maximum impact. I didn't know it could ever be like that. That I could come while actually *having* sex. And oh, how I'd come. It was explosive and addictive and more amazing than anything I'd ever felt. He hadn't stopped at one orgasm, oh no, the man was a show off. Not that I was complaining. He could demonstrate his talent all he wanted to, and continue to make me shatter into a million euphoric pieces. After all, what's the point of a fling if you can't indulge in mind-blowing sex?

My body ached in places that had long been forgotten, and while I was probably going to need an icepack and a good dose of Tylenol, I was happy. Happy. It's such a funny word, with such a wide range of meanings, but for me, it was a place of contentment and calm, and that's what I felt while I was with Dan. I know it was going to be short-lived and it probably meant a lot more to me than it did to him, but I didn't want to stop feeling this way until I absolutely had to. I would deal with that when the day eventually came. He was so unfiltered but real, which is not what I expected from a rock star. Sure his ego was huge and the things that came out of his mouth were unpredictable and dripping in innuendo, but he was so genuine I couldn't help fall for him. Therein lies the danger. The falling part. A little was to be expected. He was larger than life, ridiculously attractive, funny, and unsurpassed in the bedroom, but too much would mean heartbreak.

I wasn't sure if what I was feeling was infatuation or love. To be honest, I didn't really have anything to compare it to, but I couldn't deny I had actual feelings for him. I just needed to keep them in check and not get caught up in the fantasy. Dan Evans didn't date, he said so himself. I was never going to be his girlfriend.

"I Want Your Sex" blared obnoxiously from my cell, I didn't have the heart to change it and honestly, he was right, it was what I was thinking.

"Couldn't live without me, huh?" I smiled as I pressed the phone to my ear. "Really, Dan, we're going to have to get this dependency problem under control. I'm going to have a real job soon and not have time to listen to your heavy breathing and jerking off."

"Why must you say such hateful things? My heavy breathing and jerking off should be prioritized, woman. I expected you to carve out at least twenty minutes of your day for it. If you won't participate you can at least be my audience. Masturbation is important."

I giggled into the phone, this man was all kinds of wrong but I really, really liked him. "So did you call for a purpose or just to remind me how vain you are?"

"I was actually calling to make plans with you. I was thinking we should do something Saturday. Celebrate you landing this big shot job offer."

"Dan, I've only got an interview, there is no guarantee they'll offer me the job. Let's not get ahead of ourselves."

"Please, we both know you've got this in the bag. They are going to love you. You're going to roll in there being all badass with your fancy degree, wow them with S&P indices, and they will probably offer the job on the spot."

"Dan, are you trying out your big boy words again? Where did you hear about S&P indices?"

"Wall Street Journal and for your information, that paper

sucks. There are no pictures of girls in it at all, just a bunch of crusty old men. Lame if you ask me. I can't believe you have to pay money for this shit."

"Aw, you're reading the Wall Street Journal for me. Be still my heart."

"Well when it's done being *still* can we make plans for Saturday? I'll even let you pick the place."

My heart fell. Saturday was my birthday and I had already committed to going out with Megs and a few of our friends for drinks. It wasn't going to be a huge event but because I worked most weekends, I rarely got to spend any time with them, and I would hate to cancel. I didn't want to be *that* girl, the one who blew off her friends just because the sexy rock star she happens to be sleeping with snaps his fingers. No, I had to honor my commitments. That's who I was. Dependable and reliable. God, I sounded like a Toyota. In any case, the only option would be to invite Dan but I had already discussed it with Megs and ruled that out. It was too much, too soon. I didn't want to rock the boat. Not now when things were going so well.

"Dan, I'm sorry but I can't. I've got plans already." I shook my head knowing I was probably going to regret it. "Maybe we can do something another day?"

"What plans do you have Saturday? Lifetime channel tele-movies don't count, Ash."

"I'm not staying at home and watching TV, you moron," I laughed. "I'm meeting up with a few friends. It's nothing import-ant but it's been planned for a while and I just can't cancel. I'm sorry, Dan. I really would love to come out with you."

"Okay. Yeah. No biggie. We can do whatever, some other time."

"Of course, any other day."

"Okay, well I'll let you get back to your boring shit. I'm going to go hang with Troy. Later."

"'Bye."

Had he actually sounded disappointed by my inability to meet him Saturday or was I projecting? I'm sure it was more likely he couldn't believe I would actually say no, as I doubt he heard the word very much. Yes, that was it. He was probably annoyed he had wanted me to do something and I wasn't available. I'm sure his ego would recover by noon. Dan wasn't the type of guy who let disappointment sit with him for long. I wondered if he would ever ask again or if I'd blown my chance. Not that it had been a date. At no point did he imply it was going to be a date, he was just trying to be nice. Still, I'd really liked him asking me out. More than I cared to admit.

I sighed, walking over to my beat-up desk and sat in the recycled office chair that had come with the apartment. Well, came with the apartment in the sense that it was placed next to the outside dumpster. Either way, it was functional and unwanted so I hauled it back up the three flights of stairs and it became mine. I fired up my outdated laptop waiting for the operating system to kick in, it was just one of the many things that needed to be replaced and had been added to the when-I-have-the-money list.

My email menu flagged unread messages and I scouted through the endless irrelevant crap that seemed to fill my inbox to find the one from Matthew Burns, Lexi Reed's senior PR manager. He gave me a basic run down on Simon Jennings. He was a New York born and bred real estate broker who had made some wise investments just before the housing bubble burst in 2007. A self-made millionaire, whose office was located in the financial district, was looking for an analyst for a twelve-month contract with scope for ongoing employment. Standard. It sounded perfect.

I also had an email from Simon Jennings, asking me to call his office to make a time for an interview. My heart thumped loudly in my chest as I picked up my phone and dialed the numbers. I hoped Mr. Jennings didn't have crazy sensitive hearing and assumed I had a heart condition.

"Good afternoon JenCorp, Joanna speaking."

"Hello Joanna, my name is Ashlyn Murphy. I received an email requesting I call so we could set up an interview time."

"Ah, Yes. Ashlyn, we've been expecting your call. I have your resume in front of me. Mr. Jennings requested I set up a time for you."

"Sure, I'm flexible with my schedule so I can almost do any time." I hoped I didn't sound too desperate. I was flexible because I was mainly working nights in a bar. Not that they needed to know that. Selective resume listing I called it.

"How about tomorrow at eleven?"

Crap. Not a lot of time to prepare but I could run with it. It would mean I would be up all night but if I could land this job it would be worth it.

"Tomorrow at eleven sounds perfect."

"Wonderful, I will forward you a confirmation of your appointment. It will include directions to our offices and any additional information we may require."

"Thanks, I'll see you then."

"Goodbye."

My stomach flipped. I felt sick. I was so nervous I couldn't stand it. Job interviews were hard enough for me to get through; they always put me on edge. But an interview for a job I wanted? That was hard-core pressure. I squeezed my eyes shut. Concentrating on my breathing. It was my time. I could do this.

"Dude, sit your ass down. You are going to wear a hole through the floor." Troy tapped out some rhythm with a pair of sticks onto a chair. We were about to head out to rehearsal; Alex and James had some new material they wanted to test run.

"She flat-out lied to me, dude. She totally dissed me on her birthday. What the fuck is up with that?" The more shit rotated in my head the more it pissed me off. I never gave the whys of the situation much stock, but now...now it was all kinds of important.

"Dan, you going to give me some context or am I supposed to just fill in the fucking blanks? What are you talking about?" He lifted the sticks, twirling one in his hand as he stared at me, grinning like an asshole. Of course this would be amusing for him. He wasn't the one being dodged.

"It's Ashlyn's birthday Saturday. When she left her purse in the Suburban, I checked it for ID and I saw her date of birth." I don't know why it bothered me so much. It sure as hell wasn't the first time a girl had lied to me, but this time it really bugged me. It was also turning me into a whiny bitch. If it had been anyone but Troy

I'd have shut my mouth and pretended it was business as usual, but with the big guy, I didn't have to fake it. He always seemed to know when I was ate up about something anyway, so I was just saving time by coming clean.

"I wanted to take her out for her birthday. Thought we could go out to dinner or something. She said she had plans." I pushed my ass into the couch beside him. He was right; I was going to wear a hole through my carpet. Besides if we were going to get all Dr. Phil with this, I might as well be comfortable.

"So? It's not like the girl didn't have a social life before she met you, numbnuts. It's short notice, of course she is going to have plans for her birthday."

Fucking Troy, trying to be Captain Fucking Obvious. Of course I knew this. Hell, of course she had a life before we'd met, no doubt, with a steady line of douchebags trying to crawl into her panties. A fact I was trying to get out of my head before I put my fist through a wall.

"So why didn't she just say she was going out for her birthday? She made up some bullshit about it being no big deal, and that she was going out for drinks with friends but couldn't cancel. If it's no big deal why the fuck can't I go?"

Was she going to try and hook up with some other mother-fucker or was it that she didn't want me around? Both of these scenarios pissed me off, the first more so than the second, and I was cool with neither. I pushed my hands through my hair wishing I had some way of knowing what was going down in her head. Mind-reading powers would be good about now.

"Dude, you are starting to freak me out. If you are going to start menstruating we are going to have serious problems." Troy laughed, slapping me hard on the back. Clearly he was enjoying the situation.

"Fuck you, asshole. I'm serious. This shit is messed up." I punched him in the arm. This was no laughing matter. I wasn't spilling my guts for Troy's enjoyment.

"Have you fucking asked her?" He relaxed into his chair, putting the sticks down and clocking me with a look. "Or is this just you pulling shit out of your ass?"

I waved him off as it was bad enough I was talking about it with him. I wasn't about to lay it out on the line with her. "I'm not going to ask her, numbnuts. A man has his pride."

"Can I ask you where you left your fucking balls and who the fuck is this dude standing in front of me? 'Cause I've got to tell you, Dan Evans has never given two fucks about what a girl did or didn't do and he sure as shit didn't care what she thought."

"Don't fucking start." I pushed out a breath, leveling him with a stare. "I don't know why but I fucking care and it pisses me the hell off." Shit, I'd gone this far I might as well just let it fly. "I fucking want to be with her all the time, dude. It's like a sickness. It's not just about the fucking. It's about her. She doesn't take my shit but she doesn't try and change me either. She's cool, dude. We can just hang and she isn't trying to score free shit or be on the cover of some bullshit magazine." She was the first girl I had been with in a long time who hadn't tried to selfie and tag herself while she was with me. Hadn't even hit me up for tickets or a backstage pass. Hell she hadn't asked for anything.

"Sounds like to me you've got yourself a girl."

"Asswipe, it's not like that. She's got some weird ten-year plan or some shit. She's not interested in dating, made that quite clear early on. We're just chilling."

"So is it just fucking?"

It pissed me off that Troy would talk about her like she was just some groupie. "Dude, don't talk about her like that. She's not that kind of girl."

"Dan, newsflash. If you are so ate up about this chick and it's more than just fucking, then I hate to break it you, but you have yourself a girlfriend."

"Asshole, did you hear what I just said? She isn't interested in dating."

"Dan, brother. You know I fucking love you but you are seriously fucking dense sometimes. If you two are doing stuff, other than just fucking, you already *are* dating."

"Are you sure, man? I'm thinking there needs to be some kind of agreement or some shit. People don't just start dating."

"If she is spending time with you of her own free will, then she is agreeing. I'm telling you. You're dating, man."

"How the fuck did I start dating and not know?"

"'Cause you're a dipshit with emotional issues? How the fuck should I know? What I do know is you need to get some sack and sort that shit out."

"You're right, dude. I think I have feelings and stuff. I haven't even thought about another girl since meeting her, not even to jerk off." I scrubbed my face with my hands.

"Sounds pretty serious. I can't remember the last time you were with just one girl." Troy surprisingly wasn't being an asshole about it. "I think it's a good thing. James and Han have been happy for years and Alex and Lexi still dig each other. Maybe it's time. I know I'm getting sick of groupies and band whores. Ash seems like she has a good head on her shoulders. I can't see her being in it for the money or the fame. Fuck, if she has to put up with your sorry ass, I say she deserves a pay out."

"Yeah, I think I want to try, man. I know I'm probably going to screw this up, but the thought of her being with another dude makes me want to gut him like a fish. No seriously, I want to grab a knife and fillet the motherfucker and I haven't even met him yet."

"Easy there, Hannibal Lector. Just concentrate on your game plan, the rest will take care of itself."

"True. We should probably make tracks. I want to try and catch Lexi before we start jamming."

"You solid? You need a hug or something? We can swing past the drug store and grab you some Tampax if you still need it."

"Whatever, man. Just grab your stuff. We'll take my car."

The drive out to James and Hannah's was always a great ride. We got to leave the traffic and noise behind and hit the open road. The afternoon sun was pooling on the dash and even though the weather was starting to turn, we still had a couple more weeks of fall before shit got nasty.

James had this estate just outside of the city. When he'd bought it I thought it was kind of douchey, but now it made sense. Big house with a massive yard, tucked away from the world, plus James had a state of the art studio built into his basement. We could rehearse or lay down tracks whenever we wanted without having to worry about booking studio time. It was actually pretty sweet. Han was awesome, too. She didn't come down there and bitch and moan, she let us do our thing and most times kept us supplied with snacks and beer. James knew what he was doing when he brought her into the fold.

We pulled up the drive and parked up front. Alex's Escalade was already there, which meant he had his ladies in tow, with Jase's 'Stang parked beside it. Looked like we were the last ones here. Not that it mattered, they were all probably shooting the shit; it had been a while since we had all been together.

Troy gave me a shit-eating grin as he opened the door and ejected from the car. I knew him well enough to know he would probably be riding me about the Ashlyn thing for the rest of the day. Not that I gave a shit, 'cause even just thinking about her gave me a case of the warm and fuzzies. Fuck. Maybe I was getting a period? Screw it. Whatever the reason, I was bear-hugging the hell out of it, because letting it go wasn't an option. I pushed open the door and joined Troy at James's front door.

"Hey!" Hannah pulled open the door before we had a chance to ring the buzzer. "I was wondering when you were going to make it? Everyone's already here." Her face lit up as we stepped through the doorway.

"Hey, Han." I gave her a hug, "We ran into traffic. How's the little dude? When's Noah going to pick up the mic and give his old man a run for his money?"

Hannah smiled. "Noah is playing with Grace. Everyone is out in the living room."

She led us through the hallway to where everyone was gathered. Alex and James were on the floor playing with the kids while Jase was sitting on the armrest of the couch deep in a conversation with Lexi.

"Is Noah macking on my girl?" I walked over to where the boys were sitting, our entrance getting their attention.

"Might have some competition there, buddy. Noah's pretty sweet on Grace." James laughed, lifting himself off the floor.

I gave James a thump on the back. "Lucky for him he got his looks from his momma so he stands a fighting chance."

"No man is ever going to get close to my daughter so you're both SOL." Alex brushed off his ass as he stood, Grace stretching out her little arms wanting to be picked up. No denying that little sweetheart was daddy's girl.

Lexi alternated hugs and hellos with Troy and me as Jase lifted his beer in acknowledgement.

I cleared my throat, hoping not to make an ass out of myself as I moved over to the side of the room for some privacy. "Hey Lexi, can I have a minute?"

Truth was, when Lexi came into our lives I was more than skeptical. Being who we are and doing what we do, you meet a lot of people. People who want to get their claws into you for what they can gain out of it. No point bitching about it, it comes with the territory, but Lexi had been different. Not to say I wouldn't have jumped at the chance at fucking her, she was all kinds of sexy, but I was glad the way things had ended up. She had more than earned her place with us, she was kickass handling our shit and you could always count on her.

"This is a little cloak and dagger, Dan." She smiled as she joined me. "What did you need?" She might be a ball-buster but man, whenever I asked for something, even if it was for shit she didn't want to do, she always came through.

"Yeah, I just wanted to thank you for hooking up that job interview for Ashlyn. I was with her when she got your call and she was seriously stoked. I know you went out on a limb and I just wanted to say thanks." I scratched the back of my neck feeling like a douchebag. I don't know why I bothered to try and do this privately, the way Hannah and the boys were eyeballing us, I knew I was going to get twenty questions the minute we were done.

"Wow, Dan, look at you with manners and everything. You've really got it bad for this girl." Lexi gave me a big shit-eating grin, no doubt pleased she was making me feel like I'd just put my nuts on a chopping block. Did I mention what a ball-buster she was?

"Not you, too, Troy's already giving me shit." I didn't expect anything less, Lexi and the rest of them would probably ride my ass, but I didn't care. Ashlyn was worth it.

Lexi grinned, she was clearly enjoying this. "I think it's great. Really I do. Just wondering if strip clubs are going to survive without your business."

"Yeah, have your fun. I don't give a shit. I like her and I'm not hiding it. Not saying we're going to run to Vegas and get legal or anything but yeah, I'm going to be with her." They could make fun of it all they wanted. I'd take it. Being with Ashlyn was important to me and if all I had to do was listen to these dickheads joke about it, then I'd do that, happily.

Lexi smiled. "Devil must be pissed that Hell just froze over."

"Thought he would've been used to it after *your* marriage to Stone." I reminded her of how quickly she'd waltzed down the aisle even though she swore ever since she met us that she wasn't the marrying type. Firstly with their impromptu Miami wedding, and then again on Alex's birthday. "Two times no less." Probably not wise to poke the bear but I was on a roll.

"Well, well. Manners *and* quick off the mark. Impressive." Surprisingly she didn't seem annoyed. "But it's not me who you should be thanking. Sydney organized the interview. Her father is a close friend of Simon's. Apparently he's been looking for someone for a while but hasn't found the right candidate. He was excited by Ashlyn's resume and we had a quick chat over the phone, but it was Syd who put it all into play."

Wow Sydney had gone to bat for me? I mean we were friends and she had been working her ass off with Lexi, but she didn't owe me anything. Syd and I had fucked and unlike most girls, she hadn't gotten all weirded-out after. In the beginning it kinda made me want her more. I even asked her out a few times, but she just said that we'd had our fun and it was time to move on. She didn't avoid me or anything. Ain't going to lie, she was pretty badass.

"Well I guess I'll give her a call. I know she didn't have to do it."

"No, she didn't, but she's awesome, and quite frankly, she was as surprised as I was you cared so much. She was happy to help." Lexi rubbed my arm and damn if this whole exchange wasn't making me a feel a little emotional. Maybe Troy was right; perhaps I was turning into a girl.

"Dan, you done monopolizing Lexi? I thought we were actually going to play?" Jason tossed a pillow at us, the stupid grin on his face evidence he'd heard at least some of the conversation. Not that I gave a shit, hell they were bound to find out sooner or later, so might as well word them up now.

"All right, assholes, let's go make some magic. But before we do I have an announcement to make. I don't give a rat's ass what you think, or what trash-talk you are going to throw my way. I'm dating Ashyln and that's how it's going to be."

"Good one, numbnuts." Troy twirled a stick in his hand. "Maybe tell her first though next time."

SPENDING A NIGHT AWAY FROM DAN HAD BEEN HARDER THAN I thought. The idea was to use the time away to focus and prepare for my interview without the sexy distraction that he was, but when I finally went to bed I couldn't sleep. I spent most of the night tossing and turning. It was strange that on some level having him beside me calmed me. I didn't understand it because the man was more hyper than a child who had OD'd on too much sugar. If I were honest with myself, I'd admit that just his physical proximity made me sleep better. It was nice. Actually, it was better than nice. Lying with him in bed was amazing. Not even thinking about the sex, which had surpassed every expectation I'd had and more. It was how being in his arms made me feel while I slept. It did things to me, things that both confused and elated me. On paper, Dan and I made no sense, but being with him, felt right. God. I needed more coffee and a lobotomy.

The interview itself had been flawless. Well flawless if I you don't count the dry heaving in the bathroom thirty minutes before I walked into the boardroom. After I'd gotten over my mental and physical freak out, I was able to pull it together to actually present a rather intelligent and well-rounded front. I didn't even seem to be the slightest bit nervous which even surprised myself. I wasn't delusional enough to think I had it in the bag but I knew I had performed well and would be a serious contender. It pleased me to know I could actually have a shot at this. To get off the treadmill I had been on for months and start making progress in my life. It was as if things were finally falling into place. Like somehow, I had paid my dues and now I could start reaping the rewards. Who says karma is a bitch? Sometimes, it's just plain wonderful.

"I Want Your Sex", Dan's ringtone blared from my purse, making me smile. I really should change the ringtone but for some reason I didn't. I would get around to it one of these days.

"Hello, Dan." I couldn't help purring into the phone. Just knowing I was going to be hearing his voice excited me. Yeah, I know. I had issues.

"Well hello, babe. What are you wearing?" His words rumbled in my ear.

Dan was so unapologetically sexual and sleeping with him only reinforced it. It wasn't just a case of big ego. Well he had a *huge* ego, but with Dan, what you saw was what you got and what you got was high-octane sex. If you weren't careful the fumes alone were enough to make you dizzy.

"A latex bustier and crotchless panties." I bit my lip to stop myself from laughing.

"FUCK! Where are you? I'll be there in five minutes," Dan hissed and I heard the telltale jangling of keys. He was so easily baited and it thrilled me to know that on the flip of a dime, I could get a reaction out of him.

"Relax, Dan, I was kidding. I just got home from my interview. I'm still in my corporate gear." I slid out of my jacket and surveyed the rest of my boring and unsexy get-up. This was not what dirty dreams were made of - that's for sure.

"That's just hurtful, Ash. I got hard instantly on that image alone. To find out you were joking, well I'm actually wounded." The disappointment in his voice was real; I could hear it in his tone.

"Oh poor, baby. Do you need a hug?" I kicked off my heels half wishing I could do just that. Hug him. What was wrong with me?

Wanting sex from Dan was one thing, but wanting hugs? That was dangerous territory and I needed out of it. Now.

"By *hug* do you mean my dick in your pussy? 'Cause those are the hugs I prefer." I didn't need to see his face to know he was grinning. Predictable Dan, any concerns I had of things between us being anything more than sexual was clarified. There was no gray area as far as he was concerned; *dick in your pussy* was pretty black and white.

"You are such a charmer. How I manage to leave your bed at all with lines like those is a mystery to me." I undid the zipper of my skirt letting it fall to the floor.

"Well you know, if you didn't have anything on for the next few hours we could test that theory." He wasn't joking. Dan rarely joked about sex and he would think nothing of spending hours in bed. I wish I could be so flippant, pushing aside responsibility to take care of the primal need that seemed to ache between my legs. One that intensified the longer I considered it. In truth, I'd never found a lover who I *wanted* to spend time with in bed. Dan took that idea and turned it on its ass. He made up for everything I'd ever missed and possibly what I'd never have with anyone else.

"As tempting as the offer is, I need to get ready for work." *Because if I go to bed with you right now, feeling the way I do, I will probably tell you how much I need you. How much I don't want to let you go and how much I want to be more than just a fling to you.* My mouth thankfully clamped shut after saying the word *work* so I didn't embarrass myself by spilling what was tossing around in my head.

Deep. That's how far I'd tumbled. No matter what I cared to admit to myself, to Megs or to Dan, I wanted more. I craved more. I wasn't wired for the fun-time-no-strings-attached rendezvous. There was a very real possibility I could fall in love with Dan. Okay, maybe I had already started. I cringed at the world of hurt I knew would be in my future if I pursued this path. It was like waiting in line for a rollercoaster. I was going to end up a mess by the end but I wanted to ride it anyway.

"You working late tonight?" Dan broke the silence and

thankfully, derailed my train of thought. The one where he would tell me he felt the same way about me.

"Yeah, but Megs is picking me up so I don't need a ride." I lied. Flat-out lied. It's not that I didn't want to see him. I craved that more than anything. But not tonight. Things were finally starting to go right for me and I didn't want to screw it up. Not with him. I felt needy and I needed space. As pathetic as it sounded I still wanted him, even in the limited capacity in which he was available. That meant regrouping and a serious pep talk. And somehow flushing these crazy ideas from my mind.

"Why is Megs giving you a ride? I thought we were going to hang out tonight. We can even stay at your place if you prefer, though I have to tell you, your place is kind of a dive."

"There is nothing wrong with my place and it's within my budget. I just thought I'd come home and sleep tonight. You must have something else to do." Distance. That's exactly what I needed. Distance and someone to beat some sense into me.

"Other than you? Nope, nothing. But if you really want to sleep, I can be a good boy." Dan refused to make it easy for me. I wasn't expecting him to be insistent.

"Dan, you want to come over and cuddle? We both know that is not what you want." I said it more for my own benefit, to reinforce how stupid I was being for considering more.

"Can we cuddle naked? I like feeling my cock against your ass." Dan's voice dipped seductively. I tingled like someone just hit the hot button to my girlie parts.

"Um that's not cuddling, Dan," I clarified, unable to stop the grin spreading across my face.

"Listen, you might be smarter than me but unless I'm sliding it in, it's still only a cuddle."

"Sounds like to me there's a lot of scope in your kind of cuddles." I slowly undid the buttons of my blouse. Undressing and talking to Dan was a bad idea. The cool air hitting my skin gave me goosebumps reinforcing that notion. Why was I avoiding the mind-blowing sex I knew he was going to give me? Oh, that's right. 'Cause I was dumb enough to start having feelings for the man. I only had myself to blame. I felt my libido glaring at me all judgey. Ass. I wasn't sure if that was directed at me, or my libido.

"See, you aren't the only one who's smart." Dan apparently was not buying my let's-spend-the-night-alone suggestion. "So let's just stop arguing about it. What time you get off?"

"Is that a trick question?" I responded a little too quickly, wondering if I'd accidently moaned or something, tipping him off to my current state. Confused and aroused. I was such a catch.

"Ah, babe. Did you just think dirty thoughts?" His laugh was sexy and husky. Yep, totally not helping this situation.

"Clearly I've been spending too much time with you. Anyway, as much as I would love to sit here and talk dirty to you, I need to put some clothes on." I shivered, the rusty old radiator in my apartment not even coming close to warming the room.

"Sooo does that mean you are currently undressed?"

Why did I have to open my big mouth? "Not for long, I'm about to get dressed for work."

"Hold on a second. When did you get naked?"

"Dan, I've been getting undressed while talking to you. I told you, I needed to get ready for my shift at the bar." I looked at the pile of discarded clothes on my bed.

"You start undressing, you need to tell me. In fact, let's make it a rule and it supersedes anything else in the conversation."

"What if I start touching myself?" I breathed heavily into the phone. It really was just too easy to tease him. "Do you still want to know about the naked thing first?"

"Fuck, Ash. You start touching yourself you lead with that." His breathing deepened and followed by the noise of a zipper being lowered. "By the way, now *I'm* touching myself."

"Dan, I actually wasn't. I was just playing." I swallowed hard as my heart thumped loudly in my chest.

"Play all you want, babe. I encourage playing of all kinds." He half-moaned into the phone.

"Dan. I'm not." At least not yet. Should I start? I'd never had phone sex before. Not that I was against it but if I was going to be making myself come, what was the point of trying to maintain a conversation. Clearly, I'd be missing out.

Dan's lowered voice reverberated against my ear, "Suit

yourself, babe, doesn't mean I'm going to stop."

"Okay. I finish at two a.m. You can spend the night." The words leapt out of my mouth. All on their own. I had no control over any of my body parts it seemed, as I squeezed my thighs together. Traitorous body. Obviously seeking revenge for the earlier name-calling. This was clearly my libido's doing.

"Glad you saw it my way. So what color were your panties?"

"Goodbye, Dan. I'll see you later."

That night had been like every night that week. I stopped fighting it. I was too far gone anyway, so I might as well surrender myself to it. It was more than just wanting him, more than just sex, more than just an infatuation. Whether I tried to distance myself or not it was too late. I'd been infected. Like a test lab monkey with some rare communicable disease, it was already in my blood. It was already in my heart.

He came into the bar about an hour before the end of my shift and waited through last call. Most people had no idea who he was; it's not the kind of place we got celebrities, so they would assume he was just a random good-looking guy. The whole hiding-in-plain-sight thing was not as stupid as it sounded. He watched as I closed the bar, paying close attention to my ass as I loaded the under-the-counter dishwasher. We'd walk out to his Benz and he would drive me home. Well, his home. He'd complain about not wanting to go to mine and honestly, his place was a hell of a lot nicer. I'd make him work for it though, just because despite me being desperate (yep, that was the word I was using these days) to be with him I wasn't about to let him in on it. He was an excellent negotiator. The things he could do with his tongue... Well, needless to say we both got what we wanted.

Part of me felt like I was holding my breath, waiting for the most epic crumble of all time, and another part felt like the only time I could breathe was when I was with him. Make sense? No, of course not. None of it did. And yet, every night I found myself in the same place, my hands tearing at his sheets as he owned my body and then wrapping my arms around him as I drifted off to sleep.

The closer it got to the end of the week, the more antsy I got. Firstly, I still hadn't heard from the job interview and that was making me seven different shades of nervous. I know it hadn't even been a week yet but still, put me out of my misery already and let me know. I had convinced myself I had rocked the interview, so not even getting a call back for a second interview was seriously messing with my head. Not like I wasn't already on a permanent vacation to Crazyville, but still. The other issue that was causing me anxiety-inducing, mental dry-heaving was my birthday. Sure, I had told Dan I had plans on Saturday but I had been more than a little evasive about the occasion. Not much I could do about it though, an invite at this late stage would be insulting, not to mention raise questions as to why I'd lied about it in the beginning. No, stay the course. Celebrate my birthday, move on, and forget it ever happened. It was going to be a totally low fanfare event anyway. Technically so insignificant, it wasn't worth the mention. That's what I was telling myself. Jury was still out on how good a liar I was.

My phone buzzed early Thursday morning. I say early, but it was actually nine forty-five. However considering my shifts didn't finish until the early hours of the morning, and then there was my nightly sextivites with Dan, it would be five or six in the morning before I'd enter la-la land. I untangled my body from Dan's heated core—he was literally hot like a furnace...yeah I didn't understand it either—and reached across to answer my phone, mentally taking a roll call of any potentials who could be on the other end of the line. Most of whom I'd yell at and demand they call at a more reasonable hour. Like lunch time. With promises of coffee and pastries. Certainly not now.

"Hello," I mumbled, not offering anything more intelligible in greeting. It was surprising the word *hello* could still be identified as English. Small victories, and in the mornings, I'd take what I could get.

"Ms. Murphy?" the voice on the line questioned, "Ms. Ashlyn

Murphy?" Huh, maybe high-fiving my linguistic skills had been premature? I tried not to smirk thinking about what Dan would say about the word *linguistic*. I-do-have-a-college-degree, I-do-have-a-college-degree, I silently chanted as my mind played in the gutter.

"Yes, this is she." This is she? Was I on the set of some turn of the century drama? Had I mistakenly swallowed the spirit of Jane Austin? This is what happens when you try and live rock star hours without actually *being* a rock star. I should not be allowed to interact with the world until I had ingested my first coffee. It was for their protection as much as mine.

"I'm sorry, Ms. Murphy, I didn't recognize your voice. This is Joanna Miles, from JenCorp. Have I caught you at a bad time?"

"No." I shot out of bed like a kid who inhaled a fistful of pixie sticks, earning me a disgruntled groan from a still sleeping Dan. "This is a perfect time. Sorry, I'm a little under the weather." I tried to shake the remnants of *Ms. Pride and Prejudice* from my psyche or at the very least from my vocab.

"Sorry to hear that, Ms. Murphy. Hopefully it's nothing too serious. I was just calling regarding the position you interviewed for here at JenCorp." And here it was, the part where Joanna told me I'd been unsuccessful. Another thanks-but-no-thanks, good-luck-with-your-future let down. I had been so sure I had been in with a chance. My chest tightened as I slumped onto the edge of the mattress.

"It's okay," I found myself whispering. "Thanks for the opportunity." I couldn't hear it again, deciding it was better to anticipate the pain rather than hearing the words, *you're not good enough.*

"Um, Ms. Murphy? I'm actually calling to let you know Mr. Jennings would like to offer you the position. He just needs you to come back in so you can negotiate the terms of your employment."

"Huh?" I wasn't sure if I'd actually said it out loud or if I was just thinking it. What was all that about a college education? Yeah, I'm thinking I was going to need a refund.

"Yes, sorry it's taken me a few days to get back to you, but Mr.

Jennings has been out of town. However, he was incredibly impressed with your presentation and interview and is very enthusiastic about welcoming you to the team." Joanna was polite to ignore my momentary inability to talk. Other than random sounds that served more to embarrass me than contribute to the conversation.

"Oh my god. YES. Yes. Thank you. Thank you." All composure and control evaporated as I listened to Joanna's words. They wanted me. I was done tending bar. This was it, what I had been waiting for. My plan was finally coming together. I felt dizzy.

"Well I'm glad you feel that way, Ms. Murphy." Joanna giggled, her professionalism cracking slightly. Not that I could blame her. "If you would like to stop by tomorrow at ten, Mr. Jennings will be able to work through your offer and you can counter with any terms or conditions you may have. Does this suit?"

"Yes. Thank you. See you tomorrow." I nodded into the phone. The reality that she couldn't see the nod was lost on me. I didn't care. If I could've conveyed it telepathically I would.

"Goodbye, Ms. Murphy. Welcome to the JenCorp." Her friendly voice ended the call.

Dan slowly raised an eyelid. "Babe, I thought you told me you weren't into phone sex? Kinda rude to do it right in front of me though. At the very least you could hit the speaker and let me join in." I couldn't be sure he wasn't serious. He was smiling, so either way, not annoyed.

"Like I would have phone sex with an audience." I crawled back over to where he was positioned on the bed, his arms folded behind his head. His flexed muscles highlighted his intricate tattoos, and that smirk, which meant trouble, was plastered all over his face. He undid me. Each and every single time.

"It was a job offer." I scooped up my tattered thoughts enough to start forming sentences. "They offered it to me. A real job. As an analyst. No more working at the bar. I get to play with the big boys now."

"Of course they offered it to you. I knew you had it in the bag." He unfolded his arms and pulled me onto his chest. "Best you learn now, babe, I'm always right. And as for playing with the *big boys*, pretty sure I already took care of that."

"Could your ego get any bigger? Is there even a shred of humility that lives within you?" I nestled into the crook of his arm, falling into my own little happy place. My distaste was purely superficial. His self-assurance didn't bother me as much as it usually did. Desensitization and all that. His attitude was sexy.

"It's not my ego that is getting bigger babe, that's my cock," he whispered into my ear.

I tried to resist laughing. Honestly. I even bit my lip, but it was futile. Between floating on clouding freaking nine from the amazing news I had received and Dan's predictable but well-delivered response, I didn't stand a chance. Instead I dissolved into a fit of laughter, wrapping myself around his firm, warm body like a vine.

"I'm really happy for you, Ash." Dan's finger traced the edge of my jaw. "I love it when you laugh."

It was official. My long-term plan was going to need modification. I was too deliriously happy to walk away from Dan. Whenever that kick in the gut came, I would take it. I would accept whatever misery came after this. The days I would spend in my PJs crying into a pint of Ben and Jerry's after he had eventually broken my heart. It will have all been worth it, just for this. This moment, right now.

"YOU KNOW, I'M NOT FEELING WELL. WHY DON'T WE GRAB THE CHECK and I'll head home." I swiped the screen on my phone. It was nine thirty and as far as birthdays went, this one kind of blew. I wanted to go. Find an excuse to ditch my friends and go see Dan. I knew it was wrong and one night apart wasn't going to kill me, but it was my birthday so surely I should be able to do what I wanted to do.

It was almost impossible to get a booking at The Mexican Cantina, the wait unusually extending months. They had the best Mexican food in the city and how Megs had been able to secure us a table on such short notice was still a mystery. Maybe her dad had called in a favor or something? The food was amazing. I almost died when I saw the prices, but the atmosphere was fantastic and the margaritas delicious. Still, I was dreading the bill.

"Ash, there is nothing wrong with you, unless you count being a bad actress. You are going to go straight to Dan's." Megs took a sip from her frozen margarita. "And if you check your phone one more time, I'm going to have to confiscate it. Seriously, I've seen people waiting for kidney transplants less anxious."

"Oh, ha-ha, Dr. Winters." I twilled the stem of my still full margarita glass. I wasn't feeling it. Not even a little. Pathetic.

"C'mon, Ash. Give us one night, you can see him tomorrow." Kyla waved over a waitress. "Besides, when are we going to meet your new guy? I can't remember the last guy you dated."

"He's not really *my* guy. It's complicated." My hand moved from the stem of my glass to the napkin in my lap, anything to help distract me from these questions. Complicated was an understatement.

Megs knew the full story but Kyla and Brianne had no idea. As far as they knew, I'd met some guy at a job interview—not a lie—and we were kind of seeing each other. They also knew his name was Dan, and they had assumed he was a businessman of some sort—also technically not a lie. Being that I hadn't dated anyone recently or shown any interest in dating, they were more than a little excited to meet this mystery man. The idea made me nauseous. How would I even introduce Dan? While I was happy with our *arrangement*—that was the best word I could think of to describe it—I didn't want to complicate this situation with labels or lack-there-of.

"Not fair trying to keep him all to yourself." Brianne pouted. "Boyfriends need to be vetted. It's girl code."

"Guys, I already told you. He's not my boyfriend. We're just trying to keep it casual right now, which I'm fine with. He travels a lot. For business," I qualified, hoping my lame explanation would stop the questions about Dan. Questions I didn't want to answer.

Megs rolled her eyes at my poor attempt. Secretly, I think she was enjoying it. "Well, it's obvious Ash isn't going to play nice. I say we hit a club and dance until we can't stand up."

"Yay." "Yes," Brianne and Kyla both chimed in enthusiastically. My opportunity to escape slipped further away. I was going to have to remember to kill Megs and her bright ideas when I got her alone.

"I don't know. I'm tired and I start my new job on Monday. I should probably get an early night so I can spend the rest of tomorrow preparing." I threw out my last ditch effort to derail Megs's plans. Plans that had not been discussed nor agreed upon. She knew I hated surprises.

"Yes of course. The fancy-schmancy new job." Brianne's brow lifted suggestively. "Does Dan work there too?"

"No." I shook my head, knowing it was going to take a lot to get them to let this go. Another reason why tonight had been a bad idea. "I've been offered a twelve-month contract with JenCorp as an analyst. Of course, Mr. Jennings explained they have room on their staff if they are happy with my performance but he's pretty conservative which I completely understand."

The twelve-month timeframe had initially disappointed me, but I understood why a company would take that route. It made smart business sense, and the package I was offered was more than generous. No, seriously. I hadn't even dreamed of the kind of cash they were throwing at me. Not to mention a company credit card for expenses and use of the company car service. It was like a fantastic fairy tale come to life, but better because it was real.

I knew that within the year I would be able to prove my worth and secure a more permanent position and during our follow-up meeting yesterday, Mr. Jennings had made it clear he was pleased with what I was bringing to the table. While our interaction had been very formal—he'd sat behind his desk the entire time and didn't crack a smile once—he didn't seem cold, just cautious. I could deal with cautious. Hell my middle name was cautious. Well, at least it used to be. Ashlyn Cautious Marie Murphy had been a bit wordy, so I guess my middle name was now back to being plain old Marie. Not sure if the relinquishing of the title was a good thing. Time would tell.

"You have all of tomorrow to get responsible," Megs unhelpfully added. "It's your birthday and your last weekend of freedom before you become a slave to the corporate machine. You owe this to yourself. Besides, *Dan* would want you to have a good time."

"Okay." I let out a long dramatic sigh. I wasn't going to get out of this easily so I might as well use it to my advantage. "I'll agree to get incredibly drunk and go to whatever club you all want to go to on one condition. We don't talk about Dan. No one can mention him or ask anymore questions about him?"

The waitress who Kyla had waved over a while ago finally made her way to the table and brought the check. Not that we'd asked, and given we still hadn't finished our cocktails, it was kind of rude.

"Here." She placed the leather folder containing our bill on the table before disappearing.

"What a bitch. She is totally getting minimum tip." Kyla seethed as she opened up the folder and surveyed the damage. It was a fancy place but we'd been sucking down cocktails for a couple of hours. It was bound to be brutal.

"She is probably having a bad night. It's busy. Don't be too hard on her." I couldn't help but feel an affinity with that poor girl. I'd been there too many times myself.

"But what's the point in getting you drunk if we can't get you to divulge juicy information?" Brianne completely avoided the situation with the waitress, preferring to obsess further about Dan and me, and the possibility of finding out more. Not likely.

"Those are my terms, ladies. Take it or leave it." I was serious, too. If I couldn't be doing what I wanted on my birthday I would at least have some level of control over it. "So am I getting in a cab and heading home or we going to drink overpriced shots and fend off unwanted advances?"

Brianne drained what was left in her glass. "Fine. He's probably boring and wears a sweater vest."

Megs spluttered loudly as she bit back her smile from across the table. I knew what she was thinking. Dan and boring didn't even belong in the same hemisphere let alone in the same sentence. I coughed, taking the opportunity to finish my drink. Just thinking of Dan in a sweater vest was hilarious. I should totally buy him one for Christmas. Assuming we are still seeing each other.

Megs pulled out some cash and waved the waitress over. It was a lot of cash. Enough to cover the entire check, and a sizeable tip. Two problems with this: one, there was no way I was allowing her to foot the bill for my birthday dinner and two, Megs rarely carried cash.

"What are you doing?" I asked pointing to the leather folder.

"Ash, it's your birthday. I've got it covered." She waved me off like it she hadn't just put a stack full of fifties into the folder.

Kyla gave Megs a pointed look. "We'll sort it out later." I knew that at the very least both the girls would be covering their share. Money wasn't an issue for Megs. We all knew it, but no one was about to take advantage of her generosity.

"Yeah, yeah. We'll work it out." Megs pushed out her chair doing little to convince me she was going to be accepting any money from anyone. "Let's get out of here. I'm nowhere near drunk enough and I have our names on a door."

"Oooo name on the door. I like it. Megs is in charge of my birthday party next July. Just sayin'." Brianne smiled as we left our table and made our way to the door.

I had no idea where we were heading and to be honest I didn't really care. It might have been my birthday but Megs was running the show, and for whatever reason, this seemed important to her. Maybe it was to show me I would be okay post-Dan, maybe it was to show me I could still have a good time with my friends, or maybe she was just being a good friend and making sure I had a happy birthday. Any of those reasons would do. What we needed now was to start drinking. Let go and enjoy the night. Without Dan.

"You took us to a bar?" Kyla looked horrified as the cab pulled up to a plain looking brown and red building on Lower East Side. "I thought you had an in at a club?"

"Oh stop being so snobby. This place is great. I've heard good things." Megs smiled as she pulled out even more cash and paid the driver. What was with all the cash?

"I don't know, Megs." I looked at the large arched windows. This was not the kind of place I imagined spending my evening avoiding thoughts of Dan. It didn't look like the kind of place I'd spend my time, period. At all. Ever.

"You getting out?" The driver opened the window divider, his engine still running.

"Yes, of course." Megs popped open the door and all but

pushed me onto the sidewalk. "Give it an hour. You hate it and we'll go somewhere else. Okay?"

"Sure. Okay. Whatever." I didn't even try and hide the fact I wasn't onboard with her choice in venue. What the hell was this place and would I need a Hep C shot after leaving?

Brianne and Kyla followed us toward the bar/pub/dive/ whatever. As we got closer to the front of doorway, I saw a bright red sign with the word *Tommy's* on the front. The name of this fine establishment I assumed. There was a long line, not that Megs seemed too deterred. She smiled as we walked to the front of the line. She'd already told us that she'd organized our names at the door so I guessed she wasn't worried about the people who were eyeing us off as we walked past them.

Megs gave the door guy our names and he immediately let us through, shooting us an overly familiar smile. I'm sure in his head he was mocking us. While most people were dressed in denim and leather, the four of us were wearing short skirts and heels. Sure there were other women whose barely there outfits rivaled our skirt lengths, but they were on a different spectrum. A trashier one. Only calling it like I see it.

"Sixty minutes and counting," I tried to scream over the music, hoping Megs heard. A wall of bass hit us square in the face as we walked into the venue. It was loud and gritty. Some DJ was playing some music I'd never heard, and god willing wouldn't have to hear again after tonight. Realistically I wasn't going to need fifty-nine of those minutes, I had already decided. We were out of here the minute the counter expired and the clock was ticking.

"Let's get closer to the stage." Megs moved us deeper into the throng, her hand wrapped around mine giving me no way out. Fifty-seven minutes. Brianne and Kyla were looking just as horrified as I was. Good, so it's not just me.

"I hope you know this is the worst place ever," I all but yelled into Megs's ear. "Is this punishment for not talking to Troy about you?" I was joking of course. At least I think I was. She couldn't honestly be mad at me for that. It's not like Troy and I were friends. I barely counted Dan as a friend, and I was sleeping with him.

"This isn't a punishment. So self-absorbed." Megs laughed back. "One might question the company you are keeping." Her smirk widened.

Oh smart. She hadn't exactly mentioned Dan so therefore technically not broken any rules but the implication was there. Not that the other girls picked up on it. They were too busy looking around with wide-eyed expressions. We looked like tourists and we weren't fooling anyone.

"Hello Manhattan." The music had stopped and a voice pierced through the blackness on the stage. That voice. I knew that voice. I swallowed, trying to place it. Think, Ash. The stage remained dark, forcing me to play more mental guessing games.

"I was wondering if it would be okay if we hijacked the stage for a while," the voice continued, the toned dipping slightly, teasing the audience seductively.

The crowd around us seemed to have clued in and had started screaming and yelling excitedly. I was assuming it was their way of saying yes, they didn't mind. Either way, I was glad the mysterious voice meant DJ whoever had quit spinning whatever crap he'd been spinning at ear-bleeding decibels. I guess there was a silver lining. Crap. How much longer did we have left?

"I'm going to take that as a yes." The voice chuckled sending the crowd into an even bigger frenzy.

A spotlight fired across the stage, lighting up the area to reveal five men standing ready to play. My heart stopped. I think I forgot how to breathe as well as the room around me started to spin. My eyelids peeled back so far away from my eyes I'm surprised my eyeballs didn't fall right out of my head. Holy shit. Is it really? Yes, it is. It is Power Station, standing four feet in front of me.

Dan stared right at me, shrugging before attempting to give me an innocent-looking smile. Not even close, buddy. I knew this was more than just some freaky coincidence.

James—the now identified owner of the voice—smiled, dazzling the crowd as their screams got louder. Their suspicions were clearly confirmed as to who had been taunting them from the dark. He had a nice smile. James, I meant. I could see why girls loved him.

"Our bass player has a few words. Have you guys met Dan Evans?"

The screams got louder as Dan stepped into the center of the stage. His smile grew bigger the more the crowd hollered, his ego no doubt expanding as well. He was clearly enjoying himself. He looked down at me, as James handed him the microphone and he brought it to his mouth. "Hello Manhattan."

The crowd erupted.

"Wow, it's Power Station. Dan is fucking hot." Kyla grabbed my arm and shook me. You know, in case I wasn't sure of who was standing in front of me. She had no idea.

"So you see, ladies and gentlemen, I have a problem. I have talked it over with my brothers and they agree with me that this shit cannot stand. So we're going to need your help here tonight." I take back what I said about James's voice being seductive. It was nothing compared to what was coming through the speakers now. Raw, hot, and demanding attention. I couldn't stop watching him if I'd tried and there was no way I was going to try and stop. Not even for a minute.

"I met this girl." Dan grinned as he looked directly at me. I had no idea what he was about to say. None. Not a clue. I needed to remember to breathe.

"And while she was fucking drop-dead beautiful and smart and has an attitude like no other, I couldn't date her."

My heart stopped. Again. No this time I was serious. I think I was actually dying. Was Dan seriously and very publicly telling me I was not his girlfriend? Did he have a soul? The disruption to my cardiac rhythm was short-lived. I unfortunately wasn't going to die. Not from a heart attack at least. If ever there were a case of someone dying of embarrassment, I would probably be it. I was mortified.

"You see, for all her fucking perfection, she has never been to a concert. How does that even happen? I mean, I can't be with someone who hasn't been to a concert. Troy, can you believe that shit?"

Dan smirked as he continued, looking back toward the drum

kit. Troy seemed amused as he glanced back, shaking his head. I couldn't understand whether this was some bad, bad joke or a bad dream. Neither seemed plausible and both seemed horrible.

"So because it's her birthday and because I'm not willing to walk away from her, we are going to rectify that situation tonight."

What? What did he say? My head whipped around to Megs who was grinning, obviously in on whatever the fuck was going on. All of which was still unclear right now other than the fact that Dan Evans was standing on a stage talking about me.

"I need you to be loud, and I need you to rock this joint off its foundations so my girl can see what she's missed."

Did he just call me his girl? The crowd roared, giving Dan exactly what he wanted. Loud. Fevered. Crazy. I, on the other hand, stood stupefied. Wondering if I'd actually heard him correctly. Now would be a good time for that intelligence he spoke of to kick in.

"Ashlyn Murphy." Oh fuck he said my name. Kyla and Brianne whipped their heads toward me, reflecting the shocked, bewildered look I was wearing. At least now I wasn't the only one who had no idea. That was a positive surely, no longer alone in oblivion.

"Ash," he repeated in case anyone had missed it the first time. "You have no idea how much it turns me on to be your first, and trust me, babe, I'm going to pop your cherry like it's never been popped. Happy birthday." His voice rumbled low through the microphone as he eyed me with intent. Intent to blow my mind and ravage my body. Although probably in the reverse order. And while I was still clueless as to what was happening, I was almost one hundred percent sure if he touched me right now I'd orgasm on the spot.

The noise around me was insane, the crowd engulfing us as Dan handed the microphone back to James and they launched into the first song.

The people around us started jumping in unison with the beat. Bodies pushed and pressed up against us as they carried us closer to the stage. I looked around at Megs, Brianne, and Kyla and their expressions matched those around them. They had experienced this before. They knew what awaited them. The anticipation of greatness was written all over their faces. I was the one who didn't know what this would be like. To have them with me as I experienced this made it that little bit sweeter. That and having one hell of a live band be your first.

It was amazing. The sounds of the instruments and the vocals meshed seamlessly. It was uncanny. Flawless. It was exciting. It was thrilling and it was more emotional than I could have ever anticipated. I didn't know what I felt just that I was feeling. Excited, elated, exhausted and they were just the E emotions. I totally got it now. What the appeal was. Why people lost their minds. Why people would line up for hours in those hopes of being this close to the band. It all made sense, and I took back whatever I may have thought or said about Power Station. They were amazing. Each of them worked their asses off. They moved through the set, each song pulling just a little bit more from the crowd. The crowd seemed to know every word, they sung it back to the band with so much passion, their arms outstretched hoping one of the band members would reach out and touch them. Girls dissolved into a puddled mess if Alex, James, Jason or Dan made contact. Troy was even able to evoke the same crazed reaction with just a look and smile, being hidden behind a drum kit not hindering his contribution to the mayhem. The temperature of the room and the excitement rose to a maddening level. I was awed.

The music stopped and the lights dimmed, plunging us back into darkness. The band left the stage but the noise continued to ring in my ears, disorientating me for a few minutes. I had no idea what I was doing or where I was. If asked, I would have been lucky to remember my own name.

"Ash." Dan wrapped his arms around me materializing from the rowdy crowd. Wow. It was like magic but cooler, and with no cheesy bikini-clad assistant. His body, saturated from sweat, coated my skin as he embraced me. I loved it. He was so raw. I want to rip his clothes off and fuck him. The fact we had an audience didn't even bother me. I just wanted him and I didn't want to wait.

"Dan," I moaned as I attacked his mouth with my own. I kissed him. Hard. I settled for my tongue doing the fucking for now. At least I could have that immediately.

"Whoa, Ash." Dan's hand's reached down to my ass and pulled me up, grinding me against his cock. He was hard and obviously just as turned on as I was.

"So I take it from that reaction you enjoyed the show?" He smirked, squeezing my ass as he pulled away from me slightly. "Hey, Megs. I was beginning to think you weren't going to show up."

"Well your *girlfriend* was being difficult and wanted to go home. Like a spoilsport. On her birthday. I had my work cut out for me." The word girlfriend rattled me to my core. Her choice of words or his? Megs had been in on the plan from the beginning. The fact that this whole night had been orchestrated was slowly coming together.

"How? What? When?" I waded through random thoughts unable to make my mouth function properly. How did Dan know it was my birthday? I hadn't mentioned it. Did Megs go behind my back? I know she had good intentions but I couldn't see her deliberately telling Dan when we had discussed not telling him.

"Hi, I'm Dan." Dan peeled one of his hands from my ass and shifted me to his side so he could greet my friends.

"Kyla."

"Brianne."

They took turns in answering, still playing catch up as to what was going on.

"Nice to meet you, ladies. Thanks for coming out for the show. I swore Megs to secrecy." Dan winked at Megs before dazzling the girls with his smile. He was charming them. It wasn't hard.

Brianne nodded, unwilling or unable to speak.

"So the *Dan* you are seeing is Dan Evans?" Kyla pieced together, the penny finally dropping.

"Ah, she mentioned me. Be honest, did she tell you I'm the best sex she's ever had?" Dan couldn't help himself. Not sure if he was trying to embarrass me or he got some wild kick out of it, but there was no way we were going to be talking about our sex life with my friends. In a public bar. On my birthday.

"Actually I believe the words that were used were boring and sweater vests. Sorry, Dan." I tried to steer the conversation away from anything sexual. And I was in fact telling him the truth. Granted they hadn't been my words to describe him but they had been used while we had discussed him.

"Don't make me fuck you in front of your friends to prove a point, Ashlyn. You know I'll do it." He wasn't joking. I think we had established that when it came to sex, Dan didn't ever joke and if given the chance he probably would have sex with me in front of all these people. Hell, I'd considered it not even twenty minutes ago.

"You crazy, crazy man." I kissed him, knowing it was the only way I was going to shut him up. And because I wanted to kiss him, *really* wanted to kiss him.

"I don't understand. You guys look like you are together. Who's the guy you aren't *really* dating?" Brianne found her voice finally in time to make things awkward again. I guess it was better just to get things out in the open.

"We aren't dating? I'm kind of crushed, babe. I hope you haven't been seeing someone else." Dan pouted holding his hand to his chest, but I wasn't sure if he was playing it off like it was no big deal or it actually was no big deal. It's not like I had this thing worked out and deliberately tried to complicate things, and by the sound of it, he had no idea either.

"No, of course I'm not seeing someone else. You said you didn't do girlfriends and I didn't want to assume..." It had actually tormented me. He had put the idea in my head that what we had wasn't a relationship. I had wanted it to be but I'd figured he'd made himself clear and I wasn't about to beg. No matter how much I cared for him. No matter how much I was falling in love with him.

"Well just so there is no confusion. We're dating. You are my girlfriend. This is a done deal." He gestured between us. Well I guess it was. There was no way I wanted to fight it. It's what I had wanted him to say. I just never believed he'd actually say it. Those words sent me even further into an emotional tailspin. Elation replaced the uncertainty I had been feeling. Every cell in my body tingled with excitement as he held my hand. We were dating, and I never thought I could feel so relieved.

People had started to surround us and while I hadn't noticed before, it was painfully obvious now. Sharing this private conversation with my friends, while not ideal, was one thing. Sharing the conversation with a bunch of random people with camera phones, that was something entirely different.

"Hey, let's get you ladies backstage." Dan seemed to come to the same conclusion as I had. "You can meet the rest of the band."

Everyone agreed, especially Megs who hoped to speak to Troy. I don't know why she didn't just go ahead and ask him. Actually I know why. The same reason why I hadn't asked Dan for clarification on what *we* were. The promise of maybe was better than the disappointment of no.

Dan walked ahead through the crowd, leading us to the edge of the stage where they had played. A security guard let us through the minute he saw Dan. He didn't ask any questions. I guess he just assumed Dan had hit the groupie lottery. Either that or he'd been sent off to hunt and gather for the rest of the band. I hated someone might think of me in that way, like I could be disposable. I pushed it from my mind not willing to let someone's possible perceptions of me ruin a good thing.

We walked along the narrow, dark hallway until we got to a room hidden in the back. Dan didn't bother knocking, instead swinging the door open wide to reveal the rest of the band. It was surreal. Seeing them all there. Together. Sweaty and spent. In front of me.

"Hey, Ash. Happy Birthday." Troy was the first to come over and greet us. He gave me a hug and a warm smile. I heard Megs's breath hitch beside me. No doubt she was hoping the hugging would extend to her.

"Hey boys, this is Ashlyn." Dan pulled me close against his side. In case they hadn't got the memo we were together. "These are her friends: Megs, Brianne and Kyla." He held out his hand pausing and gesturing to each of the women as he introduced them. The girls each stood silently, managing a slight wave at the mention of their name.

"And this is the band, Troy, Alex, James, and Jason." Dan pointed around the room to the corresponding band member.

Alex Stone strolled over and smiled, all six foot four of rock god sexiness. "I believe we've already met. Nice to see you again. Happy Birthday."

"Thank you. It's a pleasure to see you again." While I still thought he was a good-looking guy, I wasn't tongue-tied like I had been the first time I'd met him. Nor was the compulsion to lick him pulsing through my veins.

"Back off, Stone. You can stop being so charming, she's not interested." Dan playfully punched Alex in the arm.

Alex's smile twitched. "Stand down, Dan. I'm just saying hi. Not trying to be charming."

"Well whatever you're doing, do less of it." Dan gripped my waist possessively. He was jealous, which was absurd but kind of cute.

Alex moved on and introduced himself properly to my friends, each of them struggling with saying hello. All except Megs, who was ignoring Alex entirely and making flirty eyes at Troy.

"Hi, I'm Jason. We met at the club a while back. Not sure if you remember. You were a little lit up." Jason laughed as he offered his hand. It's not like I could have forgotten that night if I'd tried. The night that had started this adventure. It was also the first night I'd spent with Dan. Not that I'd been conscious enough to know at the time and not that anything sexual had happened, but he had spent the entire night by my side. I was a little mad at myself I hadn't seen how sweet it had been at the time. Hindsight is twenty-twenty.

"Yeah. Not my finest moment." I shook his hand. Mentally shaking myself.

"Are you kidding? That night was spectacular," Troy chimed from the other side of the room.

"It truly was." Jason agreed. "Happy Birthday by the way."

"Thanks." I shuffled a little awkwardly. This was so weird. Being around the band and pretending they were just regular people. I hope I wasn't giving anyone any crazy looks and at least I was still able to string sentences together.

"And I'm James. Happy Birthday." The charismatic lead singer moved closer, his smile even more dazzling up close.

"Thank you." I felt like I was repeating myself, unable to think of anything else. Lame.

"So how was it?" James cracked open a bottle of water Alex had tossed him.

"Huh?" I stared at him blankly. Oh please. At least repeating *thank you* was better than random sounds. I swear I'm not a moron. Not that I was doing a good job of proving it.

"The show." James paused and took a large swallow of water before continuing. "Dan tells us it was your first time seeing a live act. Did you enjoy it?"

"Yes. It was great. Really good." I avoided tacking on a *thanks* to the end.

James smiled politely, ignoring the fact I didn't contribute much more to the conversation.

"I saw you watching me while I played." Dan kissed the base of my neck and I had to stop myself from moaning loudly.

Unable to stop myself, I turned into him, my body seeking even more contact. "You like girls watching you play with yourself, don't you?" I mumbled against his skin. It felt so good and yet so strange. The public display of affection. We were outside of our bubble.

"I'd rather watch you," he answered predictably, moving me to a more secluded area of the room. Not that there was any privacy. This was as good as we were going to get for right now. It sort of disappointed me.

"Are you thinking about touching yourself?" Dan smirked when I didn't answer right away.

"No." I rolled my eyes, shaking my head.

"Thinking about touching me?" He didn't even try and hide his excitement.

"I was just taking stock." I answered benignly not really able to make much sense of the mess of thoughts inside my head. Was I really his girlfriend?

"Snore." Dan faked a yawn. "Did you enjoy dinner?"

"Um, yes. It was great." Had Megs told Dan our dinner plans? "Actually we went to this Mexican place. I think you'd really like it." I leaned against the back wall needing some physical support.

"Who do you think chose it, babe?" Dan licked the shell of my ear. That was not helping.

I stopped. Dan had chosen the venue? "How much of this was you?" I sucked in a breath and held it. How had he known?

"The whole thing." Dan pushed me up against the wall. "I saw your ID when you left your purse in the car that first night so I knew it was your birthday. I don't know why you didn't tell me, but I decided I was done being a whiny bitch and sitting on the sidelines. It seemed I hadn't made myself clear."

"I thought you weren't interested in me. In that way." I reached up and touched his face. The room around us dissolved. For all I knew, and cared, we were alone.

"Oh, babe. I'm interested in you in every way." Dan pressed up against me. "So I called your friend Megs, got her to help me hook this up. Just so you know she flat-out denied shit for a solid twenty minutes, and it was only after I called bullshit and told her I saw your ID that she bent a little."

I was silently relieved. Glad she hadn't just rolled over on account it was Dan who was asking. Of course had he enlisted Troy, she probably would have given my social security, bank account details, and blood type. Thankfully it seemed like it had been a Dan solo mission. "Megs is good people. Loyal. She's more like family than a friend."

"Yeah, she's great." He rolled his eyes, hinting there was more to the story. "I had to fight her for this, you know. She wanted to plan your birthday. Take you to dinner and all of that, but I argued she'd had you all those other birthdays and this was my first one. I wanted to make it perfect even if I didn't get to spend all of it with you."

My heartbeat thumped out of control as the gravity of his words hit me. This was my first birthday with him and he wanted to make it memorable. Most of all, it hinted to the fact he wanted there to be others, that we weren't as temporary as I had initially thought. "I thought you said you weren't romantic." Okay, maybe not in the traditional way but organizing all of this? For me to be so important he would go out of his way? It was better than any romantic gesture I'd ever received. "So you paid for it all too I supposed." The truth was slowly coming out.

"No... Maybe..." He was such a bad liar. "Would you be mad if I said yes?"

"When I saw the roll of fifties Megs was packing I knew something was fishy. She doesn't carry cash. That was a major flaw in your plan." I wasn't the slightest bit pissed. It had been sweet and I was glad Dan had bankrolled the evening and not some unknown criminal activity that would explain the cash.

"She wouldn't take hundreds, said it was too obvious." He shrugged, not comprehending that most people didn't kick around with hundred dollar bills in their pockets. It definitely would have tipped me off sooner. "I have to give her a pair of Troy's sticks as well. Fuck if I know what she's going to do with them. I got them signed in case she want to throw them on eBay."

There was no way those sticks were going on eBay or any-where else outside Ms. Megan Winters's possession.

"Thanks for an amazing birthday, Dan, and thanks so much for the show. I loved it. Every second of it." It was so much more than I had anticipated. The dinner. The concert. Our official *coupling*. That was by far the standout.

"The night ain't over yet, sweetheart." His eyes darkened as he licked my neck. "Not even by a long shot."

I DON'T KNOW WHEN I TURNED INTO A BIG FUCKING SAP, BUT I HAD decided there was no way I was going to miss Ashlyn's birthday, regardless of whether she told me or not.

Talking over with Troy had put things into perspective. We were seeing each other and there was no one else. At least not on my part, and Ash didn't seem like the kind of girl who'd juggle two guys. Not by a long shot. So there was absolutely no reason why we shouldn't just bite the bullet and get with the program. The one where she was my girl and I didn't have to pretend that spending nights away from her didn't gnaw at my brain. I slept better with her tucked up beside me and I loved waking up and finding her ready and wet. It's a wonder I'd let her leave.

I'd tossed it around in my head for days and came up with the same conclusion. Fuck the reasons we shouldn't be together, fuck her ten-year plan and fuck the fact we are different. She made me happy and as far as I could tell, I made her happy too, so that's all that should matter.

The concert idea seemed cheesier than a hallmark commercial

but when I suggested it to the band they had been eager to get onboard. We didn't get the opportunity to play smaller venues anymore. Not that I was complaining, but there was something magical about playing a bar and having the audience right in front of you.

James jumped on the phone and made it happen. We kept it tightly under wraps so the place wouldn't be swarmed beyond capacity and we agreed we would only play one set. Tommy Zampelli, the owner, was one of the guys who had let us play in his bar when we were starting out. He'd retired and his kid Ritchie was running the show, but they were happy to have us and jacked up security for the night just to make sure it ran smoothly.

Getting Megs onboard had been a challenge but hadn't been impossible. I flat out told her there was no way I was going to let my girlfriend celebrate her birthday without me. The word had just kind of fallen out of my mouth without even thinking about, but the more I thought about it, the more it fit, and I wasn't about to take it back. Hell, no. So it hung there for a while, like a pair of big hairy balls, and when Megs saw I wasn't about to drop or forget it, she agreed. Only took thirty minutes of sweet-talking and the promise of a pair of sticks from the big guy. What the fuck she wanted to do with those was beyond me but I couldn't give a rat's ass. The important thing was she would take her to the place I had originally wanted to take Ash—before she blew me off—and bring her to me when they were done. The whole money thing was another fucking headache. Seriously, I could see why her and Ash were such good friends. They were both fucking stubborn. The fact she was a shrink made me edgy though. They start pulling that lateral thinking bullshit on you, and before you know it, you agree to something maybe you shouldn't have. In any case, I stayed on course and stood my ground. Megs finally agreed.

Waiting for her to show had been a whole other hell. Megs had texted me a few times saying Ash had been trying to make excuses to bail and it was making me fucking antsy. The whole point of this show was for Ash to see it, and for us to be the first live act she saw. The fact we were even dealing with this still baffled me. It was like finding a unicorn in Queens. That shit just didn't happen.

When she finally walked in looking all kinds of miserable, it was like being clocked in the nuts. I hated it and I hoped this little stunt didn't blow up in my face. Either way, we were locked on for target so it was too late to abort now. I had manned up and whatever the outcome was, I'd deal.

I never expected to see the look on her face when she saw me. Fuck. Her smile made me feel like Superman and I'd challenge anyone who didn't think I could've outrun a train. Playing for Ash rocked my world. Watching her move to our songs, reckless and unrestrained, I knew she had it in her. She didn't know any of the words, which was amusing 'cause everyone around her did. But damn, seeing her covered in sweat, having a good time at my show was better than any porno I'd ever seen. I had a killer fucking hard-on to prove it.

I couldn't get off the stage quick enough. I bypassed the backstage area and jumped off the front of the stage and into the crowd like a fucking rookie. Some girl grabbed my ass but I was able to get free of her pretty quick, just as well I did 'cause it's hard to make a play for one girl when you have another trying to get into your pants. I know this first hand. It gets ugly.

So I grabbed Ash, pulling her from the crowd in the dark. Her face was priceless. And after some appreciated mouth action and our dance floor confessional, it seemed like we were finally on the same page. I'd taken the girls backstage to meet the rest of the band which hopefully would mean we could call it a wrap, and I could get my girl back to my place.

Troy, Jase, and TJ had made sure Ash's friends got home; all of them too liquored up to drive and thankfully smart enough to cab it in. They loaded up into the Suburban and hit the road. Alex and James said their goodbyes and went home to their wives and kids. They didn't hang around much these days, not that I blamed them. Why bother when you have a sweet deal waiting for you at home?

"Where's your car?" Ashlyn giggled as we walked along the

sideway.

I insisted Ash do a few shots before leaving the bar. Tequila on your birthday is mandatory, and I'm a stickler for tradition.

"Just in the parking garage up the street, babe. Just a little bit farther." I wrapped my arms around her tight little body. She shivered despite me giving her my jacket to wear. I liked it on her. The leather dwarfed her tiny frame.

"Dan," Ashlyn purred as she nuzzled into my side, my dick responding by punching out against my jeans.

"Yeah, babe." I kept my feet moving, taking her along with me. Stopping wasn't an option. Not unless she was planning on spending the rest of her birthday in lock-up for a public indecency charge.

"Am I really your girl?" She looked up at me. Her eyes were full of fucking need and want as she breathed on my neck. She undid me.

"You sure are." I tried to concentrate on the words coming out of my mouth instead of the pain in my balls. My body was not on the same page as my brain, arguing whether or not we were going to have to wait until I got her home to my apartment. A few more steps till we reached the car. A few more steps too fucking far.

"I like that." Ashlyn ran her hand down my back so that it rested on my ass. Yep, I was probably getting a speeding ticket on the way home. I didn't even give a shit. I just needed to get inside of her. Like five minutes ago.

We rounded the corner into the multilevel garage and I handed the valet my ticket. The kid looked about twenty, he didn't even try to hide his shit-eating grin when he saw Ash all sweet and relaxed, no doubt a result of the tequila. Yeah, a little less time checking out my girlfriend and a little more getting my ride, asswipe.

He took the hint the way it was intended and didn't waste any time flapping his gums making small talk. Good thing too, 'cause I wasn't interested in the "how-are-yous," just wanted my keys and my Benz so I could get the fuck out of here.

"Dan," Ashlyn mumbled into my chest, her hand slowly traveling down the front of my shirt. And fuck if I wasn't torn between asking her to stop and begging her to keep going. How the hell long does it take to get a car? Where did he park it? Vermont?

"Hang in there, almost home." I don't know if I was saying that for her benefit or for mine. Hoping my balls would get the memo and yank on the brakes.

The douche who'd been ogling my girl finally pulled up in my wheels and not a second too soon. I peeled off a twenty as I took back my keys. His tip had been decreased when I caught him checking out my girl's ass. Not cool, dude. Not even close.

I slid into the driver's seat and made sure Ash was buckled in tight, my hard-on dictating we get home and get busy ASAP. Time to see what the 5.5 Liter, twin turbo V8 under the hood could do. I revved the engine and tore out of the parking garage like a bat out of hell. Ashlyn laughed as I pulled onto the secluded side street surprisingly not running her mouth about my driving. That had to be a first.

"Dan, pull over." Ashlyn grabbed my arm before we had a chance to get onto the main road.

"You going to be sick?" I looked over at her as I slammed on the brakes. God, I hoped she wasn't going to puke all over my car; that would really kill the mood. Not that it would stop me from fucking her. There wasn't much that could right now.

The sudden stop punched us both back into our seats, Ashlyn breathing heavily as she fumbled with her seatbelt. Yep, she was going to be sick. Probably could have skipped the last few shots. I put the car into park and engaged the emergency brake, just in case she needed me to hold her hair back or something.

The belt restraint flung back and she wrangled herself out of her seat, but instead of opening the car door, she flung herself at me.

"Whoa," was the only response I managed as her lips covered my mouth. The taste of salt and tequila was still fresh on her tongue as she swirled it around in my mouth. It tasted like heaven. Well, if heaven had a bar, I bet it would taste just like that.

I reached down and unhooked my seatbelt and eased back the driver's seat, keeping my mouth firmly locked on hers. I needed more room but there was no way I was stopping this. Not a fucking chance.

Ash climbed over the console and into my lap, my hands finding their way onto her ass. She straddled me, her short dress creeping up her thighs and flashing me a peek at the black satin panties she was wearing.

"Fuck," I groaned, sliding my hand underneath her dress as she rocked up against my cock. The car might have gotten from zero to a hundred in four-point-eight seconds but I just got there in under three.

"Dan, fuck me," Ashlyn moaned in between kisses, my brain misfiring on the fucking words coming out of her mouth. Was there even a possibility I wouldn't? Was she meaning now? In the car? On the fucking street?

"Babe, I want nothing more than to have sex with you but you sure you want to do it here?" I looked around at the deserted street, knowing this wasn't her. Maybe it was the booze talking.

"Isn't this what you used to do?" She giggled into my ear as she reached down in between my thighs. "Have sex in your car?" She unzipped my jeans as I struggled to hear the words she was actually saying.

"Not really. Maybe the Escalade or the Suburban but never in my car." My brain was able to get my mouth to come to the party and answer her. My dick wondering why the fuck we were still talking.

"Well then, it's going to be a first for both of us then." She threw her head back and laughed, hitting it on the windshield.

"Fuck, are you okay?" I rubbed the back of her head, Ashlyn still laughing despite bashing her melon on the glass. Alcohol is a great pain neutralizer. Been there myself.

"I'm fine. But I'm horny and I want to have sex with you." She moved forward, leaning against my throat. "Here. In your car. Knowing you haven't done that with any other girl and I haven't done it with any other guy. You said you were going to pop my cherry." She teased, clocking me with her fuck-me eyes.

Well you weren't going to have to tell me twice, if she wanted this then I was all about it. After all, it was her birthday and I'm sure there's some law or some shit about not disappointing a girl on her birthday.

I pulled her onto me, wrapping a hand around her neck and threading it through her hair. I kissed her hard, and she gave me as good as she got. She was so wild. Crazy. Out of control, and I loved it. I grabbed the top of her dress, the stretchy fabric was no match for my fist as I pulled it down, her tits spilling out of the top. No bra. What do you fucking know? Not only is it her birthday but must be fucking Christmas as well.

My mouth moved to the tip of her tit, flicking it with my tongue before swirling it around her nipple. She moaned as she let me lick her, her pussy rubbing up against my crotch sending me into overdrive. I wasn't going to last long.

"I need to be in you, Ash. This is going to be fast." I reached down to her panties and tore them straight from her body. There was no way I was going to wait for her to slide them off. Fuck that. We were on a schedule, one that was dictated by my dick.

She yelped as the cool air hit her ass, my hand moving from her neck, down across her tits and over her belly. She was so hot I couldn't stand it. She proved what a team player she was by pulling out my dick and jerking me off. I bunched up her dress around her waist giving me unrestricted access, just the way I wanted it. I slid a finger inside of her while my thumb played with her clit. She was already wet.

"Fuck, Ash. You are so wet. How long have you been thinking about fucking me?" I pushed in another finger, and damn if my dick wasn't getting all kinds of jealous of my hand.

"Since I saw you on stage." She groaned as I fingered her, my hand fucking coated in her wetness.

"Ash, I'm usually all about the foreplay but if I don't fuck you right now I'm going to blow my load like a fucking teenager who just watched his first porno. I promise I will take care of you later." I pulled her hand from my dick knowing a few more pulls was going to make me come.

"Fuck me, Dan. Fuck me." She moaned as I continued working her with my hand, her pussy riding up against me.

"Babe, I need to get a condom." This was one of those times

where it honestly sucked only having two hands. I know I had a condom in my back pocket, but that meant moving and stopping what I was doing. Neither of these options made me happy. I slid my hand out of her, both of us cursing under our breath.

"Dan," she moaned as she rubbed her pussy up against my shaft, bracing herself against my seat as she traveled up and down the length of my cock.

"Ash," I groaned. Her hot, wet pussy teased the head of my cock as I lifted my ass off the seat, hoping Ash might be able to reach the condom and we wouldn't have to stop. The inside of the car proving not as *spacious* as the douchebag car salesman had claimed. "Can you reach into my pocket, babe? Left side, grab my wal—" I wasn't able to finish my sentence as I accidently slid inside her.

"Fuck," I groaned, as I couldn't stop myself from pushing in deeper. Holy shit, this felt amazing. Her hot pussy wrapped around my bare cock. I'd never had unprotected sex. Too fucking scared I'd get some disease that would make my dick fall off or I'd end up being someone's dad. No fucking way. But feeling how good it felt, I completely understood why a man would roll that dice. Right now we could play Russian roulette, and you could pull the trigger of that loaded gun as long as I got to keep sliding inside of the tight pussy.

"Ash." I pumped harder, waiting for her to tell me to stop. One of us needed to think straight and I didn't think it was going to be me.

"I'm clean. Don't stop. I trust you." She pushed down hard against me, giving me the green light.

I wanted to tell her I was clean. To reassure her I wasn't putting her at risk, but I couldn't fucking talk. What I needed to do was fuck. Hard. I palmed her ass, guiding her up and down as I pushed inside her. My dick so fucking hard I impaled her with each thrust. She screamed as she rode me, her fucking pussy fisted me like a vice then milked my dick as she came. I pumped into her as she shook, those pussy pulses sending me over the edge as I shot my load into her. We collapsed against each other, our breathing out of control like freight train barreling down the tracks.

It was one of the most intense experiences of my life. It was like every single part of me shot out through my cock. It was amazing.

Oh, Shit. I just came inside of her. The reality of the situation started to poke its ugly fucking mug, as soon as the high from the awesome sex started to fade. I had meant to pull out. What the hell was I thinking?

"Fuck, Ash!" I pulled her close against my chest. "Please tell me you are on the pill or something." I had already been an asshole by jacking into her like a fucking nympho so I guess a little slide further down the dickwad scale wasn't that big a deal.

"A bit late now." She half-laughed as she kissed my neck. "You think you may have implanted the seed for a little Dan in there?"

I couldn't laugh. This was not funny. I tried to swallow but it got stuck in my throat. The thought that I could have made her pregnant was as serious as shit got. It had been stupid. I'd been thinking with my dick and not my head. Whatever happened though, I was going to be a man about it. I would not be one of those deadbeats who cut and run, no fucking way. I would take care of my business.

Ashlyn pulled away from me, studying me when I didn't speak. "Oh my god. You should see your face. Of course I'm on the pill. I'm not ready to be a mom." She gently shook my shoulders.

The near miss still rattled me a little. I'd never been so careless. "Babe, I should have asked first. If shit went down," I swallowed, "I would have still stuck around."

I wasn't sure exactly what I should say but I knew I had to say some-thing. I hadn't even pulled out of her yet. My fucking cum started spilling out of her onto my jeans. As far as romantic got, this wasn't it. Still, I wouldn't have traded it for anything. Feeling her like that.

"I know, Dan." She smiled sweetly, like I hadn't just fucked her brains out. Her voice mellowed as she moved in to kiss me. "I think I'm in love with you."

I'd heard girls tell me they loved me all the time. Usually while I was either fucking them or while I was on stage. To me it was a throwaway line, it didn't hold much weight. No one really meant it and hearing it did little for me. It was sweet they felt that way, but it wasn't going to change anything. People fall in and out of love all the time. Hearing it from Ashlyn though was a whole new ball game. It was like a punch in the gut, knocking the wind right out of me.

I blinked, dumbfounded. This five-foot-six, hundred-thirty pound redhead just knocked me on my ass. I'd just fucked her. In my car. The windows still fogged up from our heavy breathing. Her dress still hiked up around her waist. My semi-hard cock still inside her. There was nothing romantic or gentle about it, and she told me she loved me? This was not how I ever imagined this moment would go down if it ever happened for real. I'd never felt like a bigger asshole than I did at that moment.

"You don't have to say it back." She moved her mouth on me before I had a chance to answer. "I just wanted you to know."

"Ash." I closed my eyes and rested them against the headrest. "I love you, too."

"Please don't say it just because I did." Ash grabbed my chin forcing my face forward. "I'd rather you didn't say it, than say it just because you *think* you should."

My eyes flung open. She had no idea. No clue as to how far gone I was, and whether I said it or not it wouldn't change the fact I'd do anything for this girl. I'd walk through fire for her, and it wasn't 'cause she said three words to me. It was 'cause of what was going on in the blood-pumping organ in my chest. I guess I hadn't looped it back to the whole love thing, not in a serious way. I've been in love before. Or at least I thought I had. But it never felt like this. Nothing like this.

I pulled her head closer, resting her forehead against mine. "I'm not saying it because you did. I'm saying it because it's what I feel. I do love you, Ash. I fucking love you."

"Then let's do this. I mean seriously do this." She wrapped her arms around the back of my neck.

"You're mine, babe, and I'm yours. It's already done."

The street outside was dark. Not a fucking a car or person insight. The inside of the car was another story; it was a mess.

Bodily fluids spilling all over the place and I just handed this woman my fucking balls. And, I regretted neither of them.

22

Ashlyn

FIRST DAYS USUALLY BROUGHT A JUMBLE OF NERVES, BUT I WAS MORE excited than anything else. Exciting to be starting this amazing new chapter.

I had just had the most amazing weekend. My twenty-eighth birthday had been so much more than I could have ever hoped for. Ever since I'd left Boston, I'd dreaded birthdays, celebrating them more for everyone else's benefit than my own. It's not that I didn't enjoy the occasion but I missed my family. We spoke on the phone, emailed, Skyped, you name it, but it wasn't the same. It wasn't the same as having your workaholic dad take the time to hug you, wish you happy birthday, and tell you were always going to be his little girl. I'd never really thought about how much I had missed home, not wanting to derail my plan, but I guess if I was honest, I missed it a lot. And Dan and his crazy surprise concert reminded me of that. Of pushing everything aside for a few moments to wish someone you loved a happy birthday. He had orchestrated the whole thing, dinner, Megs, the show. All for me. Then he told the world I was his girlfriend. Not just the room, literally the world. Dan's little speech had already been uploaded to twitter and YouTube and the number of hits just kept climbing. Then we'd had unprotected sex in his car and I'd told him I loved him. I'm not sure why I picked that moment. I guess I got caught up in the fact I truly trusted him. Letting myself be completely bare with him. Literally and figuratively. Not that I planned it that way. He had accidently slid in. Into my vagina and into my life. That, or I'd been moved by the totally hot car sex. In any case, the road map for my plan just got a reroute. I was now happily part of a pair.

"Your first day?" A smiling good-looking stranger watched as I wrestled with the swipe pass I had been given only a few hours before. He was wearing the typical suit. His hair just a little longer than unspoken corporate regulation. Clearly a rebel.

It *was* my first day. My first day as an analyst at JenCorp. Starting a new chapter in my life with a kick-ass boyfriend and kick-ass new job.

"That obvious?" I laughed, as I pressed the errant plastic card against the white scanner. Maybe they haven't activated it yet?

"The trick is a light touch." He gently removed the card from my hand. "May I?" He looked at me for permission.

There was a look I hadn't seen in the work place in a long time. I almost had to grab a wall to stop myself from fainting. Someone who actually wanted to help me? And not holler at me for a beer, or try to touch my ass? Wow. I had the best life. No, I wasn't being dramatic; these little things rocked my world.

"Please." I nodded my head to the scanner that refused to *scan* me.

"See if you just tap it like that," he gently touched my pass to the wall and it lit up green, "it works first time." He handed my swipe pass, a pleased grin on his face.

"Thanks for the tip." I held out my hand, wondering what else was an appropriate form of greeting. Handshakes seemed a little out dated and honestly I felt kind of lame but yeah. I was still going with it. "I'm Ashlyn Murphy and you already know it's my first day."

"Rob Sawyer. The new analyst?" He took my hand without hesitation. If he was thinking I was a loser he wasn't showing it. Maybe he was too polite or he wore a killer poker face.

"Yes. Am I wearing a sign?" I was only half-joking, wondering if it was written all over my face I was fresh meat. It usually only took a day or two until I found my feet in a new job but I would hate to think I looked like I didn't belong. Not after it took me so long to get here. This is exactly where I should be.

"No. I am going to be working with you." Rob laughed. "I was told you were starting today. I had meetings this morning so I missed your induction, but by all accounts you had no issues." He had a nice smile and seemed genuine but I was cautious. Was he fishing? Or just being friendly?

The corporate world could be brutal; it had spat me out the first time without a second thought. If Rob was sizing me up as competition, I wasn't going to make it easy for him. "It was a lot to take in, but nothing I can't handle."

"Good, then you'll do well here." He was so collected and well put together. It wasn't just the way he looked it was his whole vibe. This was his world and he was comfortable in it. It was like the Discovery channel. He was a tiger in his native environment, just wearing a different kind of striped suit. I wanted to be that majestic.

"That's the plan."

I figured I'd probably filled my quota for awkward conversations for the day so best move on. Besides, I should probably head back to my office. That's right. I had an office. I was still pinching myself this was real and if it wasn't, I didn't ever want to wake up.

"Well, I better get back. Thanks again." I waved my swipe card over the sensor lightly and it immediately flicked green. I actually stepped through the doorway this time. "I'm sure I'll be seeing you soon."

"You sure will be." Rob smiled as the automatic door closed between us.

Was he hitting on me? No. What was I thinking? This wasn't a bar where people just hit on some random person they just met. This was a work place. I was just out of practice and reading way more into his kindness. Right? Right. Geez I'm beginning to think being with Dan was giving me his ego as well. It's not like every man who sees me wants to sleep with me. It sounded so conceited in my head; thank god I wasn't repeating it to anyone else. I laughed at myself as I walked to the elevator and pressed the button for my floor. The metal doors opened immediately and I stepped inside. It was empty, giving me the opportunity to take a few extra moments to collect myself and get my head out of my ass.

My phone vibrated silently in my purse. I said a silent prayer of thanks I had switched off the volume when I saw who was calling. I didn't need explicit lyrics announcing my arrival.

I didn't answer. I wanted to, but taking personal calls on company time was the easiest way to get fired. It killed me to let it go to voice mail, but the last thing I needed was Dan getting me into a hot mess. He did that often and usually I liked it but now wasn't the time. Which kind of sucked. We would make up for it no doubt tonight. I sure as hell was going to need it.

I had spent the morning in the conference room with Mitch, my new supervisor, getting the run down. It was typical, very dry, but necessary. There was no easing into the position, it was very much a sink or swim kind of deal. They didn't have time to handhold and I hated to be micro-managed so it seemed like a perfect situation, albeit intense. The afternoon was an overload of information. Account names, departments, and clientele listings. It was made marginally easier by the fact I had my own office, something I hadn't had in very long time. It had a door too, it wasn't just a cubbyhole or cubical. It was a real office. Little things obviously excited me, and this was one.

I had tried to contain my excitement when Mitch had showed me where I would be working. Breaking into over enthusiastic squealing seemed so inappropriate. So I squealed on the inside and gave a reserved nod instead in response. It was a compromise.

Rob's office was right next to mine so it seemed I would be seeing him quite a bit. Seeing as there was only the two of us in the department we would be working closely together. Mitch, our boss and the CFO's right-hand man, made it clear they expected me to hit the ground running and I wasn't going to give them an opportunity to be disappointed.

I was mentally exhausted by the end of day. Parts of my brain I hadn't used in months had to limber up and get back into the game. It was scary and exhilarating all at the same time and five o'clock didn't come a moment too soon.

The minute I stepped out from the revolving glass doorway of JenCorp and onto the sidewalk, I saw Dan's Mercedes. We'd never discussed him giving me a ride home, but I was glad I wasn't going to have to brave the subway in peak hour. I couldn't help smiling knowing he had cared enough to come. The whole relationship was so new; the fact he seemed as invested as I was, floored me.

He was out of the car the minute he saw me, wrapping his arms around my waist and pulling me up against his body while his mouth attacked mine. There was nothing sweet about his kiss, it was desperate and heated, and obviously I'd been missed.

"Dan, not on the street." I half-heartedly pulled away not wanting anyone I worked with catching me making out in front of the building.

"You seemed to have no problems with public displays of affection on the street last Saturday." His satisfied grin leaving no doubt he was remembering my birthday celebrations. His hand snaked around behind me and opened the car door.

"True but there wasn't the possibility of my boss seeing me either. Keep it in your pants long enough to get me back to my apartment and I'll make it worth your while." I unwrapped myself from Dan's grasp and slid into the car. He didn't miss a beat as he stalked around the driver's side and jumped in. The car roared to life as we pulled away from curb.

I laughed like a five-year-old, throwing my head back against the headrest as Dan tore onto the street. He then had to jam on the brakes not soon after when he realized we were in downtown Manhattan and not the interstate.

"You want me to pull over so we can reminisce?" Dan shot me a grin that did crazy things to my body. The tingling parts thought pulling over was a good idea.

"Just keep your eyes on the road and get me home in one piece." I reached over and squeezed his thigh. I had never been this into a guy. It was intoxicating. Made me dizzy. I loved it.

"I wanted to talk to you about that." Dan grabbed my hand in his lap and gave it a little squeeze. "I had a key cut for you today. Figured it makes more sense for you to stay at my place 'cause it's closer to your work. Plus, your place. Well, it ain't great."

"Dan Evans, you are such a diva. My place not flashy enough for you?" I laughed. Not that I blamed him. Given the choice; I wouldn't want to stay at my place either.

"Babe, if the only thing wrong with it was *no flash*, we wouldn't be having this conversation. I'm pretty sure I saw a rat running across the kitchen floor. Son of a bitch even had the nerve to stare me down."

"I'll call the Super and get an exterminator organized." Rats happened from time to time. I wasn't proud of it, but the drainage in the building probably predated Christianity, so rats unfortunately found their way into apartment.

"Ash, you don't need an exterminator, you need an exorcist for that place."

"You sure you aren't a girl? One little rat and you want to run back to your penthouse?" I enjoyed teasing him. I loved we could do this. Play. With Dan, I didn't have to think. I could just say what I thought. It was like riding around without a seatbelt. Dangerous, but thrilling.

"Don't even start with that shit. It wasn't a *little* rat. The fucker was huge, even had a tattoo."

"Fine, let's stay at your place then. You're lucky I'm in an incredibly giving mood." It wasn't a hard sell. His place was nicer. It was also larger, more luxurious, and, as he rightly advertised, was closer to work than mine. Not to mention it didn't need to be bug-bombed bi-monthly.

His smile tugged at the corner of his mouth. "You think the goodwill could extend a little further and you can maybe unbutton that coat? Your tits look sensational in those tight little business shirts."

"Dan. It's a business shirt. It's not supposed to be sexy."

"Well then their marketing team failed 'cause just thinking about you in that shirt makes me want to jerk off." His hand moved to the top of my coat and flipped open a button. The man had a sickness. Sadly, I think I too was infected.

"You say that about everything I wear, Dan. I'm surprised you don't have RSI."

Dan let out a huge laugh. "Babe, for you it would be worth it."

Things fell into a rhythm as the weeks wore on. While I hadn't moved in with Dan, more and more of my stuff seemed to find its way into his apartment. I was surprised how easy it all was. There had been no real discussion; it just kind of evolved. I had always assumed that when I made that leap into cohabitation there would be a strategy meeting. Pros and cons would be weighed, parameters drawn up, expectations and even personal require-ments exchanged. After all, living with someone was a big deal. You don't just start living with them. Or do you?

Work was amazing. I was on a steep learning curve but I loved the challenge. Rob was great, too. He was friendly and easygoing. Rob had mentioned Dan a few days in. It seemed our sidewalk displays hadn't gone unnoticed. I cringed hoping no one else had seen.

Streaks of gray clouds stretched across the sky, their wispy latitude hiding the sun. The thin sheet of rain hit the glass of the office window before tumbling onto the busy street below, and yet none of it bothered me. My smile widened as my thoughts of the day turned to Dan. I leaned back against the leather chair absorbing it, as the case study I should have been reading sat open on the boardroom table in front of me.

"So the guy with the AMG, he's your boyfriend?" Rob glanced up from the file that had our attention. We were working in the conference room, trying to see if there was any value in acquiring a small flagging company in Reno. My gut told me no, that absorbing it under the JenCorp banner would actually have a negative effect on the market share but we were being thorough.

"AMG? Is that an acronym for something?" I tried to work out what the letters might stand for. Nope. Coming up with nothing.

"It's the type of Mercedes. Very nice car I might add. Sorry. I was walking out behind you yesterday, I saw the two of you." Rob looked down at his papers and shuffled them.

"Oh?" I hadn't seen anyone behind me as I'd left the building but then again, I had been too fixated on Dan to notice anyone else. My lips tingled just thinking about the kiss. His kiss. "Oh." While I hadn't wanted to be give my co-workers a show, Dan it seemed, had other ideas.

"He's the guitarist from the band, Power Station, right?"

"The bass player. But yeah, he's in Power Station."

"That must be difficult for you. Having a boyfriend with such a high profile. I'm a little bit surprised; you seem so down to earth and normal. Nothing like what I imagine those people to be."

I'm sure he was saying what a lot of other people didn't have the courtesy to say to my face; I didn't look like I belonged in his world anymore than he belonged in mine. I'd had the same thoughts initially but for whatever reason, the two of us fit. Strip away all the hype and Dan was still just a man. Well, not just *a* man. *My* man.

"They are just regular people, Rob. Just like you and me. Sure they work different hours and wear different clothes, but they aren't that much different than us. James and Alex get most of the media attention, so overall, we get left alone, but occasionally there is someone sniffing around. It's not as bad as you think."

I wasn't annoyed. I was glad he had asked rather than just assuming. Or gossiping. That would be worse. Besides over the last couple of days, we have talked about all different things. Family. School. Friends. I had told him I was in a relationship but didn't elaborate further. It was bound to come up sooner or later, and no one was forcing me to answer his questions. They weren't even overly personal, he just seemed curious.

"I'm sorry, I shouldn't have said anything. I didn't mean to offend you. It's none of my business." He reached out and gently ran his thumb over the back of my hand.

"You didn't offend me. If I didn't want to answer, I wouldn't." I smiled. It was forced but I didn't want him to feel bad, especially when he'd done nothing wrong.

"So do rock bands still have groupies or is that no longer a thing?" He winced. I guess he had been working up to that one - the inevitable question about women throwing themselves at my boyfriend. Women who didn't care what his relationship status was.

"Unfortunately, yeah, they do. I hate it, but it isn't going to change anytime soon. Short of carrying around a big stick and beating anyone who looks at him longer than five seconds there isn't a lot I can do to dissuade anyone." I tried to laugh it off. I imagined eventually Dan would go on tour and that whole scenario would get very real. It's not like I could pack up and leave, follow him around the world like some obedient poodle. I pushed the notion out of my head. What was the saying about borrowing trouble? Leave that shit for another day.

"That must be hard. Seeing someone you care about being pursued by other women."

The last bit stung. I hadn't really seen it. Not yet anyway, but I guess I should be prepared for it. It would come. Inevitably. Like the winter that was sneaking in, every day a little colder than the last. Burying my head in the sand wasn't going to make it any less a fact.

"I try not to think about it. I trust Dan." I tried to sound convincing. More for my own benefit. Like hearing the words would reinforce them. I did trust Dan. It was everyone else I had a problem with.

"Of course you do. I'm sure he loves you very much. I should probably shut up."

"He does. It's fine, really. I'm fine." I shifted uncomfortably in my seat. I guess I was going to have to get used to this. People assuming because of who he was, he would screw around. He wouldn't. Why would he ask me to be his girlfriend and then turn around and be unfaithful? It didn't make sense. Dan meant what he said. I was his and he was mine. No one else's.

"Sorry. I was out of line." He raked his hand through his hair, for the first time giving me a glimpse he didn't have it all together. "Ashlyn. I was insensitive and I really am sorry. You shouldn't have to defend your relationship, least of all to someone you barely know. The curiosity got the better of me. It won't happen again."

Rob spent the rest of the afternoon apologizing and overall being very sweet. True to his word, he didn't mention groupies or the trappings of being a celebrity again. Even later in the week, whenever the subject of Dan did come up, he was always respectful and let me set the tone. He didn't have a girlfriend, so I paid him the same courtesy in not asking too many questions as to why a good-looking, smart, and successful guy was still single. None of my business.

Dan hated Rob of course. He was convinced that Rob had ulterior motives, which I thought was ironic. I didn't give it airtime. JenCorp had a predominately male workforce. So I was either going to be friendly with men or I was going to be enjoying a very lonely existence at work. Not an option.

Secretly it made me a little relieved Dan was jealous. Not that I wanted him to throw down for me or anything like that, but at least I felt like I wasn't a forgone conclusion. I guess we both had a few insecurities. It just meant we were human and made what we had more real.

23

Dan

ASHLYN WORKING FULL TIME SUCKED BALLS. I WAS GLAD SHE WASN'T at the bar any more dealing with douchebags who no doubt wanted to fuck her, but I hated she was gone so much. I had convinced her to spend most of her nights at my apartment. It made sense seeing as it was closer to her work than traveling in from Brooklyn, plus it meant we got to spend the nights together. I gave her a key to my place so she didn't have to worry about getting in if I wasn't home, and I was hoping we could make the shacking up arrangement more permanent, but I wasn't going to push it. She didn't say as much but I could tell how much this new job was taking it out of her. She had to be up at five a.m. What kind of lame-ass time is that? Of course, I made the sacrifice and would wake up early too, making sure there was no need for her alarm. A Dan wake-up was so much better. Rather than being pulled from sleep by some random piece-of-shit noise coming from her iPhone, she woke up with me between her thighs. Personally, I can't think of a better start to the day than morning sex and I couldn't start my day properly until I'd heard her scream my name while she came beneath me. It was the breakfast of champions.

The whole sex without a condom thing was fucking mind-blowing. It took sex to a whole other level. It had never been this good with any of those other girls. I didn't know if it was the skin on skin that made it seem like more, or whether it was because I was in so deep with this girl, I couldn't see straight. But I knew there would be a cold day in hell before I would be walking away from this. I totally got the whole monogamy thing now. When you find that one person who is perfect in every way, it's not that you *can't* fuck someone else, it's that you don't *want* to fuck anyone else. I used to think those poor assholes had to make this huge sacrifice to keep their women, but it had been us poor losers who didn't know what we had been missing who had been doing the sacrificing, and I wasn't willing to anymore. Not a chance.

Sure it wasn't all morning sex and rainbows. Ash was tired when she got home, and sometimes the band would have a late session which meant I'd miss picking her up from work, but they were just teething issues as far as I was concerned. Ash was happy and I fucking loved seeing her smile.

Of course there was this dickwad she worked with who I was convinced was trying to put the moves on her. Rob. While he seemed like a nice guy, I didn't trust him, and there was no way I'd be letting my guard down around him. I knew his type. I'd seen it play out a million times. Hell, my sister had even tangled with one of those sons-o-bitches, and Troy and I had broken his fucking nose. His name was Brad. Same-same as far as I was concerned. Girls think those douches are their best fucking friends and then boom, one night when they are feeling vulnerable, good old Rob has his pants down around his ankles and asks her to suck his dick. I might not have been a choirboy, but I never played women like that. Fuckers like Rob were predators, some just more patient than others.

Ash thought I was just being jealous, so I didn't push the issue. I sure as shit didn't want to rock the boat seeing as everything had been perfect the last couple of weeks. So I kept it on the down low, knowing if that asshole even breathed on her in the wrong way, I'd fuck him up. Some things were worth jail time, if you know what I mean.

The knock at the door pulled my head back to where it needed to be, away from thinking about shit going wrong between Ash and me. I knew who it was, a conversation that needed to happen, and I was going to man up and have it.

I opened the door and saw Sydney standing out in the hall. It felt like an eternity ago since we'd been together. I had to remind myself it actually happened.

"Dan." Sydney walked through the doorway and into my pad.

"Hey, Syd." I gave her a hug. We hadn't had a proper conversation in god knows how long. It's funny how I'd always thought it would be weird between us after the sex, but it just wasn't. I liked that about Sydney; she didn't say one thing and mean another. She was a genuine kick-ass chick, and I had a lot of time for her even if from here on out, it was going to be solidly in friend-zone.

"Let's take a seat in the lounge room." I didn't want to have this conversation in the fucking hallway. I was probably going to need to sit down anyway.

"So what's got your kickers in such a twist that you couldn't talk to me over the phone?" She took off her coat as she followed me through to the main living area of my apartment, her heels clicking on the polished floorboards.

"Shit I needed to say wasn't for the phone, Syd. I wanted to speak to you face to face and I didn't want to bug you at work. I know Lexi still hasn't found a new assistant yet." I gestured for her to take a seat on the couch. Syd draped her coat over the arm of the chair before settling in.

"Well thanks for the consideration. I'm sure Lexi thanks you, too. Not that it ever really stopped you from bothering me before."

"Yeah well, sometimes I just can't help myself." I shrugged.

"So what is so important? I know we're not here to talk my work schedule." Sydney was smart. Not much got by her, it's one of the reasons I respected her so much. I think that is why her and Lexi were so tight and probably one of the reasons I was attracted to them both at one stage. Clearly I have a thing for mouthy women.

"No, we're not." I grinned, taking the armchair opposite her. "I wanted to thank you for hooking up Ashlyn with the job. She needed a break, and it really made a difference. I know thank you doesn't cut it but, yeah I wanted to thank you."

"Do my ears deceive me? The great Dan Evans being all sweet and thankful. My, my, I'm not entirely sure what to do with the gratitude."

"Take it for what it's worth. A thanks. You know, I really didn't expect that. You, helping me. Helping her. I mean it's not like you owe me anything."

"Why wouldn't I help you if I had the opportunity? If I have the means to assist a friend, I'll happily lend a hand. And before you make some innuendo about hand jobs, you know I don't mean that."

"Wouldn't take it even if you offered. I got myself a girl now, and she's the only one whose hands are getting on me. But all jokes aside, I'm glad you see me as a friend."

"Well of course I see you as a friend. I'm not in the habit of sleeping with people I can't stand. You know we both went into *that* with our eyes open. I never expected anything more from you than that night, and at the risk of inflating your already ridiculously large ego, it was probably the best sex I'd ever had. I don't regret it. Still, I never thought I'd see the day where you would be happily off the market. I have to say, I'm half expecting an asteroid to come hurtling toward Earth, taking us to our deaths. At least I can say I've seen it all."

She always was a wise-ass, but I was glad she was cool about the whole thing. Not all the women I'd slept with shared Syd's carefree philosophy. I never promised them more, but some assumed what was only a fuck would turn into a *beautiful* relationship. I had probably been a bigger dick than I needed to be, but I never really cared enough not to be. Guess it didn't really matter now. That shit was well and truly in my rearview.

"Yeah, have your fun, Syd. I've been getting it from Troy for weeks now. Jase too. I'll take whatever you guys got."

"I think it's marvelous you've found a lady. It's obvious she's captured your heart. Now, just don't do something stupid and cock it up." Syd smiled as she moved off the couch. "Come on then, let's do this properly." She held out her arms in front of her.

I laughed as I lifted my ass off the chair. I wrapped my arms around her and gave her a hug, "Thanks, Syd. You're pretty awesome."

My eye caught the reflection of the door. Ash was standing there. Her coat still on, like she'd just walked in. "Hey, babe. I didn't hear you come in. This is Sydney, she—" I didn't get a chance to finish to explain before Ash cut me off.

"We've already met. At my interview with Lexi." She seemed annoyed. I guess she had seen me with Sydney and had gotten the wrong idea. Sort of like when Ash had come to my apartment and my sister and nephew had been there. We would probably laugh about it like we did then. I mean, as if I would cheat on her. That would never happen.

"I was just on my way out. Nice to see you again, Ashlyn." Sydney smiled but Ash didn't respond. Syd shot me a concerned look, "Dan, good seeing you."

It wasn't looking good. I was probably going to have to do a lot of groveling. Although, I was confident that once I explained Sydney was just a friend, Ash would come around. She could sometimes fly off the handle but she wasn't unreasonable. And we were finally in a good place.

"No probs, Syd. 'Bye." I walked her to the door while Ashlyn stood simmering in the hallway, her arms locked across her chest. Not sure how much she heard but whatever it was, she was pissed.

"Listen, Ash." I had no idea what I was going to say other than whatever she was thinking, she had it wrong. I felt like I had to say sorry, but I had no idea what I was supposed to be apologizing for.

"Don't," she whimpered. "Please, just don't." She didn't take off her coat or put down her purse. She just stood there. I fucking hated it. Seeing that look on her face and knowing that it was because of something so stupid. There was nothing going on.

"Ash. I'm not sure why you are mad but, whatever it is, you

have the wrong idea. Sydney and I are just friends."

"Just friends? Really?"

Fuck. Well, I guess this was going to be harder than I thought. Granted, I had my arms around Syd but it's not like I was grabbing her ass.

"Ash."

"What, Dan? I knew you had a past, but it's a little different when it is flaunted in front of me. Are you telling me you haven't had sex with her?" She dared me to deny it, probably guessing I couldn't. How could I? I *had* slept with Sydney.

"Babe, I'm not going to lie to you. I did sleep with Sydney. But, it was before I knew you, and it was only one time." How could something I did before I met Ashlyn come back and bite me?

"Only one time?" she repeated, her eyes were filled with hurt. I hated knowing the *hurt* was because of me,

"It was insignificant, Ash." I took a step toward her. "It didn't mean anything. It was just sex."

"How could you say that? *It was just sex.* Goddamn it, Dan, is there anyone you haven't slept with?" Despite being angry, she didn't yell.

"What do you want me to say? I can't take it back." I couldn't change my past. I couldn't un-fuck all those women. Even if I could, it wouldn't make me love her any more than I already did. It was in the past. Ash was my future.

"Why?" Just one word, but the way she said it made it sound so much worse.

"Why, what?" I wanted to go and touch her but her arms across her chest made it clear that was a no-go. I knew that if I could put my arms around her, I could show her how much she meant to me.

"Why did you sleep with her if it she didn't mean anything?" Her voice was almost a whisper.

"I don't know. It just happened. I wasn't trying to sleep with her." I moved closer and she stepped back. I blinked. Did she just move away from me?

"So I should feel better about the fact you had sex with her even though you weren't *trying* to?"

"No. I'm just saying. I don't know what I'm saying but I can't feel bad about something I did before I even knew you." I needed to get through to her. So she could understand how much this shit didn't matter. Why wouldn't she fucking see this wasn't important?

"I knew there had been lots of women, but I didn't think I would have to see them, that they would still be in your life. Is that what will happen to me? When we're done?"

"Ash, I swear to you on my mother's life, it's not like that with us. Do you think I'm just going to be done with you?"

"Then why was she here and why were you hugging her if it was just one night that meant nothing?"

"Ash, she was telling me she was happy for us."

"Please, stop." Ash held out her hand. "I need to know. I need to know the truth. Why. Was. She. Here?" She paused between each word. I could see the torment on her face, second-guessing what we were. She still hadn't moved. Her body radiated an invisible force field of don't-fucking-touch-me.

Part of me wanted to go over and drag her into the living room and make her listen to reason. Prove to her this was all fucking bullshit. She would never be just another fuck to me, and as for the situation with Syd, she was looking for something that wasn't there.

"I was thanking her, okay? That's all. There was nothing shady going on. Do you honestly think if I was going to go behind your back I'd do it where you'd find out? I know you have a key. C'mon, Ash. Don't let these doubts ruin shit for us. I can't change the fact I slept with her. I am not denying it, but I am telling you that is in my past and I would never hurt you."

"What did she do for you?"

"What do you mean?"

"Why did you need to thank her?"

"She just worked something out for me. Trust me, Ash, just let it go." This was another can of fucking worms I was not ready to open. I knew if she found out about the job she would take it the wrong way. She just needed to let it go.

"You're asking me to trust but you won't tell me what she did.

What are you hiding?"

"Nothing. I'm not hiding anything."

"Dan, I know you aren't being honest with me. If you care half as much as you say you do, you will just tell me."

Hearing her say I didn't care, fucking lit a fuse. I didn't mean to yell but I couldn't believe she would think I would lie to her, cheat on her, and fucking throw what we had away.

"She gave Simon Jennings your resume. She set up the interview for JenCorp. That's it. I was thanking her for that."

"You asked a girl you used to fuck to get me a job?" She looked disgusted and no matter how bad it had been, it was so much fucking worse now.

"No. Look, it wasn't like that. I know you are mad, and probably a little hurt, but Sydney isn't just some girl I've fucked." Syd wasn't just some groupie, and she had done nothing wrong here. If anyone was an asshole, it was me, and I wouldn't let someone who had been a friend take the fall.

"I thought you said she didn't mean anything? You can't have it both ways. I thought Lexi recommended me for this job?"

It was just getting worse. It was like a runaway train I couldn't stop from derailing. My mouth just saying anything to try and make it better

"The sex didn't mean anything, but that doesn't mean Sydney isn't a good person. She's a friend. I'm sorry you had to find out this way. I went to Lexi because I wanted her to hire you. When she said you didn't make the cut, she agreed to help find something else." The minute I'd said it I realized how bad it sounded. I couldn't find a way to make her understand the way I had seen it in my head. It wasn't supposed to hurt her.

"You did *what*? You went to Lexi and asked her to hire me? Holy shit, Dan. Did you have any faith in my ability? So this whole job has been a big pity fuck?"

Her eyes watered and I could tell she was trying not to cry. I fucking hated seeing her like this, and knew I was the cause. I would do anything to make it better for her. I hated this distance. Standing in the same place in the hallway.

"I was trying to help. You wouldn't let me help any other way.

Lexi asked Sydney and she just passed on the resume. I figured if I could do this, help you find something else, then you would be happy." It was starting to break me, too. Maybe my execution was shit but my intentions weren't. It was supposed to make it better. Why had it turned into a big ball of shit?

"I knew when I started having feelings for you that it was going to be hard. Reconciling myself with all the women. Wondering if I measured up. I wanted to believe that I was different. That you loved me *because* I was different. What I never thought I would have to doubt is whether or not I was good enough. *You* didn't even have faith in me to find a job. You can't just change people's lives, Dan. I should have known from the start I didn't fit. We didn't fit. I don't belong in your world. I was happy before I met you. I was happy with my shitty apartment, in my shitty job with my shitty life because as shitty as everything was, it was real. And right now, I have no idea what is real anymore."

She didn't mean that. I know she couldn't mean that. I got that she was hurting, and I would jump through whatever fucking hoops I needed to put shit back together, but what we had was the realest thing I'd ever had. I knew this wasn't one sided.

"This is real, Ash. What we have, it's not a lie. The other stuff, Sydney may have set up the interview but *you* got that job on your own." I moved closer and she stepped away again. Every single time she did that I wanted to put my fist through a wall. That *I* was what she was trying to get away from.

"Tell me one thing, Dan, and I want you to tell me the truth." She had wrapped her arms so tightly around her body if I hadn't clued in that she didn't want me to touch her, I was fucking getting the hint now. She was losing the battle with the waterworks, too. Her eyes were red and she was blinking really fast, trying to stop them from spilling over.

"Ash, I know this is fucked up and I know I kept things from you, but you can't doubt what we have." I looked at her right in the eye. She had to believe me. I'll be the first person to put my hand up and say I may have omitted some details and maybe I fucked up. Okay, so I *definitely* fucked up, but I've never lied to her. I would never hurt her.

"That day…in Lexi's office." She swallowed hard as the first tear dropped from the corner of her eye. She tried to wipe it away before I could see. "When I met you the first time. Why were you there?"

She looked like she was in so much pain. I couldn't make it worse. Why couldn't we let go of that shit and concentrate on what we had. On what we had built. Nothing else mattered.

"I was with Alex, he had to see Lexi."

I remembered that day like it was burned into my brain. We had been rehearsing at James's. Hannah had been looking after Grace, and Noah had helped keep her entertained while her daddy played rock star with her uncles. We had wrapped and Alex had said he was going to stop by and see Lexi. I thought it would have been the perfect opportunity to see Sydney, maybe ask her out. It wasn't supposed to be a big deal. She would shoot me down like she always did and I'd move on. It was almost like a game. I never expected to find something else there that day. *Someone* else. Someone like Ash.

"Dan, from the little I know of Alex, I know he does not need a babysitter to see his wife. Why were *you* there that day?"

I couldn't lie to her. I promised I wouldn't. I wasn't sure if this was some sick fucking test I had to pass or what, but whatever happened from here on out was going to be the fucking truth.

"I was there to see Sydney."

It was as if the words had smacked her hard in the face. Her hand flew to her mouth as she let out a gasp.

"Why?" she barely choked out.

"I was going to ask her out." The truth, no matter what happened she was going to get the truth.

"So I was the consolation prize?" The pain in her eyes tore through me. I'd swallow broken glass before I had to see it again.

"No. Ash. No. I swear to you." Fuck the consequences. I needed to hold her. To put her in my arms and for her to feel it. To feel us. I moved to her, toe to toe. We needed to make sense of this and the only way I knew how was to touch her.

"I can't." She pushed me away, her hand hitting me square in the chest. "This is too much. I can't."

"Ash, don't fucking leave. Do not walk away from this." I grabbed her hand. Did she want me to beg? Whatever the fuck she needed, she just had to say the word.

She held my stare, her green eyes annihilating me as I watched her fight against the tears. "I need to be enough, and I can't be that with you. The girls, the job, being your second choice? It's too much. We never belonged together, Dan. We were a mistake that just went on too long. Neither of us was going to admit it, but you and me, it was destined to fail. We are just too different, and I can't be anyone else anymore than you can. Goodbye, Dan."

She didn't yell and somehow that was so much worse. It fucking scared the hell out of me. I wanted her to scream, to slap me and tell me what an asshole I was, but she didn't. Instead, she turned around and walked out. She didn't even slam the door. Nothing. She was just gone. I kept staring at the door. Hoping it would open and it was all a big mistake. Like what just happened, didn't actually happen. But it didn't. Nothing changed and I was left standing there with the biggest pain in my chest I'd ever known. All that shit about feeling like your heart was tearing in two was a lie. That didn't even come close to the pain I was feeling. It felt so much worse. Like having your heart ripped from your chest, tossed on the floor, and forced to watch it helplessly while you slowly die. That's what it felt like. It felt like dying.

24

Ashlyn

MEGS KEPT ASKING ME HOW I FELT AND I DIDN'T KNOW WHAT TO SAY. Hurt. Sad. Angry. Tired. Sad. Hurt. It was everything wrapped up in a huge indescribable fuck-you emotion. I felt betrayed. I felt stupid but most of all I felt an overwhelming sense of pain and loss that compared to nothing I'd ever experienced before. I'd experienced break-ups before. Nothing even came close to this. This was some kind of medieval type pain. Epic. Sustained.

It was like a hole had been torn through me, letting the cold seep in and I could never warm up. My body shivered. I felt empty. I felt lost. I felt so incredibly sad I couldn't stand it.

"Ash. I've never seen you like this. Sweetie, I don't know what to do to make this better." It's a sad sorry state of affairs when one of my best friends, who happened to be a psychologist, didn't know what to say. That's where I had ended up. Pushing the boundaries of even professional help. Go hard or go home, right?

"Nothing, there's nothing." I was curled up on my couch in my pjs. It was the weekend so therefore it was my go-to attire. I wasn't leaving the apartment. Not unless I had to. Like if the place was on fire or something like that, and even then I'd probably seriously evaluate the size of the flames before actually leaving.

It had been exactly one week and one day since I'd walked out of Dan's apartment. He had been calling me relentlessly. I didn't answer. Letting every single one of those calls go to voice mail, and deleting them before I had a moment of weakness and listened. I couldn't. I couldn't go back. It had hurt too much.

I had made it through in a daze. Faking it through the days when I had to see people, going to work and pretending it hadn't happened, but allowing myself the luxury to fall apart at night when I was alone. It had been three days before I'd finally confessed what had happened to Megs. I had a feeling she already knew, maybe through Troy, or maybe even Dan trying to gain an ally, but she didn't say a word. She just held me and let me cry on her bedroom floor.

I wanted to pull myself together. To stop it. But it was something I just couldn't manage. Part of me didn't want to. Like finally letting go of the pain would be letting go of that last piece of Dan. How stupid was that? That even after all of this, I still loved him. I was insane.

"Ash, maybe you should talk to him. Even if it's just for closure." Megs sat beside me. She was grasping. Looking for anything to pull me out of it.

"No, I have all the closure I need." I didn't even look at her. My eyes fixed on the television screen in front of me. Not that it was actually playing anything. Staring at the black focal point just helped me not to cry.

"Ashlyn Marie Murphy, you are full of shit. You aren't anywhere close to closure." Megs pulled on my arm, forcing me to look at her. We both knew she was right. One of us was just not ready to deal with what she was suggesting.

"I'm not calling him, I don't want to hear his voice. It will hurt too much."

"Ash. I get that you are hurting right now, and I'm not going to pretend I know what you are going through, but anyone can see you are still in love with him. Maybe there is a way you can work through this."

I loved Megs, and usually her optimism was welcomed, but today I wanted to ask her *what the hell was she thinking?* She had to be kidding, trying to get me out of my funk with shock treatment. Like delivered pulses into my brain by electrodes, this was her mental equivalent.

"Megs." Where to even start? "He made a play for me while interested in another woman. Then he went to Lexi, a potential employer, and asked her to give me a job, obviously not having any faith in my own ability and making me look desperate. Then failing that, he went to a girl who he'd had a one-night stand with and got her to pull some strings. The same girl he had been trying to win over when he met me. See where I'm going with this? My pride is about all I have right now." The words come out in a jumbled rush. I barely took a breath before continuing, "What's worse is that I don't even know if the job is still mine. Like if now the gig is up, will JenCorp pull the pin? After all, they don't need to do me any more favors now I'm no longer screwing Dan. The whole week I've been waiting for someone to come into my office and hand me my walking papers. My world has dropped out from under me. None of it was real. It had just been an illusion."

"Ash, take a breath. I don't care how or who got you that interview at JenCorp, you earned that position. You are more than qualified, and you are doing an outstanding job. Even assuming they hired you as a favor, which they didn't, but assuming they did, they wouldn't keep you if you sucked. It's a business, Ash; you look at their bottom line every day. Do you think they going to sink money into you as a charity case? Even you have to admit that regardless of how you got there, you have more than proven your worth."

If I gave it some proper consideration, what Megs said was logical. JenCorp had thrived on ruthless business decisions. Simon Jennings wouldn't think twice about firing me if I didn't perform. That man was only interested in what I could do to expand his net worth, rather than who my boyfriend was. Not that it mattered now. I had no boyfriend.

"Even if I could find a way to work through it, he didn't believe in my ability to get a job on my own. I'm not sure if I could somehow find peace about possibly running into one of his past and numerous conquests. Or even, believing that if we had met under different circumstances, he still would have wanted to be with me, it doesn't change anything. All those problems did, was highlight one major flaw. We didn't belong together. We were too different."

"Ash, you were happy. I saw it. I know that those feelings you had for him were real. He was a manwhore and he had slept with a lot of women, but that was before he met you. He wasn't with anyone while you were together, right?"

I pulled my knees to my chest and wrapped my arms around my legs. "I don't think... I hope he didn't." In my heart, I believed he had been faithful even if my head, the jury was still out. I hated that either way, I just wasn't sure.

Megs rubbed my arm as she continued her dissection of our break-up. "The job thing, perhaps his methods weren't great, but I think his heart was in the right place. We've already established you got the job legitimately; all he did was get your foot in the door."

"I know it doesn't seem like a big deal, but I need to know that I'm good enough on my own."

"Oh sweetie, you are. He was just trying to help. He wanted you to be happy because he loves you."

"It doesn't matter. Whether he loved me or not, nothing changes. I mean really, what the fuck was I thinking? A rock star, Megs. A fucking rock star. What kind of future was I going to have with him? Maybe we'd date for a few months, a year at most? Then, what? We move onto *friends* like he did with Sydney? Is there some special club of girlfriends past, where we all gather and commiserate? I can't do that. It would hurt too much. He was larger than life, and I got caught up in the madness. When I met him, I knew that it wasn't going to be forever. I just stupidly forgot, and then went and did something dumb like falling in love with him."

It felt like the room had become suddenly larger, or I was smaller in it. The overwhelming hurt hung in the air above us. It had consumed me, and I knew there was no going back. I wasn't that strong.

"Please think about this. Please, talk to him," Megs begged, pulling me closer into a hug.

"You are supposed to be my friend. Please don't try and make me feel worse than I already do." I couldn't understand why she wouldn't let this go. My heart was broken into a million tiny pieces and I wasn't even sure whom to blame.

"I'm not. I promise. Ash, I really believe he loves you. I know he is hurting just as much as you are. I'm trying to help."

"Well if you want to help, stop trying to convince me that I've made a mistake. Help me get over him, and help me move on." Help me to forget how much I love him. I couldn't say that last part. Not out loud. Not ever again.

"Okay. If that's what you want." Megs sighed. Her expression was sad but resigned, like she was finally going to let it go.

I closed my eyes and let out a long, slow breath. I didn't want to feel like this, I didn't want to hurt. I'm not sure what part cut me the most, maybe it was because I had felt like a consolation prize. He had admitted he didn't do long-term, and perhaps he wasn't wired for that. Either way, even if I still loved him, and he me, I needed to look after my heart.

"It's what I need."

"**DUDE, GET YOUR HEAD IN THE GAME. I'M PLAYING A C SHARP MAJOR,** and you aren't even in the same scale. What the hell key *are* you in? Did you forget how to play? Did you tune at all?" Alex flung a guitar pick at me as I looked up from my bass. I actually had no recollection of what I played, and we'd gone over this progression at least six times.

"I'm fine, asshole. Just making sure you're paying attention. You just worry about making sure your part is tight. I can handle mine." I stretched out my fingers before flipping him off. Fucking Stone and his perfect-ass playing.

"Hey, why don't we take five?" James put his mic back on the stand and walked toward me. If there was a mediator in this band, that guy sure as hell fit the bill. Sure, he was a tough business guy and when it came to music, he knew that shit inside and out, but he was too smart to let that go to his head. Whenever things got hairy, James was always the first one to step up and take control.

"What's going on, brother? I've never seen you this edgy before a show." James clapped his hand around my shoulder. Now I felt bad about letting him down. Another heaping spoonful of disappointment.

"The show isn't the problem. I can play this shit sideways. Just got some other stuff clouding up my gray matter."

Ashlyn still wouldn't take my calls. I had left maybe forty voice messages, and I was half expecting the sheriff to show up and issue me with a restraining order.

"We can cancel the gig, dude. It's no big deal." Troy rested his sticks on his snare and popped out his in-ear monitors. "It's just an exhibition show. No tickets have been sold. No harm, no foul."

If anyone knew what private hell I'd been living with for the last two weeks, it was the man sitting across from me. He had found my sorry ass, a bottle and half of bourbon later, on the floor of my fucking apartment where Ash had left me. He didn't even say anything, just parked his ass on the floor beside me and helped me finish the other half of the bottle.

I'd fucked up. I got that. I should have told Ash right off the bat about the job. But I knew if I did, she would take it the wrong way, which she did anyway. The whole Sydney thing was a kick in the nuts. I had gone back and forth a million times and still didn't know what else I could have done differently. I came up blank each and every time. I had slept with Syd, but that shit was in the past, and the minute I fucking laid eyes on Ash, Sydney wasn't even on my radar. Ash was never a consolation prize. She was the fucking jackpot. She was The World Series and Superbowl rolled into one and no girl had even come close. The fact she didn't get what a big deal she was made me feel like I'd had my dick slammed in a car door.

"Ash and I aren't together anymore, but I'm fine. We're doing the show."

"Dude, I'm sorry. I didn't mean to blow up at you like that. I was a complete dick." Alex put down his ax and walked over. He looked all regretful and shit. "Why didn't you say something?"

"Nothing to say." I shrugged. There really wasn't. 'Cause talking about it just made it harder, and it was bad enough running through it in my head. It was a car crash, and yet I couldn't stop the fucking loop.

"We're here for you, brother. Whatever you need." Jase joined the improv therapy session.

Jase already knew. He had joined Troy and I in one of my post-break up drinking sessions and listened to me in my misery, but like the stand-up guy he was, had kept his trap shut and didn't tell James and Alex. It's not that I didn't want them to know, I just didn't want to have to say the words. Like maybe some miracle would happen and she would come back. But all the hoping in the world didn't do jack.

I was not willing to let down my brothers. It was bad enough I'd let down the only woman I'd ever loved. Yeah. There was that. I fucking loved her. Still did. The fact she'd bailed did nothing to change up that sitch.

So, I guess I knew. Knew what it felt like to have your heart broken, and knew what it felt like to live with the fact that the only person you want to be with didn't want you. It was a kind of suck that you couldn't even begin to understand, or explain. Unimaginable pain.

"I'm going to need a minute." I pulled the strap from my chest and rested the bass on the stand. I needed some air.

The guys looked at each other before looking back at me. I didn't need to be a mind reader to know what was going on in their heads. They were wondering how long I was going to be able to keep my shit together. I couldn't even clue them in, 'cause the truth was, I had no fucking idea.

I walked out of James's studio and into his backyard. It was the tail end of fall and the chill factor was getting good and cozy with the day. I wasn't wearing a jacket but I didn't give a shit. I welcomed the cold air hitting my skin like an ice bath. Gave me something else to concentrate on other than this pit of emptiness I was dealing with.

I pulled out my phone and flicked through my contacts. I stopped at her name; my finger hovering over it like it did every single time. I didn't call. Not this time at least. I reserved the calling for when I got good and worn down. Usually late at night or the early hours of the morning, hoping her automatic reflexes would kick in and she'd just pick up. But she didn't. It always diverted to voice mail where I'd get to live a different type of hell and listen to her sweet pre-recorded voice tell me *she can't come to the phone right now*. I fucking hated it, but it was my only connection to her, and like a fucking junkie, I wasn't willing to go cold turkey. For those few precious seconds, with her voice in my ear, I could pretend that she was still mine and that was I going to hold her again soon.

I scrolled down the names in my phone a little farther, and before I could stop myself, I hit call. It was the other number my brain liked to wrestle with before hitting dial; today I was all out of fight.

"Hey, Dan. You really need to stop calling me. It feels wrong going behind her back." I knew it was only a matter of time before she said it, and today those words had finally come.

"I know, Megs. I'm sorry. I just miss her and I need to know she's okay."

I closed my eyes and tried to reconcile with the fact this was probably the last time Megs would take my call. Not that I blamed her. Her loyalties were with Ash, and I was thankful she'd been so patient up to this point. A lesser person would have told me to fuck off the first time I'd called. We'd both been surprised. Me, for the fact I'd actually let the call connect, and Megs that I'd kept the number after planning Ash's birthday celebration.

Maybe it was 'cause she was a shrink, or maybe 'cause she was just a decent person, but she listened to what I had to say with no judgment. She let me spill my guts and lay myself bare with no need to censor. Her advice was sound and she was kinder than I fucking deserved, but I lived for those rare fucking moments where she'd let down her guard and tell me about my girl. Anything. Even if it was just to know she'd finally slept. I wanted to know. I needed to know.

"Dan, I've tried to be impartial, but this whole situation is really fucked up. You are both in so much fucking pain. It's horrendous. Maybe it's for the best if you let her go."

"I wish it was that easy." I swallowed, cursing the fucking lump forming in my throat. "She's always going to be with me, Megs. I love her. She's deep in me now, and even if I never see her again,

I'm always going to love her."

"Fuck, Dan, you're making me cry." Megs's voice cracked and I heard her breath hitch as she tried to hide the tiny sobs.

"I'm sorry, Megs. Seems like making girls cry is all I'm good for these days." I balled my fist up against my eyes. "I know I've got no right to ask, but I'm going to need you to do me one more thing."

"What is it?" Megs hiccupped, having lost her battle with the water-works.

"Take care of my girl for me, will you?" I tried to pull it together so I could finish what I needed to say, my body fighting a losing battle with my fucking emotions. "You or she ever need anything, I don't care what it is or when, you call. No strings. She doesn't even have to know it's from me. I don't ever want her without."

Megs cried into the phone and shit got real quiet on my end while I tried to absorb the pain. I listened. Listened to Megs's tears and let the misery wash over me. If she could do this for me, then I'd give her a blank check for whatever she wanted. She could call on favors for the rest of her days, and I'd shut my mouth and pay up with a fucking smile. I couldn't let go and I'd never stop loving her, but if I knew someone was looking out for her, I was willing to step away. She deserved a chance at being happy, and I'd obviously fucked that up. It wasn't about me, or what I wanted anymore, and I'd give my last fucking breath to make sure she was happy. Even if that meant saying goodbye.

Ashlyn

IT'S FUNNY HOW I NOW MEASURED TIME. IT WASN'T DECEMBER TENTH. It was three weeks post Dan. It was cold, brutal and unrelenting. The gray sky fought for slivers of sunshine, not usually successfully. And it had already started to snow.

Dan had stopped calling and I didn't know what was worse. Knowing he'd finally given up, or realizing I wish he hadn't. Not that it was his fault. He stuck it out a lot longer than I thought he would. I just had been too scared to give it another chance. The gamble. Not knowing if he had loved me as deeply as I had loved him, or if it had been an illusion.

I had stopped crying, too. Well mostly. There was still a night here or there when I'd slip from the wagon, but overall I was doing better. Work kept me busy which helped, hard to be sad when you're neck deep in property analysis. I was still cautious online, avoiding any website that could potentially spill gossip, and I ran past newsstands like they contained a life threatening disease. I was okay, but I just couldn't see it yet. Dan with other women. Even though I knew I had no right to think it, I just couldn't stand the thought of him with someone else. He would have moved on by now. Found someone else, perhaps more than one. Maybe one for every day of the week? I don't know why I tortured myself.

If it weren't so tragic, it would be funny. That I had been the one to end it, and yet here I was, obsessed over whether I'd been replaced. I really needed a hobby. I'd heard knitting had suddenly become cool; maybe I'd knit myself a scarf. Or I could cut out the lead-time and just become a crazy cat woman now. Except that I hated cats and wool made me itchy.

"Ash, we're heading out for lunch. You want to join us?" Celeste from marketing knocked at my door. I'd tried to make friends around the office, thought it would help. But it didn't. It just added new names to the list of people I had to fake it for. So much for intelligence. I was clearly a dumbass.

"Thanks, but I think I'm going to work through. I have a vicious deadline," I lied, not wanting lunch or the company.

"Maybe some other time."

"Yeah, another time." Like when I stopped being a downer. I forced a smile back.

She was kind enough to leave without pushing it further. It wasn't the first decline she had received from me. Honestly, I'm surprised she kept asking. Maybe she was going for sainthood. Or, I just looked really pathetic.

I turned my head back to my monitor, the sound of her heels heading down the hall marking the end of the conversation. What was I doing again? That's right, reworking this email for the hundredth time, and hopefully making it seem like someone who was college educated wrote it.

"Hey." Rob rapped his knuckled against the doorframe. Not sure if it was a knock or a call to attention, but it got me to stop shooting daggers at the computer screen for the minute.

"Thought you might be hungry." He held up the plastic bag of non-descript containers. "Got some lunch. You want to share?"

My stomach growled on cue, shooting down the anticipated *I'm-not-hungry* my mouth was working on. Both of them, my stomach and my mouth, were assholes.

"I'll take that as a yes." Rob grinned, strolling into my office. The bag of takeaway waved like a victory flag. "I hope you like Chinese. There's enough here to feed an army."

"Thanks," I conceded. Busy or not, I had to eat. My body was only going to tolerate the lack of fuel for so long before it turned on me. My stomach's vocal protest proof it had already started the revolt. "Chinese is great," my asshole mouth offered. It sounded like a shitty tagline. Something a second rate advertising manager would come up with. Thank god I was in the numbers business instead of words.

Rob pulled up a chair, seating himself opposite my desk and started unpacking the takeaway bag. "Sooo." It began. The small talk. I should have known the Chinese would come with a side of conversation. Hadn't we already established that words were not my friends?

"I'm not trying to pry," Rob held up his hands in mock surrender, "but it's hard not to notice how sad you've been." While he was still oozing sympathy, his hands moved to a more important task, like spooning out the General Tso chicken.

"I'm okay." I shrugged. It wasn't complete bullshit. I was definitely better, and at least I hadn't said *I'm good*, which would have been a total lie.

"I liked it better when you weren't just *okay*." He handed me some chopsticks, the look on his face telling me he wasn't buying it - that I wasn't anything other than miserable.

"Dan and I broke up." I might as well tell him. He probably already knew. The absence of Dan and his fancy car would have been the first tip off. Followed closely by recent overtime and my reluctance to go home.

"I figured as much. I'm sorry." He looked genuinely sorry for me, which I couldn't decide if that made him a nice guy or me pathetic.

"It was for the best." Sure, it's been a while since we've tried this explanation on. Let's walk around in it and see how it fits this time around. "We were just too different." Nope, it still didn't feel right, even though it was the truth.

"Ash, if there is anything I can do... ," Rob paused like he was shifting through what he was about to say, "I know it can't be easy to lose someone you care about."

No it wasn't. It was the opposite of easy, and I didn't just care about him, I loved him. Which made it even harder. Which got me wondering if Rob was talking from experience, or just commiserating.

I knew he dated, I'd seen the odd female friend stop by the office, although never the same one twice, and I had ruled out him being gay. He didn't seem like a player, but he'd never spoken about a significant other, and from what I could see he didn't have any major flaws. He was polite, well spoken, and good-looking. A winning combo. And assuming he was earning at very least what I was, although probably more, he ticked the box for steady job and good income. Rob being single didn't make sense. Unless he was rocking some deep, dark secret? Or he had a tiny penis.

"What about you?" I heard myself say it before my brain had a chance to back out. "No girlfriend?" I stuffed a spoonful of fried rice in my mouth before I could do anymore damage. I guess it was only fair, he knew about my love life.

"Not recently. In the past, sure. Some I even thought maybe could be the one. But none of them really filled the criteria, and as conceited as it may sound. I just didn't want to settle."

"I used to have criteria, too." I had to smile as I remembered my old list of requirements. "Before Dan. He blew it all out of the water though."

"Do you think maybe that's why it didn't work out? That even if your heart wanted something your head knew better?"

"Is that the way it was for you?" I stopped eating, suddenly interested in his response.

"Yeah. I know this sounds a little messed up but, what the hell, right?" His easy laugh was a nice sound and I realized that I was having a conversation, and wasn't thinking about running away. Or crying. Or wanting to cause someone or myself physical harm. He took a deep breath. "I have it all planned out."

There were no sparks between us, Rob and me, but we were so similar it was impossible to ignore we would make an amazing team. After our lunchtime confessional, he'd asked if I'd consider going out with him. I wanted to say no, that there was no way, but I agreed anyway. Better to move on and move forward right? I had no reason not to, unless you counted that I was still in love with someone else. There was a perfect guy, with the perfect criteria right in front of me, and we were both single. I should at the very least give it a chance. See if maybe something can grow. Make me happy. Six months ago I wouldn't have even had this debate. I would have been giving thanks to the relationship gods and high-fiving my good fortune. Sadly, it wasn't six months ago.

Megs was trying to be supportive, but her lack of encouragement told me otherwise. She hadn't spoken about Dan or suggested I call him, but I think deep down she thought we'd get back together. We weren't though, so sitting around and avoiding men didn't make sense. Even if things didn't work out with Rob, at least it would get me back in the game.

"So where's he taking you?" Megs sat on the edge of my tub and watched me get ready.

"A play. Off Broadway." I applied a layer of mascara. I was supposed to be excited. Why wasn't I excited?

"Wow. Could he be any more pretentious? Off Broadway? Why doesn't he just take you to a jazz club and call it a day." She yawned. She wasn't tired, and I knew sarcasm when I saw it.

"Megs, give him a chance. He's a nice guy." I moved the mascara wand to the other eye. I wonder if he's going to try and kiss me. I really hope he doesn't.

"Nice and boring. Come on, Ash. You don't even like productions." Megs's support had come to an impasse.

I wasn't sure if she was anti-Rob, or if she'd have reservations about anyone I would be dating. Strangely, I would have assumed she would have welcomed this. A return to my old self now my course had been corrected.

"Well if I recall, it was you who said I should try new things. This is new. Besides, it's what grown-ups do. He's exactly the kind of guy I should be with."

"Ash, he's the perfect guy, except that he is all wrong for you." Megs took my face in her hands. Forcing me to stop applying another layer of mascara. Probably just as well. I didn't want to look like a hooker.

"He won't make me cry." This was the only reason I could offer.

"Ash," she wrapped her arms around me, "I love you." She hugged me closer and I tried not to get emotional because a, we had talked about me *not* crying and, b, I had just applied mascara.

"I'm going to go to this boring-ass play, and I'm going to learn to like it. There are worse things in life."

I think we both knew I was no longer talking about the play. I was happily resigned. Accepting that while I had gone slightly off the rails, I was done with that chapter. The one where I made out with guys I barely knew in nightclubs, and let them hold me all night, the one where I got into relationships I didn't understand and had crazy unrestrained sex, and the one where I fell in love with a larger-than-life rock star, who turned my world upside down. Yes, done with that.

"DAN."

Troy yelled over the noise, as I passed the waitress another fifty. She'd been a sweetheart and kept our glasses full. Not that I'd been doing much drinking tonight. I was still nursing the same Jack and Coke I had palmed an hour ago.

"What's up?" I handed him a fresh beer as he closed the gap between us.

"How long we going to keep doing this?" He took a swig of his long neck.

"What you mean? This is what we do." I was wondering if the music wasn't fucking with his head. The DJ was spinning this bullshit techno shit, and it was making me seriously angry. I could understand the big guy wanting to bail.

"Dan, you want to feed yourself those bullshit lines 'cause it makes you feel better, go right ahead, but this is *not* what we do. We haven't done this shit in a long time." Oh, we were back to that again.

The asshole was trying to get his Dr. Phil on, and start

dissecting the whys or the whats. What he didn't understand is right now, I had a huge case of the I-don't-cares, and just wanted to feel good. I wanted to feel something, even though I knew it wouldn't be a hundredth of what I had with Ashlyn.

"Fuck, Troy. Stop being a whiny bitch already. You want to go home, go home. No one is keeping you here, but I'm staying and getting laid."

Or so was the plan, not sure my balls had got the memo though. It seemed I'd had the ghost of limp-dick past wave its wand over my crotch and no amount of tits or ass was getting me hard. Even jerking off had become a chore. I wasn't entirely sure I wasn't permanently fucked up. I should've probably been more worried about it, and yet, I couldn't find the motivation to give two fucks. Pun entirely intended.

"Like last night? Or the night before? Or what about the night before that? Those times all good for you? Funny, 'cause my recollection is you ending up going home alone." Fucking Troy pointing out the obvious.

Maybe we *had* been beating this dead horse, a little too much. We'd been out every night since Tuesday. Different clubs, different parts of town. The end result always the same.

"I'm just biding my time. Just waiting for the right girl." More like trying to forget her.

"Well then, you are in the wrong place, 'cause the right girl is in a piece-of-shit apartment in Brooklyn, not trying to score in some shady club." Troy had to go there and state the fucking obvious. Again. It wasn't enough how much it killed me to try and forget her, like that was even a possibility, but he had to fucking bring her up too. Throw a bit more salt in the fucking wound. 'Cause I got to tell you, it hurt plenty without the reminder.

"You really going to come at me with that? What the fuck, dude? She doesn't want me. It's finished. Done. Don't be playing like I didn't fucking try."

If she had even given me the slightest hint of a chance, I would have toughed it out. But all I seemed to do was make her cry, and she made it clear she wanted nothing to do with me. Short of embracing my new stalker status, and getting cozy with an orange jump suit, I had no choice but to let it go.

"Dan, seriously, what are we doing here? We both know if you wanted to fuck someone, you would have done it already. This shit was never my scene, so you can't be telling me this is for my benefit."

"I don't know what I'm doing, but I have to do something. Something that will hopefully get me back to where I don't feel like beating the living shit out of everything, and everyone. This is what I know. This is what I should be doing."

I couldn't think of anything else to do. At least nothing that made sense.

"So do it. If you think that going back to what you were doing before is going to make shit all fine and dandy, then why are you sitting around with me, drinking watered down bourbon and Coke, instead of getting your dick sucked. You like redheads right, there's one right over there." Troy pointed to a chick that'd been trying to catch our attention all night. She'd been pushing up her tits and playing with her hair for hours. Her efforts wasted. I almost felt sorry for her.

"Watch it, Troy. I'm giving you a pass right now on account you've gone above and beyond for me in the last couple of weeks, but don't think that if you keep running your mouth, that you and me ain't going to have problems." I stood up and got in his face. The fucking reality of the situation at breaking point.

Troy didn't back down, instead meeting me toe to toe.

"You wanna take a swing at me, brother, be my fucking guest. At least it's a fucking reaction. Something. You've been on the cruise control for too long. I'll take you mad any day of the week, rather than indifferent."

"Troy, I know what you are doing, and you know I love you for it. But I'm fine."

"Fine you say?" He eyeballed me hard. "You still have her number?"

"Nope. Deleted it." I tipped my chin toward him. I had deleted it, a safeguard to stop me from trying to call her. Only issue was, I'd dialed the number so many times the digits were permanently burned into my brain.

"How many times you drive by her place?" He tilted his head, testing me.

"I don't, she could have moved, and I wouldn't know." Well if she'd moved anytime *after* Monday, then I'd have been oblivious. Just another reason for our repetitive, late night excursions, it stopped me from getting my car, and cruising by her neighborhood.

I know all this shit was making me sound like a contender for creeper of the year, but I was worried that she was going to throw in the towel at JenCorp, and go back to the bar. While I couldn't give a rat's ass where she worked as long as she was happy, the thought of her coming home late at night, by herself, was enough of an incentive for me to get familiar with her nocturnal activities. Thank fucking Christ, she liked her job more than she hated me. I figured if she hadn't left by now, she probably wasn't going to, so I relaxed the after-dark tail.

"So you don't know anything?" Troy gave me a cocky look, like he knew something that maybe I should.

"What should I fucking know, Troy?" I looked him dead in the eye, this wasn't playtime, and if she is in any kind of danger or trouble, I didn't give a fuck what promises I'd made about staying clear of her. All bets were off.

"Just thought it was interesting that she'd recently start seeing someone, and you hadn't mentioned it."

It's like someone pulled the fucking pin on a grenade. Even though I hadn't been drunk, I was immediately sober, my reflexes razor sharp. I couldn't even hear the music anymore, the backdrop of the club completely off my grid.

"How recently?"

"Two days ago. I have it on a good authority that your girl is fucking miserable. And about to make a mistake with an asshole, 'cause for some messed-up reason, she doesn't think she has a choice."

Seemed like pretty specific intel for a dude who played drums for a fucking rock band. So, unless Troy had been moonlighting as the new *Gossip Girl* of the Upper East Side, he had been swapping late night whispers with one Megan Winters.

"You've been talking to Megs?" The fucking smile on his face was enough of a yes. "Please tell me it's not that motherfucker she works with."

"Bingo. Give the boy a prize."

"Troy, don't fuck with me. What did Megs say, and do not paraphrase for my benefit. I want you to be real clear about it."

My heartbeat had jazzed up to double what it had been clocking before. The thought of Ash unhappy made the blood ring in my ears.

"She's given up, Dan. Lost the fight in her. Decided she'll settle for mediocre, and that douchebag she's dating, she doesn't even like him let alone love him."

That's all I needed to hear. Shit was already in motion, and I couldn't stop it if I tried. "You know where she is?"

"I do, but before I give you that information I need to know what you plan on doing with it."

I fished my phone out of my pocket and texted TJ to bring the car around. We were out of here.

"There's no plan about it. I love her and I'm getting her back."

28

Ashlyn

"I'M REALLY GLAD YOU SAID YES." ROB GAVE ME A SATISFIED SMILE AND gentle hug as he walked me to his car.

Megs had given him the stare down at the door, not even pretending to try and like him and given me the eye roll when he showed up with a single red rose. It was cliché and maybe a little boring but still sweet nonetheless.

I nodded, not able to think of anything to say in response. *"I'm really glad I said yes, too,"* wasn't coming out of my mouth. I was with him and I was smiling and that was about as *glad* as I was going to get tonight. Though I really hoped this production we were heading to didn't bore me to tears. I never did fake enthusiasm well.

"This is me." The lights flashed on a navy Chevrolet Impala. It had just been cleaned. The fact I noticed shiny chrome on the car, but couldn't tell you what my date was wearing was already a red flag. Damn Dan Evans. No man would ever compare.

"Great." My smile tightened as I mentally kicked my own ass. I'd gone exactly ten minutes without thinking about my ex-boyfriend. We were already off to such a stellar start.

Rob opened the car door and I ducked inside, trying to calculate how many dates it would take to convince myself this was fun. Maybe I need to reward myself with chocolate, build up some learned psychological response. Go on a date with Rob, treat myself a box of Godiva. My mood improved just thinking about the promise of the gold box, so maybe it was a viable option.

The drive was quiet and slightly awkward. He didn't seem nervous at all, which annoyed me a little. He didn't have to be so cocky. I hadn't agreed to sleep with him yet, and that sure as hell wouldn't be happening tonight.

"Are you hungry? We can grab a bite to eat before the show."

"Sure."

What I meant to say was, no, I've changed my mind. I don't think this is going to work out, so let's get me that box of chocolate and I'll get back to my solitude. Maybe I could wait until intermission, and fake a headache. That was about as cliché as the rose he'd brought me, but I figured we were reading from the same playbook, so not entirely unexpected. I still got chocolate though, right? Half dates most definitely counted.

Dinner didn't yield any surprises. A quaint little café near the theater. Trendy and overpriced. Nuevo French cuisine. It helped me learn about myself that I really didn't like French food. Who knew? Well at least the date hadn't been a total loss - the lesson in self-discovery and the promise of Godiva rewards.

The conversation was just as contrived as the meal I hadn't been able to finish. Rob asked about college, family, and my hometown, but it felt more like a survey than actual interest. I reciprocated, even nodded and smiled in all the right places. Proof the performance had started well and truly before the scheduled show. I was so fucking bored.

A short walk later and we were standing in front of a small playhouse theater, and I was looking for a sharp object I could stab myself with. Even the allure of Godiva wasn't cutting it. My planned headache replaced by a mid-performance bathroom dash, where I'd-obviously-eaten-something-bad-and-needed-to-go-home. It's not like it couldn't happen. People got food poisoning all the time.

Rob put his arm around my waist as he walked through the doorway and suddenly the idea of being sick wasn't so much of a hypothetical. My stomach gurgled uncomfortably. There was a lot to be said for psychosomatic. Megs could totally do a case study on me.

"Hey, babe, I think you're lost," a voice whispered into my ear. "Unless you are looking for douchebags, and then you've totally come to the right place."

"Dan?" I turned around to see him standing behind me.

He looked good. A little more tired than usual, like maybe he hadn't sleep, but other than that, he was perfect. He was wearing a pair of jeans, heavy boots and Black Flag T-shirt, his inked arms on display. My mind barely registered the fact he wasn't wearing a jacket. I was too overwhelmed to be standing before him. He didn't even flinch at the attention he was attracting, not sure if it was because he looked out of place, or if the crowd had guessed who he was. He didn't even acknowledge them as he moved in closer, getting so close to me I could feel my skin tingle. My stomach doing some Olympic-inspired flip as he refused to take his eyes off me.

"Listen, Dan. Let's not make scene." Rob tried to step in. *Oh, he was still here?* "Ashlyn doesn't need the drama right now. Why don't you give her some space?"

"See, hearing stuff like that convinces me even more what an asshole you are." Dan turned to Rob. "You know nothing about her, and you know even less about what she needs. So how about you don't embarrass yourself any further, and you let me make shit right with my girl."

Hearing him call me *his girl* knocked the air right out of my lungs. I wanted to be mad at him. I wanted to yell at him and tell how much he hurt me. But I also wanted to wrap myself around him, and lose myself in his kisses, until nothing else existed. If it was a vote, the last option was most definitely winning.

"Dan." I found that I could actually open my mouth, and words showed up to the party.

"I'm not..." There was no way I could finish that sentence, not convincingly anyway. "Maybe we..." Nope, that wasn't going to work either. "What are you doing here?"

"Doing what I should have done weeks ago." He threaded his

arm around my waist, pulling me closer, and my body of its own volition moved against him. It was like I had no control of it. I wanted to stop but I just couldn't. It. Felt. So. Good. We ignored the crowd and moved outside the theater. I left Rob open-mouthed and red-faced in the lobby. A better person would have been more concerned about him—my date—but I wasn't that person. Not today.

I followed Dan silently into the alley that separated the old brick buildings. I thought if I spoke this would evaporate, so I kept my mouth shut, needing to see where he would lead me. The Suburban's flashing lights marked the end of the alley. Troy was leaning against the doorframe of the truck until he saw us, and then he disappeared into the dark cabin, leaving us relatively alone.

"I'm sorry, Ashlyn. I'm sorry I was an asshole, and I didn't tell you the whole truth. I should never have kept shit from you. You deserved better than that but I don't regret helping you. I don't regret giving you an opportunity to be happy, even if it meant I would lose you."

"Dan—"

I wanted to speak but I wasn't sure what I wanted to say. Whether I would ask him to keep going or ask him to stop. But he took that choice out of my hands.

"No, wait. Let me get this out." He held his hand gently over my mouth. "You don't want to be with me, I'll hate it but I'll accept it. What I won't fucking accept is you settling for anything less than perfect. Being with *him* 'cause you think you should, 'cause it conforms to this idea in your head, this plan? It's bullshit and I won't let you do it yourself."

"Dan—"

"Ash, I'm not done." He cradled my face with his hands. "I don't deserve you. I never did. I've fucked a lot of women, some I didn't even know their names. It was something to do, a distraction, and I never really thought about the consequences. I can't change what I did, or who I was back then, but I can only tell you that now, that man no longer exists. I never thought in a million years I'd meet someone whom I wanted to be with forever, so I never cared enough about what I was bringing to the table. I never cared enough to stop myself from giving it away. There's only one piece of me that all those girls I've slept with have never had. And that's my heart. Only you, and whatever happens now, that shit is not going to change. I know I can't quit loving you even if I tried. I've been trying, and I'm not even close to being able to stop.

"I love you. I am in love with you, and I'm going to love you until the end of time. We're not done. We'll never be done. There isn't anything in this world that will convince me otherwise, and I'll do whatever I need to do to make this right. 'Cause now that I've got you in my arms, I ain't never letting you go."

He brushed his finger gently along my jaw. Being that close to him, having him touch me, and to be intoxicated by his delicious scent, it overwhelmed me. I knew I was fighting a losing battle, my body had stopped fighting the minute I had heard his sexy voice. Looking into his beautiful eyes, seeing how much this had hurt him and how much he still loved me, tore away at any of my remaining defenses.

"Shut up and kiss me already." I had barely got the words out before he sealed my lips with his. The world fell away beneath me. Nothing else existed. Just us in that perfect moment where the man I couldn't live without, couldn't live without me. And I loved him. So much. So whatever we needed to work through, we would get past, because being apart wasn't an option. We'd tried it. We both failed. We belonged together.

I had spent my life up until this point planning for perfection, avoiding the extraordinary, and playing it safe. I thought it would make me happy and give me a good life. What I couldn't have planned for, was meeting a man who was so exceptional it would redefine my expectations.

Life isn't about the perfect plan. It's about the perfect storm that engulfs you when you're busy living it.

CRASH RIDE

1

My head was fuzzy. I'd definitely drunk too much. Christmas parties were the work of the Devil. Under the guise of holiday cheer, you were suckered into swallowing punch that had a higher alcohol content than the city of Tijuana. It burned going down, but unsurprisingly the more you drank; the more appealing it tasted. I was going to be pissed if I threw up all over my new Gucci boots.

Some guy I barely knew invaded my personal space and almost spilled his drink on me. "Oh … hey, Megan, how's your dad? I sent him a study I'm trying to get published." I wasn't drunk enough to see his thinly veiled attempt at conversation was a chance to use me to get to my father.

"Wouldn't know." I took another sip of the demon elixir from my cup. "He and my mom are in Vale at the moment."

"Too bad." Random guy shrugged before trudging off to go find someone else to talk to.

This was typical of my work situation. My dad, Dr. Mitchell Winters, was one of the head cardiothoracic surgeons at New York Presbyterian and even guest lectured at Cornell; he was highly respected and very influential in the medical field. My mom, Dr. Mary Winters, was a pediatrician and my older brother, Dr. Thomas Winters, was an ER attending physician. Yeah, you guessed it; there was a definite trend in my family.

Don't get me wrong, I loved my job. Being a clinical psychologist at Mount Sinai was an amazing opportunity, but I knew that my dad had been instrumental in me securing my position. People either wanted to be my best friend or give me a wide berth because of my last name; I was like the *Harry Potter* of the hospital world. Unlike Harry, I didn't have magical powers and I could sure use some magic tonight.

Use some of that magic on Troy Harris. The mohawked, hazel-eyed drummer from the band Power Station that did things to my girlie parts.

Troy Harris. Ah, he who cannot be named. Well, I can name him; I just can't *do* anything with him. Why am I even thinking about him? I'm supposed to be getting loaded and possibly hooking up with that cute guy from radiology. See—*that* guy—he was a guy I could actually have. That is where my energy *should* be focused, not on a rock star that only saw me as a friend.

Troy Harris. Damn it, the more I tried to stop, the more I thought of him. He was permanently burned into my brain. I had shamelessly thrown myself at him the night we met. My judgment had been clouded by one too many Long Island iced teas and years of pent up lusting. I'd had that longing from way back, but I never imaged our paths would cross. Not in real life at least. I had gone to the concerts, but I wasn't the type of girl who got invited backstage. Not that it bothered me, it was what it was.

I had always been a fan. Power Station was an amazing live band and their music was more than just good, it was something else. It was real. They had purpose. They gave hope. They evoked emotions. It was one of the best therapies I knew and *therapy* was my line of work, so I should know.

Meeting Troy had felt like a dream. No, really. Like an actual altered state of lucidity. Ash, my best friend, and I had been celebrating. Not that I fully remember the occasion and all of which seems inconsequential now. My sobriety had taken the Staten Island Ferry, sailing away from me without a second thought. That is when, in a noise-filled nightclub, that my stumbling introduction to Troy was made.

Ash had previously, albeit briefly, met Dan and it was this link which had been our *in*.

Troy Harris was nothing like Dan Evans; while the latter had celebrated his status as of one Manhattan's biggest manwhores, his BFF did not share his reputation. Rumors swirled of his bedroom talents, but for the most part no one talked.

Those girls were like a vault. Either he paid them off or he was *that* good. No shady ex's had come out of the woodwork selling their nighttime confessionals, and no hidden camera money shots had shown up online. Not going to lie, the lack of intel on Troy's *goods* had disappointed me slightly—purely from a research point of view of course.

Instead he was touted as the comical, smoldering, nice guy who didn't take himself too seriously. This mixed with his genetic windfall of good looks made him ridiculously attractive. Let's face it, I was going to need someone who wasn't intimidated by my particular brand of enthusiasm. Sounded to me like Troy Harris might just fit the bill.

His jokester reputation for making waves with his fellow band mates was also proven to be true when he caught us trying to sneak into the VIP section where they had been holed-up.

With Ash having been very vocal about her dislike for Dan, Troy was ready to be our best friend.

I liked this. A lot. So much so that after our drunken introductions were made, I wrapped myself around him like a vine. After all, chances of seeing him again were probably low and he was ripe to be climbed. I was too intoxicated to care about the implications and not coherent enough to care what he thought. I wasn't going to possibly miss the only chance I had to lay my hands on him, and I very much liked what my hands discovered. Troy Harris was most definitely not photoshopped.

Unfortunately my clingy, juvenile routine wasn't my only misdemeanor. No. I was *allegedly* defeated by a pair of Louboutins and an uneven sidewalk. I say allegedly because I actually have no recollection, though regardless of the finer details, I ended up with a bad ankle sprain and Troy Harris taking me home. Sadly, he didn't nurse me back to health

Ugh, my cup was empty. The paint stripper I had been drinking had sadly been drained of its last drop. Unlike Troy Harris, the empty cup was an easy fix, so I strolled over to the makeshift bar and helped myself to another drink.

Mmmmm … much better. The warm alcohol spread through my body like a wildfire and prompted me to giggle. The subject of what I found so hilarious eluded me but whatever it was, was funny. I was funny. Hey, you know what else would be funny?

Without properly thinking it through, I reached into my purse and pulled out my phone. Saved within in its memory banks was a number I had acquired for a previous and unrelated exercise and wisely, not deleted. Who cared if holding on to it made me seem creepy? I dialed before I'd had a chance to reconsider. I felt brave. Like a gladiator, but with better shoes.

"Hey, Megs." He answered almost instantly; my hand gripped the phone tighter upon hearing his voice. I fumbled as I tried to play it cool.

"Oh hey, Troy Harris, it's Megs." I cringed realizing he had already said my name.

"I know." His low laugh rumbled through the phone.

"I saved your number. From before. I'm not a stalker." I doubt he was convinced, the words coming from my mouth sounded slurred and chaotic. It had not been a good sell.

"It's okay, I don't mind you calling me." I heard the smile in his voice.

"God, you're sexy." It leapt out of my mouth before I had a chance to stop. "I can't believe I actually called you. Can you just sit on the phone with me a while and breathe."

"Er, Megs? Are you okay?"

"Yeah, I'm good. *Really good.* I love it when you say my name. Say it again," I slurred into the phone.

Did I sound as lame as I thought? I tried to regulate my breathing so I didn't sound like a complete creeper. Speaking to him short-circuited my brain. It was like being star-struck, only amplified. Nervous didn't even cover half of it.

"Megs, are you drunk? Where are you?"

"At work, Troy Harris. Mount Sinai. You need any medical

attention?" I giggled.

Who knew I was a comedian. How he was able to resist me was a mystery. "Shhhhh don't tell anyone, but I'm Harry Potter, the movie version. I haven't read the books."

"Jesus. Megs, stop drinking. You sound really loaded, so unless you tell me that you have a ride home tonight, I'm coming to get you."

I brought my cup to my lips and took another swallow. "You're going to let me ride you tonight? Santa must have got my Christmas list early." The thought alone was deserving of another drink.

"Wow. Can you do me favor and stay out of trouble? I'll be there soon."

"Boooooo. Stay out of trouble? How is that any fun?"

"I'm getting into my car. Please, just sit down or something. I'll call you when I get there."

"Fine, Troy Harris, because you said please."

"Bye, Megs."

I ended the call and tossed the phone into my purse, unable to suppress the huge smile on my face or stop my excited victory dance. Lucky for me the blaring music meant that my rhythmless hyperactive shuffle was not out of place.

He—Troy Harris—was coming for me. For *me*. The thought looped in my head. It was something that I never thought would happen and fully expected my interactions with him being tied to a third party. Yet, Dan or Ash were nowhere in sight, and Troy Harris was on his way to see *me*. How quickly my luck had turned. I was king of the world, or at the very least Manhattan. I resisted the urge to outstretch my arms to celebrate my newfound sovereignty. That would be overkill, as would be a tiara.

Rather than wait until Troy called me again— like a regular person would—I decided to go wait for him downstairs. Smart. In case I missed him or something, there was no way I would risk that. Besides, I had spent enough time with my drunken coworkers to be polite; no one would even notice I was gone.

And just like, I slipped out of the room. Probably *not* with the stealth and coordination as the word slipped implied, but I didn't fall on my ass or twist an ankle. I was out the door and down the wide and empty corridor as fast as my designer boots would carry me.

The cold air hit me like a punch in the stomach as I opened the main outside door. Every breath I inhaled felt like tiny daggers in my lungs. Why, was I so damn cold? Oh, crap. I had been so excited to leave I'd forgotten my coat inside.

Oh well, hopefully he would get here before hypothermia set in, so I'd just suck it up and wait. I didn't need something as silly as warmth. Pfft. Didn't I say I was a gladiator? I would be brave.

Okay, so five minutes outside with snow flurries swirling around me and I'd decided I wasn't that brave and it was freakin' cold. I ran back inside the building and into the room where my coat had been slung over a chair. I was in and out like a ninja, grabbing what I needed without making eye contact with anyone. I followed my previous path back down the corridors and out the main doors again.

Not sure in which direction he would be arriving, I walked out from the main entrance way and onto the street, keeping a look out for his souped-up '74 VW Baha Beatle. Not that I'd stalked him or anything, it was like common knowledge. Any self-respecting Power Station fan would know what set of wheels they drove; unfortunately my research didn't extend to the license plate.

The noisy activity of the emergency department was on the opposite side of the building so the howling wind was the only sound that broke the silence. Two large headlights pierced through the darkness, the huge black pick-up truck they were attached to rolled slowly up the road toward me. Shit. I was alone. This was not good.

It was probably just a dude who was lost, or at least that's what I told myself.

I decide to walk in the opposite direction, away from the truck. Sure, that's the smart thing to do, walk *away* from the main entrance. I was paranoid, alcohol delusions messing with my head. The truck had nothing to do with me. My heart thumped hard as I looked down the road. Troy would show up any minute, I just needed to not freak out.

The pick-up stopped, its engine idled before it performed a K turn and started to drive toward me. Shit. I was *not* paranoid. I was being followed. If this was fate's way of giving me a big fuck you by dangling Troy Harris in front of me only to have me mugged or killed moments before I got to enjoy him, then fate was a fucking asshole. I wouldn't die, not tonight.

The truck got closer, flashing its lights and I did the only thing I could think of—I ran. My arms pumped as the cold wind lashed at my face, my footing unsteady in my heeled boots. My feet screamed in agony as they pounded against the pavement. I promised my feet if we survived the night I would buy more sensible footwear. Just not Birkenstocks, I mean, comfort can still look good, right?

I heard the noise of the engine close in behind me, the beast of a vehicle picking up speed. Okay, okay—I prayed to whatever deity who would have me—I'll buy Birkenstocks, just let me not die. It was too late; tires screeched as the truck mounted the curb and cut me off. I was a goner. I didn't even get to kiss him. Life was so unfair.

"Megs, what the fuck are you doing and why are you running?" Troy jumped out of the still idling truck and grabbed me around the waist.

He pinned me against the warm hood as I stared at him in confusion. "Huh? You drive a VW Baha." The most intelligent thing I was able to utter.

"I have other cars; I blew the transmission in my VW last week. I haven't had a chance to replace it." He moved his face closer to mine. "How do you know what kind of car I drive?"

"Google. It's a sickness. Don't hate me." The uncontrolled words spilled from my lips. His eyes were like truth serum. I couldn't lie when I looked directly into them. Which is what I was doing. He had such amazing eyes.

"You Googled my car?" He laughed, a big throaty laugh. "What *else* did you Google?"

Look away, don't look into his eyes, it's a trap. It's a TRAP. "Shoe size, favorite food, taste in women." I swallowed as my subconscious self cowered in horror. Now I actually *wanted* to die.

"Size thirteen, Mexican, as for women—varied. I don't have a type. Anything else you want to know?" His face was inches from mine; I could feel his breath tickle my neck. The sensation intoxicated me further, awaking every cell of my body as his frame pressed against mine.

I closed my eyes, saving myself before I asked him, *why won't you kiss me* and shook my head.

"Okay, let's get you off the street before you hurt yourself or someone else." His fingers wrapped around my arms and peeled me off the hood. "I flashed my lights at you, to let you know it was me."

"Gangs do that. I'm sure I've read it somewhere," I explained as I righted myself on my feet. "They flash their lights at you so you think they're friendly and then they kill you. I am pretty sure it's for initiation."

"Do you realize how crazy that sounds? Why would they warn you if they are going to kill you?"

"I don't know, Troy Harris; do you see me flashing gang signs? They're gangsters. I wouldn't argue with them."

Troy chuckled as he moved to the passenger side door and opened it. "You are so funny when you're drunk."

I stared at the space between the doorframe of the car and the floor. It was so high up. Was I supposed to take a running jump? "Do you have a ladder?"

"Here." Troy smiled and tapped the black steps along the outside of the car. "One foot here and the other here. I'll stand behind you, just in case."

It wasn't pretty, but I managed to haul myself into the beast without incident despite contorting my body into a weird angle to get into the cab. Why I made things harder than they had to be, I'll never know.

Once I was safely inside and buckled in, Troy moved to the driver's side and hopped in. He was able to do so in one swift, graceful movement —something I had been unable to do—and I couldn't stop myself from staring.

He cocked his head to the side. "You good?" He fastened his

seatbelt.

I nodded slowly as he dismounted the curb and pulled back onto the road.

Suspended reality was the best way I could describe it. The surprise and the shock of the situation I found myself in stunned me momentarily. Had I ever been alone with him before? I'd imagined it so many times but now that I was sitting beside him, I had no idea where to even start.

It was quiet. His stereo was off and the only noise to break the silence was the hum of the engine.

"Hey, so I never thanked you for your help." It was the first thing that came to mind. "With Dan and Ash. I know you were skeptical about stepping in, but they needed us. So thanks."

Troy didn't take his eyes off the road as he answered me. "I'll admit getting involved in Dan's business was not high on my agenda, but you made a solid case. Doesn't mean I want to play interference on a regular rotation though."

"I think they are going to be fine now." Ash and Dan would no doubt have their ups and downs like any couple, but I had faith they were in it for the long haul. "You can probably go back to playing drums and being sexy." Did I actually say that last bit out loud? I wasn't even looking at his eyes this time. I had no excuse.

Troy glanced at me and laughed. "I think I'll just stick to the drum part of your proposal, being sexy sounds like too much work, but thanks."

Little did he know, he didn't even have to try. Oh no. In fact, the only thing the man had to do was show up and sexiness took care of itself. It was in him. The way he walked. His I-don't-give-a-fuck attitude. The haphazard fashion sense—no other man over thirty could wear a *Hershey's Chocolate* tee and rock it. It all cumulated into a simmering vibe. Like one big melting pot of *yum*, I involuntarily licked my lips.

"Soooooooo," I fumbled, twisting my hair nervously around my finger. My mind and my mouth were at odds as to which statement would come barreling out next. "We should go out and celebrate. Both of us returning to our respective fields of expertise." It was worth a shot. Not like I had a lot to lose. My dignity had checked-out a while ago.

The truck stopped in traffic as we approached a red light. My eyes kind of stared off into the distance in a state of semi-disbelief. Was I really in this car or was it just a dream? Having him close felt like a fantasy. I wonder if I just reached out and... The loud blaring of a cab's horn punctuated that it wasn't a dream.

"Megs, do you really think that is a good idea?"

"What idea?" I tried to untangle the lock of hair that was cutting off the circulation of my finger as I mentally retraced the steps in the conversation. Oh. Right. I had asked him out. This was the part where he gave me the gentle brush off. It's not like I hadn't alluded to my interest for weeks. We had been playing this little flirty game since I met him and while I'm not the hang-from-the-chandeliers kind of girl, I'm certainly not a wallflower either.

"Us, going out." He took a breath, the playful vibe of the conversation evaporated, taking along with it any chance of the two of us dating. "Megs, you are an amazing girl. You're funny and beautiful, and when you aren't repeating my name five hundred times, I dig spending time with you. But Dan and Ash. They just got back together. I know you and Ash are tight, and I think it goes without saying that Dan and I are... well he's my brother. I just don't want to complicate things, you know what I'm saying?"

I pushed back my errant hair and bit my lip; forcing myself to look at him and smile sweetly. "Troy Harris, it was just a night out. It didn't have to be complicated." I didn't bother trying to hide my disappointment. It wasn't a maybe, it was a definitive no.

"Megs. What happens if we go out and I do something stupid like not call you or some shit? Then it gets awkward and people have to choose sides. People we both care about. Before you know, it's like we're on a fucking reality show. No matter how many times people say they won't let shit get complicated, it ends up complicated. I like you, I think you're awesome and I don't want to screw it up. I want us to be friends."

Wow. Friend-zoned. He was pretty clear. Perhaps he was looking for a commendation, for his honesty and all, but rejection is still a rejection. Even one that made sense. It still stung. He was right about one thing. If we did go out, and things went bad, either for us or for Dan and Ash, then it would inevitably spill into a big cesspool of suck. Of course, common sense didn't ease the disappointment of the situation and solidified the fact my nighttime illicit fantasies would be staying just that...fantasies. Can't blame a girl for trying.

My teeth toyed with my bottom lip as I closed my eyes. I couldn't believe I was being so brazen. "Can we at least be friends with benefits?" It couldn't hurt to put it out there, even if I assumed the answer was probably going to be a no. Nothing ventured, nothing gained. I was still stunned I was having this conversation and I wasn't sure if I was thankful I had alcohol to blame or I was going to hate myself in the morning. Probably a little of both.

"Wow, Megs," Troy laughed. "I'm going to pretend you didn't say that, 'cause we've already established I think you are awesome and that situation would not be a hard sell. Maybe we could just be *regular* friends."

"Okay, Troy Harris. Let the records show that you *had* the opportunity to sleep with me, and you turned it down." Who the hell says that? If he hadn't turned me down before, that sure as hell would be the nail in the coffin. Crap. That freaking punch I'd been drinking had a lot to answer for.

"Noted, your Honor." He pulled up to the curb beside my apartment. "Do you think you are ever going to just call me Troy?"

My heart sunk, my excuse for being in the car was over as we stopped in front of my building.

"We'll have to wait and see I guess. I should let you go, thanks for driving me home." I knew I had to get out and go up into my apartment, even if what I actually wanted to do was try and convince him further. I wouldn't be one of those desperate girls who asked him to come upstairs, even though I wanted nothing more than to throw my self-respect out the window and beg. Beg for one night with him. Toe-curling red-hot sex. That's what that body promised and I was going to have to walk away. It sucked. Big time.

He let out a long steady breath, and if I didn't know better I'd assume that maybe it hadn't been so easy to turn me down. "Yeah, you should be safe enough from gangstas and uneven sidewalks from here." His voice softened. "Oh, and Megs ..."

My heart pounded so loudly I was sure he'd hear it. "Yeah, Troy Harris?" I looked into his eyes. Throwing caution to the wind with the powers they held over me.

"Just 'cause we aren't sleeping together doesn't mean you can't call me sometime. You know. If you need something... or if you just wanna hang."

I closed my eyes and smiled. The intonation of his voice was so seductive it hurt, even if the words weren't sexy. "I'd like that. Can you sometimes take your shirt off?" I laughed as I slowly reopened my eyes.

His chuckle reverberated through the cabin. "Ha. I'll see what I can do."

"Bye, Troy Harris." I turned and jumped out of the car, my feet landing heavily on the sidewalk.

"Bye, Megan Winters."

Troy

6 Months Later/Present Day

"SO YOU WANNA COME UP WITH ME, MAYBE HAVE A DRINK?" SHE smiled, not even trying to hide what she had on her mind, and a beer was not it.

"Thanks, but I'm going to pass." The engine idling should have been a big tip off. Not going there. There were many places my dick was not going tonight and inside of her was at the top of the list.

"Oh? I can go down on you right here if you like?" She didn't take the hint, her hand sliding up my thigh. Seriously, what did I need to do to clue this girl in I wasn't going to fuck her?

"Going to have to pass on that, too. Thanks for the offer though, that was sweet." Or desperate, we could go either way. The asshole in me was leaning toward the latter, but I didn't care to find out. No point. Getting her out of my car and gone were my priority right now, not working out the finer points of this chick's seduction technique. If my dick was any less hard I was going to need to pop a Viagra just to take a piss.

"Well… I guess I should go then?" The look of surprise on her face floored me. Seriously? She hadn't joined the dots yet? Clueless. Fucking perfect.

"Yeah, I need to meet Dan. We have a band thing." A lie, but an easier let down than *I have no interest in you, please get out of my fucking car.* Being an asshole was one thing, being unnecessarily cruel was something else. "See ya, Lacey." The I'll-call-you or let's-do-this-again-sometime wasn't tacked onto the end. There was no chance I'd do either of those things.

"Okay… Thanks." She leaned in and kissed me, no doubt in a last ditched effort to change my mind. She was persistent, I'll give her that but still no cigar.

"Yep. Thanks." My hands tapped on the steering wheel as I pulled my mouth away.

If Lacey wasn't up to speed before, she sure as hell was then. Her fingers snatched her purse from the console and stormed out of my ride. The slamming of the car door behind her, muffled the "fuck you" as she left. It was deserved and yet I couldn't make myself care. At least she was gone, even if it meant I would probably lose a friend on Facebook. Once again, care factor, zero.

It was nine-thirty on a Friday night and I was heading home. Living the fucking dream.

My fist tapped against the big wooden door. "Douchebag, Open up."

"Hey, asshole." Dan smirked as he cracked open his front door. "Nice shirt. Brings out the color of your eyes." He stepped aside so I could walk in.

"I'm glad you approve. I wore it especially for you." Wiseass. I hadn't bothered to change, still wearing the bullshit button down and jeans I'd worn to dinner. "You and Ash got plans? I'm so fucking bored, taking a nap looks like a good time."

Ash moved into Dan's apartment pretty soon after they got back together. Not that there was any doubt of what their zip code was going to be, her place had been a shit hole in a bad part of town. So being that Dan and my real estate shared the top floor of a high rise, it meant I was now kicking it with a new female neighbor.

"Didn't you have a date?" Dan looked over his shoulder as we walked into the living room. He silenced the dipshit on his large screen television before tossing the remote onto his fancy, new distressed wooden coffee table. His pad recently overhauled at the hand of his girl.

"Yep, Lacey. Masturbating with a cheese grater would've been less painful. I called time early and bailed." It wasn't an exaggeration. I was so done with airhead bimbos, I didn't give a fuck how well they sucked dick.

"Sounds like a fun night." Dan laughed as he disappeared into the kitchen, emerging a few moments later with a couple of ice-cold long necks. "Beer?"

"Hell, yes." I snagged a bottle out of his hand. "So, you never answered my question. You wanna do something tonight?" The leather of the couch creaked as I sunk my ass into the chair.

"Ash is going out. With Megs. Just the two of them." He took a swallow of his beer, but his face said it all. He wasn't cool with his girl hitting the town without him in tow. I'm convinced Dan missed all those classes in Pre K when we all were taught to share.

"Interesting." My grin widened. I couldn't help myself. He was too much of an easy target.

"Don't even fucking start, Troy. This whole girls' night out thing is fucking bogus. I just know some motherfucker is going to try and hit on my girl. I'm not cool with this, not at all." Dan planted his ass in the opposite matching leather two-seater. Edgy was the understatement of the century. Poor bastard, looked like he was ready to gut some poor SOB.

"Earth to neanderthal, she's coming home to you. Even if some douche hits on her, you know she's probably going to tell him to go fuck himself or knee him in the nuts. Don't you remember how *charmed* she was when you hit on her?" I hated to admit it, but Dan pussy-whipped was kind of fucking nice. He had given James and Alex so much shit when they'd done the ball and chain thing. It was poetic justice that he was tied up in knots.

My pep talk fell on deaf fucking ears as he continued to sulk like a two-year-old. "You know, we could go out too," I suggested, knowing he was going to be a moody asshole whatever the location was.

"You want to go out?" Dan lowered his beer, carefully placing the bottle on a coaster. Yep, well and truly whipped!

"Sure, why not? We can go shoot some pool, or go see a band?" It had been awhile since we'd been out. The band had been holed-up in James's studio for the last three months while we laid down the new album.

"Dan, can you zip me?" Ashlyn appeared in the doorway, wearing a tight blue dress. "Oh, hey, Troy." Her eyes widened, as she grabbed at the material exposing her back. I couldn't help noticing the amount of skin she was flashing. No wonder Dan looked like he had swallowed glass.

"Hey, Ash, what's shakin'?" I tilted my beer in greeting, unable to suppress my grin. "You look great."

"Shut up, dickwad." Dan got to his feet and yanked at Ashlyn's zipper. His effort to hurry the process made it snag. "Fuck!" He shook his finger, obviously coming off second best against the teeth of the zip. "Babe, seriously, why don't you and Megs hang here? We'll go to Troy's if you want have a girls' night. I'm pretty sure there is a Zac Effron movie on *Showtime*, and there's ice cream and cookie dough in the freezer."

"Aw, Dan, are you jealous?" Ash smiled as Dan finished fucking around with her dress. "You are just going to have survive without me for a night. Megs is working some tough cases and she needs a night out. You understand don't you, baby?" Ash wrapped her arms around Dan's neck and it didn't take a genius to work out where this was heading.

"I don't want some asshole trying to touch what's mine." Dan tipped Ash's chin and he clocked her with a look that claimed her more than his words.

"No one is going to touch anything." Ash moved in closer, her mouth getting cozy with the side of his face. I wondered if I shouldn't leave the room and give them a moment. Not that either of them seemed to give a shit I was still around.

Like the big guy upstairs was listening to my silent prayer, there was a knock at the door that gave me an out. I'd seen enough of Dan getting busy to last me a lifetime and even though I dug Ash, I preferred to leave some shit unseen.

"I'll get it, anything is better than listening to you two clowns." I don't think they even noticed the knock or me leaving. I moved off the couch and made for the door, hoping the lovin' feeling wasn't going to spill into the hallway as I walked out of the room.

My gratitude went to whoever was on the other side as I grabbed at the solid wooden door and yanked it open. And there she was, the five-foot-four blonde bombshell that made my dick twitch every time I saw her.

"Megs." My grin got wider as I looked down at her next-to-nothing outfit. I didn't have to imagine too hard to guess what was underneath her tight black dress, her perky tits straining against the material. Once again, I was throwing my thanks to the man upstairs.

Megan Winters was straight up beautiful. Long, wavy blonde hair that went half way down her back with the sexiest, clearest, blue-green eyes I'd ever seen. Topped off with a knockout fucking smile. Her body was nothing short of perfection, with the right combination of tits and ass that would force even the strongest man onto their knees. Add to that her wicked sense of humor and her ridiculous fucking IQ, and you had a girl that most men would give their left nut to call their own. Not that it would ever go beyond the silent appreciation I had for her, still it was hard not to notice. No matter how many times I saw her, it did nothing to diminish the punch in the gut I got every time I laid eyes on her.

"Hey, Troy Harris." My name rolled out of her mouth with a smile, and damn if it didn't make me stand up a little straighter. Her little quirk of tacking on *Harris* after *Troy* didn't bother me anywhere near as much as I pretended. Her eyebrow lifted as she moved through the doorway, "Dan and Ash making out again?" Like me, it wasn't her first rodeo with those two boneheads.

"I'm sure they've moved on to dry humping by now." I stepped aside so she could stride past me, which also treated me to the most superb view of her ass. Total scumbag move, but I couldn't help myself. I had already decided she was a no-go zone, a decision I was having a hard time reconciling with at the moment.

"Ha, remember the good old days when they could be together in a room and not be all over each other like a rash?" She glanced back at me as she made her way to the lounge room.

"Preaching to the choir, Megs." My eyes glued to the sway of her hips as she moved in front of me. Yeah, not creepy at all. I shook my head as I tried to focus on something other than trying to imagine what kind of underwear she was wearing.

Putting the brakes on the chance to bed Megs was not an easy task. At first, I considered it —more like my dick demanded it— but I wasn't going to be a douchebag. I knew too well what it was like to get caught up in the misery that came with fucking around with a friend of a friend.

High school, junior year, I had dated Quinn Sinclair who happened to be the best friend of Kim Evans. Kim and Dan hadn't only shared the same last name but they also shared DNA. And while I would never have dated Dan's sister, Quinn seemed like fair game.

Shit had been fine and dandy while things were going well, but it all went to hell the minute we broke up. Kim constantly gave me the stink eye anytime I went around and saw Dan, and Dan was catching heat from his sister, and from Quinn. What I had thought was a mutual break-up, Quinn had seen as me breaking her heart. Enter drama, stage right. Needless to say, I avoided the Evans house like the plague for a solid three months and Dan threatened to kick me in the nuts if I even looked at one of his sister's friends again. Granted shit died down eventually, and last I heard Quinn was still in the old neighborhood, happily married to her accountant husband with her two-point-five kids, but that pact I made to Dan, still stood.

"Why don't you two just make a porno already?" Megs laughed as we walked into the lounge room; Dan and Ash still lip-locked like a pair of freshmen.

"Don't encourage him," Ash giggled as she rubbed lipstick off

Dan's mouth.

"Megs." Dan tipped his chin as he looked over at us. "You know I'd never share my girl with anyone. And I got all the footage I need locked up here." He tapped his noggin with the hand that wasn't wrapped around his girlfriend.

"Ever the romantic." Ash rolled her eyes. "It's a good thing I love you." She squeezed Dan's chin in another loved-up exchange. Fuck, at this rate we'd never get out the door.

"Right, so if the two of you are done being adorable, maybe we can get out of here. I have had the worst week at work, if I don't get to lose myself in a good time in the next thirty minutes, I'm going to be rocking manically in a corner." Megs smiled but I could tell there was something else underneath it. Something in her tone didn't sit right, made me all kinds of uncomfortable.

"Is everything okay, Megs?" I had to ask. Rationally I chalked up my concern to Megs being a friend. While technically not part of this circus of crazy, her connection to Ash justified me taking notice.

The excuse also meant I didn't have to advertise my other interests. The ones that were less about who she was friends with, and more about the woman standing in front of me. The whys of the situation were still unclear, but it wasn't just about her ability to get me hard. Nope, it went deeper than that, and if there was something going down, then I wanted in on that intel.

She shrugged it off and it didn't take a genius to realize she was holding shit back. "Nothing I can talk about, just a rough case load. I can handle it though, just need a night out."

"You girls want a ride in? Dan and I are thinking of hitting the town as well. That is, if I can convince cry-baby to stop bitching into his beer and get out the door." Extra time with Megs would be a bonus. Hopefully I could get a bead on what was clouding those beautiful eyes. Yeah, it made no sense for me to be protective of her, but it was a lost cause pushing down the urge. I'd learnt not to fight it.

"We were going to get a cab. You guys are going out too?" Ash asked, as she turned to look at Dan who was still weighing my offer. Like it or not, he was riding shotgun. I wasn't going to be sitting here all night with his miserable ass. Lord knows, I'd paid him that courtesy more than just a few times.

"Yeah, guess so." Dan got on the same page, not like I'd given him much choice. "Give me five and I'll change." He pulled off his T-shirt as he walked toward the bedroom.

I grabbed my cell and started dialing. "We'll get TJ to drive us in. He can take you ladies wherever you wanna go, and then we'll come get you when you're done."

"Well if we're all going out, why don't we just go out together?" Megs volunteered, and I'll be damned if her face didn't light up at the suggestion.

Ash played devil's advocate; her concern was an easy read. "Megs, are you sure? I thought you wanted it to be just us." She'd made a point of not being one of those girls who was constantly under thumb. Just as well too, 'cause that's sure as shit not what a *real* man wants. All that yes-sir-shit was great in the bedroom, but outside of that, they needed to be able to think for themselves.

Megs's lips curved into a smile. "Ash, I know you. You're going to be thinking about Dan the whole time anyway and he is probably going to be texting you every five minutes. It's fine. We can go out as a group. That is, if Troy Harris is okay with it?" She turned to me, nailing me with a single look.

Wow, did the temperature of the room just raise a few degrees since she'd walked in? There wasn't a lot she could ask me for and I'd say no. Her suggestion—us hanging out tonight— had zero chance of me not being on board. "Oh, I'm more than okay with it. I'm immediately a fan of anything that means I won't have to deal with Dan being a whiny bitch the whole night."

"So it's settled." Megs flicked her hair from her shoulders, her spectacular tits getting my attention as she breathed in and out with excitement. "I get to pick the venue though. If Dan has his way, we're going to end up at Hooter's."

"Hooter's? What are you guys talking about?" Dan was back, freshly changed into a clean pair of jeans and Misfits T-shirt. "Megs, you know I like you and all, but talking shit about that fine establishment is blasphemy in this house."

"Dan, no one was talking shit about your tits-n-wings haven.

Relax." Ash shot him down pretty quickly. That right there was one of the biggest reasons I liked her. She picked up my slack, so to speak, where Dan was concerned. "Megs has decided we should turn girls' night into a foursome."

"Wait. What? Is this some kind of test?" Dan looked confused, the color draining from his face.

I threw back my head and laughed, putting him out of his misery. "Not that kind of a foursome, you moron. Fuck, man, seriously. We're tagging along on Megs's magical mystery tour."

"Well, hells yeah!" Dan grabbed Ash around the waist, looking at her like she was dinner. "That mean I get to be down and dirty on the dance floor with my baby?"

"I'm already regretting this decision." Megs sidled up close to me, rolling her eyes.

"Oh no, Megs. You've already committed. No take-backs." I slung my arm around her shoulder and pulled her into a hug. Hmmm. I liked the way she felt against me. Very fucking nice.

"Well, if everyone's agreed what's say we get out the door and see if we can't get Megs to forget her shitty day," Ash offered, putting a stop to Dan's wandering hands. "Dan, shouldn't you change? I'm not sure they are going to let you into a club wearing a T-shirt."

"Oh Ash, I love you, babe." Dan's mouth curled into a grin. "But green supersedes dress code every time, sweetheart. Besides, name a club and I know most of the dudes at door. I could walk in wearing a chicken suit and they'd still let me in."

Ash gave him a friendly shove. "You are so conceited, you know that?"

"I know, babe. It's part of my charm." His fucking grin getting wider.

The man was an idiot, but he wasn't wrong. Call it unfair or social unjust, but along with the fame we attracted, we got one hell of a free pass. People just gave us shit and treated us differently, even if we didn't want it. Fuck, I couldn't even remember the last time someone told me I couldn't do something. As for establishments, short of taking a piss on the bar, we could pretty much wear, do or say anything we wanted if it meant that it got people through their door.

I moved my arm lower, feeling Megs's soft skin under my calloused fingers and my cock stirred, all kinds of interested in what my hands were doing. Yeah, not going to happen buddy. We needed to eject ASAP or it was going to be really fucking obvious what my thoughts were about. "As much as I'd like to see Dan in a chicken suit tearing around Manhattan, I think we should make tracks. You good?"

"Ready." Dan tucked his arm around his girl's waist, the shit-eating grin on his face a dead giveaway he was ecstatic with the development of the evening. Great.

Megs smiled, her face happier than a kid in a candy store. "Okay, so I'm feeling sentimental. Let's go back to where it all started. Let's head to *Panic*."

3

Megan

IF ANYTHING WAS GOING TO MAKE ME FORGET MY CRAP-TASTIC DAY AT work, it was Troy Harris. Ah, sigh. He was like the Holy Grail of good times wrapped up in one badass package. Not that I knew, it was all assumptions and measured guesses, but surely a man built like that wouldn't disappoint. And disappointment is one thing I didn't need tonight.

It wasn't like I didn't have an amazing life. My quota of *great* was straining against the maximum. A loving, supportive family, a beautiful apartment, wonderful friends and a fulfilling job, how did I get so lucky? Sure, Prince Charming hadn't shown up yet, but I hadn't had to give up one of my shoes either, so it wasn't all bad.

Not a lot of people understood my career choice, but working with troubled kids was something you could never attach a dollar value to. While angels didn't cluster around me like a renaissance painting—I'm still partially bummed about that— what I did, mattered. There was no greater reward than seeing one of my *kids* weather the storm. Nothing even came close.

My latest *kid* was Brad Hemsworth. A sixteen-year-old who, despite coming from a middle class, well-adjusted family, was dealing with adolescent depression. He was struggling to find his place, not fitting in with the jocks or smart kids at the school and generally spending most of his time alone. He had tried to commit suicide once before and he was admitted into the ER yesterday after another failed attempt. This time with pills. His reasoning, it was neater than slitting his wrist like he had done the time previously. I tried not to take it personally, but a part of me felt I'd failed him. Tonight, I needed a night to just forget. Selfish, I know, and I hoped that feeling this way wasn't going to guarantee me a place burning in Hell, but I needed distance. Distance from the sadness and distance from the guilt.

Panic was the club Ash and I had fatefully found ourselves in so many months ago when we were trying to cheer up Ash. It wasn't a coincidence that I chose this place, hoping it would rework its magic. Troy Harris, along for the ride, well that was the cherry on top.

True to Dan's word, dress code hadn't been an issue with the bouncers falling over themselves to raise the rope for both he and Troy. Not even a look was thrown in our direction as we breezed right in. They didn't even check ID. I could have been a sixteen-year-old runaway with a purse full of blow and I would have received the same nod and smile. Lucky for them I *was* of age and *not* packing narcotics—they had dodged that bullet.

"You going to get drunk and fall over?" Troy playfully bumped my shoulder as we entered the club, the light sweeping through the room in an erratic wave. The noise wasn't any less obnoxious since our last visit, but strangely, that excited me. My senses exploded with the familiarity of the room; the darkness and the light were at war with each other as a soundtrack of destruction played in the background. Panic was an appropriate name for the place, the thumping of my pulse matched the bass booming from the speakers.

I playfully nudged him back as we waded through the crowd. My hands probably lingered a little longer than was necessary, but it was crowded and dark, so the touching was totally acceptable. That was my story and I was sticking to it. All that was needed was a suitable justification for my hand wandering to his ass and my night would be complete. Just putting it out there and if the universe wanted to reward me, then what could I say? I would be grabbing that opportunity with both hands—pun totally intended.

"If I fall, will you promise you'll nurse me back to health, Troy Harris?" Seeing as sleeping with me was out, a little TLC from those strong capable hands would be worth another tumble.

Dan and Ash were a few feet in front of us, Dan's arms wrapped protectively around Ash's waist. No one would have missed his territorial vibe, and short of actually marking her, he was doing a fine job so that no man would think twice about approaching her. It was kind of adorable.

"I've got an icepack waiting in the car, just in case." His lips teased into a smile.

I liked that. His smile. It was so contagious and it did amazing things to those hazel eyes. It also managed to do other amazing things, *tingly* things to parts of my body. He didn't even have to touch me. Look Mom, no hands —just that smile and those eyes. It was his superpower. I wasn't entirely convinced he was human.

The stress of my day had already started to evaporate. This was definitely one of my smartest decisions. Troy had a kindness in his face that contradicted the roughness of his body. All those hard lines converged into big walls of flesh. He was solid and I wanted nothing more than to rub myself up against his mass.

Wearing a fitted, black button-down he left undone at collar and at the sleeves, he was looking particularly good tonight. He'd teamed it up with a pair of black jeans and black heavy boots, the pop of color coming from his intricate and artful tattoos that poked out from the fabric. His tats were beautiful, covering both arms, most of his chest and back. Not that I'd actually seen all of them up close, but I'd stalked enough pictures to know. Have we discussed my Google habit? Yeah, it wasn't a coincidence that when you typed "TR" into my search bar, *Troy Harris* was the first thing to pop up. If he ever checked out my computer's history, I would be totally screwed. Mental note— clear my cache when I get home.

My want for him, that hadn't diminished despite him telling me it wasn't happening. Masochism was the only explanation for it. Because despite our flirting back and forth, I knew he didn't feel for me what I felt for him. Did I stop? Nope.

The lust I had ran deep; it was an itch I just couldn't quite reach no matter how hard I scratched. No one else seemed to satisfy it either. Not like I hadn't tried and not like I bet he could. And I needed that more than I cared to admit, especially tonight. To help me forget the thoughts that were unrelenting in my mind, and to help me remember the pleasure that my body had long been denied.

A couple rushed past, almost knocking me over. They didn't even notice I'd almost fallen on my ass as they pushed through the crowd. Too busy laughing and wrapped up in their own excitement to worry about the fact they had shoved me. My body swayed as I tried to regain my balance.

Troy instinctively pulled me to his side. "You okay?" His hand moved around my body, forming a protective barrier around me as he tried to right me back onto my feet. His concern for me dissipated my anger at the couple for being rude assholes. I actually might thank them —Troy's hands on me as a result of their handy work; that was a serious positive.

"I'm fine, thanks." My hand brushed up against his arm, hoping he would hold me a little longer. Sadly, I needed to get my thrills when they came and Troy touching me definitely fell into that category. If only I could convince him to touch me a little lower, and possibly while we were both naked. Too much?

"Maybe I should hold on to you, just to be sure. We wouldn't want for you to end up injured so soon. You can't even blame the booze this time around." He lowered his hand so that it circled my waist and I had to remember to breathe. My body pressed against his side as he guided me through the crowd. Instinctively, I reciprocated and wrapped my arm around his waist. After all, I wouldn't want to seem rude or ungrateful; manners were a big part of my upbringing. I sure wasn't going to argue. He could keep his hands on me for as long as he wanted. Not that I would vocalize that encouragement, I still had my pride.

"I can assure you, I'm going to do everything I can not to end up on my ass." I leaned against him, his scent intoxicating me. I had to stop myself from actually pressing my nose against his chest and sniffing him. It would not be something that would have been easily explained even though the pleasure would have been worth the embarrassment. He smelled good too. All that masculine-sexy- whatever it was spliced with cologne. Yum. I actually had to stop myself from licking my lips. I seriously needed to get laid, and preferably by someone who knew what he was doing.

It's not like I had spent the last six months pining after a guy I couldn't have. No, I had brushed myself off and went full steam ahead in trying to find a distraction. Any distraction. Not that I started bedding strange men and having one-night stands, but I was certainly more open to a *casual* relationship. I was actively dating and I'd always had a healthy sex life, but the last couple of months... well I was a little bored with what the life buffet had offered me. Maybe it's the bad-boy hang up or the allure of the forbidden, but the reasons why Troy and I shouldn't sleep together were making less and less sense. After all, we were adults. Rational ones even. Well, for the most part. Feelings wouldn't even have to come into it. Who says it has to be a relationship? It could just be just sex. Maybe once we'd *had* sex, the whole forbidden fruit issue would be gone, thus remedying the situation. Maybe, it would be like a vaccination, sort of like when they give you the live virus of something to prevent a full-blown outbreak. It would definitely cure the sexual frustration I had going on.

"Um, Megs? Where did you go?" Troy's raised eyebrow hinted at the fact I'd zoned out again. It seemed to be a real hazard when I was around him. I hadn't even noticed we reached the stairs that lead to the VIP area.

"I was just thinking..." I swallowed. My heartbeat raced as I contemplated what I was about to say. Best not to over thinking it, I didn't want to lose my nerve. I was also stone cold sober, as Troy had helpfully pointed out, so there was no way I could blame my future actions on inebriation. Still, there was a sure fire way to stop the loop of crap rolling around in my head and *that* way was standing in front of me. Sue me if I sounded desperate, I really didn't care about public opinion, what I needed was to lose myself for an hour or two. And the person I wanted to do that with was

Troy. Here goes nothing. I was about to test my theory once and for all to prove that honesty is in fact the best policy.

"We should have sex."

"Whoa. Um. Megs. Maybe we should get a drink first. Maybe sit down?" Troy smiled but didn't act shocked. After all, the flirting was nothing new so he probably assumed *this* was just an extension of *that.* Turning it up a notch, if you will. I could tell he didn't think it was a legitimate proposition. I would fix that.

"No seriously. The more I think about it, the more I'm convinced we should do it."

He lowered his face inches from mine. "Megs, didn't we already agree dating would be a bad idea?"

"Who said anything about dating? No, I'm talking about fucking. Just sex. Purely physical," I clarified in case there was any confusion. I figured if I was going to sell this baby, I had to do it justice and leaving wiggle room in the interpretation would not do.

His eyes narrowed, realizing I was serious. "Were you drinking *before* you got to Ash and Dan's?"

Laughing would be inappropriate, and would not help my cause, so I tried not to. It wasn't easy. Sure what I was asking was slightly out of character—scratch that, extremely out of character—but I had suggested it in the past. Granted I'd been drunk, and my lets-have-sex had been off-the-cuff, but a proposal had been made. What did I have to lose? "No. I'm completely sober. Actually, this is the clearest my mind has been in a long time."

"So we're just supposed to *fuck* and then stay friends?" His eyes were a mix of contradiction and confusion. Strangely, it just made him even more alluring. "I really don't think that works out that way for anyone."

While I admired his integrity on the issue—really, give the man a round of applause—it was his other attributes I was interested in tonight. It wasn't going to turn into some long and romantic love story. I was okay with that. I was surprised I hadn't come to this conclusion sooner. Sex was definitely the answer. "No, not if they go in with other expectations. Of course, we know better. No emotional attachment, just fulfilling a primal need."

His mouth curved into a grin and despite my indecent proposal, he didn't seem pissed. "Megs, think about what you are saying. Once you go there, you can't un-go there. We both know it's not that simple."

"Are you two coming up or what? I thought we were going to party tonight, not have a PTA meeting on the stairs," Dan called from the top of the stairs, his arm around Ash. I guess they had finally noticed our absence, or potentially heard the whistle of the crazy train threatening to take me away.

"Shut up, asshole. We'll be there in a minute." Troy turned and called back to him over the noise. Secretly I was glad he hadn't just shot down the conversation. It would be premature to high-five myself just yet.

Dan rolled his eyes but didn't seem overly concerned as he allowed Ash to pull him away. She gave me a quick wink and a smile just before they disappeared from view. I would have to thank her for that later; her intuition guessing it was a conversation that didn't need an interruption. She didn't need to know the finer details, especially seeing as I had no idea what I was actually doing.

I leaned in closer to Troy, needing to know if I was fighting a losing battle. "Aren't you even the slightest bit turned on by me?"

"Megs, my dick is about to get choked out by my jeans. Trust me, not being turned on is *not* the issue here."

So I wasn't imagining it. He was interested. Or at the very least his *dick* was, and lets face it, that was the only part we really *needed* to be on board. Yep, we can officially declare me out of control. Maybe the stress really was getting to me? Whatever the excuse, I was going with it. I'd come this far, might as well jump off the cliff. I had always been an overachiever.

"I think you are over-thinking this. Here is the way I see it. I have had a really bad week, horrendous even. And what I would really like right now is sex. Just to lose myself in a raging, screaming orgasm. Nothing fancy, as long as we both get off. Now, I know I could find some random guy and take him home, but I would really prefer for it to be you. Who gives me the orgasm, I mean."

Troy cocked an eyebrow as he considered my offer. "And you think we can just have sex and shit won't be awkward later?"

"I know so. Besides, I think it might actually help us." At the very least help me. Possibly even cure me of my crazy obsession all while helping me forget my mental baggage. There really wasn't a drawback as far as I was concerned.

"How do you figure?"

I took a deep breath. This is what I like to call my finishing maneuver. The final wrap up. The end argument. "Well, I've always had a thing for you. I'd go to shows and see you on stage and secretly wonder what it would be like. Knowing you hasn't really stopped me from thinking about it. If we did it, then maybe I could stop looking at you and wondering what it would feel like to come with your cock inside me."

His jaw tightened, as his eyes raked up and down my body. The intensity of his stare made me feel naked.

"Fuck." He hissed out a breath.

"That's what I'm trying to facilitate here—"

"Seriously, douchebags. What's the hold up? You stand on that step any longer and the club is going to start charging you rent." Dan reappeared, his timing horrible. Fortunately he was alone, but he was descending the stairs toward us. Well, this was about to get interesting.

"Give me a minute, Megs." Troy eyed me intently before turning to Dan who was now standing beside us. "Dude, what the fuck is your problem? Can't you see we're talking?"

Dan rubbed his neck as he looked between us. "Yeah I see, what I don't get is what's so important you can't talk up here?"

"I've had a shitty week," I began to explain. Not a lie. My week had been horrible. "Worse than normal, and I just needed to offload some steam. I know Ash will worry if I talk about it up there. Troy was just lending me a friendly ear. Trust me, it's not the kind of conversation you want to hear." There was the understatement of the century, if ever I'd heard one.

"Why? Are you ok?" Dan's face turned serious. "Megs, if you are in some kind of trouble, you need to tell me and we will handle that shit. You're Ash's best friend; I don't give a fuck what's going down, Troy and I will to be front and center on it." His concern was endearing. Granted he could be conceited, but underneath it all, he had such a good heart. Sadly, this was not something I wanted him front and center on, however impassionate the plea.

"Stand down, asshole. I've got it covered." Troy tapped Dan across the chest and shot him a look in warning.

"I'm fine, really." I smiled. I really didn't want to explain to Dan that the real reason we were standing here was that we were deliberating the finer points of Troy's cock giving me pleasure. It sounded so crude when I said it like that, so it definitely shouldn't be repeated.

Troy placed his hand on the small of my back, asserting *he had this under control.* "We're just going to take a walk around the club, okay? Just tell Ash we're dancing or something."

"Fine." Dan's eyes darted between us, somewhat appeased. "Go do what needs doing but if you need reinforcements, I'm your first port of call." He poked Troy in the chest.

Stopping myself from getting my hopes up was not an easy task. The what-did-it-mean dominated what thoughts while the tugging in my lower belly prayed I wasn't getting ready for another brush off. Not after I'd laid all my cards on the table. Surely, that would be too cruel.

Troy laughed, tapping Dan on the shoulder while his other hand stayed glued to my lower back. "Always. Now stop busting my stones and go hang with your girl before she wises up and realizes she can do better than your sorry ass."

Dan flipped Troy the finger and wisely retreated back to the VIP area, where no doubt he would make out with Ash until we returned. If we returned. Was he actually considering doing this? He easily could have had an out, citing that we would attract too much attention if we slunk off into the darkness. Could it be that this sexual tension I had been feeling was not just one-sided?

He lowered his head and whispered in my ear. "You called me Troy."

"Huh?" That was not where I thought this conversation was

heading.

"When you were talking to Dan, you didn't tack on my last name."

"Oh, yeah I guess I didn't." I hadn't really noticed, but I guess now that I thought about it, I had just called him Troy. Though I didn't see how this piece of information was conducive to us getting horizontal.

His lips rested against my ear, his breath tickled my skin. "Hmmmm, so now that has me curious."

His beautiful eyes seared me. My body wondered if he was going to touch me in a way I needed, and my brain needed to know what he had meant. Internally, I was mess. I was both turned on and confused. "Curious about what?"

"About how you are going to scream out my name when I fuck you."

I swallowed, hard. "Are you going to fuck me, Troy Harris?"

"You bet your ass I am. Let's go."

I HONESTLY TRIED TO FIGHT THIS. NO, REALLY, I DID. IT'S NOT LIKE I hadn't fantasized about the five hundred ways I could fuck Megs. Hell, just seeing her and knowing the possibility was off the table had been torture. Of course, I'm not a fucking deviant who can't think with anything but his dick, so I kept that shit locked down and pretended like my cock didn't get hard every time she walked into the room.

See, apart from my pact with Dan, I actually really liked Megs. I mean *genuinely* liked her, and the last thing I wanted to do was make shit weird between the two of us. So, while I *wanted* Megs in the biblical sense of the word, it was the other shit she offered that actually made me sit up and take notice. She was funny and smart and wasn't scared to stand up for herself. She had also been a sweetheart to Dan when Ash had broken up with him. That brand of kindness, the kind that doesn't attach strings, it isn't just rare in our world— it's almost non-existent. There's always something, some fine print bullshit that came with the preverbal *free lunch*. Megs, she was one of the exceptions. As I said rare, and there was no way I would do anything to disrespect her.

However, she was now offering herself to me on a fucking

platter and as pathetic as it sounded, I didn't have the fucking strength to turn her down. Telling me that she wanted to come with my cock inside her flipped a switch in me that I had no hope of controlling. Shit, now it was all I could think about and I couldn't even remember all those reasons for *not* having sex with her.

I should be saying no, be a better man and tell her this would be a mistake but my mouth wouldn't say the words. My dick …well it was already wondering why the fuck it had taken us this long to get to this point. I tilted her chin so I could get a better look at her, see if maybe there was some indecision in those drop-dead gorgeous eyes. Nothing. Not even a hint of freaking hesitation stared back at me.

Her perfect tits heaved up and down as she breathed heavily, and if I had any willpower left in me, that vision alone ensured that it took the expressway out of here. Without talking, I snaked my hand around her waist, her eyes widening as I pulled her close to my body and lead her down the stairs back to the Gen Pop part of the club. She didn't fight me, keeping in step as we sifted through the bodies that lined the space between the blood red walls.

"Where are we going?" she asked, her eyes darting between the crowd and me as we continued along our way.

I could tell from her tone she was uninitiated in what was about to go down.

She may have talked a good game, but the quick-fuck-thing obviously wasn't her usual speed. Megs was different and I liked that she probably hadn't done this before with someone else. It shouldn't have mattered, but it did. Juicing me up even more with the prospect.

She wasn't looking to advertise what we were about to do for status points. Nor was looking to sink her claws in and get a ring from me.

It excited me that she wanted to go there with me, knowing she was about as far from a groupie as I could get.

Fucking me right now, in the club hadn't been her suggestion. I was being an asshole and I knew it and yet, the chance to change her mind was not an option. I'd given her that, and she hadn't seemed keen, so now it was all about doing what both of us seemed to be starving for. And no, I'm not being fucking dramatic. Starving is how I felt.

She was beautiful and sexy and I'd stared at her for months, pushing down the urge to kiss those lips and sink my cock into her. Months, I'd convinced myself not to go there, needing a cold shower after seeing her and a fucking pep talk as to why we weren't going down that road. There was no fucking way we *weren't* doing this.

"You're playing with fire, Megs; and I'm not feeling very gentlemanly right now." I hissed through my clenched jaw, my balls so tight I thought for sure they were going to explode.

"Are you going to fuck me on the dance floor, Troy Harris?" Her eyes lit up in a weird excitement that made me almost consider it as a possibility.

"Not interested in giving anyone else the pleasure tonight, sweetheart, just you."

"Oh." Her beautiful lips formed an O to back up the wide-eyed expression as the penny finally dropped.

We walked past the security and straight out the front door. I spied the Suburban parked up against the curb, TJ leaning up against the hood shooting the breeze with one of the bouncers.

"Hey, Troy, you looking to leave already? Ms. Winters, you ok?" TJ looked at us suspiciously, like we'd suddenly grown extra heads.

"Yeah man, just need the keys." I gave him a look not to argue with me and held out my hand. It wasn't the first time one of us had commandeered the ride for something other than transportation; it just had been awhile.

TJ eyed my hands around Megs's waist and hesitantly pulled out the keys from his pocket. He didn't give me any lip, but he was far from liking the idea. His death stare translated the you-better-know-what-the-fuck-you're-doing without the need for an audible. It didn't take a brain surgeon to work out what we were up to, but he was smart enough to keep his trap shut, even if he thought that it was a bad idea.

Of course it was a bad idea, it was full-blow idiotic. Megs and I were about to get down and dirty in a fucking car while our two best friends were ignorantly partying no more than five hundred feet away. This wasn't going to be some hit-and-run. She wasn't just a girl who I wanted to fuck, we'd already established that when it came to Megs, it went beyond just the physical. Not that my dick wanted to hear the argument right now. We were both going to have to play nice after the fact, and pretend we hadn't seen each other naked. The fall-out if shit went bad had the potential to be fucking huge and yet none of those reasons seemed good enough to stop me.

I hit the keyless entry on the remote, the door lock popped open as I guided Megs to the passenger side door.

"You ready?" I pulled open the door and waited for her to climb inside the cabin. Part of me waited for her to tell me she'd changed her mind and to take her back inside the club.

She slid her toned legs into the car as her ass sunk into the seat, biting her lip seductively. "Let's go." She yanked the door I had been holding open and shut it. I watched through the glass from my place on the sidewalk as she fastened her seatbelt.

Ok then, no second thoughts. Good to know. I walked around to the driver's side and climbed in. My ass barely hitting the soft leather seat and I cranked the ignition.

I shifted into drive, reaching around for the seat belt as we eased away from the curb into the flow of traffic.

"Are you taking me home?" Megs shot me a sideways glance as the lights of the club faded in the rearview.

"Nope, we aren't making it that far." I hung a right and pulled into a narrow one-way street. I wasn't even sure if it was a legitimate street or if it just an alley used to facilitate deliveries for the businesses that backed onto this narrow strip of asphalt. My care factor on the matter was less than zero, other than thanking God that it existed.

The car jerked as I hit the brakes and shifted into park, stepping on the emergency break as the car continued to idle. My head swiveled to Megs, her eyes wide as she surveyed the alley before she turned and looked at me, her hand slowly moving down her side to unfasten her restraint. *Good idea.* I hit the eject button on mine and let the seat belt slide off as I killed the engine.

"You want to go into the back?" I leaned over the console and brushed her cheek with my thumb. Translation. You sure you want to do this? While my balls had reached Defcon 1, I wasn't going to be a complete asshole. It was bad enough I was about to fuck her in a car on some dead-end street, I wasn't going to do this without giving her one last out if she wanted to take it.

She didn't answer, instead she moved closer and slammed those sweet lips on mine. Well fuck me. No seriously, fuck me. My dick punched out in protest against the fly of my jeans as she opened her mouth and allowed my tongue to slide inside. It was better than I imagined. Her hungry mouth opening wider as her tongue wrestled with mine, my hand having a mind of its own reached up, palming one of her tits. She whimpered as I thumbed over the material of her dress and teased her nipple, the peak rising to the occasion with very little encouragement.

"In the back," I groaned against her mouth. I wanted unrestricted access to that body and the front seat wasn't even close to cutting it.

She pulled back, her hand reached up against mine as I kneaded her tit. "That feels so good." Her eyes watched me closely as I continued to play.

"I can make it better. C'mon Megs, jump into the back." I reluctantly moved my hand away and cracked open the driver's side door. My already rock-hard dick throbbed in my pants, wanting to know what the hold up was.

Megs followed suit, both of us exiting the front seat and moving into the back. The car's back doors slammed in unison as we scrambled onto the bench seat. My hands sliding up her legs at fucking warp speed as they made their way to her ass.

She was just as enthusiastic as she clawed at my shirt as I hauled her onto my lap and attacked her mouth. Her lips opened, allowing my tongue to slide inside, the invasion far from gentle. She moaned into my mouth as she rocked against my hard-on, my hands slid from her ass to her naked thighs as I tried to lift her dress.

Megs continued to writhe in my lap, the friction making my eyes water as I hovered between sweet pleasure and motherfucking torture. I wanted to tear the clothes from my body and torch them purely on the fact they were hindering shit right now.

Her nails clawed down my chest and abs with enough pressure I was sure it was going to leave a mark, and damn if the prospect didn't make me even more excited. We made out like a pair of fucking teenagers under the bleachers, dry humping each other with enough intensity I wasn't sure if I was going to blow my load or get the worst case of chafing known to man. Either way, I wasn't stopping. With her dress pulled up out of the way, my hand once again moved to her ass, my fingers making contact with bare skin. Fuck. I moved a little further along her skin in my quest to discover if she had decided to go commando or not, and came across a thin strap of fabric. G-String. Very fucking nice. I yanked the strip to the side, allowing my finger to slid down the seam of her ass and watched her shudder as I travelled further down. The nails that were previously embedded in my skin were now wrestling with my belt; the leather flicked me as she violently tore it from my jeans. She didn't stop, ripping open my fly while we remained lip-locked and I teased her ass.

My cock sprung free as she pushed down my boxers, my hard-on hitting my stomach. I was so turned on I could barely speak, but there was no way I was ready for this to be over without tasting her first. I lifted her off of me and Megs yelped as I tossed her down onto the seat. The confusion on her face priceless as I smiled and then gently parted her thighs.

"Oh!" The tension in her legs relaxed as my tongue lapped at the edge of her G-string. "But I want to touch your cock," she half-moaned as I pulled across the material and flicked across her hot, wet center.

"You can touch it all you want." The edges of my lips curved before I lowered my mouth back down and sucked gently on her clit. "You want me to stop?" I asked, slowly sliding a finger inside her. "Megs, holy hell, you are so wet." My finger was instantly coated as I slid in another. It was a challenge not to throw this game plan out the window and just move to a bootleg play, the one where my dick got involved. It had been screaming to get into the game since she mentioned the word "cock" and was wondering why the fuck it was still on the bench. Easy there buddy, you'll get your chance to play, but not until I fucking make her come with my mouth.

"Don't stop," she moaned, her hips lifting closer to my mouth as I resumed licking and sucking her clit while I gently finger-fucked her. "Oh God, please don't stop." Her plea unnecessary, 'cause I had no intention of stopping. I continued to work her over with my mouth, her body bucking against me as I tried to ignore the pain in my balls. They too, like my dick, begging to get in on the action.

"Oh fuck," screamed Megs, her voice echoing around the car as I moved my other hand to her ass, gently thumbing over it while my fingers stretched her pussy. One last flick of my tongue was all it took and her legs clamped around my head and she screamed. Her body convulsed as I felt the orgasm rip through her, her pussy pulsing around my fingers while I continued to gently lick her. Each pass of my tongue made her body shake as I teased every last inch of pleasure from her. Not going to lie, watching her pant with my head between her thighs was even better than I'd imagined.

"Oh. My. God." She paused between each word. "That. Was. Amazing." Her chest heaved up and down as she sucked in air, both of us still mostly clothed despite my dick poking proudly out of my boxers.

"I think it's time these came off," I gently slid my fingers out of her and pulled at her G-string taking it with me as I moved my hand down her legs. I threw them onto the other seat as I spread her legs open and got a better look. Her glistening, wet pussy was fucking beautiful and I had to stop myself from going down on her again, my fingers circling her opening as I shuffled up onto my knees.

"Holy shit!" Her eyes widened as she stared down at my crotch. A slight look of fear flicked through her face as she caught sight of my cock.

"Well, you do know how to make a guy feel special, don't you?" I laughed as held it for her to get a better look; my cock jerked the minute it made contact with my hand.

"Is that metal? In your—?" She couldn't peel her eyes away as she stared at the thick metal ring that circled the tip to just below the head of my cock. It wasn't the first time I'd caught a girl off guard. It's not like I'd broadcasted that shit in *Rolling Stone* Magazine, nope. It was on a purely need-to-know basis. Sure, the rumors were out there, so on more than one occasion, girls had asked to see it backstage. Their eagerness to see my dick had almost convinced Dan to take the plunge. We got right to the piercing shop too, but he chickened out when a dude tapped the chair and told him to pull down his pants.

"It's a piercing. Trust me, I think you'll enjoy it." I shoved my jeans down, reaching into my back pocket and pulling out a condom.

"Did it hurt?" she asked, genuine interest flicking through those beautiful eyes.

"A needle getting driven through the head of your dick sure didn't tickle, but it wasn't that bad." I was beginning to wonder if show-and-tell was as far as we were going to get.

"Can I touch it?"

"Well, I was hoping you would." I grinned, gently stroking the length of my shaft as I brought it closer, sitting on the seat beside her.

So maybe we weren't just going to be playing show-and-tell. Excellent.

Her fingers tiptoed up the length of my shaft before she curled her hand around my length. "That's so fucking sexy, Troy Harris." She grinned as she slowly stroked me.

I eased back into the chair, her fingers around me felt so fucking magical, I had to fight the urge not to blow my load all over her hand. "Megs, you just came on my mouth. I think we're on a first name basis now."

"I want to lick it; I want to feel it in my mouth." She moved closer, not bothering to wait for permission. She bent down and took me into her mouth in one big thrust.

"Jesus, Megs," I hissed as she wrapped her lips around the head of my cock. Her tongue flicked around my shaft before circling around the tip, her teeth gently pulling on the ring. I'm not sure which deserved the greater applause, her initiative on the blowjob or that fact she was sending me into outer space with that sweet mouth of hers. The jury was still out, but what I did know is — the deeper she took me into her mouth, and the more she sucked me, the harder it was for me to maintain any type of control. Fuck, at this rate I was going to *need* her to repeat my full fucking name 'cause I sure as hell was having trouble remembering it.

Caught between wanting to ask her to stop and begging her to keep going, I gently pulled on her hair and freed my cock from her mouth. There was no way I was going to come without making her eyes roll back into her head at least one last time. I grabbed the condom that had fallen out of my hand and onto the seat beside me and tore open the foil. She watched as I pulled out the rubber and rolled it down my hard-on, licking her lips as her eyes followed my hand, smoothing the latex over my piercing and all the way down to the base. Damn, if there wasn't a part of me that regretted pulling out of those beautiful lips.

"Do you know how long I've wanted to do this?" She moved onto my lap and straddled me. "I almost want to pinch myself to make sure it's real." Her face inches from mine.

With my hand firmly around my shaft, I teased her pussy with the head of my cock. "Does this feel real?" The ball from the ring hit her clit and made her whimper.

"Troy," she moaned. "Please don't stop." Her eyes closed as I slowly pushed into her. Not a lot— just barely an inch— trust me, that was a fucking exercise in restraint if ever there was.

"Holy shit!" Her eyes flew open and I felt her pussy clamp around the head of my cock, the only part of me which was actually inside of her.

"You ok?" I asked, steadying her hips to stop myself from pushing any deeper.

"Yes, I'm ok. It just feels... So amazing."

"It will feel a lot better once I'm all the way in, but I'm going to need you to relax. I don't want to hurt you."

Megs dropped her head so that her forehead rested on mine. "I don't care if it hurts, I want it all. Deep. Hard. I. Want. It. All." Her voice so full of fucking want, it was like I'd been smacked in the jaw.

That grand plan I had —to take this slow—yeah that shit just sailed right out the window as I pulled her down onto me and sunk deep into her in one hit. She moaned and I blew out a curse as her tight wet pussy clamped around me like a fist. So fucking tight.

"Fuck, Megs." I slowly breathed out as I started to move, my hands on her hips guiding her as I picked up the tempo. She quickly got on the same page and met each one of my thrusts with one of her own, twisting her pelvis as she lifted up before slamming back down hard. I grabbed the top of her dress and pulled it down, needing to suck on one of her gorgeous tits. The bra she had on underneath was some sheer fucking mesh that I was sure I could rip just by looking at it. I pulled down the front, rolling her nipple between my fingers and guided it to my mouth. We were panting so much, the windows had fogged up.

I slammed into her, harder and faster each time. The gloves were off, and I couldn't have been gentle if I'd tried. The fact we'd both wanted this but had kept our distance had just made it that much more intense. My mouth moved from her tit to her mouth and I slammed my lips on hers. I felt desperate, like I couldn't get deep enough into her, it was fucking euphoric and maddening at the same time. She bit my lip as I pulled her down, my hands once again around her perfect ass. She bucked against me, wild with each thrust and I knew she was close.

"Touch yourself, Megs. I want to see you finger that amazing pussy of yours while I fuck you."

"Oh," she moaned as her hand moved from behind my neck, to slither down her body and between her legs. Some girls got weird when you ask them to do it, but Megs didn't even miss a beat as her fingers twisting over her clit while I continued to pound her. It was fucking beautiful, watching her touch herself with my cock inside her, the tips of her fingers making contact with my dick as I moved in and out. I couldn't look away. It was the hottest thing I'd seen in a long time, more so 'cause she was so into it. The fact that it was Megs elevated it to eleven.

"Troy, I'm going to come." Megs closed her eyes and her fingers moved faster, her body tense as she rode me.

"That's it, Megs. I want to feel how hard you come." I moved my fingers across the crease of her ass, teasing it before slowly sliding in a finger. Megs's eyes flung open as I invaded her ass, her pussy milking my dick as she came hard. The pulses she sent up my shaft giving me no hope to hold off any longer as I exploded into her. "Fuck." I groaned as my load hit the tip of the condom and I wasn't sure it didn't tear the fucking thing in half.

Megs collapsed against me, her head on my shoulder as she sucked in each breath. "Wow, that was incredible." Her muffled voice sent tiny vibrations against my skin.

My finger slowly slid out of her ass, her body shaking as what was left of her orgasm rode its way out. "That was more than incredible." I tried to rein in my own breathing as I wrapped my arms around her. "Megs, you're fucking amazing."

"Aww, Troy Harris, you'll make me blush." She hid her face against my chest as she giggled.

"Really? After what we just did, me talking is what makes you blush?" I couldn't help but laugh. She was definitely not the *good girl* I had her pegged for. Hell no. She was one of these girls who looked all straight laced and turned into a nympho in the bedroom. Shit. Just thinking about the crazy things she might be up for made my dick twitch, which conveniently was still buried inside of her.

"We should get back." Megs sighed as the reality of the situation hit us both. Sure, this isn't awkward. We now had to go pretend like we *hadn't* just had fucked each other's brains out and be social. Yep. This was going to suck. Hard Core.

"Yeah. You're probably right." I rubbed her back wondering if I should say something. I mean, we hadn't really discussed what was going to happen after. Sure, she had said all it was going to be was sex, but I still felt like an asshole fucking her in the car, in some alley. Shit, we hadn't even gotten totally undressed, screwing like two crazy animals in heat. Not my best moment, that's for sure.

Megs lifted off me, her teeth biting down on her lip as I slid out. "You don't regret it, do you?" I guess she felt the weird vibe as well.

My eyes were firmly locked on hers. "Are you kidding me? Hell no. I'm just trying not be a complete douchebag and ask if that was a onetime deal."

She smiled, obviously pleased I was looking for a repeat. "You would do it again? With me?"

My hand moved up and down her thigh, her skin so soft it almost didn't feel real. "Megs, I'd do it again right now if we had the time. You were incredible. I know I'm probably breaking all kinds of rules right now but yeah, I really want you to come home with me tonight."

She relaxed, sinking into the seat beside me and smiled. "I'd like that. A lot. I guess if it's the same night, technically it's still the same one time. Right?"

"I'm all about the technicalities." Especially ones that meant I was going to be able to do *that* again.

"Good, so we do this tonight and then we both move on." She fished her underwear off the seat and started to smooth out her dress. "No one has to know, nothing has to get weird and we can just go back to the way things were."

So that was the plan. One night. One night to fuck each other's brains out and then we'd go back to friends. I didn't even care how fucking shady it sounded, I wanted it. I wanted her. One night and then maybe we both could get over this twisted infatuation we seemed to have. One thing was for sure, I was going all out and making it count. Tonight she was going to scream out my name so many times she was going to be sick of it and I was going to enjoy every second of it. And while we were both going to be moving on, she would never forget it.

5

Megan

HOLY—EXPLETIVE-EXPLETIVE-MY-BRAIN-IS-SO-FRIED-I-CAN'T-THINK
—Hell, I just had sex with Troy Harris. Yep, the use of his first and last name was still required, if only to try and get my head around it. Did a twister suddenly pick me up and transport me to OZ? The absence of ruby slippers told me no. It was like the ultimate crime and I had gotten away with the robbery of the century. I've been a bad, bad girl, officer go ahead and take my prints.

The whole trip back to the club I couldn't even think straight. My thoughts jumped in a suspended state of what-the-fuck-just-happened. Oh, and I couldn't sit straight either, but that was on account of his HUGE cock.

The size-thirteen shoes should have probably been the tip off; his hands were big too, so it would stand to reason... And yet I was still unprepared for what he was packing.

Damn. Was I going to be walking funny? It would totally be worth it. And while we were on the subject of "ta-dah" moments, that big giant ring in the head of his aforementioned huge cock just about made me choke. Literally, as in I couldn't freaking breath. Me and my friend, *Google* were going to be having some serious words when I got home. How the hell could I have not known about that? And more importantly, how could I have ever orgasmed without it in the past? What would possess a guy to pierce *that* part of his body, I'll never know, but I am saying a silent thank-you to the person who had the balls—no pun intended— to start that trend. If the talented penis wasn't enough to get me on my knees and sing Hallelujah, the *other* things he had in his bag of tricks, sure did.

So, the anal play. Yeah, didn't see that one coming. Sure, guys had asked me to go *down that road* before, but the answer had always been a resounding, oh-hell-no. Wow. Boy, was I wrong. I'm not going to lie and say that at first the invasion didn't make my eyes bug-out like an old school cartoon character, but that uncertainty lasted about a quarter of a second till the freaking mind blowing orgasm rolled in. It was less like a wave and more like a tsunami. If I'd had pockets, I would be checking them for sand.

I'm not sure if that was some kind of signature move, or if he just felt inspired, but the man had some serious talent when it came to pleasuring a woman. Between his hands, his mouth and his cock, I was seriously wondering how the hell a man like that was legal. Maybe the ultimate crime was his. There sure as hell would be no police report filed by me.

"You doin' okay?" Troy stopped the Suburban in front of *Panic*, the short ride back to the club over.

"Uh-huh." My head nodded slightly more enthusiastically than I would have liked.

"You just look a little…" His truth serum eyes seared me. There would be no controlling my mouth.

"Well-fucked?" Was what I'd offered. Not like it was a lie, but I could have been a little smoother. Nothing else seemed to fit, so I was going to stick with that.

His low laugh rumbled through the cabin of the car. "I was going to say *antsy*. I'm not good with you being so unsettled. Makes me think I didn't take care of what needed to be taken care of, you get me?"

He leaned across the console all cool-and-unaffected as the smell of sex and his cologne assaulted the air around me. It just didn't seem fair. He wasn't allowed to be talented, good looking, able to produce mind-blowing orgasm *and* be cool. Greedy much?

"Oh, it was taken care of. Twice." My head bobbled like an idiot as I tried to play off the goof-ball grin that was plastered across my face. No one was fooled. "We should get back inside." Thank you mouth for finally kicking in. Look at me acting close to normal. He'd never know it was all an act. Move along folks, nothing to see here.

"Yeah, they've probably noticed by now." Troy eyed TJ who had walked around the passenger side door and opened it for me.

"Ms. Winters." TJ spared me the judgmental stare down or the cold shoulder. I nodded my appreciation, as a gigantic hug thanking him would have been overkill.

"Ready?" Troy appeared beside me as TJ helped me from the car to the sidewalk. For that, the big burly security-guard-come-driver deserved another thank you. The length of my dress hem not conducive to climbing in and out of a tank-like vehicle.

Who can get out of a car *that* size *that* quickly? Seriously, was he Batman? "Yep." My mouth popped on the P as I adjusted my dress and added *stealthy* to Troy's list of attributes. The list was extensive.

"Here you go, man." The car keys flew out of Troy's hand and landed in TJ's steady palm before he pocketed them. The extent of the exchange limited to a few grunts and a nod as Troy lead me back to the main entrance of the club. Maybe they had a code? Whatever, it was a mystery that didn't need solving tonight, certainly not by me.

"Just so we're clear on our story." My voice rose to compensate for the loud mayhem we had stepped into. "Crappy week at work. We went to the bar, had a few drinks and then I need to step outside for some air." Sounded plausible. Yeah, let's go with that.

"Sure, but we never did discuss your *crappy* week." Troy's hand pressed into my lower back as he guided me up the stairs. The same stairs we had neglected to climb earlier. He leaned into me, "I'm not buying it's just a tough case load." His hot breath in my ear was making all kinds of parts of me tingle and I had to remind myself not to press myself up against his body and bury my tongue in his mouth.

"I'm fine." The rehearsed response was automatic when it

came to work talk. The added shrug wasn't. I couldn't have been any less convincing, and for once it hadn't been my mouth that let me down. Kudos traitorous body, you are now on my shit list.

"You know you can talk to me, right? I'm pretty good at keeping secrets." Troy's lips spread into a grin as he reached the top of the stairs.

Well then. So, my plan to inoculate myself with a good dose of Troy Harris and be cured was a bust. It certainly didn't help that he was being so sweet, and that grin he had going on just made me want him more. Maybe I needed more exposure. Like I literally needed to fuck him out of my system? I certainly owed it to myself to explore the options.

"I'm fine, promise." I made a cross-my-heart motion over my chest and walked to the entrance of the VIP lounge area. The bouncer waving us through the minute he laid eyes on Troy.

"There you are!" Ash rushed to greet us. Her eyes were red and puffy, her mascara *less* enhancing her lashes and *more* giving her smudgy panda eyes. And unless you are *Courtney Love,* that look is not intentional.

This was certainly not the welcome I thought we would be walking into. Dan followed slowly behind her. He looked guiltily responsible; the hands shoved into his front pockets and the dopey look on his face a dead giveaway.

"Ash, are you ok?" I grabbed her hand and shot a death-glare at Dan. "What did you do?" So help me if he'd made her cry by doing or saying something stupid, I was going to end him. I don't think I could go through another one of their break-ups. The last one had almost sent *me* into therapy.

"Relax, Megs. It's not what you think." Dan circled his hands around Ash's waist and pulled her against his body, she didn't fight him so I'm guessing that's a good thing. Someone needed to start talking.

Ash dried the corners of her eyes with the tips of her fingers. "Dan asked me to marry him."

Huh? All muscle control of my mouth was lost as it fell open in disbelief. My eyelids peeling back to their capacity was also a nice touch. *Wow.* Did *not* see that one coming. Marriage? How long were we gone? Had Marty McFly shown up in his Delorean and we'd somehow time travelled? Maybe Troy's penis had an in-built flux capacitor and zipped us through the time-space continuum. His talented cock knew no end.

"What? Just now?" My shaking head complemented the attractive facial paralysis I had going on as I tried to wrap my brain around what I'd obviously missed.

Troy, who obviously hadn't shared my stunned reaction, moved in front of me. "Congrats, man. Good move on making it legal, it will be harder for her to dump your sorry ass when she finally realizes she can do better." He shook Dan's hand and gave Ash a warm hug.

Dan was unmistakably pleased, the smile barely contained on his face as he patted Troy on the back. "Thanks, man. You know you're going to have to be suited up and stand beside me as my best man, right?"

"Wouldn't miss it for the world, dude. Whatever you need."

My brain kicked into gear and demanded I say something. My best friend just announced she was getting married and I had been standing there speechless while the revelry went on around me. *You're happy for her. This is a good thing. Congratulations.* All acceptable responses, pick one...any one! "Wow. Congratulations, Ash. I'm so happy for you." Thank you, sweet baby Jesus.

Ash beamed, her excitement and happiness palpable as she tugged on my arm. "And Megs, I need you to be my maid of honor. I know it's kind of soon, but I know Dan's the one. There's never going to be another guy for me."

"Of course I will. I would love nothing more than to stand beside you." It was a given that I would be there in whatever way I was needed. Being partnered with Troy? Time will tell if that was a blessing or a curse. "I'm so glad you're happy, that's all that matters. Who cares how long it's been? When you know, you know. So which one of you two is going to spill the details? Is there a ring?" My mouth spewed every random thought as I grabbed Ash's left hand and noticed a sparkling diamond was absent from her ring finger.

Dan held up his hand as he entered the *ring* debate. "There ain't no way in hell I'm choosing an engagement ring without Ash's input. I know Stone and James took a knee with a box full of carats, but I wanted to be sure that whatever she wears is something that she loves." He punctuated his stance by pulling her in close and kissing her neck.

Ash smiled. "The ring isn't important. I don't even need one."

"Yeah, you do." Dan made it clear where he sat on the *no ring* stance. "No future wife of mine is going to be without an engagement ring and don't even think about the money. So you can either choose a ring you like or you get one the size of a baseball when I go buy one myself."

"I don't think he's bending on this one, Ash; might be easier just to take the hit and get the bauble." Troy winked with a laugh. Ash nodded, agreeing it was probably a losing battle.

While their touching exchange was endearing, I was still no closer to know how or why Dan decided to pop the question in a club. That information was something I needed to know. Not that it was any of my business, but that had never stopped me before. I was an information girl. It was a sickness and I was very unwell. "So... getting back to the proposal. You know I need details."

"Well, to be honest I hadn't really planned it." Dan took the reigns on this one as he explained how he decided they needed to become husband and wife. "But being here reminded me of that night and how it all started."

It was evident in the telling how much he loved her. My heart swooned despite the absence of rose petals and sunsets —and probably no bended knees either—but he was a fly-by-the-seat-of-your-pants kind of guy so I wouldn't expect his proposal to be anything less. I felt my eyes water as I looked at my friend, so happy and in love with a guy who adored and loved her like she deserved. It was fitting that she was finally getting her little slice of happily ever after.

"I'm not sure if that's romantic or kind of creepy." My eyes blinked rapidly, trying to keep my tears at bay.

Ash joined me on my journey to Tearsville, her fingertips trying to salvage what was left of her eye make-up. She needn't have bothered. It was a lost cause. "Oh hush, Megs, it's beautiful and it's perfect."

"Ok babe, you're going to need to stop crying." It had been a long time since I'd heard Dan sound so serious, he stroked Ash's arm with concern. "I know you said you're happy, but the tears are starting to mess with my head. Last time I made you cry, you left me."

"Aww Dan, stop. You're going to make me cry now." His words plunged my own make-up at risk as my eyes started to water. Damn him for being so incredibly sweet.

"Ok, ladies," Troy waved over a waitress and ordered some champagne. "No more crying. What we need to is celebrate."

He was a God. Troy, I meant. His intervention saved me from a full emotional outburst that would have unleashed my unattractive crying face. No one needed to see that. He would *so* be getting a blowjob for that act of kindness; I was a really ugly crier.

We moved over to one of the vacant couches, coupling off as we sat down. It should have felt weird— sitting next to him, acting normal—but it didn't. Instead we laughed and chatted about the impending nuptials as the waitress handed out our champagne.

"To my best friend, who's been more like a brother to me." Troy held up his glass. "I'm so freaking glad you didn't waste time and asked the best woman who ever walked into your life to marry you."

His smile made my heart skip a beat before he continued. "Ash, I know we haven't known each other long but I can tell you are the real deal, and I couldn't be happier to have you as a sister-in-law. Sorry to tell you, but you marry this loser, you get us as well. It's all good though, 'cause it means you can stare at Alex's ass anytime you want now."

We laughed— Ash and I. She *had* stared at Alex's ass so it was funny. Dan didn't share the amusement as he shot Troy a dirty look and flipped him the bird. "I hate you, asshole."

"Back at ya, sunshine." Troy grinned back.

"To Dan and Ash." Troy paused before adding, "Nothing but love for both of you. Congratulations."

"Dan and Ash." The words left my mouth with very little effort. Troy had said it all so I showed my support by taking a drink. It was the least I could do and would keep me from declarations of how amazing Troy was. I was thinking it but the world didn't need to know. Best I pin that thought for later.

The drinks flowed freely, which could have been dangerous. My hands seemed to spend more and more time on Troy Harris; his arm, his knee, his thigh. No one noticed and more to the point, no one stopped me. I would have stopped had he asked, but he didn't so I didn't. Did that sound right? Probably not. Oh look, another glass of champagne.

"So you wanna team up, beat the two of them into submission if either of them fucks this up?" Troy gently bumped my shoulder—*he* was touching *me*— as we watched Dan and Ash move from the couch and onto the dance floor.

"Yes. I think that's part of the job description when you sign up for the wedding party." My voice came out breathier than I would have liked, possibly on account that I wanted to nuzzle against his chest.

Troy's arms stretched out over the top of the couch, his skin making contact with my back. The shiver travelled down my spine, all the way to my toes. "Funny how we worried about them noticing us being gone and they couldn't have cared less."

Yes, no one had noticed. Let's go back to car was what I had wanted to say but instead the watered down version of, "Yeah, I guess we lucked out," was what I actually said.

It was a compromise and it meant I didn't sound like a nympho, so positives all around. Yay! "Did you still want to... get together...later?" My voice was unsteady, either champagne or concern that our night of debauchery was going to be put on a permanent hold, to blame. Best to be prepared.

Troy's hand slid off the couch and gently caressed my back. "Of course I do, why wouldn't I?" His smile convinced me that he had no plans to sleep alone.

I stifled a moan, allowing more skin to connect with his hand. "I just wanted to be sure you hadn't changed your mind."

"Changed my mind? I'm the best man, you're the maid of

honor. I'm pretty sure there is some unwritten law that we have to sleep together." There was a smile but no humor in his voice.

"I'm fairly sure there is no such law." My eyelids may have fluttered; I couldn't be sure as the silliness of my words made me giggle.

"Going to have to disagree with you, Megs, respectfully of course." Troy's hand slowly slid down the couch to rest on my hip. "I'm not going to be held accountable if you doom their marriage 'cause you didn't follow the rules."

"Oh, so that's the reason?" My chin tilted as my body relaxed against his. Cooling it would have been the smart thing to do. Dan and Ash could walk up at any moment, we were in a public place and I was practically in his lap. Did I care? Nope, and I couldn't make myself either. He was intoxicating. My lips moved closer to his ear. "You afraid we're going to curse them if we don't sleep together?"

Troy turned his head, his lips hovered above mine and I was sure he was going to kiss me. "No." He paused, his voice husky and low. "The reason is 'cause I want to own that body of yours tonight. I couldn't give a rat's ass about anything else other than making sure that happens."

IT WAS SOMETIME AROUND TWO IN THE MORNING WHEN WE FINALLY
wrapped it up and piled into the Suburban. That was about three
hours later than I would have liked. Patience and virtue—yeah I
didn't get the memo. Instead I concentrated on what it would feel
like to have my hands on her ass while she rode my cock; it gave
me the incentive to hang back and let the night play out.

Dan and Ash got cozy on the row of seats in front of us while
Megs and I took the ones in the back. Two things it had been good
for. One, the two lovebirds didn't get an eyeful of my hard-on. And
two, my hands were able to stay busy on Megs without any raised
eyebrows or suspicion. And busy they were.

That dress she was wearing deserved a standing ovation,
'cause other than looking outstanding on her, it didn't hinder my
access. My fingers got on a first name basis with her thong while
she rubbed the front of my jeans with her hand. It was a beautiful
thing.

The little moans she had going on didn't help either. They
weren't loud enough for our audience to hear. Nope, she'd saved
that privilege for me alone. Almost made me forget where the
fuck I was, reaching for her mouth with my own on more than one

occasion. That probably would have required some explanation. My tongue down her throat? Yeah, really no way getting around that unless she needed mouth-to-mouth resuscitation.

Both Ash and Megs had both consumed their fair share of drinks at the club. If the collection of champagne bottles hadn't been a clue, the giggling sure was. Sober? Not likely. And while they weren't loaded, they were fairly lit up.

Of course being the stand-up guy that I am, I kindly offered Megs the use of my guest room so she wouldn't have to go back her place alone. She happily accepted. The brownie points I'd won from Ash were a nice touch, my concern for Megs's well-being, commended even. I know, I'm a regular fucking saint.

The elevator ride up to the Penthouse had been excruciating. Being in such a confined space and not being able to do anything, yeah that was brutal. I had to mentally recite the batting order for the Yankees to try and calm the raging hard-on I had going on.

The minute we'd said our goodbyes and Dan and Ash disappeared through their front door, I grabbed Megs and pushed her up against the wall. I'd waited as long as I cared to and I wanted her mouth, and every other part of her on me.

She gave me zero resistance as my tongue continued to fuck her mouth. That was the preshow as I fumbled with my keys and opened my front door, both of us ready for the main event.

The door slamming behind us was all we needed to take it to the next level, clawing each other like savages. We didn't even make it to the bedroom. Instead we dropped onto the hardwood floor of my entranceway and tore our clothes from our bodies like they were on fire. I'd take her to my bed later, what I needed was to get my mouth on her— every part of her.

Her neck, her tits, her thighs— my tongue got real familiar with it all, and she was almost begging by the time my mouth hit her pussy. Her back bowed off the floor as I continued to tease her, invading her, making her squirm. She twisted beneath me, changing her position and demanded to suck my cock. I wasn't about to argue as I turned to give her access, her hot lips wrapping around me made me lose my damn mind. I'd had my fair share of blowjobs, but the way she worked that mouth of hers had me convinced I'd been dealing with amateurs all these years. Good to know.

My thumb circled her clit as I pushed a finger inside her, my cock muffling her pleasured moan. The charge coming off our bodies would have been enough to power a small country. Energy crisis solved.

I felt her body tense as her pussy tightened around my fingers, her breathing erratic as she thrashed beneath me with my dick in her mouth. She was close, and so was I. The heat in my body rose as I fought a losing battle to prolong the inevitable. My dick made the decision that it had gone on long enough. "Megs, I'm going to come."

Her body convulsed as she beat me to it, every inch of her shook as I shot my load into her mouth. She continued to suck and swallow as I pulsed into her. Little muffled whimpers escaped from her lips as I drew out the last of her orgasm. My hands and mouth still busy between her legs.

It was awhile before we actually made it to my bedroom. Moving? That shit was obsolete for a good ten minutes while we both came down from the monumental sixty-nine in the entranceway.

Taking her to bed was high on my agenda, but it turns out all the good intentions in the world didn't count for shit. 'Cause after getting cozy on the floor for a while, my hard-on came back, interested as to why we weren't fucking yet. The bastard was out of control. Megs didn't seem to mind.

We'd made it about thirty feet. Which considering the backtrack to my discarded jeans by the doorway; it had been a fair effort. The condom was fished out of the pocket and onto my dick in record time. It was the rug on the living room floor that got pleasure of hosting *that* action. The couch had just been too fucking far.

That was followed up by a blowjob in the kitchen to which I happily reciprocated by going down on her in my study. Being that she was a psychologist, I'd assumed she appreciate the house tour with positive reinforcement. Who said I didn't pay attention in school?

By the time we eventually crawled onto the bed, the alarm clock on my nightstand was hinting the sun would soon be playing peek-a-boo. What hadn't changed with the flicking over of those florescent green digits was my need to take her again. She was like sexual heroin and I was a junkie with an unrelenting addiction.

We were both covered in sweat, panting, as I pounded into her from behind. Megs was on her hands and knees in front of me, my hands locked around her waist.

"That's it, fuck me," she screamed. "Harder, Troy Harris. I'm so close."

My thrusts deepened as I picked up speed. "Hard enough for you?" I pushed every inch of me into her, my finger once again sinking into her ass as she clawed the sheets.

"Oh. My. God," she screamed as her pussy gripped my cock, the pulsing sensation sending me over the edge as I came with her. Her body shook uncontrollably as muscle fatigue set in and she collapsed onto the mattress, pulling me down with her.

"Fuck, Megs." I rolled on to my side, taking her with me so I wouldn't crush her. "I can't believe you are *still* calling me Troy Harris." I laughed in between sucking breaths, pulling my finger from her ass.

"Yeah, that kind of slipped out." She shrugged. "I got caught up in the moment."

Her body shivered as I moved my hand up her side. "You cold?" I kissed her neck wrapping my arms around her. My A/C had kicked in at some point and was blowing cold air through the room.

"A little." She shuffled back against my chest. I liked it. A lot.

My dick slowly slid out of her and I pulled off the condom. The used latex reunited with the foil wrapper in the wastepaper basket beside my bed. More of their friends would probably be joining them later.

The comforter that had been kicked off the bed—courtesy of either her foot or mine— was quickly snagged by my hand and wrapped around us. My plans for not moving changed as my hands rubbed over her body. Goosebumps covered her damp skin. "You want to join me in the shower? Warm up a little?"

She turned to me and smiled. "Is this your attempt to fuck me in the shower?"

I couldn't help but laugh. It hadn't been my game plan but I liked her thinking. "Megs, I think we've got a good ten-fifteen minutes before I'll be operational again. No fucking. Just a shower."

"Sure, I'd like that."

The shower had been as promised— just a shower. We'd stood under the spray of the warm water, my cock stirring the minute my hand started soaping her. Up her body, down her body, other side, repeat. It was mechanical but necessary if I wanted to keep my word. Lathered up and shut up, I even washed and conditioned her hair, which had been a first.

Girls in the shower were usually a precursor to shower sex, so the experience had been a new one for me. Megs sure as hell wasn't making things easy either, the little noises she made while I massaged her head were putting my resolve to the test. Got me wondering if I couldn't make her come purely from washing her hair. It seemed she'd gotten almost as much pleasure when she'd washed my 'hawk, her fingers twisting through my hair while her wet, slippery body pressed against me. It was driving me insane and while the plan had been to get clean, all I could think about was getting dirty.

Done fantasizing about screwing her against the tiled wall of the shower, I cut the water and put myself out of my misery. The only rub she received was courtesy of a couple of over-sized towels. Her hands, not mine.

When it came to blow-drying her hair, I opted out. Sure, I would have loved to stay and watch a re-enactment of a *Whitesnake* video play out in my bathroom. Tits and hair flying wildly sounded like a good time, but my dick was having serious problems with the *look but don't touch* scenario I had us locked into.

So while she took care of *that,* I ripped the sheets from my mattress and freshened it up with a pair that weren't sporting our DNA. Managed to get in between them as well, leaving the dirty sheets I'd stripped piled in a corner. A run to the laundry wasn't on the cards. Not if it meant I'd risk missing the view. And what a view it was.

Megs stepped out of the bathroom, her hair doing that floaty thing around her shoulders, and the best part —she was naked. She didn't even do that lame-ass hand-wrap manoeuver to cover her tits or her pussy that some girls do. Thank Christ for that. She just strolled out with her head high and a smile on her face, crawling back into bed beside me. Oh, she also shot me a look that clued me in that the *hands off* thing I had going on was no longer working for her. This was not a problem for me and I was more than happy to continue playtime. Her lips tightly wrapped around my cock was a very nice start.

I wasn't sure how many times we'd fucked. It was irrelevant, but I do know I spent more of the night/morning inside of her than out. Not one of those times did the thought *I shouldn't be doing this* cross my mind. The sunlight cracked through the drapes, flooding the room, before we finally admitted defeat. Exhausted, I wrapped my arms around her and we both fell asleep.

I'M AN IDIOT. THE PLAN HAD BEEN— I HAVE SEX WITH TROY, I GET HIM out of my system and I move on. Simple. It's what I had convinced myself would cure this borderline obsession. It was basic psychology, like craving chocolate the minute you go on a diet purely because now you *can't* have it. My initial approach hadn't been affective. My taste of Troy had only stimulated the craving, not diminished it, which is why I decided on another approach. Binging. Getting my fill of Troy Harris so I would be sick of the sight of him. Literally screwing him out of my system. Sounds like a reasonable theory. Turned off by saturation. So binge I did. All. Night. Long.

It didn't take.

What the hell was wrong with me? Not only had I *not* cured my addiction slash infatuation, but I'd also reinforced how much I was attracted to him. It hadn't helped that he had been so freaking awesome, and funny, and sexy. Not to mention his amazing, long, hard co... Damn it! I was supposed to not be thinking about it and now all I can do is think about *it*. I wonder if I asked nicely if he'd let me take a mold for a dildo? Everyone is so DYI these days. That wouldn't be creepy at all. Yep. I was a self-diagnosed deviant nymphomaniac with addiction disorder. Glad all those years at Georgetown paid off, my parents must be so proud.

Reality check. It was not going to be so easy to just move on. I had even started to look for reasons why we weren't compatible. Surely that's the way to get over this silly crush. My investigation had been fruitful.

Troy Harris was a closet *Star Wars* fanatic. You heard right. Star. Wars. He had one tattoo dedicated to the *Dark Side* as well as one to the *Rebel Alliance* and they reflected each other on opposite parts of his arm. A representation of his inner light and dark. Kind of like a nerdy yin and yang. I should have been weirded out by this sci-fi, cult classic revelation; instead... I found it adorable.

The life-sized R2D2 in his kitchen, that was not cute. In fact, it had scared this shit of me. Who has movie memorabilia in their kitchen? See, there was something I could work with. Robot in the kitchen kicked off my mental tally of "cons."

And another thing, the man had no coffee in his apartment. None. Who doesn't have, at the very least, a rogue tin of *Folger's* hiding behind a prehistoric box of crackers? What if the Zombie apocalypse hit? I can tell you that the people *without* coffee would be the first suckers turned. Have you seen people in the morning before their cup of Joe? The caffeine would be the only thing that would distinguish *us* from the Walkers. Apparently Troy is not a coffee drinker. Gasp. I didn't know these people existed. Who doesn't drink coffee? I'm still trying to get a handle on that.

So two— flimsy at best— excuses as to why I shouldn't sleep with him again. And when was the last time I had achieved that many orgasms in one night? Never. My argument as to why we shouldn't be *back in the saddle again* was very quickly negated. He had even very sweetly offered to take me to breakfast, apologizing for his lack of coffee. I had to decline of course. Showing up to a coffee shop in last night's dress and heels? No. Just No.

My morning-after coffee was when I did my post mortem. A break down of the night that was, and I had a system. Go home, shower, change and *then* you go get coffee. The side order of a muffin was standard— the heart-to-heart with Ash, was an added bonus.

Yeah, that would NOT be happening. How would I even start that conversation? *So Ash, remember how I've wanted to sleep with Troy in like forever? Remember how we decided it's probably for the best if I don't because let's face it, other than hot sex, nothing good will come of it? Well, funny thing. You're going to love this. I disregarded all that common sense nonsense and threw myself at him... with my vagina. Yep. That's right. While you and Dan were busily planning your happily-ever-after, I was getting some sexual healing in the back of the Suburban.*

Yep. Some things really are best left unsaid.

So after kissing Troy goodbye —I lingered, sue me — I hailed a cab back to my Greenwich Village apartment. I quickly showered, changed into my favorite sundress and took the short walk to my favorite coffee house.

Jilly Beans was always bustling with activity, the recycled wooden tables and chairs crammed in between cotton candy pink walls and the checkerboard linoleum floor. It was in the tiny corner café where I sat with a half-full latte trying to stop myself from going back to Troy's apartment and tying him to the headboard. Or he could tie me. We could take turns. That would be fun.

"Hey!" Ash pulled out a chair and sat down at my table. Fresh-faced with her red hair pulled back into a ponytail, she looked gorgeous without even a hint of makeup, casually dressed in jeans and cotton tee. "Why did you run off? I went over to Troy's this morning and he said you'd already left. I would have thought you would have been trying to steal his bath towels or rub yourself on his bed sheets." Ash laughed, reminding me of previous conversations where I had threatened to do just that.

She had no idea.

"Yeah, I didn't want to over stay my welcome." I picked up my cup and took a swallow of my now lukewarm coffee. "Besides, the man had no coffee in his place. Did you know he doesn't drink coffee? He must be some kind of freak." I contorted my face in mock horror trying to steer the conversation away from me being alone with Troy.

"Definitely a freak if he doesn't drink coffee," she mused sarcastically, rolling her eyes. Unlike me, she didn't need to play the pick-Troys-flaws-so-I-don't-sleep-with-him-again game. It was quite a mouthful.

A lot like Troy.

I needed to stop.

Ash's smile lit up her green eyes. "I guessed this is where you'd be after I checked your apartment and no one answered. So predictable." She was right; this is where I could be found most mornings.

Whether it was a quick stop for a takeaway or a more relaxed sit-and-sip, my day didn't start until I'd stopped at *Jilly Beans*. God knows if for some reason I happened to miss a couple of days in a row, the staff would probably file a missing person's report. They understood my caffeine addiction and happily enabled me. "I like it here, they know my order and the baristas are cute. I'm thinking of asking the dark-haired one out on a date. Good looking and knows how to make good coffee. That's husband material right there. I could potentially beat you to the altar."

I wasn't seriously thinking of dating him, it was a throw away line. Our witty little banter just made my day more interesting. I'd flirted with him for the last few months, but he wasn't my type. My type was rockin' hot drummers who inspired scorching hot drive-by sex. Clearly I had a specific palette. I was in so much trouble.

Ash looked over at the tall, lanky, and shaggy-haired man standing behind the counter. His smile was barely visible beneath a neatly manicured beard. The attention we were suddenly throwing his way caused him to adjust his large, thick-rimmed glasses.

Ash laughed. "I think he noticed us staring."

"Good." My lips twitched into a flirty smile as I gave him a friendly wave. He waved back discreetly before he turned his attention back to the important task of working a milk jug and a steam wand. A man making coffee was sexy.

Maybe I should ask him out. It wouldn't hurt. He seemed to be good with his hands, expertly having made a smiley face in my coffee foam. Perhaps I was looking at this all wrong? Maybe Troy actually wasn't *that* good.

It had been a while since my last sexual encounter. It's not like I had accumulated tumbleweeds in my girlie bits, but in recent times I had been spending a lot more time with my vibrator than with a living, breathing penis. Seeing other people would prove that it had been the break in my man-drought that had made last night so toe curling. It probably didn't even matter that it was Troy. I could have had sex with Jimmy, the creepy emo/goth EMT guy, and today I'd be sitting here fantasizing about white skin and eyeliner. Ugh. I shuddered. I dodged a bullet with that one. I mentally made a note to avoid the ER for a while, at least until I was able to scrub that image from my mind.

Ash disregarded the conversation of my dating future with the wave of her hand. "Well, you're a big girl so you can date who you like but I need you to put off your rendezvous with nameless-coffee-dude for one night. Please come over for dinner tonight. Dan has rehearsal; we can eat ice cream and talk wedding stuff."

"Tonight? I guess I can postpone my date with destiny for one night." I squeezed her hand. It was hard to believe my friend, who had seen marriage more as an amicable merger not twelve months ago, was happily living her own fairytale.

"Thanks, Megs." A slight blush crept up her face. "You're not only my maid of honor, but with my mom and my sisters being back in Boston, I don't really have anyone else to get excited with me. Unfortunately you've drawn the short straw. Besides, who else can I trust to kick my ass if I turn into Bridezilla?"

"Aw, sweetie, I love that you've chosen me to share this with, and you couldn't be a Bridezilla if you tried. Although I think this is a good time to tell you, if you make me look a pink marshmallow, I will kill you." I laughed. Not that there was any real danger of that, Ash hated pink but I figured it was best to put our cards on the table. I was still haunted by the nightmare that had been my senior prom. I really wish I could go back in time and tell my seventeen-year-old self that Barbie was not the fashion icon I'd believed her to be. God help me if those pictures ever got out.

Ash grinned, fully aware of my aversion to large bouffant-ed ball gowns. "Damn, I had the pink tulle tutu already picked out."

"Ha. Ha. Very funny. Just remember karma's a bitch and I'll be the one planning your bachelorette party." I threatened, only half kidding. "Have you told your folks yet?"

"Yeah, this morning. Mom cried and Dad got quiet. I could tell he was emotional. Can you believe Dan asked for my dad's blessing? Apparently while we were home for Christmas he told Dad that he wanted to make me his wife and would ask me when the time was right. I know he can be an ass sometimes, but God I love him." The smile on her face reinforcing how happy she was.

I couldn't help myself. Dan was entirely too easy a target. "That's beautiful, Ash. By the way, you should totally call him an ass like that in your vows. I think everyone would love that."

"Are you kidding me? Troy already suggested I work in douchebag and numbnuts. If I didn't know them better, I'd swear they hated each other."

Just hearing Troy's name sent a shiver down my spine. For five minutes I had successfully not thought about him and yet, as soon as he *was* mentioned, I was back imagining bad, bad things. *Good* bad, bad things. Things we had done and things I would love to attempt.

Not helping. Think of something else. I drained the last of my cold coffee from my cup as I realigned my thoughts with Manolo Blahnik's new season's sandals.

Black, strappy patent leather. They would complement that Marc Jacob dress I loved so much but rarely wore. This was good. Positive reinforcement. Shoes. Shoes would be my savior.

"So what time do you want me tonight?" The smile fixed firmly on my face as thoughts of those strappy Blahniks resting on Troy's shoulders while he fucked me, now dominated my mind.

I was in. So. Much. Trouble.

I had returned to the scene of the crime. Well, close enough to it anyway. Criminals not being able to resist the urge? It was all true. A weird sense of curiosity taunted me. Compelling me to walk out of Dan and Ash's apartment where I sat, surrounded by Bridal publications, and revisit the location of one of the most erotic nights of my life.

I didn't.

That's why murderers always got caught on CSI shows. It wasn't the killing that did them in; it was the poking around after the fact. The compulsion to relive the act. I understood it now. Morons. Both me, and them.

My limbs stretched out in front of me as I made myself comfortable on the floor, rolling onto my stomach. The plush area rug underneath me was soft as I propped myself up onto my elbows, oblivious to my surroundings. I heard the faint sound of murmuring in the distance, probably Dan saying goodbye to Ash before he left to go be a rock star. Best left ignored. Spoiler alert, they were probably making out.

My head lowered into the glossy pages of whatever bride magazine I had been flicking through as I pushed a spoonful of *Chubby Hubby* into my mouth, and tried not to think about fact that Troy was only a few feet away. Just through the doorway and down the hall. The ghost of him haunting me, I could almost *feel* his presence and *smell* the sex.

"Megs," Troy's husky voice startled me, almost making me choke on the spoon still in my mouth.

There he was. Like a conjured-up dirty dream. Except he wasn't an apparition, instead he'd walked in, crouched beside me and rested his hand on my bare leg, all while I was blissfully unaware in my self-imposed oblivion.

The spoon was hastily removed from my mouth as I yanked it out. If I was going for seductive, I'd failed. "Oh. Hey, Troy Harris." Quickly swallowing as I scrambled to my knees. Sure, *that* wasn't a more compromising position.

He grinned as he wordlessly took the spoon from my hand and dug it into the pint of ice cream that sat on the coffee table. His hand brought the ice cream loaded spoon to his mouth and his lips closed around it. Hot. Oh hell.

He pulled the spoon from his mouth, with the seduction I hadn't managed. The surface licked clean before scooping more ice cream. "You want some?" His smile widened as he held the spoon inches away from my lips and waited for my response.

"Yes." It was almost moaned, the word clearly too difficult for me to speak. My mouth opened wide like a freak-show clown at a carnival, and he lowered the spoon inside. The ice cream spilled across my tongue that played against the cold metal. Delicious.

It had nothing to do with the ice cream. Just so we're clear.

He slowly pulled the spoon from between my lips, my resistance making him grin.

He raised an eyebrow, "More?" Whatever he was offering, I most definitely wanted *more* of it. Every. Last. Drop.

"Dude, you ready to go?" Dan called from off in the distance, shattering my iced confectionary erotica. I could have wept at the loss.

Troy eyed me intently and then licked the spoon—the one that had just been in my mouth, God that was so fucking hot— and placed it beside the pint on the coffee table.

And like he hadn't just mind-fucked me, he slowly rose to his feet, his lips curled into a sexy smile and he strode to the doorway. "See you later, Megs." He waved as my eyes stayed glued to his sexy ass as he walked away.

He didn't even look back. Just left me there. Frustrated. And it had nothing to do with my so-called man drought, and everything to do with him. I wanted him. I. Was. In. So. Much. Trouble. I seemed to be saying that a lot lately.

"Alrighty. Boys are gone!" Ash cheerily bound into the room carrying her own pint of goodness. Ice cream would never be the same again. "So, I'm ready to make fun of all these crazy wedding dresses while feeding my face." She giggled as she slunk down onto the floor beside me. "Hey, what's wrong? You look weird."

Weird? Or sexually frustrated? It was a fine line. In either case it was not a conversation I wanted to be having. "I'm fine." I lied as I picked up the same bridal magazine I had been flipping through when Troy had waltzed it. Not that my brain connected with the pictures that were in front of me. It was all a blur.

Ash joined me, picking up her copy of *bride-something* monthly and I forced my head to nod in all the right places as she pointed out dresses. My mind was M.I.A.

Right. So what were my chances of being able to stay away from Troy Harris? Slim to none at best. Not great odds. So, maybe one more time? Yes, just one more time and then I'll stop. Promise. At least that's what I told myself.

Denial. It wasn't just a river in Egypt.

RECIPE OF DISASTER. THAT'S WHAT LAST NIGHT HAD BEEN. JUST because shit hadn't gone pear shaped didn't mean given half a chance it wouldn't. Did I want to go there again? Abso-fucking-lutely.

My head was not in the game, pretty sure it was on the smokin' hot blonde who'd walked out my door this morning. My dick got instantly hard just thinking about her, which given the amount of times I blew my load in the last twenty-fours was ridiculous. How she was still walking this morning was also a mystery. I hadn't been gentle.

"Hey, asshole, you channeling your inner Don Johnson?" Dan's face scanned the length of my new ride as we entered the undercover garage. "Fuck… Miami Vice just threw up all over this car."

"Don Johnson drove a Ferrari not a Lamborghini, douchebag." My morning had been busy. Impulse shopping wasn't usually my thing. I'd survived my thirty-two years without a set of Ginsu knives or an Ab-Cruncher. Then again, I'd never needed the distraction.

"Magnum P.I.?"

"Ferrari."

"So you just woke up and decided to buy a car?" His mitt hit the handle and raised the scissor door on the passenger side. The action repeated by me on the driver's side.

"I wanted to go fast." More like needed the rush. The junkie high from Dr. Winters wouldn't be happening anytime soon. It was a substitution. My hands fisted the steering wheel as I slid into the seat.

"This thing is a fucking dinosaur. Did they run out of new Lamborghinis?" His ass sunk into black leather seat.

"The Countach is a classic, show some motherfucking respect." New cars weren't my style and I had a thing for the classics. This one came in the form of a wedge-shaped aircraft-grade aluminum sports car with a V12 that sounded like Armageddon. My latest throw-back was going to be leaving one hell of a carbon footprint, best start planting trees or some shit to try and even the score. My boot kicked the gas pedal, the rev of the engine reverberated off the garage walls. Fuck that. The environment had no hope.

"Mike Lowry. Bad Boys 2." Dan snapped his fingers, shit-eating grin on his face.

"Still a Ferrari."

"Fuck it. Just drive this fucking thing and don't kill us." Dan buckled his seatbelt and thankfully shut his mouth. Not that I was worried about him flapping his gums, the roar of the engine would drown anything out.

The session tonight had been my saving grace. A last minute addition to the album, and we were skating pretty close to the wire on production time. It was either record it now or forever hold our peace. James wanted a song included and had floated the suggestion. Everyone gave the nod, so Casa Bowden is where we would be kicking it for the evening. Fucking brilliant because hitting the skins is exactly what I needed. Help me work out some of this shit I had looping around in my head. Not going there.

Megs being at Dan's was unexpected. My plans had been simple, pick up the douchebag, get in the car and leave— things hadn't worked out that way. Ash casually mentioned that Megs was in the living room and I suddenly got very interested in saying hi.

It would've been rude to not at least stick my head in, considering she'd spent the night in my guest room the night before. All about appearances, right? What was the harm?

Seeing Megs splayed out on the living room floor was like a punch in the balls. Yep, I was a goner. Let's blame it on impulse, or the fact all the blood from my brain had drained into my cock, but all I could think about were those sweet fucking lips and owning that mouth. That shit we had spoken about, being friends and *not* fucking, yeah that went right out the window. So maybe licking her spoon was playing dirty, but I didn't give a fuck. What I did care about was making my intentions clear, and I wasn't subtle about it.

Megs and I, that shit was not over.

We pulled in along Jason's Mustang and ejected from the Lambo. The drive had been pleasurable even if the occasional conversation interjected wasn't.

"I swear, dude. The vibrations in that car when you drive—you could jerk off with no hands." A sample of what I had to endure.

We walked in, said our hellos and got down to business. Getting the track laid down was the priority, getting Megs off my mind, an added bonus.

"Hey man, you wanna go over that last bit again? It sounds kind of tired." Alex stopped mid strum, the new song not sounding right.

"It's missing something." James ran his hands through his hair. "The verse is okay but the chorus fucking blows."

"I don't think it's the lyrics, dude," Jase added to the mix. "I think it's the timing. It's too slow."

"You know my feelings on this," Dan piped in. "Every song should be faster."

"We're not playing death metal you tool." Alex threw a guitar pick at Dan.

"Don't be jealous, asshole, it's not my fault I can play faster than you."

Alex rolled his eyes. "Does your future wife know she's marrying a child?"

Dan's claim was laughable at best, just yanking Alex's chain like he always did. Usually the back and forth amused the hell out of me. Tonight, not so much.

Before Dan had a chance to respond, I picked up my sticks and started playing the chorus again. This time faster on the snare and giving the double kick a little more love. Beside the obvious benefit of drowning out any further bitching, it released some of the tension I'd been feeling.

What came out was aggressive but catchy as fuck. Jase was right; it was a timing issue. Sped up, it sounded amazing.

"That's wicked, dude." James grabbed the mic off the stand, his excitement almost as big as his grin. "Play it again, exactly like that. Alex..."

"On it." Alex turned up his amp and sped up the tempo. His fingers owned the fret board as he moved through the complicated progression. The smug watch-me-shred-like-a-demon look he shot Dan wasn't missed by anyone either. Jase snorted a laugh, punching Dan in the arm before they both joined in and rounded out the sound. It was magic.

James was more excited than a kid on Christmas morning as we hit record. The track was cut and polished a few hours later. And while my poor DW kit took the mother of all poundings, at least I wasn't thinking about the pint-size blonde who'd been dominating my thoughts and making my cock stir.

It was late by the time we made it back to the apartment, and Megs would for sure be tucked up in her bed at home. That piece of information both pissed me off 'cause it meant not seeing her, and made thankful as fuck my torture session for one day was over. It was a fifty-fifty split.

The minute I walked through my front door, I pulled off my boots, tossing my keys on my kitchen counter before I stripped off my T-shirt and socks. It was easier to dump my gear in the laundry on the way through, so I peeled off my jeans and boxers as well and walked to my bedroom, naked.

The place was dark but the layout had been permanently locked away in my brain so I didn't bother hitting the lights. Instead I navigated through the hall, allowing my eyes to readjust.

This was a journey I'd made a million times — sometimes drunk, sometimes sober, and sometimes with a girl around my waist. Yeah, only one girl I was interested in at the moment and we were not going there. My dick showed interest even though there was no prospect of that happening. Not like I blame him.

By the time I'd reached my bedroom, I was seriously contemplating skipping the shower and collapsing into bed. Not like I couldn't get one in the morning. Who the fuck cared that I smelled like last week's gym socks? The sooner my eyes closed, the sooner I would stop this fucked up fantasy I had. The fantasy where I call Megs and tell her to get her sexy little ass over here, and let her ride me until the sun comes up. If my cock wasn't complete awake before, he was sure as hell taking notice now. My hand was tempted to reach down and at least give myself some relief.

"Holy fuck!" My voice bounced off my black bedroom walls, yelling a little louder than I'd meant to, My eyes shut and then reopened just to confirm it wasn't some fucked up optical illusion that I was looking at as a naked and shocked Megs shot up in my bed, pulling the sheets up around her.

"Is this some crazy fucking dream?" My hand raked through my mohawk. Hadn't it been like two minutes ago I'd wished for this very thing? If I'd somehow managed to score three wishes or some shit, they could keep the other two. Megs, in my bed, more than enough for me.

"Shit, Megs. I didn't mean to scare you." I moved closer to the bed. Not sure if her look of surprise was over the fact I'd yelled or the fact I was standing there naked with a hard-on.

"Hey, Troy Harris." Her eyes dipped down to my cock. "I was waiting for you to get home." She gave me an appreciative smile when she saw that part of me was already good to go.

There were a million important questions I should've asked. Starting with "how did you get in?" You know how many I asked? Zero. I didn't give a fuck if she picked my locks or teleported into my bedroom. What I did care about was the fact we were both naked, alone and still not getting busy. "Come here." I ripped the sheets off my bed and exposed her beautiful body. She was so fucking perfect.

She gasped but I didn't buy into that shy bullshit as she moved off the bed and strode over to me. She opened her mouth to talk, not sure whether it was to explain or something else, but I claimed her mouth before she had the chance. All that crap we spoke about last night, about the one-time deal? I was no longer on board. From the looks of things, neither was she. Good, 'cause while that bullshit made all kinds of sense, as far as I was concerned, it was still fucking bullshit.

Her arms wrapped around my neck as our kiss deepened. Never in a million years had I thought *this* was what I'd be coming home to. Hell, had I known, I might've blown off the whole recording session. I palmed her ass and lifted her onto me. She was all about it and wrapped her legs around my waist, little whimpers escaping her mouth as I kissed her. My mouth was too busy to ask, so I made an executive decision and carried her to my bathroom. Last night's shower might have been relatively tame but that was not going to get a repeat performance tonight.

"Troy," she moaned as pushed her against the cold tiled wall. Her hands travelled down the length of my chest.

"You want me to stop?" My mouth moved down her neck, kissing her naked skin. It was going to take a hell of a lot of restraint to stop right now, so I prayed she wasn't going to tell me to put the brakes on.

"Don't stop. I want this. I want you." Her tits heaved up and down as she sucked in a breath.

I pulled her body back against me and into the shower stall. Our lips and hands busy with each other as I turned the faucet and let the cold water hit our skin. It was like a million needles poked us simultaneously but even that wasn't enough to stop us, my skin on fire with fucking need. Megs unwrapped her legs and slithered down my body, giving me a free hand to adjust the water temperature.

She sunk to her knees in front of me, her hands pushing me against the shower wall as her tongue trailed down my abs to my cock. She smiled as she licked the ring, her tongue swirling around the head of my dick. My hands fisted her hair as she took me into her mouth, her blue-green eyes looking up at me as she sucked me hard. It was more than I could stand.

I pulled my dick from her mouth and joined her on the floor of the shower. She protested until my tongue flicked her nipple and then she arched her back and let me do whatever I wanted. What I wanted was to put my mouth on every part of her. My teeth gently teased her pink peak while I snaked my hand down between her legs. She lowered herself down onto her ass and gave me better access. Fucking amazing. Her legs spread and my fingers teased her clit. She was wet and not from the water that was raining down on us from the showerhead.

She reached out and grabbed my shaft, her tight hand moving up and down my length while my fingers rubbed circles around the opening of her pussy. I plunged two fingers inside her; Megs's grip around me —both her pussy around my fingers and her hand on my cock— tightened.

I wanted to be deep inside her but with the closest condom in the nightstand, my hand and tongue were going to have to be the only parts that got that pleasure. The other part, the one that was about to blow its load into her hand, would sink into her the minute we were out of the shower and suited up in latex.

We didn't talk; moans seemed all we were capable of as our hands got each other off. I was torn between wanting to watch her get worked up with my fingers moving in and out of her sweet pussy, or watching her jerk me off, both had its benefits. Her back arched toward my hand and I knew that she was close, I was trying to hold off, wanting it to last just a little longer. It felt so fucking good. In the end, biology took over and my mouth slammed down on hers as we both came hard on the floor of the shower stall.

"Hey," I whispered against her shoulder as I wrapped my arms around her.

"Hey," she giggled back, slowly opening her eyes. God she was beautiful.

"You going to spend the night with me so I can do that properly?" My fingers traced little circles on her back.

"It felt pretty good the first time."

"You know it can be better."

"I can probably stay."

"Good. Let's get cleaned up so I can get you into my bed."

"Aren't you curious how I got into your apartment?"

"Well, it crossed my mind for about a second until I saw you were naked and then I no longer gave a fuck. You could've busted my locks and I'd still have a smile on my face."

I'm sure there was a story, and in truth part of me was curious but currently it wasn't *that* part of me that was running the show, so whatever the explanation was, it could wait.

"I didn't bust your locks."

"You have a life of crime you've been keeping under wraps? Vandalizing and boosting cars when you were a teenager?"

"Would that turn you on, Troy Harris?"

Her smile would've knocked me on my ass if I weren't already on it. "Megs, you just have to show up and I get turned on. Anything else is just gravy."

While the first time had been frenzied, the second time I would be taking it slow. I wanted to feel every inch of myself inside her and get familiar with every part of her body. There was no way I would be wasting the opportunity, even if I knew when the morning cracked through my drapes, it would probably be the last time.

Megan

OKAY, SO *THAT* HAD TO BE THE LAST TIME.

I would go cold turkey and there would be no more slipups. Yeah, because *that's* what happened. We accidently found ourselves naked and his penis *slipped* into my vagina—again.

So what if he was incredibly hot and made me orgasm like it was an Olympic sport. I refused to accept there was more to it than that. That just being around him didn't make my heart squeeze a little. Or that his smile didn't make my shitty day infinitely better. No, it was purely sexual. It had to be, and there were other attractive guys, ones who had talent. Men who didn't have a connection to any of my friends or their partners. I just needed to find them.

So how did it come to pass that I ended up in Troy's apartment, naked? Well, watching Troy Harris lick that spoon bordered on obscene. He might as well have just licked me between my legs. The same effect was achieved. Who could have resisted that? Certainly not this girl. I needed to sleep with him again. More so to prove to myself that it wasn't as fantastic as I remembered it, so I could move on. Like a reality check of sorts.

The first time—all right, the first six times— we had sex, I was caught up in the fantasy. It was Troy Harris for God's sake. I'd fingered myself to his image so many times I should have been embarrassed. It had to be the hype that had made it so out-standing. No man was *that* good. Of course the theory needed testing. It meant overlooking the fact that my theory testing hadn't worked out for me so well in the past, but it was a hardship I figured I had to endure. What? Everyone makes mistakes. Moving on.

The plan had been to wait with Ash until Dan and Troy got home, and then knock on his door.

I hadn't really thought beyond that brilliant idea. *Winging it* was going to feature heavily. But the hours ticked over, and Ash yawned a few too many times so I said my goodbye.

Hope had almost been lost.

When I got Ash's front door I *remembered* that I had left my bracelet in Troy's apartment. Which was a lie. It was sitting at the bottom of my purse with a broken clasp.

I was going right to hell; sadly at this point, I didn't care.

Ash very kindly offered to let me into Troy's apartment with the spare key he kept at their place—something I'd hoped for. Cue me exiting Troy's bathroom with the bracelet triumphantly dangling between my fingers. We left, with me pulling the door shut behind me, and said our goodbyes in the hallway.

Two things didn't happen. One, I *didn't* pull Troy's door all the way shut.

I gently eased the door just enough into the jamb to catch but not enough for the lock to engage. The second thing was I *didn't* leave.

Instead, I pretended to walk away and then promptly returned to Troy's door. My relaxed strut probably making me look like a catwalk reject from fashion week, but at least I wasn't sprinting.

God, I hoped no one actually watched the surveillance footage.

Once I was at Troy's front door, all that was required was a gentle push and *boom,* I was in.

My rap sheet now included wild sex with a rock star *and* breaking and entering. There goes the neighborhood.

So I was inside; now, what the hell I was supposed to do? Pacing nervously only held my attention so far before I gave up to the magnetic pull of his bed.

I was discreet at first, kicking off my shoes and crawling slowly over his covers to his pillows. Their intoxicating scent overwhelmed me as I nuzzled them.

Insanity—the only explanation as to why I was on my hands and knees, ass in the air with my face in his pillow. Thank you sweet baby Jesus no one walked in sparing me the *what-the-fuck* moment.

Somewhere in between taking off my clothes and rubbing myself all over his sheets — yeah I did it, don't judge me—I fell asleep.

Maybe it was the tension, or perhaps pure exhaustion, but instead of a light doze, I fell into something close to resembling a coma. It wasn't until I heard a very loud "Holy Shit" that I was awakened from my peaceful slumber.

No need to guess what happened next. My oh-it-can't-be-that-good-I-must-have-imagined-the-toe-curling-orgasms was blown right out of the water. How could it keep getting better? How could he know exactly what to do and when to make my eyes roll back into my head? How was I ever going to willingly give this up? Whatever trouble I thought I had been in before had doubled in magnitude now.

So my fate had been sealed. I would be damned to mediocre sex with other men because that had been my last hurrah with Troy. He made me come so hard, I actually cried. Mourning the orgasms that would no longer echo through my body and overwhelmed by every nerve ending in my body feeling like it was on fire.

It had never been like that, not like *that*.

And it hadn't been just the sex. The seemingly bleak caseload I was juggling, and the mountain of guilt I was battling had me on a hair trigger and I was primed for an explosion. It should have been awkward—crying after sex in front of Troy Harris— but strangely, it wasn't. He made me feel safe and he was cool enough to not get all weird after. No questions were asked, he just held me in his arms.

Which is why it could never happen again. I couldn't lose him. Never feeling him again inside me was a horrendous thought, but what would be so much worse was if we ended up hating each other. I *really* liked him and it wasn't just sexual, and there was no way I would jeopardize that.

Cold turkey, I repeated my mantra. It was the only way.

Avoiding Troy wasn't going to work. Apart from the fact he was deeply involved with my best friend's soon-to-be husband, he was also going to be the best man to my maid of honor. What was I going to do? Pretend he had cooties? I *could* be around him, *not* strip naked and drop to my knees. It just took practice.

I buried myself in work. Even though I missed his beautiful enigmatic smile, the time away made me stronger, more prepared to deal with the attraction I was denying. It could totally be done. Totally.

"My parents are assholes. This whole therapy shit blows and I don't need you. I hate them for making me come here. Am I supposed to sit and cry like a fucking loser?"

All thought of Troy vaporized as I looked over at the skinny, fair headed boy who sat in the chair opposite me. Brad Hemsworth had been discharged yesterday into the care of his parents. His release had hinged on regular therapy sessions with me, as well as very close monitoring by his folks. It was either that or he would be admitted to a facility. He flat out refused to stay in the hospital.

He was angry but hopefully not beyond reason. "Brad, I know you don't want to be here and no one is going to make you talk about anything you don't want. Why don't we just get to know each other a little better? This is your time and we can talk about whatever it is you want to talk about."

He got out of his chair and started to pace around the room. "How about we talk about *you* convincing my folks I'm not going to slit my wrists or take a bunch of pills. I made a mistake. I'm not taking your mind-altering drugs either. I swear it's a way for them to control me. I'm not about to be dumbed down on Ritalin."

My eyes followed his agitated, twitchy movements as he paced, while I remained in my chair. I stayed calm, neutral. "Brad, first of all, I'm a psychologist not a psychiatrist so I can't prescribe you anything. We just talk here, no drugs involved at all. And secondly, Ritalin is used for treatment of attention deficit disorders; it wouldn't be effective treating depression."

He balled his fist at his sides; his face flushed with anger. "I'm not depressed. God, you are just as bad as my fucking parents. I wasn't going to actually kill myself. It was a fucking mistake. Like I told the shrink in the hospital, it was a moment of weakness, I'm fine now."

"Brad, depression can take on many forms. Let's not worry about the label right now, let's talk about making you feel a little less angry."

It was a balancing act, knowing how much to push and when to back off, and he was putting me through my paces. I worried about him. He was severely in denial but I needed to win his trust, to get through to him. Today, however, that breakthrough wouldn't be happening.

I spent the rest of his appointed hour trying to coax him to a safe place, one where he felt comfortable talking to me, a place with less anger. But at the end of the sixty minutes, I wasn't entirely sure that any of it had broken through.

"So, we done yet?" Brad impatiently kicked the chair leg with his Converse-covered foot. He yanked at his *30 second to Mars* T-shirt that looked as if it had seen better days. The worn-out jeans he was wearing were frayed at the hem. "Can I go?" he asked again, flicking his long blond bangs so they covered his tormented brown eyes.

"We're done for this week, you can go," I responded, lifting myself out of my seat, smoothing out my tailored skirt as I stood. "I'll see you next week."

"Yeah, whatever." Brad sunk his hands into his pockets and walked out of my office.

His exit gave me permission to sink back into my chair and let my head drop into my hands, mentally and emotionally exhausted. The blue painted walls of my office were not as bright as they used to be, my large wooden desk was filled with notes and files that would take at least another hour or two to put in order. Some days were harder than others, and today had been a difficult day.

My cell buzzed silently on my desk and I welcomed the distraction, reaching across and answering it without bothering to check who was on the other end.

"Megs," Ashlyn's excited voice broke through my mental fog, "tell me you have no plans tonight."

"Ash, it's a Wednesday. What plans would I have?"

"I wasn't sure if you'd set up your hot date with coffee boy yet." Ash laughed, I had almost forgotten about him and my faux dating interest.

"I'm playing hard to get," I joked. "What's up?"

"Hannah, James's wife, is having a little engagement dinner for us at their house. Nothing fancy, just the band really and their significant others, but you have to come."

Great. That would be a perfect punctuation mark to an already crappy day. An evening spent avoiding Troy and pretending like hanging out with Power Station was no big deal. No one was that convincing. I mentally waved my fist in the air and mouthed, "Fuck you" to the universe.

"Ash, I don't really know her that well. Besides, you said it yourself. It's a band thing."

"Hello? I'm sorry but where is my friend Megs?" Ash sarcastically slurred into the phone.

"Very funny. I just think maybe that you should probably go without me. Besides, my laundry hamper needs some serious attention." I cringed at my bogus excuse. Why hadn't my brain manufactured something better? A case report that needed to be written or a patient review that needed to be read, anything other than laundry. I might as well have said I was washing my hair.

"Did you fall and hit your head?" She almost shouted through the phone. "This is *Power Station*. I'd have thought you'd be so excited that you would be humping my leg, not making lame excuses not to go."

She wasn't wrong; a few months ago that very reaction might have been accurate. "Ash, I'm not going to start using you to get to the band, that wouldn't be cool. It's fine, go have a good time."

"Okay, stop that. I know we joke about your love for the band, but I have never felt used nor do I think you would ever do that." She took a breath before continuing. "Is there something else going on? I know I have been a bit wedding obsessed lately; I'm sorry if there is stuff that I've missed."

I weighed her words for a minute, glad she had missed the change between Troy and I, the subtle glances between us. No one else needed to be tied up in that mess. Seems you can't play the it's-only-sex game with someone who is so intimately woven into your life. Troy had tried to convince me of that very idea early on. I hadn't wanted to hear it. Well, it was really fucking obvious now.

Humor was my go-to in my bag of tricks, that and sarcasm. I employed them both in equal measures. My dad, in the past, accused me of using them as diversionary tactics; he wasn't wrong. "Well, I didn't want to say anything, but your perpetual happiness is kind of annoying. You think you can kick it down a notch?"

Ashlyn laughed, thankfully not pressing the issue any further. "I promise to be less happy if you come. I might even manage a frown."

"Now who is sounding like they hit their head?"

"Well, Dr. Winters, I didn't want to have to pull out the big guns but you've left me no choice. I need you to be there. I love Dan, but being in his world still feels kind of awkward. Pretending that those guys weren't a big deal was a hell of a lot easier when I didn't have to see them up close. I'm a realist and it's tough being in love with someone that comes with all of *that.* I know it's my hang up and whatever weirdness I feel is worth it, but I need you in my corner. I also need for you to know just because I'm with him it doesn't mean I'm no longer with you. I'm not going to join the rock-star-wives-club the minute I marry Dan and forget who I am."

"I knew there had to be a club. It's probably for the best you aren't joining though; organized groups were never your thing."

"So are you going to quit being a dumbass, and help me even out the ratio of people featured on *MTV* verses people not featured on *MTV?*"

The magic words *"I need you"* was all Ashlyn had to say. All jokes aside, there wasn't a lot I wouldn't do for her, even if it meant making myself uncomfortable. She was like the sister I'd never had, balancing out my crazy as I pushed her out of her comfort zone.

"Sweetie, if it's that important to you, of course I will come. Although, I will say it's rather hurtful you think I'm not going to be on *MTV*. I can play the *hell* out of the recorder and that shit is poised to be the next big thing."

"You know you're leaving yourself wide open here for jokes about oral skills."

"Wow, Ash, I think you've spent too much time with Dan and he has burrowed inside your brain. If you start calling me a douchebag, I'm telling you right now, I'm going to stage an intervention."

"Deal." Ash's tone did little to hide how delighted she was. "We can come and pick you up around seven."

While I was prepared to sit across from Troy Harris and not sleep with and/or pretend I hadn't slept with him, I also needed the means for a quick escape. Sure, in a perfect world things wouldn't get weird but if they did, at least I could say my goodbyes and privately berate myself for my stupidity.

"Actually, it might be easier if I borrowed my mom's car. It's just sitting in the garage since Dad whisked my mom to Providence for some romantic mid-week getaway. I cringe at the thought of them having sex, so I have convinced myself all they will be doing is antiquing and exploring lighthouses." *Thank you parents for having a healthy relationship, which has taken you out of state.*

Not that it would have been a problem to use either of their vehicles; it was just easier without the third degree. My father still couldn't wrap his head around the fact that I didn't own one myself. I lived in Manhattan. Enough said.

"Blissful ignorance, huh?" Ash laughed. Having been around my parents, she knew they were more likely to be holed in a charming Bed and Breakfast enjoying adult time, rather than scaling a narrow, winding staircase of a decrepit lighthouse. "Okay, I'll text you the address."

"Awesome." It was so *not* awesome. "I'll see you there."

We ended the call and I closed my eyes. The soft leather of my office chair cushioned my head as I leaned back against it. It was time to get over myself and do what I said I was capable of doing. Remain calm, unaffected and enjoy my evening regardless of Troy being there or not. It was ridiculous. I was ridiculous. I was not going to let a moment—okay, several moments— of weakness ruin my night. I would pull up my big girl panties, put my money where my mouth was, practice what I preached, and any other cheesy analogies I could use to tell myself that I would be okay.

The breath I had unconsciously been holding slowly spilled from my lips and I felt my body slowly relax. It would be okay; I repeated it in my head. It had to be, because the only thing worse than seeing Troy Harris and it being weird would be to never see him again. That would crush me more than I cared to admit.

MEGS HADN'T CALLED, SENT A MESSAGE OR SHOWN UP NAKED ON MY doorstep in days. All of that —especially the last part—really fucking sucked. Yeah, we both knew we had to cool it and get back to *friend zone*, but it agitated me.

Why? Who the fuck knew. What I did know was the past few days while we were on radio silence, I was pissed off, worked up and so fucking edgy I was wondering if I should just sit down with whatever Oprah's latest book club recommendation was and feed my face with Ho-Ho's.

The more I tried, the less I was able to get her off my mind. Thinking about what a cool chick she was and wondering what she was doing. Yeah, all the bullshit what-ifs weren't helping; instead it was giving me an even bigger head fuck.

We'd had sex. Big deal. True, it had been monumental sex, but we agreed that's all it was. It's not like I was never going to have that again. Well obviously not with *her*, but my dick hadn't fallen off and I hadn't suddenly turned into a fugly mutant.

I could get laid any time I wanted. As much as I wanted. With anyone that I wanted. I was living the fucking dream, and I needed to remind myself of how good my life was. There were men who would kill to be in my place. I couldn't even begin to describe how awesome things were.

Right, just keep telling yourself that buddy and you might actually believe that shit.

Megs. Yep, and we were back to that. Should I have called her? I'm not the kind of asshole who fucks a girl and then doesn't call. That had been Dan's M.O., pre-Ashlyn days of course. We were in some lame ass limbo of being friends but not talking to each other. It made zero sense to me.

Fuck. This call-or-don't-call bullshit was giving me a headache. I pinched the bridge of my nose and closed my eyes, wishing I had a magic eight ball or something.

"Yeah." My phone had been blowing up all morning and I'd finally decided to give it reprieve.

"Hey, man." It was James, not Megs, and fuck if I was disappointed. Wanting to hear from her more than I cared to admit. "Hannah has decided we need to have a dinner to celebrate Dan finally putting a ring on it. My place, tonight."

"Funny, I didn't hear that as a question."

"Probably because it wasn't."

"Dude, I still remember the last time your wife was pregnant. That Jekyll and Hide thing fucking scares the crap out of me."

"Good, we'll expect you then. Seven o'clock and Hannah said don't be late."

Not even going to pretend to know how a chick can turn from happy to murderous on a dime, but one thing was for sure—you do not mess with it, ever. No, seriously. That's some prehistoric survival shit. It was easier to agree than have my balls ripped off.

"Yep, I'll be there at seven." Guess my evening was set.

My new Lambo slid in beside Stone's Escalade and Jase's Mustang. Sure, it got like five miles to the gallon and probably elevated me to douchebag status, but driving it got my mind off all things blonde and beautiful. I'd take the win when I could.

Dan's Benz was parked on the other side of the driveway along side a flash, high-end red Lexus sedan. Huh? Who the hell drove a Lexus? Fuck it. The owner of the corporate coffin didn't rate high on my give-a-shit meter. Snagging the large white box that had been sitting on my passenger seat, I climbed out of my car and strolled to the front door.

"You're late." Hannah stood in the open doorway. The hands on her hips clueing me in she was less than pleased.

"Sorry, Han, traffic was a bitch until I got out of Manhattan." My head dipped and I gave her a kiss on the cheek. "I brought dessert. Dan's favorite." I grinned, tapping the box in my hand.

The peace offering seemed to thaw the chill Hannah was throwing at me. "Aw, Troy. That is so sweet. Come in, everyone is waiting." See what I mean? Mood swings.

I followed her through the hallway and into the back end of the house. From the back, you'd never know she was in the family way, the only clue the small basketball-sized belly you got an eyeful of when she turned around. The baby was due just before we went out on the road, which was cool.

Noah, James and Hannah's first, had been on the road with us in the past, and I was almost certain Grace, Alex and Lexi's little girl, was tour bound as well. Long gone were the days of wild parties and drinking till dawn. It was a different kind of backstage party these days, one that involved juice boxes and *Nick Jr.*

Thinking of the tour gave me something to smile about, even if it was going to be dominated by kids. The sooner we got on the road, the sooner I could stop acting like a moody asshole. Put some distance between the Megs situation and me. Who knows, maybe find someone out there that would happily be my distraction. It certainly was worth a try.

"Sweetheart, I'm just trying to get Noah off to bed." James met us in the hallway; trying to wrangle Noah, who wasn't convinced it should be bedtime. "Oh, hey man. You made it." James tipped his chin hello given his hands were tied up with a defiant two-year-old.

"No. No Bed." Noah pushed against the arms of his dad, his face red from the effort. Poor little guy was giving it a shot but was no match for James's strength.

"Hey, buddy." I tickled the back of Noah's neck. "You giving your old man a hard time? That's Uncle Troy's job. You wouldn't want me to lose my job would you?" Hoping it didn't turn on the waterworks, I gave the kid my best puppy dog eyes.

Noah looked over me, giving it some serious thought. "Nu-uh Uncle Troy."

"Okay, so why don't you let your dad get you off to bed." I planted a kiss on his forehead and rubbed his back. "And I promise I'll make sure your dad gets a hard enough time for the both of us."

"Okay, Uncle Troy, night-night." Noah waved his little hand then curled his arm around his old man's neck. James mouthed me a silent thank-you as he carried Noah to his bedroom.

Hannah's hand went to her belly and gave it a little Buddha action. "You boys are so sweet with him. He's been impossible lately. He refuses to do anything I say, and everything is *no*." Thinking I dodged the waterworks bullet might have been premature as Hannah's eyes started to water.

"He's just pushing your buttons. I would've thought that after all the practice you had with us, this would be a walk in the park." I put my arm around her and gave her a hug. "Han, you are an amazing mom."

"Thanks." Her fingertips mopped the tears that were pooling in the corner of her eyes and gave me a smile. "Hormones are a bitch."

"Preach, sister." I shot her a grin. "Just the other day I was telling Dan about this fucking water retention I had going on. You should see the size of my feet."

She sucked in laugh. "You are an ass, but I still adore you."

"Back at ya, Han. Now let's go celebrate my best friend being off the market." We walked in to dining room, my box of goodness still in my hand.

"Hey, Troy Harris." Megs walked slowly toward me with a big ass smile on her face. "Fancy meeting you here."

Fuck.

So there goes my quiet evening not thinking about the sexy

blonde who can get my dick hard just by walking into the room. It felt like I'd been sucker punched as she moved toward me in slow motion. She looked fucking amazing too; the short green dress she was wearing was showing most of her tanned legs. Her long hair hung loose. She was stunning.

"Hey, Megs." I quickly recovered, thanking my mouth for getting with the program. "Yeah, big surprise. It's good to see you." Not a lie. It was really, really good to see her.

"Do you need a hand with that?" she asked, her eyes dipping down to the box that I had completely forgotten I was carrying.

Yeah, your hand around my cock would be nice, thank you very much.

"Nah, I got it. You look... good." Good didn't even come close to covering it. Mouthwatering was more accurate.

"Why thank you, Troy Harris." She gave it a little *Scarlett O'Hara*, her voice taking a stroll below the Mason-Dixon line. "You look mighty fine yourself."

What's mighty is this hard-on I'm packing, let's talk about that.

Shit. I was a fucking pervert. Thank God she couldn't read minds.

"Whatcha got there?" Dan moseyed over, all kinds of interested in the box. The dude had perfect timing, pulling my ass from the fire. "Fuck, yeah! This is why you are my best man." The dozen frosted cupcakes inside the reason he was grinning like an idiot.

"I don't get it?" Alex shook his head, walking over to join the party. "What's so special about cupcakes?"

"Hi, Troy." Ashlyn waved, rolling her eyes before playfully nudging Dan's shoulder. "Alex, don't even get him started."

"Heathens, the lot of you." Dan waved them off dismissively taking the box into the kitchen.

The exchange in front of me did little to change my view. The one that had my eyes glued to the knockout blonde in front of me. Megs stayed and watched it played out; her interest in it seemed on par with mine. Non-existent.

"Here." Jase handed me a long neck, ignoring Dan and the staring competition I obviously had going on with Megs.

"Thanks." Nod. Swallow. Just what I needed to put these

flames out.

"Megs, want a beer?" He offered her the other.

Don't take it. Not sure I'd be good with sitting on the sidelines watching you swallow.

Her eyes dropped to the frosty bottle before they came back to me. "Thanks, but I'm fine."

Yes, you are.

Pin. Drop.

Neither of us able to tear our eyes from each other but our mouths staying clamped shut.

Well, that wasn't awkward. Not one little bit.

"Okay then. Good times, guys." Jase slapped me on the shoulder. The asshole decided to bail. "Going over to chat to Alex, can't get a word in edgewise over here." He walked. Didn't even look back.

"I might go see if I can help Hannah or Ashlyn." Megs followed Jason's lead and hightailed it to the other side of the room.

Awesome. This was going well.

"Hey, Troy." Lexi gave me her usual warm smile, her eyes a little more tired than I was used to seeing.

"Lexi." I welcomed the distraction and noticed we were one Power Station rug rat short. "You leave the little lady home alone? Hope you gave her enough vodka and cigarettes to get her through."

"Ha, very funny. Grace is having a sleep over with Alex's mom." She gave me a smug smile that meant trouble. "So... you and Megs."

"Don't start." My sideways glance was also a warning. "There's nothing there. We're just friends."

"Oh, really?" She clearly wasn't letting it go. "Huh, because I could have sworn that when you walked in and saw her your eyes almost bulged out of your head. Followed by your tongue hitting the floor. That's the way I always react when I see my *friends*." The sarcasm on the word friend wasn't missed.

While shit might have slid past Dan and Ash, Lexi didn't miss a thing. The clearing of my throat didn't help either. "I thought the matchmaker bullshit was Hannah's deal; don't tell me having a baby has made you soft." I deflected hoping she would let it go, the situation not needing the heat or the attention it was getting.

"Not soft, just more invested in what's important."

Megs was on the other side of the room, laughing with Hannah and Ashlyn. No less beautiful than the last time I'd looked. "Yeah, well regardless of any of it. It ain't happening. That's a whole lot of fucking complication no one needs."

"I'm not really the person you should be talking to about avoiding a complicated relationship." She glanced to where Stone was deep in conversation with James and Jason. "I think Alex and I covered about every aspect. Long distance, crazy exes, miscommunication, misunderstandings and more baggage than the Parisian flagship store of *Louis Vuitton*." She laughed. "But when the right person comes along, complications... they just make it more worthwhile."

"Thanks, Lex." I wrapped my arms around her and pulled her in for a hug. "Hey, if this gig with us doesn't work out, you know can always go write cards for Hallmark."

"Whatever, Troy." She smiled, her arms wrapping around me. "You guys would fall apart without me."

"True." It's not like I could disagree.

Hannah waved her oven-mitted hand and called everyone to attention. "Okay everyone, grab a seat. It's time to eat."

The rowdy group that we were moved to the table. Asses found their seats with no real thought given to the seating plan. Conversations not interrupted during the process.

Rather than pussy out, I pulled out a chair and gave her a nod. "Megs."

It could have gone either way, but I was glad when she took me up on my offer and sat down. Keeping my hand from running down her bare arm while she took her seat had been fucking difficult. Although the bigger challenge was not looking down the front of her dress, which was doing a wonderful job and showcasing her perky... not fucking helping.

Megs shuffled back in toward the table, rewarding me with a big smile. "Thanks, such a gentleman."

"For pulling out your chair?" I took my seat beside her;

surprised she'd had been so easy to impress. I know the whole pulling-out-the-chair thing was a bit cliché, but when the mood took me, I could play nice.

"Nope." Her eyebrow rose as she leaned in to whisper. "For not looking down my dress."

Uh-hum, had it suddenly gotten warmer in here? "Oh, I looked; I'm just good at not being caught," I lied, and apparently I was a comedian because my response had made her laugh. Like a real laugh— not some half-assed chuckle. It was a nice sound too and I really liked the way it made me feel. I was going to need to hear more of it.

A bunch of separate conversations zigzagged over the mountain of food that sat in front of us. Alex and James were talking shop. Hannah, Ash and Lexi were talking babies, and Dan and Jason were in a fierce car debate about whether American muscle was more superior to European design. No one paid us any attention.

"Have you been good?" I leaned over and picked up a plate of some kind of chicken and offered it to Megs.

She smiled and helped herself to some food before answering. "Yeah, I've been buried in work but I've been okay. How about you?"

This felt good. We were having a normal conversation, and look we weren't fucking each other senseless up against a wall. Who knew?

"I've been doing band stuff. Same old, same old." I grabbed a spoonful of potato salad and slapped it onto my plate. "I'm glad you came tonight."

Megs scrunched her nose up at the potato salad, opting for the garden salad instead. "I'm glad too. I'll be honest, I didn't want to."

I froze. She didn't want to? Not sure I wanted to know the answer, but I had to ask anyway. "Why? Because of me?"

"Yeah," She shrugged. "We said we wouldn't let it get awkward and it got awkward. I wanted to call you; I just thought it would be easier if I didn't."

Yeah, not happy with that. Last thing I wanted was for her not to wanna be around me. How was that a good thing? Nope, that was not okay. The only way the stupid hell of not being with her would make any sense was if I could still be sure she was okay. Wow. When did that happen?

"We both probably could have handled it a little better; I mean, I didn't call you either. But, Megs, you want to call me, call me. We said we'd stay friends and we can't do that if we are avoiding each other."

"You're so wise, Troy Harris."

"Well playing drums only takes up so many hours in the day, everyone needs a hobby."

She laughed again, this time the light hit her eyes and made them sparkle. If I hadn't already been sitting down, I would have needed to. She was so freaking beautiful and when she laughed she did things to me I just didn't understand.

So this was our deal now, laughing and talking but no fucking. Yep. This was going to blow.

Megan

THAT FIRST POST-SEX ENCOUNTER HADN'T BEEN SO BAD. AFTER THE initial, hey-let's-pretend-I-don't-know-what-you-look-like-naked, we were actually in a good place. Not to say that I didn't wish things could be different and that we could see each other naked again—with everything else that comes with that— but friend-ship is where we seemed poised to stay. So I kept telling myself.

Because I couldn't leave well enough alone— really, I'm a hazard to myself— I suggested we should *probably* date other people. The conversation went something like this: "So, Troy Harris, seeing as you aren't dating me, and there's no hope of that happening, you should let some other lucky lady have the privilege. It will help me move on and this is, after all, all about me."

Okay so maybe the conversation didn't go exactly like that, but it was mentioned we should see other people—by me, the idiot — and Troy, who seemed to have no problem with it, readily agreed. I'm not even sure how it was interjected into the conversation. Clearly I suck when it comes to making my mouth not say stupid stuff, so it really wasn't surprising.

At least we'd finished the evening on a positive note, promising to stop avoiding each other and work our way to a decent friendship. More than sleeping with him again, it's what I desperately wanted. Just to be able to call and see him again without it being weird would be a start. Okay so not weird was a tall order, maybe less weird than it had been was what I should be aiming for.

Troy and I became somewhat of phone-buddies—yeah I know it sounds like some obscure anime themed App— but we often called each other and had lame-ass conversations. Ridiculous even, but I looked forward to them. Completely nonsexual and everything. At first it was a challenge trying to not picture him naked but we eased into a friendship that was actually kind of nice.

The person to make the first call had been me, when on Monday I dialed his number.

"Megs." Troy answered the phone almost immediately.

"So, I was thinking." I didn't even bother with formalities like hello.

Troy laughed. "Sounds good to me, I usually like it when you get thinking." I didn't need to ask where his mind had wandered.

"Awesome, so can I sign you up to be on the next season of *The Bachelor*?" Genuinely curious as to what he would say.

"No, you can't." He shot me down, not even entertaining the idea.

"You are no fun, Troy Harris." I pouted, despite him not being able to see it. I'm sure he heard it though. I had a very pouty voice.

Troy laughed. "Goodbye, Megs."

The next volley came from Troy on Tuesday.

"Hey, Troy Harris." I smiled as I placed the phone to my ear. Did I mention how much I really liked seeing his name on my caller ID?

"Hey, Megs, I heard one of the Jonas brother's is single. I have no idea which one it is, but they all pretty much look alike. You want me to set you up?"

"Please. Like I'd date a Jonas brother." I exaggerated my displeasure.

He chuckled. "Right, you like your men a little more rock and roll, got it. Ummm let me check TMZ and see who's available. I'll call you back."

My follow up had happened on Wednesday and the conversation had turned from dating to something else entirely.

"Hey, Troy Harris." His name left my lips as soon as he'd pick up the receiver.

"Hey, Megs, I hope this is important. The Vampire Dairies reruns are on and that Nina whatever-her-name is hot."

"Oh, I love Vampire Diaries. Damon Salvatore is so misunderstood. This is important. Does your cock ring set off metal detectors at airports? I mean, do you need like pull your pants down and let them wand you?"

"Er, no. Why?"

"Oh, I was bored and thought we could take a drive out to La Guardia and mess with some TSA people. Back to square one I guess. Bye."

By Thursday I was not only expecting his call but also anxiously waiting for it. My pulse racing a little every time my phone went off.

"Megs." I heard the smile in his voice. "I hope you found another satisfactory way to amuse yourself yesterday."

"Oh I sure did. I bought a huge dildo online instead, and I'm going to pack it in my carry on for my next trip." It took everything I had to suppress my laugh.

"That's awesome; remind me never to fly with you. Anyway, I got a new Tat today and while I was there I picked up a gift certificate for you. Figured we could get a *return to* label inked on your ass, you know in case you fall down again."

"Aw, you shouldn't have. You are so sweet."

"My pleasure, Megs. There was also a discount on *Ace* bandages at *Walgreens*. I know I shouldn't spoil you, but I couldn't help myself."

"Goodbye, Troy Harris."

"Bye, Megs."

Friday had me buzzing with anticipation over his call.

"Hey, Megs."

I loved hearing him say my name. "Hey, Troy Harris."

"I used your address to do some internet shopping. I know I should have asked first, but we're so cool with each other, I figured you'd say yes. I really hate it when people see my name and address and then before you know it...boom a stalker."

"Sure, no problem at all. What did you buy?"

"Chinese throwing stars and a sword. Hopefully it doesn't get flagged by the FBI; you don't have an existing record do you?"

I couldn't even respond I was laughing so hard. Those calls had been the highlight of my day. It wasn't just phone calls; there were voice messages as well. At the end of my workday, there would always be a missed call and message from Troy. I'd put my headphones on and would listen on my cab ride home from work. It almost became a sort of therapy for me, a way to unwind.

The mix of feelings that I was experiencing for him was new and exciting. They confused me slightly, not being able to package them up neatly, but I knew my days were better with him in them; even it was just phone calls.

It was official— apart from being sexy and so incredibly funny— Troy Harris was also very sweet and sincere. It was so unexpected. One more thing to add to the list of his perfections; I'd stalled greatly on his imperfections after those original two. Hated coffee and the R2D2 in the kitchen (in case anyone needed a refresher) and even now, those two didn't seem so bad. The no coffee thing could actually be a positive. I would never have to compete with him for the last cup.

Saturday's call had been a little bit different. Rather than wait until later in the day, I instead gave him a five a.m. wake up call and played Britney Spear's "Oops!...I Did It Again" at ear-splitting decibels through the phone. Even though I had also been affected by the sleep deprivation, it had been worth it to hear the expletives that spewed from Troy's mouth while he tried to work out what was going on. It had taken me at least ten minutes before I had been able to catch my breath. Tears streamed down my cheeks, I had been laughing so hard.

After Troy warned me that we were now at war, the conversation took a more serious turn.

"So, are you dating anyone?" The words leapt out of my mouth before I had a chance to stop them.

"Not really, Jase and I hung out with a couple of girls on

Wednesday but nothing really serious."

"Oh, okay," I managed to say without choking. My voice almost sounded normal, indifferent. There, something to be proud of.

The thought of him with someone else made my blood run cold. Did I want to know any of this? I should have stopped, but of course I didn't. I had to dig a little bit deeper, maybe torment myself a little more. It would have been too much to ask to just end the call on a happy note.

"Why didn't you tell me?" It wasn't any of my business and I had no right to ask.

I heard a small sign. "It wasn't important. It wasn't some hot date or anything. What about you? You dating?"

What about me? I hadn't even looked at a guy since I'd slept with Troy, not seriously anyway. I mean, I'd appreciated the guy in his underwear on the billboard in Time's Square, but it would have been rude if I hadn't. The poor guy was in his underwear, demanding attention.

"Me? Sure, there's this guy I've kind of been interested in. Who knows, we might even go out tonight."

"Really? Well that's good."

What did that mean? He wanted me to date? Why couldn't *he* be jealous? Not that I was jealous. Nooo, of course I wasn't. I was just curious. "What are you doing tonight?"

"Not sure yet. I'll probably go out."

It was his non-committal reply and lack of jealousy that was responsible for my next move. Rational Megs would have never suggested what I was about to suggest. A time machine would have been good. So I could've either gone back and kicked myself for being so stupid or clamp my hand across my mouth so the words didn't come out.

"Well, you know what would be fun," I said. The world moved in slow motion as I finished the last part. "We should go on a double date."

It was like a car crash. The minute it left my mouth, I regretted it and prayed that Troy would shoot down the idea. Who even suggests something like that? You didn't have to look too far to get your answer. This was by far my dumbest idea.

"Sure." His words had sealed my fate.

Panic set in as the reality hit me. I needed a date, like now. That guy I had kind of been interested in—Fictional. Non-existent. It was something to say so I didn't sound like a pathetic loser who had been sitting at home waiting for someone who wasn't interested in her. Yeah, all right. I'll admit. Me being cool with Troy and I not dating wasn't entirely the truth. I was fine with it as long as he wasn't dating someone else. Now I was not only going to have to be *okay* with it but watch it, all night long. Damn it.

So was there dial-a-date service? I sure as hell could use that right now. Trust me, at this point hiring an escort was not off the table. I had no shame and I would rather turn up with Juan Pablo on my dime, than show up alone.

It also didn't help that I was working against the clock. Assuming I could find someone who would be bearable, what would be the chances they were available on a Saturday night?

I could do this. It was one night. It would be fine. Troy and I were fine, now. I could even look at him and not need to stick panty liners under my armpits to stem the ridiculous amount of perspiration he seemed to induce. See? Totally, fucking, fine.

Was it too late to fake an illness? Something contagious but not so grotesque he would never want to see me again. I paced nervously around my living room. Fuck. I was in deep shit. Think. I willed myself to come up with some master plan but nothing happened, other than giving myself a headache and the possibility of an angina attack from the stress.

The walls were closing in on me as the first two hours ticked over with not even a possible name of a willing victim I could ask. I pulled on my runners and left my apartment for the solace of *Jilly Beans,* my lack of caffeine adding to my distress.

It was there while I ordered my extra large, extra hot latte with an extra coffee shot from hot coffee guy that inspiration struck me. Or was it desperation? Which ever it was, I was thankful. And if I didn't think it would have earned me some seriously judgmental stares, I would have gotten on my knees and praised God.

"Hi." I handed over a twenty-dollar bill and gave my best flirty smile.

"Hi," hot coffee guy responded. His cute smile teased beneath his neatly manicured beard.

"I've been watching you for a while..." What the fuck was I saying? I've been watching you for a while? I sounded like a freaking stalker. Had I suddenly lost the ability to flirt?

"I meant, I've been coming here for a while and I've noticed you." Not much better but we were going to work with it. "And..." I continued hoping that at some point the seductress in me would kick in. "I was wondering if you had any plans for this evening?" Not my best work and probably too direct, but I was on the clock.

"Are you asking me out?" Hot coffee guy leaned against the counter, amused.

Look buddy, this isn't a sideshow. It's a yes or a no. "Well, sure. I mean, if you want to. I understand if you have plans. It's short notice."

"Do you even know my name?" He raised his eyebrow as his grin widened.

"Um..." I looked down at his apron hoping to find a name badge but was disappointed when my search came up empty.

"I'm sure I'll find out, if you go out with me tonight." Lame. Why didn't I just hang a sign around my neck that read desperado? I swear I had better moves than that.

Thankfully hot coffee dude had a good sense of humor and didn't laugh his ass off at my feeble attempt. After he whipped up my order, he took a break and sat with me while I enjoyed my coffee. His name was actually Callum and he was incredibly sweet. The thirty-three-year-old New Jersey native took the trip across state lines with dreams of opening his own retro-style coffee house. I didn't want to crush his spirit by pointing out his business venture was probably better suited to New Jersey than New York, so instead I smiled and promised to be one of their first customers when he opened. That wasn't a hard promise to make, regardless of my feelings for Callum, my love for the liquid God of caffeinated goodness would stand the test of time.

So with my coffee all consumed and Callum's break over, we exchanged numbers with a promise from me that I would text details sometime that day for our hot date that evening.

It was with this new found relief that I floated back to my apartment. I had a date, he was cute *and* he wasn't on an hourly rate. So many positives, I could barely contain my excitement. I texted Troy and told him that *Project Double Date* was a go and because I had been cocky, told him to name the time and pick the place. Clearly I hadn't learnt from my earlier overconfident idiocy.

Callum—like most residents of NYC —didn't own a car, so we decided it would make more sense to meet at *Jilly Beans* and split a cab to our destination. Troy had picked a club—standard— in midtown and silently I was glad it was somewhere noisy that lacked intimacy.

We stepped out of the shiny yellow cab sometime around nine. It was a Saturday night and the streets were filled with excited locals and tourists ready to party away the weekend in the city that never slept. Smoke bellowed from a grate in the ground; the heat of the day not willing to give anyone a reprieve.

I'd worn a short black backless dress that teased at my upper thigh—no bra. I knew it was sexy but if I had any doubts, they had been put to rest by Callum's eyes almost bugging out of this head. My strappy Manolo's —the ones I had purchased while trying to manage my Troy obsession— were the perfect compliment. Callum had dressed nice too, black skinny jeans, black pointy-toed shoes and a blue and red checkered button down shirt, rolled at his biceps. I still hadn't decided whom I was trying to impress.

There was a short line, but Troy had informed me that my name with a plus one would be left on the list to ensure I would be allowed entry quickly and with no trouble. Sure enough, after the mention of my name, the rope was lowered and we were ushered inside. No cover charge was demanded, nor were our IDs checked, such was the power of celebrity.

The inside of the club was like a hundred others in the city. It was as if all the designers had all compared notes or they'd been styled by the same person. A marriage of industrial and modern, the walls had been painted to look like exposed cinder blocks. Lights swirled randomly from the exposed metal truss that hung from the celling. The bar, metallic and mirrored. Even the music sounded the same. Wash, rinse, and repeat.

"How did we get in so fast? Are you famous or something?" Callum naïvely asked.

It had been mentioned, in passing that we *might* be catching up with a friend or two of mine. Sure, the boundaries of honesty had been stretched, but telling him it was a double date right off the bat would have sent him running a mile.

"Oh, those friends I told you we may run into? They come here a lot, they said they'd leave my name at the door." My web of deceit became more intricate.

"That's cool, Megsy." Callum smiled and slung his arm around my waist. I wasn't crazy about the *Megsy* thing but didn't set him straight. His overfamiliarity felt weird, like an ill-fitting belt that ruined a good outfit.

"Megs." We'd barely travelled five feet when Troy's smiling face greeted us, his arm around the shoulder of some blonde skinny whore.

Okay, maybe she wasn't a whore and I was being catty, but the smug look she wore on her face was enough of a reason to hate her. And did he have to pick a blonde? He couldn't have diversified and picked a brunette or something?

"Troy." I forced the smile on my face and tried not to hiss out his name through gritted teeth. I hated seeing him with someone else. "Fancy meeting you here."

"Yeah, big coincidence." Thankfully he continued my rouse though his smirk very plainly showed he was enjoying making me squirm.

"Callum, this is my friend, Troy." I childishly sidled up closer to my date as I made the introductions. "Troy, Callum."

"Hey, man. Good to meet you." Troy shook Callum's hand amicably. It annoyed me how easy it seemed for him.

"Wow, are you Troy Harris? The drummer for Power Station?"

Callum's smile widened.

"He sure is." Skinny whore weighed in, tightening her grip on Troy. Oh look, she speaks. I had been worried she wouldn't be able to move her exaggerated collagen-inflated lips.

"Yeah. Guilty as charged, and this is Amber. " Troy nodded and gave his cheerleader a squeeze. Amber, she even had a stripper name. Perfect.

"Hi," Amber squeaked. "And you are..." She deliberately left her voice trailing as she looked me over.

I am the woman who made the guy whose arm you're clinging to come so many times he could barely walk two weeks ago. "Megs." I compromised. "A friend of Troy's," I added, not entirely content with my amended introduction.

Amber, obviously bored with me, turned her attention back to Troy. "Are you going to take us to the VIP section?" she whined, sounding like a toddler pleading for candy.

Troy shrugged. He didn't seem as excited as he had been when we walked in. "If that's where everyone wants to go."

"Sounds good to me. Megsy? You cool with that?" Callum's hand moved down the exposed skin on my back, dangerously close to my ass.

Troy's eyes followed Callum's wandering hand and his jaw tightened. "Megsy?" His eyebrow raised at my new found nickname. "Any objections?"

"None here." I smiled brightly and pretended like the hand on my ass or the nickname wasn't bothering me.

Amber clasped her hands together excitedly. "Great, follow me."

We tried to squeeze through the crowd but had to stop every ten steps when someone recognized Troy. Every time he was polite, spending a few moments with each fan before moving forward. Amber seemed to enjoy the extra attention and always made sure she was tightly on Troy's arm at every photo opportunity.

The VIP area carried the same theme as the rest of the club, metallic, industrial. What was different were the plush bright blue chairs that spliced through the harshness of the place. It was either some nuevo style technique I wasn't cool enough to understand or the designer had been colorblind. The glass-topped coffee tables that were randomly scattered through the room were also a mystery.

When I had suggested this double date thing, it had seemed like a bad idea. The reality was so much worse. Amber poured herself all over Troy; her hands, legs, mouth, tongue on him at all times.

It was enough to make me sick.

My hands were balled so tightly that my fingernails had cut into my palms. I smiled politely while Callum spoke passionately about different Columbian coffee beans and his aspirations to open a coffee house. Amber commandeered the conversation when she could, chatting excitedly about who had been ostracized from the catwalk in Milan— The fact the coffee table legs were wider than her thighs should have been a tip-off that she was a model. I hated her even more.

We sat and drank, the smile fixed to my face while I lived out my private hell. Troy seemed relaxed, his arms draped around the back of one of the plush blue chairs —they might look like an eyesore but at least they were comfy— with Amber perched in his lap.

Despite having a fairly decent buzz from the copious amount of alcohol I had consumed, I was still far from having a good time. Mentally I made the decision to keep a handle on my inebriation. Drunk Megs was not as diplomatic as sober Megs, and also lacked the filter between her mind and her mouth. The last thing I needed was a slurred and emotional purge of my feelings or alternatively, to grab Amber by the hair and tell her to *back the hell off*. I'll admit that the last part made me smile.

As the warmth of the alcohol spread through my body and made more me relaxed, my body discovered it had other needs— ones that required a bathroom. I had already filled my quota of listening politely and was skating to the end of my self-control. So rather than sprout the drunken, emotional confessional I had been avoiding, I decided I needed to get away from there.

"I'm going to the bathroom," I announced loudly as I stood up, my body swaying unsteadily on my feet. Not sure why I felt compelled to broadcast my bodily need, but I didn't wait for a response or an acknowledgement. Instead I opted to turn my back on the farce that was my night, both literally and figuratively and stalk to the nearest bathroom. The trip somewhat reminiscent of the first time I'd met Troy.

The private restrooms of the VIP area were extremely luxurious. The white tiled walls and chrome accents made it feel like I'd stepped into a private utopia. Luckily for me, I was the only occupant, which allowed me the ability to explore. My high heels echoed off the white marble floor as I inspected the space that featured a large, white leather chaise and an old-school bureau filled with designer lotions, soaps and colognes.

It was in the bathroom that I could finally breathe. The noise of the club and the memory of my horrendous evening could be shut behind the large metal door. It was heaven. I wondered how long I could stay here. Or if I slunk off without saying goodbye, if anyone would notice? I had been okay with not dating Troy, or at least I thought I was. What we had now was great, he made me laugh and I loved spending time with him either on the phone or seeing him briefly when I went to visit Ash. But I wasn't prepared to see him dating someone else. To see another woman touching him, going home with him. It was selfish and unreasonable and I knew that, but I would give anything for that the girl he took home tonight to be me. News flash. It wasn't going to be. Great. I was emotional, confused, far from sober and hiding in a bathroom. I had reached a new level of hell.

AMBER—MY DATE—WAS AS DUMB AS TWO PLANKS. ACTUALLY, THAT would be insulting to the wood—she was probably dumber than that, and the only interest she had in me was my ability to get her into the restricted VIP area and continue to pay for the overpriced pink cocktails she was sucking down. In all honesty, that situation was perfect with me, so I didn't feel like a complete and utter asshole in having zero interest in her.

Her number was randomly selected from the collection of crumpled napkins, matchboxes and scraps of paper I had accumulated over the last couple of weeks. Not that I called any of them before—I wasn't interested in dating— but Megs's bright idea had required me to play the number lottery.

When Megs had suggested this double date thing, I thought she was kidding. No shit, I fucking laughed. Firstly, because we weren't in junior fucking high— who the hell went on double dates, and secondly, 'cause the last thing I wanted was to see her with some other dude. Fuck that. NO.

We'd played it cool for the past few weeks, doing the friend thing. It seemed like every day I got a little bit deeper, and even though we saw each other and spoke all the time, it was never enough. Our phone conversations were hilarious and the highlight of my day. I even pretended like shit was all fucking fine even though I was less than happy that I couldn't touch her. Yeah, and it wasn't just about not being able to fuck her either. I missed the weight of her against me. Her smile. Her laugh—made my world go around.

Tonight had been its own special brand of hell. She strolled in looking like sex on legs, and I had to spend the night hiding the hard on I'd been rocking since she walked in. God, she was beautiful.

While there was no denying Amber was pretty, the girl had yet to take a breath since the minute we'd sat down. No seriously, I was surprised she hadn't passed the fuck out. She had been running her mouth about a bunch of bullshit I had no interest in. The hipster douche from the wannabe *Starbucks* that Megs had walked in with was fucking riveted. Awesome, maybe those two should get together seeing as neither of them had even noticed when Megs left to use the bathroom.

My quota with sitting around and pretending like I gave a shit was full. So rather than listen to the mundane world of those two morons, I excused myself to go take a piss. Besides, Megs had looked a weeble-wobble when she'd stood up and I could smell the disaster.

The idea of her going home with Callum fucking pissed me off. He had the nice guy routine down, but I knew nothing about this kid other than he had a Jersey accent and he had a hard-on for coffee. The thought of her sleeping with him— that put me on a whole different level of rage.

The bathroom was tucked away in the back right hand corner, and was found with very little effort. I debated whether or not I go in, or earn myself creeper status by standing outside and waiting for her to come out. The decision was made for me when after a two-minute internal debate she came barreling, bull-in-a-china-shop, through the doorway and slammed right into me. I caught her.

"Hey, Troy Harris, do you need to use the little boy's room?" Those big beautiful eyes clocked me as her tits pressed against my arm.

I bit back my grin. "Come on, Megs. You know there is nothing little about me."

"True, Miss Stripper USA is in for a treat tonight," she slurred sarcastically. She sounded drunk and maybe a little jealous.

"She's a model not a stripper," I corrected. Not that I wanted to talk about any girl other the one in front of me.

"Model, stripper—the girl needs a sandwich." Megs waved her hands animatedly in front of my face. "You might want to spring for a burger or something. It would be kind of awkward if she passed out while you were having sex."

"Thanks for the tip." My grin got bigger. "Would you like me to get your date a burger while I'm at it? My forearms are bigger than the dude's legs. Incidentally, you might want to check your wardrobe when you get home. I don't think the pants he is wearing are his own."

"They are called *skinny* jeans." Megs rolled her eyes. "They're supposed to look like *that*."

"Skinny jeans? When did real men start wearing girl's pants?" Horrified! It would be a cold day in hell before I'd be rocking a pair of pants like that. How the man hadn't spoken three octaves higher had me dumbfounded.

"Oh, you are just jealous they don't make them in your size." Megs poked me in the chest, big ass grin on her face.

"You're right, I'd be lucky to get a fucking toe in a pair. How do those pants not strangle his sack? Oh, I know *you* probably have bigger balls than he does." I laughed as I pulled her closer, her body up against mine.

"It's not the size of his balls I'm interested in." She smirked as she breathed into my face. "It's whether or not he can make me come."

Right, now she had my attention. I lowered my head and whispered in her ear. "Well it's a good thing you bought that huge dildo early in the week, 'cause it looks like you're going to need it tonight."

"Wow, thanks for the great idea." She turned her face, those beautiful lips almost touching mine. "I can get myself off with the dildo while I blow him."

Detonation. Something inside of me snapped. Like a fucking avalanche of sexual tension unleashed all at once and there was no stopping it.

My mouth slammed down on hers, my hands grabbing her ass and hauled her onto me. She got with the program, wrapping her legs around my waist and I walked us back into the bathroom she had just walked out of. My tongue got to know every inch of her mouth as I pinned her against the cold tiled wall. My hands busy palming her ass.

She moaned my name as I used the bulge in my pants to rub up against her hungry pussy, her head thrashing from side to side as I worked the length of it up and down between her legs.

I reached out an arm and slammed the bathroom door shut. My hand fumbled for the lock, twisting until I heard the telltale click of the metal sliding into place. If I weren't so fucking turned on right now, I would have thanked the club management for their progressive stance on public fornication by installing a lock. But the only thing rocking my thoughts was touching every part of the woman whose tongue was currently in my mouth.

"Megs." I pulled my mouth away; my hand brushing the hair out of her eyes. "We're in a whole world of trouble right now."

"Oh God, stop talking and touch me. That feels so good." Megs's hands clawed at my back and pulled me closer toward her.

"You going home with him tonight? You and Callum, is this a thing?" This shit wouldn't go down if she was with him. No fucking way. She moaned against me trying to get the friction she needed. "Megs, I need to know."

"No, he's just a guy. Coffee shop. Needed a date." Her mouth on me making her words come out jumbled. "Amber?"

"You're not her type, sweetheart, and neither am I."

Green light. Her eyes widened as my hands moved to her inner thigh and pulled aside her panties. She was soaking wet, the tips of my fingers coated as I circled her opening.

"Yeah, is that what you want? You want me to make you feel good?" The pads of my two fingers stroked her while I thumbed her clit.

"Yes." She circled her hips in rhythm with my hand. "It's been two weeks and I need to come so fucking bad."

Fuck, I wanted her. I wanted her to yell my name so loudly that even with the fucking music blaring in the club they'd hear her. I wanted to make her pant and pulse and come so hard she wouldn't be able to walk straight in the morning. She had me by the balls and I didn't give a fuck, my sole mission was to give her what she was begging me for.

"Megs, you have a dirty little mouth when you're horny." My hands palmed her tits, pinching her nipples through the material of her dress. "You want me to make you come with my hand?" My thumb got cozy with the opening of her pussy.

"No, Troy." She leveled me with a stare and looked me dead in the eye. "I want your cock. Fuck me."

I'd lost the ability to think.

I ripped the tiny black thong from her body and tossed what was left of it on the floor. It had no business covering what I wanted. Her legs unfurled from around my waist, sliding them down so she could stand. Not that she was going to be able to do that for long if I had my way. Her hands went straight for my belt. Fuck. We were going to do this.

Fingers wrestled with my buckle and my zipper, as my thumb rubbed circles around her clit. I was so hard, it fucking hurt. My objective, get suited up and inside of her. Like five minutes ago.

She pushed down my jeans and boxers below my hips. My dick springing free was her reward. Her hands palmed my shaft, giving me a stroke or two while I plunged two fingers inside of her.

"Yes." She writhed against the wall as I continued to play, her head flailing from side to side as I slid my fingers in and out.

It killed me to stop touching her, my cock punched out in protest to let me know he wasn't happy either. From the minute I'd seen her walk in, this is exactly what I wanted to be doing. Sadly the condom wasn't going to magically fly out of my pocket and land on my dick all by itself. And not having sex with her was *not* an option.

"No, don't stop." She grabbed my wrist as I moved my hand. Trust me, I didn't want to either.

"I need to get a condom on, Megs. Give me a second."

"Hurry, Troy. I need you in me."

I yanked the condom from my back pocket, ripping open the packet with my teeth. The packaging was tossed to the floor as I fought with Megs's hands, needing her to let go of my cock long enough to slide the latex down my shaft.

As soon as I was suited up, her hands went straight back to my dick, gripping me so tight it bordered on pain. "Fuck," I hissed, as she continued to jerk me off. It felt freaking amazing but there was no way this was going to end in a hand job.

My mouth was once again on hers as I pried her fingers from around my cock and captured her hands. She protested, bucking against me as I raised them above her head. My lips moved to her neck as I sucked against her skin. Knowing it would probably leave a mark made me even harder.

I grabbed her wrists with my hand and held them steady against the wall. "I need to be in you." My other hand rubbed the head of my cock against the opening of her pussy. She arched her back to get closer and making me feel like king of the fucking world, she was just as desperate for this as I was.

She wrestled her hands out of my hold and gripped my ass, pulling me toward her. I met her half way and slid into her in one, swift stroke.

"Megs." It was halfway between a moan and a prayer. She felt so tight and wet that I had to stop for a minute and just let myself feel it. My lips panted against her neck. This girl was going to be the death of me.

Not one to sit around and wait, Megs starting moving. Restricted by my body caging her up against the wall, she swiveled her hips from side to side, which created some crazy-good twisting sensation. It was like be jerked off—by her fucking pussy. My mind almost exploded.

I grabbed her legs and locked them around my hips, needing to get in deeper. She gasped as I gave her everything I had. I pulled out slow before sliding back in fast, my finger marks indented on her ass. She fought against me each time, not wanting me to pull out.

"Holy Shit." Megs scrunched her eyes tight as I plunged into her, her pussy clamping around my dick.

Yep, playtime was over. I slammed into her deeper and faster, her hips meeting my every thrust. It was out-of-control crazy and unrestrained, pumping into her while I kissed her hard. God, nothing should feel this good and be legal. I wanted every part of her.

"Don't stop. I'm so close," she mumbled against my lips.

"You going to come for me, Megs? I want to feel it."

"Troy."

One word. That was all she said.

It was more a muffled scream than a word, but it was clear she had said my name— and then I felt *it*. Her body tightened before it finally let go, and she shook in my arms as I rode out the rest of her orgasm. I'd been holding back, wanting to see her face when she'd finally come, not allowing myself to finish. That look alone tipped me over the edge. It was like chasing down a runaway train as I continued to pump, my load shooting deep as I panted against her throat.

We didn't move. Her legs still pinned around me with her face buried against my shoulder, both of us breathing hard. She didn't say a word, which made me edgy. Had me wondering if she was going to give me the we-shouldn't-have-done this speech. But I couldn't make myself regret it, being with her.

She tilted her head toward me and whispered. "Fuck."

Yep, that was pretty much an accurate description of it.

I released her legs and she slowly lowered them to the floor. Her body was still unsteady as she tried to smooth out her messed up hair. Her make-up? I was wearing more of her lipstick than she was, but she still looked like a knockout. Keeping away from her had been impossible, and what's worse was now I didn't want to. Not just to get my rocks off, this girl was different. Things were different.

"I told you we were in a world of trouble."

13

Megan

What the hell had I done? Who has sex in a bathroom with one guy while on a date with someone else? I was some kind of freak. What's worse is that if given the same chance, I would do it all over again. All that rhetoric about having wisdom in hindsight is bullshit. I take your hindsight and raise you one mind-blowing orgasm with the guy I'm obsessed with. Obsession, that's what it was.

That's how the whole mess started. He was the unattainable guy who looked like a sex God. He was famous. It would be fun. One time wouldn't hurt anyone. Ok, so maybe just a few more times, but I could stop at any time I wanted. What does that sound like to you? Yep, I was going to need a twelve-step program and a sponsor.

Troy and I had fucked each other senseless while the two people each of us walked in with sat maybe twenty feet away in blissful oblivion, awaiting our return. Sure, technically neither of us was dating either of them but still, that was a very slippery slope. I mean, who does that? It's like I couldn't control myself— not at all.

Was it a mistake? That was a massive trick question. My brain was telling me yes, but something that felt that good could never be a mistake. Herein lies the biggest problem. Not the fact I had crazy, bathroom sex with Troy while I was supposed to be on a date with someone else i.e. the issue that I *should* see as the problem, but that we couldn't seem to be able to be alone together and not end up naked.

How is that healthy? It's certainly not a relationship. We weren't dating, we were just fucking and while at the start of this little arrangement that had been fine, it didn't sit well with me anymore. No, I didn't think I was a whore or a pervert. Highly sexed with compulsion issues? Okay, so no one was perfect.

"Hey, we should get back." I straightened my dress and picked up my shredded panties. They weren't going to be much use to me so I tossed them in the trash and made the conscious effort to remember I was now sans underwear. Suddenly I had a new found affinity toward *Britney Spears.*

Troy pulled off his condom and tossed it the trashcan, ironically where it would lay with my discarded G-string, a tribute to our *good time.* "Are you okay?" He looked at me, concerned—probably wondering if I was going to start crying hysterically or insist he declare his intentions for me.

It was his lucky day, because not only did he just *blow his load,* he wasn't going to be getting any emotional drama from me. Nope, not doing it. Not after I had told him shit wouldn't get complicated, and I was capable of sex without emotion. There was no denying things had changed. Or at least they had for me. This wasn't just about him being sexy and us having a good time, this was about the way he made me feel. Emotions—that dirty word— were most definitely involved.

"Megs, do you want to talk about what just happened?" Troy grabbed some paper towel and handed it to me before taking care of himself.

The clean up —the stark realism of the situation. It's not like we could walk out back into the club with goo everywhere. I prayed no one would be murdered in the bathroom in the near future and it got swabbed for DNA.

"We had sex. We seem to do that a lot when were alone," I responded drily as I turned on the faucet and washed my hands. Act normal I told myself and for God's sake keep it together.

"Yeah, so..." Troy cocked his eyebrow looking for me to continue.

"So... we should probably try harder not to?" It was the best I could offer. What else could we do? Short of locking up my vagina, there wasn't a lot it seemed. One of us was the weakest link and I couldn't be sure it wasn't me.

"Yeah, probably." He nodded as he took his turn at the sink. It was all so civilized.

"Good, we agree. That was the last time." The paper towel I was using went sailing into the trash. I got the distinctive feeling of déjà vu. We've been here before and I had been just as convincing, hopefully this time, it would stick.

"Okay." Troy dried his hand. The zipping of his pants and adjusting of his T-shirt happened soon after. "So we're good then?" He looked skeptical, liked he expected more. Maybe he honestly did believe I was going to cry.

"Yep, we're perfectly fine." I was amazed at how easy the lie passed through my lips.

We did our best to tidy ourselves up so we didn't look like we just had sex, but there was only so much I could do with a compact and a lipstick. I already had a massive hickey developing on my neck, the thrill of explaining that to friends and co-workers was something I hoped to avoid.

Troy walked out first and then I followed after the obligatory five minutes. It was ridiculous really, the cloak and dagger routine. No one in the club gave us so much as a secondary glance and the only people who may have shown some concern were our *dates*, but even they didn't seem to wise up.

When I had gotten back to our little awesome foursome, Callum and Amber were laughing hysterically about some joke they had shared. The two of them discovered they both had *so much in common*, how nice for them. Troy looked bored as they generously got me up to speed on everything in the conversation I had missed. They needn't have bothered, it was plainly obvious Troy and I had been replaced.

Sitting across from Troy after just having had him inside of me was weird. There was no getting around that. Oh I gave it my best shot, playing it off like I had sex in club bathrooms all the time, and this was no big deal, but the truth remained—it was a big deal. He gave me a few concerned looks from time to time, but each time I met his eye I gave him my best it's-all-good smile and calculated when would be a good time to make my exit.

Another drink later and I had reached a respectable arbitrary length of time for me to leave. I did the whole I-have-work-in-the-morning excuse and said my goodbyes. Troy offered to call TJ for me but I declined. I'd already received one ride courtesy of Troy Harris that evening. I didn't need another.

Callum walked me outside so I could hail a cab. His hug goodbye warm but noticeably less familiar than when we'd walked it and just like that— I'd been friend-zoned.

"Hey, Megsy, thanks so much for asking me out tonight. I had a ball. Your friends are awesome."

I smiled as I returned the hug. "Yeah, well I really only know Troy. Amber, not so much."

"She's pretty great." His sheepish grin alluding to the fact he thought she was more than just *great.*

It should've been awkward, his interest in another woman while he was speaking to me, but it wasn't. Let's be honest, I was in no position to judge. He hadn't been the one to sneak off for a quickie in the bathroom.

"Yep. So I guess I'll see you at *Jilly Beans.*" There was no need to see each other socially again. It was clear he was interested in Amber and the connection between us was non-existent.

"Extra large, extra hot, extra shot." He rattled off my usual order.

"That's me. Just want a little extra of everything." I laughed but it was so *not* funny. Extra trouble is what I would be getting whether I'd ordered it or not.

No more sex with Troy Harris.
Ever.

It can't happen.

Not again.

It was like my daily mantra reminding me that the *casual fling* hadn't worked. Hold on to your seats folks, I had feelings for Troy Harris. Not just the ones that make your girlie bits tingle, I'm talking about the ones that make your heart ache.

I had stopped seeing him just as someone to be lusted over and craved for him to be my *one*, and I wanted to be his.

When that actually happened, eluded me and honestly it didn't matter—what mattered was we weren't good for each other.

The intensity we had would eventually burn out, and then what? You can't sustain a relationship on sex alone; you would eventually have to be regular people and do normal stuff. We lacked that capacity.

He had made it clear from the start; he wasn't interested in dating me. Stupidly I had convinced myself that it didn't matter. Like this girl could suddenly be ok with having feelings for a guy that weren't reciprocated. Not likely.

We were friends, and I had to push it and open my big mouth. *Sleep with him; get him out of your system, have your fun and you will be strong enough to walk away.* That is what I had told myself. Yeah that was all a big fat lie.

So do I tell him —*hey remember when I said I could handle this and wouldn't ask for more? Yeah, I take that all back, I'm asking for more.* Or do I pretend nothing has changed, try and move on and really—and I mean *really* this time— try to date someone who is going to fulfill all my needs, and be available in the boyfriend sense of the word. I wouldn't beg, not for a guy to want me, so that left only the latter option.

Troy had called the next day and I had pretended it was business as usual. I avoided talking about *us* and asked him where the tattoo voucher he'd bought me was. We fell into our usual rhythm of daily, nonsensical fodder with the plan that I slowly wean myself. Eventually I wouldn't have to fake the we're-just-friends thing, it would just be. And what a glorious day that would be.

The wedding was a good distraction. Ashlyn and Dan had

finally set a date. A few months from now, in November. The bridal party was limited to two —Troy and me. Yeah, it took me a few minutes breathing into a paper bag to calm down.

Forget. That's what I needed to do.

IN MY BID TO FORGET, I TRIED TO AVOID SOCIAL SITUATIONS WITH ASH and limited our contact to a few phone calls and coffee catch-ups. I blamed work— it was a believable excuse.

I hated keeping my distance but couldn't risk running Troy, so I stayed away.

So what does a person do when they are trying to forget? They go and get a permanent reminder etched into their skin. Just like that.

Oh look, a tattoo parlor.

Tattoos had always fascinated me, but I had always chickened out. First, because I knew my parents would freak out and later because I couldn't choose something I could live with for the Rest. Of. My. Life. That tramp stamp isn't going to just wash off when you decide it's no longer cool. The pressure was too great.

It was a whim and I assumed that my feet would *hit* the door before the needle *hit* my skin, but then I met Josh—the tattoo artist. He made me so comfortable, I actually wanted to do it. We talked about what I wanted and placement and before you knew it I was laying on his table in my panties, getting a stunningly, beautiful gray-scale feather etched above each hipbone. They were soft and feminine and just for me. My own little private rebellion.

The tattoos had hurt. A lot. I couldn't even imagine the pain ink-work like Troy's would have caused. I just closed my eyes and absorbed it. It was real, tangible and in a crazy way actually made me feel better.

Josh the tattooist was hot. His tall muscular frame was covered with intricate artwork. His black hair that was shaved short and tight against his skull made his stunning blue eyes stand out. He made me laugh, which helped considering the world of hurt I was in, and was a consummate professional while inking me. He didn't look at my rack once. Well, not that I saw anyway.

After it was done, he suggested maybe we could go out—if I was interested. No pressure.

I said yes.

Not that I wanted to, but figured it was best to get back on the horse and at least pretend I was interested in other men. Besides, he'd already seen me in my panties.

Our first date had been relatively low key— a new fusion restaurant in Chinatown. The usual first date conversation followed, favorite foods, movies and uh-hem... music. He was a Power Station fan too— sure, that wasn't weird at all.

I steered the conversation away from all things Troy Harris to talk about my work at the hospital. He didn't cut and run the minute I'd told him I was a psychologist, *or* ask me to read his future. Oh it happens and *psychic*, I am not. But I'd known in the first date he was never going to be my forever.

The second date was a little more fun. We watched the goofy classic, *The Rocky Horror Picture Show* at *Landmark Sunshine Cinemas* on the Lower East Side. Josh joined me in the aisle for a loud, off-key rendition of "Time-Warp" —neither of us would be quitting our day jobs.

It was on the second date when he'd kissed me.

After the movie we'd stopped in at my old work place *Garro's* for a drink. Our waitress had just sauntered off with instructions to load us up with cheese fries and soda when Josh leaned across the table and kissed me.

While unexpected, it wasn't all together horrible. More of a savor-my-lips than tongue-down-my-throat kind of kiss and when it was over, I smiled and said thank you. Thank you! Like the man had just handed me a napkin or a bottle of ketchup.

After that second date, I told Troy about Josh.

It was the right thing to do. Sure we'd never dated and were no longer sleeping together, but I still felt I needed to tell him. If I was honest with myself, I told him hoping to illicit some reaction. Maybe a *hey, don't date him* or *I really miss sleeping with you* —the second response probably more likely than the first— but I just thought he might, I don't know, have an opinion.

He didn't. Well, at least none he shared with me. He instead let me talk about my dates and didn't even make a wise-ass remark about the guy kissing me. Part of me was disappointed. Whatever Troy and I had shared romantically, it was now the past.

With the third date came a certain amount of anticipation. He'd already kissed me and while it had been very PG-13, he would probably want to up that rating. Possibly get some hands on action.

Usually not a problem for me— a good make out session with some dry humping was good for the soul. Like chicken soup for your libido. But, my soul and my libido were playing a solid game of hide-and-go-seek when it came to tattoo guy Josh. I was attracted to him; I just wasn't attracted to him *enough*.

So the third date was the deal-breaker. Either some magic started to happen or we said our friendly goodbyes and saved ourselves the trouble. To test the chemistry, I decided to go all out— sexy outfit, sexy shoes, a venue that would be conducive to *the mood* and alcohol. Lots of alcohol. Might as well give poor Josh a fighting chance.

Josh arrived at my apartment around seven. He looked great, dressed head to toe in black —black baggy jeans, black button down shirt and black heavy boots; his tattooed arm sleeves and neck on display. He smiled with appreciation at the plunging neckline of my new red dress. Discreetly readjusting his man-bits as we got into his Jeep Wrangler. Objective of the dress—met.

For this monumental make-or-break date, I'd pick a little

basement bar in Soho. Not the typical eye-rolling ultra trendy club that usually graced the sidewalk of that locale, no, it was a bar. Like a speakeasy but without the jazz band or moonshine.

Donavan's was a hidden gem. With no markings or signage—word of mouth was the only way you found this dirty little secret. It promised a plethora of liquor, dartboards, pool tables, and good music at the hand of the hottest DJs in town.

"You sure this is the right place?" Josh followed me down the narrow, rickety stairwell.

"Relax, where's your sense of adventure?" I tapped on the dilapidated door.

"Do we need a secret handshake?" Josh grabbed my hand and gave it a squeeze.

"'Sup." The security guard was huge. His large menacing body filling the doorway he'd opened.

"Hey, umm is there a code word or something?" Neither my cheesy grin nor my attempt at humor impressed the giant in front of me. My bad.

"IDs?" Amazing how that small demand translated into *show me your IDs and stop wasting my time.* Powerful and scary. It kind of excited me. The night was definitely not going to suck.

"You really know how to pick a place." Josh slung his arm around me, his pleased smile teased at the corners of his mouth.

On the inside, the place was huge. It expended into a large but slightly uneven rectangle. And like a Steampunk wet dream, it featured celling to floor matte black walls with gold gilded cornices.

"Rumor has it, anything goes in this place. Don't ask, don't tell." I pulled his arm playfully.

"Is that why there's a dude smoking a joint in the corner?"

"Could be medicinal. So judgey."

"Want a beer to go with the contact high?" Josh wrapped his arms around me and nuzzled my neck. Okay so the touchy-feely stuff was going to happen sooner than later. In that case I was definitely going to need that drink.

"Um, can I have a Long Island Iced Tea instead?" Beer wasn't going to cut it.

"Sure, baby. You can have whatever you want." Josh brushed the hair away from my face. Calling me *baby* was a new development.

We made it to the bar through the maze of people and ordered our drinks. Josh handed over some cash as the disinterested bartender prepared my Long Island and twisted the cap off Josh's Coors Light. He didn't look up at us once. Perhaps this was the anti-*Cheers* of the bar world— "where everybody knows your name" didn't apply. They didn't only *not* know it, but they didn't care to either.

"Have I told how great that dress looks on you?" Josh's smile hinted he was more interested in what was under the dress, as he leaned up against the bar.

"Thanks." Smile. "It's new." Smile. Why was this drink taking so long to make? Next time, order shots.

"Megan."

He refused to call me Megs, preferring to use the name that graced my birth certificate. It all stemmed from a previously owned pet cat named Megs that had died when he was eight. I wasn't sure if I should be horrified that someone had named their cat *Megs* or if I should book this guy in for therapy. You were eight, dude—she is in a better place, move on.

"Are you nervous?" His hand grazed across my cheek.

"No." My exaggerated laugh didn't fool anyone. "Yes."

"It's the whole third-date-third-base expectation. I'm not sure I am ready to sleep with you." What the fuck was I saying? My mouth spewed words my brain was convinced I should not be saying.

"Baby, you are far from a foregone conclusion." He smiled; it was a nice smile. Just not as nice as Troy's. "Have I done anything to make you think that?"

Thank you, sweet baby Jesus, my drink was finally ready. I snatched the highball the minute it hit the bar, sipping the icy alcoholic goodness through a straw. Smile. "No, of course not." Smile. Hiding emotions was something I clearly sucked at.

"Megan, we're not going to do anything you're not comfortable with. No expectations here, okay?" He grabbed his beer from the bar and took a sip.

"I don't usually suck this much at dating." It was more of an apology than an explanation. My *game* was very much missing in action.

"Why don't we go shoot some pool or something?" His head jerked to the direction of the back left hand corner where we were told we'd find a couple of tables. "Get the ball action out of the way so you can relax." The smile lit up his blue eyes.

I laughed. And not the fake kind. "I'd like that." God he was sweet. That alone deserved a kiss.

He looped his arm around my waist and led us to the back end of the club. The pool tables were situated in little secluded alcoves, almost like little hidey-holes. Kudos management — it was a cute way to give the players privacy and probably facilitated more than just a blowjob or two. Things were looking up; I was thinking about blowjobs and not having a full-on panic attack. Awesome.

As we rounded the corner and stepped into the pool-cave the brighter light of the gaming area distorted my vision momentarily.

"Megs?" Troy's eyes widened as he stood from taking his shot at the table. Every curve of his chest was displayed through the tight fabric of his white *Nirvana* T-shirt.

Wow. He looked *good*. Wearing faded blue jeans and black boots; he was his usual mix of unpretentious sexiness. Why tonight did it seem so much more... sexier.

"Megs, aren't you going to introduce us to your friend?" I was guessing from his tone I had been staring and unresponsive. It had been a while since he had affected me like that. Usually, I had time to prepare myself to act normal. Psyche myself up to see him and play my usual game of pretend. This was something else, I had been blindsided. I had also been drinking, so we can put some blame on that. I ignored the fact the couple of sips I had taken wouldn't qualify as drinking.

"Yes, of course." My brain kicked into gear as I peeled my eyes away from Troy's chest. Jason, who I hadn't noticed up until now, gave me a friendly wave.

"Troy and Jason, this is Josh. He's a friend. Josh, this is Jason and Troy." I stopped short not knowing how to explain my affiliation. *Here are two members of Power Station, my best friend's fiancé's band and before I forget to mention it, I slept with one of them,* didn't seem like a good idea.

"Hey, dude." Jason stepped forward and shook Josh's hand, Josh returned the handshake with a mix of shock and genuine awe on his face. I was wondering how long it would be before he broke out the you-didn't-tell-me-you-knew-Power-Station speech. Jase gave me a huge hug and a cheeky smile before adding, "Megs, you look like you're going to start some trouble in that dress tonight."

"She sure is." Troy eyes steamrolled over the length of my body and I had to remember to breathe. "Josh, nice to meet you." He took his turn to do some handshaking.

"Wow, Megan. You know Power Station? How could this have never come up?" Strangely even though this conversation was directed at me, Josh was too busy shaking Troy's hand and smiling at the guys to actually look at me. "Jason, Troy. I'm a big fan."

I rolled my eyes. I couldn't help it. While Josh had been a *fan,* he wasn't a *big fan.* He didn't have every album like I did and certainly hadn't been to the number of shows I had been. But no, put a couple of the band members in front of him and suddenly he becomes star-struck and is instantly their biggest fan.

"It didn't seem like a big deal." I lied, not sure what would be an acceptable excuse seeing as we had actually spoken about the band. The time when we compared musical tastes on our first date and their name had come up probably would have been an excellent time to throw in there, oh yeah, I know them. "I didn't want to name-drop like I was bragging," I added, figuring it would redeem me slightly.

"Oh, Megs, you're such a sweetheart not wanting to exploit us like that." Troy leaned in and gave me a hug, his hands pressed against me making me feel like I was on fire. "This isn't your usual hang out, *Megan.*" I didn't miss the emphasis on my name.

To say it was horrible to see Troy was a lie. I had wanted to see him, but I couldn't trust myself. Being close to him when I didn't have my emotions in check would be dangerous, with reasonable thought thrown out the window. I would want him— to touch, to taste, to savor. It wasn't just the instant arousal the minute I'd walked in the room; it was my thumping heartbeat I couldn't rein in. My inability to be near him without telling him how much I wanted him to hold me.

"No, not my usual hang out." I suppressed the urge to press my lips against his neck. "I thought I would try something different." I didn't just mean the club. Josh was also neatly pigeonholed in the *something different*. Or maybe it was just the same but different. Having a stand-in bad boy for the one I couldn't have. The one I desperately wanted.

"Wow, so how do you all know each other?" Josh seemed oblivious to the fact I wanted nothing more than to throw Troy across the pool table and kiss him.

I usually had my shit more together than this; we had been talking and seeing each other for weeks without incident and now I was willing to throw away our perfect unblemished record. What the hell was I doing? I was here with another guy. One who had asked a question that I still hadn't answered.

"My best friend, Ashlyn— the one I told you about who used to work with me at the bar," I explained turning back my attention to Josh, you know the guy I was considering kissing or perhaps maybe sleeping with tonight. "Well, Ash is engaged to Dan, so I kind of got acquainted with the band through her."

It felt dirty after I'd said it, like my friendship with Jason and Troy was an incidental after effect of Ash and Dan's relationship, which wasn't true. I don't know why I didn't say, we'd met in a club one day and all become friends. Maybe I was worried that my real feelings for Troy would be revealed unless I kept it light and uncomplicated. I hated myself for saying it all the same.

"Really?" Jason laughed. I was petrified by what he was going to say next. "I don't think Ash can take all the credit for it. Megs made a pretty memorable first impression." Busted! I prayed the walk down memory lane would end there.

"Yeah, that was a great night," Troy added, his voice tight but his face unreadable. "You might want to keep an eye on her, buddy; she has a tendency to fall down if she has too much to drink." Okay, that was a cheap shot. He hadn't reacted this way on our disastrous double date *or* after our numerous sexual encounters. The tension in the air crackled between us.

"Um, did I miss something?" Josh looked awkwardly between us. It was obvious that *something had been missed*. Even Josh in his post-Power-Station-appreciation glow could spot it a mile away.

Troy answered before I had a chance to open my mouth. "Miss something?" He let out a huge laugh. "We're just messing around. I'm not used to seeing Megs so serious, that's all."

While Josh seemed satisfied with Troy's explanation, I didn't miss the edge in Troy's voice. My heart was beating so fast I was positive that any minute it was going to leap out of my chest and land on the pool table. Was Troy trying to prove a point? And did he have to do it so publically or so sarcastically? It seemed I hadn't been the only person who caught the things-are-getting-strange vibe with Jason studying both Troy and I carefully before stepping in.

"Hey, Josh, why don't you let me buy you a beer while these two rack up the balls for the next game." Jase tapped Josh on the shoulder. "They have this awesome microbrew that is off-menu, I'll get us hooked up."

If it wouldn't have attracted too much attention I would have thrown myself at Jason and kissed him, his plan to give me and Troy *a moment,* an answer to my silent prayer that this eyeballing contest we seemed to be playing would come to an end.

Josh looked genuinely pleased that Jason had extended a private invitation. If he'd suspected it was anything more, he wasn't letting on. "Sure, as long as Megan doesn't mind. You want another drink, baby?"

"No, I'm fine." I gave him a polite smile and lifted my mostly full Long Island. "Thanks for asking. Go ahead with Jason. I don't mind." Pushing him out the door and telling him not to hurry right back would probably raise alarm bells, so I went with nonchalant.

"Awesome, thanks, baby." Josh gave me a squeeze before

walking off with Jason, his voice trailing off in the distance. "So you guys are releasing a new album soon huh?"

"Your new boyfriend I assume." It wasn't a question; Troy tipped his chin toward the direction that Josh and Jase had left. He didn't smile as he folded his arms in front of his chest.

"He isn't my boyfriend, just a guy I'm seeing," I snapped, wondering why he was acting so cagey. "I don't know why you are being weird about it. I told you I was dating someone."

I didn't trust myself to be near him, knowing how twisted he made my emotions.

Troy didn't have the same concerns about getting closer to me it seemed as he took a step in my direction. His hand tilted my chin to look him in his beautiful eyes. "You might want to clarify that with him. How many more times can he call you baby?" I could feel his breath on my skin as he spoke. "And I'm not the one being weird, *Megan*."

It was much harder to be strong when I had to look at him, to deny that I wasn't making a huge mistake by being with someone else. "What do you want me to say? You want me to tell him we slept together? I didn't think that would help our cause of keeping *that* in the past."

"Jesus, Megs, there is a lot of room between not knowing me and fucking me." His hand grazed across his chin. "You didn't think to pick somewhere in the middle?" His forehead crinkled in confusion.

"I panicked. I wasn't expecting to see you here. I wasn't prepared to answer questions about us. I just thought it would be easier..."

"Questions about us? Aren't we supposed to be friends, I don't understand why that's so complicated. You had no problem telling *me* about *him*." I saw the hurt flicker through his hazel eyes. "You introduce me as your friend, not just some fucking dude you happen to know because of Ash."

"I don't know what to say. You were never just some dude. I'm sorry that I said it and more than that, I'm sorry that I implied that you weren't my friend."

Sorry didn't even begin to cut it. I felt horrible, there had been no need to lie about how I'd known Troy and yet, I had. It was the guilt. As ridiculous as it sounded, I felt like I was cheating. Cheating on Troy and cheating on myself by being with someone else. It took seeing them together in the room to put that in perspective. Troy wasn't some guy I could just forget by dating someone else. He wasn't someone I could just replace. I had been stupid to assume that I could, and even more stupid for falling in love with him. Yeah, I had avoided the word, danced around infatuation and lust, but what I felt was beyond those.

"Fuck, Megs, when you give those puppy dog eyes, it's really hard for me to be pissed at you." Troy rolled his eyes and he gave me a smile I didn't think I deserved. He moved in closer and rubbed my arm with the tips of his fingers.

I shook my head softly and whispered. "Don't be pissed at me, I'm already pissed at myself."

"Yeah?" Troy raised an eyebrow. "And why are you pissed at yourself?"

A slow breath escaped my lips as I closed whatever distance there was between us. "There isn't enough time to list all the reasons right now, Troy."

It was instinct. I couldn't be this so close to him and not touch him. It felt natural, like where I belonged. It wasn't about sex or lust, it was a comfort I couldn't describe and it's what I needed. My head fell against his chest as my arms strained to wrap around him.

"Megs, what are you doing?" Troy chuckled against my hair.

My eyes closed as I absorbed him, savoring the moment. If I could have stopped us both from talking I would have. "I just need you to hold me right now. I know they are going to be back really soon, just hold me for a minute."

"Megs, if there is something wrong you would tell me, right?" Troy gently ran his hand through my hair; there was a concern in his voice that hadn't been there before. "This guy isn't being an asshole is he?"

I signed as I answered honestly. "No, the only asshole here is me."

He held me close to his body for a while and I let his warmness envelop me. It was selfish and I had no right to the comfort it afforded me, but I wanted it anyway. He wasn't mine, he had never been mine and there would never be a time he would be. I'd tried to forget him, get over him and even talk myself into the fact that what we'd had was purely a sexual connection. What I had completely ignored was the truth, that I'd fallen for him—God it was so much more than that—and I wanted to have a relationship with him. Any other guy that came into my life was never going to measure up. It hadn't been fair to anyone, least of all not to Josh.

I reluctantly peeled myself away from Troy's chest, giving him my best smile to reassure him I was okay. The last thing Josh deserved was to come back and see me in the arms of another guy, especially when he'd held such high hopes for tonight. It was bad enough my heart already belonged to someone else; I wasn't going to lie about it as well. Maybe Josh didn't want a relationship, maybe he was looking for a good time; in any case, I wasn't the girl for either of those things. The only fair thing would be to tell him.

Troy studied me curiously as I moved to the opposite end of the pool table and racked up the balls in the triangle. I had no intention of playing but it gave me something to do, something to take my mind off the mess that I had apparently got myself into.

Troy edged closer to me, his hand resting next to me on the pool table. "Megs, don't go home with him," he pleaded, my heart fracturing with the sound. His beautiful eyes were focused and serious. It hurt to look at them.

"Hey, baby. This beer is the *shit.* You want a taste?" Josh waltzed in, a half consumed bottle of beer in his hand and just like that, whatever moment Troy and I had had was over. Josh's eyes flicked over the racked-up balls on the felt and grinned. "Awesome, you set up. Who's breaking?"

Never had a more appropriate question been asked. *Who's breaking?* I was, and I didn't want to. My feet miraculously took a few steps in front of the other and ended up by Josh's side. "Would it be okay if we didn't play. I'm a little tired."

"Come on, Megs." Jason looked disappointed as he grabbed a pool cue from the wall. "Stay and play a game."

Josh put his arms around me and I tried not to flinch. "You sure you don't want to play for a bit?" He was disappointed. His chance to rub shoulders with the rich-and-famous sabotaged by a moody date.

"You can stay if you want, you don't have to leave." Honestly at this point it didn't matter. I was going home alone, so regardless if I walked out the door by myself or not, our date was coming to a very quick finale.

"Sorry boys, looks like Megan wants to call it a night." Josh looked hopeful as he waved to the guys. "Maybe some other time?"

Troy leaned against his pool cue and gave us a tight smile. "Sure, anytime." I was almost positive that offer was not genuine.

"Bye, Jase, Troy. I'll see you soon." I gave them both a half-hearted wave and let Josh put his arm around my waist.

He quickly swallowed what was left of his beer and placed the empty bottle on a nearby table. "See you, Troy, Jason. Thanks for the beer."

Jase nodded and gave us a warm smile. "No problem, enjoy your night."

I forced my way back though the maze of bodies, just needing to get out of the club. It felt like I couldn't breathe, a condition made worse by Josh's hands around my waist. I was almost dizzy by the time we made it to the front door.

"Hey baby, what's the hurry?" He eyed me curiously as the bouncer who had let us in earlier opened the door to let us back out.

I didn't answer, instead I climbed the stairs that lead to the sidewalk, all my concentration on putting one foot in front of the other so I didn't fall on my face. A trip to the emergency room was not on the agenda for tonight.

Relief flooded me once I'd finally made it to the top, the street still brimming with night traffic. "Megan, slow down." Josh grabbed my wrist as I tried to hail a cab. "You want to tell me what that was about?" He spun me around and forced me to look at him. He didn't seem mad, which was a plus, but he wasn't going to let me get into a cab without some kind of explanation.

Words eluded me. What did I even say? He was a fun guy, sure, we weren't a perfect match, but he'd been so incredibly nice to me. He had been a distraction and that hadn't been fair. So rather than continue the lie, I went with the truth and hoped it would stop me from feeling like a total jerk.

"Look, you're a nice guy but we can't see each other any more. I thought I was ready to date someone but I'm not. I don't want to give you the it's-not-you-it's-me line but it really is *me*. I just can't do this."

He slowly let go of my wrist. "Is this because you're running away from *him*?" His head jerked to the direction of the rickety stairwell.

"Huh?" My mouth dropped open. How did he know? Did one of my subconscious thoughts actually come out of my mouth or had he seen us together? Did I deny or confirm it? Now would have been a good time for some random act of God. In the end, my silence had been enough.

"Megan, you and me, we're in a similar line of work. You'd be surprised how much you learn about a person when they are lying in your chair, waiting for you to tattoo them. Some get chatty, some stay quiet like you did; either way, you can read all you need to read from their body." There was a kindness in his eyes when he spoke, it made me hate myself even more. "There are usually three different types of people who come and get ink."

He held up his fingers and started to list them. "One. The living canvas. For these people their skin is blank pages that they use to tell their story. There is no separation between the art and them. It's a part of them as much as an ear or a toe. It's an addiction as well as an expression. Two. The weekend warrior. They go under the needle to earn cool points or to follow trend. These are the people who usually get some lame tribal band around their arm or a tramp stamp. They get tats that are highly visible and often cheesy. I don't judge, but I assume that five to ten years down the track they will be spending time with a laser. Three. The tortured soul. They use the art as therapy, to memorialize something or a loved one. They mark their skins with tributes and dedications or a connection to something or someone. It's just for them;

displayed or not displayed it wouldn't mean any more or less.

"I knew when you came into my studio that you weren't a weekend warrior and you had virgin skin so it just left the last option. That's why I asked you to sit down and let me draw something. I could tell you needed it."

"They are beautiful." My hands involuntary brushed across my hips where my tattoos were safely hidden.

"Like the girl who's wearing them." He smiled. "I didn't know it was a guy, but I sensed your head was elsewhere. You're *really* pretty though and I just thought I'd take a chance. Hoping whatever demon was chasing you would hopefully quiet down and we could get to know each other a little better. You seemed like you would be a lot of fun. The not wanting to kiss me should have tipped me off that you weren't interested, but you know..." He gave me an adorable smile. "I figured I'd keep trying."

"I'm sorry." I swallowed. "I feel so fucking terrible right now."

Apparently the pedestrians on the street didn't care for my heart felt apology, nor did they seem invested in our chat; their heated stares glared as they jostled past us as we stood in the middle of the sidewalk. Josh gently took my hand and guided me away from the foot traffic and onto a nearby stoop.

"Why? 'Cause you went out with me?" He rubbed the base of his chin, his eyes confused like he could comprehend why I'd felt bad.

Because I used you, because there was never going to be anyone else other than him. The words I eventually said were softer but no less true. "Because I let you believe there was more than there was."

"You didn't do anything like that." He laughed. "I had a ball, didn't you have fun? Cheese fries and drag queens, I don't think I've ever had a date like that."

"Yeah, it was nice." I agreed, for the most part it had been pleasant. It certainly wasn't terrible and as horrible as it sounded, he had been a lovely distraction.

"Megan, I really like seeing that beautiful smile and it's been cool hanging out with you over the last week or so. But a man can't really compete with a memory, especially one that is still very much in your life." He gave me slight shrug of the shoulders.

Did I explain further or did I let it go? I'd never met a guy who'd seemed so relaxed about the fact his date wasn't actually interested in him. It confused me a little but most of all, I was glad. Josh had been right about one thing, we *were* in a similar line of work. He knew exactly what to say and exactly how to say it. There was going to be no dramatic showdown on the street and I was glad that I had walked into his shop that day. He'd given me so much more than the beautiful feathers that now graced my skin.

"Do I owe you any extra money for the counseling? I feel like those tattoos were hugely under priced," I asked cautiously, thankful that out of all the tattoo shops in all of New York, I walked into his.

Another shrug, another smile. "Nah, you were a nice canvas to work on. I got to look at your beautiful skin for hours instead of a big sweaty biker. You also smell a lot nicer than they usually do."

And just like that it was over. It had been almost anticlimactic. We both knew we probably wouldn't be seeing each again, not unless I decided to get another tattoo, and there was an easy sense of calm around the end of it. If I didn't think it would send the wrong signal, I would have given him a big hug but instead I opted for a shoulder bump and a smile. "Thanks, Josh, I showered that morning and everything. I'm so glad I didn't stink."

He playfully bumped me back and smiled. "I know the date's pretty much a bust, but will you let me drive you home?"

"Yeah, I would like that."

15

Megan

I can't believe she just left with the asshole. She had asked me to hold her, and then she turned around and left with *him*. One thing was fucking clear— she still wanted me as much as I still wanted her. I felt it and I saw it in her eyes when I'd wrapped my arms around her. It was not fucking one-sided and all she had to do was *not* go home with him.

I didn't say a fucking word when she told me she had started dating some dude. The chair I threw at the wall, well that couldn't be helped. She was so cagey about how they'd met. He wasn't even her type as far as I could tell but if she was happy, then I'd keep a lid on it. I'd even kept my trap shut when she mentioned he'd kissed her. Yep. That had been a fun night. I'd gotten into my Lambo and redlined the shit out of it before I calmed down enough to finally go home. There was no reason why she shouldn't be kissing some other guy, not unless you counted the fact that I didn't want her to. Nope, those lips I only wanted on me.

Seeing his hands on her, calling her *baby*, was more than I could fucking stand. But the kicker was her playing it off like she barely knew me. The fucking icing on the cake.

I'd been ready to tell her to forget it; I wasn't really interested in being some chump who sat on the sidelines. But those eyes, when she said she was sorry, there was no way those words would come out of my mouth. She didn't just look fucking sorry, she looked sad. Tore me up. I didn't care if it was me or the situation— I wanted it to stop. The hug; it was the beginning of the end.

My hands on her were something I'd avoided. Why torture myself? But the minute that I had her, there was no way I could pretend she didn't matter, that I didn't want her. That I didn't think about her, each and every fucking night.

So what did she do? She turned around and left with some other guy who, as far as I was concerned, hadn't proved he deserved her.

"Dude, that vein in your neck bulges any more than it is now, you're going to spring a leak." Jase's stare nailed me from across the table.

"I just think she can do better than him. C'mon, Jase, even you can admit she doesn't belong with him." The pool cue in my hand was probably getting a little more pressure than it would have liked.

Jase shrugged. "He seemed okay." He pulled the cue out from my death grip before it snapped. Smart move.

"Okay? Are you serious, brother? He called her *Megan* the whole fucking time. Everyone knows she prefers Megs." None of this shit was even close to being okay.

Jase took a swig of his beer, his smirk poking out from behind the bottle. "So it's her date's tendency to use her *real* name that has you in a mood. Good to know." His shit-eating grin got wider. Smug bastard.

Too juiced up to stand still, I paced around the room. "And what the fuck is up with calling her *baby*? He's known her for like five fucking minutes. Maybe he should've just pulled his dick out and taken a piss on her, it would have been less obvious."

Jase eyeballed me hard, planting his ass on the beat-up couch beside the table. "So you going to tell me how long you've been sleeping with her or we going to insult the poor dude some more?"

"Fuck."

I thought it as well as said it. No point denying it now, I'd been acting like a moody asshole since Megs had walked in. It was only a matter of time before he wised up and put two and two together. Must've been why he asked Josh to go have a friendly beer with him at the bar, not his hard-on for the off-menu microbrew. He'd clued up that we needed to talk, and like the stand-up guy that he was, he made it happen. I parked my ass on the chair next to him and slowly let out a breath.

"I'd suspected as much." Jase casually took another mouthful of beer. "Dan might have his head up his ass, but I've noticed your little secret squirrel meetings with Megs, and your lack of female company."

"We thought we'd kept it under wraps." I pinched the bridge of my nose and hoped no one else had caught the vibe.

"Trust me, dude, I'm almost positive no one has noticed. James and Alex are so focused on the album and we've already established Dan's main concern is making Ash his Mrs."

"Why didn't you say something?"

"I figured if you hadn't mentioned it, you probably didn't want to talk about it. I wasn't going to push the issue."

That was the big difference between Jason and Dan. If I'd been sitting here with Dan, he would have run his mouth for the next few hours demanding to know the how's and what's of the situation. Jase on the other hand, had no interest in the details. He just sat back and relaxed, and if you wanted to spill your guts then he'd happily listen. No pressure, either way. It was the main reason why I'd called him and asked to shoot some pool with me tonight. I didn't want the fucking twenty questions that usually came with a night out with Dan.

"Megs had said she had a date tonight, I had no idea she was coming here. He'd already kissed her, third date and everything. Do the math. I wasn't going to sit at home like a fucking little bitch."

"So I'm your rebound. Nice." Jase tipped his chin with a grin.

"Well getting loaded and other women were off the table so... No one gives a fuck who we are here. I just wanted to shoot some pool, maybe have a beer without someone trying to crawl into my lap."

That had been the plan at least. Then she'd walked through the doorway; looking so hot I'd had to nail my feet to floor so I didn't walk straight over to her and attack her mouth. The fact she was with a dude meant jack shit to me. As far as I was concerned, the asshole was touching what didn't belong to him.

My head fell back against the couch, wondering if while I was sitting with my dick in my hand, the tattoo king of NYC was rounding second base. "This is so fucked up, man." And wasn't that the understatement of the fucking century.

"So, I'm guessing this was more than just a sex thing." Jase proved how smart he was by reading between the lines.

I shut my eyes and let out a breath. "Yep."

"You love her?"

Jase's simple question was like taking a bat swing upside my head. Did I love her? I didn't want to be without her, and if that's what love was then yeah, I was there.

Well, fuck me. I wasn't just being a jealous asshole, nope. It went much deeper than that, but there was no way the first time I would be saying it would be to Jase. It would be to Megs, or not at all.

"What I do know for sure is, that I like her a hell of a lot and I don't want her with someone else."

Jase drained the rest of his beer and cracked his knuckles. "Sounds like we have problem."

"Yep."

"You want to go get a burger or something, talk some of this shit out?"

"Should we paint each other's toenails as well?"

"Well I sure as hell ain't going to try and braid that shit you call hair."

"Let's get out of here, I need some distance."

"Right behind you."

While we'd decided against painting each other's nails, we did end up back at my place. Somewhere in between throwing a few hands of poker and tossing back a few beers, I'd given Jase the rundown on the Megs dilemma. It didn't solve shit but it kept me from punching holes in the drywall. I didn't even want to think about how Megs had spent her night. Nope, not going there. I was pushing that shit to the side of my brain that had a big do-not-disturb sign hanging off it.

We must have crashed at some point because when I woke up in the morning there was a half spilled bottle of beer on the floor and a passed out Jason Irwin snoring on the rug.

"Dude." I reached down and gave him a shove. "How much did we drink last night?"

Jase peeled open an eye. "Fuck, man. Your floor sucks." He scrubbed his face with his hand. "I have the mother of all headaches. I need about ten Excedrin and five gallons of coffee."

"On it." I fished my phone out of my pocket and sent Dan a text to bring some coffee around. The day wasn't going to be pretty for either of us. The empties of the floor gave me a hint we'd drank more than a case between us.

My stomach rolled as I made it my feet. "Grab the door when he gets here. I'll get the Excedrin so this sucks a little less." Not that I was convinced they were going to make a shit of difference, nothing in my medicine cabinet was even going to make a dent.

I needed out of here. The place, the situation and the mind frame. At least that's what I kept telling myself as I snagged the bottle of pills from the bathroom cabinet and went back to the living room.

"Fuck, you both look like shit. Rough night?" Dan tossed me the what-the-fuck the minute I walked back in.

Awesome. My morning hadn't sucked enough.

"Don't start asswipe. I have zero mood for your shit."

"Wow. You seriously need to get laid." Dan handed me his usual response as he parked his ass on my two-seater.

Yeah, *that* was the fucking solution. Not likely. "Thanks but I don't think any amount of pussy is going to cure the migraine." I tossed the bottle of Excedrin to Jase.

"Shit going down I need to know about?" Dan eyeballed me as I collapsed into the chair beside him. He didn't need to say he had my back— the look was enough.

"Nope, just need to sober myself up so I can drive." That's about as much as I was willing to share. My head fell back and I squeezed my eyes shut, willing my liver to kick in and get the show on the road.

"You taking off?" Dan asked.

"Yeah, a couple of days. Maybe Atlantic City?" My eyes rolled back into focus as I lifted my lids. Who knew where I'd end up. The location was irrelevant. The distance was what mattered.

"You want some company? I've got no where to be." Jase swallowed his pills followed by his Java chaser.

"Fuck it, we should all go. We'll be like the Wolf pack. Let me square things away with Ash." Dan didn't bother to check if I wanted the tag along. I guessed this was his version of trying to make me feel better.

"No offence, but I don't need my hand held."

"Stop being a buzzkill. We'll even find someone to suck your dick while we're there. Trust me, it will improve your *zero mood* bullshit. Bring your suit too, I want to play the tables and I'm going to need a spotter," Dan added, not giving a fuck that he hadn't been invited.

"Fuck me, this isn't about your scheme for counting cards is it?" Jase lowered his cup.

Dan folded his arms across his chest not willing to admit his plan was bogus. "Hate all you want, but that shit is full proof."

"Hey Rain Man." I didn't even bother addressing how much we weren't going to be getting my dick sucked. "You get caught doing that, a big scary asshole takes you into a little back room and messes you up so badly you're going to spend the rest of your days shitting into a bag."

"Seriously, Troy." Dan rolled his eyes. "I'm going to need to hook you up with Megs with some therapy. That is just messed up."

Silence.

"Okay. Someone want to tell me why we're eyeballing each

other and don't give me some bullshit excuse about being hung over." Dan shot us a both the start-talking look.

"We saw Megs last night." This was going to be fun. Of all the things I didn't want to talk about, *Megs* and *last night* were at the top of the list. "I was less than polite to her and her date."

"Megs was on a date last night? Huh, must have been the last one. Anyway, you need to jump on the horn and make that shit right." Dan poked me in the chest. "No need to be a pussy about it, just tell her you're sorry and move on. She'll forgive you. That girl is a sweetheart."

Ain't no way things would be smoothed over by a phone call but the dude wasn't to know that. How would that call even go? Hey, I know you were with some other dude last night but I wised up to the fact I'm in love with you and need you to be my girl. Too little, too late on that one. And what the fuck was the rest of the stuff he was talking about?

"Wait a minute. What do you mean by *last* one?"

Dan waved it off, already bored with conversation. "I mean she called Ash last night, she isn't seeing the tattoo guy anymore. Something about it not working out. I didn't pay too much attention."

"Dan, I need you to focus." I grabbed him by the shirt and leveled him with a stare. My heart thumping like the fucker was keeping time to Metallica. "Are you sure that's what she said?"

"Lay off asshole, fuck." He pushed off my hands and straightened his shirt. "Yes, that's what she said. What's the big deal?"

The big deal was that last I saw of Megs she was upset and needed to be held. I didn't know the why's or the what's, but shit wasn't right. I'd asked her not to go home with the asshole she'd walked with, but she left anyway. His fucking hands on her as they walked out. She didn't fight him so I assumed any further attention was going to come courtesy of the guy who kept calling her *baby*. They didn't look like they were heading for splitsville.

"When we saw them, they didn't look like they were about to break up." I was still trying to wrap my head around it.

"Well maybe after you saw them they got into a fight or maybe the kid found Jesus and was no longer interested in pussy?

Whatever the reason, they ain't together anymore." Dan clapped his hands together and rubbed in anticipation. "Now let's talk AC."

There was no way I was getting in a car and going anywhere right now unless it was to Megs's apartment. I didn't give a fuck if I had to bang her damn door down, she was going to talk to me and tell me why she'd been so sad, and then I would tell her that this bullshit about keeping away from each other was just that—bullshit.

"Yeah, that trip ain't happening." I needed to see her. "Dan, you're right. I need to go make this right."

"Oh fuck, man. I was looking forward to taking down the house." Dan whined like it was an actual possibility. Poor fucker didn't stand a chance at a legit casino.

"Please go home before you hurt yourself. I have genuine fear for you, brother." It was bewildering to me how he had managed to skate through life without doing jail time.

"With pleasure." Dan smirked before flipping us off. "Unlike you two morons, I have an amazing woman to go home to."

Dan headed to my door and I followed him out. The clock was ticking and I was still pissed I was standing in my apartment and not on my way to her.

Dan stopped in my doorway. "Troy, smooth over whatever needs smoothing. I don't want to have to punch you in the sack 'cause Megs won't talk to you at the wedding."

That wouldn't be happening. Her and me, we were going to work this shit out, and she was not going to be dating or kissing any other douchebags. Nope. I was done sitting back and pretending that what we were doing made sense. Whatever the chances were, I'd be taking them, and short of her telling me she felt nothing, I wouldn't be walking away, any time soon.

Maybe I was a cocky son of bitch, but I had zero hesitation in looking at Dan and telling him, "I've got this."

WHAT TIME WAS IT? MY EYES SLOWLY OPENED TO SUNLIGHT BURNING my retinas. Like a dumbass, I'd forgotten to close my drapes last night before I'd collapsed into bed. It was too early and I had no reason to be awake. Ugh. I needed coffee.

Josh had driven me home, given me sweet kiss on the cheek and then said goodbye. He even waited until I was safely inside my apartment before leaving. He wasn't even weird about. I hoped this didn't mean the next guy I dated was an asshole, not that I would be dating anyone anytime soon.

Rather than going to bed like a *normal* person and trying to forget my horrible night, I instead voted to stay up watching cheesy RomCom reruns. With a box of Kleenex and obviously no common sense, I watched as time after time the hero found his way to his heroine and they walked off into the sunset together. It was enough to make me want to hurl my snotty, scrunched up tissues at the screen. But instead of doing that—which would have been totally reasonable— I just sat there and watched another. The definition of insanity is repeating the same action and expecting a different result. I was clearly insane.

Damn it. I tried to squeeze my eyelids shut and hoped to

ignore the happy beams of light that danced on my comforter. Assholes, I didn't want to be awake, and I sure as hell didn't want to be happy. Yet, ironically, my eyes were wide open and I didn't feel so bad. Maybe it was a new day's perspective or maybe my fatigued brain was giving me a reprieve, whatever the reason, I was grabbing onto it.

Ugh, my legs kicked off the covers —it was too hot. Wordless pictures played on the television, the same screen that had tormented me. While I had been smart enough to mute the stupid thing, I hadn't turned it off. The remote nestled within the mess of crumpled tissues —the graveyard of fallen tears on my bedside table. Tragic.

The buzzer from my front door demanded attention; the relenting sound meant my fantasy of staying in bed was not going to happen— my second disappointment for the day.

I assumed it was Ash. She had wanted to come over last night after I called her. No amount of telling her it was unnecessary would appease her. I was just glad she waited until the morning, letting me have my pity party undisturbed. Hopefully she had a really big coffee and maybe a muffin.

Reluctantly, I swung my legs off the mattress. My feet hit the floor heavily as my hands scrubbed my face. I tried to not imagine what I looked like. Nightmare came to mind. Or possibly, one of those scary zombie walking dead dolls. Ash was going to have to overlook my bad hair day and my puffy eyes.

Slowly I trudged to the door, the buzzer continuing to sound. Geez, Ash, give me a minute. My finger hit the release on the lower external entry and I cracked open my front door, waiting for her inevitable arrival. I really hope she brought that coffee, I needed the caffeine hit like no other.

The sounds of footsteps echoed up the staircase, my door flew open to reveal... Troy Harris? Huh? My head couldn't reconcile what I seeing.

"Troy? What are you doing here?"

He didn't answer.

Instead, he kissed me. *Really* kissed me. Like those stupid, sappy movies I'd watched, he wrapped his arms around me and he lifted me off the floor. His mouth was on mine like he needed me to breathe.

I didn't care I hadn't brushed my teeth or that I looked like shit, none of it got any airtime. I wanted the kiss to last forever, for him to hold me with the desperation that he was...forever.

"You've been crying." He peeled his lips from mine and lifted my chin to look at me. "Did that asshole hurt you?"

"He wasn't an asshole, and no, he didn't hurt me." Josh had been far from being an asshole. He should have hated me for using him as my rebound guy but instead had been sweet and kind. I shook my head and repeated. "He didn't hurt me."

"Did I hurt you?" Troy's finger trailed against the edge of my jaw.

"I hurt myself." I shrugged. "You did nothing wrong." He hadn't. He had just followed my fucked up diagram on how to screw up a friendship, relationship, whatever it was. I still have no idea what we actually were.

"That's bullshit. I did plenty wrong." He lowered his lips and kissed me on the mouth again. I guessed that was the end of the conversation and as long as he kept kissing me, I didn't care.

Troy's hands threaded through my hair, his fingers tangled in the messy waves as the kiss intensified. He moved his hands down my neck and then across my shoulders like he was trying to remember me by touch. It was erotic and sensual and sweet baby Jesus— it was really turning me on.

While my mind was currently being dictated by the throbbing need between my legs, it had occurred to me in a small window of clarity that we were standing in the entranceway of my apartment with my front door *wide* open.

That would *not* do. I pulled him closer and kicked the door closed, the wooden doorframe shaking under the force of it being slammed shut. Troy responded by pushing me back into my living room, my feet doing their best not to trip over my rug.

We should probably have moved to the bedroom—that would have been the smart thing to do— but we had already established that when it came to sex, Troy and I weren't very smart. So rather than fight it, I gave in as we tumbled onto my large sofa.

Our bodies were pressed together as we clawed at each other, our mouths too preoccupied with kissing to be worried about something as silly as words. I didn't want to speak. Not at that moment anyway.

I'm not sure how it happened but I pulled off his T-shirt. One minute I was grabbing at the soft cotton fabric, bunching it in my hands and the next minute it was off his chest and on the floor. It seemed like a better place for it.

He seemed to have the same idea, with my thin cotton tank top magically being pulled over my head and disappearing over the back of the couch. His hands moved to my naked breasts, he grunted in appreciation over my lack of a bra. It also meant less to take off, which was another plus.

Troy laid back across the cushions of the sofa and pulled me with him. His hands alternated between rolling my nipples between his fingers to palming my breasts.

I wiggled on top of him as my hands moved down his chest, my fingertips feeling each curve and ripple of his defined torso. The bulge in his pants got harder as I straddled him and rocked against it.

His hands left my body and I whimpered a protest but was quickly pacified when I saw they were getting busying unzipping his fly and pulling down his jeans. Ok, then. He toed off his shoes and reached down to yank off his socks, my body rocking against his erection while he tried to undress himself underneath me.

He had only managed to maneuver his jeans half way down his thighs when he'd lost his patience, lifting me off his hard cock and moving me to the other cushion of the couch. The jeans that had been giving him so much trouble were kicked off violently as I watched beside him. His boxers, they were the next to go—a casualty in our desperation to get naked.

"Get them off," he growled as he tugged at my sleep shorts. My clothing, the next victim, his attention focused on getting me as naked as he was.

His body was so toned and defined; the way his muscles flexed when he moved made him look lethal. The tattoos that covered his chest and arms enhanced an already spectacular view.

"Megs?" He stopped the desperate tugging of my shorts as my feather tattoos came into view. His finger gently traced the delicate outline. "When did you get these?"

The confusion in his eyes was an easy read. Skin that had previously been bare had two small but delicate feathers marking it. "A couple of days after we last..."

"Why?"

"Because I thought we'd never have this again." The emotion was thick in my throat as I tried not to cry. "I needed the memory. When I was with you it felt like feathers in the wind. Crazy, flying out of control—exhilarating. But when it stopped— when we stopped, they floated away. It was the only way I could get them back."

"Fuck." He cradled me, running his hand over my skin. "They're beautiful. You're beautiful and I've never seen anything more perfect."

"Troy Harris." My lips gently kissed his chest.

"Yeah?" His hands played with my hair.

"I don't want to talk anymore about things that make me sad. I'm still wearing pants and you're naked. You want to do something about that or—" I didn't get the chance to finish.

Hands, fingers, lips and a tangle of limbs, he pressed his body back to mine. My sleep shorts and panties quickly left my body and joined the pile of discarded clothing. I wasn't sure if it had been by my hand or his, but I was thankful we were now skin on skin.

The head of his cock teased at my opening as I wiggled beneath him, it felt amazing as I arched my back using friction to rub against me. The mental piercing hit me in just the right spot.

"Easy," he warned as he reached down in between my legs and thumbed circles around my clit. "I'm not suited up yet."

"I can't wait." I bucked against him, wanting to be filled with him. It felt like I had been waiting for an eternity. "I want you in me."

His jaw tensed as he lifted off me, his eyes raking up and down my body as he fished for jeans on the floor. I couldn't look away, the shine of the metal in his cock catching the sunlight each time he moved.

Success, he held up the small foil packet with his fingers that he'd dug out of his jeans pocket and all I could think of was that shinny ring that I wanted so desperately inside of me. I couldn't wait. Moving across to him I placed my lips around the head of his cock, my mouth closed around him and I flicked my tongue along the length. "Megs," he hissed out as his hand went around my head, his body thrusting with each and every suck I gave him.

My teeth pulled gently against the ring and I saw his eyes roll back from pleasure, the throbbing between my legs almost unbearable.

His fingers wrapped around his cock and pulled it from my lips, his grip travelling along his length as I watched him rip open the condom wrapper with his teeth and the slide it out with his fingers. It was mesmerizing as he quickly went to work, the piercing carefully encased in the latex before it rolled down the rest of his cock.

And then, in one thrust he was in me. Yep, just that quickly. One minute I'm sitting down watching him stroke himself, and then the next minute, I'm on my back. It was hard and fast and my body tightened around him. Had it always been this good?

"Troy," I moaned, my head flying back in ecstasy as my body welcomed the invasion. "I need you." And I meant it. I needed him in every sense of the word and I didn't want this to ever stop.

"You've got me." His hands found my hips as he moved in and out of me with long, deliberate thrusts. "You've got me," he repeated, getting deeper with each time.

It wasn't going to take long, the anticipation had worked me up into a state that was making me feel crazy. I wanted this, wanted him, so badly that I hadn't even explored what this meant. Had we returned back to the let's-have-sex-but-not-date or was this something else? At that moment, I didn't care.

Our bodies crashed into each other, his thrust countered by mine. The movements of the frenzied pace getting me so close that I teetered on the edge of bliss.

"Touch yourself. I want to see you play with yourself with my cock in you." He groaned as he bit down on his lip.

I reached down to the slickness between my legs, twisting my fingers over my clit as I exploded around him. Tingles travelled up and down my arms and legs as the wave of my orgasm rode out. One more thrust was all it took, his cock pulsing inside of me as he came hard.

He collapsed against me, panting as his heavy body almost crushed me beneath him. I loved it, the heat and his weight on me. It felt real, tangible. Raw. It's what I needed.

Troy's arms covered me, wrapping around my body as he shifted to the side. His large frame wedged between the back of the couch and my body. Our legs intertwined at the knees.

It was at around that point that my post-coital buzz started to dissipate, and my common sense kicked in. I had slept with Troy again. After I had promised myself I wouldn't do this anymore.

Did I have any self-control? Like, at all?

Troy's lips tenderly kissed my neck and in a moment of braveness —or possibly fear— I asked what I had never had the courage to ask before. "So... where does that leave us?"

It was probably too ambiguous a question but I needed to know what it was we were doing. I would leave the scary *are we dating now?* chat for at least a few minutes, following up with *so does this mean you're my boyfriend?* And my pièce di résistance would be *oh and we have to be exclusive.* That would be a fun conversation that would surely send him running out my door. Still, what choice did I have? I couldn't do the sex and no commitment thing. Even if Troy Harris was the provider of that sex, it just wasn't enough for my fragile heart to handle.

Troy's fingers lightly circled my skin, sending chills up my spine. "It leaves us right here. Together."

"*Together*, together or just together and not together?"

There was a lot of gray area that needed to be clarified and now was probably a good time to do that. You know, before we did something stupid like have sex again without discussing it. Sure, like that could happen *again?* Every single time I was around him alone, I swear I ended up naked. If we were going to continue to get naked, we would have to be in some kind of, I don't know, commitment.

"It's going to be complicated. You said so yourself." I expected him to start running any time now. Complicated was usually like mood cyanide. Things going well —here, add some *complicated* to it—boom good feeling gone.

"Turns out, I was wrong. It's actually really simple." Troy's fingers tiptoed down my arm and across my stomach. His voice had no hesitation. "I want to be with you, you want to be with me. No one else needs to come into that equation."

I took a breath and really had to concentrate not to hold it. "Troy, I know I said we can just have sex and be casual." I slowly exhaled. "But I don't think I can do that. Not anymore. I need more."

Yeah me! There you have it. I finally said it. Who claimed I couldn't admit when I was wrong, and I was clearly *very* wrong about my earlier judgment.

"Look at me." Troy stopped toying with my naked body—which I had to admit was slightly distracting in the most delicious sort of way—and positioned himself so he could face me. "You think you are the only one who's wanted this for the last few months? This isn't just about sex."

"I still don't know what that means?" I whispered quietly as I looked into his eyes. Tell me, I wanted to beg. Tell me exactly what this means. Tell me that you are only mine.

"It means that we do the couple thing. Exclusively. No more talk about dating other people. That was a dumb idea."

The world's problems that existed an hour ago still existed. Sickness, hunger, war etc. they were still very real, present. But in my little world—the bubble I was in— there was only a Zen-like bliss I couldn't have even imagined.

Can a heart actually fill with happiness? Because if it could, mine was about to burst. I would stop short of chasing rainbows and unicorns but to me, this was the best-case scenario multiplied by a hundred. It was my half-time shot at the free throw, and I had nothing but net.

"You know," I giggled, loving the lighter conversations we were familiar with. "I don't want to ruin the moment because I like where this conversation is heading—but this is sort of your fault." I bit my lip and looked up at him under my lashes. Yeah, it was a total cheesy move and I didn't care.

"Oh yeah? How do you figure?" He raised his eyebrow and grinned. "It kind of feels like a two person mess to me."

"Well... if you had just dated me in the beginning." I shrugged innocently.

"What? And missed out on that stellar seduction in between." He chuckled "Not a chance."

"Do we need to tell people?" Ok, that was probably a bit sudden and didn't need to be said at that point, but my mind and mouth had this impulsive thing going on since it had been unleashed a little while back.

"We don't *need* to do anything." Troy gave me a pointed look. "It's up to us, we're making the rules."

So maybe it could wait— the telling everyone we were together part. Would our friends even care? It could definitely be left for a day or two. Or not. I pushed the thought to the side to dwell on later.

Sadly the next thought that floated into my cerebral cortex was not pleasant. The trivial *do-we-tell-them* problem that concerned me five seconds ago seemed wonderful in comparison and I desperately wanted to go back that.

The silence ate away at me as it tumbled in my head. Did I want to know? Would it make a difference? I opened my mouth before I was able to answer either of those questions definitively.

"Were there other girls? Like, after me?"

"You really want to have that conversation, now?"

I nodded silently, it would kill me but it would be worse not knowing. Like a Band-Aid, I just had to rip it off.

Troy sighed and I prepared for the worst. "No, I didn't have sex with anyone else. I was hung up on *someone* and had no interest in fucking around. I'm not a scumbag, Megs. I am more than capable of keeping my dick in my pants."

I had no right to expect him to *save himself* for *me*, but I'd secretly hoped for it. The relief to hear that he had, flooded me in a rush. My words bubbled out erratically.

"I didn't either. Sleep with anyone I mean. Obviously I couldn't keep a dick in my pants because I didn't have one to keep there. And with vaginas it's more about whether or not the pants are on them or not…they are so much more tidier."

"You are so weird."

"Why thank you, Troy Harris."

His grin widened and lit up his eyes. "I missed hearing that."

"I thought you hated it?" I coughed out a laugh.

"Not even close. It was like foreplay." He smirked.

"Troy Harris." I whispered as low and seductive as I could manage.

"You know I'm going to have to fuck you again, right? No complaints from you if you can't walk."

I brought my mouth up to his neck and parted my lips, my tongue trailing up to his jaw. If he was trying to scare me off with his threat, it didn't work. There would be no complaints for me and I would say his name, every single syllable of it every opportunity I got. My hand moved leisurely down his chest as I tilted my head to look at him.

"Well then, take me, Troy Harris."

"SO THE TATTOOS." WE HAD EVENTUALLY MADE IT TO THE BED. HER body laid on mine. "Josh?" The mystery of how she met him, solved.

"Yeah, he did a great job." She didn't lift her head. Didn't need to. I liked feeling the vibrations on my skin as she moved her mouth.

"Not sure I liked the idea of his face being that close to your pussy, but as much as I want to hate the guy, he obviously has skills." The detail on the feathers so fine, it was obvious one kickass artist was handling the needle.

"You're cute when you're jealous."

"Can we think of something more manly than cute?" In truth, I didn't fucking care what she called me as long as we were done with the let's-be-friends shit.

People rarely surprised me and yet with Megs, the surprises didn't end. I loved the way she felt against me. Her hair fanned out across my chest and her little quirk for hooking an ankle around my calf when we curled up after sex. It was adorable even though my leg would go numb after a while. There wasn't one thing I didn't like about her. Not a fucking thing I would change and while I'd I had my hesitations for doing this from the start, none of it made sense to me now.

"This feels like a dream, being here with you. I'm almost expecting to wake up and find out I'm hugging a pillow. It wouldn't be the first time." She giggled, not sold on the smooth-sailing-from-here-on-out.

"Just so you know." I lifted her head so she could look at me. There wasn't going to be any misunderstandings on this. "There isn't going to be a break up between the two of us. We're not going to fuck this up. I'm not being a cocky son of a bitch—both of us are capable of doing stuff that is monumentally stupid—but we're going to always work it out. There isn't an alternative. We'd tried being apart. It sucked. So we aren't going to do that anymore."

The more time I spent with her, the more I knew it. Nope. Together is where we belonged. Whatever it took, and however fucking difficult it would be. Complicated? Hit me with your best shot, I'm ready.

"Troy, I don't want to fuck up Ash's big day." Megs scooched up the bed, the smile she had before no longer there. "If we are doing this then we have to keep it quiet until after the wedding. I don't want her worried about us fighting or something happening. It's only a little while longer. Besides, think of how much fun we'll have sneaking around." The smile was back but a little uncertain.

"That sounds like a recipe for trouble, Megs." She pouted before I had a chance to finish. "But as long as we're finally seeing eye to eye on the being together part, I'm not going to argue." Saying no to her wasn't in my vocabulary. Besides, if it made Megs happy then it was an easy ask.

Leaving Megs's apartment that afternoon wasn't easy and not for the reasons you'd think. Sure, I would have loved to have stuck around and worshipped her body— we had lost time we needed to make up— but more than that, I just hated not being with her. Funny how just knowing she was tucked up beside me was enough to put me at ease. Still, she had some patient reports she needed to write and I figured she'd get them done sooner without me trying to pull her into bed.

I wasn't bound to the ball and chain that was the nine-to-five, but she worked some hella long hours at the hospital and I wasn't going to be an inconsiderate asshole. So I kissed her goodbye in a way she wouldn't forget in a hurry, and I booked it back to my place before I could change my mind. Chances were I'd probably be finding myself back there anyway.

We started our old game of phone tag, with me hitting the call button the minute I got back to mine.

"Hello, Troy Harris," she purred as she answered. Made me want to get back into the car and drive right back.

"Megs." I did my best to keep it together and not suggest she talk dirty to me while I jack off. Jesus. I was turning into Dan. "I have to say I'm a little disappointed in you.

"Oh, really?" The intonation of her voice clued me in she was digging the role-play. "And why is that? The blowjob I gave you in a shower not deep throat enough?"

The memory alone forced me to swallow, *hard*. That had been one hell of a blowjob. "No, the blowjob was fantastic. It's your tattoos that's upset me."

"I thought you said you liked my tattoos, you liar," she answered defiantly.

"They're beautiful." No way I could lie about that. "But I had already spent money on that gift certificate for you. What's the chances of getting my name tattooed on your ass?" I cursed the fact I wasn't able to see her face.

"Oooo can we get matchy ones?" She didn't miss a beat. "With an arrow going through a heart?"

"I'll get your name but I'm not getting an arrowed heart. That shit is so fucking cliché it hurts." No way would I get a fucking heart. Power Station wasn't a fucking hair band.

"Fine, barb-wire it is." She sighed. "Make a booking."

"Bye, Megs." I hated saying those words to her, but I knew I had to let her go.

"Bye, Troy Harris."

She was so fucking precious, I hated that she was going to be spending the night alone. Megs wasn't the only one I was worried about.

That first night alone I didn't sleep worth a shit. I tossed and turned until I just gave up and turned on the television. Ironically

"The Vampire Diaries" was on and my curiosity got the better of me.

Two vampire brothers fight over a human girl who happens to have a vampire doppelgänger. Or maybe the human is the doppelgänger? How can these vampires go out in the sunlight? Is it like "Twilight"? No one is sparkling. Someone needed to draw me a fucking diagram 'cause I didn't understand any of that shit.

The early morning phone call waking me meant that at some point I had eventually fallen asleep. I reached for the phone and answered it without even bothering to open my eyes.

"Yeah." I didn't waste my time with hello. Anyone who was calling me this early would have to deal with me not being Mr. Happy.

"Aw, did I wake you Troy?" Megs giggled into the phone. My mood took a really quick upswing at the sound of her voice.

"Yeah, not everyone has to be up at the ass crack of dawn. You could do me a favor and sound a little bit sympathetic." She could wake me anytime and I'd never fucking care.

"Poor, Troy Harris." She didn't even try and hide how pleased she was. "This should cheer you up though. I watched part of Star Wars last night."

"Wow, Megs, that's kind of hot. Was it "A New Hope"?" Not gonna lie, the thought of her watching Star Wars turned me on.

"I didn't really hold any hope for it, I'm not really into Sci-Fi but it wasn't all bad."

"Fuck, you're adorable." Her confusion was so cute, I laughed so hard I could barely breathe. "The name of it, was it the episode four, "A New Hope"? The first one of the original trilogy."

"Okay so you've already lost me. How can it be episode four, if it's the first one? That makes no sense." She took a breath before continuing. "Anyway, I'm not sure which one this was, but *Luke Skywalker* finds out that his dad is *Darth Vader*. Their reunion wasn't pretty, his kid didn't even give him a chance."

"Oh my God, we need to have some serious words, sweetheart. I think I might actually cry. That was "Return of the Jedi"; you can't watch them out of order."

"See this is why I shouldn't watch these things. Although that light saber thing, tell me that wasn't some nerdy way of comparing penises."

"Okay, hanging up now. You've crushed my soul and desecrated the force enough for one day."

"So be it, Jedi." Megs laughed, her off-the-cuff quote from the movie proved she paid more attention than she led me to believe. If I had any doubts before, they'd just incinerated. This girl was it for me.

"Bye, Megs."

"Bye, Troy Harris."

One night alone was enough; I wasn't willing to do it again. We could go to bed early so she could sleep but it would be with me by her side. Besides, I was scared if she watched any more episodes of *Star Wars* by herself, I wouldn't be able to undo the damage.

Given that we weren't advertising being together just yet, it meant I was spending my nights at Megs's apartment. The chances of being caught less likely when we didn't have to worry about Dan and Ash living across the hall. I couldn't give a shit where I slept as long as it was in the same bed as Megs.

So that's how the week went. Megs would go to work and I would head back to my apartment. Shower, change and then fill my day with shit I needed to get done so I could spend the nights making sure Megs came so hard her voice would echo off the walls.

It wasn't all sex, though it seemed to take up most of our time. We'd talk for hours. Sometimes it would be just about the stuff we'd filled our hours with, it didn't matter that it wasn't important. I just wanted to know about her day or how many times she'd laughed. It was hearing her recount of the hours I wasn't there that made the time away from her bearable.

Jase knew where I was spending my nights. There was no point hiding it, he hadn't missed my feelings for her before we started dating so I came clean and told him we were doing the couple thing. He wasn't surprised and was glad we'd sorted out whatever it was that needed sorting out. It was good thing too, he'd pulled my ass out of the fire a couple of times when Dan wanted to hang out by making up some shit about us going to get laid at clubs. Jase was a fucking team player.

"Hey asshole, are you just getting home now?" Dan had opened his door as I'd stepped into the hall from the elevator.

"Yep, I was busy last night." Not a lie, my night had been spent getting very busy.

"A skirt?" He strolled over to me obviously wanting to continue the conversation.

"Yep." I nodded, pulling my keys from pocket. I wasn't in the mood for show and tell, especially not with Dan.

He grabbed my arm, pulling my hand away from the lock of my front door. Perhaps my one word answer wasn't satisfactory enough. "You've been doing that a lot lately. You haven't been home all week."

It was so freaking weird being on this side on the fence. Dan, playing the role of concerned friend, me, the man-whore. "I'm sorry, Mom." I barked out a laugh. We must have stepped into some parallel universe. "I didn't realize I missed curfew."

"Very funny." He rolled his eyes, the irony of the situation not lost on him. "Is this one girl in particular or you playing the field? Looks like you're going for some kind of record."

Dan giving me the third degree was almost touching. He'd changed and I had to say, I liked this version of him a hell of a lot better. It sucked that I couldn't tell him shit, and that all his worry wasn't necessary but Megs and I agreed to wait and I'd eat my own hand before I'd break a promise to that girl.

"Just 'cause you're reformed now don't pretend like you weren't out every fucking night for years getting tail." Deflection. Easier than telling him stuff that wasn't true and at least I wouldn't feel like a total asshole.

"Fuck, Troy. I don't care if you are fucking two girls at once if that's what you want to do." Dan let go of my arm and ran his hands through his hair. "I'm just saying it's not like you. Look, I'm not going to pretend I didn't screw more than my fair share of women, but I know now that it's 'cause I had no idea what I was missing. Trust me, all the pussy in the world doesn't hold a candle to what I have with Ashlyn."

The heart-to-heart hadn't been necessary; the reality of *that* had already hit me. His delivery was flawed but the man spoke the truth. There was no other girl that would compare to Megs.

"That's fucking beautiful, man. Alex and James should really let you write some lyrics on the next album." My hand cupped the back of his neck and I laughed. "Oh, by the way, don't ever compare the love you have for your woman to *all the pussy in the world*. Not if you want to keep your balls." For most guys it was a give-me, but I'd hate to see a domestic dispute arriving 'cause the man could sometimes be an idiot.

Dan backhanded me across the chest. "I meant it in a positive way."

"Yeah, it will still piss her off. Trust me on this one."

"Point taken." Dan shrugged it off, hopefully having learnt his lesson. "So you doing anything today?"

I didn't have plans, well none than that went beyond the first hour or so. "Just getting a shower and then maybe watching the tube, why? What did you need?"

"I'm bored." Dan shrugged. With the album recorded and no tour dates set, the days were kind of slow for both of us. "You wanna go buy dirt bikes and ride through Central Park?" he suggested.

"You feel like getting arrested today? How about *no* on the dirt bike riding through Central Park." I shot down his idea, not wanting to spend my afternoon in lock-up.

"This is why you don't have a girlfriend, dude. You are so fucking negative."

"Yeah, that's exactly why, asshole. If you're really that bored why don't we drive to Jersey and go ask Jon Bon Jovi is he's still livin' on a prayer."

"Shit, that's brilliant. Hurry the fuck up and get ready. I'm driving."

It was just after eight when I climbed the stars that lead to

Megs's loft. Having been with Dan all day and most of the evening meant I had barely spoken to her and I wasn't sure if I was going to ask her how her day was or kiss her.

Buzzing me up minutes before, she was standing in the doorway waiting for me. She looked fucking beautiful. Her face had been scrubbed of make up and she'd changed out of work clothes and into her sleep shorts and tank top. No bra. It didn't get much better than that.

The debate I'd been having— about whether to kiss her or talk— was over. I crossed that last step and took her mouth right there. She let out a little whimper as I circled my arms around her and lifted her off the ground. I couldn't get close enough to her— holding her, kissing her— I'd never get tired of that.

"Well, hello to you too." She smiled wrapping her arms around my neck.

"I missed you today. I'm just trying to catch up." I lowered her to the floor as my hands got reacquainted with the rest of her body.

"We going to move this inside or you want to give my neighbors a show?" She looked over my shoulder signaling to the other doors in her hallway.

I grinned looking down at what she was wearing. The tank top she had on, showcasing the curve of her tits. "I think you already gave them a show." My hand reached up and gently squeezed one of her nipples.

She jerked on my arm, pulling me inside. The door got a kick from her foot and closed behind us. "Be thankful I'm wearing clothes. I could have answered the door naked."

"You would have received no complaints from me." We moved through the hallway and into her living room as my mouth went back to work, this time making its way down her neck. I pulled down her tank top as I continued my journey, her beautiful tits popping out the top.

"Troy." She closed her eyes as my tongue circled her nipple.

"Shsssh, I'm trying to have conversation with your breasts." Any other conversation would have to wait.

"I want to give you something first." She pulled her body away from my mouth, and had she not added the next part I would have been extremely pissed off. "Something... sexy."

"Well now you have me interested." I smirked as I moved my mouth away from her body. I'd finish that later.

She gave me a gentle shove in the direction of the couch. "Sit," she demanded, placing both her hands on her hips.

No idea where this was going, but it was kind of hot. My grin got wider as I sunk into the chair behind me. "Is this where you slap a collar on me and pull a whip out of your ass? We both know I'd make a terrible submissive."

"I don't want you as a submissive." She joined me on the chair and curled up in my lap. "I want you naked."

Her arm reached across to the coffee table and picked up a file that had been sitting there. Her eyes were full of excitement as she handed it to me.

"If that was your goal, you would've got me naked quicker my way of doing things." I kissed her neck before looking at the folder she was pushing against my chest. "What's with the paperwork? I thought you said it was something sexy."

She smiled, opening the folder and insisting. "Read it."

"Urrrr... Female. Caucasian." I started to read off the notes. "If this is to confirm you're a female, it's okay, I worked that out myself. But thanks, I appreciate the reassurance." I glanced up from the pages of words I wasn't interested in.

"It's my blood work, silly. I had a sample taken on Monday and I got my results today. Screenings for STDs and other stuff. See? I'm all good." She pointed to the part on the page that revealed not only her blood type but also a list of potential nasties, all which read negative.

"This is your health screening? Why are you showing me this?" I placed the folder beside me, it's purpose having been served.

"Because I wanted to feel your cock in me without the condom." She smiled sweetly liked she'd just asked me to take her to the mall.

How she was able to say those things with a straight face bewildered me. I loved that she was unfiltered and that she could say the word cock without getting all embarrassed. There was something so fucking hot about a woman who knew what she wanted and wasn't afraid to ask for it.

"Jesus, Megs. You keep talking like that and you're going to get your wish sooner than later." My already hard dick concurred on my assessment. Both of us down for the skin on skin action.

"So does that mean you want that too?" She looked up at me, a patch of vulnerability shining through all that bravado. It just made me want her more.

Did I want to have sex with her, bare? Hell-fucking-yes, I did. We hadn't had the are-you-on-the-pill talk, and I didn't want to assume she was. But the prospect of slipping inside of her with nothing between us got me so hard my balls ached. "Of course I want to. That's not even a real question. But you could have just told me. You didn't have to show me all this." I tossed the folder back onto the coffee table.

"I wanted to make it official." She smiled as she nuzzled against my chest. "I'm on the pill as well so you can come inside me and everything."

FUCK. Well then. I guess we've now had *that* talk.

"Wow. I'm going to need a minute to stop visualizing if we want *that* to actually happen. I'm dangerously close to coming in my pants right now." I wasn't even kidding. One sweep of a hand on my dick, and it was all over.

My reaction obviously satisfied her, the grin evidence of that. "See, I told you it was sexy."

I liked that look on her face, her being happy and knowing I had something to do with it.

"We're screened every six months for insurance purposes." It was my turn to do the I'm-all-good talk. "My last one was two months ago and I always have used condoms. I'm good. I can pull the paperwork if you want to see." Seeing as she had produced paperwork, it was only fair I offered to do the same. I didn't carry personal medical records around with me but they wouldn't have been hard to get.

"No, I don't need to see." She shook her head and smiled. "We can get to the sex part now, you kissing my nipple at the door made me so freaking wet."

"Do you practice these things before you say them to me? I swear every word out of your mouth is hotter than the last." I brushed the hair off her shoulder wondering how the hell I got so lucky.

"It's a natural talent, now come here and kiss me again." She brought her lips inches away from mine. "I need things that only you can give me."

I tiled her chin so that I could look at her, her lips parted, waiting for me to take her mouth. I loved her. I'd never been more sure of anything in my life.

"I'll give you everything you need, and things you didn't even know you did."

I WAS IN LOVE WITH HIM. I HAD FLIPPANTLY USED THOSE WORDS TO describe my feelings for Troy Harris in the past, having seen him on stage but *those* feelings, they hadn't even come close to what I felt now. Even having known him for months still hadn't prepared me and, while we hadn't said the words out loud, he had my heart. Completely. Every part. I wanted Troy. I needed Troy.

"Troy Harris." I managed to moan in between kisses. "Why are you still wearing clothes?"

There was a sexy laugh against my neck. "I can fix that." He pulled away from me for a second to remove his T-shirt, his beautiful sculptured chest on display. Every time I saw it, it was just as impressive. His arms came back around me. "Now let me see how much wetter I can get you."

A loud buzz from the speaker beside my door broke through my lust-filled fog. Whoever it was didn't stand a chance. Not. A. Chance.

"I'm not answering it. It's probably someone who's got the wrong apartment." My hands moved to his belt and started to fumble with the buckle. It felt like I was going to explode.

"Megs, if we're going to do this, you need to be naked too." Troy pulled at the edge of my tank top. He was such a smart man, and one hundred percent right. Naked was an awesome plan.

My fingers moved from trying to undo Troy's pants to lifting off my top, I tossed it onto the couch without a second though. The warmth of his body on mine was mind blowing.

My cell started ringing loudly from beside me, the illuminated screen doing its best to attract my attention. What? What was so important that needed me to be taken away from this moment? Was the world trying to conspire against this happening? Screw it. It could go to voice mail.

"Fuck, this cannot be happening." Troy laughed as once again my buzzer started being obnoxious. I hated that thing. Where was a baseball bat when you needed one?

My phone once again lit up, the buzzer and my cell at war with each other as to who would get my attention. It was clear that getting Troy's naked cock into me would need to wait. I kid you not, I almost cried.

"Yeah?" I palmed the phone and pressed it against my ear. The cell won out because I could still straddle Troy and neither of us had to put our clothes on.

"Megs," Kyla huffed into the phone. "I know you're home. Let me up."

Kyla Heatherington was one of my closest friends and she lived about a block away with her bestie, Brianne. Ashlyn and I had been working at *Garro's* sports bar for about three months when the two of them waltzed in and poured a pitcher of beer over Brianne's cheating boyfriend's head. Turned out it had been the same guy who had been hitting on me since I'd started, so we bonded over a mutual distaste for him. One margarita-filled evening later and the four of us became instant friends. Some things were just meant to be.

Noooooooooo. I bit down on my lip to stop myself from screaming it. That would be rude, right? As much as I loved her, now was not the time for a social call. My eyes closed as my fist tightened around the phone, I needed to keep my voice light.

"Kyyyylaaaa." Ok, too light, you sound high. Try backing off a bit. "You're here?" Now you sounded stupid. Of course she was here, she just said that. "What are you doing here?" Better, but was still going to get questions. Maybe I should have stuck with sounding high.

"Are you high? You sound funny." Kyla's voice snapped back. See, told you. A career in espionage was something I could safely rule out.

"Umm. I was just..." My brain searched its recesses for something plausible. I had nothing. "Give me a minute and I'll let you up." I ended the call and tossed my phone onto the couch beside us.

My eyes glanced longingly at Troy's naked chest— it wasn't going to happen. Not until I could get rid of her. "Fuck. I have company." My teeth clenched so tightly I'm surprised any words got out.

"Okay, I'll put my shirt back on." Troy calmly reached for his T-shirt hanging of the arm of the couch.

"No." My head shook as my voice rose. "No, you can't be here." My wide eyes went with the rest of the crazed expression I had going on.

"Megs, she knows we're friends." Troy pushed the tee over his head. "Just tell her I stopped by." He shrugged calmly.

"Stopped by?" My voice rose yet again as I tried to rein in my panic. "Are you kidding? She will smell the sex on you." My discarded tank top was retrieved and shoved back over my head.

"Ah, Megs we haven't had sex yet." Troy smirked as he kissed me.

"That is so unhelpful right now, I'm going to ignore it. You need to hide." I jumped to my feet and yanked on his arm. Yes, that was solution. Where could I hide him? The closet wasn't even a contender.

"What the fuck?" He laughed it off; my incessant pulling of his forearm did nothing to move him. "I am not going to hide." He stood up defiantly and made for my front door.

"Yes you are." He had to. Kyla had a big mouth and a tendency to gossip. If she knew—everyone knew. And I wasn't ready for everyone to know. This was so not good. I raced him to my door, flinging my arms across it like a barrier. Ha! Like that would stop him if he wanted to get past.

"She can't see you. Please go to my room." My plea sounded

desperate. I wasn't even trying to hide how freaked out I was.

"Megs." He rolled his eyes, saying my name like I was being ridiculous. Maybe I was being ridiculous. We could argue later, right now I needed him to hide.

"Please," I begged, my arms still stretched out either side of me, barricading the door.

"Fine." He relented, and my body relaxed a little. "But know this, the minute she is out the door, your ass is mine and I'm not going to be gentle about it." He didn't sound like he was kidding.

"Sure, sure." I nodded so furiously I hoped it didn't result in a brain injury, and pointed toward my bedroom door. "My room. I'll be quick and take the file with you, I can't have her seeing it."

Troy muttered something under his breath and huffed a few times but thankfully turned and walked toward my room. He picked up the file from the coffee table, more muttering, and closed my bedroom door. Thank you God, I mouthed silently as I released the external lock and opened my front door.

"Oh hey, Kyla." I leaned my body lazily against the jamb as I tried to sound casual. Kyla took the final few steps before she reached the landing. "What brings you here?"

"Why aren't you answering your door? What took you so long? You're already in your pajamas? It's not even nine o'clock." The barrage of questions had started and she hadn't even entered the apartment. This was not going to be easy.

"I'm tired. I had the music on. I didn't hear the door." The answers rolled out of sequence from my mouth, and with very little conviction. The wave of my hand ushering her inside as I shut the door behind us.

"What the fuck happened to your hair?" She looked around my apartment like it would yield an explanation. I silently prayed Troy would not pick this moment to come out, thinking the jig was up. "And why is your face so red?" Her raised brow hinting she wasn't going to be easily fooled.

"I was exercising." The lame excuse leapt from my mouth before I had a chance to think of something better.

"In your pajamas? I thought you said you were tired." Another raised eyebrow, with the folded arms thrown in for good measure. This wasn't going well for me.

"Yeah I was, from the exercising." I bounced in place to demonstrate like an idiot. You know, in case she didn't know what exercising was.

"Okay, this is weird even for you, but whatever." She waved and started wandering around my apartment. Being that throwing my head between my knees would attract attention, I tried not to have a panic attack.

"Ash called, said you'd had a few rough days at work so I came by to drag your ass out. Get dressed, we're going out." She picked up the latest edition of *Cosmo* that was sitting on my coffee table and started to randomly flip.

"No, I can't." I almost shouted as she went to sit down on my couch. The same couch Troy had been on moments before.

"Why not? Have a shower if you need, I can wait." She ignored me, sinking into the seat as she thumbed the glossy pages.

"No, I have an early start tomorrow," I stuttered. "I can't go out tonight."

"Tomorrow's Saturday. You don't work tomorrow. What's so important you need to be up?" Once again it earned me a raised eyebrow, the magazine was also tossed aside in disinterest.

"I have plans." Once again my mouth opened without proper thought.

"Doing what?" She folded her arms across her chest, giving me her full interest.

"Tae Bo." There was no hope. My ship was sinking fast when *that* was the best I could come up with. It was only a matter of time before it all unraveled.

"Tae Bo? Is that still even a thing? Didn't it go to fitness heaven sometime after the 90's? Megs, seriously, I'll ask you one more time. Are you high?"

"No! Of course not." The giggle and the indignation intertwined wildly in my tone. Did I mention how much I sucked at this?

"I'm not judging you, who hasn't had a *special* brownie or two. Just saying if you were, it would be nice to share." Kayla shrugged like it was no big deal.

"Well you're out of luck because I've got nothing."

"Okay, so stop being lame. Go get changed. We won't be back late."

"I really can't."

"Why the hell not?"

"Because there is a man in my bedroom I'd really like to have sex with."

The truth startled us both into silence. Well then. This wasn't going to be an easy fix.

Kyla opened and shut her mouth a few times, words obviously eluding her. Her eyes flicked to my closed bedroom door. "You have some man holed up in your room?"

"Yes. It's new. I'm not ready to share him yet." It was the most honest thing that had come out of my mouth since she'd walked in.

"Are we going to get to meet him?" She didn't even try to lower her voice, probably hoping to flush out my hidden guest.

"Eventually, just not now. Can you keep this to yourself for a little while?" Not sure why I even bothered to ask, she was going to be on the phone to Brianne and Ashlyn before she'd even left my building.

"Fine, but you know I'm not good with secrets." She huffed impatiently before lowering her voice. "When the hell did you hook up with this one? Weren't you dating Josh like not even a week ago?"

"Yeah, I was. It's..." There was no other word I could think of that was better suited, "...complicated."

"Honey, you know I love you, right?" She planted her hands on her hips and I prepared for the I'm-worried-about-you speech. "But your life is complicated enough with your work, maybe you need to find some guy who isn't going to add to that. Find a nice guy, someone you can...I don't know, settle down with. Oh, there's this nice guy I work with. He'd be perfect for you."

"Kyla, thanks but this guy *is* a nice guy and I don't need anyone setting me up."

"Fine, just don't let him break your heart." She gave me a hug before raising her voice intentionally. "And make sure he treats you right because we have friends that can take care of it if he doesn't."

I cringed knowing Troy would have probably heard. "Thanks for that. I'll call you." My arms returned the hug before I pushed her toward the door. "And don't worry about me, I'll be fine."

She wasn't happy about it but she left, the door slamming punctuating her exit. I assumed I'd have about a ten to fifteen minute grace period before she caved and told someone. If anyone was going to make those ten minutes count, it would be me.

"Troy Harris, it's time for you to make good on that promise." I almost ran to the bedroom and flung the door open. My hopes of a happy reunion were crushed as I was greeted by Troy's pale face.

"Megs, you need to sit down." He tapped the bed beside him and not in sexy kind of way, in the we-need-to-talk kind of way.

"Look, I know you probably heard Kyla be all protective but she is just looking out for me. She doesn't know it's you and trust me, she doesn't have friends who can take care of *it* if things don't work out, she was being dramatic." The words bubbled furiously as I made my way to the bed; I wouldn't let Kayla's good intentions ruin what was supposed to be an amazing night.

"Besides, I know you aren't going to hurt me and you already said this was for the long haul and I believe you, truly I do." My mouth refused to be still, the look on his face putting the fear of God into me. Please don't think this is all too much work, please don't regret being with me. "And as soon as the wedding is over, we'll go public and it will all be fine and this will be just—"

"Megs, shut up." He placed his hands over my mouth as I sat down on the bed beside him. Probably for the best, it didn't show any signs of letting up. "I need you to tell you something and I need you to listen to me."

My head nodded being my mouth was still covered, not that I think words would have been able to come out right now, I was so afraid of him ending us, I couldn't talk.

Troy took a deep breath but kept his hand over my mouth. "I love you. I know we have only been together officially for a week but those feelings have been coming at me for a while. Nod if you are on the same page with me." I nodded wondering if it was declarations of love we were sharing, why I couldn't be free to declare mine.

My heartbeat starting thumping wildly as I waited for the "but" that was inevitably coming, the look in his eyes too intense, too serious to be simply wanting to tell me he loved me. Perhaps my self-assurances that he wouldn't break my heart had been premature.

"So there is something else you need to know."

I braced myself, wondering if he was going to go the this-isn't-going-to-work-out or love-doesn't-conquer-all route, either would hurt just as badly.

"We're pregnant."

"What?" My mouth mumbled against his palm as my brain screamed what the fuck. How the fuck can I be pregnant? I'm on the pill for fuck's sake. We've been using condoms. We haven't had unprotected sexy time yet. I don't feel any different. When was my last period? Oh my God, I'm going to pass out. The garbled noises continued from underneath his hand.

"Megs, I'm going to take my hand away. Don't freak out on me." He slowly unpeeled his hand from around my mouth.

"What! What? How can I be pregnant?" My head shook in disbelief, I was no virgin so divine intervention was out. Not that I thought I was a suitable mother for the second coming but... "How?"

"I have no idea, but this file." He picked up my blood work and opened it to the second page. "Says that you are."

And there it was a *pregnant* followed by the letters hCG and a bunch of numbers I didn't understand.

"I—I..." I had no idea what to say, my brain went into free fall.

"No, no I." Troy took my chin in his hands. "*We*, do you understand me? Us— together. This is our baby."

"I got pathology to take the blood but submitted the samples to the lab anonymously." Words had started to come out but the voice didn't sound like mine. "I said it was a patient of mine, a minor. They didn't ask questions. My brother works in the ER and my dad... I didn't want my name on the sample and people asking questions." It seemed so harmless. It wasn't the first time I requested an anonymous sample. It happens a lot when a minor is scared they might have an STD or knocked up (trust me the irony was not lost on me) and didn't want their parents to know. Patient, doctor privilege meant it could happen. We used a coding system instead.

"You didn't read it all the way through I take it?" Troy pulled the file from my hands, the papers scrunched at the edges underneath my death grip.

"I wasn't looking for that. It's on the second page. It wasn't even a possibility, I just wanted to prove I didn't have gonorrhea."

"Well, good news — you don't have gonorrhea." He smiled like it was no big deal.

"This isn't funny." His calm or his smile didn't reassure me this *wasn't* a big deal. "How can I be pregnant when we have used condoms and I've been on the pill? That's like zero chance. Do you have like super sperm or something?"

"Megs, we need to get you to a doctor. I don't know what these numbers mean and we don't know how long junior's been cooking in there. You're also going to need stuff, vitamins and shit." He put his arms around me, pulling my body closer to his. "We are going to work this out, you're not in this alone."

"Do you want to keep the baby? This is a big decision, Troy, like a *life long* decision. We can't just decide we're done— we'll be parents." My fingers wrapped around his forearms tightly like I could some how extract the definitive reassurance I needed. This wasn't playtime, this was real life.

"What part of we're not breaking up did you not understand? You think even without the baby, I could just be done with you?" He took my face in his hands. "I said I loved you and I meant it. Marriage, kids, that was always in our future. Someone just hit the fast forward button."

"You are too calm, why aren't you freaking out? I'm freaking the fuck out. You know how crazy I can be, I'm going to be someone's mom. That's insanity of the highest level." Holy shit, there is a baby inside of me. Puking right now would not be out of the question.

"You're not going to be someone's mom, you're going to be our baby's mom. And I'm calm 'cause life throws you a curve ball every once in a while, big deal. It's not like we're sixteen with no futures ahead of us. Money isn't an issue, we're both healthy and we love each other. So maybe the timing sucks a little, we've got to roll with it."

He was so sure, not even the slightest hesitation. Part of me was mad that I was the only one about to hyperventilate, granted he had a few more minutes to adjust to the news before I did, and *he* wasn't the one who was going to be blowing up to the size of Shamu.

"I love you." I realized Troy had been the only one who'd said it, my wordless nod not really qualifying. "I want to have this baby— *our* baby." It sounded so weird saying it but he was right, this wasn't mine or his— it was ours.

To think my plans for the evening were a night of unrestrained sex, without a condom and then boom, I'm knocked up.

"Good, let's get some sleep and see if we can't get you an appointment tomorrow. I need to hold you." He turned and pulled off his boots. The socks came next and then the shirt.

Woah. Sleep hadn't been the plan, who was going to be able to sleep?

"Wait, sleep? But we were supposed to have sex. The whole getting pregnant is a non issue so there's no concerns there." Look at that, a silver lining. Let's concentrate on that and stop with the no sex talk.

"As much as I want to, and trust me— I really want to— we need to wait until a doctor checks you out." He stood and unbuttoned his jeans. They dropped to the floor, as did my hope for action tonight.

"People who are pregnant have sex all the time." Valid argument, thank you brain for stepping in. Was good of you to finally show up.

"Yeah, but they knew they were pregnant and were taking care of it. We can wait. As soon as we're given the all clear, I promise I'll make it worth the wait." Troy moved back on to the bed and pulled the covers aside and waited for me to crawl in.

"But I'm going to get fat and moody and then you won't want

me." It was childish but I pouted, shoving myself into bed like an errant child. The moodiness had already started; we were in for a treat in the next nine months or so.

"You're not going to get fat, you're going to be carrying our baby and it doesn't get sexier than that. Trust me, it's going to be you who turns me down, not the other way around." Troy crawled in and rolled me onto my side. We laid face to face, his arms around me, and his hard-on pressing against my leg. The danger of hyperventilation was back.

"I was wrong, you're the one who's crazy." Or maybe we were both crazy. This poor kid didn't stand a chance.

"We'll see. Now shhhh, I need to love on my woman." His hands moved up and down my back as he kissed my neck.

"Troy, I want our baby to have your last name."

He stopped kissing me. "I was kinda hoping you both would."

"Do you mean?" Tonight was not the night for misunderstandings.

His eyes said it loud and clear even before he opened his mouth. "Yeah."

"Just so we're clear, you're talking about getting married, right?" Again, clarification was needed.

"That's exactly what I'm talking about, but we're not doing anymore talking tonight. Go to sleep, Megs, I promise you this will all be okay."

He kissed me and with that kiss I believed him. Believed that it would all be okay.

THE ONLY THING MORE RIDICULOUS THAN HIDING IN MEGS'S BEDROOM, had been sitting around with nothing to do but listen to her stumble over herself like an amateur. I loved my girl but she couldn't lie for shit. So it was either crack open the file and find out what blood type she was, or walk out there and put her out of her misery. I never found out what blood type she was. The word pregnant had put the brakes on my future reading.

Wow. A dad. Mind blown. There you go, my life was about to change.

"Megs, I think you should probably lay down. The pacing is making me edgy, and I can totally see your ass from the split in your gown. Don't think the doc is going to appreciate my hard-on if you catch my drift." Nervous? Megs was about as close to a breakdown as I'd ever seen her.

"I can't sit down. Sitting down does nothing." She continued wearing a hole into the floor, her gown flapping open with each stride. We'd been here for a couple of hours, running tests and trying to find out answers, she'd been done with the sit still routine after thirty minutes. "What's taking so long? I'm losing my mind." The statement wasn't necessary, I'd kind of guessed that on my own.

"You need to calm down. All the stress isn't helping either of you." Now she was making me nervous. The look on her face was not one I wanted to be seeing. I tried to coax her back to the bed and lay down. Yeah, that wasn't going to happen.

"On top of everything else I've done? Troy, I've been drinking. I've taken birth control pills. I've been in smoked-filled rooms. I think the stress is the least of the baby's problems. God, I'm a horrible mother and he or she isn't even born yet." She threw her hands up in the air as her feet kept moving. Nothing I said stuck, her head hell bent on thinking up worst-case scenarios.

"For fuck's sake, you didn't know." It was an effort not to drag her to the bed and make her lie down. The guilt she was putting on herself was enough for me to want to toss the chair I was sitting on through a wall. "It's not like you went out and did crack. It will be fine, let's just wait and see what the doctor says before we go off the deep end."

The sooner they gave us the all clear and we got out of here, the better. Seeing Megs like that did something to me I didn't like. Like chest-thumping-macho-caveman shit that demanded I made it right.

"Good morning, Miss Winters." The doctor strolled in the room with no fucking urgency and placed her files down on the desk. Wonder how long I can be polite before I tell her to hurry the fuck up and reassure my girl.

"Yes. That's me, but you can't tell anyone I've been here." Megs's feet had stopped moving but now her hands were getting the attention. Her fingers twitched as they locked and unlocked with each other. If a baby hadn't been involved, I'd have suggested a double dose of Xanax.

"Miss Winters, I assure you, your confidentiality is safe." Dr. sorry-missed-her-name-the-first-time-and-didn't-care-enough-to-ask-again sat down. Once again, no fucking urgency. "You know that I couldn't talk about anything that goes on here without your written consent."

"She's freaking out, Doc. Safe to assume anything you think she knows might need to be reiterated." Figured I needed to light that fire under her ass and maybe get some intel on what we were dealing with.

"You're the father I assume?" Wow, the woman was a genius, was her first clue me putting my hand around my girl and trying to get her to calm down?

"Yep, Troy Harris. I'm the father."

"Megan, can I call you Megan?" She waited for a go ahead before she continued. "You need to relax and let us get all the facts before you start getting too excited okay? The unnecessary stress isn't healthy for you or the baby."

And where had I heard those words before? Oh, I know. They'd come out of my mouth not five minutes earlier.

"I just... I don't understand. How could it have happened? I didn't know. I didn't suspect. Were the tests wrong, there can be false positives right?" Megs pushed her hands through her hair, still hanging on to the thread of denial.

It had been a fucking ordeal to convince her to call in a favor and get an appointment on a Saturday, but waiting till Monday wasn't an option. The private clinic was happy to accommodate us for the right amount of green. It was a no brainer.

"Megan, I looked over your initial blood results and compared that with the blood samples we took this morning." The doc looked at the paper work almost as if to prove her point. "Your hCG levels are consistent with you being five weeks pregnant."

Any hope I had of calming Megs went out the window. "Five weeks? I've been pregnant for five weeks. I haven't been sick. I had a period. I've been on birth control."

"Let's start with addressing the birth control issue. Have you taken it uninterrupted? Been on any other medication? Been sick? Any one of those factors would reduce the efficiency of that method of contraception." The doc eased back into her chair as we played the how-did-it-happen game.

"I take it...." Megs swallowed before continuing, "...when I remember. I mean, I mostly remember. Sure there was some missed day here or there but only a few."

"Megan, missing one pill is enough to start your cycle. Ovulation can happen at anytime. As far as condoms, yes they are reliable but accidents happen. Heat can damage the latex or it can break, and there can be leakage. Penetrative contact with no ejaculation can also result in pregnancy."

Well that took care of my hard-on. Talk of penetrative contact with no ejaculation. Don't even get me started on the condom leakage. Still not that it fucking made a difference, what mattered was it was official. There was a baby. Ours.

"Looks like we were that one in a million chance, Megs, lucky us." I hoped the squeeze I gave her was enough to offset the dry heave that looked like was about to happen.

"What about the fact I kept taking the pill? What about my period?" Megs refused to sit down; instead we played the twenty questions while we stood up.

"Obviously it's not ideal that you continued to take them but these things can happen and in most cases have no long term effects. As far as your period, some women menstruate right through to deliver. It might have also been an implant bleed. We'll know more as you progress."

"Are you sure I haven't screwed up my baby? Tell me he or she is okay!" Megs demanded, her voice tight.

"Doc, put us out of our misery here. I'm not good with seeing her like this." That was the watered down version of what was pumping through my head, but this didn't seem like the kind of place that I could slam my fist on her desk and demand answers. It wasn't the rent-a-cops that worried me; it was that they'd refuse to help us.

"Megan, what you are experiencing is normal. Even a woman who is fully prepared and who has been actively trying to conceive will have moments of fear. But your results look great and no sign of any complications. We're going to do an internal ultrasound to get a better look, is that okay?" She moved from behind her desk and pointed us to the bed I'd been trying to get Megs on since the start of this conversation.

"Okay." Megs shuffled up onto the bed, her eyes no less scared than when this visit started. "Will you hold my hand?"

"Never going to stop, Megs, never going to stop." One of the easiest promises I'd ever had to make.

She laid back and squeezed my hand so tightly I was sure she was going to crack a bone or two. Did I give a fuck? Not even one. My girl and my baby would be worth a broken hand.

A tiny blip showed up on the screen, small and blurry but there was definitely something there. The little dude or dudette who hadn't cared that his or her parents were behaving like a bunch of loony tunes. Seems to me like junior was already smarter than the both of us, knowing what we should have fucking known from the start.

"That's our baby, Troy." Megs started to cry and I had to swallow hard a few times myself.

"Yeah, sure is." Damn if my eyes didn't get wetter the longer I looked.

There were more questions and answers but for the most part, there was a bunch of wait-and-see shit that needed to happen. We grabbed a script for some vitamins that Megs needed and left with a grainy picture of what looked like a whole lot of nothing but meant everything to us.

"Can we go get a milkshake? I really want a coffee but it's on the bad list. " We'd barely made it out the door as Megs reread over her lists of dos and don'ts.

"She said you can have it moderation." The way Megs sucked down her coffee, the avoid was going to be a hard ask. "Maybe down grade to a small or switch to decaf."

"Decaf? I'm going to assume it's the shock of impending parenthood that has made you say such horrible things to me. Yuck, no way. It's the real deal or nothing, and a small one is just going to make me want more. I have poor impulse control."

"Yes, I've noticed."

We rounded the corner to where my Lambo was parked. The car didn't seem like such a good idea now and would probably be gathering dust after a few months. Guess I would be Escalading like James and Alex. There were worse cars I could be driving.

"Oh and you are so much better. I don't recall a lot of times you said no." She folded her arms in front of her chest which happened to give me a superb view of her tits. The distraction causing my car key to almost hit the paint as I tried to open her door.

"Probably because I loved your lack of impulse control, made my job a hell of a lot easier." I braced my arms on the roof of the car, her body in the middle as I leaned in for a kiss.

"You." She mumbled against my mouth, not having the chance to finish her sentence.

My body cursed me as I pulled away and popped open the door, watching her slither into the seat. That erection that had sailed away earlier was back and it meant business. I jogged to the driver's side of the car and jumped in and tried to concentrate on the more important things we needed to deal with, other than getting me inside her.

"So you want to go tell your folks? I think that should probably happen soon." We eased into the flow of traffic, the road doing its best impression of a Manhattan parking lot.

"I think we should wait a little bit longer. There's no reason why we have to tell anyone." Her hands got busy doing that wringing action again. My brain flew into overdrive.

"Megs, come on. You're pregnant. You don't honestly think we were going to keep pretending like we weren't together did you?" I'd assumed the baby would have put the final nail in the sneaking around BS we had going on. Surely, that was done and dusted.

"Well, yeah. I did."

"No. No more."

"Troy, but…"

"No, Megs, this is bullshit." My hand slamming on the steering wheel made her jump and my regret was immediate. She was scared enough as it was without adding my frustration to the mix.

"People are going to say shit I don't need to hear right now. Some are going to say I'll be too emotional to do my job, some might even say I trapped you. Why does anyone have to know?"

"Who gives a fuck what they say. I know different and that should be the only opinion that matters." That thought had never been given any airtime.

"No, I love you, but it isn't the only opinion that matters. Do you know how hard I've worked to establish myself? It's hard enough being Mitchell Winters's daughter, everyone thinking that you only got where you did because of your last name. Add in pregnancy and it will kill any professional respect I've earned. They will think I'll be checking out soon, off to go shack-up with my *rock star* boyfriend and have little *rock star* babies."

"That's bullshit, they can't judge you 'cause you're having a baby or because you are dating me." The car inched forward before having to stop again, the break in the flow giving me the opportunity to look at her.

"It's bullshit, but it's what will happen." Her eyes convinced of what she was saying. "Trust me. We will tell people when the time is right. Now is not that time."

"Fine but you're killing me, you know that right?" Me letting go would only be carried so far. But the minute she looked like she was in the family way, I would be making it clear that I was the man responsible for that.

"Looks like we both have something that will be worth waiting for." She smiled; no doubt pleased she'd gotten her way.

"So you going to shack up with your rock star boyfriend and have rock star babies?" My grin got wider than the one she was wearing, the idea of us being a family rocking my fucking world.

"Considering I'm already knocked up, I'd say your chances are pretty good." She nodded, looking a lot less stressed than when we'd left the clinic. I liked that. Seeing her happy and knowing that while she wasn't totally cool with everything, she was slowly coming around.

"Let's go get you that milkshake and then you're heading to bed." That shake better be quick too, we'd have to get it to go. I needed to get her home.

"Bed? I'm not tired. It's the middle of the day and I'm pregnant, not sick." Her tone let me know that she had no intention on doing what she was told. Not that I expected anything less.

"You won't be sleeping, trust me." Not if I had anything to with it.

"Do you mean sex?" She sat up in her seat, it seemed like she was no longer interested in fighting me. It was a good thing too.

"Oh yeah. Doctor gave us the green light which means I need to make good on my promise."

“Screw the milkshake, take me home.”
“Done.”

20

Megan

"Troy." My head rolled back onto the pillow as my hands gripped his strong, muscular arms. God he had sexy arms, just look at that definition. Rope like almost. He must go to the gym…like a lot.

"Yeah." Troy lifted his mouth from my nipple; the way he licked me made everything feel so good.

"No, don't stop." My hands gently pushed his head back into position, I hadn't meant for him to stop. He had a very, very important job to do.

Troy laughed against my breast, his mouth closing over the tight peak. It was insane to feel this happy.

"Yeah… Like that." My eyes closed as my chest rose to meet his lips. God he had a talented mouth, almost as good as his hands—almost.

"Megs." Troy rumbled against my skin, moving the talented lip-action to my neck. He body slid higher and wow his erection pressed against me in the most delicious way.

There was urgency and yet a sweetness in the way he kissed me, almost like it hadn't been there before. He was careful and controlled, like bringing a pot slowly up to boil. It was driving me crazy yet I could find the words to make him stop.

We had arrived back at the apartment and predictably it was

an epic free-for-all of hands, fingers, and lips. Clothes were hastily removed— not like we needed them anyway— and we kissed and touched our way to my bed.

What had been unpredictable was that once our bodies had hit the mattress, the gears were heavily down graded and everything slowed the hell down. Like really slow.

I had fought it, needing the instant gratification, but Troy had simply ignored my rather vocal protests and continued on his merry way of obscene oral pleasure. No, not licking in between my legs— which is where I'd wanted him—but everywhere else. Teasing me, drawing every last inch of sanity out of me— assuming there was any left.

Hours—okay maybe not hours, but it felt like it—he owned my body, barely allowing me to touch him. My skin felt like it had been licked by a million fireflies with my core ready to explode.

"Troy, please," I shamelessly begged, "this is borderline torture, don't be so cruel."

He chuckled against my neck, "Why don't you tell me what you want then?" Oh he knew what I wanted, he just wasn't done playing with me yet.

"You. In. Me." I mumbled as his lips moved to my mouth.

"Here?" His hand swept tight little circles around my opening, teasing me more. You could have asked me my name at that point and I wouldn't have been able to tell you.

"Yes." It was a moan or maybe a groan, possibly a hybrid that sounded more like dying than sexy but I didn't care. I didn't care about anything other than having him stop the fire that was consuming me.

He shifted his body again, and then he was there. The sweet relief didn't come; instead he kept with his theme, moving inch by inch into me before slowly dragging himself out. Each time he filled me, my body tightened around him, fighting his retreat.

"Look at me, Megs," he whispered slowly as he continued the agonizing assault. "I love you."

"I love you too." The words automatically spilling from my lips, which was just as well because I couldn't have conjured up a conscious thought to have saved my life.

It was then, as we stared into each other's eyes, that I saw what he was doing. Our relationship had started off as *fucking*— intense and out of control. It had been fun and had fulfilled every physical need I had, but this... this was something else. A connection that went beyond what our bodies wanted. Went beyond the orgasm. It went beyond a good time. This, this is what I had waited my whole life to find.

In his eyes I saw the love, I saw his commitment and I hoped he saw the same in mine. There was no mistake on what *this* was, there was no misunderstanding on what it could be. It was home. Mine. His. Ours.

"Troy." My arms wrapped around him tightly as my body finally got what it had craved, my nerves tingling as pleasure ripped through me. I clung to him unable to speak anything else. His release came soon after, murmuring my name and I-love-you's as he filled me, gently raining kisses down on my face as he held me.

I hoped we would still have times where we'd fuck—because no one fucked like Troy Harris— but making love to him was so much better. Lucky for me, I hadn't had to choose. He was mine, all of him.

"Wake-up, sleepy head, your phone is being an asshole." Troy kissed my neck as his hands looked for another part of me to keep him amused. My breasts ended up the lucky recipients. Well good morning to you too, Troy Harris. "I've ignored it the first five times but whoever it is, isn't giving up."

"Ugh..." I hadn't remembered falling asleep, but I obviously had seeing as now I was trying to open my eyes. "It might be the hospital, I should probably get it."

The mattress moved as he lifted himself off and then compressed again under his weight as he returned. "Here. It's Ash." He placed my phone in my hand as he resumed holding me against his warm body. It would be so easy to drift back to sleep.

"Megs, you need to actually answer it. Holding it isn't going to help you any." Troy chuckled against my ear.

"Hello." My voice sounded groggy, thick from sleep. "Hello." I tried again, slightly less scary sounding the second time around.

"Megan Katharine Winters." Uh-oh. Three names, it couldn't be good if she was using all three names. "You are seeing someone and you didn't bother to tell me?"

Kyla had lasted exactly two days. Better than her usual record, but still I'd secretly hoped for more. "Ash, it's...."

"Complicated. Yes I've already got the down low from Kyla. What's so complicated about it? Why can't we meet him? What does he do? It's not that coffee guy again is it? How long have you been seeing him?" The questions tumbled out of her mouth without even a breath or an opportunity to answer. "Is he good to you? Tell me, he's good to you. Have you told your folks?"

"Ash, slow down." If I wasn't awake before, I surely was now. And here comes the Spanish Inquisition. "He is very good to me and I didn't tell anyone because I wasn't ready yet."

"Well, are you ready now?" She didn't give me the opportunity to answer. There was a definite theme for this phone call. One where Ash talked and I listened. "You are bringing him over for dinner. Tonight. I promise Dan will be on his best behavior and so will Troy and Jase. Kyla and Brianne, I have no control over."

"Wait, what? Troy's coming?" My eyes shot to Troy who could clearly hear the phone conversation beside me. He just shrugged innocently. I didn't buy it, not for a second. Oh shit, I had shown way too much interest in the Troy part of with that sentence. "I mean Troy *and* Jase are coming." I tried to recover. Cringe. It was a bad cover-up if ever I heard one.

"Nice try." Ash didn't miss my slip. Damn it. "Does your new guy know you have a secret obsession? And yes, they will *both* be coming."

"I'm not obsessed and tonight is kind of short notice. He probably has plans." The nervous giggle that came from my throat didn't make me sound any more convincing than I had been.

"So use that magic vagina of yours to get him to change them. Just tell him it's important because your *friends* need to make sure he's not an axe murderer."

"Oh, 'cause that's going to make the invitation so much more appealing. Look, I'll try. My magic vagina can only do so much. No promises."

What could I say? Flat out refusing would have invited too many questions. At least the promise to try would buy me a few hours to work something out.

"Make it happen and no calling me later today with some mysterious stomach bug or headache." Ash nixed the other option I had been considering. Foiled! "So unless you are in an emergency room, you are going to come to dinner. And FYI, I have your brother's number. I'm sure he'd be interested to hear some guy is bedding his sister but refusing to be seen in public with her. Can't think he would be too pleased."

I sat up in bed in a panic. "You wouldn't. I thought we were friends?"

"We are, and you would do the exact same thing if I were dating some guy who no one knew about." She wasn't wrong, not to mention I had involved myself very much so in her relationship not so long ago. Karma wasn't just a bitch; she was giggling her ass off too. "See you tonight. Seven o'clock."

Resignation. I had no other choice. "Fine. I'll see you then." I ended the call and tossed the phone onto the bed.

Fuck. Fuck. Fuck.

"Dinner plans?" Troy asked innocently, like he hadn't heard ninety-five percent of the conversation.

"Yes, ones you apparently already agreed too?" My finger jabbed him in the chest. Not like it would even make a mark on that solid wall of muscle, but it made me feel better so I did it anyway.

"Hey, don't look at me. I didn't know I was going there for dinner. Dan text me this morning and asked me if I could go over later this evening because he needed help with something. He didn't say anything about dinner." Troy put his hands up in defense.

"Fuck." My head fell into my hands. There wasn't going to be a quick fix.

"We can do that, but I don't think it's going to solve your problem." He smirked before kissing my shoulder—which incidentally was so not helpful. "Tell me, beautiful, how you are going to talk your way out of this one?

My mind ticked wildly with possibilities. "Maybe I can ask Callum..."

"No." He shot the idea down before I even finished the sentence. "I don't give a fuck if it's pretend or otherwise, no other guy gets to date you. That shit was hard enough to take before—now that you're mine and have my baby inside you—I'd probably rip the guy's head off."

The vibe he was throwing off was one dictated by pure testosterone. Let's forget to mention that I had dated Josh while I was unknowingly pregnant. There were some things best left unsaid.

"Fine, then I'll go alone." There was no getting out of it. "I'll say *he* had to work or something." Plausible. Short notice. I was liking my idea already.

"Do you know how bad of a liar you are?" Troy's voice softened as he kissed my neck. "I mean, like horrendously bad. I love you, sweetheart, but if I'm ever going to hide a body, you are the last person I'm going to call."

"I'll have you know I would totally rock body disposal. So that would be *your* loss." With my arms folded defiantly across my chest I tried to look insulted.

"We'll see." The smirk was back, the laugh added in for good measure. "Should make for an interesting evening."

"You know, you could enjoy this a little less. It wouldn't kill you." I gave him my best death glare. His smile told me, it had been less than convincing.

"Where's the fun in that?" He laughed, rubbing my arms affectionately. He was going to need to stop that if I wanted to continue to be mad. "I'm assuming you won't be travelling with me to Dan's or with your *boyfriend*."

"You assumed correctly." Showing up with Troy would look suspicious. No, I would catch a cab. That would give me more time to create a backstory. "I might make him a fireman. And he got called away, he's a hero you know."

"So many pole jokes, and so little time."

"Please don't make fun of my fictional boyfriend, it's not classy." I rolled my eyes.

"Fine, I'll leave your fictional boyfriend alone, but your *real* boyfriend is sending a car to come pick you up." He held up his hand anticipating my rebuttal. I was more than capable of getting around by myself. "Don't get all feisty on me. Dan has probably already organized TJ anyway."

"Okay. I won't fight you." At least the ride would be one thing I wouldn't have to worry about.

"Good. Now come here and let me give you a proper good morning." My body was yanked back onto the mattress; an involuntary yelp accompanied me on the way down.

While my concerns for the evening weren't solved, not yet at least, I lost myself in Troy's kiss. It was easy to do and it was definitely the best way to wake up. Whatever stress the phone call had caused was washed a way, and as luck would have it, it *was* a good morning. A very, very good morning.

"BEER?" JASE HANDED ME A LONGNECK WHILE I MILLED AROUND IN Dan's living room. I was edgy as fuck. "Just a pointer, you checking the time every five minutes is probably not the best way to play it cool." He took a swallow of the beer in his hand.

"It's seven thirty, she was supposed to be here half an hour ago. Where the fuck is she?" My mind got caught up on possibilities I didn't like as I took a swig from the bottle. I was already over this bullshit game and the night hadn't even started.

"Maybe she got held up with her *boyfriend*." Jase grinned and took another swallow.

"Very funny, asshole. Do you know how much this bullshit is pissing me off?" Jase was one of the few people I could talk to about Megs. At least while I was pacing like a caged dog he could help run interference.

"What's pissing you off?" Dan joined us, leaving his wife-to-be to fuss in the kitchen. "What are you two ladies gossiping about?"

"Oh nothing important." I wondered how much he'd heard. "Just that I'm going to have to get into a monkey suit for your big day. It's like wearing a straight jacket." The excuse of the suit gave me a save. Not like I could tell him the fucking truth.

"Damn right you are suiting up. You aren't going to bitch about it either." His eyeballing told me he meant business. Not that there was any doubt. "Wonder where Megs is? You wanna give the loser a hard time?"

"Probably not one of your better ideas. Maybe give the girl a break, huh?" Jase thankfully took the reins on that one; saving me from telling Dan I'd punch him in the sack if he made her cry. Yep. It was going to be a long ass night.

"Fine." Dan pouted, pissed his source of entertainment had been taken for the night.

I pulled my phone out from my pocket. No texts, no missed calls and thirty-three minutes later than when Megs said she was going to be here. Another minute and I'd be getting TJ on the horn— someone had some explaining to do.

Since finding out I was going to be a dad, it was insane how fucking protective and territorial I'd become. It was straight up caveman shit, I didn't understand it but I knew well enough to know there was no fighting it either. And no shit, if I could wrap Megs in cotton wool for the next eight months, I'd do it.

The door buzzer sounded and it looked like I was finally going to be put out of my misery. Thank fucking Christ.

The relief, however, was short lived 'cause when the door swung open it wasn't Megs. The two chicks whose names I didn't quite remember were busy squealing over Ash's newly acquired engagement ring in the entranceway with no sign of my girl.

I'd waited long enough. "Need to make a call, guys. Give me a sec." Neither Dan nor Jase asked questions as I turned my back and put some distance between us so I could get busy giving JT the where-the-fuck-are-you.

"Oh, hi Troy." One of the pair, who'd just walked in, popped up in front of me—her smile was more than just a little friendly. My phone that had barely made it out of my pocket was still in my hand as she gave me a wave to go with the smile. I hadn't even had a chance to dial.

"Hey…" I search my mind for her name. It had to be in there somewhere; both Ashlyn and Megs had introduced us a couple of times. I'd never been interested enough to take notice.

"Brianne." She let me off the hook, adding another little smile at the end. Well at least I hadn't pissed her off, not that she was high on my list of priorities but being out and out rude to a friend of Ash and Megs wouldn't win me any favors either.

"Right. Brianne. How are you doing?" My phone got shoved back into my pocket as I mentally calculated how long I would have to talk to her. One minute? Five? Surely Megs would show in that time. If she didn't— polite or not— I'd be giving Brianne a friendly shove and making that call.

"I'm good. Really good." More smiles and I had to wonder if the girl hadn't taken some happy pills before she'd shown up.

Ash flicked her eyes over to us and gave me a nod. Not sure if she was glad 'cause I wasn't being an asshole to her friend or Brianne talking to me meant one less chick pawing at the rock on her hand. So guess I was stuck a little while longer. Jase and Dan were no help either; the two of them not even giving us a second look as they stood where I'd left them deep in conversation.

"Great." I forced my mouth into a smile. Great? Not even close.

Brianne continued to talk, but a bunch of words was all I heard. My limit for waiting had just been reached when another loud buzz came from the door. And if that door opened and Megs wasn't behind it, there would be some serious hell to pay.

"Hey, everyone. Sorry I'm late." Megs burst through the doorway, her face more pale than when I'd left. My need to be polite put on a back burner as I moved closer to where the action was.

"So where is he?" Ashlyn asked, her head poking out the doorway looking to see if someone else was with her. Not fucking likely.

"Ash, I'm sorry. It was late notice and he had to work." Well what do you know, she sounded genuinely sincere, she must've been working on the act in the car ride over. Maybe that's why she'd been late.

Megs shot me a look but didn't hold it for long, instead giving Ash her attention as the questioning continued.

"It's Sunday, what does he do?" Ash wasn't letting it go that easy, not that I'd expected anything less.

"He's a fireman." Megs smiled like she'd just been given a puppy. I wasn't sure if I should be proud she was really trying to pull it off or pissed that she was pretending she was with someone else.

"He let you slide down his pole?" The expected Dan response didn't take too long to show up. I had tried to warn her about pole jokes— she hadn't listened.

"Dan, really." Ash planted her hands on her hips and gave her head a shake but no one seemed surprised. Megs relaxed a little seeing the heat was off her, at least short term.

"Sorry babe, it kind of needed to be said." Dan shrugged, the shit-eating grin showing how *not* sorry he was.

"So, your fireman." Ash turned back to Megs, the twenty questions far from done. "Does he have a name?"

The more I watched, the more juiced up I was getting. Fuck it. She was clearly not herself, I could tell just by looking at her, and I wasn't sure if it was the fucking stress of sprouting bullshit or if she was genuinely not well.

"So Troy, are you done with the new album? You will be touring soon I'm assuming?" Brianne shoved herself in front of me again, stopping me from hearing Megs's answer.

"Huh?" The words she had said not fully registering in my head because I'd been worried about my girl.

"Touring? The band will be going on the road, right?" she repeated, her body so close to me I had to take a step back.

"Rory's so busy and sort of shy. Maybe some other time...." Bits of Megs's conversation floated over to me as Brianne waited for a response. Hinting that her interest in the Megs show was done and dusted.

"Yeah, next year sometime," I answered, not bothering to look at her, my eyes focused on Megs who was looking paler by the second.

"Would love to see a show. You guys are fantastic live," Brianne continued. Stepping in front of me when I tried to get closer to where Megs was standing. This dance was getting old.

"I'm sure we can manage to float you some tickets. No big deal." I threw it out there hoping that the promise of free tickets would get her off my ass. I had been done with this conversation five minutes ago.

"Rory sounds like a douche if you ask me. What kind of guy can't get his shit together for his girl." Dan weighed in, adding to my already short fuse.

"Really? You would give me tickets?" Brianne smiled and side stepped in front of me again.

"Yeah, like I said, it's no big deal." I moved again finally getting past her.

"Oh, thank you, Troy, you're the best." She threw her arms around me stopping me from moving forward, her hands getting familiar with my chest.

"Heyyyyyyy. Wow. Easy there." I got to work quickly trying to peel her arms off my body, but she was persistent, tightening her grip as I tried to move her fingers.

My eyes shot to Megs, who because of my edging to get closer, now had a front row seat to Brianne's little show. The seething eyes and the tight mouth enough of a hint she wasn't happy.

"You smell nice, is that some special cologne you're wearing?" She moved her head closer, sniffing my neck as I tried to maneuver out.

"Brianne, hey." I was done being nice. "How about you let go. I don't want to hurt you." I was completely ready to rip her hands off me if she didn't fucking remove them herself.

"I like it, you smell manly." She completely ignored me, like I hadn't just asked her to get her fucking mitts off me.

"Get your hands off him!" Megs seethed as she stormed over to us, yanking on Brianne's arm.

"Megs? Oh hey, sweetie, I was just chatting to Troy." She patted my chest like I was her fucking pet as I freed myself from her.

"Yeah, I saw how you were chatting to him. Any closer and you would be giving him a lap dance." She planted her hands on her hips, her voice full of venom.

"Ah-ha. I fucking knew it!" Kyla pointed at us both, her eyes and grin just as big as each other. "I knew it. I told you we would smoke them out."

Kyla and Brianne high fived each other and the pieces came

together. The whole fucking thing had been a set up and we'd both been played.

"Knew what? What?" Dan looked around, confused not knowing what the hell was going on.

"Oh lord, here we go." Jase laughed, knowing the shit storm had just been unleashed.

"Megs and Troy are together." Brianne smiled, proud her little performance had outed us. If I hadn't been so distracted with concern with Megs, I would have seen this shit a mile away.

"Megs and Troy are together? Does the fireman know?" Dan looked between Megs and me, trying to play catch up.

"There's no fireman, you moron. Try and keep up." Jase smacked him on the shoulder.

"Fuck it." I did what I should have done from the start. I grabbed Megs's hand and gave it a squeeze. "Yes, we're together. We were trying to keep it on the DL and not make a big deal about it but now it's out there, we're seeing each other. We're a couple. Whatever you wanna call it, I'm done with this hiding shit."

"Waaiiiiiitttt a minute." Dan held up his hands, giving me the eyeball. "What about all those broads you've been screwing?"

"There weren't any other broads. It was just Megs." I slung my arm around her and tucked her in close. It's what I had wanted to do from the minute she'd walked in. It felt good and I made a fucking promise that from now on, I wouldn't be holding back.

"Fuck, it's like Lexi and Alex all over again. Seriously, I'm fucking offended. Why the hell wasn't I in on this memo?" He threw up his hands in disgust.

"Dan, not now," I warned.

"People are fucking, left, right and center and I'm none the wiser." He continued to run his mouth at the risk of a beat down from me. His attention turned to Ash who didn't look all that surprised. "Did you know?"

"Not until Kyla came to me with her theory. Although I'm really not surprised." She tucked her arms around Dan and gave us a smile.

"So you played us? You weren't really flirting with Troy?" Megs looked at her friends, apparently needing confirmation on what I already knew.

"Come on, Megs, girl code. I would never go after a guy you've been lusting over for years. But Kyla and I decided that you would probably need the incentive to come clean." Brianne gave her a smile, her delight fucking obvious.

"I hate you both."

"No you don't. Look how awesome it is. All in the open." Kayla smirked, giving Brianne a hug. The pair of them, pleased.

"Whatever." Megs waved them off and turned her attention back to me.

"Well now everyone knows about us, can you give me a minute so I can kiss my girl?" Not that I needed the permission, my mouth on Megs was happening and the fact I'd waited this long was a fucking miracle.

"Oh, so sweet." Brianne clapped her hands together, giving us her endorsement.

"I mean, literally everyone is fucking and not telling me." Dan was still stuck on the same old tune.

"Shut up, dickwad. You are spoiling my mood." I flipped him off as I slowly edged Megs back into the living room.

I didn't give her much time, my hands around her jaw tilting her head toward mine so I could taste her. She parted her lips and let me inside, her hands pulling me closer as I sealed my mouth with hers. It was like being in heaven. I would never get sick of it.

Megs pulled her mouth away from mine; her smile telling me it had been just as good for her. "You don't have to look so pleased with yourself and don't you dare say I told you so."

"Wouldn't dream of it but the pleased look is staying. I am very, very pleased." Not a lie, I was ecstatic about the turn of events. Happy that people knew that we were together and what did you know? Nothing bad had happened.

"Let's not mention the baby just yet, okay?" Megs pulled against my shirt, her eyes flooded with please-don't-fight-me. "I think we've reached our quota for crazy reveals for one night."

"Deal." I could live with that. We had all kinds of time to announce junior. "Why were you late? You feeling okay?"

"I think my easy run might be coming to an end." Megs gave

me a tight smile and my inner caveman got very interested in the conversation. "I was feeling weird and puked a bit, but I'm fine now."

"Should we go back and see the doctor?" I cursed myself for not being there to take care of her when she was sick. That shit would be changing, very fucking soon.

"No, from all the reading material they gave us, it sounds normal." She gave a shrug and wrapped her arms back around me.

"Alright you two, come sit down." Ash smiled from the doorway. "We are actually eating dinner tonight."

"Ash, I'm sorry I didn't tell you. I just ..." Megs wriggled out of my hold and started to explain before Ash cut her off.

"Megs, I'm happy for you. Really I am. It doesn't matter, I'm just glad you got your guy." She didn't seem pissed which was a plus. While I knew eventually everyone would get over it —even Dan— the last thing I wanted was Megs upset.

"Thank God, I'm so relieved. I thought for sure you would be mad and worried our relationship would screw up your wedding plans." Megs grabbed Ash's hand and gave it a squeeze.

"Megs, you're crazy." Ash smiled, giving Megs's arm a little shake. "How much trouble can you get into in a couple of months?"

"True." Megs laughed. "I mean I can only get knocked up once, right?" She slapped her hand across her mouth as soon as she realized what she'd said. So much for not telling anyone about the baby.

"What?!" Ash looked at Megs before looking at me, obviously putting two and two together.

"Yeah, that's the other bit of news we were keeping on the quiet." There was no hiding my big ass grin. "It's early days, but we're going to be parents."

"Oh my God." Ash's eyes got wide as she got caught up to speed.

"Ash, please don't tell anyone. I can't believe I let that slip. It's so early, we just found out ourselves."

"I swear I won't tell a soul, but no more fucking secrets, okay?"

Ash pulled Megs in for a hug, both of them pretty emotional.

"I promise." Megs hugged back, no doubt part of her glad she wasn't hiding more shit from her friend.

"Alrighty, you think I can have my girl back? Have some lost time I want to make up for." And make sure she's okay. The sickness thing still worried me a little.

"Sure, sure." Ash released Megs and I pulled her back to my side. "Five minutes you two."

"Thanks." I tipped my chin as Ash scooted out of the room.

"Now," my hands went to her jaw again, clocking her eyes with mine, "let me do that one more time so I can make sure you are okay."

22

Megan

"UGH, I FEEL SICK." MY STOMACH ROLLED AS I RAN TO THE BATHROOM. My morning ritual about to be performed for the second time as I heaved whatever contents my stomach had left into the toilet. "God, this is so fucking gross." I heaved again, hoping to God it would be the last.

"Megs, what can I do?" Troy asked helplessly from the door, the one I'd tried in vain to close before doubling over and puking my guts out. It was bad enough I had to witness it; I didn't want an audience.

It had been two weeks since we'd found out a little life was growing inside me and within that two weeks, my body had already started to change. The biggest change seemed to be the relationship I was now in with the bathroom. I'd contemplated changing my status on Facebook; we were inseparable these days.

"Please don't watch." I waved him off, mortified. "I'm almost done." My hands braced either side of the cold tiled wall as my body hovered in limbo, waiting for the next wave of nausea to rip through me.

"You think I haven't seen anyone get sick before? Megs, I spent most of my teenage years watching underage kids puke their parents' liquor cabinet out onto their lawn."

Obviously the view hadn't been good enough from the door,

because despite my protest he came and sat on the tub beside me. I grabbed the washcloth from the sink and wiped my face.

"Awesome, thanks for the visual. It doesn't change that I don't want you to see me. God, could this be any less sexy? I wouldn't be surprised if you never slept with me again." Oh God, please don't let me cry. Cry for the ghosts of orgasms past. I'd had a good run, I shouldn't be so greedy.

"Going to take a little bit more than vomit to turn me off, sweetheart. Do I need to have sex with you right now just to prove a point?"

I grabbed my toothbrush from the holder and squeezed on some toothpaste. It was probably going to make me gag but at least my mouth would be minty fresh. Got to take the victory when you can. "I'd probably throw up on you and ruin your *New York Dolls* T-shirt." I pointed to his vintage Tee before shoving the toothbrush in my mouth.

"Fine, we'll do it in the shower, easy fix." He stood up and pulled off his T-shirt, his face deadly serious. "Let's go, get naked."

"You're insane." I mumbled spitting the toothpaste into the sink. Wow, it didn't get any less sexier than this. How was he still standing there?

"Nope, just know that no matter what happens my feelings aren't going to change." He walked over to the sink while I rinsed.

Things would change. He would go on tour and meet women who weren't moody or emotional and whose boobs didn't sag to their knees. Not that mine did yet, but I was prepared— I've read *Cosmo.* When did I become so fucking insecure?

"They'll change after the baby, when you'll be able to park your car in my vagina."

Troy's face animated as he barked out a laugh. "Seriously, do you rehearse this shit?" And yet again more laughter at my expense. This was so not funny. "You are killing me."

"Stop laughing at me, this is not funny." The damp washcloth I had been using went flying toward his face. My throw wasn't great —I had never been good at sports—and he ducked, the washcloth hitting the wall in a rather defeated splat.

"Look at me, Megs," Troy closing the gap between us and I gave silent thanks I had brushed my teeth. "I am not going anywhere. I love you. We've got this, okay?" He wrapped his arms around me, capturing me in a Troy prison of sorts. It felt nice there. Safe.

"I love you, too," I mumbled against his chest, breathing him in.

"Well then, we're more than half way there, yeah?" His hand played with my hair as he held me close. He showed no signs of letting go, which was awesome seeing as I didn't want him to.

"I hate that you're the one making sense when I'm acting crazy. Worst thing is I know it's crazy talk, but I can't make myself stop. You know I graduated cum laude from Georgetown? I should be the one making sense."

His chuckle vibrated through his chest. "So, even smart people get to fly off the handle. If it makes you feel better, most my twenties were spent *acting crazy*. I've done my time."

"God, you're sexy, Troy Harris." I peeled my head from his chest to admire the view. It was a view that I would never get tired of.

"Must be the company I'm keeping." He flashed a cheeky grin. "I would also like to point out that shower sex is still very much on the table."

"We have to be at my mom and dad's in an hour." Of all the craziness I'd been sprouting this morning, now was when I decided to be responsible? I was so appalled.

"So? I have a Lambo, Megs. I'll drive the thing sideways to get us there in time."

He was making a solid argument and I almost caved, except thoughts of having to sit through a meeting with my parents after just having had sex was probably a little too skeevy, even for me.

"Just kiss me now."

It was a compromise and probably one that would see us being late anyway. Me and impulse control left a lot to be desired.

"Always."

Nerves. They didn't help the nausea I'd been dealing with, nor did the eggs benedict my mother had placed in front of me. Mental note. It's easier to introduce your boyfriend to your parents *before* you get knocked up.

"Troy, would like some more juice?" My mother hovered with a pitcher full of orange juice. Her bright smile thawing some of my nerves. Oh hell, my parents were going to freak the fuck out.

"Thank you, Mrs. Winters, I'd love some." Troy held my hand under the table as I counted backward from ten and tried to regulate my breathing.

"So, you're a rock star." My dad took a sip from his coffee cup, his brow raised in the I'm-not-making-this-easy-for-you position I hadn't seen in awhile. It was his talent—along with being a brilliant heart surgeon—the ability to make me feel like I was sixteen and got caught sneaking out.

"With all due respect, Mr. Winters, anyone who calls themselves a rock star is an ass...." He caught himself before adding *hole* and corrected himself. "...is conceited. I'm a musician and I'm lucky enough to be successful in a pretty difficult industry." Troy obviously wasn't feeling the same fear I was. Good. Only one of us was allowed to freak out at a time and currently I was definitely freaking the hell out.

"Yes, very difficult industry but no career paths are safe these days are they, Mitchell?" My mom sat back down in her seat and gave me a wink. Her support was something I could always count on, and besides I blamed her for some of my quirky antics. Sitting right there in her chiffon blouse and playing with her strand of pearls was an original member of the *KISS* army, I kid you not.

"Of course, I was merely trying to establish what it is you do." My dad took another slow sip from his cup. "You play in the same band with that Dan fellow, Ashlyn's rather taken with?" I didn't correct him that Ash was *marrying* him, slightly more than *rather taken*.

Troy's calm veneer didn't shatter, answering my dad respectfully with a calmness I clearly didn't possess. "Yes, sir. Dan Evans is my best friend; we are both in the same band."

"Do you do drugs?" My dad lowered his cup nonchalantly like he'd just asked if Troy flossed after brushing.

"Dad." I barked out, horrified he'd subscribe to such a clichéd stereotype.

Troy looked my father dead in the eye and answered. "No. No drugs."

"So, how did the two of you meet?" My mom tried to lighten the mood, not like it could get any tenser, mention of drug use will do that to a conversation.

"I had the pleasure of meeting your daughter last year. Just took me a while to wise up and ask her out." Troy smiled and thankfully went with the censored version. I didn't need for my parents to know about my extra circular sextivities.

"Are you alright sweetie, you haven't touched your brunch?" My mom touched my arm, the plate in front of me, untouched.

"I'm just not very hungry, Mom." I gave her my best smile, the lopsided half-grin didn't do much to help my cause.

My dad eyed me up and down, no doubt gathering intel from my lack of appetite. I swear the man had x-ray vision or something. He could always *tell* when something was wrong.

"So, are you getting married or are you pregnant?"

"Dad!"

"Mitchell!"

My mom and I both snap simultaneously. He must definitely have x-ray vision.

"Look, I know I'm an old man but I'm not completely ignorant." He wiped his mouth with his napkin. "You both look like you've been told you need a triple bypass. So which is it? Oh, and I will remind you son, while I am doctor, I still maintain my second amendment rights."

"Mitchell, stop." My mother waved my father off before reaching across and touching Troy's arm. "He doesn't have a gun."

"I didn't say I had a gun, I said I maintain my rights— which means I could get one," my father clarified.

"I'm pregnant." It was time to come clean, after all that's why we were here, right? "We love each other, and we're having the baby."

"Mr. and Mrs. Winters, while this pregnancy wasn't planned, I love your daughter very much and we're going to be a family."

Troy took over, not willing to let me face the music by myself. "We're getting married as soon as she agrees. Hell, I'd marry her tomorrow, if she'd let me."

"Is this what you want, darling? I need you to know that your mother and I will respect and support you, whatever decision you make but I don't want you to get married out of obligation. That will never work out. Baby or no baby, this has to be something you need to be sure of."

My dad reached out his hand and touched my arm.

"Dad, of course I want this. I love him." My eyes watered as I nodded my head and Troy squeezed my hand even tighter.

"Sir, me not marrying Megs is not really an option." Troy moved his arm around me.

"Our Megan is an exceptionally bright girl, and usually a good judge of character so the fact that you are sitting here in our home means she obviously thinks very highly of you. But I held that baby girl when she came into this world. I loved her first, and I'm always going to love her, so when I give her away, I'm going to make damn well certain that the man is worthy of her."

"I don't think there is a man alive who is worthy of her, but I can tell you now that I would give my last breath to make her happy.

"Right answer." My dad nodded.

"Dad?" Was this some test Troy was supposed to pass?

"When the two of you eventually have children you will understand. No one will ever be good enough for them; all you can ask for is that they find someone who will give it their all to make them happy."

I was already an emotional mess—hearing how much he loved me—just about sent me over the edge. I should probably buy shares in *Kleenex* for the rest of this pregnancy.

"Does this mean we have your blessing?" I knew it was old fashioned and I would be with Troy without it, but I desperately wanted for my parents to be okay with this.

"Beautiful girl, you will always have our blessing." My father smiled. "Troy, if you mess this up, I know ways to kill you and make it look like natural causes."

"Mitchell!"

"Dad!"

"I'm not going to mess this up." Troy grinned, no doubt or hesitation in his voice.

"Good, now tell me when we can expect this grandbaby."

"SO YOU GOING TO MAKE ME BEG, IS THAT HOW YOU WANNA PLAY THIS game?" I kissed her neck in the spot I'd knew would make her squeal. Our bodies lying on top of the makeshift pallet bed I'd made out of blankets and pillows on my living room floor. The bullshit movie we'd been trying to watch no longer holding our interest.

"Troy Harris, stop that! You're playing dirty." She threw her head back laughing, but made no attempt to move—not that my arms locked around her would have let her.

"Last time I checked, that's how you liked it." I nipped at her shoulder, loving the noise that was coming from her mouth.

"I do, I do." She laughed as she tried to wiggle out of my hold.

"See, it's not that hard to say. Now, just let me get you in front of a preacher and you just need to repeat that again." I moved my arms from their strong hold and maneuvered her onto her back, my legs caging her in as I hovered above her.

"Who knew you were such a traditionalist." She raised her hands to my face. "God, could you be any more adorable?"

"Can we quit calling me adorable? I thought we agreed on calling me bad-ass, fierce will also work." My hands worked their way up her sides, tickling her.

"Whatever— you are just a big teddy bear, Troy Harris." She threw her head back in a laugh; the smile she was wearing rocking my world.

"You're lucky I'm secure in my manhood." My fingers traced the lines of her body, part of me not believing that she was actually mine. "I thought the idea of a shrink was to make people *less* crazy not give them a complex."

"I'm off duty, so messing with your mind is allowed." Her grin got bigger. Jesus, there was nothing I wouldn't do for this girl.

"Is that why you are refusing to set a date? My mind not pretzeled enough for your liking?" My head dipped down, my mouth deciding it had something better to do than talk.

"I want to marry you, I do —but it's so soon." Her thumbs moved over my lips and her eyes clocked mine. "Like sooooo soon. We have just started telling people we're dating, we get married— everyone is going to know it was a shotgun wedding. Besides, Dan and Ash haven't even had their wedding yet."

"Fuck what people think, and the only shotgun will be the one I'll be lugging if we end up having a daughter. No one is forcing my hand, but I want a ring on yours."

Marrying Megs was not something I needing to think about. Not sure when I'd wised up, but her carrying our baby wasn't the reason. Sure it might have sped up the process, but there was zero doubt that it was what I wanted. Her and me forever, I was more than okay with that game plan.

"But I'll be fat in the wedding photos." Megs screwed up her face in disgust. "Is that what you want to look back and see? Me being poured into a wedding dress like the Stay Puft marshmallow man?"

"You will look fucking perfect, like you do everyday."

"See, you don't need me to mess with your head, you're already delusional." She rolled her eyes not understanding that for me, her body changing was a turn on, not a fucking turn off.

"I sure as hell was in the past. Looking at you and pretending that I didn't want to be with you, yeah —it doesn't get more delusional than that." Ain't that the truth.

"Aw. You're being adorable again." Her smile was back, this time even bigger than before.

"I'm motherfucking fierce I told you." My mouth attacked hers, trying to prove my point.

"Fiercely adorable," she mumbled against my mouth.

"Killing me. You are killing me." My lips moved to her neck, kissing their way down.

"Tell me you love me." Her hands locked into my hair, pulling my head back to look at her.

"I love you, marry me," I said with zero hesitation.

"I love you too. Not yet." Her eyes got glassy as she nodded her head.

"Then I'm going to ask you every day until you say yes."

And so started our game, everyday a new proposal.

Monday I went with funny and got a huge ass teddy bear delivered to her office. No shit, the thing was easily six-foot and had a sign around his neck that said his name was Fierce. In his huge paw I'd taped a card that said *Marry Troy*. Sure I wanted to be the one doing the asking, but I wasn't scared to call in some help if it meant we got to take the walk down the aisle sooner.

She'd jumped on the horn and giggled for ten minutes straight.

"Troy, I love Fierce. You are so sweet."

"Just don't love him more than me; I didn't pay all that money for the bastard to steal my woman," I warned, glad I'd been able to make her laugh.

"I don't know— it's a coin toss right now as to which one of you holds a bigger piece of my heart." She teased as if she was trying to bait me.

"Did he give you my message or was he too busy putting the moves on?" I'd hoped that she hadn't missed the message he had in his hand.

"He did and I'll think about it." It was a step up from the *not yet* I'd gotten yesterday, so as far as I was concerned it was a win.

"Awesome. I'll get the ball rolling for tomorrow's surprise then."

"I can hardly wait. Hey, Troy. Is it okay if I take Fierce to the children's wing to play? I think the kids would really love him."

"Yeah, I think that would be the best place for him seeing as I've obviously got things covered at home. Besides, it will mean I won't have to worry about him hitting on you when I'm not looking." This earned me more giggles.

For Tuesday I went with romantic.

I woke up at the crack of dawn and placed a trail of rose petals from her bed all the way to the kitchen. Then I got busy making heart-shaped pancakes, trying to not set off the smoke alarm while I cooked them. Avoiding third degree burns was also a challenge—accidently grabbing the fucking heart shaped cookie cutter I was using with my bare hand while it was still in the skillet, wasn't my smartest move.

"Rose petals. Awww, did Fierce sneak in last night or was it my other teddy bear?" She yawned as she took a seat at the kitchen counter.

"Oh no, that fucker isn't getting credit for my moves." I swooped around, kissing her neck before placing the plate of pancakes in front of her. *Marry me* written in maple syrup across the top.

"Is this your way of getting me to eat my words?" Her finger slid along the edge of the plate collecting some *Aunt Jemima* before popping it into her mouth.

I moved around to the other side of the counter to where her feet were dangling from the barstool, sinking down to one knee and pulled a candy ring out from my pocket. If she wanted me on my knees, she'd have it. Whatever it took to make her say that three letter word, and I would keep asking until she said yes. There was no one else for me.

"This is just a stand in till we find the right one." I slid the ring onto her left hand. "But I've already found the right woman. Marry me, Megs. I love you."

"Troy." She teared up as she cupped my face. "I love you too, but maybe we should wait until the baby's born. Do it properly? The baby will still have your last name even if we're not married, I promise you."

This wasn't about our baby having my last name; this was about having the woman I loved as my wife. "When we do it, either before or after the baby is born, it will be properly. I'll keep asking you. One of these days you are going to say yes." And I wasn't giving up.

Wednesday I hid Post-It notes in all of her stuff. So throughout the day she found little yellow squares that said *Marry Me.* I had been busy and stuck them in shoes, her laptop bag, bathroom cabinet, underwear drawer, in her purse and even managed to hide a few in her office. This hadn't been as hard to coordinate as I'd thought. I had been picking her up from work all week and every time, without fail she would need to use the bathroom before we left. So I'd used the time Tuesday evening while she was answering her call of nature to stuff a few in her drawers and push some under her keyboard.

"Troy Harris." The call had come around noon.

"Megs, what a nice surprise." I grinned into the phone like an idiot even though she couldn't see me.

"Did you buy shares in *3M* and not tell me? It's like Post-It notes threw up all over the place."

She was exaggerating, but I hadn't been shy about how many I'd hid. 'Cause I couldn't be sure she'd see them all, I played the numbers game and boosted the amount I'd left.

"I figured killing a few trees was less conspicuous than a billboard in *Times Square,* but give me a week and I'm sure I can get it together."

"Oh just make sure you don't replace Mr. tighty-whities in his Calvins, I really like looking at him."

"You look at him all you want as long as you come home to me." Some dude with his junk on display didn't threaten me, as long as he stayed on a billboard.

"Bye, Troy Harris."

I would never get sick of hearing her call me that, sure as hell meant more to me than calling me baby.

"Bye, Megs."

And so went the rest of the week. Thursday I dialed it down and went with simple. A big bunch of flowers with a card that said *TH Loves MW* was delivered to her office. There wasn't a *will you marry me* on there but it was kind of implied. She called and told me that they were beautiful, and then warned me her receptionist might try and snap me up herself— like that could ever happen. Friday, I surprised her and took her out to lunch. I got a local deli to get together a picnic basket for us and we walked to Central Park where we ate on the grass.

We had made the trek to Yonkers on the weekend and we'd told my folks we were together. My mom cried with excitement, firstly that I'd brought a girl home—something I hadn't done in a really long time, and secondly that we were going to be parents. The whole out-of-wedlock thing hadn't bothered my parents so much, they knew I was going to do the right thing by Megs and my son or daughter, so they did even ask if we were going to get hitched. Besides, my sister had gotten knocked up when she was eighteen—so me being a dad in my thirties —was a walk in the fucking park.

Not surprisingly they loved her and I did tell Megs that she was stuck with me now; my mother would probably disown my ass if I let her slip through my fingers. I'd even managed to ask her to marry me two more times on the weekend.

Everyday we moved a little bit closer, with my calculation being that by end of next week we would be in the courthouse — either getting a marriage license or her filing a restraining order.

It was worth taking the risk.

24

Megan

YOU KNOW WHAT ELSE COMES WITH HAVING YOUR HEAD DOWN A toilet and peeing every five minutes? Fatigue. Like a black cloud, it rolls in and sucks your energy right when you need it most, i.e. having your shit together at work.

"I hate my parents. I wish they'd never had me." Brad fidgeted in his chair; progress with him was going at a snail's pace.

"Why don't we talk about why you have these feelings. Has something happened recently? Have they mistreated you in any way?" It was the same story every session. He was filled with so much hate.

"They are trying to ruin my life. I didn't fucking ask to be born. It's all their fault my life sucks. They don't give a fuck about me." The venom spewed out of him, his feet tapping nervously on the floor.

At some stage something had to get through to him; a tiny *in* was all I needed.

"Brad, I can see you have a lot of hurt and anger, but your parents love you very much. I know things are hard for you to see right now but they are doing everything they can to help you. They care very much; they want you to be happy and well. I care Brad, I need for you to know that."

"I'm not crazy, I know you and everyone else thinks it, but I'm not." He flicked his ruffled bangs out of his eyes and looked at me, his eyes pleading with me to take away some of his pain.

"No one thinks you're crazy, you just need help. Please let me help you." My thoughts flicked to my own child and the things I would do to save them, save them from this pit of despair. "Please Brad, we can do this together."

"I don't know where to start." It was the first crack—the tiny, tiny step to moving forward but it was all I needed.

"We start slow, by being honest." I wanted to weep with relief. "We are going to write some scenarios down, triggers." My hand flew to my desk drawer and pulled out a blank piece of paper. "Things that make you feel not so great." I handed him a pencil. "It can be anything."

Brad leaned forward in his chair and tentatively started his list. "Anything? Like if I hate butterflies and they make me mad, I can write that?"

"Yep, you can write anything." I reassured him as I leaned back in my chair.

Uh-oh. That didn't feel good. The sudden movement back made me feel weird. Now was not the time for morning/afternoon sickness. I shouldn't have skipped lunch—you would think it would be easier on an empty stomach but it just made it worse.

"Dr. Winters? You okay?" Brad looked up from his list as I felt a heat come over me. Yep, this wasn't good. I was probably going to puke.

"Just a little upset stomach." The heat slowly travelled up my body as beads of sweat started to glisten on my forehead. "I just need a glass of water."

The water was a crapshoot—it was either going to settle the urge or accelerate the process, either way, I couldn't leave. I slowly rose out my chair, feeling clammy all over as I slowly walked away from my desk.

My hand started to shake as I poured myself a glass of water from the water cooler in my office. Just keep it together a little while longer, I told myself as my unsteady hand brought the paper cup to my mouth.

"Just keep writing, Brad." My breathing started to hitch as a different kind of feeling washed over me. "I—I'm okay." My voice wavered as I took another swallow of water.

Something was wrong, it wasn't just nausea—the heat, the shaking—it felt like the flu. I felt weak, like I could potentially pass out.

Abdominal pain gripped me—like period pain but worse— as I literally lost my breath. No. Another cramp took hold as I fell to my knees in pain. No.

"Dr. Winters!" Brad leapt out of his seat and joined me on the floor, his face filled with fear. "What's wrong? I'm sorry I was so mad."

"No." I whispered as yet again I felt the contraction of my abdominal wall. This couldn't be happening. My panties becoming wet as I felt the tell tale drip from in between my legs. "No." It was barely audible, my voice gripped by pain and fear as I clutched my stomach.

"Dr. Winters, please tell me what to do? Please?" Brad begged on the floor beside me, I had almost forgotten he was there.

"You need to grab my phone, Brad. It's on the desk. Then I'm going to need you to run outside to Mrs. Bennett in reception and wait with her, okay? Can you do that?" I harnessed whatever calmness I had in me, making sure I didn't raise my voice. He was just a kid, seeing me on the floor was bad enough—freaking out, that would scar him for life.

Brad ran to my desk and retrieved my cell, planting himself back on the floor with me. His shaky hand handed the phone to me as he stayed beside me on his knees.

"You need to go wait outside, Brad. Mrs. Bennett will look after you until your parents come to get you." I forced the smile as pain shot up my back.

"Something bad is happening to you, isn't it?" His eyes were so wide with fear.

"Please wait outside, Brad; I promise I am going to be okay." I wasn't sure if I believed it but I needed it to be the truth.

My fingers started dialing the ER department as I watched him reluctantly move to his feet. His scared eyes looked back at me from the doorway before he finally disappeared through it.

"Hi ER, Ronda speaking." The call was answered on the second ring.

"Hey Ronda, it's Dr. Winters from Psych room 3, I need a wheel chair and some assistance. I think I'm miscarrying my baby." I breathed through the pain as my hand squeezed the phone.

"Dr. Winters, I'll get someone up to you A.S.A.P. — just hang tight."

It's not like I had a lot of options other than *hanging*, there wasn't anything I could do but sit there.

"Okay, Okay." I nodded even though she couldn't see me, my eyes welling as I ended the call.

"Jesus, Mary and Joseph." Carrie Bennett ran through the door, sinking to her knees beside me. "It's going to be alright sweetie, just hang in there."

It wasn't going to be all right. No doctor or nurse would convince me of that.

"Please go out and stay with Brad, he's scared. Please go sit with him." My breathing was labored as I stared down at the floor. I couldn't raise my head.

"He's with Lani, sweetie. He's fine. I promise you." Her voice softened as she told me he was safely waiting with the other receptionist.

"Then please go wait with them. I just want to be alone." I couldn't do this and be strong for an audience. I was about to fall apart.

"Dr. Winters..." She started to protest.

"Please, Carrie." I interrupted forcing my head up to look at her, "Please."

Carrie slowly rose to her feet, her eyes flicking between me and the door. "I'm just going to be outside."

I nodded as I maneuvered the phone back into my palm so that I could make another call. My fingers were barely able to hit the number keys the pain was so intense.

"Megs." Troy answered; in his voice I heard a smile. "You going to try and sneak out early? I think we should definitely eat in tonight."

"Troy." My throat was thick with emotion as I tried to speak. I just needed to hold it together for a few more minutes, just a few more. "I'm losing the baby. I'm sorry."

It was all I could say, unable to explain or talk anymore as I pulled my cell from my ear, Troy's desperate voice echoing my name over and over before I hit end. He deserved more but I just couldn't give it.

"Megs!" My brother ran into the room with another attending physician, the stretcher behind them rattling into the room. "Stay calm, Megs, we're going to take care of you."

Our schedules rarely synced and I wasn't sure if it was a blessing or a curse that the stars had aligned today.

My head shook as he and the other doctor placed their hands on my elbows as they tried to ease me up.

"It's too late, I know it's too late." My body shook as they helped me to my feet. Blood trickled down my leg as I stood.

"Tom, she's lost a lot of blood. We need to get her lying down." The other doctor moved the stretcher closer to me as he held onto my arm.

"It's too late." They were the only words that seemed to come out of my mouth.

"Lay down, Megs." Tom nodded to the stretcher. "We need to move you."

My legs were on automatic, my body being controlled by the men whose hands were around my arms. I don't remember lying down, or my back hitting the gurney. The words of my brother and the other doctor were jumbled above me as my eyes flashed open to the passing fluorescent lights in the ceiling. The gentle rocking meant we were moving but I didn't care where we were going. ER or the parking lot, the end result would be the same.

"Megs, as much as I want to be in that room with you, I can't treat you. Blake is going to take it from here. I promise you, I'll be outside the whole time. Can I call Mom and Dad?"

I think I nodded, but I couldn't be sure; the thought that he would tell them was somewhat of a relief. The words were just too painful to say over.

"Megs." Tom's hand stayed locked on mine till they wheeled

me into the exam room, "Have you called Troy?"

"Yes." It was barely a whisper but he nodded so I'd know that he'd heard.

And then he let go. Pushed out and swallowed by the noise as the curtain was drawn behind him.

"MEGS! MEGS!" I SCREAMED INTO THE PHONE, MY VOICE GETTING nothing but air. "Megs!" It was no use. The line was dead, the call —over.

"What the fuck, dude?" Dan killed the sound on the *Xbox*, the game of *Call of Duty* we'd been playing, well and truly over.

"I need to get to the hospital, I can't talk right now." I tossed my controller onto his couch. So much shit going through my head that I couldn't even focus on where the fuck I'd left my keys.

"Is Megs in trouble?" Dan got to his feet, throwing his controller to join mine while I patted my pockets like a fucking moron.

"Troy! Let me come with you. I'll drive." Dan held up my car keys. The bastards had been sitting on the coffee table right in front of my face the whole freaking time.

"No, I have to do this alone." I snatched the keys from his palm and sprinted to the door. I had no fucking idea what I was walking into, but I couldn't do this with back up.

"Brother, do whatever you need to do but for fuck's sake call me later. Whatever it is." He called after me as I yanked open his front door, his eyes full of I've-got-your-back.

"I've got to go." Were the only words I bothered to give him as the door slammed behind me.

My heart pounded as I jumped into the elevator and hit the button for the basement, the fucker not moving anywhere near fast enough.

"Come on!" My fist slammed against the mirrored wall, willing the metal box to speed the hell up. Every second, it dragged its feet until the steel doors opened at the underground parking garage.

My feet pounded, making my way to my car, cursing the fucking thing for not having keyless entry.

"Fuck." I fisted the keys to unlock the door.

My hand wrenched at the door, sinking my ass into the driver's seat before the thing was fully open and shoving the key into the ignition.

The engine roared as I pumped the gas, pulling the door shut as I tried to make some fucking sense of what was going on.

Megs had sounded so calm, so fucking calm it scared the fuck out of me.

My boot hit the accelerator, fishtailing onto the street as I tried to put on my seatbelt with one hand. Getting a ticket, yeah—didn't give a fuck—too juiced up to focus on anything other than getting where I was going.

Cars jammed on their brakes in front of me, the Lambo hitting a wall of fucking traffic as we pulled onto the main road. "Goddamit." My fist punched the horn as I tried to weave between the lanes to move this shit along faster.

Nightmare. It was a motherfucking nightmare as the minutes ticked by and I was still no closer to where I needed to be. Drivers beeped their horns and flipped me off as I cut them off, driving like an asshole with a death wish.

I punched it on Madison Avenue, making the turn onto 99th and skidding into the parking garage.

"Hey, buddy, slow down." The asshole attendant called from his glass box like I give a shit what he thought.

Muscle memory steered the car into an empty spot, hauled my ass out of the seat and got my feet moving to the E.R. Thank fuck for the auto switch that kicked in because my brain had checked out the minute Megs had killed the call.

"I'm looking for Dr. Megan Winters." My palms slammed on the info desk making the chick behind it shoot up like a Pop Tart.

"Sir, I'm going to need you to calm down." Ms. Not-fucking-helpful rose to her feet and gave me the once over.

"I'll calm the fuck down when you tell me where she is." There was zero chance of me being calm until I found where Megs was and got to see her. The way I saw it, the lady should be grateful I wasn't tearing the place apart.

"Sir. Please, I don't want to have to call security; please refrain from using profanity."

Seriously. She's going give me shit over the word *fuck*? Why the fuck were we talking about what words I was using and not about where the hell my girl was? My fists balled tight to stop myself from ripping the fucking headset she was wearing off her fucking head.

"Lady, I'm not trying to start anything, but my girl and my baby are in there somewhere and I'm not in the mood to be pleasant. So, sorry if your feelings got hurt but I need you to quit eyeballing me and get on that fancy computer and tell me where she is." My fists primed by my sides ready to punch the computer if she didn't start giving me answers.

Her hands went to the two-way that was sitting on the desk near the phone, bringing it to her mouth without breaking eye contact.

"Security, we have a code gray..."

No! I could not get hauled out of there. Not without seeing Megs first.

"Don't call security, please." I prayed she would give me a chance to explain, forcing myself to lower my voice. "I just need to get to her."

"This is security, please advise the location of the code gray." The voice spewed out of the box in her hand.

My eyes flicked to the two-way, then to her. If there was a fucking God, this was when I needed him to get into the game. Every muscle in my body was wound tight as I relied on this stranger to help me. "Please. I'm begging you."

"Disregard the last transmission. False alarm." Her eyes stayed locked on me as she lowered the hand-held. She looked like she wasn't a hundred percent on board with listening to me, but whatever the chance was, I'd take it.

"Thank you. I'm sorry." I held up my hands in a peace offering and to prove I wasn't going to bitch-slap her desk anymore. "Dr. Megan Winters." I said her name slow. "Where is she?"

"Give me a moment." She sat her ass back down as she hammered the keys on her keyboard.

"She was brought in, but only immediate family can go back through. Are you related to Dr. Winters?" Her face told me she already knew the answer, her fingers easing off the keys and inching toward the two-way.

"I'm her boyfriend."

It sounded so fucking insignificant and didn't come anywhere near close enough to describing what she was to me. "She's pregnant and she is losing our baby. I know you have protocol, but I can't let her go through that alone. I need to be there with her."

"Sir...." The sorry-I-can't-help-you, about to be thrown on the end.

"Look, I swear to you, if she doesn't want me there I will leave. There isn't going to be a fight from me and you won't need some asshole rent-a-cop to haul me out, but I can't wait out here. I need to see her."

"Please wait." She sighed and picked up the phone. It was promising but until I was in the same room with Megs, I was still going to be edgy as fuck.

"Hey, are you Troy Harris?" Some blond-headed kid edged toward me.

Not sure if he was a fan or whatever, but there was no way in fuck I was going to do a meet-and-greet. "Listen kid, seriously haven't got time for this shit right now. I'm not interested in being your big news of the day so please just leave me the hell alone."

"O-Okay." The kid shuffled back into his seat like I'd just punched him in the face.

"Troy?" A dude in scrubs came up beside me, his hand landing on my arm.

"Yes. Are you her doctor? I need to get back there." I wasn't sure if this was the new person that I needed to be convincing. I didn't care whom I had to talk to as long as they let me through.

"I'm her brother, Tom." He tipped his head toward the double doors he'd walked out of. "Take a walk with me."

We were supposed to have a sit down sometime during the week. Her brother worked crazy long ass days, making it hard to nail him down; so while I'd known about him, we hadn't done the hi-how-are-yous yet. Not that it mattered now.

"I have to know, man; I need to know she is okay." My nerves were jangling so much I could barely get the words out straight.

"Megs is resting, they have her on an IV for fluids and some pain meds." He directed us through a corridor.

"That's not what I asked." I stopped walking. I needed to know the truth, not hear shit being sugar coated.

"I'm going to be honest with you, she's not doing great."

It wasn't easy to hear it but at least he'd finally come clean.

"The baby?"

He almost didn't need to say it; the look he was giving me told me there was no chance.

"I'm sorry. At eight weeks there is nothing we can do."

It was like a wave washed over me and dumped me on my ass. Or maybe it was a truck that had come and collected me in its grill. My chest hurt so much I was surprised I could still breathe, the lump in my throat also not helping the cause. I blinked fast, my eyes not doing real well with keeping their shit together. Guess they'd been following my lead.

"Can I see her? She can't do this by herself. I need to be there." It wasn't about me anymore, whatever I was feeling, it had to have been doubly worse for her.

"You can go back for a second but if she wants you out, you're going to have to leave."

He was talking as her brother, not a doctor and I had to respect that even if it was unnecessary. There was zero chance of me walking away from Megs, but I wasn't going to let my stupid need to see her make shit worse. I would sit in the waiting room until she was ready but I wouldn't leave. Not ever.

"I swear to you." I looked him in the eye and held out my hand.

He shook my hand and gave me a tight smile. "Hell of a way to meet, huh?"

We started ambling down the hallway again, people in curtained-off areas wailing either side of us.

"Yeah— no offense—but this wasn't how I saw this shit going down." I shoved my hands in my pocket as he rounded the corner.

"She's in there." He stopped short, his chin tipping to the curtain on the right. "Just don't... don't expect too much of her. She might not want to talk about it, you have to let her take the lead on this one."

I took a big swallow, once again fighting the lump in my throat. "Dude, she's had the lead from the start. I'm just the lucky bastard who's trying to keep up."

He gave me a nod and then wandered off, giving me the space to do this on my own. No doubt he wouldn't be far and ready to haul my ass away if Megs asked him to.

My hand hesitated as I pulled the curtain across, the zipping noise on the rail making Megs turn toward me. Her eyes were so red from crying, I didn't ever think they'd be right again. "Hey." I pulled the thing closed behind me and took a step inside, my heart fucking breaking with every stride.

"Hey," she responded, her voice shaky as she unwrapped her arms from around her chest.

There was so much about this situation that I hated. My chest felt like it was tearing in two but the pain that I saw in her, that was the fucking worst. I didn't even know where to start to make this right.

I pulled up a chair and planted it beside the bed. "I'm just going to sit down beside you and hold your hand, if that's okay with you?" My hand stretched out and linked with hers.

"Troy..."

There was so much hurt in that one fucking word that I literally hated my own name.

"Megs, we've got nothing but time, sweetheart. The only thing I need right now is to be here, we don't have to talk."

"I'm so sorry." She sucked in a breath as her eyes started to leak.

"Sorry?" My fingers stroked the back of her hand. I wanted to hold her but I didn't dare push it. "What have you got to be sorry for?"

"It was my fault." She whispered, the torment ripping through her like a freaking knife.

"Megs, no." This was not going to land on her. No fucking way. "It was no one's fault. Shit happens, it just wasn't our time yet."

"When you told me—that day when you read the report— I wanted it to be a mistake. I didn't want the baby. What kind of person does that?" Her eyes flooded.

"You were in shock, it was a surprise," I reasoned. Neither of us had been expecting that the sheet of paper was going to tell us we were about to be parents. Fuck, I'd had to re-read the stupid thing before it sunk in.

"The first five weeks of our baby's, life I put our baby at risk by not knowing and then when I finally did find out, I wished him gone." She ripped her hand out of mine and covered her face. "I'm the reason why. All my complaining about morning sickness and getting fat, I had wanted it to be over and now it is."

"Megs, this isn't on you. Do you hear me, this isn't on you." My feet pushed out of the chair and I sat on the bed, my hand rubbing circles on her back as I tried to comfort her. The pain I'd had before, nothing on what I had now. It killed me that she owned it, like she was in some way responsible.

"I'd changed my mind, Troy. I really did. I wanted our baby and I was sorry, but it wasn't enough." She pulled her hands away from her face and looked at me. Her tear stained cheeks and bloodshot eyes nailing me in place. "God, I'd do anything right now to feel sick again. I would have my head in a toilet all day long if I could just have the baby back. I don't care how fat I get. I don't care how our lives are going to change. I just want..."

"Come here." My arms wrapped around her as she shuffled up the bed, her head buried in my chest as my T-shirt got wet from her tears.

"I wanted our baby. I really did."

"I did too." My eyes once again fought the tears but I needed to keep it together. "I love you, Megs. I love you so much."

"I love you too." She whimpered against my neck as I stroked her hair.

"Marry me." I'm not sure why I said it and I knew that putting it out there wasn't what she needed right now, but the thought of her not being my wife was tearing me apart. For me—what we had—was as real as it got, and going through life without her wasn't an option. Not now, not ever.

"But there's no baby now, we don't have to get married." Her big blue-green eyes were wide as she shook her head.

"Wanting you to be my wife had nothing to do with the baby, and everything to do with not being able to live my life without you." I tipped her chin, needing her to really look at me. "That hasn't changed."

"We were worried that our relationship would be complicated, but every step of the way has been crazy, Troy. We don't have the best track record for easy."

Complicated, crazy —none of it mattered to me. "Where's the fun in a smooth ride? I'd take crashing and burning with you than easy with someone else."

"I just can't right now." Her lip wobbled as I wiped her tears.

"I know, and I'll wait, but I'm not walking away."

Forever, I'd wait forever.

The curtain pushed open again, Tom filling the space with his hands still gripped tight around the fabric.

"Hey, Megs, sorry to interrupt. Mom and Dad are here."

Megs nodded at me him before she looked up at me. "Can you wait outside? While I talk to my parents."

"Megs, you don't have to do this by yourself. We can talk to them together." It wasn't just me manning up, I didn't want to bail—not yet.

"I know, but I would rather do it by myself." She laid her hand on my chest and gave me a weak hug.

No matter how much I wanted to stay in that room, I couldn't find it in me to say no to her. "Whatever you want, sweetheart. I'm just going to be outside."

Walking back through the corridor, the space filled with activity. Bodies crashing into each other, doctors and nurses talking over each other but it felt like a piece of my heart had been ripped out. It didn't matter that I hadn't met our baby yet; I still felt the loss all the same.

I pushed through the door that led out into the main waiting room of the E.R., some of the same people were there waiting for their turn. The blond-headed kid I'd blown off was still there too, his ball cap pulled down to cover his eyes.

Seeing him got me thinking of what an asshole I'd been. He wasn't to know my world had been fucking falling apart. He was probably looking for an autograph or a photo or five minutes of my time. I'd have punched the SOB who spoke to my son the way I'd spoken to him.

"Hey, kid, I'm sorry about before. It was just a really bad time for me."

My apology was bullshit but it was the best I could do, nothing would make up for being a total cock. My head hadn't been right but I never should have pulled that shit. The kid was maybe sixteen? He had no idea that he had just picked the wrong time to talk to me.

"Oh, it's okay. No it's fine. I'm sorry." He pushed his cap back, his Cons kicks tapping nervously on the floor.

"No, it wasn't fine. No matter what I was going through, I shouldn't have bit your head off like that. I was a complete asshole and I'm really sorry." I took the seat beside him.

"I overheard you." He took a swallow and nodded. "You and Dr. Winters lost your baby?"

Hearing it didn't make it easier the second time. I didn't know what to say, saying the words out loud weren't an option.

"I'm not going to tell anyone, I swear," the kid quickly added. "I didn't even know she was dating you, honest." He stopped, clocking me with an eyeball, his voice shaking so much I couldn't help but know he was scared. "I was with her. It's 'cause of me."

"What are you talking about?"

None of it made sense. This kid being with Megs or thinking he was the reason why in seven months I wasn't going to be holding my son or daughter.

"She's my shrink. I've been such a fucking shit." He pulled the cap off his head and rolled the bill nervously his hands. "I'm just mad a lot, you know? I'd come and talk and I didn't mean to but I always ended up giving her a hard time. I'd cuss her out even though she was nothing but nice to me. We were in a session, and it just happened. I didn't know what to do, I didn't know."

Fuck. No one deserved to see that, let alone a kid. On top of that, he was thinking that his problems were the reason Megs had lost our baby. It was a mess I honestly didn't know how to fix but I needed to try. Megs would have known what the say, I owed it to her to at least try.

"There's nothing you could have done, nothing any of us could have done. It didn't happen 'cause of what you guys talked about, sometimes bad shit just happens."

He concentrated hard on his cap in his hands, not lifting his eyes from their mark. "Bad shit happens a lot in my life. It follows me around, like a curse."

He was way too young to be battling those kinds of demons, way too young to be carrying that load. Were all the kids Megs saw like this? How was she able to do it and not have it mess with her head? In that moment, I fell in love with her all over again.

"What's your name kid?"

"Brad. Brad Hemsworth." He flicked his eyes sideways to me.

"Brad, I'm not a doctor but I can tell you that there is no way you had anything to do with what went down." I had a feeling that talking to him was probably breaking all kinds of rules— but it was one small thing that I could do, hopefully it would make a microscopic difference. "I'm sorry shit isn't going right for you, but Dr. Winters—she really cares. She's changed my life, if you give her a chance she can change yours too."

Brad nodded like he understood but I had no idea if any of it stuck. A fair-headed lady with a panic stricken face bolted toward us from the opposite end of the room.

"Brad! Honey, we've been searching the whole building for you." Her hand gripping her handbag so tight her knuckles had turned white.

"I just wanted to make sure Dr. Winters was okay." Brad shoved his cap back on his head, his eyes nailing themselves to the floor.

"I know, sweetie, but you shouldn't have run off. I was scared half to death." She looked it too; her fingers twisted her wedding ring nervously as she stood in front of us.

Brad lifted his head and gave the lady a good look at his face. "Mom, I'm sorry."

"That's —That's alright." The lady looked shocked, like maybe she hadn't heard it in a while. Her eyes doing the mist over as she looked at her boy. "We should go home now."

Brad stood up, shoving his hands in his pockets as he shifted on his feet. "Hey, I know I'm not supposed to contact Dr. Winters outside of my appointments, but can you tell her— tell her I won't be a shit anymore."

"How about I tell her you said hey, and that you'll be looking forward to the next session." My version was the only version Megs would be getting.

"Yeah, that will do." Brad gave me a nod as he looked to his mom.

"Take care, Brad." I shoved out my hand, the kid clapping it with his own.

"See ya, Troy."

The mom looked on nervously, not wanting to rock the boat as we said our goodbyes and I watched them leave.

My ass sunk back into the seat and I started my game of hurry-up and wait. If I had to sit there until tomorrow, then that's what I'd do. Eventually she would have to come around and let me in— the alternative was just too hard to take.

26

Megan

DR. BLAKE WHEELED ME BACK INTO THE ROOM WHERE MY PARENTS had been waiting. I was still a little groggy from the anesthetic, but the added meds they had pumped into my IV had taken the pain away. The pain in my body, that was, the pain in my heart was still there.

"Megan, as long as you have someone to stay with you over the next twenty-four hours, there's no reason why you can't go home." Notes were scribbled onto my chart, ones that probably said the "clean up" was all over and I was no longer pregnant. It was over so quickly—done, finished.

My dad was doing a horrible job at being discreet, trying to read over poor Dr. Blake's shoulder. "Of course, she can come home with us. Either myself or her mother will be with her the whole time."

It didn't matter that I was a grown woman; my father would always want to take over. He didn't do out-of-control, he wanted everything nice and neat —organized. Something I wasn't right now, and didn't aspire to be.

"Dad, don't take this the wrong way but I want to go to *my* home. It will be easier for me to get back to normal in my own surroundings. Whisking me off and putting me into my childhood bedroom isn't the answer." Neither was pretending what happened, didn't just happen but I didn't bother vocalizing the last part.

"Darling, you've just suffered a trauma and you need time to heal. I think it's best you are around medical professionals who are able to care for you." My mother moved the hair out of my face, her eyes filled with worry.

"I don't need medical professionals, I'm not sick —I lost my baby. I know everyone is tiptoeing around the words but that is what happened. Calling it a trauma doesn't make it easier, so please don't fight me on this. I think that I am more equipped than anyone to make the decision on what's best for me."

"Well, I'll let you guys sort it out, shall I? As long as you promise me you won't be alone, I'll sign your release papers." Dr. Blake looked over at us from his chart, no doubt wanting to avoid the drama of our family politics. Can't say I blamed him—at that moment— I wanted out too.

"I won't be." I promised Dr. Blake who gave me a nod and walked off. Hopefully to fill out the paperwork so I could go home.

Tom pulled the curtain across filling the space that the doctor had just vacated. What do you know? It was Grand Central station in my little cubicle.

"Megs, Troy is still outside and he looks terrible. Can I put the guy out of his misery and let him back in?"

Troy. I had shoved him out of my room when my parents had arrived and then a nurse had come and wheeled me to the O.R.

He'd been here the whole time? I probably shouldn't have been surprised, he'd said he wouldn't leave but it had been so long. I assumed he would have gone home.

I'd lost our baby and then told him to leave. He must hate me. If I was him, I sure would.

"He's been waiting the whole time?" It was stating the fucking obvious but it came out of my mouth anyway. To be honest, I had little control over what I was saying or feeling. My heart almost bursting that he was still here, for me, despite me sending him away. No man had ever loved me like that.

"Yeah, in the waiting room. He hasn't left." The corners of Tom's mouth slightly curled at the edges. The smile he gave to soften the blow when regular smiling wasn't appropriate. I wondered if they taught that in medical school? I sure as hell hadn't mastered it.

"Please let him in." I nodded to Tom and then turned to my parents. "Dad, Mom. You can go, I've got it from here."

"Megan, are you sure, sweetie?" The protest already started to bubble in my mother. "We can stay, or give you a ride home?"

"I can take her home." Troy moved into the crowded space, his face tired and drawn. He looked destroyed. I had done that. That look was there because of me.

"Hi, Troy." My mother rubbed his arm gently.

"Hi, Mrs. Winters. Mr. Winters." He answered robotically but didn't move any closer.

"Well, alright but if you need us for anything, just call. Day or night, just pick up the phone." My dad admitted defeat and gave my mother the we-should-go look. I silently thanked God they weren't going to fight me on this.

"Thanks." Please don't cry, please don't cry. "I love you both." I didn't even attempt a smile—I wasn't delusional enough to think I'd be able to pull it off.

"We love you too." My mother blew me a kiss with my dad ushering her out of the cubical.

"I need to get back to patients, Sis. If you need anything, just buzz." Tom also excused himself, giving Troy a nod on the way out.

"Troy..." What to even say? I was coming up a blank.

"Megs, please. I know you are hurting right now but please don't shut me out. I lost our baby too." He moved quietly to the chair beside my bed and sat down. There was an unmistakable sadness in his face.

"Do you hate me? I assumed you left. It's been hours."

"Why would I hate you? I told you I wasn't leaving and I'm not. My place is here, with you."

"Because..." I couldn't finish. How many tears could one person cry? Surely I'd exceeded my limit, not that my leaky eyes had received the memo.

"Megs, I love you." He was out of his chair and up on the bed before I'd had a chance to wipe away the tears, cupping my face in his hands. "I really, really do, and nothing is going to change that. What happened is no one's fault. I'm mad as hell that it happened, but not at you, never at you."

"Will you stay with me tonight? Will you hold me?" I didn't care how desperate I sounded. I was desperate, desperate for this ache in my chest to stop.

His mouth gently brushed against mine. "Always."

The time alone back at the apartment had been horrible, we both cried and held each other, but most of all we talked— really talked. Nothing was off the table and in some ways, it was almost liberating.

"You know, we never talked about kids before and then I was pregnant." My hands were tucked under my pillow as I faced him.

"I want kids, Megs, not like a basketball team, but I want a family. What about you?" His pose mirrored mine; his face just inches away.

"I want two." It was late and I was tired, but I didn't want to stop talking.

Troy smiled and gave me a nod. "Two's a good number, makes riding roller-coasters easier."

"You can't decide the number of kids you have based on that." The smile teased at my mouth.

"Sure you can." He threw some further conviction behind his voice before he continued. "You try going to Disney World with an uneven number, someone is missing out."

"I can't even argue with that logic." How could I argue? It was adorable, even if it was somewhat crazy.

"Because you know I'm right." He grinned; probably pleased I hadn't been able to come up with a counter argument.

"Moving on, Troy Harris." I waved him off casually. It felt good to be talking about normal things again, both of us even managing a smile. The guilt wasn't lurking too far away as I tried to shove it to the back of my mind and asked another question. "Did you have pets growing up?"

"You mean your detailed Google search didn't give you that information?" His grin got wider as he raised an eyebrow.

"Shut up." I gently shoved his chest. "You make me sound like a stalker." Besides, I hadn't Googled him in a *really* long time.

"Nah, stalking is more like watching me through my bedroom window, so unless you did that..." He left his sentence trailing, waiting for my response.

I winced, giving him a guilty smile. "Well."

"Megs?"

"I'm joking." I laughed, amused by the slight concern that was on his face. "I've never watched you from your bedroom. Although I totally would have done it but— you know— you live on the top floor of your building, and hiring the abseiling equipment would have raised too many questions."

"Okay, it's my turn." He shuffled closer, his hand resting on my hip. "Did you always want to be a psychologist?"

"When I was younger I wanted to be one of the ladies on the high-wire at the circus. They looked so glamorous in those sparkling costumes." I sighed remembering my childhood fantasy.

"Let me guess, you had issues with your balance?"

I fell over one time and the man assumes I'm a klutz. "No, smartass. I found out you had to live in a trailer." I grimaced. "Ughhhh."

Troy barked out a laugh and it was too hard not to join him. It felt wrong to be happy but also kind of right. We hadn't forgotten what happened, but we were finding a way to be okay with it.

"I have a question." It had been something I had been curious but hadn't ever asked.

"Well go on, it's not like you to hold back." He smirked, clearly loving our session of truth or dare.

"So that first night you met me, it was pretty clear what I thought of you, but what did you think of me?" My heart pounded as I waited for him to respond.

"I was kind of pissed you were so drunk." He answered honestly with a little shrug.

Well, that had been unexpected. I was thinking he was going to go with I thought you were annoying or maybe—in my fantasies—I thought you were so incredibly sexy. But pissed because I was drunk? There had to be more to it than that.

"Because I was all over you and fell over?"

"No, because it meant that if I tried to kiss you, I would feel like a complete scumbag." His voice was low and so very sexy as his smile curled at his lips.

"You wanted to kiss me?" Had I heard him right? That night when I'd wrapped myself around him like a boa constrictor, he had wanted to kiss me?

"I wanted to do more than just kiss you." He moved his mouth closer to mine. I guess to give me a visual interpretation seeing as I seemed to be having trouble with his words.

"Woah!" My hands pushed against his chest in surprise. "Define more."

He cocked an eyebrow. "Megs, seriously?"

Oh hell yes, seriously. He wasn't getting out of it that easily. "No, no. You have to answer. I confessed about my secret aspirations of being a trapeze artist; you need to come clean, bubby."

"Fine." He took a breath before he continued. "I wanted to take you home and have sex with you. That dress you were wearing wasn't doing a very good job at keeping that hot body of yours under wraps, and watching your beautiful red lips calling me Troy Harris made me instantly hard. The car ride home was brutal; your legs were in my lap and I could totally see your panties. In my head I'd fucked you three times before I'd gotten you settled in your apartment." His are-you-happy-now face waited for my response.

"It's probably warped and twisted, but knowing you wanted me back then really excites me." And made me feel like less of a pervert for having been so obsessed with him. It was reassuring to know it hadn't been one sided.

"Well, I did. The first time you called me, I had a hard-on for hours. And the time I picked you up from your Christmas party after you drunk-dialed me, yeah that was another fun night," he mused sarcastically.

"Oh I remember that, I wanted you to kiss me so badly." And hadn't I almost begged for him to sleep with me? Ugh. Not my finest moment. Thank God, the memories are fuzzy. There is bliss in ignorance.

"Trust me, one of the hardest things I ever had to do was say goodbye to you that night, and you sure weren't making it easy for me."

Yeah, obviously my suspicions had been correct.

"Good." I smiled; it pleased me to know he had been just as sexually frustrated that night as I had. "I'm glad you suffered."

"Well I'm glad my *suffering* stopped." He nipped at my shoulder before kissing my neck.

He had been so gentle— affectionate without trying to turn it sexual. It's like he could read exactly what I needed.

"It feels like a lifetime ago." Or more, so much had changed during those months.

"It kind of was." Troy shrugged. He was right, it was. We were different. *Things* were different.

"So where do we go from here?" We couldn't go back to the way things were. That never would have worked.

"Where ever you want to go, as long as it's together. I can't lose you; I think we've both lost enough." He held me tightly; there was no doubt in my mind that he would never let me go.

"Troy Harris." I whispered against his skin, kissing his chest before bringing my face up to meet his."

"Yes." He gave that smile that meant he would humor whatever lame-ass idea I'd come up with.

"Will you marry me?"

Every reason I had that had been holding me back was no longer relevant. In that moment—just being with him— I'd fallen in love with him all over again.

He dipped his head and kissed me—hard.

"Yes."

"HEY, BEAUTIFUL, IT'S TIME TO WAKE UP."

Watching Megs sleep had been the first time I'd been able to catch a breath since leaving the hospital. Her tired lids peeled opened as I kissed her neck before slamming them back shut.

"Come on, Megs. Let me off the hook here. I feel like an asshole trying to wake you, but it's time." The small shake I gave her earning me a groan.

"So tired." She yawned trying to bury her head in the crook of my armpit.

"I wouldn't be hiding there, if I was you." I warned her, the last time I'd spent any time under a shower at least twenty-four hours ago. Sure I'd hit it with some *Old Spice* but it still wouldn't have been pretty, that's for sure.

"Just five more minutes." She waved me off as she tried to chase down some more Zs.

"Five more minutes and we're going to be on the runway." The plane banked, making its finale approach into JFK. "You want me to carry you off the plane, I have no problem with that— but the attention we were trying to avoid— yeah that will probably be history."

"Troy Harris, I love it when you get all logical on me." Her beautiful eyes stayed hidden behind her lids but she treated me to a smile.

"And here I was thinking you married me for my last name. I know how fond you are of saying it, Megs Harris."

"That sounds so freaking weird." She laughed as she sat up in her seat. "I still can't believe we did it."

"Well it's kind of fitting with our history— impulsive and unconventional. Besides you'd finally agreed. I sure as shit wasn't giving you the opportunity to change your mind."

We had both laid it out on the line when had gotten back from the hospital. Stuff we'd never talked about suddenly got airtime and it went a long way to heal us both.

Megs asking *me* to marry *her* was the icing on the cake. I had been fully prepared to wait and I'd even decided that I'd lay off on the proposals, but her saying those words to me was like being punched right in the mouth.

Being that fast forward had been kind of our speed, we jumped on a late flight to Vegas and made it to *Van Cleef & Arpels* just before they shut their doors. A couple of rings and a seedy Vegas chapel later, we walking down the aisle to the tune of "Don't Stop Believin'" by *Journey*. Yep, the cheese factor was high but it was either that or Shania Twain. So *Journey* it was.

There was no dress, no flowers and no friends. Just the two of us and a preacher who was older than kerosene, but it was legal and we were married, and that was all that mattered.

It occurred to me getting on a plane so soon after Megs had lost the baby wasn't the smartest decision, but she insisted that the risks were minimal. And her wanting it as much as I did was enough to convince me not to wait. I'd waited long enough and if one good thing could come out of the nightmare we'd been through, then I'd take it.

"For the record, I wouldn't have changed my mind but last night was perfect." Megs stared down at her wedding rings, the diamonds doing the twinkling thing they did when they hit the sun, and I didn't doubt for a second that we'd made the right choice. Staying in Vegas wasn't an option. We had no intention of hiding out, or avoiding the shit storm our quickie wedding was going to attract, so we high-tailed it back, ready to face the music.

"Technically it was this morning. Our marriage license says two forty-five a.m. so guess it's still our wedding day." The plane shook as the landing gear was lowered, the runway in sight.

"Well seeing as it's my wedding day, that means I get to choose what we do and my vote is breakfast." Megs squeezed my arm as the plane dropped altitude, my stomach lunging from the dip and the lack of food.

"Megs, it's almost noon. I think breakfast is a bust." While breakfast was out, food was definitely on the agenda. I could murder a burger and fries I was so hungry.

"But I want pancakes and bacon and the biggest coffee we can find. Oh my God, coffee. I missed it so much. I'm going to get two." Her eyes got wide with the promise of caffeinated goodness.

"Then if my wife wants breakfast, we'll get her breakfast." She would get whatever she wanted, whenever she wanted and I would spend my last breath making sure of that fact.

She grinned as the tires on the plane hit the tarmac, the plane knocking us around on the touch down.

"We should probably tell our folks as well." We were back in NYC and the fact we eloped was hanging over us like a big neon sign. No regrets, but we sure as hell had a lot of explaining to do. "No doubt the chewing out we're going to get is going to be massive. Let's hope your dad didn't make good on his threat of getting a gun."

"I'll handle my dad." She undid her seat belt as the plane rolled to the gate. "Do you think our friends will be pissed?"

"They'll get over it." I unhooked my belt too, ready to get off the plane. "If you want to do the wedding thing, we can make that happen. Alex and Lexi did a redo a few months after."

"You know it's funny, I always pictured my wedding a certain way. You know, wearing a *Vera Wang* gown, the fancy shoes and possibly the Plaza, but I just don't want that now."

Not that I knew what a Vera Whatever was, but she had rocked the jeans and T-shirt she'd worn, and I'd never seen her look more beautiful.

"It's up to you, I'm good with the way we did it."

"Mr. Harris, Ms. Winters you can disembark the plane now." The airline chick smiled as she directed us to the jet bridge.

"Thanks." I nodded and grabbed Megs's hand. "Let's get out of here."

Knowing Vegas was going to be a drive-by, we hadn't packed shit. Not even carry on. We were there long enough to say "I do" and for me to add a tiny bit of ink to my collection. We had almost spent more time in the air than we had in the desert, which had suited me just fine. I was glad to be back and pleased we weren't going to be wasting our time at baggage claim.

JFK was freaking pumping, people running to gates and the loud speaker demanding attention. I was glad I'd sent TJ a message and organized a pick up. Getting a cab would have probably been a nightmare. We moved from arrivals to the curbside area, my fingers getting busy letting the big guy know we were waiting.

"Troy, Ms. Winters." TJ rolled up in the Escalade, the two of us piling into the back.

"I just sent you a message." His phone pinged from the front seat. "You have ESP or somethin', dude?"

"Watched the flight schedule and was doing laps. It's easier than having you sitting out there unattended." He kept the engine idling as we climbed into the back seats.

"Thank you, TJ." Megs smiled as she snuggled into her seat.

"No problem, Ms. Winters." He gave her a chin tip in the rearview.

"Yeah, about that." Fuck it—might as well start telling people and TJ was as close as family got without being blood or the band. "She kinda has the same last name as me now but keep it on the down low until we break it to everyone else."

"I figured you probably went and got legal. Not too many reasons for you to be inbound from Vegas when you were in New York yesterday. Congratulations." TJ grinned, giving us a good look at his grill as we pulled away from the curb.

"Thanks, man. It was spur of the moment. Maybe take us to Megs's first. We should probably make a few calls." And maybe get a shower as well, I also still had the promise of breakfast I needed to make good on.

"Yep, can do." TJ nodded as he changed lanes and put us on the road, Greenwich bound.

Megs pulled out her cell and powered it up, the phone having been stuck on airplane mode for the last six or so hours.

"Holy shit!" Meg's hand vibrated with the cell blowing up with a bunch of missed calls and unanswered texts. "My parents are freaking out. They've been calling for hours."

"You want me to talk to them?" I held out my hand ready to take the heat. Fuck, they could unleash whatever they wanted on me, nothing was removing the shit-eating grin I was wearing.

"No, I've got it." Her voice wavered a little like she wasn't all that convinced that she *had it*. Her fingers punching the keypad as she dialed the number.

"Just remember, anyone starts giving you a hard time, you hand that phone to me. I won't have anyone making you feel bad about what we did." Not to mention that the happy-happy-joy-joy was still arm wrestling with the grief of losing our baby. Sure we were smiles and rainbows but that didn't mean the minute we walked back into the apartment that the reality of the situation wouldn't rear its ugly mug.

"You are too sweet, Troy Harris." She bit her lip as she raised her cell to her ear as we navigated through the shit storm that was Manhattan traffic.

"Hey, Mom. No please don't cry. I'm fine." The smile Megs had been wearing slipped from her face. "I'm sorry you were worried. I just..."

She took a breath, not seeming to get a word in edgeways. "Mom, I'm fine. I was on a plane, I had to have my phone off." Megs got defensive as she continued. "Well the doctor didn't say I couldn't fly, I wasn't flying the plane myself."

I was just about to grab the phone off her when she finally broke the news. "Because Troy and I went to Vegas and got married." I stared at Megs waiting for a reaction and hoping her parents weren't going to give her a hard time. My primal need to protect her from anything bad was making me twitchy.

"Mom?" Megs waited. "Oh, hey Dad. Yeah, that's right we eloped. No, no one pressured me. I wanted to. Because I was tired of waiting to be happy and this made me happy." From the one-sided conversation I was hearing, I was getting the gist they weren't pleased. Megs stood her ground though, not going the I'm-sorry-don't-be-mad route. "I don't care about a big cele-bration; it's what I wanted and it's done."

She pulled the phone from her ear obviously done with defending our actions and brought it closer to her mouth. "Dad, I'm hanging up now. I love you both but I need you to be happy for us." And with that she ended the call.

"Did that go as well as it sounded?" I didn't need to hear the other side of the phone call to know they weren't going to be welcoming us to Sunday lunch anytime soon. I was probably on the top of their shit list as well. Still them being pissed off didn't change that we were rocking matching rings, and that us being married was as permanent as the tattoo I'd gotten an hour after.

"Yeah they are freaking out, they think I'm suffering post traumatic stress disorder and somehow jumped into making a decision. They already knew I wanted this, sure it was sudden but it's not like we hadn't talked about it." Megs switched the phone to silent and threw it into her purse. No doubt her folks would try and call her back, maybe to try and talk some sense into her.

"It's a valid concern, Megs, they are just worried. Let's give them a few days and then maybe go see them." Not saying that they were right, but they were only worried 'cause they loved her. If my kid ran off and married some dude, I'd probably have words to say about it myself.

I reached across and held her hand, my thumb rubbing over the back of her knuckles. Megs gave me a weak smile as I stroked her skin. "What about your parents? Are they going to freak out?"

"Ha! My mom will get down on her knees and thank God I finally came to my senses and married you; she won't care too much about missing the ceremony. She kind of got used to the idea that I wasn't going to settle down, so this is like her Christmas and birthday all coming at once."

And wasn't that the truth. My mom had given up on the pipe

dream of me being shacked up. She wasn't an idiot, and knew I had female company but she ignored the press for the most part. And other than a lecture telling me to be respectful and me not being too big for an ass whooping if she heard about me being a scumbag, we had the whole don't-ask-don't-tell thing going for us.

"Troy Harris, the perpetual bachelor?" Megs laughed, obviously my dating history amusing the shit out here.

"Well, considering before I brought you home, the number of girlfriends my folks had met, stood at three—all of which were while I was in high school—she hadn't counted on sitting in a church watching me put a ring on it."

"See, why can't my parents be that cool?" She leaned her head back against the headrest, her eyes getting sleepy with the rock of the Escalade.

"Probably 'cause you haven't been on tour since you were seventeen."

We rode the rest of the way without any further commentary, TJ turned on some jams and Megs dozed off and on till we got to her apartment.

"You good? Need me to hang around?" TJ pulled over to the curb not far from the entrance of her building.

"All good, brother. My car's chillin' in the underground garage. You can go do your *Driving Miss Daisy* thing with someone else." I popped open the door and my feet hit the sidewalk.

"Thanks, TJ." Megs rubbed her eyes, obviously the Zs she'd snagged in between traffic lights not enough for her liking. She ambled out of the car and joined me on the curb.

"Yep. My pleasure." TJ gave us a two finger wave as we shut the door. The tail lights of the Escalade easing back into the gridlock we'd escaped from.

"Come on, Mrs. Harris." I tucked her in close to me. "Shower, change and then I'm going to caffeinate you." My lips landed on the top of her head as we walked through the doorway of the apartment building.

"Mmm. You are such a smooth talker." She nuzzled closer into me as he strolled to the elevator. I liked having the weight of her body tight against mine, and being able to see the rise and fall of each of her breaths. It made me feel like a better man, like a piece of my puzzle was in place. Losing the baby had been bad enough, but if I had lost Megs— not sure I could have come back from that.

The elevator pinged once we got to her floor, the metal doors sliding open to reveal a deserted hallway. Just as well—neither of us was in the mood to socialize.

Megs fished her keys from her purse and twisted them in the lock, the door springing open from the effort.

"Hey!" Megs squealed as I hauled her up into my arms. "What are you doing?" Her feet gave a half-hearted kick in protest.

"Threshold." The one worded explanation enough for her feet to give up. I grinned as I carried her through her doorway.

She slithered down out of my arms, her feet hitting the floor in front of me. The last twenty-four hours had been a rollercoaster of emotions for both of us, and being in the apartment brought back some of the ghosts of yesterday with it.

"Troy…" Megs's eyes got serious, the blue-green pools losing the shine they'd had no five minutes ago. "I can't have sex yet. I'm still…" She didn't need to fill in the blanks. The stash of *Kotex* in her purse gave me all the info I needed.

"Look at me." I tipped her chin so her eyes were on me. "There will be plenty of time for that. When you're ready, you let me know."

"I want to, but…" My finger on her mouth stopped her talking. She wasn't going to be wearing more guilt than she already had. Hell no. End of discussion.

"Megs, I waited for months to have you for the first time, and months for you to be my girl. Going without sex for a few weeks isn't even on my radar as an issue. We've got nothing but time, sweetheart, and neither of us is going anywhere."

"Stop, you'll make me cry." Her chin did the wobble as her eyes blinked real quick.

"No crying." My arms wrapped around hers. "Not over that. Now, let's get cleaned up and go get breakfast for lunch before my stomach cannibalizes itself." No shit—the threat was real, my last meal having been hours ago.

"And coffee." She reminded me, her lost smile creeping back.

"Whatever you want."

"You know, Troy Harris. That's a dangerous promise to make a girl. I could start demanding all kinds of crazy shit." She wiggled her eyebrows, her threat making me laugh.

"Bring it. It's either a done deal or I'll spend my last breath trying." I gave her a quick kiss and unwrapped my arms, the vibrating from her bag getting my attention.

"Trying to amuse yourself with the TSA again?" I raised my eyebrow. "I thought you bought a giant dildo not a vibrator." My grin got wider.

"It's my phone." She elbowed me in the ribs as she pulled out her cell. "Shit, there's a missed call from work." Her eyes floated down to the number displayed on the screen. "It must be urgent if they are trying to get a hold of me. I have a couple of patients that are high risk."

Work— shit. I'd completely mind dumped the run-in I'd had with the kid in the waiting room. I had meant to tell her, but I was waiting for the right time and then it just kind of slipped. I'd promised him I would give her his message, so I needed to make good on that.

"Yeah, I forgot to tell you. I met one of them, one of your kids. Brad Hemsworth. He was waiting outside of the ER."

Megs looked up from her phone, her face getting pale. "Oh my God, was he alright?"

"Megs, he was just worried about you. Said he was with you when it went down." Part of me still was torn up that I hadn't been there. Not that I was delusional and thought I could have changed the outcome. I got that there was nothing anyone could've done— but that didn't put to rest the shit floating around in my gray matter that at the very least, I could have made it easier for Megs.

"Yeah, unfortunately I was in a session." Megs focused on me, her mind probably getting a reboot courtesy of the memory. "I tried to get him out of there as soon as I could. I should really book him into a relief counselor."

"Megs, listen." I had no idea if talking to the kid had made shit worse or better but it still didn't change the fact I'd done it. Last thing I wanted is for her to be blindsided when she went back or worse, think I was hiding shit. "I know we probably shouldn't have, but we talked."

"You talked to my patient?" She didn't seem mad; more surprised and super curious. Her eyes on me as she waited for me to join the dots on how I came to be have a D and M with one of her patients.

"Yeah, he was feeling guilty and I was trying to tell him that shit wasn't his fault. He overheard what happened. We didn't go deep or anything, but he came clean about probably not being the easiest kid to get along with. He thought that had something to do with it."

"Oh my God, no." She shook her head and sunk into an armchair. "I can't have him taking that on. He already has enough."

I dropped to my knees beside her, there was more to the conversation than what needed to be said. Not that I was a shrink and hell, who knows if I'd made things better or worse, but I'd opened my mouth and I was fessing up.

"Which is what I told him. I don't know, Megs— I don't know this kid and maybe I saw something I wanted to see. But he seemed to understand that you were only trying to help him. He even told me that he was looking forward to next time when you guys had a session."

Her eyes got wide, almost like she hadn't bought my version of events. "He said that? He actually said he was looking forward to our next session? He hates our sessions."

"Well not those exact words but we agreed my version was probably what he meant. He even apologized to his mom for making her worry." The paraphrase was a definite improvement, no way was I ever going to say the kid was a shit.

"You got him to say sorry? Troy, that's huge. I know you don't understand but trust me... it's massive." She scooted forward in her seat, her excitement earning me some lip action as she pressed her mouth against mine.

"So you're not mad? I know there is all kinds of gray area there about talking to kids and shit." Yeah as in, don't fucking do it.

"Troy, you weren't impersonating a psychologist, and from

what you said he approached you. As long as you weren't talking about our therapy sessions or giving him prescribed treatment there's nothing unethical with you having a consensual conversation. Besides, it sounds like talking to you was exactly what he needed. Sometimes, all it takes is one thing to set off a chain reaction of change."

"Well, I just didn't want to fuck anything up." Not for the kid and not for Megs.

"You didn't fuck anything up." She gave me one of my favorite smiles. The ones where the corners of her mouth pull up so much it lights up her entire face. The kind of smile you couldn't fake.

"Awesome." I leaned in and gave her a kiss on the forehead. "Why don't you return your call and I'll hit the shower. I can't do anything about a change of clothes but at least I won't smell."

Maybe I had a clean T-shirt lying around somewhere? In any case, our living arrangement needed to be sorted at some point in the very near future, and one of us going to be relocating. Best we could save that dilemma for after we fed our faces.

"Yes and then foooooooood," Megs added, seeming to read my mind.

I shot her a wink before strolling off into the bathroom, not forgetting the promise I'd made to her. "And coffee."

28

Megan

TROY HAD BEEN RIGHT ABOUT ONE THING—HIS PARENTS HAD BEEN ecstatic when he broke the news to them about our impromptu I-do's. He had called them after his shower and even put the phone on speaker so I could hear. There weren't any shocked gasps or tearful accusations— so basically the opposite of my parents— and they were both just so lovingly supportive that it made me teary all over again.

My work emergency had turned out to be just Carrie checking in on me. All my appointments had been postponed with all my high risk patients being re-allocated for care in the interim. It made things a little easier that there was one less thing for me to worry about.

Breakfast for lunch, as Troy had called it, had been sublime. While the pancakes had been delicious, it had been my extra large, extra hot with an extra shot of coffee that had ricocheted me straight off the planet and into outer space. It was like welcoming back an old friend and went a long way in making me feel less zombiefied. I pledged my renewed fealty to the caffeine master and tried not to sound like I was having an orgasm when taking the first sip. Not going to lie— it hadn't been easy.

"They know about the baby, right?" My palms were sweaty as we loitered outside Dan and Ash's door. I hadn't seen or spoken to either of them since it happened and really wasn't up for detailed run through.

I shouldn't have had that second coffee; I was so jittery my teeth were rattling.

"Yeah, I had been with Dan when you called me so he knew something was up. I gave him a call and filled him in while I was in the waiting room." Troy gave me a sideways glance, like he was unsure of what my reaction was going to be. My lack of an emotional explosion prompted him to go on.

"I didn't know if it was going to leak out or not, and figured it was better they heard it from me. I told the rest of the band too, and Lexi—she made sure that nothing showed up in the press."

I hadn't even thought about the press and how much worse it could have been with a camera in my face asking us about our loss.

"I'm glad you told them, they should know. It's not like we can pretend it didn't happen." That would have been so much worse.

"You ready to go in? We can go hang at my place for a while." Troy jangled his keys temptingly.

It would be easy to run away, but it was only a matter of time before our Vegas jaunt made news. I was surprised *TMZ* hadn't been at the airport, no doubt *MTV* would have the story by the evening. Ironically, Ashlyn's prediction about me never being featured would be a bust, however it wouldn't be my recorder prowess that would earn me headlines, but the sparkly new finger wear I was sporting. In truth— I sucked at the recorder.

So my new philosophy was to *own* being Mrs. Troy Harris, consequences be damned. Besides, I really liked saying his last name.

"No, I'm good." My head bobbled a little too enthusiastically, the full effect of the caffeine running havoc on my nervous system.

Troy didn't look convinced as he knocked on the door. His concern evident as he wrapped his arms around me and pulled me closer to him. It was either that or he was expecting me to drop to the floor and have a cardiac arrest— not out of the realm of possibility given how much I'd been buzzing.

"Megs!" Ash screamed, pulling me out of Troy's arms and into her own as she opened the door. "Oh, crap. I didn't hurt you, did I?" She eased her hold on me as she led me through the doorway, Troy walking in casually behind us.

"I'm fine, I'm fine." Well, as fine as I was going to be. Certainly not about to fall apart, which was a plus.

"Troy." Ash gave him a slightly less emotional hug than the one she'd given me.

"Hey, Ash." Troy returned her hug before lifting his head to address Dan. "Hey, douchebag."

"Hey." Dan tipped his chin hello. It wasn't just his subdued greeting weirding me out a little, it was the absence of the trailing "numbnuts" which was also odd. He was almost like an anti-Dan, respectfully standing back and observing without insults or innuendo. I hadn't been the only one who had noticed, his scaled down behavior earning him a raised eyebrow from Troy.

"Soooooooo." Did I launch into our big announcement or did I let things be awkward a little while longer? I wasn't sure what the protocol was. "Troy and I got married." My mouth made the decision for me, with my left hand flying out in front of me. The big rock on my ring finger to serve as exhibit A for submitted evidence.

"You got married?" Ashlyn's eyes widened as she snatched my hand and examined my ring. "When did you have time to get married?" She continued to talk to my *Van Cleef and Arpels* diamond rather than address me directly. Not that I blamed her, I had a hard time not breaking into a *Gollum* impersonation and stroking *my precious, my precious* myself.

"When did they have time? They've been dating like ninjas since God knows when, I'm surprised we're only celebrating their wedding and not their freaking first year anniversary." Thankfully the Dan I remembered came back with a vengeance, leaving behind whatever the previous reincarnation had been. Better the devil you know I say.

"Dan, you promised you wouldn't be an ass." Ash gave him a gentle shove in the shoulder. The mystery of anti-Dan solved.

"I didn't even call Troy an asshole, even though he called me a douchebag. Can't I get credit for that?" He rubbed his shoulder with his hand indignantly, no doubt annoyed his sacrifice hadn't been acknowledged.

"Ash, thanks for the sentiment but it feels weirder if he tries to act normal. Just be yourself, Dan."

"Thank you, Megs." He shot his wife-to-be a smug grin. "See, I'm a regular freaking delight, babe. Don't know why you were worried."

"Anyway," Ash rolled her eyes ignoring Dan's now inflated ego. "When did this all happen?"

Troy took over and explained our snap decision to go rogue and elope.

"I'm so fucking disappointed, dude." Dan paced, his agitation showing as Troy recounted the story.

"I'm sorry, man. No one was there. We didn't even tell our families." Troy's apology attempted to ease Dan's disappointment. Both of us genuinely touched that Dan had been bummed about missing out on the wedding.

"No, not about not being there. I totally get that. You wanted to get married, you got married. I can respect that." Dan waved off Troy's apology.

"So what's the problem then?" Troy asked, neither of us closer to working out why if it hadn't been his lack of attendance that had upset him, what he'd got worked up over.

"That fact that you two idiots weren't married by a fat Elvis wearing a satin jumpsuit. You were in Vegas, dude. That's like going to the Coliseum and not seeing the Pope. The King is rolling around in his grave right now. I hope you two fuckers are satisfied." He passionately informed us of our squandered opportunity as he pointing his finger at us accusingly.

"The Pope lives in the Vatican, you moron, not the Coliseum and The King didn't need our business. It's fine." Troy laughed off Dan's concerns of us ruffling the deceased rock star's blue suede shoes.

"I'm just sayin' next time you're in Memphis you should probably head to Graceland and apologize to the Velvet Elvis just to be sure."

Velvet Elvis would probably be waiting a while, but I didn't bother informing Dan.

"Yeah, we'll get right on that." Troy rolled his eyes, pretending to humor him.

We stayed and chatted for a while, Ash giving me concerned looks but I remembered to nod enough and give her the I'm-okay smile. It wasn't a lie; deep down I knew I would be. The laughter certainly helped, but our adventure-filled night had left me tired, so Troy and I wrapped it up and said our goodbyes, talking the walk across the hallway. Our destination—his apartment.

"You want to lie down?" Troy tossed the keys on his kitchen bench; it had been awhile since we'd been in his apartment. The venue for our late night rendezvous had been usually my place.

"Yeah." I smiled as I pulled him toward me. "I think we should live here." It was sudden— my snap decision on where we should call home—but it seemed to fit. Everything about our relationship had either been out of sequence or fly-by-the-seat-your-pants, why change it now?

"Megs, we can live anywhere you want. I can move to yours or we can buy something new. It's just space, it's what's in it that counts." Troy kissed the top of my head.

"I know but it feels right that we move here. Beside, this is where we spent our first night together and our second. It's where the craziness began."

Troy shot me a sideways glance. "That a good thing or a bad thing?"

"It's an *us* thing."

It had been two weeks and I was back at work, my routine slipping into something resembling normal. Normal if you took into account I was married to Troy Harris— I still wasn't used to it, the Zsa Zsa diamond on my hand a constant reminder.

My parents had also come around, which was another win. Once the shock of my changed marital status wore off, they not only accepted both the marriage and Troy, but also actively welcomed him into the family. My dad and husband had even scheduled a man-date on the green. Troy had been quoting *Caddyshack* all week and I had bought a pair of suitable hideous pants I had planned on making him wear, the laugh alone worth every penny I'd spent on them.

"Dr. Harris, your three o'clock is here." Carrie buzzed through my intercom.

"Thanks, Carrie, send him in."

Oh and another thing, I totally did the name change. The freedom from the legacy of my father's last name, liberating. No more having to endure *Harry Potter* stares when people met me for the first time, or whispers about who my parents were behind my back. Their wonder in me— moving forward —would be on my merit alone. Unless they were Power Station fans and then I was shit out of luck.

I stood as I waited for my patient to arrive, the door opening to reveal my three o'clock appointment.

"Hi, Brad, take a seat."

He quietly slumped into the chair opposite my desk as I retook mine.

"Look, before we start I just wanted to talk to you about our last session. I know you followed up with Dr. Meyer and spoke about what happened, but I just wanted you to know that I'm okay now."

It was a fine line in talking about something personal with a. a patient and b. a minor, but as long as I kept the details out of it, ethically I could reassure him that I was okay without crossing any lines. It's not like we could ignore the elephant in the room either— he knew about Troy and the baby.

"I'm really glad, Dr. Winters...I mean, Dr. Harris." Brad fidgeted nervously with the drawstring of his hoodie.

"You can call me Dr. Winters if it makes you feel more comfortable. I don't mind." Change could sometimes be a trigger, and the last thing I wanted to do was have his progress pushed back on something as trivial as my name change.

He shrugged. "Your name is Dr. Harris now, so if it's cool with you, that's what I'd like to call you."

"Of course. I'd like that. So I read over your notes from the last two weeks. Seems like you and your parents came to an agreement about school?"

"Yeah, it's no big deal. I promised my mom I would graduate high school even though it's fucking lame." He shifted uncomfortably in his seat, his hair flicking into his eyes.

"That's fantastic. I'm so proud of you." The fact he'd made the commitment, massive progress in itself.

"Like I said, no big deal." Another shrug.

"Would you like to talk about something else?" I shifted gears, not wanting to push too hard on our first session back.

"I started playing drums." His eyes met mine.

Drums? It was too strange to be a coincidence and I had to wonder if a particular drummer hadn't influenced the decision to pick up the sticks.

"Interesting choice of instrument. Was there any particular reason you chose drums?"

"Yeah, a set showed up at my house one day, with a note."

Drums just showed up on his doorstep? That was even stranger. My gut told me the responsibility of this random act of kindness fell at the feet of someone whose name began with *Troy* and ended with *Harris.* Of course it was all purely speculation, but if I'd been hedging a wager, I'd be going all in.

"You wouldn't happen to have the note would you?"

"Yeah, it's here." Brad pulled the folded piece of paper from his pocket and placed it on the desk in front of me. The deep lines and wear on the paper indicating it had been read and refolded numerous times.

Dear Brad,

When I was younger I'd sometimes get mad too, but instead of beating myself up, I'd take it out on the skins. Maybe it's worth a shot? It doesn't have to be musical, just make some noise. And don't be scared to hit them hard — trust me, they can take it.

The note was incredibly sweet and had all the hallmarkings of Troy. I could almost hear him reading it to me himself. It seemed that Brad and I then embarked on a game of let-me-say-one-thing-but-I-actually-mean-another. I was actually really good at this game, and short of have telepathy; I could read the subtext pretty damn well. This is how the conversation went and what was my interpretation.

"It's not signed?" Translation— Do you know who sent it?

"Nope, no return address either." Translation— someone obviously hiding their identity.

"Well it's a really nice gesture, who ever sent them." Translation— let's dance around the fact that it was probably Troy who did it.

"Yeah, he must be pretty cool." Translation —I know it was your husband.

"Yeah, he must be." Translation — yeah okay, so we both know it was my husband.

See. It's a great game and anyone can play. Now let's get back to therapy so I can find out whether this grand gesture was just a social experiment or if it actually helped the kid.

"Has it helped?" I leaned forward in my seat, already knowing the answer to what I was asking. "Playing the drums?"

"Yeah, I feel less angry." The evidence of that in his less explosive responses and the massive drop in expletives used when talking. "I'm even taking lessons."

"That's really great, Brad."

We spent the rest of the time we had discussing strategies, but I could tell by the change in him already that he would make it. It wasn't going to be a cakewalk, and he had a long road ahead, but for the first time since that angry boy had stepped inside my office, he seemed to want the change.

We said our goodbyes and I instructed Brad to make another appointment and he'd barely shut my office door when I reached for my phone.

"Megs." He answered on the second ring.

"Troy Harris, do you have something you need to tell me?"

He had to have known I'd eventually find out. I mean, Brad's my patient, talking is what we do.

"Okay, Megs, I'll come clean. All the people on *Lost's* Oceania flight 815 were dead the whole time." He barked out a laugh.

"Ha, ha. Very funny. No something else."

"Is this about the lingerie in the back of the closet?"

"What? No. You bought me lingerie?"

"No it's for me actually, but sure I guess you can wear it."

He was having way too much fun with this. There was something about the two of us on a phone. I don't think he had the capacity to have a serious conversation with me.

"It's not about underwear." My fingertips massaged my temples as I calculated how much longer to let this play out.

"Can I buy a vowel?"

"Troy." Okay so obviously not very long. "Did you buy a drum kit?"

"As in ever?" He laughed, my question clearly ridiculous.

"Okay, you're going to make me ask, aren't you?"

"I say we keep playing this game. It's fun and kind of like charades with audibles. Sounds like…"

This conversation was going nowhere fast. "Troy did you send Brad Hemsworth a drum kit?"

"That's odd, did he say I did?" He didn't sound half as surprised as he was trying to.

"No, the note was *anonymous*." The emphasis on the last word for his benefit, not mine.

"Oh see, I'm *Harris* not *anonymous*, both end in *s* so I can see how you got confused." He annunciated the words— both his last name and anonymous— slowly for effect.

"Troy!" I actually huffed into the phone.

"Megs!" He mimicked, but with less huff and more chuckle.

"Tell me," I demanded. Did we establish eons ago, I have an acute need to know?

"Assuming I did and I'm not saying I did but purely for this exercise let's work on the hypothetical." There was finesse in Troy's voice that was smooth and un-frazzled. Clearly I hadn't been the only one who'd watch CSI.

"Fine," I humored him. "Say it *might've* been you."

"Okay, so based on that assumption if I had sent a drum kit wouldn't it stand to reason that you best not know anything about it, where it could cause a conflict of interest in your treatment of him?"

Of course he was right. His silence was protecting me from a wading through an ethical minefield. I mean technically it wasn't breaking any rules but Troy contacting one of patients? Even if his intentions were pure... Yeah, let's file that under *it would probably have given me a nervous breakdown had I known at the time.*

"Troy, I know it was you. How did you get his address?"

There was no way he would have been able to access my patient information. Not unless he was moonlighting as a computer hacker.

"Well, *hypothetically* you're not the only person who knows how to use *Google.*"

"Even though I can't sanction what you did, it was a really good thing and I love you." My heart swelled for this amazing man who never ceased to amaze me.

"I love you too." His voice oozed sweetness. "Oh, but while we're doing confessionals." He paused and I had no idea where he was going with it. "You want to tell me how a pair of my auto-graphed sticks found their way into one of your storage boxes?"

Ooooooooohhhhhhhh. Yeah. Those. Totally forgot about the sticks I swindled from Dan when he'd pumped me for information for Ash's birthday. Probably should have hidden those.

"Is that kind of creepy?"

Did I really need to ask?

"Nah, the photoshopped picture of us at the *AMAs* is waaay creepier."

Huh? What photo? I cast my mind back to try and recall if I'd ever done that. Let's face it. It did sound like me.

"I did not photoshop myself into a photo with you at the AMAs."

Or at the very least I was ninety-nine percent sure I hadn't.

"No, I did. It looks great too." Troy chuckled. "Thinking of making it our Christmas card."

The smile spread across my face. Yeah, we were made for each other.

"Bye Troy, love you."

"Bye Megs, love you more."

"**Dude, we are so lame. Can you believe we went to *Scores* and** spent more time talking to each other than checking out tits? I got bored half way through the lap dance and actually paid the chick fifty bucks to stop." Dan and I stepped out of the elevator and into our shared hallway. Times were definitely a-changin'.

"It's where you said you wanted to go, douchebag. Did you not specifically ask for a strip joint for your Stag party?" If I'd had my way, we'd have gone and shot some pool at *Donavan's*, maybe smoked some cigars. Watching chicks bump and grind the pole was not my idea of a good time, and it hadn't been in a long while.

"Yeah but it's no fun any more. I mean—if anyone is going to be rubbing my junk, I want it to be Ash." Dan swung his keys around his fingers, ready for us to do the catch-ya-laters.

"You are such a romantic, dude. Brings a tear to my eye."

"Hate all you want to hate. Going inside to my girl."

"Later."

The key went in and the lock turned, the door creaking slightly as it opened. I cursed under my breath, it was late and I didn't want to wake Megs.

We'd been out to celebrate Dan's last few weeks of freedom

but I'd been lucky if I'd had three beers. It wasn't the ring on my finger that was stopping me from having a good time; it was the zero desire I had to look at any other woman that wasn't my wife.

My wife. Best fucking thing that ever happened to me was that blonde powerhouse that was tucked up in my bed, and not a day didn't go by that I couldn't believe my luck that she was mine.

Trying to keep the noise to a minimum, I did my usual strip on the way through routine, dumping my clothes in the hamper before heading to bed. The smell of stripper's perfume and cigarettes left behind as I made the familiar walk to my bedroom.

Megs was naked, sprawled out on our king size bed, her hair all over her face with her head on my pillow. The big-ass grin spread across my face as I watched her sleeping, her legs kicked out taking up most of the room, her hands lying on the space I'd usually be occupying.

I quickly hit the shower, rinsing off the stench of my ordinary night out. I toweled off and headed back into our bedroom, hoping the water hitting the tiles hadn't been enough to disturb her.

Still sleeping.

My eyes focused on Megs's body, which had inched over slightly while I'd been getting clean, giving me just enough room to crawl onto the mattress. The smell of her got me instantly hard the minute I'd slid in between the sheets.

"Holy Fuck." My voice echoed louder than I'd meant. Megs wrapped her hand around my cock as soon as my ass hit the bed, barely giving me enough time to turn and see her huge smile.

"Hello, Troy Harris." Her voice purred, clueing me in that maybe she hadn't been sleeping the whole time.

"Did I wake you, sweetheart?" I tried not to focus on her hand slowly moving up and down my shaft.

"Tell me, Troy Harris." She ignored my question, instead shuffling up the bed, giving me more wrist action as she continued to talk. "This hard-on, is it for me? Or did you see something else you liked tonight?"

"Only you, Megs." My eyes nailed her as she tightened her grip around my cock.

"I've missed you." Something in her tone had me guessing that she hadn't meant just tonight. The last time I'd been inside her had been over three weeks ago.

"I've missed you too." My hand itched to touch her skin as it moved over her tits. "You sure about this?" I asked, needing to know this was exactly what she had in mind.

She didn't answer, instead dipped her head into my lap and swirled her tongue around the head of my dick, her teeth gently pulling on the ring on the tip. So I'm assuming that would be a yes.

"Fuck, Megs." I cursed out a breath, the feeling of her mouth on me better than I'd remembered.

"That's what I'm trying to facilitate here." She mumbled as she pulled my cock out her mouth. The words familiar, kicking us back to our first time.

"Yeah? Well who am I to deny my wife what she wants."

My interest in the blowjob was superseded by the need to get my mouth on her, my body moving quickly as I splayed her out on the bed. The green light had gotten me so juiced up I wasn't sure which part of her would be getting my attention.

She yelped as her ass hit the mattress, my mouth making the decision as it licked her nipple, my hand palming her other tit.

"Troy." She moaned as my tongue got reacquainted with her pink peaks, moving from one and then other. It wasn't like me to play favorites, making sure each of them got enough of the loving feeling.

Being the dedicated guy that I am, I continued the mouth action down her body; the echoing of my name acting as my soundtrack as I gently parted her thighs. She was so fucking wet.

She arched her back, giving me better access as my tongue invaded her pussy. The "Holy Shit" while she bunched the sheets beside me all the encouragement I needed as I sucked and licked her clit.

"Don't stop." Her hands locked around my head holding me in place as she twisted her fingers through my mohawk.

If I could have told her that telepathically and not by actually stopping what I was doing, I would have let her know that there was zero danger of that.

She thrashed as I slid two fingers inside her, my tongue keeping busy as it circled her clit.

"Troy," she moaned as her hands moved from my head to her body, her fingertips kneading her tits as her legs started to shake.

She was close, and with one last flick of my tongue, she was pushed over. Her beautiful tits heaving up and down as I teased out the rest of her orgasm with my fingers.

"Mmm. I love watching you come." The fingers that had been buried in her pussy found their way to my mouth, my lips closing around them, as I tasted her one last time. "You want to go to sleep now?" I teased, with no intention of putting the brakes on. Nope. Not until I'd sunk my cock deep into her and felt her come at least one more time.

"I want you in me," she panted, her hands fixing on my shoulders and pulling me down onto her. Her mouth clamped over mine as I tried not to crush her.

My arms wrapped around her body and I rolled her on top of mine, adjusting her so my cock hit her in all the right places.

"What part?" I palmed my hard-on, circling the opening of her wet pussy.

"That, I want that." She moaned as she rubbed herself against my hard-on

"What's that? You need to be clear with me. I'm having a hard time understanding," I hissed out not sure who was I was torturing by holding back— her or me.

"Your cock. I want your cock," she all but screamed.

Well then, you heard the lady. My dick got into position, demanding I put us both out of our misery as it slid in an inch.

It was quick—way quicker than I had meant to —but I sunk into her in one fluid thrust, her pussy fisting me as I entered her. The skin on skin contact drove me insane as I moved slowly out, and then pushed in again. It was like I was on autopilot as my cock slid inside of her.

"Megs." I pulled back, my drive to sink into her giving me temporary amnesia, and the fact we hadn't done this in a while not getting the attention it deserved. "Did I hurt you?" I couldn't see her face, her head buried in my neck as she breathed heavily.

"I said." She kissed my neck as she shuffled up my body, her knees hitting the mattress as she straddled me. "I want your cock."

"I love your fucking dirty mouth," I hissed through clenched teeth as I pulled her back down onto me.

She didn't give me a chance for another thrust, linking her hands into mine, using them for leverage as she pushed down to bury my cock deep inside her.

She writhed on top of me, my mouth no longer capable of talking as she met every one of my thrusts with one of her own.

"Troy." She begged me, her body not quite there as she rode me.

"Right here, sweetheart. Feel me?" I pushed deeper inside her as my hand reached down and thumbed her clit.

"Yes," she screamed, the extra attention my hand was giving her enough to tip her over. "Oh. My. God." Her pussy milked my cock as she exploded on top of me. Her body collapsed onto mine as she rode out the rest of her orgasm.

"Megs, I need to come." I couldn't hold out any longer, the pulsing that was travelling up the length of my shaft driving me fucking insane. One more thrust was all it took and I shot my load into her, kissing her hard as I emptied into her.

Movement was obsolete, my arms the only part of me still operational as I snaked them around her body and held her, both of us still shaking.

"Are you okay?" My hand brushed her hair off her shoulder, slightly pissed at myself I hadn't been able to rein it in and give her more *making love* and less *fucking*.

"I'm fine now." Her giggles vibrated against my chest, her face still pressed against my body.

Her fingers traced the lines of my new tattoo, the one that I'd gotten just an hour after saying "I do."

"I love this." Her lips kissed the gray-scale tiny feather that sat just above my heart, a smaller replica of the ones that decorated her skin. A tribute not only to Megs but also to the little life we'd lost.

"Yeah, me too." It made it a little easier knowing that they would both always be with me.

"Megs." Thinking about the baby gave me a different kind of wake up call. "I wasn't wearing any protection and you're not on the pill anymore."

Sure we were both sporting matching rings and the same last name, but I assumed we'd need to have a sit down and discuss whether we were going to try for another baby or not. Have the second time around happen with a little less of an OMG moment. Probably a conversation we should have had thirty minutes before we'd started fucking.

"I kind of realized that once I felt the ring inside me, but there was no way I could ask you to stop." She rested her head on my shoulder, those blue-green eyes owning me as she smiled.

"So how would you feel if we just made a baby?" I didn't know what the chances were— but sex without any barriers—it was a definite roll of the dice.

Her wide eyes blinked as if the realization had finally hit her, the possibility higher than average.

She didn't give any words, instead pushing her lips down on mine, my mouth getting on the same page as I kissed her.

"Megs, do you want to make a baby?" I rephrased the question, thinking that the new improved way of asking had a nicer ring to it. My cock that was still buried inside her, stirred with renewed interest.

"Yes, Troy Harris. I want to make a baby." Her eyes started to glass, rapid blinks chasing down her tears.

"Well then, Megs Harris, let's get you knocked up."

EPILOGUE

Megan

"**Dan, stop touching my ass. My dad is right over there.**" **Ashlyn** very unconvincingly smacked away Dan's hand. Her lips curved into a smile as her other hand brought the glass of champagne to her mouth. Despite being manhandled, there was no hiding how happy she was.

"Oh come on, babe, I'm dying here. Can't we sneak off for a quickie?" Dan almost pleaded. His eyes filled with lust as they raked over his new wife. I would have thought Ash should be more worried about the come-sit-on-my-face vibes he was throwing off rather than hands on her ass, but who was I to judge.

"No, we have a few more hours of the reception and then I'm all yours." She giggled as she lowered her champagne glass back to the table.

"Hate to break it you, babe, but you're all mine now. I'm just being respectful by not having sex with you right here and now," Dan not so quietly whispered into her ear. His hands disappeared under the white table linen of the bridal table. The grin getting wider hinted that they weren't sitting idle in his lap. My role as maid of honor earned me a front row seat to the shenanigans, catching an eyeful as I sat to their left.

The wedding had been beautiful. My dress had even been a stunning slate grey chiffon full-length gown. Not a pink tutu in sight. The whole vibe was traditional and simple, with the bride and groom exchanging vows in a catholic church in Manhattan before a stunning reception in the Manhattan Ballroom of the Grand Hyatt hotel. The ornate tables all but deserted as guests danced to a live five-piece band. They weren't anyone famous, but knew just about every chart topping song from the last thirty years.

It was all very low key considering whom the groom was. Although given that the night wasn't over, there was still time for a bunch of bikini-clad babes to jump out of a cake or something.

"You should probably do the flower toss and call it a day. Save us and everyone else from an indecent display." Troy popped open a button on his tailored tuxedo jacket to reveal a fitted charcoal vest as he sat down beside me. The contradiction of the mohwak he was rocking, making the suit look even more delicious.

"Did I tell you how sexy you look, Troy Harris?" My arms snaked around his broad chest. God, he looked good. Maybe Dan had the right idea? Holy hell. I'd just agreed with Dan. Maybe it was best we called it a night.

"Yeah? You got a thing for the monkey suit?" Troy gave me a suggestive look, his grin widening as he leaned back in his chair. The power of his smile making me tingle all over.

"I have a *thing* for you." I tiptoed my fingers along the seam of his vest.

"Yeah we know." Dan laughed, apparently done with fondling his wife in time to eavesdrop on our conversation.

In fairness, I hadn't been quiet about it. I had a couple of rings on my finger than told me I didn't have to be. Oh, and I didn't have to worry about stalking charges now either. I was able to ogle Troy Harris all I wanted, and it was total legal. It was winning all the way around.

"Wow." Jase nodded, taking a swig from his beer as he pulled up a chair beside us. "I feel like I should be busting out a rendition of "Can you feel the love tonight?" That, or cry into these expensive napkins at the beauty of all of it. The struggle is real." His voice dripped with sarcasm as he joined us at the bridal table.

"Yeah, whatever, asswipe. You're next." Dan tipped his chin, giving him a pointed glare. Jase being the only member of Power Station not with a significant other.

"Nah, someone has to keep us on the most eligible bachelor lists." Jase's smile widened as he brought the bottle back to his lips and took another drink. With his dark suit fitting snuggly against his toned body, he could have easily been a model for GQ.

"Five large says he ends up in knots over a girl within the next three months." Troy smirked, his hand resting on the back of my chair.

"I say let's make it ten, but Jase likes putting in the ground work. The guy isn't even dating anyone, so I think it would be closer to six," Dan piped in, Ashlyn giggling by his side.

"You know I'm right here, assholes." Jase rolled his brown eyes. "And I can't believe you are gambling on my relationship status. I feel so fucking cheap."

"Done." Troy agreed, his wager with Dan apparently decided as they both ignored Jason.

"I'll drink to that." Dan raised his glass of champagne before pausing. "Hey, why aren't you drinking?" His eyes floated over to the lack of alcoholic beverage in front of me. I'd been sipping water all night.

"Wait. What?" Ashlyn's attention now also directed on my apparently offensive glass. Obviously her being busy getting married had distracted her enough to not notice. "Why are you not drinking?" She pointed a finger at my glass accusingly, her eyes peeled wide as she looked down at the glass of water and then at me. "Megs!"

"Wow, Ash. No need to yell at her, babe. It's only a drink." Dan rubbed his wife's arm oblivious as to why she was getting excited.

"Megs. Don't you hold out on me." Ash showed no signs of letting it go.

Let's face it. When it came to keeping secrets, I sucked. Also in the list of things I didn't do well was lie. So combine the two, and I was pretty much a goner when it came to hiding that just two days ago, peeing on a stick had given me two very clear lines.

"Okay." I admitted as I slowly rose to my feet, Troy's arms

circling me as I continued. "It's early and we just found out. We're being cautious." Not to mention petrified, but elated and crazy happy. Oh and I'd had cried about fifteen times in the last forty-eight hours. I was sure that wasn't normal either.

Ash squealed, leapt out of her chair and gave me a hug, her display of affection drawing curious stares from people close by. Lucky for us they didn't give us much more interest. A bride squealing on her wedding day wasn't exactly a surprising occurrence.

"Nothing bad is going to happen this time." Troy gave my hand a subtle squeeze being that Ash was still dominating my personal space. They were same words he had been reciting to me since I'd held the EPT test in front of his face. My vocabulary had been limited to "Oh my God" as the significance of those two lines sunk in.

It's what we both wanted, had hoped for but it didn't mean that I didn't freak the hell out. It seemed to be my natural reaction so this time around I didn't fight it. Troy was his usual calm self and even though I suspected he was just as scared as I was, he was wearing an ironclad poker face.

"Congrats, man." Jase clapped Troy over the shoulder. "So happy for you guys." He turned his attention to me and pulled me into a warm one-armed hug. "Awesome news, Megs. Oh and thanks for the heat off my love life. I owe you one."

"Thanks." My eyes started to leak again. I swear, by the end of this pregnancy I was going to be hospitalized for dehydration via tear ducts. Could that even happen? Crap. I needed to drink more water.

"You're knocked up?" Dan shot us a sideways glance, clearly needing the clarification.

"Yep." Troy grinned not even trying to hide his excitement. "We sure are."

Dan gave us his excited congratulations like everyone else had and I gave up trying to stop from crying again. Ash joined me, proving what a team player she was, not leaving me to ruin my mascara all by myself. So much for my initial concern about bringing drama to her wedding— yeah that ship had sailed. I know there was a saying about even the best intentions going down the tube, but I couldn't remember it, and in the end it didn't matter.

Troy and I, we didn't know how to do ordinary, and that was okay, because like he'd told me months ago, where's the fun in an easy ride? I was buckled up and ready to go.

No one needed to give me a guarantee this was going to work out, I already knew. Why? Because I had Troy Harris.

BACK STAGE

PROLOGUE

Angie

Ten Years Ago

GOD, HE WAS SEXY. ALL THOSE TANNED MUSCLES, POPPING OUT proudly. I had to fight the urge not to give the man a standing ovation every time I looked at him. Which was a lot. And I was thankful. Every. Single. Time.

He was different, and I'd known that from the second I'd laid eyes on him. He wasn't a boy, not like any I'd seen. It wasn't just that he was older; there was something in his face, the way he walked, that set him apart. He was a man, and he wasn't shy about showing it.

A black '72 Mercury Montego fastback had pulled up just before dusk sometime in late May. The rumble of the V8 had me at the window before the car had even been parked in front of Troy's house. And while the car had initially captured my attention, it was what stepped out of it that made me stand up and take notice. The way he strode to Troy's door was almost erotic, his movements so fluid and sure that his body screamed sex. He was so hot.

He spent the summer living with Troy and his family, and I had found a renewed sense of religion spending most of my days thanking God for the creation that was Jason Irwin. Having just separated from the Army, his hair was starting to grow out of the regulation high-and-tight, while his body was still in that be-all-you-can-be shape. I whispered my silent thank-you's to the US Government when he'd pull off his shirt.

It wasn't just his GI Joe body that had my brain feeling like it had been blended, it was the way he would talk to me when I finally stopped being a chicken-shit and introduced myself. He didn't treat me like a kid nor did he try and weasel himself into my panties like Dan. He seemed genuinely interested in what I had to say. Those times when he'd give me his attention, my world would stand still and before I could stop it, my heart wanted him more than my hormones.

The temp hadn't dipped below a hundred in four days straight, with the last days of August proving summer wouldn't give in to fall without one last fight. Which had encouraged him to be outside a lot, which is where I also seemed to be. I prayed every night the heat wave would never end. It was heaven on Earth. The heat, the night, and him.

"Angie." His voice rumbled, his eyes slowly opening.

Sleep had been near impossible. After weeks and weeks of hoping, he finally kissed me.

Except it hadn't been just a kiss.

His mouth had owned mine. His big strong hands around my head brought me in closer as his tongue teased the inside of my mouth. It was hot, my body almost combusting in the overload. I never wanted it to stop.

The flirting back and forth wasn't new. Every time we spoke, my heart thumped so loud I was convinced a marching band had taken up residence. It had been the same since the moment I saw him, getting to know him had reinforced what I had already guessed. He was perfection. Beautiful. Smart. Sexy. But there was something else, a lingering darkness that I didn't understand. He was quiet. Not rude, just held back. And damn if he wasn't a nut I wanted to crack. Last night I had gotten that chance.

"Hey." The smile on my face threatened to split apart.

This was my favorite view. Jason Irwin lying naked beneath

me, his rugged arms holding me close—those dark eyes of his giving *me* their full attention.

That kiss—the one that would forever be elevated to the best kiss of my life—didn't end with just some heavy petting. After asking me repeatedly if I was sure, he finally made love to me.

At first he seemed like he hadn't wanted to. Mumbling something about not being good enough for me. He had always been so concerned about me, so kind, but he didn't have to worry. It was *exactly* what I wanted and when I finally convinced him it was okay, he gave in.

Under the moonlight, in the backseat of his car.

It couldn't have been more perfect.

"Are you okay?" His fingers gently moved over my shoulder and down my arm.

It tickled but I didn't dare ask him to stop. I'd never ask him to stop. Not when we'd *finally* gotten together. This was going to be the start of something fantastic. I could just feel it. There were going to be so many more nights like this. Him and me. Holding each other. Loving each other.

"I'm fine," I breathed against his skin, nuzzling myself closer to his neck. Our legs were twisted within the confined space of his car, the leather sticking to parts of our skin. Did I mention how perfect it had been? It could have been a penthouse bedroom at the Waldorf Astoria and it wouldn't have been any better. His body knew exactly what to do with mine. Who knew sex could even feel like that? That I loved him, well that just made it better.

"We should probably get dressed; everyone is going to be waking up soon." His body shifted under mine, the leather creaking in protest as he moved. I didn't blame it. I wanted to protest, too.

"Yeah, we should." I fished my bra out of the pile of clothes on the floor and sat up to slide it on. "My dad is going to be heading to work in a few hours; I could make us breakfast as soon as he leaves." My smile hopefully hinted that he could repay me by taking care of dessert. It was my birthday after all, and I knew exactly how I wanted to spend my day. Naked, with Jason—in case anyone was wondering.

"That's not such a good idea." With a flicker of panic in his eyes, he threw water on whatever flames I had going on, his lack of a smile making me nervous.

"Uh?" The word had shot out of my mouth, wondering if he had something better planned. Naked on the beach could also work. It might be a bit sandy, but okay. In any case, we were still going to need to eat.

"Yeah, I think it's best if we just … did our own thing."

He wanted to play it cool. Smart. I mean I had *just* turned eighteen and while I had no issue with the seven-year age gap, my dad would probably lose his shit. He was worried. Of course he was. We'd have to keep it a secret for a while, just until everyone got used to it. Jase moving away meant it would be easier. We could date and not have to worry about prying eyes and judgmental stares. Troy might be a little weird about it at first, being that he was usually so protective. But he had to think Jason was a decent guy if he'd invited him to stay an entire summer. Plus, once he saw how in love we were, he would come around. How could he not? We wouldn't have to mention that our first time had been in his backyard while he was blissfully asleep a few feet away. Nope, that piece of information I would take to the grave. And hopefully now Dan Evans would finally get it through his head he didn't stand a chance. Not now that I had a boyfriend.

"Sure. Did you want to meet up with me later? When the coast is clear?" My panties were next on my redress mission. Difficult, seeing Jase was still naked and not making any effort to cover up. My eyes inadvertently floated down to see his cock was very much awake and ready for me now, rather than later. The surge between my thighs concluding we were very much on the same page. This was going to be the best birthday ever.

"No, Angie. I'm leaving." He swallowed hard, shaking his head like he was finally convinced. "What happened last night was a mistake."

"Huh?"

It had been more of a sound than an actual word. My mouth no longer being controlled by my brain as I processed the words he had said. "Leaving" and "mistake" being the loudest.

"We shouldn't have done that. It wasn't smart. In any case, it won't be happening again."

It was as if a switch had been flicked, the interior of the car immediately chilling despite the sun threatening to rise at any moment. His eyes darkened, emotionless, as he threw on a T-shirt over his head. The amazing guy I had fallen in love with, gone and in his place ... someone else.

"I—I know you're moving. But we can still see each other." I purposely ignored the other part of his statement. The one where he'd said I had been a mistake.

"No." He reached down and shoved his legs into his jeans without bothering with his boxers. "We can't."

I don't understand. I wasn't sure if I had said it out loud or if it was just on a constant loop in my head. What had gone wrong?

"Hey." He looked at me, I wasn't sure if it was regret or pity in his eyes. "It's just better this way. Maybe we should just pretend it didn't happen."

"But it did happen." I blinked, wondering if it was a joke.

"Yeah, it did. But it was a mistake. You understand that, right?"

I felt like I was going to be sick. That word again. Mistake. The bile from my stomach surged uncomfortably as I scrambled to pull on my cotton, crumpled sundress. The one he had told me last night looked so hot on me. Shoes, they weren't an option as I all but threw myself from his car, the dress barely covering my skin as my feet hit the dirt.

"Yep, no biggie." I nodded, praying if there was any god at all he would help me not to cry. Not now. Not in front of him while he looked at me so impassively.

"Hey, Angie. Are you okay?" His eyes widened as my shoeless feet hit an overgrown tree root in the Harris backyard.

Pain.

The one in my foot nothing like the one that was going on in my heart. I needed to get away. Now.

"Sure. Dumb tree." *Please don't cry. Please don't cry.* My legs doing their best to keep me upright and get me out down the side path to the front of the house. "See you, thanks." My back turned before the first tear fell.

In my head, he'd call after me. Run from his car and tell me that the mistake was this stupid conversation, and not last night.

But that didn't happen.

And as I made it the short distance next door to the safety of my house, I'd heard the rumble of his V8.

I wished I'd been stronger. Asked him why. But I felt so dumb.

Dumb, that I'd been stupid enough to allow myself to be played.

Dumb, that I'd fallen in love with some guy who had only wanted to fuck me.

Dumb, that I'd fallen for the oldest trick in the book.

By the time I'd pulled my key from my pocket, his black Montego had already driven past.

He was gone.

And he had taken my heart with him.

Present Day

"THANK YOU NEW YORK AND GOOD NIIIGGHHHHHHT!" JAMES, OUR front man, pumped his fist in the air as the techs killed the lights, plunging the stage into darkness.

Opening night in our hometown, and the air was mother-fucking electric. Two encores and fans were still chanting for "one more song", our three-hour set not long enough apparently. And damn if that shit didn't make me feel bullet proof.

"Jase! Here, dude." A towel flew through the air toward me as I stepped out from behind the keys; my hand grabbed it and slung it over a shoulder. Was going to need more than that to mop up the sweat that was pouring off me. The excitement wasn't going to wash off even *with* the shower.

"Thanks, man!" I said to no one in particular, not sure entirely which one of the roadies had been my hook-up.

My muscles ached, tightly coiled from exhaustion, but even still it would be a hard task to wipe the smile off my face.

"Fuck, that felt good." Troy toweled off his face as he fell into step beside me, our feet taking us off the stage and down the stairs. "It's been too long. Recording is one thing, but playing in front of a crowd. That shit never gets old." Big ass smile on his face was the hint he was feeling the same way I was.

"Truth, right?" Dan jogged up beside us as we made our way to the back of house area. "I don't give a shit how many times we play Madison Square Garden. Every time I get on that stage, I almost blow my load."

"Save it for your wife, asswipe; no one wants to hear about your jizz." Troy's stank-ass towel flew over my head and clocked Dan right in the mouth. He had it opened too, so that got extra points. I ignored the subsequent name-calling that erupted as a result. It was a case of the same *fuck you, asshole* I'd been hearing for the last ten years. While the others got vocal with their appreciation, I did what I always did, and kept it locked down.

Not because they weren't right on the money—that euphoric feeling of playing live for a crowd—nothing else compared. But because big, showy and emotional wasn't my thing. Not any more at least, and not because I didn't care. It was just better to keep an even keel. For me, unstable wasn't a good look. Didn't mean good things either, so I kept my shit in check. Better for everyone.

We were just five guys playing our tunes. It had always been about that. Difference now was the crowd and the venues were bigger, but if shit went down tomorrow and we were back playing a dive bar in Queens, we'd still be showing up every night and rocking its ass off.

"Awesome show guys." James clapped his hand around my neck. "This tour is going to be our best yet."

Our fearless leader was always the last one off the stage, Alex, our badass guitarist, usually leaving a second or two before him. They were our Lennon and McCartney, the drivers of the crazy train, and they usually got more time in the spotlight. None of us gave a shit, far as the rest of us where concerned, it was deserved.

It was the usual back and forth after a show. The high-fiving and us talking shop was our way of unwinding as we made it back to the dressing rooms. Roadies took care of securing the gear while security made sure we kept moving; us hanging around only made their jobs harder. They weren't assholes about it, but they made it clear that the hallway was not the place for us to get warm and fuzzy.

"Great show." Lexi Reed, our PR manager, greeted us as we rounded the corner. "Get showered and changed. There's no meet and greet tonight, but there's a few people who want to show their personal adoration." She'd barely gotten the words out when Alex put his mouth on hers. Lucky for him there would be no sexual harassment charges, being that Lexi was also his wife.

The PDA was all now par for the course with every one of the band members hooked up with a significant other. Well, all except for me, and that was more than fine as far as I was concerned. While it all worked out for them, I'd learnt my lesson early on, and I'd rather piss out razor blades than go through a relationship again. Still, I wasn't raining on anyone else's parade. Evil son of a bitch was also something I'd left in my past. The cool, calm and collected Jase version 2.0, definitely the better of the two.

A loud bang echoed through the hall; it was followed up with a piercing and vocal "motherfuuuuuucckkkkkerrr!" stopping any further high-fiving and/or lip action. James looked to the door where the commotion was coming from with the same what-the-fuck look on his face as the rest of us. Seemed ground zero was our support act, *Unhinged Throttle's* dressing room.

"Hey, maybe we poke our heads in for a sec," James nodded to the door, "make sure shit isn't getting too out of control."

Wise choice, support bands had a tendency to let the excitement go to their heads, especially ones who weren't seasoned. It was like bringing a virgin to a gangbang— unpredictable, volatile and usually escalated quickly. Taking a look was definitely on the cards.

We let James take the lead as he rapped on the door a couple of times; a loud "come on in" shouted back in response. Good sign; meant at least they were still conscious. Calling 9-1-1 on opening night would have been a buzz kill.

"What the fuck?" Alex's voice boomed across the room, the door opening to what could have been a scene from a bad movie. Two of the band members were on their knees doing lines of coke off a mirror. The gaping hole in the drywall that looked to be the same size of the reflective surface, a tip-off it hadn't been an accessory they'd walked in with.

They had company as well. Three naked girls giving *blow* of a different variety, while two other charming ladies finding an interesting use for a champagne bottle—obviously bigger fans of each other rather than the actual band.

"Hey!" Wade, the lead guitarist waved us over as the girl in his lap kept up her Dyson action. "Welcome to our kingdom. You guys want some H? It's clean, my dealer is a stand-up guy."

"Wow, didn't think when I got out of bed this morning I'd be hearing *drug dealer* and *stand-up guy* in the same sentence." Dan's eyes widened as he checked out the scene. Had to admit, he was saying what we all were thinking.

Hardcore drug use hadn't been part of the Power Station history. And while that shit was straight up reminiscent of my teenage years, thankfully I'd separated myself from those fucktards a long time ago. Most of them either in a cell or underground— I couldn't make myself give a crap either way. I was just glad it hadn't been my footnote. Which brought us to the dipshits currently in front of us.

"You losers have drugs in here? Are you motherfucking insane? There are kids on this tour." The anger rolled off James like a tidal wave. If the words that jutted from his mouth weren't enough of a clue, the bulging veins in his neck would have cleared up any misunderstanding.

"Relax dude, we're just partying." Wade held his hands up defensively, smug-ass grin on his face. "This is how we do our come down."

"You come down by getting high?" I coughed out a laugh. "Yeah these guys are fucking geniuses."

What the poster boys for Dumbasses of the Year didn't realize was that we weren't interested in the irony. The rage kicked up to we're-going-to-bust-some-heads level as they were told to pack up their shit and get the fuck out.

Oh, and mention of the five-o made the girls who had been deep-throating suddenly take an interest in the conversation.

The motley crew of assholes got ready to clear out with Wade throwing in there, "We'll see you tomorrow," while he pushed his dick in his pants and zipped up.

It really shouldn't have needed to be said. Their contracts, crystal freaking clear. Drugs on tour equaled do not pass go, do not collect two hundred dollars. Buh-bye. It didn't matter it wasn't my woman or child that needed protecting; they were *my* family and this was a hundred percent united front. And if I got to limber up and break out some old school moves with the bastards, well that would just make the evening more interesting. My guess was the collective douchebags in front of me had never seen any real action. As for me, I'd been in more street fights than I'd cared to remember. Not that the press ever got a hold of that information. Nope, my bio was sold as an Army vet who played keys and liked to knit. The knitting thing was complete bullshit of course, but it just goes to show how nobody was taking notice. FYI, no one gives a rat's ass about the keyboard player.

"No, I don't think you understood me." James settled into an eerie calm. "You're done."

"You're firing us?" Oh look, one of the other band members, Pete, suddenly decided he wasn't mute and joined in the conversation. "You can't just fucking fire us." The unsteadiness of his voice not giving the statement the confidence he'd possibly hoped for.

"Read your contract, asshole." Alex stepped in, the edge in his voice enough to chill the room a few degrees. "I think we can all agree a piss test at this point isn't needed." His raised eyebrow dared them to prove him wrong.

What happened next I could only describe as stupid-ass shit. Because clearly you should know better than to argue with a bunch of guys who were sober and not only outweighed you in muscle, but freaking brains as well. That right there should have been an advert for an anti-drug campaign. Look kids, if the drugs don't fuck you up, the stupid shit that will come out of your mouth will finish the job.

Wade had opened his mouth, and I really didn't care much for what he had to say. The conversation had already taken too long. Cue my fist grabbing the front of his shirt and tossing him out the door while Troy threatened to go Scorsese on the other douchebags who weren't moving fast enough. And just like that, we'd pulled some abracadabra type shit. Boom—place cleared.

"We solid, big guy?" I clapped my hand around Troy's neck hoping to help him rein in some of the rage. My time with the dark side had taught me some pretty handy tricks in talking people down from the ledge. And this guy, I'd easily take a bullet for.

He shook his head, the look in his eyes enough to convince me he was exercising as much restraint as he knew how. "I don't want Megs exposed to that, especially not while she is knocked up."

"Agreed." James sunk his ass into one of the vacated chairs. "That shit doesn't go on. I'm not expecting them to be sitting around holding prayer meetings—I expected blowjobs and weed, not fucking heroin and coke."

The high we'd been on from the show took a very quick downswing; the reality of the situation hitting home. I took a seat beside James and cleared my throat. "Not to be an asshole and state the obvious, but we just fired our opening act day one of our tour. Any ideas on how we're going to play this?"

Not that I didn't concur with said firing, but tomorrow we were going to be hitting the stage again. A big gaping slot where the warm-up band should be. Going on without a pre-show was unheard of, so it was either get creative or hire some record spinner from Soho.

"Everyone decent is already booked. We can probably put out a call, see who's around?" Dan grabbed his phone from his back pocket. His creased brow the tip-off he wasn't entirely convinced, that even with his connections, he could pull off a miracle and fill the spot.

"No, this just perfectly illustrates why we need to do this in house. It isn't just us on the road anymore. We don't need the kids finding a fucking needle 'cause some jerk-off thinks it's the 90's." Alex planted his ass beside James; Troy and Dan following suit in chairs opposite them. Well wasn't this warm and fucking cozy? Pity the situation itself blew hardcore.

"Alex is right," James agreed, "we need someone we can trust.

Now would be a good time for any ideas."

"Hey what about Angie Morelli?" Troy rubbed his hand through his mohawk, the mess of crap he called hair.

Angie Morelli.

Yep, just saying her name was enough to send a chill up my spine. It had been ten years, and still not long enough. Her long, black hair and dark-brown eyes, something that had taken a while to wipe from my mind. That body. Yeah, I still remembered every curve. So freaking sweet, too. Unfortunately it wasn't only her attributes that I remembered, one of my biggest asshole moments was also front and center getting the trip down memory lane. So you would have to understand why I didn't immediately start doing backflips and welcoming her. The idea was to avoid the drama, not to give it top freaking billing.

"Dude, no. No fucking way," Dan chimed in, his words echoing exactly what was rattling around in my head.

Thank you, douchebag. An Angie reunion was bad news. There had to be someone else. Hey, was Charlie Manson out of prison yet? I mean if we were thinking up bad ideas to take on tour, we might as well put them all on the table.

"She's still playing?" James tipped his head toward Troy, taking way more interest in the topic than I would have liked. The itch to shut the conversation down danced with the need to keep my mouth shut. Delicate act. Wasn't sure which one was going to win. Honestly, it was going to be trouble either way.

"Sure is. Lexi is trying to sign her band, Black Addiction; saw them last week at a club in Brooklyn. She said they packed the house." Troy threw some more weight behind the cause. The conversation continued around me, even as the mother of all headaches took up residence in my frontal lobe.

"I saw her stuff on You Tube, they're tight." Alex nodded, the bastard not having any idea on what he was signing us up for, and I wasn't going to be neon-signing it for him either.

"C'mon! Angie?" Dan rolled his eyes, throwing his hands up in disgust. "Troy, did you snort some of Wade's nose candy before he left? She doesn't have the chops for a stadium. Besides, she hates us."

Had to admit, this was one time where I was happy for Dan to be running his mouth. Giving him a round of applause would have been too conspicuous, so I kept it on the down low, but I was a hundred percent behind his stance. The fact it wasn't me who was leading the anti-Angie movement was a fucking bonus.

"No, she hates *you*." Troy smirked. The Dan v Angie battles common knowledge.

"No, she fucking hates Jase, too."

The motherfucker had to go there. He couldn't have left it with his own reasons for not wanting her around. He had to go ahead and drag me into it.

"Hate is a pretty strong word, let's go with a strong dislike." I eased back into the chair knowing well enough that it wasn't going to be the last on the topic I was going to have to volunteer. Fucking Dan.

"Dan I understand, but why you, Jase?" Troy's raised eyebrow proving he had no idea what had happened between me and his sexy, barely legal neighbor before we'd hit the big time.

At least Dan had managed to keep a lid on it for longer than I'd ever imagined; I'd always had my suspicions that he'd spilled one time or another, but seems to be those concerns were unfounded. Who knew he had it in him. In the end, the violence was still happening. I'd just make sure I didn't punch him above the neck, keep the SOB pretty for the fans.

"Long story." Well at least it wasn't a total lie. "Let's just say I'm not her favorite person and move on, shall we." The less I said about the subject the better. Besides, it was fucking years ago. Why the hell were we dredging it all up now?

"I heard she has a voodoo doll of you." Dan stretched out his arms, anchoring them behind his head, his grin splitting off the side of his face. "Tell me, asswipe, do you feel any stabbing pain in your cock?"

"Dude, seriously. Can we focus here?" My shut-the-fuck-up vibe via the eyeball hopefully coming in loud and clear.

So remember how we talked about Jase version 2.0? It turns out some stuff can't be wiped away even after an upgrade. A one-night-stand seemed part of this system failure. Not that I would take it back. The memory of her, and that night, worth the grief I was catching now. God, she'd been perfect. Fuck. Maybe I had snorted Wade's nose candy. Would explain the crazy talk.

Thankfully Dan's tendency to say stupid shit was enough for the band to overlook his current hard-on to bring up the past, namely mine. His comments about me, Angie, and all things to do with my cock were left ignored as they moved on to the problem of no support band. Once again, I resisted the urge to fucking applaud. Seemed someone upstairs was throwing me a Hail Mary.

My thanks to all things holy took a strong and steady nosedive as Alex sold her virtues some more. "Ain't gonna lie, someone from the old neighborhood would be a fucking godsend right now. She knows us, we know her and last I checked isn't attending AA meetings."

Awesome, was he selling the band or nominating her for sainthood? James's head action telling me he'd already made his decision.

The recon went further, with someone stalking Black Addiction's Facebook page and mentioning they were playing a bar in Long Island. Someone else chimed in suggesting we jump into our ride and put this to bed ASAP. Whose voice was whose really didn't matter. It all spelled trouble.

"Angie fucking Morelli. I can't believe we are even considering this." Dan gave it a last-ditch effort to stop the insanity.

"Dude, she will probably say no." Or at least I'd hoped she would.

"Well we can stand here with hypotheticals or we can go fucking ask. Do you not remember her back in the day? She had killer pipes and played wicked guitar. I say we at least have to consider this." Alex squared off, his no-bullshit meter running overtime.

My problem was I remembered *exactly* how she was back in the day. I remember how I was, too. Bringing that on tour. A lit match in a fireworks factory stood a better chance. And I wasn't sure if I was more worried about her or me.

"Fine, let's go fucking ask and get shot down." Dan sunk his hands into his pockets as he reluctantly planted his feet on the floor.

"Awesome, should feel like old times for you then." Troy bucked out a laugh. "Let's just go see where shit lands. And keep your mouth shut."

Yep, where shit would be *landing* would be right in my fucking lap. This night could *not* get any worse.

2

Angie

THE MONEY I WAS MAKING WAS PATHETIC. SINGING MY ASS OFF FOR AN hour, working up a sweat, and I'd be lucky to cover the gas money it cost us to get to the gigs. Studio time? Ha! Only way we afforded that was courtesy of the day jobs we all were working, but I wouldn't have it any other way. On stage is when I could finally exhale, when I could finally be myself, and no amount of coin would ever be worth more than that.

"Angie, you want to go grab a burger or something?" Joey loaded the last of his kit into his beat-up Chevy Blazer.

"Nah, Pops needs me to open the shop tomorrow morning. I need to get home." The night air hit my skin. Even though I'd be jumping into my bed soon, it was going to be a while before I came down from my buzz. The crowd had been great, even more people than last time. Maybe soon we could talk Big Al into giving us a cut of the bar. We sure could use the extra cash flow if we were going to self-produce an album.

"You need a ride to your car? Where you parked?" Rusty lit up a cigarette, the blaze of the ash brightening as he inhaled. With his guitar slung around his chest and his amp in his hand, he was relegated to giving Joey a chin tip as he drove by us.

"See ya guys. My shift starts early." Max jumped into his

weathered Thunderbird, tossing his bass across the backseat. Both the car and his instrument had seen better days.

"See ya." I waved, my feet restless in my boots as I stood on the side of the road and refocused on Rusty. "I'm good, just down a little ways down the road."

Rusty gave me a look over, his finger flicking ash as he glanced down the street to where I said I was parked. His hesitation a hint he wasn't sold on me walking alone. "Alrighty. Be safe." He knew better than to argue.

"Bye." I gave him a wave as he hauled his guitar and amp into his Camaro and then slid into the driver's seat. The roar of his engine muffled our goodbyes.

Walking the streets didn't scare me. I'd grown up in New York, would probably die here too. But I wasn't some tourist with a death wish—just knew my way around. Happens when you spend most of your nights around the seediest part of town. Sadly, the *Rainbow Room* wasn't looking to book a rock band with second-hand instruments and fuck-you attitude. Who knew?

There she was, my most prized possession. The glow of the streetlight hit the cherry-red curves of my '69 Corvette as I'd made my short trip down the road. Pops and I had pulled her from the junkyard and rebuilt her from the chassis up. Took us years, but was worth every single minute. The car, and the time we spent together kept us sane after mom died. Poor man had no idea what to do with a teenage girl with an attitude. It was that car and the Harris family that saved us from all-consuming grief.

A hand grabbed my shoulder as I fished for car keys in my purse. It had been a dumb move, ignoring my surroundings while I took a trip down memory lane. I should have known better.

My body swung around, throwing off the hand on my shoulder as I faced my would-be attacker. He'd picked the wrong girl to mess with.

"Holy shit, Angie, put the gun away." Troy's eyes widened as he stared at the muzzle of my nine-millimeter. I'd flicked off the safety as I'd pulled it from my purse. The business end of my Glock pointed square at his chest.

"Troy? What are you doing here?" I lowered my gun and took

my finger off the trigger. Troy Harris, my old neighbor and drummer for a now famous rock band, was not who I was expecting to see on the dark, deserted streets of Long Island. "Didn't you have a show?"

"Yeah, we did." His eyes followed my hands as I flicked the safety back on and tossed my gun back into my purse. "When did you start carrying?"

"Since always." I shrugged. Like I said, I knew my way around.

"Hey, Angie, how you doing?" James slowly walked toward us, his band of merry men following close behind him. Great. Jason fucking Irwin. I resisted the urge to reach back into my purse and palm my weapon. Not to kill him, maybe just let a bullet wiz by. Scare him a little. The thought alone made me smile.

"Well, well, it's Power Station." Did they expect me to fucking bow down before them? Not likely. "You get lost on your way home from the Garden, boys?"

Even if I hadn't grown up next door to their drummer, there weren't many people in the city who didn't know who they were. The constant rotation on the radio took care of that, the billboards promoting their current domination of nationwide stadiums, a nice exclamation point.

Their still idling SUV was parked in Big Al's parking lot not far up the road. At least I wasn't totally losing my edge; Troy's footsteps had been masked by the residual noise spewing from Al's as the last drunkards left for the night.

"We actually came out looking for you. You'd already left the bar and some guy named Eric said you wouldn't be too far. Thought we could catch up for a chat." Troy flashed me a grin, the smile a peacekeeping effort if ever I saw one.

Mental note. Punch Eric right in the kidneys for giving out information about my whereabouts. I didn't give a fuck how famous anyone was, he needed to keep his big bartending mouth shut.

"It's almost midnight." My weight shifted on my feet, my hip leaning against my 'Vette. "Last time I checked I didn't owe any of you money, what's so important?" Their impromptu visit had my interest piqued more than I cared to admit.

"Can we go out for a drink?" James offered, his head tilting toward their waiting SUV.

Was he joking? The serious look he was giving me led me to believe he wasn't, but the fact none of the other band members had said anything had me worried. Even Dan was standing there giving his best rendition of a mime. Jason had kept his eyes glued to me the whole time, despite me not even glancing his way. Peripheral vision unfortunately meant he crept into my line of sight. Damn, he still looked good. No. Fuck that. Where the hell was that gun? I need to coldcock myself for even mentally going there.

"I have an early morning, not all of us made the cover of *Rolling Stone*." My keys jingled in my hand, signaling they should probably get lost. That was a cheap shot and I knew it. They'd deserved their success and I was just annoyed. At what? Well the jury was still out.

"Give us an hour, for old times sake." Troy flashed another grin. Crap. He knew I owed his family big time for everything they'd done for Pops and me. Saying no? Not an option unless I wanted my father to disown me. Goddamit. I'd hear him out, but whatever it was, I could already tell I wasn't interested.

"Fine, an hour." Which was sixty minutes too long as far as I was concerned if Jason was going to be present. The night had been so promising, too.

"*Tuesday's* is still open, let's head there." James tilted his head to their waiting ride.

Um. No. *Not* getting in a car with them was on the top of my to-do list.

"I'll drive myself thank you very much. My 'Vette doesn't need to be on the street any longer than she already has."

"Okay, see you there." James gave me a wave as I cranked open my car door.

An hour. I could do an hour.

"What are you having?" the bartender asked the minute we'd sat down. The Power Station express arrived a few minutes after I walked in. I had opted for sitting at the bar. It was less personal than sitting at a booth.

"A double of the twenty-year-old Macallan. Neat. He's buying." I pointed squarely at Dan, barely able to contain my smile as he shot me daggers.

"I'll buy." Troy rolled his eyes as he pulled out his wallet.

"No, *he* buys." Not going to lie, it gave me an irrational sense of pleasure to annoy Dan. Sure it was childish, but at least I could get some sense of enjoyment from this ... whatever *this* was.

"For fuck's sake, here." Dan pulled out a roll of cash and peeled off a hundred and slammed it on the bar. The distaste in his voice making me smile even wider. "Give her the fucking scotch."

"Thanks." I cracked my knuckles as the bartender poured the overpriced liquor into an old school tumbler. "So, gentleman. I'm assuming you're not here to reminisce about the good old days in the 'hood." Might as well cut to the chase, we were still on the clock as far as I was concerned.

"You're right." James once again took the lead. "We have a business proposition for you."

"Yeah, thanks guys but ..." I hadn't even had a chance to give them the no-thanks-there'd-be-a-cold-day-in-hell before James cut me off.

"We want Black Addiction on the road with us. Opening act. All dates, all cities." He didn't flinch. Was he actually serious? Offering an opening slot for a stadium tour like he was asking me to split an order of chili fries? He had to be high.

"Your opening act?" Cue my mouth hitting the floor and my eyes widening to unprecedented proportions, hell even my voice sounded weird. My effort to sound cool, calm and collected taking a back seat to freaking shock. "Don't you have those assholes from Tampa on your lineup?"

Their smug smiling faces had been featured on the tour billiard, and no it wasn't a case of sour grapes. *Unhinged Throttle* were *genuine* assholes. Their drummer had once gotten into a bar fight with Rusty over a look he'd apparently given him. A look, people. That's as dumb as starting a war over a Facebook status.

Alex's mouth spread into an amused smile. He'd always been a good-looking guy and the years had definitely not hurt him. Shame I'd never been into that. "Yeah that didn't work out, we want someone else. Someone we know." His voice just as smooth as I'd remembered.

"Sorry boys, not interested in being your feel good project." My ass slid off the bar stool in one fluid movement. I wasn't, nor would I ever be, a pity fuck. Any success and adulation we had coming to us would be earned, not because of a fence line that had once been shared. My feet pointed toward the door as I got ready to give them the see-you-later. Flipping them off would have been too bratty, even for me.

"Hey, aren't you going to drink your scotch?" Dan looked at the glass of amber liquid that sat on the bar untouched.

"Please, it's almost midnight. I have to be up in six hours. I'm not a raving alcoholic." I laughed, flicking my dark hair back for good measure. "I didn't want to drink it; I just wanted you to pay for it."

"Fuck, you're still a bitch." Dan grinned, almost as if he was glad I still was.

"And you're still an asshole, so we've established not much has changed." My brow arched, daring his comeback. Our game of tit-for-tat was juvenile, but it sure beat the hell out of thinking about the guy who was standing not more than five feet away. Despite not even throwing a greeting in my direction, his eyes had been boring holes into me since we started this little pow-wow. Another reason why I wanted to get the hell out of Dodge.

"Angie, come on. Give it some serious thought. This could open up a whole new world for you and the boys. Think of the exposure." Ever the salesman, James tried to negotiate. He didn't need to put in the effort; I knew what an opportunity like this could yield. Still—the offer—not one I wanted to consider.

"We don't need to ride anyone's coattails, thanks very much. We can do this shit on our own."

"Maybe you should let the band have a say? Instead of letting your emotions dictate your decisions." Jason unwisely opened his mouth for the first time.

Oh. My. God. Did he just accuse me of being emotional? Would he even know what the fuck that was? The man was soulless as far as I could tell. If he even tried that are-you-on-your-period bullshit, I was for real going to need to be held back. Did the motherfucker forget I had a gun? God, I'd been a dumbass when I'd gone there. Young and stupid—they were my excuses and I was sticking to them.

"My emotions?" I tried to rein it in, not wanting my *emotions* to get out of hand. "You think because I'm a woman, I'm being emotional? Head up your ass much? We have day jobs, asshole. We can't just quit and go on tour with you. Think about it. What happens after the tour, and we need to go back to our *regular* lives, pay our *regular* bills? Somehow I don't think I-played-with-Power-Station-three-months-ago will be enough to keep my lights on."

Our game of eyeball chicken continued with neither of us looking away. There was so much I wanted to do to him. Sadly, not all of it bad, and that just made me angrier.

"Okay, that's fair." Typical. James tried to diffuse the situation, ignoring the stare down Jason and I were playing. "What about you open for our next four shows, all the Garden? It won't interfere with your day jobs and we will more than make it worth your while. Gives us time to find someone else or alternatively you and the boys give us a number that will compensate for your time."

What was being offered was a chance of a lifetime. Seeking us out and telling me to give them a number was insane. No one got that lucky, certainly not girls like me. I wasn't sure if this was the break I'd be praying for, or if it would be selling my soul to the devil.

"Why us?" My head turned to James. I hadn't wanted to look away but it was going to be difficult to have a conversation *and* shoot the death glare, sadly I wasn't that talented. As far as I was concerned it wasn't conceding though, more just being polite. "There's a million dipshits out there who would kill to play with you. Why do you have a hard-on for us?"

"Because we need someone we trust," James sighed. Curiously, it seemed more than just fatigue wearing him down. Hard to believe that someone who was living their life could have problems that would lead to that kind of sigh.

Troy edged closer toward me, my feet still undecided if I was walking out the door or sticking around. "You've known us since before we made it, and never once have you tried to capitalize on that. Hell, lord knows you've got enough dirt on us from the early days, would have set you up for awhile."

"Yeah, well I'm not in the habit of selling out." And wasn't that the truth. "I'm not interested in that kind of singing."

"Which is why we want *you*. Angie, it's four shows. You hate it; you take the cash and walk. No questions asked. Worst case scenario you get to play stadiums instead of bars for a few nights and make a truck load of cash, best case you get put on the map." Troy joined James on the wear-Angie-down parade.

"Fine, but only because it's you asking me, Troy. But the band does its own thing. We play what we want." The only way I would be stepping on that stage was on our own terms.

"Your set, your rules. Complete creative control." James held up his hands in a show of his word.

"Well ..." My eyes measured them as I looked around at each member of the band. "I guess it looks like you've got yourself an opening act."

"You won't regret this." Troy pulled me in for hug, my heartbeat already ringing in my ears as the reality of what I agreed to hit me.

"Let's hope not."

ANGIE MORELLI.

She hadn't changed. Well, of course she was older and displaying a hell of a lot more ink than I remembered, but she could still get me from zero to one hundred just from looking at her. The multiple piercings up her ears were new, as was the edgier wardrobe. Those doe eyes she used to look at me with were gone though. Now, those big brown eyes were filled with attitude and hate. Not that I blamed her. Still, the piss-and-vinegar routine she had going on did nothing to hide how beautiful she was. She had to have noticed me staring at her, my eyes on her the entire time. And *time* had definitely been good to her. The way she filled out that T-Shirt and jeans was definitely enough to cause a re-rack in my pants. She looked good, and not in a way I wanted to leave alone.

"So what's the story?" Troy had paid me the courtesy of waiting until after we'd dropped off Alex and James before giving me the third degree. "I know she had a crush on you back in the day, but that was some evil eye she was throwing your way." Troy's sideways glance a hint he hadn't missed the arctic chill she was blasting in my direction. Not that she'd been trying to hide it. Hell, even the bartender felt the need to relocate to the other end of the bar, and we'd been the only people in the joint.

"Yeah Jase, what's the story?" Dan's shit-eating grin needling the situation. Unlike Troy, he *knew* the story. I'd stupidly confessed to him one drunken night early on, the guilt eating me up. And while he'd promised to take it to the grave, now it was out in the open, and he wasn't doing me any favors in trying to keep it buried. The asshole pleased that it wasn't him who was at the top of her shit list. Bad news for him was he was now located at the top of mine.

"No story. Just a misunderstanding. Not my finest moment." Yep, let's go with that. It wasn't only the stupidest thing I'd ever done but sadly, I'd kill to do it over.

Seeing her had lit a fire under my ass that I had been sure no longer existed. The stirring up of old emotions giving me a reality check. It was a knife's edge. And I wasn't just talking about the sex either. Although—yeah, let's not go there.

Well wasn't this just freaking great. My keeping-it-together shit about to be unhinged by a blast from the past. My nerves jangled with the need to get physical. The thought of having sex— not appealing, despite the hard-on I'd already worked up. Punching stuff suddenly sounded good. Wonder if Wade had checked out of his hotel yet?

"You wanna clarify that for me, brother? Angie is like a sister to me, and I'm not liking where this conversation is heading." The hard look he shot me was enough of a warning, the tone—exactly what I'd wanted to avoid.

Annnd here we go. I could dress it any way I wanted, but it was still going to be like entering RuPaul into the Miss America contest. All the fucking glitter in the world wasn't going to hide the fucking dick. In this case, the dick was me.

"Then best you stop hearing it now." Dan eased back into his seat, his grin getting even wider.

The motherfucker was enjoying himself and while he hadn't broken out the popcorn just yet, he was settling in for some payback. The karma bus had my name it and currently sitting behind the wheel was Dan fucking Evans.

"Angie and I have some history. Not all of it great."

Wow. That didn't sound bad. Not at all. Excuse me while I go kick my own fucking ass.

"Define, history." Troy's words were measured, controlled. Not good.

"I dated her once, nothing serious."

Sure, let's fucking pretend like it wasn't a monumental fuck-up on my part. Lack of judgment? Try, dumbest move I'd ever pulled. She was waaaaaaayyyyy too good for me, and like an asshole, I went there anyway. Of course the minute I came to my fucking senses, I did my best to fix the situation. Having her think she meant nothing was better than me ruining her life. Because that's what hitching your wagon to me meant.

"Translation, he fucked her." Dan piped in, freaking beaming with his addition to the conversation.

"Goddamit, Dan!" I slammed my fist on the inside of the door panel causing TJ, our driver, to turn around and give us the eye. It wasn't like me to lose my temper, but Dan talking about her being a fuck, well, she had never been a *fuck*. The bastard should be glad it wasn't my fist meeting his face.

"Fuck, dude." The loud exhale from Troy killing the silence we had going on. "When was this?"

"Before we all moved into the shady POS apartment in Harlem."

The memory had been buried but hadn't gone anywhere. I still remembered everything about that night, the way she smelled, how she smiled, the way she felt. Hardest thing I ever had to do was look at her after. Looking at myself? Try couldn't stand the sight of my own fucking face for weeks. Only thing I did right was walk away. Everything else was a fuck up for which I deserved to rot in hell.

"Wait a minute. Before we moved? She was like seventeen. I'm not liking this intel." The raised eyebrow and the tight jaw an added hint he wasn't cool with what he was hearing. No surprises. I wasn't cool with it either.

"Nope, she was eighteen. Might have been twelve-oh-one on her birthday, but she was definitely legal."

Like it mattered either way. Legal or not, my hands should

never have gone there, and yet they did. Not the nice guy everyone thought I was, because a nice guy would have regretted it. And as much as I wanted to, I couldn't make that happen.

"Jase was the gift that kept on giving." Dan tapped me on the shoulder because apparently he was done being annoying; we had to add patronizing to the mix.

"Dan, seriously stop." My fist connected with his arm. He even had the fucking balls to look surprised.

"You slept with her?" Troy's voice dripped with disappointment, and straight up I wished we didn't have to have this conversation. "How could you just sleep with her? That wasn't just some piece of ass, it's Angie."

"She wasn't a piece of ass." That control I had locked down all but splintered as I white-knuckled my fists. "She was never that."

I clocked Troy dead in the eye. "Look, I'm not proud of myself. She was sweet, and the flirting back and forth was cute, but she turned it up a little, and *cute* was no longer the word I was using to describe it."

"Keep talking."

"I swear to you, I wasn't going to go there, but it was the night before her birthday and we were drinking in your backyard."

"Okay, maybe stop talking."

She had been pure.

Not in that she'd been a virgin, as in she was untouched by the world and all its evil. I could tell just by looking in her eyes. It was like looking out on a calm lake on a warm day. The sun hitting the surface, the tiny ripples across the top. Inviting, calm and a fucking peace I'd never known could exist. It had been for that reason, in addition to me not wanting to do jail time, that I'd kept away from her for so long.

That kind of beautiful, that kind of purity, didn't belong with me—in any capacity. I knew it. I knew it every single time I was around her, and still, I wanted her. Not just sexually—although she was the hottest thing I'd ever seen—but because I wanted to feel that peace, even if it was just once. Complete dick move, selfish and fucking uncaring, but I needed it. Just to prove to myself that it was actually real.

That night, the night I caved, I'd been worn down fighting it. Talked myself into believing that all she was after was a fun night. Her mouth had been sprouting silly, drunk talk about needing a man to kiss her properly and that's all it was supposed to be. A kiss. Problem was that when I started, I couldn't stop. I didn't want to stop and figured that if I made her come hard enough it would even out the fact I was an asshole that didn't deserve to lay with her, much less have sex with her.

I used her that night—not for sex like I used other women— but for warmth. To feel the sun on my face again.

"Anyway, the reality hit the next day. Waking up with her. She was so damn sweet, dude. You knew who I was back then, that man was not for her. So as much as it made me an asshole, I told her it was a mistake and that it couldn't happen again."

"Let me guess, she didn't feel all warm and fuzzy after you slept with her and then dumped her."

"It wasn't like that." The anger surged in me again. *She was never like that.* "I never wanted to hurt her in that way, which is why I had to end it. No way did I want that for her. I'd rather her think the worst of me than *know* it. Trust me, any hurt she felt would have been a holiday compared to reality."

Troy and Dan knew my history. They'd both seen it with their own eyes. Sleeping with her had been a mistake, trying to have a relationship? We're talking fall out of biblical proportions.

"Still, dude." Troy shook his head. "This is not the kind of shit I would have expected from you. Dan, maybe. But not you."

Dan's face contorted in horror. "Why am I being dragged into this? I didn't screw her."

Mention of Dan with his hands on her, even in the hypothetical, made me move before I even knew what I was doing. Someone as sweet as her being with him, being with *anyone* made me glad I no longer carried a gun. Irrational as it was, no one would ever be good enough for her.

"Jase, what the fuck?" Dan's eyes widened as my brain registered that my hands were gripping the front of his shirt, my teeth pitbulling at his face.

"I'm sorry." My fingers let go as my eyes flicked from Dan back to Troy. The big guy ten seconds away from getting involved. "Shit, man. I'm sorry."

"You cool?" Troy watched as I settled back into my seat. My nod doing little to convince either of us I was in fact *cool*. "Everyone needs to calm down. It's Angie. After her mom died she spent more time at my house than her own. I don't want to imagine *anyone* screwing her."

He and me both.

"All I can do is say I'm sorry. It never should have happened, but I want to be clear about one thing. I never saw her as a piece of ass. Ever. She was beautiful and sweet and I wanted to be a part of that. Yeah, I was an asshole, I'll own that, but it wasn't just means to a quick fuck for me."

If things had been different, maybe it could have worked out. Who was I kidding? It still would have ended up in flames. I was even less capable then than I was now of doing the happily shacked up thing.

"I'm not the one you should be apologizing to, dude." Troy's you-need-to-talk-to-her look transmitted loud and fucking clear.

"Yeah, well I'll go see her."

It was time I manned up and had the conversation anyway. Apologize for being a dick, let her yell at me and then hopefully we could move on. I mean, how bad could it be?

"You better."

The bell jingled as I pulled open the door. The morning commute to the *old neighborhood* hadn't been pleasant, my mind churning over thoughts like clothes in a dryer. I hadn't grown up here, but it felt more like home than Albany did. If my folks still didn't live there, I'd never go back. Even my brother and sister had shipped out. My memories of that place not pleasant. The people—I'd been trying like hell to erase from my mental space.

"Well, well, twice in twenty-four hours. I'm literally giddy from the Power Station overload." Angie scowled as she leaned up against the counter, her tits straining against the *Joe's Garage* T-shirt she was wearing. Fuck, this was going to be harder than I thought.

"Can we talk?"

Her eyes narrowed, giving me her answer before she'd opened her mouth.

"I'm at work, Jason. I haven't got time to socialize." The empty shop not convincing me she didn't have five minutes to spare. Regardless, I owed her an apology and my feet weren't going anywhere until I'd given her one.

"Hey Angie, you need me?" Joe wandered in from the connecting work bays. The rag in his hand wiped off the grease as he walked through the doorway into the office space.

"All good, Pops, just an uptight loser driving a muscle car." Angie turned to open a filing cabinet and shoved invoices into a drawer. Didn't look like an adequate filing system to me, but I wasn't about to argue.

"Hey, Jason." Joe's face spread into a smile as he put out his hand. "I haven't seen you in years. You guys did good, huh? Been awhile since you've been in the old neighborhood."

"Thanks, Joe." My hand clapped against his, returning his handshake as I gave him a nod. "Yep, it's been a while. Life has been keeping us busy."

My eyes shifted to Angie curiously. I'd half expected Joe to come at me with a tire iron not a handshake. Clearly, I hadn't been the only one who'd been keeping our past on the quiet.

"Sure, sure." He loosened his grip and glanced over at Angie. "You two kids just catching up or you need something for your Mustang?"

"No, she's great." The car I meant. Angie, not so much.

"Okay, well I'll leave you to it." He shoved the dirty rag into his pocket as he moseyed back to the doorway he'd come in from. "Don't be trusting any of those fancy city boys with the car if she needs work. You bring her here. We'll take care of it, right, sweetheart?"

"Sure, Pops." The smile she gave was for his benefit, the eye roll for mine.

He disappeared, shutting the door behind him.

"You obviously didn't tell him."

For a second I thought I saw something in her eyes other than distaste. That she had hidden our horizontal history to save us both.

"You're still alive aren't you? If he *knew,* you would be laying on the floor doing a little less breathing."

"Look Ange, I'm so—"

"Save it," she hissed, cutting me off before I'd gotten a chance to finish my sentence. "I don't give a shit. It was a lifetime ago, right? You think I've been sitting in my room crying my eyes out over you? Wow, your head is even further up your ass than I thought."

The venom was real. The hostility she was throwing today about ten times what it had been last night.

"You don't give a shit?" My head tilted as I tried to get a read on her. "But you won't let me talk either. Doesn't sound like you *don't give a shit.*"

My mission had been clear. Go, say sorry and smooth it over. Let her swear at me for a bit if necessary; hell I'd even let her take a swing if she wanted. All of it, well and truly deserved. But seeing her lie to me was something else. No matter what words were coming out of her mouth, things were most definitely not fucking fine. And that didn't sit well with me.

"You can say all the words you want, just not to me." She tried to keep her voice down, but I could tell it was a struggle. "I don't have to listen. So get back in your car and drive out of here."

Two choices.

Escalate or eject.

Any other girl and there'd have been no consideration. That big pile of drama could have stayed right where it was as I waved goodbye. Sayonara. So long. Yet my feet stayed exactly where they were. And it wasn't because she was drop-dead beautiful. It was a need in me to set things right that was of unparalleled importance. Not for the band. Not for my fucking reputation. For her.

"Angie, we need to be cool with each other."

That wasn't so much a request as it was a promise to myself.

"You want us to be cool?" Her eyes got wide like I'd said I wanted to french kiss the GTO parked out front. "We're as cool as we get, Jase. Any cooler and penguins would be starting a fucking colony."

"Noted. But your water under the bridge bullshit isn't fooling anyone."

"Don't flatter yourself. Moody bitch is my resting face. You weren't that special."

There was so much I could've said and yet what I wanted most to do was kiss that fucking mouth of hers. The exact one that had been calling me an asshole. Because clearly, not only was she right on that count, but also because I was deranged. Wanting her. Wanting this.

"We're not done here."

Another promise. And one I'd be making good on soon.

"Oh, yes we fucking well are." Her hands slammed down on the counter in between us, her chest heaving as she sucked in a breath.

"No, we're not."

My eyes locked onto hers, so much being said without even opening our mouths, and she was the first to look away.

One thing was for sure. That baggage that evidently just got FedEx'd to our doorstep was being dealt with. And as for the band, none of it would land on them. Hell, it had stopped being about the tour the minute I'd walked in.

I gave her a look over before moving to the door. Her eyes did their best to try and meet mine but for the most part, she came up empty.

My hand hesitated on the handle, my body having a hard time leaving the unfinished business. *Not now, soon,* the familiar jingle of the doorbell rang as I yanked open the door ready to leave. "See you tonight," I said, looking back one last time. Her mouth opened and closed a couple of times before she settled on flipping me off.

Well that went well.

Fire meet gasoline. Let's get cozy shall we?

The 'Stang seemed to drive itself back to my apartment, which was a bonus cause my mind was in another zip code. The purr of the engine letting me know that while we'd made it back to my apartment, I had yet to cut the ignition.

Yeah, she hadn't gotten under my skin. Not. At. All.

"What's this, an intervention?"

The Troy welcoming committee was standing by my front door as I walked out of the elevator. My suspicion, it wasn't a friendly let's-hang visit.

"Did you talk to her?" Troy didn't waste any time with the inquisition, drilling me before I'd had a chance to get my keys into my door.

"Yeah, she wasn't in a chatty mood though. Wouldn't hear my apology." I neglected to mention the other stuff. His need-to-know limited to the earlier part of the conversation.

"Well, that's a problem then." Troy followed me into my apartment, not needing an invitation.

"Troy, I've got this okay. No need to worry."

Ha! Even I sounded convinced. Good job, Irwin.

"So did she talk to you at all?" Troy parked his ass on my couch as I tossed my keys on the counter.

"Just enough to tell me she wasn't my number one fan. I believe she also mentioned my head was up my ass as well. In any case, she isn't some evil vindictive bitch who's going to sabotage the tour just to get even." My butt hit the opposite two-seater as I gave Troy the only debriefing he'd be getting.

The stuff I said about Angie pulling it together, I had absolute faith in. Confident she loved that stage more than she hated me.

"She isn't the only one I'm worried about here. That shit in the car with Dan. Haven't seen you lose your cool like that for a while. You aren't feeling nostalgic are you?"

The man sitting across from me had seen me at my worst. The whole band had. My polished, have-all-my-shit together persona was a far cry from the dude they'd first met. But those days were over. The drinking and fighting hadn't been an issue in years. And while the aggression that churned through my body hadn't left, I had found a more acceptable outlet for it.

Sex.

And what do you know. Being in a rock band meant there was plenty of that on offer. Even keyboard players got lucky. Talented fingers and all that jazz.

"Oh for fuck's sake." My lack of desire for D and M at all time high. "I'm not allowed to have a bad day? I'm fucking solid, Troy."

Trust me. No one wanted a rerun of my past less than me. That cry me a river shit had more than taken up enough of my time.

"If you say it, then I'm going to have to believe you are on the level with me. But Jase, shit changes, we talk it out. Don't think for a second I won't get involved if you don't." Troy's hard stare told me he wasn't kidding.

"Listen to me, brother, I know all this Angie stuff might seem like it's stirred the pot. But trust me on this. I'm good. Now we done sitting around in my living room like jerk offs?"

"Yeah, Yeah we're done."

4

Angie

"YOU ARE A MACHINE. YOU CAN DO THIS." THE REFLECTION THAT stared back at me wasn't so sure. No, it looked like I was going to puke my guts out. "Fuck!" I paced as my nerves got the better of me. It was just a bigger stage, nothing different. Fancier, bigger stage but still a stage. When the hell did I start getting stage fright? This wasn't me; the jangling feeling that was twisting my stomach into knots was not me. It was because of *him*, it had to be.

Seeing him again after all these years had thrown me off my game. Rattled my cage. It was the only explanation. Sure, let's put the blame squarely at the feet of Jason fucking Irwin. I liked the blame there. It felt familiar, I sure had laid more than the fair share of the blame there in the past. Not that I was jaded. Of course not. He broke my heart years ago but I wasn't bitter, I was just making sure it never happened again. EVER.

Not that there was any danger of it with him. Nope. No fucking chance. I was just mad I had to see his face again. Bring all those memories back. That's why I was so pissed off. His face.

I bounced on the balls of my feet like a prizefighter; trying to burn the extra adrenaline my adrenal gland seemed hell bent on secreting. I was over him; this shouldn't even be a problem.

So over him.

So over him it was hilarious.

I was so *not* over him.

He wasn't my first—boyfriend or sexual experience. He wasn't even my first heartbreak. Nope, that pleasure had gone to Tyler Farley. At sixteen he'd broken my hymen but had forgotten to give me an orgasm. It was horrible and messy and made me want to never do it again. But, I did and the next time wasn't so bad. Of course, after six months Tyler decided to dump me for Cindy Watts. She was a cheerleader. We weren't friends.

My poor little sixteen-year-old heart thought my world was ending when I spent those nights crying into my pillow. Little did I know the real heartbreak would come later.

Jason Irwin. That's where the real heartache lay.

Asshole extraordinaire.

Who still looked amazing.

And what the fuck was with his *we aren't done?* The guy must also be insane. Good looking and insane. Top two headers on his resume. Oh, and hot. Most definitely hot.

Great, now I was insane.

"You ready to knock them on their asses?" Rusty burst through the door without knocking, pulling me from a dangerous slide down memory mountain. I was supposed to be remembering the reasons why I hated Jason, not focusing on what his chest looked like underneath that shirt.

"I could have been naked, Rus." My attention was happily diverted to the six-foot-two blond guitarist in front of me.

"So, not like you've got anything I haven't already seen before. Plus, I know you've probably been dressed for like an hour." He shoved his hands into his worn jeans while his grin of satisfaction dared me to say that I hadn't. He wasn't wrong; I'd been dressed for over an hour and a half.

"Not an hour." I lied; the smile on my lips spelling out how little his interruption had bothered me. "And just because you've seen me naked once before doesn't mean you get to see it again."

"I know, and I die a little each day because of it." Rusty laughed before pulling me into a hug.

Rusty wasn't just a guy and my guitarist, he was my best friend. I'm not sure if it was because I was an only child or because I'd grown up in a garage, but for the most part the whole girlie gene was missing from my DNA. High school had been a nightmare with girls assuming my interest in cars had been an angle to steal their boyfriends. Consequently, I didn't have many female friends, so when Rusty transferred in tenth grade from another school, we became tight.

Him being so good looking didn't hurt, but neither of us had ever been attracted to each other. Trust me, we'd tried to hook up in the early days, thinking being that we were such good friends the sex would be super awesome too. But it just didn't work. We both ended up laughing before he'd even gotten the condom on, quickest mood killer ever. So instead of having sex, we spent the night drinking beers he'd stolen from his dad's beer fridge, and jamming to a Foo Fighters CD.

"So, I'll ask you again." Rusty shadow boxed before raising his voice. "Are. You. Ready?"

"As ready as I'll ever be." I blew out a breath, convinced the pep talk I'd tried to give myself hadn't done shit. So much for the power of positive thought. Fuck you, *Deepak Chopra*.

"I give you gold and you give me some lukewarm meh ... yeah whatevs." Rusty's grin twitched at his outer lips. "You're not nervous are you, Angie?"

"Me? No. We play in front of eighteen or so thousand people all the time," I mused sarcastically, wondering if I should be fussing with something. Messing around with my hair wasn't going to make me feel any better.

"Well stop doing whatever it is you're doing and get excited." He leapt onto the couch and raised his arms above his head. *"What we do in life echoes in eternity."* I knew I was in trouble now he'd started quoting *Gladiator*. "We're opening for Power Station at the Madison Square Fucking Garden!" He leaned across and gave me a shake. "This is our time."

I wanted to be happy. Knowing how much this meant to him, and the rest of the band. Hell, knowing what this meant to me. "Yep, dream come true." I just wished it had been any other band.

One that didn't feature Jason. Damn him, and damn me too. I hated that he still got under my skin.

"Well stop jerking off and let's do this thing. Joey's had three Red Bulls and is either going to have a heart attack or fly off the stage like Superman. I'm trying to tell him the 'gives you wings' tagline is just fucking advertising. I could use the reinforcements." He tapped me playfully on the arm.

"Give me a few minutes to get in my groove and I'll meet you stage side."

"Just don't take too long, I'm itching to plug in."

"I won't. I want this too."

Rusty gave me a quick wink and eased toward the door. "Remember, Angie. They want you, they just don't know it yet."

It had been our motto since we'd started the band. Knowing that if we could get out there and play, that's all we would need. Funny how much those words were messing with my head tonight. Maybe sometimes they didn't *want* you. Ugh. That was *so* not about the band.

"You nervous?" Troy tapped at the open door; the one Rusty had conveniently forgotten to close behind him.

"Well I wasn't until everyone started asking me. You worried, Troy? Think I'm going to make you look bad?" My arms folded across my chest as I turned to face him and smile. Where Rusty was my best friend, Troy was the big brother I'd never had. Sure, we hadn't been as close in recent years, but it didn't matter. It wasn't something that could be wiped away by time.

"Nope, I've seen you play. I know you deserve the shot." The easy smile on his face proved he wasn't worried. He'd always had faith in me, even when I didn't have any in myself.

"So this a social call?" My eyes fell toward the open doorway wondering if anyone else would be joining us or if this was just a Troy-Angie heart-to-heart.

"Yeah," Troy cleared his throat and rubbed his neck awkwardly. "So ... you and Jason?"

Silence.

Well the mystery of the need for a spontaneous chat had been solved. We didn't even need the few seconds of *Jeopardy* music to get us through. How much of it he knew was still unknown, and I'd rather keep it that way. Internally I cringed; it was like your dad catching you making out in your bedroom. Not cool.

"We are sooooo not having that conversation." Like ever.

"Awesome." Troy nodded, almost looking relieved.

Yeah, let's just sweep it under the rug and forget I had sex with one of your friends, shall we.

"So you going to stand there and freak me out some more? Rusty was just in here all reciting movie lines and jumping on furniture. And Joey is probably going to need a crash cart before our first song. I'm not a hundred percent convinced you are going to want us back tomorrow." It hadn't been a smooth transition of topic, but at least we weren't talking about Jason anymore.

"Just want to make sure you know that you can come to me. You know, if you need something. I promised your dad I had your back." Troy's eyes met mine. Something uneasy flicked through those hazel pools of his, maybe concern? Responsibility?

"Troy, I'm not a little girl anymore. You left, remember? You all did. I've been doing this without you having my back for a long time."

It wasn't to make him feel bad; honestly, I just didn't need him in the same way as I did back then. I was okay with the way things were, making my own way in the world. It sure as hell made me stronger.

"Well, regardless." He didn't look away. "The offer stands."

"Thanks." His endearing words thawed my hard-ass routine. I was losing my edge tonight, all these feelings. Gah. "But can you leave now? I wasn't kidding, you standing there is freaking me out."

"Sure, I'm leaving." He laughed, pulling me into a one armed hug. "Knock 'em dead, Angie."

The door closed behind him leaving me alone in the dressing room. It's where I found the most comfort. Not having to pretend. "I am a machine. I've got this." I peered back at my reflection.

Nope, still wasn't convinced.

Faces were a blur. The lights blinding me from seeing any definition other than raised hands in the air. The noise as they chanted—deafening. Except they weren't chanting for us.

I would change that.

I'd make them love us.

The stage plunged into darkness as we moved into position. The noise got louder as the anticipation rose, and still I could hear the thumping of my own heartbeat above the crowd.

One of my hands wrapped around the mic as I peered out into the darkness, the pop of an amp signaled Rusty was ready to go. This wasn't a rehearsal. This was the real deal, and we'd finally made it to the dance.

"One, two, three, four." Joey tapped out on his sticks as a wall of fucking lights ignited above us. The sound exploded from every direction as we launched into our opening number.

There was no pretentious introduction. Fuck that. We didn't do that shit. If the crowd wanted to hear stand-up they should have gone to the *Comedy Lounge*. We were here to rock, and that was exactly what we were going to give them.

My body moved as I slipped into the familiar trance and every single hesitation I'd had of being on the stage dissolved. It didn't matter how I'd gotten here, I deserved to be there now. It was mine to own, and I'll be damned if I was leaving any of it unclaimed. I was home.

The boys were just as electrified as I was, the energy on stage, fevered. Joey thinking he was Superman was right on the money. I was right there with him, and tonight I could fly.

One song.

That's all it took and I had the crowd eating out of our hands. I didn't care if the attention was fleeting, if it was just until they got their Power Station main course. For those forty-five minutes, they were mine. Some even knew some of the lyrics, singing them back to me by the time I'd hit the chorus. It was the ultimate high and there wasn't a drug, either natural or synthetic, that could even come close.

Then all too soon it was over.

The final note echoed from the PA as we left our instruments where they stood and waved goodbye to the crowd. And as someone killed the lights and we walked off the stage, there wasn't any doubt left. The applause that was still ringing in my ears—that had been for us.

"That was better than sex." Joey twirled his stick as he walked beside me, the grin on his face a mile wide.

"You saying that just proves you've been doing it wrong all these years." Rusty chuckled as he grabbed a towel from a roadie. "Trust me, it's better when a woman is involved, not just your hand."

"It's not better but comes a close second. Sorry Joe, I'm with Rusty on this one." Max piped in, snagging a Gatorade on his way toward us. His grin just as wide as the rest of us.

"Angie, back me up on this one. You get it, right?" Joey wasn't giving up.

"Not taking sides, boys. As far as shows, that one was pretty freaking awesome."

"Nice set." Jason stepped out, seeming to materialize from the dark. It was kind of creepy if you asked me but I was in too good of a mood to care.

"Thanks." The word slipped from my lips before I'd had a chance to substitute a fuck-you or I-don't-give-a-shit-what-you-think. He'd caught me off guard while I was feeling post-show-happy.

"Was that a smile, Angie?" A satisfied grin spread across his mouth. Jerk.

"I smile, Jason, just usually after you leave. It's less manufactured that way." Ha! See, I was back in the game, my response prompting my smile to widen.

"Yeah, most girls are left smiling after I leave." He wasn't annoyed, he was smug. "You're right, nothing manufactured about that."

Asshole.

"Well, we might get going then shall we?" Joey jerked his head toward the door making it even more awkward. Clearly he didn't want to stick around for a game of verbal tennis. "See ya, Jase. Have a good show."

"Right behind you, buddy. Later, Jase." Max followed Joey down the hall as they bailed. Lightweights, both of them.

"What about you? Have somewhere else you need to be?" Jason moved closer, giving Rusty a hard look. He seemed to enjoy the fact that my other two band mates had scattered.

"Nope, I like this vibe the two of you have going." Rusty eased back onto the heels of his feet. "It's like HBO but without the nudity. Not sure if you are going to challenge each other to a duel or a dance off. Just FYI Jase, Angie does a killer running man."

I wasn't sure who cracked first, probably Jason, both of them were laughing their asses off. Jase clapping his hand across Rusty's back. "You're okay, dude."

"Yeah, you're not bad either." Rusty—who moving forward would be known as the traitor—gave him an easy smile.

Great, my best friend and the man that I despised were falling into a weird bromance.

"Would you two like a moment to make out? I can leave if you want."

"Don't be jealous, Ange. Listen Jase, as much as I'm sure you would enjoy it, I'm not into dating dudes. My heart just belongs to the ladies."

Seriously, we were going to be having words when I got Rusty alone.

"You can leave anytime, Rus. I think I've got it from here."

Instead of vocalizing my *displeasure*—which I'd already established I'd be doing later—I gave Rusty aka Traitor one of my death stares. He'd been around me long enough to know *the look* wasn't an idle threat.

"Fine, fine. Keep your hairy-eye ball for Jason. I'm leaving." Rusty pulled me into a hug. "I'll see you in the dressing room. See ya, man." The latter part of his goodbye for Jason's benefit.

"Later." Jason smiled as we watched Rusty leave.

Our earlier conversation hadn't been forgotten.

All that fantastic tension, his threats of not being done.

All still there.

But what I hadn't been able to achieve with my pep talk in the mirror had magically happened on stage. Jason on my care factor wasn't rating highly. Not now at least, with that buzz still coursing through my veins. I couldn't even stop the smile if I wanted to. See that's how good performing was, it was able to wipe away bad feelings. In the short term. And currently that was the only term that counted.

"He seems like a nice guy." Jason's eyes flicked from the hallway to where Rusty had disappeared. My smile possibly giving him false hope.

"He's the best guy."

Rusty was undeniably the best kind of guy, especially if we were talking about the present company. While I was happy, I wasn't delusional. And I did say that buzz was short term.

"Are you two together?" Jason tilted his head to the side as he studied my face.

Were we together? Did he mean sleeping together? The question had thrown me so much that I didn't even ask why he wanted to know. "Does it matter?"

"I guess it doesn't, I'm just curious."

There was no waver in his voice, no shrug, no hint of whether he wanted the answer to be in the positive or the negative.

It was a weird stalemate. Where I wasn't sure if his indifference upset me or I welcomed it. At least he wasn't trying to apologize anymore, hearing him say he was sorry just dug the knife in deeper. Thinking that night had meant more than it did was bad enough, having his pity ... No. He wouldn't get the satisfaction.

That's why I refused to hear him out earlier. It's why I refused to enter the conversation. Yes. I was angry. Yes, I was probably bitchier than I needed to be. Yes, it was a long time ago. But I'd changed that day and there was no going back to the naïve girl.

Funny how I'd practiced this moment for years, all my insults lined up in a row ready to hurl at him and now I had not a one. Was it too much to wish for some rogue occurrence to transpire? An earthquake or a freak hurricane? Anything to give me an out.

Something so it didn't look like I was running. It didn't have to be fancy. A blackout would suffice.

"Hey Jase, James was looking for you."

That random act of God I'd been praying for appeared in the form of production crew.

"Thanks, man. Tell him I'll be right there." Jase answered without moving his eyes from mine, not giving me a reprieve.

"Looks like you're being summoned. Have a good show, I've got to get changed."

The words thankfully tumbled out of my mouth. They were good words too—concise, non bitchy and not too familiar. I liked them. They made up for all the ones I couldn't formulate while I was standing there wondering if every single time I looked at him I was going to have wild mood swings.

Honestly, I'd rather not feel anything, but currently I was swaying somewhere in between stab-him-in-the-eye anger and why-did-you-break-my-heart anger. Trust me, even though anger was the common denominator, they were still very different.

"Stick around, Angie. Things have changed."

There were so many minefields in that sentence my brain couldn't compute. Did he mean tonight's show, the tour or him? Reading into it was just plain crazy, because *whatever* he meant, didn't matter. Not to me, at least.

That girl, the one who would have cared, was gone and now I was in her place.

"You're right. Things have changed."

ANGIE MORELLI WAS A LOT OF THINGS: BEAUTIFUL, ANGRY, VOLATILE *and* motherfucking hypnotic on stage. If she'd been good the last time I'd seen her perform, she blew me out of the water now. It wasn't that she could sing—she'd always had a killer set of pipes—she had a presence. The shit that you can't learn—the ability to work it and own it—she had it in spades.

So what was she going to do after this? Go back to playing grease monkey and turn her back on what she had tonight? Play some random gig in a dive bar in Butt-fuck, USA to get her thrills? Fuck that.

Her bullshit I'm-going-to-do-four-shows-and-bail deal wasn't going to fly. Not if I had anything to do with it.

Pushing the issue wasn't something I usually did. My laid back approach reaching legend status. Not because I didn't care, but because I knew there was a bigger picture. And while it was usually someone else coming up with some dumbass scheme and me sitting around watching the fireworks, my hands were rubbing together in the anticipation.

News Flash. Angie and her band were staying on the tour.

Of course she hadn't been informed yet.

We'd get to that.

Along with all the other issues.

Oh. And won't that be fun. That rumored voodoo doll was probably going to get a workout.

Did I give a shit?

Nope, not a one.

I wasn't stupid enough to think her recent thaw was going to be her regular disposition. Though I had to admit, that smile of hers, I'd forgotten how damn sweet it was. Hopefully I'd be seeing more of them. Even if those smiles weren't directed at me. Not that I wanted to see them directed at some other asshole. Yep, 'cause that made all the fucking sense in the world.

Besides, from what I could work out she was dating her guitarist. And as long as he treated her right we'd have no problems. Yeah, yeah—the fucking irony. Pot. Kettle. I'm an asshole. Let's move on.

So being that we weren't going to be BFFs anytime soon, I was going to need to enlist some help. And I wasn't above playing dirty. Not when the end justified the means. It's not like she could hate me anymore than she already did. Fuck. It. I'd take her death stares and anything else she had to throw at me if it meant giving her that happiness. Which is what she was going to get. And the first part of that was keeping her on this tour.

"Hey Rusty, you got a minute?"

Surprisingly he hadn't been too hard to find. While our original support act had taken to channeling their inner *Jane's Addiction*, Rusty, Max and Joey had been chilling with the sound engineers and lightening director at control. They'd watched our show at the desk and were shooting the breeze with our crew.

Still wasn't sold he was the right guy for her, but he seemed responsible so at the very least he had my respect. Had to wonder why he was without his girl.

Not that it was any of my business. Or at the very least *should not* have been any of my business.

"Hey Jase, isn't the stalker routine a little embarrassing for you?" He gave me a big ass grin. "I already told you we weren't making out."

The peanut gallery erupted into laughter. They were easily amused.

"Yeah, I know but you can't blame a guy for trying." I played along with his freaking rouse, not wanting to have this conversation with the rest of band in tow.

Not sure what arrangement they had but I wasn't convinced one of them wasn't going give Angie a full report. The less people knew about it the better, and given I hadn't even had a sit down with my own band, I didn't think broadcasting in front of a crowd was a smart idea. Gossip on tour spread as easily as sniffles at a kiddie daycare.

"You wanna grab a beer?" I tipped my head to the doorway, having no intention of actually drinking.

"Oh, yeah. Sure." Rusty stood up, joining me as I moved away from the group.

Responsible and not stupid. Rusty earned another nod. Still didn't mean I liked him with her.

"So aren't you supposed to be shaking babies and kissing hands or some shit like that? You going AWOL from the meet-and-greet?" Rusty wasn't wasting any time getting to the what-do-you-want. I had to hand it to him. There was no bullshit with him. I could see why he was tight with Angie.

"It was a short one, the guys have their girls and kids they were anxious to get to."

The addition of wives and offspring had dramatically changed the landscape. The fact that these additions weren't mine didn't bother me at all. I loved having the girls and the kids running around. Besides, after years on the road there were only so many sets of tits you could sign before it all became a major snore.

"So you came to find me, should I be worried or flattered?"

Because bullshitting wasn't in my bag of tricks and I had zero inclination to add it now, I figured I'd cut to the chase. The deserted hallway served as good a venue as any to have the conversation.

"Listen, you guys were really great out there tonight. Tight sound, great vibe, low on the theatrics. It was a solid show."

"Thanks. Why am I feeling like there is a *but* coming?"

"No *but*, I was just honestly surprised. Not going to lie, I expected an unpolished bar band and assumed you guys would choke. I can admit when I'm wrong."

Me being surprised wasn't a lie. While I'd assumed Angie was going to be great, the other guys were an unknown quantity. And considering they'd had no prep time and zero lead up, the adulation I was giving them was well deserved. Not that it changed my reason for this secret squirrel meeting. And as much as I manned up when I was wrong, it was more about getting Angie locked in for rest of the gigs and less about patting them on the back.

Rusty shot me a look as he tried to work out my angle.

"Ok-ay. So. Is there somewhere we are going with this other than giving me an ego stroke? I prefer them a little lower to be honest, and by a girl, no offense."

"It's not an ego stroke, I'm just hoping you are seriously considering staying on the tour." And get your lead singer to agree, because we all knew *that* would be the deciding factor.

I'll admit I left out the last part. No point to rock the boat. Just because he seemed like a decent guy, didn't mean I immediately trusted him. In fact, I didn't trust him. And yet, we were still having this conversation so I guess I cared more about this girl than I'd first admitted.

"Is this a serious offer, or you just getting me hard for when your lawyers come to fuck me?" Rusty looked like this was the first he was hearing of it. It wasn't the fake kind of surprise either; it was a genuine I-haven't-heard-this-shit-before kind. What do you know; Angie hadn't been on the level with them.

"Wait a second, what contract did you sign?"

I pulled the pin and threw the grenade. And wait for it. Three ... two ... one.

"The one that said we were doing four shows with you. A bunch of fine print BS I didn't read, but basically unless we fucked up, we are your NYC band."

Rusty confirmed what I already assumed. Four show deal. Angie had no intention of filling the rest of the dates. Why the hell would she throw away an opportunity like that? I knew *exactly* why she'd throw away an opportunity like that. Yeah, and it wasn't sitting well with me.

"So you didn't know about our offer?"

"What offer? More cities?" Rusty's shrug more evidence that he had no idea what had been put on the table.

Angie had invited them to dinner but was only going to let them have appetizers and now here I was offering them the opportunity to stay all the way to dessert. I probably should have felt bad, going behind her back. And yet, my conscience was clear. If you wanted to get technical, I was just merely disclosing information that should have already been shared. Yeah, let's pretend like she wouldn't want to rip my balls off when she found out. Honestly, the thought of her hand on my balls made me smile. I really was a sick bastard.

"All dates, all cities. The offer was the *whole* tour."

"Huh?" Rusty's eyes got wide as I saw the mental cogs in his head ticking. "The whole thing?"

"Yes, James, Alex, Troy, they hadn't had the same reservations I'd had about you guys." I figured some backstory about how they'd came onto our radar would be helpful. Shake off some of the holy-shit that was floating around. "Lexi our—"

"Yeah, we know who Lexi is." He didn't give me a chance to finish. "She is trying to get us to sign, said she can get us a deal."

"Yeah well, *her* interest in you and Troy's recommendation had pretty much sealed the deal. Of course your performance tonight spoke for itself, they were right on the money."

"So, let's go around this one more time. The offer was for the whole enchilada but we only signed on for New York." Rusty proved he was a quick study by following right along with me. No doubt having some serious questions for his front woman/ girlfriend. Not sure how I wanted *that* to go.

"Angie hadn't been as *excited* on the offer as the guys had hoped. We thought she might come around."

Oh she'd been *excited*, excited to tell us to shove it, but I didn't think that it would add anything to the argument so chose to paraphrase.

"Dude, listen. Me and you are cool, I've got no beef with you. Sure we didn't really know each other back in the day, but from what I remember you seemed like a stand-up guy. But this divide and conquer shit, isn't the way we run our band. Straight-up, what are your motives here?"

So I guess he was smarter than I thought.

"You've known Angie for a while, right?"

"Yeah, since tenth grade."

"You and her ..."

Dating? Fucking? Not sure which of the words I was looking for. Neither word seemed to want to come out of my mouth when it came to her. We'd already established that for some reason the thought of Angie and another dude poked my inner Godzilla. Seriously need a handle on that ASAP.

"Dude, please don't make me fucking punch you right now. Like for real, I know I'm a guy and stuff, but that hitting each other and other macho bullshit gives me a headache. I'm a lover not a fighter, but if you start being disrespectful about Angie I'm going to have to lay you out. I won't enjoy it, but I will fucking do it." He squared off, ready to engage if he needed. At least she wasn't dating a pussy. That was a small consolation.

"Trust me, disrespectful is the last thing I am trying to be. There's some shit that went down in our past, Angie and me. I don't want to start shit between you two if you were...a thing."

Thing was such a shitty word but what else was there? *If you two are together?* It's not like they were sharing class rings. Why the hell couldn't I just say the fucking words? Angie had every right to fuck other dudes. Why was this shit messing with my head so much?

"You worried I was going to get territorial, thinking you were going to mack on my girl?"

"Look, you don't have to worry about me trying to put the moves on your girl. Whatever happened between us is ancient history."

The chances of me putting the moves on were laughable at

best. Considering she shot me death stares every time she looked at me, I'd say us getting busy were … yeah, last time I checked it still wasn't snowing in hell.

"No, Angie and I aren't dating. Never have. She's my best friend but bumping uglies isn't our thing."

Not that the new piece of info should have ranked on my give-a-shit meter one way or another, but it did. The reason why that little nugget made me smile was still a mystery but I would tuck it away for later. Like perhaps when I came to my senses and realized Angie's dating status wasn't any of my business.

"Yeah, well then maybe you can talk her around. I'm not sure why she doesn't want to take up our offer but me trying to convince her isn't going to do it."

Well wasn't that a lie if ever I heard one. Pretty sure the reason she wasn't interested was what stared at me in the face when I looked in the mirror.

"So you want me to run interference."

Bingo. The boy had skills, let's see him put them to use and convince our girl she needed to play ball. Wait? Our girl? What the fuck? *His* girl.

"I'm not saying blindside her, just maybe talk about what the tour could do for the band. Get her to think of the big picture."

My motives were pretty clear. Angie. Tour. End of story. But I could see that while Rusty wasn't dating her, they had this whole watch each other's back thing going on. The asshole in me also knew that Angie wouldn't want to disappoint her buddy either. Two birds, one stone and all that.

"You know." Rusty took a long exhale before eyeballing me. "One thing I do remember about the good ole days was the huge crush Angie had on you. Then all of a sudden, nothing. Like she just got over you. That wouldn't have anything to do with this, would it?"

Yep, it took him about ten seconds to join the dots.

"That's probably something you should ask her."

"Yeah, sure nothing shady about that answer." Rusty rolled his eyes.

"Please, just talk to her." *And maybe clue me in when you do.*

"Oh I'll talk to her, but not because you want me to."

"Whatever it takes."

Angie

WHILE THE BOYS HAD STUCK AROUND AFTER POWER STATION HAD finished, I had high-tailed it out of the arena. Best decision I'd ever made.

After our set, Max had recognized one of the guys who were mixing the show so we had sat at the sound desk and watched the show with the crew. Not only was it cool to see it from there, but it also meant there was zero chance of running into the band. Because running into Jason once was more than enough for one night. Who cares if he still looked like he could bench a Ford Focus? I bet he was still ripped under that shirt too. The ink he'd added since the last time also did an awesome job of making those arms look hot.

Stop.

It didn't matter how much he resembled an action figure, we were not going there. *There* was trouble. I had already been *there,* remember?

Ugh! I hated him so much.

"Hey, you know that *tune and lube* sign at the front is very distracting. I'm not sure if I should be popping my hood or looking for a happy ending." Rusty pushed open the door of the shop. The bells jingled to announce his arrival as he strode through the doorway, his eyes still a little bloodshot from the late night.

"I'm pretty sure we have a shop vac out the back, the sign below it says satisfaction is guaranteed." I couldn't help but yawn. It had been next to impossible to get sleep last night. And if I was honest with myself, it hadn't only been the buzz from the concert that had kept me tossing and turning through the early hours of the morning.

"You didn't even blink. It's not the first time you've been asked, is it?" He looked disappointed. Like anything that could come out of his mouth would shock me.

"Nope, not even close."

"So let me ask you something?"

With Rusty that *something* could have been anything. He had issues with boundaries so it very easily could have been either extremely rude or ridiculous. He'd asked me for tampons once for a nosebleed.

"Sure." I hoped this conversation wasn't going to be to out there considering we were both sleep deprived.

"Do you remember that day we went out to *Coney Island* and we rode the Cyclone until you puked?"

Ummmmm. What? I had absolutely no idea where this conversation was going.

"Yeah, of course I do. It was my eighteenth birthday, and to be fair I was hung over. I can handle my coasters thank you."

"You play it out in your head however you want to, babe, but that day your ass got owned." Rusty broke into a smile.

That day had been terrible. He had assumed it had been the half bottle of vodka I had drunk the night before that had made me sick. True, I was a lightweight back then and even a ride on the bus would have made me nauseous, but the real kicker had been something else. Like waking up beside the guy you supposedly loved and have him thank you for the good time, and leave you like you were nothing special. Gah! I pushed that bullshit away from my mind.

"Okay, so, is this a weird way of suggesting we go to Coney Island? 'Cause I have to work and I'm not really in the mood."

"I was just thinking about that day." Rus leaned up against the counter, his eyes on me as he spoke. "Thinking about the reason why I had dragged your ass to Brooklyn in the first place. You had been crying that morning about the one-night stand you'd had the night before. Older guy who you thought was into you but turned out to be an asshole. What was his name again?"

Crap. Did he know? How could he know? I never told a freaking soul. It's not like the embarrassment that I had allowed myself to be used like a groupie hadn't been enough. I didn't want anyone else to know. That would have just added to my mortification.

"Ummm. I think we decided his name was going to be asshole." I had chosen some other names for him too, but those were for my private collection. They included a lot of swear words, with so many colorful variations.

"Yeah, funny how I never made the connection between asshole-one-night-stand and you suddenly losing interest in Jason Irwin of the Power Station variety. It all kind of happened around the same time, weird huh? That's some crazy ass coincidence."

He knew.

That lying, cock-sucking spawn of evil—see, variation—must have opened his big fucking mouth.

"You deduce this theory all by yourself Sherlock Holmes or is *someone* filling your head with fanciful ideas?" *Someone* being a bastard otherwise known as Jason Irwin or Dick-face, see another variation.

"So is *that* the reason why you didn't tell me that we were offered all the dates on the tour?"

He didn't blink. His focus was locked on mine as a flicker of hurt flashed in his eyes, catching me in my lie. Sure, I could dress it up in my head as something else, omission perhaps. But in the end, I had never told any of them the whole tour was a possibility. How could I? I knew the minute I did, they would be falling over themselves wanting to sign straight on the dotted line. There would be no questions asked, and they wouldn't have even wanted to hear the reason why we shouldn't. Not that any of those reasons really made any sense, not if I was really honest.

"Rus—" I swallowed, disappointed in myself.

"Look, I'm not mad that you lied." Rusty raked his hands through his hair in frustration. "Couldn't give a fuck, and I remember how much that asshole messed with your head. I was there, watching you cry because he made you feel like a cheap slut."

I blinked at his harsh words but he hadn't been wrong. That's exactly how it had felt. "And I'll owe you for that."

"You don't owe me shit. I did it because that's what we do. We're there for each other. But, we *are* going to do this tour."

There was no hesitation in his voice. And while there was no anger either, he had made up his mind, and there wouldn't be a thing I could say that would sway him.

It was lame to even attempt to convince him otherwise, but I couldn't help myself to try. "I'm not sure that's the right decision for the band. We'd have to give up our jobs. It's not even enough time to give notice—"

"Oh come on, Angie." He interrupted me, throwing his hands up in the air for dramatics. "I sell used cars for a living. You think Archie is going to give a fuck if tomorrow he has to get some other sucker to pimp his used Chevys?"

Silence.

When I didn't answer he continued. "Yeah, and they are going to miss Max at *Staples* too. Who the hell is going to run all those print jobs? I can hear the reams of copying paper weeping now. And as for Joey, I don't even know what the fuck he does." His brow crinkled in confusion. "Does he even have a job?"

"He's a valet." Well at least he was this week. He'd been a bus boy last month, and a waiter at *TGI's* the month before.

"He's a fucking valet? Fuck me, they let him park cars? Have they seen his ride? The only straight panel on that thing is the back seat. We'd be doing them a favor by taking him."

"You practice that speech on the way over here?" I folded my arms across my chest.

"Yeah I did, was it too dramatic? It's tough to find the balance." Rusty's mouth curled into a smile.

"Nah, it was ok. Throwing in the *cheap slut* was a little harsh though. You might want to work on that for next time, go for something less offensive."

"Yeah, noted. I got caught up in the moment."

My arms relaxed as I unfurled them, my hand reaching across, needing to touch him. "I know we should do this, and I know it was so long ago." No one wanted more than I did for it to be left in the past, the memories still burning me as much as they did back then. "But he broke my heart, Rusty. I thought I loved him. I chased him around for an entire summer, and it wasn't just one sided. He encouraged it. He let me believe that he felt something toward me too, and then he slept with me. Of course once he got what he wanted he couldn't run fast enough. It really messed with my head."

More like broke me. My first boyfriend had cheated on me because I hadn't been a good lay, and then the only guy I had ever really loved screwed me and left. It didn't sell the virtues of a relationship to me, or do wonders for my self-esteem. "I know I'm being selfish, and that we should do this." *Please don't make me do this,* I wanted to beg.

"We *need* to do this, Angie. You have to make it right in your head so we can." His voice was soft, but I could tell he wouldn't be bending.

"It's the best thing for the band. I know." The words felt tight in my throat. The last thing I wanted to do was punish them for my own mistakes.

"The band?" Rus screwed up his face in disgust. "You think I'm telling you we need to do this for the band? Fuck. That. The band will do what it's going to do, and we will stand behind you, always. This is about you."

"Me?" My voice squeaked in surprise. How could it be about *me?*

"Yeah, this is about you. Middle finger in the air, giving *him* a big fuck you. He doesn't get to break you, Angie. No man is ever allowed to do that." His face became more animated as he waved his hands around. "You need to *Taylor Swift* his ass. I've got a blank space, baby."

"*Taylor Swift* his ass?" I laughed. No one else but Rusty would have been able to make me laugh at a time like this. "Rus, do you even know what that song is about? It's a fuck you about how everyone fixates on her ex-boyfriends, not at the boyfriends themselves."

"Whatever, a fuck you was extended, was it not? You're missing my point." He shrugged, with a smile added for extra effect. "You get on that stage, you show him what the hell you're made of. Hell, channel that shit into a song, the crowd will love it."

"So I'm just supposed to decimate him on stage?" Had to admit, the idea wasn't entirely bad. My smile returned at the thought of telling the world how horrible he was. It's not like I was lying—he was horrible, even if he did look delicious.

"Hells yes and we'll release it on iTunes, make a ton of money. It will make you feel better, trust me." Rusty took the idea, and as usual, ran with it.

"Making a ton of money from my buried hurt isn't going make me feel better."

"No, of course not. Showing him what a dumbass he was every night in front of thousands of people, and the *fuck you* you'll be giving him, will. The money will make *me* feel better, and I make you feel better so it gets us full circle."

"You going to draw me a diagram?" I laughed.

"If it gets us over the line."

"You've got it all figured out." I sighed. He was right. I couldn't even argue with him. I needed to move on, not to prove it to Jason, but to prove to myself that I was stronger than I thought.

"Yep, so you telling the guys or am I? We all need to quit our jobs. Oh and I'm writing the rider. We need blue M&Ms at every show, and Doritos. Someone needs to make it happen." He smacked his hands together in excitement.

"I need to talk to my dad." My excitement significantly lower than Rusty's at the prospect of telling my dad I would be leaving. "I'm not sure how that's going to go."

"Talk to me about what?" Pops emerged from the work bays, his timing perfect. Or not, as the case may be.

"Hey, Pops." I forced the smile. It looked like the conversation was going to happening sooner, rather than later.

"Hey, Pops," Rusty echoed.

"Please don't call me, Pops, Rusty. It makes my ulcer flare up." He tapped Rusty across the back of the head—his usual greeting for Rus—before turning to me. "So what's on your mind, sweetheart?"

"Maybe you should go, Rus?" My head jerked toward the door, which translated into, I needed to do this alone.

"He can stay; I get the feeling he's involved." Pops eyed us cautiously.

"You know we're playing with Troy's band." A good start, but how was I going to break it to him that I would be gone for months?

"They asked you to do the rest of the tour." He answered with complete lack of surprise.

"Ummm. Yeah." The surprise that had been lacking in my father had taken up residence in me.

"So are you worried your old man can't handle himself, or are you worried I would tell you not to live your dreams?" He shot me his careful-before-answering face.

"Pops, I know you need me here and—"

"Angie, you are the most amazing kid I could have ever asked for. Your mother and I were blessed beyond measure and if she was here, God rest her soul, she would be so proud of you. But if you don't do this, I'm going to be so mad at you." He looked like he meant it too.

"Mad at me?"

"Yep, us Morellis make our dreams happen, we don't sit around settling. My dream was to have my own shop and marry your mom. You've wanted to be on the stage since you were seven years old, it's about time you start living up to the responsibility that comes with your family name."

"Dad."

"Don't *dad* me either. You call Troy and tell him you're going."

"I love you." My eyes blinked, willing myself not to cry as I wrapped my arms around him.

"I know. I love you, too." His hand gently stroked my hair as he returned my hug.

"I love everyone." Rusty threw his arms around both of us

crushing us in a group hug.

Rusty and my dad were more than just my family; they were my world. And knowing I had those two in my corner gave me the confidence to know I could do anything.

"Take care of each other, okay?" Pops warned as he shook off Rusty's affectionate embrace.

"Don't worry, Joe, I promise to look after Angie, and pull her into line if she goes all *Kayne West.*"

"I'm more worried about you, Rusty." He tapped him upside the back of the head again. "Now you think we can get some work done around here before the two of you become big shots?"

"Too late for that. We're already big shots, the world is just now starting to catch up." Rusty eased back onto the heels of his feet.

"Well *big shot* how about you get out of here and go bother your own boss. Angie has work to do." Pops' voice trailed as he disappeared back into his workspace, no longer interested in Rusty's response.

"I would, but I don't work there anymore." The sheepish grin hinted he had already given his notice or had been handed his walking papers. It was a coin toss as to which.

"You resigned already?" My mouth flew open in mock horror. "What if I had said no?"

"You wouldn't have said no to me, you love me too much. Besides, I slept with Archie's daughter last week. I was on borrowed time." He laughed.

"Get out of here." I pointed to the door.

"See you at the show tonight." Rusty's feet made for the door, his hand pausing on the handle before pulling it open. "You tell James and Troy, and I'll tell the guys. And if Archie comes looking for me, tell him I've moved to Mexico."

"See ya." I waved as I watched him walk away and reached for my phone.

I could do this.

Make the call, tell Troy the good news and not freak out. Ha! Who was I kidding? The call would be the easy part; I had a whole six months to rein in my freak out. This was not going to be easy.

7

Jason

MY BUZZING PHONE BROKE THROUGH THE TUNES ON MY PLAY LIST AS my feet pounded against the belt of the treadmill. I'd lost my shirt at the three-mile mark, sweat pouring off me as I sucked in air and I cut the power. This better be good, I had a few more miles before I'd burn off the mood I'd been carrying this morning.

"Yeah." I huffed into the phone, grabbing a towel that was hanging off the handle.

"Dude, are you fucking?"

I shouldn't be surprised; *Dan* and *fucking* usually came as a package deal. Still a simple *hello* would be a nice change of pace.

"I was running jack-ass. If I was fucking, I wouldn't have bothered answering the phone." I toweled off my face, reaching for a bottle of H2O.

"*Or* you would just say you were running so I wouldn't know."

Yeah, I was so not in the mood for Dan's brand of circular logic.

"Dan, it's too fucking early. What do you need?"

"Well seeing as you are asking, I really need a blowjob but Ash had to work."

I had to ask, didn't I? I tossed the sweat-filled towel over my shoulder.

"Well you won't be finding one here so you're SOL. Anything

else you want to share before I hit the shower?"

"Yeah, I was actually calling for a reason. Band meeting in an hour at Troy's."

"Band meeting? Everything okay?"

"Yep, the problem of our opening act has been solved. Troy is still on the phone with Angie. Looks like her band is coming out on the road with us. You going to be able handle the daily *Resident Evil* she's going to throw your way?"

"I'll be fine." Thank fuck. I squeezed my eyes shut wondering if this was the calm before the storm. "That's good news. Really, I'm glad they agreed."

"You're glad?" Dan all but yelled into the phone. "Well that's no fucking fun. This tour is going to be difficult enough without Ash on it, I was counting on the two of you going at it for my entertainment."

"We're not going to be your source of entertainment, asshole." At least that's not what I had planned.

"She still hates you though, right?" Dan asked, the amusement evident in his voice.

"Not that I've checked recently but I'm assuming she does." I let out a sigh. It was less of an assumption and more a definite, but who is keeping score?

"Good, at least *she* hasn't let me down."

"Dan, all jokes aside. This isn't a game. You're not going to fuck with Angie, you hear me?"

"Wow, you almost sounded like you liked her." Dan laughed. "Relax, asswipe, Troy's already given me the spiel. I'm going to be a regular boy scout."

"Your words aren't filling me with confidence."

"I'll handle my end." Dan took a breath before continuing. "Hers, I've got no control over."

"Okay, see you in sixty," I said, hoping to end the conversation. Talking about Angie with Dan, yeah ... really didn't want to go there.

"See ya. Oh, Jase?"

"Yeah?"

"You were really fucking, weren't you?" The douchebag

laughed.

"Goodbye, asshole."

Well what do you know? Our boy Rusty came through after all. Who the fuck knew what he had to say to convince her. Did it matter? Not one bit.

So the part of me that liked slow and systematic torture limbered up. Because that's what I had in front of me. And fuck me if the thought didn't make me smile, because ladies with a permanent case of PMS were obviously my thing.

After a quick shower and change, I jumped into my car and headed to Troy's penthouse, the destination for our meeting.

"Hey, there you are." James pulled open the door of Troy's pad, allowing me to walk inside.

"Are you the butler?" I laughed as I strolled into the living room, Alex and Dan already situated on the couch.

"Megs has bad morning sickness, Troy's in the other room with her which is why we're doing this here. He wanted to be close by in case she needed something." James helped me play catch up.

"Yeah, good call."

We were on the same page, and Troy being all protective and shit was not an issue for any of us.

"I'll let him know everyone is here." Dan's feet hit the floor as he made for the back of the apartment.

"Hey." Troy emerged looking a little worse for wear, Dan not far behind him.

"Hey dude, Megs okay?" My chin tipped in his direction as he walked into the living room and sunk his ass into the two-seater.

"Yeah, other than being pissed at me for hovering. Apparently me wanting to be with her while she pukes isn't romantic." His tone clueing us in that despite Megs's protests, nothing much would be changing.

"In my opinion, that's as romantic as it's going to get." Dan rejoined the group, his ass sinking into the leather couch.

"I can hear you talking about me, Troy Harris." Megs slowly ambled into the room, her face pale but wearing a big ass grin.

"Good, 'cause I wasn't trying to hide it. You want anything before we start?" Troy automatically rose to his feet, his usual response when his girl walked in the room.

"For you to stop hovering." Megs waved him off, the grin hinting she knew she was fighting a losing battle.

"Maybe ask for something you actually have a chance of getting." Troy's tucked her in tight against his body before kissing her neck.

Megs rolled her eyes. "I'm fine. I'm not going to break."

So with everyone roughly assembled, and rather than jerk off anymore we decided to get this show on the road. The reason for our meeting wasn't a mystery. Neither was the reason my pulse was still racing. And it didn't have anything to do with the time I'd clocked on the treadmill earlier either.

"Okay, so Black Addiction is locked in. Full commitment, all dates. They will sign their revised contract today. Everyone cool with that? Dan? Jason?" James asked, the singling out of the two of us, no coincidence.

"They're a good fit. They owned it last night, and the crowd seemed to love them," Troy added, clearly on Team Angie.

"Yeah everyone was shitting out rainbows." Dan leaned back into his chair. "I've got no problem with it."

All eyes turned to me.

"No problem here."

Well, none that was in this room at least.

"Good, 'cause if there was going to be a problem, I'd rather hear about it now." James gave a predictable warning. The raised eyebrow clueing me in that whatever I was selling, he wasn't buying.

"Shit went down between the two of us in the past. It's over; we're fine. There will be no drama." My mouth spouted the usual bullshit. Not sure if I believed it, not that it mattered at this point.

"Awesome." James didn't smile.

He didn't believe me either.

So I'd learned a few things today.

One, we were touring with Angie's band, and two, I had suddenly developed an unexplained need to watch the support act perform.

Good work, Jase, I was now stalking her.

I was edgy, too.

My fist flexed open and shut a couple of times, my hands needing something to do while I sat in the dark. My vibe was completely off.

There had been two girls that I'd ever really cared about. One, I hoped for both our sake's, I'd never see again, and other was on the stage in front of me.

Both times I'd been stupid.

Both times I'd fucked up.

Both times I'd said I'd never go back.

But only one of those times I'd actually wanted to.

So, here I was feeding my musical appreciation. Absolutely mesmerized by the woman I was watching. Straight up voodoo shit. That had to be the reason why I couldn't look away.

Of course it had *nothing* to do with the way she looked. Those deadly curves *couldn't* be what had my attention. No, I hadn't even noticed how perfect her tits were or what a stellar job her ass did of showcasing those tight black shorts. The fact she was the perfect mix of knock-you-on-your-ass stunning and real-girl beautiful could also *not* be the reason I was sitting on a road case stage side being all Phantom-of-the-Opera.

My dick getting harder the longer I looked at her had nothing to with the fact I hadn't been laid in a while either. The opportunities hadn't changed, I could still score any night of the week. But it was my motivation that was suffering the dysfunction, not my cock.

This wasn't good.

I needed to give myself a reality check and get busy doing something else. A hobby. Possibly one that didn't involve an intervention order or require night vision goggles.

"They're pretty good." Troy parked his ass on the road case beside me. His eyes darted out to the stage, nodding his approval.

"Yep." The less that came out of my mouth the better. My need to share wasn't high being that I doubted he would embrace my new creeper status.

"So you sitting out here for a reason?"

He had waited two minutes before asking the inevitable question. My guess, it was his attempt at keeping it polite. Who says we weren't gentlemen?

"Just enjoying the show." I tipped my chin toward the stage.

Enjoying it wasn't exactly accurate. None of it was actually enjoyable, not unless you loved feeling like your nuts were in a vice. Which I must, considering Troy was giving me a hard stare and raised eyebrow combo that translated into *no, really. What the fuck are you doing here?* and I still hadn't moved.

"Jase—"

"I'm solid, dude." I cut him off knowing what was coming next.

It had been a long time since anyone had to worry about me. Since I'd come out the other end from shithead to dependable Jase. Reliable Jase. It was me who usually did the watching out for. Not the other way around. Troy's concern made me uncomfortable, and not the wearing a turtleneck kind.

"No man is an island. Just remember that."

"Yeah, and you need to stop reading fortune cookies."

Continuing the conversation took a back seat as my head whipped back around to the stage as vaguely familiar chords ripped through the speakers. "Are they playing ...*Taylor Swift?*"

The dirtied up intro leading into the first verse snared my full attention. What the hell were we even talking about?

"Er ... like if *TSwift* and *Stone Temple Pilots* had a baby, it would sound like that." Troy was equally intrigued, his face wearing the same what-the-fuck as I was.

"Holy shit, it's "Blank Space" rocker-fied."

Angie belted out the unmistakable words of the chorus, putting any doubt to bed. It might have been someone else's tune, but she was putting her sexy-ass stamp on it. And damn if my dick wasn't suddenly becoming more interested. The heart-to-heart with Troy shelved for another day. Hopefully, never.

"It sounds bad ass if you ask me." Thankfully Troy had no idea where my mind was at, i.e. not on the fucking brilliance of the rendition.

"Totally bad ass."

Nice one, asshole. You sound like an inept moron. FYI, my hard-on could cut glass right now.

Angie's voice curled around each of the words, spitting them out with a little more venom than the original version. The heavy distortion on the guitars was also *less* sweet and *more* go-fuck-yourself, which was incredibly hot. I wasn't sure if I should be appalled or impressed that the song had me so turned on.

Who knew why they'd worked a cover into their repertoire, they hadn't played anything but originals the night before. And as far as unlikely song choices went, it was up there with shit-I-would-bet-won't-happen. It was fucking strange. Not that I was going to argue with it, because it was catchy as fuck and the crowd was eating it up with a motherfucking spoon.

I watched hypnotized as the last line of the bastardized pop song left her mouth, her lips settling into a satisfied grin as she lifted her hands in the air and signaled the end of their set, her confidence radiating off her like a nuclear detonation.

Yeah, that wasn't sexy.

Not at all.

The rest of the boys dropped their gear and moved to the center of the stage. Each of them wore the same pleased looks on their faces as they sidled up next to Angie and took a group bow to the deafening sound of applause.

"I'd say we weren't the only ones who liked it." Troy's laugh beside me reminding me I wasn't standing there solo.

It was also a good time to remind myself to pick up my damn jaw from the floor. I was sure my tongue had been spending some chill time down there, too.

It was hot. Not that I was going to mention that. The word and the sentiment a definite danger zone. As was noticing how her sweat-saturated top showed off her specular tits. Awesome, I was now a deviant as well as a stalker. Who says men can't multi-task.

"Hey!" Angie couldn't have stopped grinning even if she'd tried as she made her way backstage. "Hi, Troy." She gave him a hug before she turned to me. "Hi, loser."

Her attitude had shifted. There was no way I hadn't noticed that. Well at least now that I peeled my eyes from other parts of her body, I had. It wasn't just her smile—which was lethal all by itself—it was that she was freaking beaming.

"What's with the addition to your set list? I didn't think you did covers." I couldn't have given a rat's ass about her *colorful* greeting nor was I waiting to see if Troy was going to investigate. My curiosity at need-to-know levels.

"Rusty thought we should shake things up a little." Angie smirked at the man in question like they shared some private joke before her eyes returned to me and narrowed.

Huh? Was there something in that statement that I was supposed to decipher? I was a lot of things, but telepath wasn't one of them. Along with mind reader and chick-whisperer. All of which could have been an asset right about now.

"Well, the crowd loved it." Troy weighed in, not even hiding the fact he'd loved it too. He alternated between slapping them on the back and shaking hands. The rest of the band loving the "awesome show" and "well done" that was being tossed their way. All except Angie who seemed to be more enjoying my reaction.

"Sounds like Rusty is a smart man." The mouth decided to get into the game.

"Keep talking, Irwin, your praise feeds into my god complex. Feel free to use more descriptive words like *motherfucking genius* and *most brilliant guitarist alive*. We're song writers, so words are our friends." His shit-eating grin almost as big as his inflated ego. Guitarists, all the fucking same.

"So can we expect more of that?" Rusty's comments completely ignored as I focused on Angie. I wasn't entirely sure what I was asking. The song? Her attitude? The fact my cock was so hard I was starting to lose feeling in my legs?

"I have a lot more where that came from." Her blood-red lips twitched into a grin.

Okay, so now I was even more confused as to what we were talking about. Not that I actually gave a shit. Nor did I care we had an audience.

"I'm looking forward to seeing it."

What the actual fuck was I saying? Was I flirting? I resisted the urge to check if I still had my balls because of the raised eyebrows it might get me, but part of me had to wonder if they weren't tucked away somewhere else.

She leaned in, each word slower than it needed to be. "Good, I think you'll enjoy it."

No seriously, what the hell were we talking about?

"I can't wait."

It was probably the most honest thing to come out of my mouth in the last twenty-four hours. I had no damn idea what I was agreeing to, except that I freaking well wanted it. Trouble? Sure, double fucking helping, right here. All my earlier thoughts about history getting a re-run were suddenly even more appealing. Which meant I was certifiable and should be committed.

"So Jase and I are going to take off, got to get ready for our set. You guys going to hang around?"

Oh yeah, Troy was still with me. Yeah, right. Had a show to play and everything. Best I shelve the crazy for a few hours.

"We're actually heading back to my place." Rusty jumped in, big smile he'd been wearing since he'd stepped off stage. "Having a few drinks with some of our friends before we get on the road. Nothing crazy, but you guys are welcome if you want to stop by."

"Thanks, dude but with Megs being pregnant, she gets tired and—"

"Yeah, sounds good. See you there."

My mouth opened and the words came out all by themselves. Boom. Like a five-year-old doing the I-want-go. My mouth and I didn't really care for the stare-down we were getting. The biggest coming from Troy and not because I'd interrupted him.

"Awesome." Rusty clapped his hands together, rubbing them with anticipation. "Let me write down my address." He grabbed a set list that had been gaffed to the wall and located a Sharpie on the floor. His barely legible scrawl printed on the page where I would be heading the minute I stepped off stage.

This was such a bad idea. The folded paper scrunched into the

pocket of my pants.
 "Awesome."

Angie

So my giving of the *fuck you* had made me feel better. Well, it had been more a singing of, rather than a giving, but the result was the same. Rusty was right. I was stronger than I thought.

I am woman, hear me roar, and all that shit.

It was great. I was great, and I might actually get through this whole tour without an addiction to anxiety meds. At least that's how I was feeling until Rusty opened his big damn mouth.

Sure, invite Jase into my safe place. Was he motherfucking insane? I wanted to kill him. The *him* was interchangeable. Rusty, Jason—blood was probably going to need to be shed.

So my plans of easing into it were tossed out the window. Rusty giving me the "it would have been rude not to extend the invitation." Yada, yada—not helping. I needed to roar god damn it. How was I supposed to roar if Jason Irwin was invading my personal space?

New plan.

My bubble was about to burst so I need to get my game face on. I had a feeling those fuck-yous I needed to be delivering were going to be after hours.

Of course Rusty seemed pleased with the latest development. He was freaking ecstatic. It was his way of escalating the process, and if we got to hang out with big shots at the same time—well wasn't that fantastic. You can only kill a person once, correct?

Rus even had the nerve to ask me if I still loved him. Pfft. Excuse me while I laugh my ass off.

Ass laughed completely off.

I am standing here with no ass because that's how much I laughed.

There was *no* way I loved him.

Not a chance.

The appreciating of his fine form was okay though. I mean, the man looked good. I hadn't suddenly developed blindness. Besides hormones clearly had nothing to do with your brain so that was totally allowed. Touching was not. I should probably remind myself of that a few more times.

So given that Rusty always said all the best stories started with regret—he had been a regular Diane Sawyer of late, digging up shit and delivering with a smile—I was ready.

Against my better judgment—the one that told me to go home—I was doing this.

Meh, who needs judgment anyway?

Famous. Last. Words.

"Angie!" Joey pulled me through the doorway as I wandered into Rusty's living room.

Some blonde I didn't recognize shoved a beer into my hand, her smile inviting conversation. She obviously didn't know my reputation for not being a people person—or my lack of ability to *chat*.

"Hey, how are you?" I nodded in her direction. See, I can be nice sometimes and I wasn't looking to cock-block anyone. Besides, I was trying on my "being nice." A practice run. It felt like wearing new shoes—tight, awkward and slightly uncomfortable. Unlike most girls, new shoes did not excite me. So the analogy was extremely apt.

"Good, I'm so happy for you guys." The mystery blonde was still there. Crap. "This is huge. I mean, it's Power Station." Her eyes widened as she said their name. It was the typical response, her voice changing tone to almost reverent proportion.

"Yeah, it sure is." Nod. Smile. Faux enthusiasm.

"Of course I knew good things would happen for you guys. You are all so talented." Her eyes floated to Joey who was currently involved in a very serious game of beer pong. I didn't believe for a second she was talking about his ability to keep time.

"Thanks." Smile. Faux enthusiasm. Nod. It was good to mix it up.

"Angie. Come do shots with me. We need to celebrate," Max hollered from the kitchen, his shirt missing in action.

"Well, bye." I waved to the nameless blonde and silently thanked Max for saving me from any more small talk. In case you hadn't guessed, it wasn't my forte.

"Ewwww, we're drinking Jäger?" The brown liquid swished in the shot glass that had just been handed to me.

"Yep, tequila is for pussies. Tonight we drink like men." He threw the liquid down his throat as a point of punctuation. His hand reached for the bottle for a refill.

"I'm not a man, Max."

"What? You're telling me now? All this time I thought you were a dude." Max's face contorted in mock horror.

"Har-Ha." My elbow jabbed him in the ribs.

"Drink." His hand edged the glass closer to my mouth in encouragement. "I've already had three, you need to catch up."

The shot burned as it went down. The herbal grassy tang coated my mouth and I wanted to gag. Yuck.

So even though I'd said I wasn't a man, apparently I needed to drink like one. Max poured shot after shot of nasty cough-medicine tasting liquor down my throat.

Honestly, give me tequila. It might be for pussies, but considering I had one of those, surely that made the drink more appropriate for me. Although my rising blood alcohol content sure was making me feel good.

Wasn't I supposed to roar or something?

Hehehe.

That lamp was looking at me funny.

"And again!" Max's eyes glazed with enthusiasm or perhaps it was from his Jäger haze as he tried to ply me with more of the nasty, brown liquor.

"No more, just give me a beer." My limit for shots reached as I pushed Max and the offending bottle away.

My head had already started to cloud. As was probably my liver. My judgment had been gone from before I'd started to drink, so there were no surprises there.

"How he doesn't get hangovers is a mystery to me." Beth, Max's sometimes girlfriend gave me a hug.

Unlike most female company, hers was one I actually liked. Her embrace wasn't one I minded either; I generally wasn't a hugger. The feel-good juice probably played a part too.

"He goes from happy drunk to sober with no segue. It's bullshit." I hugged her back.

She flicked her short black hair out of her eyes, her smile simmering as she watched him take another shot. She got a wink back in recognition. I guess tonight they were "together".

Rusty had predictably been in his bedroom, *entertaining* a redhead from NYU. Both of them emerged an hour or so later not even trying to hide their ruffled appearance. The pleased look on her face was the other hint. By all accounts, she'd received Rusty's full service effort.

The drinking continued, as did our friends' constant congratulations and attention, which made me feel sort of weird. We were musicians, it's not like we were curing cancer. Yet somehow playing a big show had elevated us to big deals, and I wasn't so hot on the pedestal.

At some point I passed out on the couch, my legs curled up under me. My grip slowly loosened on the bottle of beer I'd been holding, waking me before I spilled any.

"Hey! There's two of you." The bottle was peeled from my hand before it had a chance to hit the floor as my eyes blinked at the body hovering above me. "And I hate both of you."

"I know you do." Jason placed my half empty bottle on the coffee table before easing back into his seat. "But the other seats are taken so you'll just have to put up with me."

He didn't even try and sound sorry. Ass.

The "fine" I huffed in response dripped with sarcasm, but I was too loaded to argue. The room was filled with bodies either dancing, passed out on the floor or occupying the limited chair space. But surely there was somewhere else he could sit, like for instance, in Staten Island.

"You really hate me, don't you?"

"Oh come on, Jason. You can't be that clueless. Don't you have a college degree?"

Ugh. I so did not want to have this conversation, and the room needed to stop spinning too. Both of those reasons contributing to my building nausea. And his sexy cologne needed to stop wafting up my nose too, that was rude.

"I should have said goodbye properly, and I should have called you. That was a dick move." He moved closer, bringing with him all that sexiness I was trying to avoid.

"Yeah, there's a lot of things that should have happened that night. Like me not fucking you." Or him not fucking me. Let's not get hung up on semantics.

"You really regret it?" His eyes did that thing where they disarmed me. I hate them. Both of his beautiful, dark eyes.

"No. Yes. No. I don't know." My mouth wouldn't behave, not sticking to the standard line we'd rehearsed. It had been a mistake; I regretted it. That's what my dumbass mouth should have said instead of babbling in indecision.

"If I remember correctly, you told me that it had been the best you'd ever had."

Of course out of everything that happened, he would remember that tiny detail. My post sex euphoria had me spilling secrets he didn't need to know.

"Well I hadn't had a lot to compare it to, the bar wasn't that high."

Lies. Even now, no one had come close, but he would never be hearing that piece of information. He could torture me and I'd still never say, which incidentally is what it felt like as he sat there watching me.

"Wow, you know how to crush an ego." The bastard smiled, not even pretending to be hurt.

"Like your ego could be crushed by lil-ole me. Crushing shit is your specialty. " *Shut up!* My brain screamed. Damn Max and his bottle of man-drink. This would not turn into another clichéd drunken confessional.

"Is that what it's all about?" His head tilted as those gorgeous eyes I hated so much stayed glued to mine. "I crushed your ego?"

No asshole, it was my heart. Thank God, I didn't say it out loud. Instead I clamped my lips shut hoping to minimize the damage.

"Angie, I'm sor—"

My hand covered his mouth. The vibrations of his voice tingled against my palm. I couldn't hear the word. Couldn't hear him tell me he was sorry. I was drunk but not enough that hearing him apologize for that night wouldn't crush me all over again. Why? Why did it still freaking hurt?

Touching him hadn't been the plan. His lips against my palm did things that confused me; it was like a memory and not one all together horrible. The familiar tug in my gut also added to the mental assault. Oh shit. As much as I wanted to, at that moment, I didn't hate him. That was not a good sign.

"Please don't. Just don't say sorry, okay?" I hadn't meant to sound so vulnerable, so small, but that is exactly what my voice sounded like. I hated it.

His eyes widened as he lowered my hand from his mouth, my fingers inadvertently interlocked with his. Great. So now my hands were against me too, my body literally rebelling.

"Okay." He nodded, and I wished I knew what he was agreeing to.

"You want more beer?" My brain scrambled for something that would get me off that couch. Yes. Drinks. Getting him a drink would give me a reason to leave without running. Because running is exactly what I felt like I was doing.

"I'm still full." His head dipped to his beer on the coffee table— the twin of the one he'd saved from my hand—a swallow or two missing from the bottle.

"Did you want to kiss me then?"

Did I just say that out loud? No, it must have been in my head. It had to have been in my head. Oh God, please let it have been in my head.

"Yes."

Fuck. I'd said it. If the yes wasn't confirmation enough, the way he was looking at me was.

"Why?"

Another thing I probably shouldn't have said but hey, why stop now?

He didn't answer, instead leaning over and brushing his lips against mine. It was slow. His touch, gentle as he moved my lips apart with his own. His tongue slowly traced the seam of my mouth, involuntarily I moaned as he nibbled on my bottom lower lip. It was my undoing.

"Yes." I wasn't sure whom I was saying it to but with the one word he moved closer, pressing my body against him as his mouth continued to invade mine. Not content with just the lip contact I was getting, I pushed him back onto the seat and straddled him, the bulge in his jeans doing little to hide the hard-on he apparently had worked up.

Still questioning my motives—and my sanity—I reached down between us and palmed him, working him with my hands. His lids lowered as a guttural "fuck" escaped through his parted lips. His body moved against my hand as I tried to reconcile what I was doing. Different parts of my brain were at war with each other as I moved my hand back up to his head and threaded my fingers through his hair.

Tension, stress, alcohol, confusion or the fact I hadn't had sex in over a month could have all been to blame. It was potluck as to why I had lowered myself onto him, using the hard-on pressing against the seam of his jeans to hit me in that sweet spot between my legs.

My brain had obviously checked out as my body took over, our mouths ending up back together. Man, he knew how to kiss. The way he pulled my head in closer was a textbook panty-melting maneuver, and he used just the right amount of tongue. If the last time we'd kissed had been good, this was off the charts. Whatever he'd been doing in those years since had obviously been working for him.

"Shit."

Like a bucket of cold water hitting my skin, my brain finally kicked in. My head snapping back as I registered what the hell I was doing i.e. making out with the enemy.

"What am *I* doing?" The question could have been asked by either of us, although I wasn't sure I wanted to know the answer. "What are *you* doing?" While my shopping list of motivators were the reasons for my mistake, he had no excuse.

"Fuck." That cold shot of reality must have hit him too. "Angie …" There was more to that sentence, but he didn't say it.

"Okay, it was nothing. I'm drunk. I probably won't remember this in the morning." My mouth fumbled with an explanation.

I was *so* going to remember this in the morning.

"That doesn't make it better." His eyes filled with an emotion I couldn't read. Hell, in another five minutes I would have had sex with him.

On the couch.

In front of all these people.

"I'm going to be sick."

And if he still had any urge to kiss me, I'm sure talk of vomit had eradicated it. My body almost levitated in the rush to climb off him, my feet desperate to get me to a bathroom. My hands that had been so interested in playing touchy-and-feely with Jason Irwin managed to not be total assholes and slam the door behind me.

My fingers fumbled the lock closed before I made it to the toilet bowl and vomited. My body contorted in a full-body heave as I lost my battle with my stomach and threw up again.

Awesome. Perfect end to the night.

"Angie, are you okay?" Jason yelled through the door, the music doing it's best to drown him out. Just as well. At least he hadn't heard that.

"Go away," I half groaned as I turned on the faucet, my hand cupping the water and bringing it to my mouth. Never drinking with Max again. Ever.

"Angie, just open up."

Had to hand it to him, he was persistent. Of course he was about ten years too late with the concerned friend routine. The *better late than never* did not apply here.

"I'm fine." I cursed through the closed door. *Will be even better if you leave,* I finished in my head.

"I'll leave as soon as I know you are okay."

Oh, so I had said that part too. I really needed to get a better handle on my freaking mouth.

"Fuck." One hand gripped the basin to keep my balance as the other shut off the faucet. My pale, smudgy-eyed reflection looked back at me from Rusty's bathroom mirror.

"I can stand here all night," he threatened when I didn't open the door. "Nowhere else I need to be."

My eyes narrowed as I flipped him off, the door unfortunately blocking his view of seeing it.

"Flip me off all you want, I'm still standing here."

Crap, did he have x-ray vision as well?

"How did you know I was flipping you off?" I pulled open the door, figuring he wasn't going to leave until he had at least seen I was fine.

"Because you're predictable." He smiled, his hands supporting his weight on each side of the doorjamb. It showed off his biceps and his stunning ink work.

Not what I should be concentrating on.

"See, all good." I fought the urge to twirl knowing it would inevitably make me hurl. Ha. I rhymed. A small giggle escaped from my lips.

"What's funny?" Jason moved in closer, the safety of the doorway no longer being in my favor.

"Nothing. You wouldn't get it." I fumbled as I took a step back to his step forward.

"I'm not going to touch you. I just want to make sure you get home okay."

Probably a little late for the no touching thing, we could have used that twenty minutes ago.

"I said I was fine. I'll just crash here." My ass hit the sink, my backward stepping getting me no further. I hadn't been convinced there was going to be no more touching. Better to be safe than sorry.

"Here? In the bathroom?" Jason looked around, eyeing off the tub.

"No, Rusty has a guest room. It's around the back."

"Well let's get you there then." Jason stepped aside; his head jerked to the side as if to say *lead the way*.

"You're not putting me to bed, I'm not a child." Sure, put the two of us in the vicinity of a bed, that wasn't a recipe for disaster.

"Tell me, when did you start second guessing everyone's motives?" He moved closer, his arms dangerously close to mine. What happened to the not touching rule? We needed to go back to that. "And I wasn't implying you were a child, I was trying to be helpful."

Like you were when you kissed me? Yeah, thanks but I think I can take it from here. "I don't need any help. Honestly, I'm good. You can leave now."

Like you did the first time.

Please if there was a God let my mouth only have said the parts I'd meant it to.

His eyes followed the length of my body up and down, his hesitation thick in the air as he took a step back from my personal space. "Okay, I'll see you tomorrow then."

"Sure thing." My forced smile strained at the corners of my mouth as I watched him walk toward the doorway.

Just a few more feet, keep going.

"Oh and Angie, about that kiss." He stopped, flushing any hopes I had of forgetting what we'd done down the toilet.

"It was nothing." My voice not sounding convincing, as I shrugged. I blamed the booze. "Already forgotten." Not likely.

"It won't happen again." He looked me over one last time and then thankfully—no seriously, praise the lord hallelujah—he left the room.

The breath I'd been holding slowly escaped from my lips as my body sagged against the sink.

"No, it won't."

WHAT THE HELL WAS THAT?

I needed my head examined.

That or some shock therapy because thinking about kissing her was one thing, following through, something else.

Dumb move going to Rusty's afterparty last night. Complete rookie mistake. Clearly I'd been thinking with my dick because going to see her was asking for trouble. Yet, there I went. Straight off stage, did our hello-how-are-yas with the fans and then I jetted out the door.

It wasn't even a debate, and it fucking well should have been. What was even worse was that I'd lied about it.

Troy had been anxious to get Megs home, standard. She could tell him she was okay until she was blue in the face, but she looked pale and Troy was locked on target. He had the caveman bullshit jacked-up to eleven. So the two of them bailed the minute the official BS was over. James, Hannah, along with Power Station's second string Noah and their kid on the block, Jesse, left soon after. Alex, Lexi and mini Lexi, aka Grace, hung around a little longer but not by much. Which left me kicking it backstage with Dan and Ash. Cue my lame excuse of being tired when they invited me to go hang with them.

It hadn't even been convincing and still neither of them suspected anything. Such was the trust they had in me. They just smiled, told me to go get some sleep and waved me goodbye. I should've felt bad, but instead I got in my car and went the one place I knew I shouldn't. To see Angie.

She was like a fucking Rubix cube. I wasn't even asking why anymore, it was enough to know that no matter how scrambled the puzzle was, I had to solve it. And that shit with the song— pulling out a *Taylor Swift* cover—that just made it more interesting.

Of course by the time I'd made it to the Bronx, the small get-together had gotten messy. It was a typical Saturday night in the old neighborhood. Even if they hadn't been doing the farewell thing, there still would've been half a dozen cars parked on the lawn and wall-to-wall people on the inside. Much like the night before we'd left. The night Angie and I had ... yeah so much for ancient history.

So, we'd established that I hadn't been thinking. Add to that a beautiful woman I'd never been able to resist, and we ended up reminiscing—with our tongues.

Fuck.

Well, at least it hadn't gotten *that* far because that's exactly where it had been heading. Her hand worked my cock like she was trying to get the genie out of a bottle; any conscious thought I had did an *Elvis,* and left the building.

Just a few more miles.

Right. I could run to Cleveland, and I'd still not have my mind right.

The T-shirt I'd stripped off thirty minutes ago multitasked as a towel. I used it to mop up the sweat off my face as I sucked air in and out of my lungs. My legs not getting anywhere close to the burn I needed to feel.

The buzz from my front door cut through the whirl of the treadmill, my stride thrown off by the knocking accompaniment. My feet hit the side guards as the belt kept moving, and I cursed the asshole who was on the other side of the door. My legs were slightly unsteady as I made my way to the source of the disturbance. It wasn't going to be a friendly greeting.

"Angie?"

My eyes flew open to match my mouth's display of surprise. That was followed up by my head flipping around the doorway to see if anyone else was in tow. "You're alone? How did you know where I lived?"

She nodded as she moved through the doorway and into my apartment. "Yep, just me. And I asked Troy; he had no problem telling me where I could find you. Seemed only fair seeing as you knew where I lived." My mind loitered in the hallway as I tried to reconcile the what-the-fuck.

Angie looked all kinds of fine as she strode in, my dick instantly taking an interest. Her jet-black hair was pulled back from her face, which was without the usual dark eye makeup. She looked better without it. The multiple studs down either side of her ears catching the light as she turned her head. The blue jeans she was wearing clung to her body like they'd been painted on, and her lotus tats stretching the length of her right arm peeked out from her faded *Nine Inch Nails* T-shirt. All put together, it cemented one hell of a vibe—sexy as hell.

She was the last person I expected to be showing up on my doorstep any time soon. And by any time soon, I meant *never*.

"Wow, you really are Captain America underneath the shirt." Angie's eyes widened as she glared at my bare chest. "Still *Army Strong*, I see."

PT five days a week had been a habit even after I hung up my uniform. Working out was as much part of my routine as was brushing my teeth. I wasn't huge, but I could hold my own.

"I wasn't expecting company. I run to clear my head."

Perspective was easy to come by when you had to slow down and concentrate on your body. Simple things, like breathing, makes all the worrying about trivial bullshit fall away. And if there was one day I needed to run, today was it.

"Well, judging by that," she waved her hands in front of her, "you've got a lot on your mind." Her lips twitched into a slight smile. She hadn't been quick enough to hide it before resuming her usual death glare. It's the look she usually gave me. The one I was most familiar with.

As much as I enjoyed seeing her smile—it made a change from the usual venom she had for me—I was still no closer to knowing why she was here, in my apartment.

"So you here to check out my suitability for *Armani's* new underwear campaign, or was there something I can get you?"

Obviously there was a point; the sooner we got to it the better. Besides, the longer I looked at her the greater chance of having a repeat of last night. Those lips were so fucking inviting I had to nail my feet to the floor. Did I mention how fucking hot she looked?

"You should totally do the underwear thing. Bieber had a billboard, so being an ass obviously isn't a deal breaker." Another smile. This time she didn't try and hide it.

"Nice backhanded compliment." My grin matched hers. "Who says singing is your only talent."

"I can also play guitar." Her smile got wider. "The bitch thing is just a hobby."

"Of which you excel at when I'm around." My feet inched forward, bringing me to stand directly in front of her. Nothing like tempting fate. It was like jumping out of a plane and then checking to see you had the parachute.

"What can I say? You bring out the best in me."

Yeah, not even going to pretend that she wasn't giving me a hard-on from hell. It didn't even make sense. Clearly she was telling me she didn't like me and yet here we were.

"You want to go back and forth some more, or we going to get to the point of why you're here?"

Before I take you to my bed and we can work out our differences there.

Her chest rose as she took a breath. "After you left, I started thinking."

"Not sure you were in any condition to have any conscious thoughts."

She could barely stand; not sure much actual *thinking* had gone down.

"Oh shut up, Jason, I wasn't *that* drunk." Her death glare was back with a vengeance.

"Drunk enough to throw up."

The taste of Jäger and beer had been on her breath when I'd kissed her, and the fact that she'd let me was also a hint she was far from sober.

"It was kissing you that made me puke, *not* the booze."

I could barely contain my fucking grin. "Wow, Angie. That's two for two where you've gone zero to bitch in three seconds."

"You interrupted me." This time it was a death glare/smile combo.

"Go on." I folded my arms across my chest, waiting to see how this was going to play out.

"So I was thinking," she repeated, her game clearly off.

"Yes you mentioned that." I leaned up against the back of my couch, settling in for what was no doubt going to be a hell of a story.

"Can you put on a goddamn shirt or something? I feel like I've stumbled into *Nick Bateman's* Instagram."

"Give me a second." I grabbed a sweatshirt that had been hanging across the back end of my couch and shoved it over my head. Not ideal but it would do. I tried to not enjoy that my being half naked threw her off her game. Because that would make me an even bigger dick, wouldn't it. Not to mention I'd rather be taking clothes off rather than adding them. Looks like she wasn't the only one losing her trail of thought. "Alright. You were thinking ..." My head nodded waiting for her to continue.

"Are you gay?"

Huh? Did she just ask me if I was... gay?

"Are you high?" That casual leaning I had going on no longer worked for me as I straightened back onto my feet.

"No, I'm not trying to be a wiseass, I mean it kind of fits."

Holy shit, she was serious. I had to fight the urge to show her how *not* gay I was.

"What the hell are you talking about? *It kind of fits.*"

She shifted uncomfortably in place before meeting my eyes. "So, that summer you were at Troy's, I didn't see you date anyone. Girls were throwing themselves at you, but you didn't do anything."

"I think I recall doing *something* with you that would disprove your theory."

Maybe I was mistaken, but I kind of thought the sex we'd had in the backseat of my car qualified for something.

"We had sex *once* and then you ran like a bat out of hell. A gay guy can sleep with a woman and it means no more than a straight woman sleeping with another woman. It doesn't mean anything. Hard-ons can be a physical response."

Well fuck, she had actually sold herself on this theory.

Like, she'd actually given it some thought. A plus B equaled I liked to suck dick.

"I assure you, I'm not gay."

I would have loved to have seen the thought process. The one where she forgot how many times I made her come. That, and the fact I'd had been ready to do it again last night. Because clearly that didn't sell my position on whether or not I preferred pussy. Her fucking extrapolation so freaking funny, it didn't even offend me. Proving her wrong, still very much on the table.

"I've rarely seen you linked to anyone." She took a breath before qualifying. "Like online. James was with Hannah for like forever so he was out. Alex and Dan, those two were all over the internet the whole damn time until they found their significant others. Even Troy, who was super discreet, couldn't escape the limelight. You? There was one mention of a chick you were seeing long distance but never any photos. Did she even exist? Oh, wait? Was she your beard? And Rusty said you were being really friendly to him."

"I was wrong. You aren't high, you are motherfucking insane."

Wow.

No idea.

She honestly had no fucking clue.

"You can tell me." Her voice softened for the first time since our reconnection. "Honestly, it would explain a lot."

She was actually being sympathetic. Like I had been stuffed all this time in a closest with a dildo up my ass. Let me be clear. Gay, straight, bi, whatever. I gave zero fucks—yeah, the word choice completely intentional—on anyone else's sexual orientation. They could fuck whom they wanted, as much as they wanted and they could all skip into the sunset.

My preference was one way—my dick in a woman. *Where* in the woman was the only part that was open for debate. There wasn't any other gray area. Not a *maybe let's experiment.* Not an *excuse me sir, can I lick your balls?*

"I'm sorry I slept with you and left you. Like I said, it was a dick move, but it wasn't because I was gay, it was because I was an asshole." And I was a coward, but I chose to leave that bit out.

"Rusty is a cool guy but I don't want to fuck him. The lack of girls in the press is partly because I'm the freaking keyboard player and no one gives a shit, and partly because I don't date women who are looking to land a role in *The Real Housewives of New York.*"

"Oh." Her face vacant of emotion.

"Look, I don't do relationships. I know some guys say that, but I've tried and every single time is more miserable than the last. I do casual hook ups but don't flash it around. I'm with them and then I leave. It's just the way I'm wired."

Not that it had always been that way, but it had been for a very long time. If it wasn't broke don't fix it, and as far as women were concerned this was the only way it worked for me. Everyone assumed it was Dan who was biggest manwhore, but they had no idea. He just ran his mouth about it, I didn't. Plus, I was careful about the women I chose. If they looked like they were angling for a feature in *Billboard Magazine*, I'd leave them to him. He could have all the publicity he wanted while I found someone who would rather fuck than have her picture in the paper.

"But what about the girl, the one you were seeing?"

Angie had obviously heard about the girl I tried to do normal with a couple of years ago.

"Erin." That was the name of my failed foray back into relationship land. She was a cutie. We met at a show but actually wasn't a fan, and what started as one of my planned hook-ups went pear-shaped when she thought it meant more. It had been a while since I'd done the girlfriend thing so I thought I'd give it a try. Shouldn't have bothered. It didn't end well.

"Erin." Angie repeated it back; it felt weird hearing that name on her lips. Almost like it was dirty. It wasn't like what we'd had. I had been with Erin because I felt obligated; I'd been with Angie because I couldn't stop myself from *not* being with her.

"Honestly, I was only with her because I figured it was something I should be doing. We should never have gotten together. It's not that I didn't like her, she was a sweet girl but she wanted things from me that I couldn't give her. Besides, she lived in fucking Pennsylvania, it never would have worked out."

Webcam dating didn't interest me, nor did jerking myself off with phone sex. It was more work than pleasure. I ended it as soon as I was able to.

"Because she's a *Steeler's* fan, right? I don't blame you, I never got that *Terrible Towel* thing either." A slight smile ghosted on her lips, it was the first one she'd given me since the whole are-you-gay discussion had begun.

"No, she didn't even like football."

"Well it's a good thing you dumped her then." Angie straightened, and I realized I hadn't even asked her to sit down. We'd been standing the whole time and I felt if I asked her to sit now it would probably be inviting trouble. I guess we'd be standing a little longer.

"Yeah, maybe."

Yes, definitely, but not because she didn't like football, because she wanted a boyfriend and I wanted sex without commitment.

"So you like women then." It wasn't a question, more a confirmation of the fact that I was very much into pussy and not cock.

"Yes, very much so." And often, just not with the attachment and dating after.

"Just casual hook ups."

"Yes, generally. It works."

This conversation was not one I wanted to be having. My bed was my business and no one else needed to hear about it. It wasn't for bragging rights. Not even the band knew the full extent of my extracurricular activities. They'd seen me with a girl or two, but for the most part it was kept on the down low. Like I said, Dan took the heat off for a lot of years.

"Do you know them? Like, know their names?"

Well, wasn't that the question of the century. It actually helped if I didn't know them too well, made it easier. I'd never paid for sex but that line of who was a whore wasn't always clear. They weren't prostitutes, but who was I to question their lifestyle, especially when I was doing what I was doing.

"Sometimes. Not always. They knew what they were getting themselves in to. I don't pretend it's going to be more than it is."

She flinched. Not a lot, but enough for me to notice. Obviously, not the answer she'd expected. Maybe the truth disgusted her, not that I blamed her. My reality was no fucking fairytale.

"Well I guess I know then." Her eyes shot down to the floor before coming back to me. "Thanks."

Any progress the two of us had made went right out the window. I felt the chill coming off her as her invisible wall went up.

"Know what?" I asked.

That I was an asshole? That I fucked around? That I was a complete commitment-phobe? Obviously, she was disgusted.

"Know ..." She hesitated before continuing. "That you're not gay."

"Don't lie, Angie. What were you going to say?"

It wasn't like her to bite her tongue; it made me uneasy. I'd rather have her say it to my face. It's not like it wouldn't be something I hadn't already said to myself.

"It doesn't matter." She shot down any further hope for discussion as she made for the door. "I should go. Rusty wants to go through another song for tonight."

"A new cover?" It was a cheap shot but I hoped if I changed the subject I could get her to stay a little longer. I just needed more time. Time to work her out.

"Yes." She tried to smile but didn't quite pull it off.

"I'll look forward to it." Lord knows I'd be sitting there watching like I had the last couple of nights, no need to pretend like I wasn't.

"Yeah, whatever." She grabbed at the doorknob and yanked it open. Her back faced me as I watched her about to leave.

"Angie, did you really think I was gay?"

She took a deep breath but didn't turn around. "No."

She stayed still in her spot as I walked up behind her and whispered in her ear. "Are you going to tell me what you're holding back?"

"No," she whispered back.

"You should go then."

"I know. I'm going."

Her feet moved and then she was gone, the door slamming behind her.

Angie

WHAT JASON HAD SAID RIPPED RIGHT THROUGH ME.

Casual hook ups.

He didn't do relationships.

Sex with lots of different women.

It's what worked.

Sex with me, didn't.

Well, he hadn't said that but that's what he meant. What did he say about his ex girlfriend? She was sweet but wanted things he couldn't give her. Is that what he'd thought about me? At least he hadn't run out on *her*. I wonder which was worse, knowing or not, that it had all been a farce. It's not like I could ask her. Not sure I wanted to know the answer.

What I didn't understand was he said they all—the hordes of women, okay maybe I was exaggerating—knew what they were getting into. I hadn't. At no time did he ever imply it was just sex, well I guess he did when he told me it was a mistake and left, but that was after the fact. He didn't get to change the rules after; that was not fair.

Perhaps I'd missed the briefing before, the one he obviously gave to these women who had no problem screwing him and not getting attached. That had been my bad, I guess. I got attached.

"Hey, you solid? You're not still hung over are you?" Rusty burst through the dressing room door. Once again he hadn't knocked. Once again, I had been dressed hours ago.

"Don't you ever knock? And no, I'm not still hung over." If I hadn't been sober before, my candid little chat with Jase earlier sure had taken care of that.

"Knocking is for strangers. I'm family." Rusty took a seat beside my illuminated makeup mirror. "You sure you want to do *that* song tonight?"

"Yeah, I ran through it today. Just make sure the band is tight, I've got the rest covered." It was most definitely the song I wanted to sing. Years later than I should have, but at least I was getting the opportunity now.

"The band has it covered, I meant the *words*, dude." His raised eyebrow hinted at his concern.

"Did you just call me, dude?" I punched him in the arm trying to lighten the mood. Changing my mind wasn't an option.

"I call everyone, dude." Rusty barked out a laugh.

"And here I was thinking I was special."

"Stop avoiding." He knew exactly what I was doing, and he called me on it. "The song."

"It's the one that I'm singing so it would be in the band's interest to be the one that you play."

There was probably a better song out there—one that better expressed my feelings—but not one I could learn in a few hours.

Closure. That's what it was about. And this felt like the best way to do it, because despite my tough exterior, I wasn't that tough. But that was my secret, and Jason or anyone else didn't need to know it.

Rusty continued his rant on my song choice, threatening to *play the fuck out of it.* Not sure that was going to be possible but it was a conversation I was more comfortable having while I finished applying my makeup and smoothed on the finishing touches.

It would have been so much easier if he had only been gay, if that had been the reason. It must have been my alcoholic delusions—trying to make sense of it—that convinced me it was even a possibility. My stupid brain pairing together his lack of arm candy reported in the press and the hope that it was *all* women that were the problem. But nope, he was straight and just not interested. Wishful thinking hadn't helped me up to this point. Not to mention how stupid the idea seemed in the light of day, while I was sober.

Never. Drinking. Again.

"So rumor is, you made out with Jase last night." He eyed me hard while I blotted my lips with a tissue. "The whole *fuck you* thing doesn't work if you kiss him later. Sends mixed messages."

"And where did you hear this rumor?" The tissue was tossed into the trash as I turned to face him, wondering which snitch had turned me in. It could have been anyone. Traitors, the lot of them.

"From the fifty people who saw you with your tongue down his throat."

He was right; we hadn't been discreet. Funny how I was more annoyed about getting caught rather than actually kissing him, yeah that's not telling at all.

"It was nothing, I was drunk. I get friendly when I drink." Not a lie, I do get very touchy-feely after a few beers. I hugged Beth remember, and I was nice to that other girl, too. See, just friendly. "Besides, how many girls did you make out with last night huh? A little late to be throwing stones."

"I made out with three girls, and each time it was a beautiful thing." He smiled at the memory. "Just make sure you know what you are doing, Angie. You want to kiss him, do it. Hell, sleep with him if it will make you feel better. But do it with your eyes open this time."

It wasn't necessary, my eyes were well and truly open this time but I appreciated Rusty being a friend. At least someone was thinking out of the two of us. Obviously last night, it hadn't been me.

"I'm not going to sleep with him." Not that there was even the slightest chance. "I asked him if he was gay."

"What? You asked Power Station Jase if he was gay?" Rusty erupted into laugher. "Oh my God, I can't breath." He doubled over as he continued giggling his ass off. "Seriously, I wonder if there's oxygen around." And still the laughter continued. "Oh fuck, that was awesome. I wish I had've been there. Damn, girl, you're killing me."

"I'm glad you are amused." I popped him in the arm. It wasn't *that* funny and had made more sense to me this morning. Not so much now.

"Of course I'm amused, who asks someone they actually have *had* sex with if they are gay. Unless they sucked, which from all accounts he didn't." He wiped the tears from his eyes.

"How do you know he didn't suck, I never spoke about the sex."

Jase had been great. Out of this world phenomenal, but pretty sure I never mentioned it. I'd been too devastated, lots of crying. Proclamations of a broken heart a-plenty but I can almost guarantee his prowess as a lover took a backseat to how much I hated him. Asshole was thrown around a lot. Talk of great sex, not so much.

"Because *if* he sucked, sweetheart, you would have been happy to see him leave. Love him or not, life's too short for bad sex. And you had your fill with Taylor Limp-dick."

"His name was Tyler." A chuckle escaped my lips.

"Yet notice how you didn't correct me on his last name."

"Touché."

"So you asked the guy if he prefers dick. How did he take it?"

Yeah, not my finest moment. It had definitely sounded better in my head on the drive over. When I was living in my fantasy world of, maybe it wasn't me, maybe it was all women. I should have quit while I was ahead.

"Oh, he set me straight by explaining to me not only is he *not* gay, but he has meaningless sex with lots of different women. He doesn't do relationships. Could have used that memo *before* he'd had sex with me." Or alternatively had sex with me *before* I fell in love with him. Not sure it would have changed much, not that it mattered now.

"So you know then."

"Yep, I know."

Known that I had just been another vagina. Nothing special.

Even worse, less than special, because no sooner had he fucked me, had he given me my walking papers. It had always been a suspicion, one that twisted and turned in my head. It was the reason I swore never to give my heart again, not fully. But to have it confirmed was something else entirely. That cut went deep. So glad to have that new level of awareness—not.

"You wanna say that out loud?"

"Rusty, don't."

I couldn't say the words. It would make it that much more real. Make me feel that much more stupid. No. Words weren't needed. My heart ached enough without them.

"Fine, sing your damn song tonight then." Rusty wrapped his arms around me. "But I strongly recommend you don't kiss him. Kiss someone else."

"Yeah, maybe I will."

"Wow, you guys were fantastic."

Our backstage crowd had grown to include not only Power Station but also some of their wives. Ashlyn and Megs, Dan and Troy's ladies, were the newest additions.

"That N'Sync song sounded crazy good. I loved it." Ashlyn, the redhead whose last name she shared with Dan, threw her arms around me in a hug.

Great. I wasn't good with touching when I was sober, although Ashlyn didn't seem to have the same trouble as she beamed at me. Rusty and the boys wandered off, leaving me to accept the adulation on my own. Bastards.

"Thanks." My hands awkwardly tapped her on the back, not knowing exactly what to do here. "Who didn't love that song, right?"

"I know. Can you imagine if that was written about you? Hey, I loved you but I'm kicking your ass to the curb and leaving. Kind of the ultimate fuck you."

Wow. She had got it. That was exactly what the song was about and even though she hadn't been my intended audience, I was glad at least someone saw my genius.

"Yeah, that sounded great." Megan aka Megs aka Mrs. Troy took her turn in giving me unsolicited affection, she received the same stiff-arm tap, tap I'd given Ash.

The two ladies, as well as being married to their rock star husbands, were also best friends. Oh and totally welcoming, didn't even look at me funny once or ask me why I had so many tattoos. Plus neither had accused me of trying to sleep with their husbands either. It was almost too normal. Could these women actually ... like me?

Of course the song they were referring to was *N'Sync's* "Bye, Bye, Bye." The message of the song, as Ash had so appropriately put it, was I love you but I'm kicking your ass to the curb. See ya. Full stop.

"Well, well, Angie. You seemed to have won over some new fans." Troy planted a kiss on his pregnant wife, which of course had her wriggling with delight. Which was not surprising considering the few times I had seen her, she seemed to be in a perpetual state of happiness. I wasn't sure she had another mood. Oh and she called her husband by his whole name, kind of adorable but mostly weird.

"Don't give her a head swell." Dan snuck up behind his significant other, Ash. "We need for her head to be able to get through the door." He not so subtly kissed her neck.

Those Power Station men did that a lot, PDA's I mean. It was as if they had decided everyone needed to be aware of how loved up they were. I wasn't sure if it was sad or sweet. Perhaps we should be breaking out in the song, "Can you feel the love tonight."

Everyone laughed.

Crap. How much of that had I said out loud? I needed to keep better track of my mouth.

"Just the part about *The Lion King*, and they are laughing because I'd said the same thing at Dan and Ash's wedding. Strange coincidence." Jason materialized from the darkness.

While making out with wives was what the other band members did, appearing from the shadows was Jason's usual trick. "I'm assuming you hadn't meant to say it. Or the bit about needing to keep better track of your mouth."

"Yeah. Sorry. No disrespect intended."

While I didn't care for Jason's opinion, I wasn't deliberately going out of my way to be a bitch. I know that's what people generally thought, my appearance and general attitude not really soft around the edges, but part of that was insecurity. Rudeness wasn't attractive and not something I wanted to be known for, even if in the past that was what I had usually come to expect from other girls. I assumed my newfound hug buddies would make the regular assumptions about me, that I was a whore or something. Then hate me, and warn me off their men.

"None, taken." Ash shrugged, her smile still sincere.

Wow. Maybe she wasn't going to automatically dislike me.

Both Ash and Megs were stunningly beautiful, confident and educated. Sassy too and it was hard not to be awed in their presence. They seemed so well put together, I on the other hand, was not. My mom had been like them. Classically beautiful, smart and so kind that I'd wondered if she hadn't been an angel all along. Sometimes I thought if she'd been around longer things would have been different. If maybe some of that might have hopefully rubbed off on me. Instead of me being, well ... me.

"You guys let her off the hook too easily. I would have totally made her sweat it out a little longer," Dan unhelpfully added.

"Oh hush, Dan. Don't be an ass." Ash elbowed Dan in the ribs.

She didn't take his shit either. I actually really like this girl.

"Thanks, I like you, too." Ash giggled.

"Yeah, I should probably go now before I embarrass myself further." I prayed the floor under me would swallow me as I resolved to staple my mouth freaking shut.

"No, hang out with us." Megs grabbed my arm, her smile just as warm as her friend's had been. "It will be fun. Say whatever you want, we don't care."

"Exactly, and Megs has a tendency to let her mouth fly so we're totally used to it." Ash laughed, Megs nodded, not even trying to disprove her statement.

They were being nice, and seeming so welcoming of me. Not

mean or judgmental, like they were actually interested in getting to know who I was. Which was completely unexpected, because along with never giving my heart away again, I'd assumed I'd never have that. Even going so far as telling myself I didn't need them—girlfriends. But, it was really kind of cool. I wondered if this is what sisterhood felt like. Sort of like peeing in the pool, I felt completely weird doing it but I really liked the warm feeling it gave me.

"C'mon Dan and Jase, we're on in ten. Ladies, we'll see you after the show." Troy said his goodbyes and rounded up the troops, all with his arms still around Megs. "You need anything?" The last bit was only for her.

He was being so incredibly sweet, even a non-believer like me couldn't help but be sucked into a sappy awww-aren't-they-just-adorable. Thankfully this time my mouth had stayed shut.

"Troy Harris, I'm fine. Go." Her small frame comically pushed him toward the stage exit. Dan laughed as he kissed Ash goodbye and made his way out.

"By the way, I love this new T-shirt with the arms cut off." Megs ran her hands suggestively over his biceps. "It's freaking sexy, you're so getting laid tonight."

"Yeah, not what you want to say to me, Megs, right before getting on stage." Troy's voice rumbled as he slowly edged her toward the back wall.

Ummmm. Hello. We're still here. Please don't have sex in front of us.

"I'm pregnant. I've got no control over it." She didn't even seem the slightest bit sorry. The smile she wore a hint that she enjoyed seeing him all revved up. "Go smack stuff, and then come back to me."

"Okay, I'll just be over here." I sidestepped a little and gave them their privacy. Well as much as they were going to be getting with a bunch of other people milling around. But I figured some pretty showy kisses were bound to happen before Troy got out the door, and I didn't need to see that.

"You're a popular girl."

Oh look, Jason was still here. Awesome.

"Oh, I'm sure I'm just a novelty. But they seem really nice."

All true. I wasn't sure how long their fascination with me would last but I was glad I was able to survive the small talk and not sound moronic. Chit-chat was not something I excelled in and I really did think both Megs and Ash were great.

"They are. Both those girls are sweethearts. Honest, loyal and genuine." His eyes didn't move from mine as he rattled off the remarkable attributes of his band mates' wives.

Jase also forgot to mention beautiful, which both of them were. "Looks like they won the wife lotto. Lucky them." Which explained the fixed state of happy their husbands seemed to be in.

Had me wondering why he would choose his sex with no strings lifestyle when he saw what he could have. Surely, it couldn't feel the same. It was the first time I actually felt a little sorry for him.

"Yep, lucky them." Jase moved closer, his big body dominating the space. "Interesting song choice." The direction of the conversation took a sharp left turn.

Avoidance, or he was just done with the other conversation? It seemed really sudden to be talking about one thing and then, boom, something else. Still I needed to remind myself that Jason Irwin was not a riddle that I needed to solve.

"Oh it's a classic, you know. We just jazzed it up. JT is a crowd pleaser."

I followed his lead, moving the conversation to a place that was probably safer—music, songs, my finales etc. The appropriateness of the song's message didn't get a mention sadly, but I secretively hoped he'd been around when Ash was making her observations. Probably not—such a shame.

"Yeah, is there a pattern to these covers? Or just random songs? You have to admit, your choices are a little left of center."

It felt like a fishing expedition, like he knew there was *something* there but he hadn't worked it out. The songs almost too random to be accidental choices. Well, I sure as hell wasn't going to tell him. Oh, no. My odes to him could be like a little treasure hunt. Eventually the penny would drop.

"We like left of center."

Really, what was center anyway? Clearly I was the last person you should be asking because despite everything I knew, deep down, I felt like I was fighting a losing battle. The one where I told myself I was over him.

"I guess I'll have to wait and see tomorrow's song. Last show in New York before we hit the road."

"Looking forward to it."

So not looking forward to it.

"Jase, don't you have somewhere to be? Stop crowding, Angie." Megs had obviously freed herself from Troy, the latter having already disappeared. "Ash and I found her first."

Oh how wrong she was, Jason had most definitely found me first, but I was thankful for the reprieve. All these warm feelings, I could feel myself softening. Just a few more minutes and I probably would have jumped into his lap. So much for my *I am never going to kiss him again*. My lips had happily screwed me over by spewing every single thought that had passed through my head; they would just as surely betray me when it came to kissing. The bastards would probably welcome it.

"Bye ladies. Enjoy the show." Jason said *ladies*, but he was only looking at me. Totally sexy move too because we'd already established what his eyes did to me and why I hated them. The reason—in case it was unclear—being the things they did to my girlie parts.

"See ya, Jase."

"Bye, Jase."

Megs and Ash took their turns in saying their farewells. Their excitement bubbling as they turned to me. I had no idea what their plans were, honestly didn't care. Whatever they were, they had to be safer than standing here with him.

"Bye." I shoved as much confidence into my voice as I could. Bye, bye, bye. I repeated in my head as my mind floated over the lyrics I had just sung.

He smiled—something else of his that I hated—and then disappeared down one of the narrow corridors.

"Let's go grab a place to watch the show, okay?" Ash's head tilted toward the mostly deserted hallway.

"Sure." I shrugged; with my band AWOL I didn't have any other plans.

"Great." Megs slung an arm around me. This time, I didn't mind the touching so much. "We're going to have an awesome night."

"We so are."

A nervous laugh escaped from my throat. This was a new start, a way to break away from my past—all of it. There was no going back. Goodbyes had been said, I was moving on and Jason could have as many casual hook ups as he wanted. In fact, I'd have a few of my own. This tour would not be my undoing. Finally, I felt free.

"WOMANIZER" BY *BRITNEY SPEARS.*

That had been the next night's song choice. And I knew for a fact she couldn't stand Britney. And it wasn't a coincidence that she had just learned about my colorful dating history and, there you go—a song about a man who couldn't keep it in his pants.

I'd had my suspicions about the random additions to their set list. First I thought it was the band trying to be edgy, an unpredicted tune mashed up with some distortion and heavy beats giving the crowd a we-aren't-a-one-trick-pony.

Wrong. While they had proved they could pull a Top 40 high-rotation song and inject it with some rock, I highly doubted that had been their motivator. I'd say the reason was more on par with what Ash had said after the *N'Sync* performance. A big, loud, fuck you. Womanizer. Well that was the smoking gun.

Was I offended? Not even close. I was intrigued beyond fucking measure.

I assumed Angie was leading the parade on the musical vendetta. The sly smile she wore thinking I hadn't clued up was almost adorable. But I wasn't that stupid. She could have left smaller breadcrumbs and I *still* would have found the trail. The fact that it pleased me wasn't right. It shouldn't please me, it should fucking horrify me. But in my twisted mind that connection was better than none. Give me a minute while I go book some therapy.

That she still hated me, or that she thought of me, was the variable. And it was a coin toss as to which of those was the one I was hoping for. She had every right to hate me; we'd already established I had been less than a gentleman. That she still thought of me; well wasn't I the sick bastard who strangely got off on that.

With New York done and dusted we'd headed to Boston. The plane ride had shown me another side to her. She seemed different, more relaxed on the short flight. Like we'd entered into a silent truce. Except for at night on stage when I was sure to get the usual burn she planned on serving up. And wasn't I just looking forward to it more than I should.

Ash reuniting with her family in her hometown was pretty sweet. While Lexi and Hannah we're on the tour for the long haul, Megs and Ash were temps. They'd join us when they could, which would be for the next two weeks before they scaled it back to weekends. Both of them had clocks to punch and jobs to be at, so following around their men on tour wasn't in the cards. Plus Megs was expecting, it was only a matter of time before her doc pulled the plug and stopped her flying altogether. That was going to be a fun day, Troy probably not going to do well with the separation.

Knowing that I was the only one who didn't have an entourage might have made another dude sad, especially seeing how happy everyone else was. But I'd resigned myself to fate a long time ago. That part of the story wasn't destined for me, and I was okay with that.

"Why don't yer drink a real beer." Ash's dad laughed as he shoved a pint of the thick brown draft he'd just pulled in front of me. Guinness. Somehow I didn't think anyone was going to be asking for *Miller Lite.*

"Thanks, Finton." I lifted my glass. "For the beer, and the hospitality."

"Pleasure." His Irish accent causing the words to lilt. "Anything for my baby girl." He shot Ash a proud grin as he mopped up the bar. His baby girl doing a fine job of proving no matter how long it had been since she'd pulled a beer, she still had what it took.

"Babe, you are turning me on right now." Dan leaned not so subtly forward in his bar stool. "Watching you do that with your hand is giving me such a hard-on."

"Dan." She didn't skip a beat as she pulled another glass. "My dad is right there." Her eyes darted to the man who had closed up shop so we could have a private reception. He probably hadn't heard Dan but the vibe he was throwing off was unmistakable, like a cat in fucking heat. No one needed to see it, especially not Ashlyn's dad.

"Keep it in your pants, lover boy." Alex gave him a friendly slap across the back. "The kids don't need to see you dry humping a bar stool." His glance shot to Lexi, who was sitting with Hannah and the collective of rug rats. The mountain of toys, coloring shit and other crap covering the table they were seated around. It was the only time the kids were probably going to be in a bar.

"The kids love their Uncle Dan, don't you kids?" Dan turned his attention to the little people who proved how smart they already were by ignoring him. Their heads buried in whatever activity that was dominating their little minds. "Not cool, children." Dan shook his head. "I'll remember this when your parents piss you off and you want to run away to Uncle Dan's."

"God, help us if that happens." James laughed, throwing back what was left of his beer. "Or when there is a little version of him running around."

"Nah, Ash has superior DNA, it will override Dan's. Their kids are safe," Troy chimed in, taking a sip from his glass. His drink, an iced tea; keeping his wife company with the alcohol avoid.

"Hi, sorry we're late." Angie walked through the side door, her long hair floating around her shoulders as she stepped into the room. She was wearing a skirt for a change; her tanned legs getting lots of view time given the length of the hem. Wow. I didn't know who the designer was, but I suddenly felt the need to write them a thank-you.

Ash's mom ushered the rest of *Black Addiction* through. Not that I gave a shit, my attention still locked on to Angie. "The cab drivers here are freaking crazy." She shot a look toward Ash's dad who was smiling. "No offense."

"Nah. None taken. The cab drivers are crazy. Take a seat." He nodded to the collection of empty tables. "We'll get yah fed soon enough." The hospitality extended to dinner and chill time for all of us at *Murphy's Irish Tavern*.

She gave him a smile that would no doubt melt his damn heart, her dark eyes scanning the room before taking a seat. My eyes shifted to the curve of her thighs, her hem riding up a little and exposed more skin as she sat. Got me thinking about what was in between them. Damn. I needed to focus, and probably get laid at some point.

And while the rest of her band sunk their asses into chairs as well, none of them held my attention like she had. The conversation flowed easy. And it turns out that they weren't only a good support band, but they were polite bastards too, remembering their pleases and thank yous, charming Ash's parents.

Max, their bass player, confessed to being a Red Sox fan, which had Ash's dad almost blow his load. Ash stirred the pot a little more by smiling at the bass player that wasn't her own, which earned the poor bastard some heated stares from Dan.

"Hey, Pa, you need a hand?"

A diagram of the family tree wasn't needed to assume that the dude who wandered in was Ash's brother. Besides the obvious of addressing his old man, the family resemblance was also pretty hard to miss.

"Liam!" Ash squealed, hugging the guy within an inch of his life. "Everyone this is my brother, Liam."

I'm sure I'd probably met him at the wedding, but obviously the introduction hadn't been memorable.

"Hey everyone." He gave us all a wave, his smile getting a little wider when his eyes settled on Angie. Bastard didn't even try and hide the fact he was scoping her out. Just stood there smiling like a douchebag with his dick in his hand.

Knowing I had no claim to her didn't make me any less edgy. We'd been through it before—none of my business, and yet there I was, wondering which fingernail I'd rip off first if he laid a hand on her. The guy was an easy read too, his attention not shifting since he entered the room. The big ass grin plastered on his face further proved where his interests lay. And they weren't on helping his *Pa.*

Angie should date. Of course she should. And she could be with anyone she wanted—just not this guy. He was probably a decent guy, truth is I knew jack about him. Except that he wanted to fuck her. That part was plainly obvious. Which of course made me instantly dislike him.

Rough introductions were made by Ash with hellos and how-you-doings being thrown at the guy as he settled in with the group; the dick taking a seat right next Angie despite his dad telling him his help wasn't required. Not obvious at all, asshole. He immediately climbed to the top of my shit list.

"So you are musicians?" Dickhead asked. The fact I knew his name was Liam meant very little to me.

"Some of us, some not so much." Dan grinned at Max, answering his brother-in-law.

"It's two bands," Ash pitched in given that Dan's explanation hadn't been adequate. "Angie, Rusty, Max and Joey are in Black Addiction. They are Power Station's support for this tour."

"And what do you play?" Loser turned his head toward Angie in what I can only assume was an attempt to flirt. Newsflash. He sucked at it.

"I sing and play guitar."

Thankfully she didn't seem to be swallowing his bullshit line, the information that she gave him stock standard and without any extra attention. Had to admit, that was the only part of the exchange I was actually enjoying.

Apart from the obvious train wreck that was poor Liam Murphy's attempt at seduction, the room hummed with conversation. The others got pulled into one exchange or another, bullshit chatter filling the air. I, on the other hand, was curious to see how our resident Casanova was going to play this out. My eyes and ears trained on them both.

"I'm sure we'll be seeing you headlining your own tour soon." Liam's fingers drummed nervously on the table.

Clueless. I almost felt sorry for the guy. He was fucking drowning in a sea of no-fucking-idea and Angie hadn't so much as given him a second look. It made me want to laugh, my body finally relaxing in the seat as I watched him fight a losing battle.

"We'd need to be signed and have recorded an album before that can happen. It's a long way off. But thanks." The brush off was gentle—who knew she had it in her—as Angie shifted uncomfortably in her chair. She really wasn't into him. A celebratory drink was definitely in the cards, my glass raised toward my smirk as I took another drink.

"Liam, Riley's here." Ash's dad gave the poor douche an out, the sound of footsteps coming toward the bar from the direction of the kitchen.

"Shit, I forgot we were supposed to hang." The disappointment on his face was real, as was my utter freaking delight.

"Hey, you ready to go?" A dude who was around the same height as Alex, strolled through the door. "Hell, man, didn't realize you had company." The new guy peeled the ball cap off of his head, and shoved it into the back of his jeans.

"Hi, Riley," Ash and Megs sung out at the same time. Seemed like the new guy had a fan club.

"Hey, Ash, didn't realize you were home, doll. Let me get your loser brother out of your hair." He shot Ash a wink, Dan stiffened beside me at the mention of the word *doll*. I guess it wasn't a good night for either of us.

"Ry, you wanna stick around? Pull up a chair and chill for a while." Liam gave his buddy the subtle head tip toward Angie, in what I can only assume was some fucked up bro-signal that he was trying to put the moves on. I'd seen Tibetan Monks with more game.

The new guy—Riley, another name I gave zero fucks in knowing—rolled his eyes before he took a few steps closer to where his buddy was situated.

"I'm Riley." He offered Angie a handshake, not waiting for an introduction. "You want me to get rid of him for you?"

Angie laughed, a real one this time, not of the lame variety she'd been giving Liam. I didn't like it.

"It's fine. I'm Angie, by the way."

All that interest she hadn't shown the first guy was directed at the feet of this one. Me wanting Liam to disappear had been premature. He wasn't the enemy; no he was the harmless decoy. Riley—I really hated saying the asshole's name—not only had Angie's attention but didn't suffer from the same deer-in-headlights his friend had been struck down with.

"Nice to meet you, Angie." Douchebag number two flashed her a grin like he was auditioning for a toothpaste commercial. "I'd love to stay and chat but we have a hot date with … exactly what could we be pretending to do tonight that might sound cool?" He looked to his clueless friend who answered with a shrug.

She laughed.

And it really, really pissed me off.

Not because her head was thrown back as she enjoyed whatever bullshit was spilling from his mouth, but that I was rationally trying to justify punching the asshole in the face.

The reasons didn't even make fucking sense. We'd established that we were barely even friends. Yet, here I was, my fist ready to get busy on the asshole's face as I watched him put the moves on my girl.

Wow. Dangerous territory. She wasn't *my* girl. I didn't have a girl, and if I did I'm pretty sure the shit I'd pulled years ago guaranteed Angie wouldn't be in a hurry to fill the role. I couldn't just flip the script now. I'd made my choices. And it was better for both of us, both then and now. *Remember the reasons, asshole. Remember why you don't do relationships.*

The noise of the room resumed as conversations picked up from where they'd left off. Power Station and Black Addiction settled into what seemed like a relaxed night of not much happening, which is exactly what had been the plan. It also became clear that douche one and douche two would also not be leaving. No one else seemed to have a problem except for me, if the motherfucking easy vibe was anything to go by.

"Hey, you cool?" Troy had ninja'd himself onto the bar stool beside me. It could have been a circus of monkeys and I'd probably still been surprised, my attention too locked onto Angie to notice. The feeling made me uncomfortable, as did the heat prickling at my neck. Animosity I had no business feeling was setting up and taking residence.

"Yeah, I was actually just thinking the about time we all got together. Back in Montreal."

Well not so much the city but more as to why I ended up in the Great White North. It was the same reason why I wouldn't tangle with that whole love game bullshit, and the same reason why I'd known I'd screwed up after Angie. No matter how much distance and time passes, there are some things you just can't outrun.

"Montreal? Fuck, dude. That was an eternity ago. That hockey game changed the band lineup forever."

"I'd say it was more the bar fight than the hockey game."

"Right? Holy shit, that was a good time. Dan had a black eye for days."

"He probably shouldn't have asked the goalie's girlfriend for a blowjob."

We both laughed. Just as we had after the fight, which not only served as our introduction but changed things for all of us.

Back then Power Station was a foursome, still finding their feet. No deals, no labels, just the music. James had managed to secure them a gig across the border, which made for a nice addition to their resumes—international gig. The fact the Rangers were playing that weekend had sweetened the pot, hell they would have played that shitty sports bar for free. My reasons for being there were very different.

Traveling alone, in the hopes of getting so drunk I'd forget the misery I'd left back in Albany, I'd found myself in the very same bar. Dan's mouth had got him to trouble; something that I would later learn was typical and expected.

Jumping into the fight wasn't something I thought about. In fact, it had been the exact opposite. I hadn't been thinking. But taking a right hook to the jaw beat the hell out of sitting in that seedy, worn booth alone feeling sorry for myself. And at that point, the reason to get up was as good as any. My assist helped even out the numbers between Canadians and Americans. I didn't even care why I was hitting people or getting hit, it just felt fucking fantastic to not be dealing with the messed up slide show I had repeating in my head. The conversation we'd had after, while icing up and swapping names, was when shit turned out to be a game changer.

Their band had been good, even in my half-hammered state I'd seen it a mile away. They just need something else—me. Who even remembered whose idea it had been, but it wasn't much of a discussion in any case. We'd all sobered up and drove back to New York, where I was crashing at Troy's till we got our plan for greatness sorted. I didn't even go home to say goodbye. There was no need and my folks more than understanding of the whys, shipped my shit to Troy's address the week after.

"So what's got you thinking about that? Getting sentimental in your old age?" Troy's sideways glance concerned about where this was leading. It had been a while since we'd taken that stroll down memory lane.

"Watch it asshole, I'm not yelling at the kids to get off my lawn just yet." It had also been a while since the three years I had on them came up in discussion. Still, it was all about the classics tonight it seemed.

"Probably because you can't hear them, maybe turn the hearing aid up. How old are you now? Forty-five? Fifty?" The bastard laughed, thoroughly enjoying himself.

"Thirty-five and I could still out run all of you every day of the week and twice on Sunday."

"No doubt." Troy nodded, the look on his face easing away from yanking my chain to respect. "You got something on your mind, brother?"

Ha. Where to even start on what was on my mind? So many scrambled, messed up thoughts, and they all were given birth to by the same fucking woman.

"Em."

Just saying her name made me want to glass myself in the face. The goddamn hate and rage that those two fucking letters came with, it was a dangerous place to be.

Not the same kind that I was in when I thought of Angie. No, while that had the capacity to make me act irresponsible and make bad decisions, it wasn't the kind that was going to see me doing jail time. Which is exactly where I would have ended up if I hadn't have left Em and my hometown behind. The band, it had been more than just a gig. It had saved my life. Saved me from a road that there would be no coming back from, and that's why I'd take a bullet of any of them.

"Not a name I hoped to be hearing." Troy's lowered voice kept our conversation tight between us. Best we didn't do a show-and-tell, especially not here.

Yeah, not a name I wanted to be saying either. But no amount of booze, women, time or fucking distance would ever jack that evil bitch from my mind. Like a motherfucking scab that could be picked off at a moment's notice and open the festering wound. There weren't many people that I hated; in fact that list was reserved for just one. Her.

"The flashback isn't intentional and my feelings of zen aren't cutting it tonight." Even Mother Teresa would have had her work cut out for her. Em, was pure evil and if the devil hadn't claimed her as his own it was because even *he* didn't trust her.

"Fuck," Troy warned, not even trying to hide the concern in his eyes. He knew how quickly it could go bad. "She's not worth it, Jase. Don't get pulled back in."

"Trust me, not going there." Not unless I was willing to give up everything I'd worked for in the time between leaving her and now, and I sure as shit was not giving her that satisfaction. The bitch had taken enough.

"You better not be. Seriously, Jase. Don't go there."

He knew. Knew where the road would lead, had seen it first hand as I busted some asshole's nose for no fucking good reason other than I was itching to get into a fight. Because of her, because of what she'd done, and because of what I had become in the aftermath.

My gaze flicked over to Angie and I felt like I was going to be sick. Her beautiful eyes sparkling as she enjoyed the fuckwit putting on his lame-ass moves. And so she should. At least he was being honest with her, not like I had been. I hadn't even been fucking honest with myself that night, fooling myself that I could sleep with her and shit would all be okay. Right, and we all lived in fantasyland where leprechauns sat on buckets of gold and assholes like me didn't use a sweet girl like her.

That's what it had been, no point pretending like it wasn't. I'd wanted her and I took her, not even giving the consequences a second thought. Her feelings, they'd also been on the backburner because if I'd given half a fuck about anyone but myself, I would have gone and screwed someone else. Anyone else but her. Yet, here we were.

"Hey, do you think anyone would care if I bailed? I know we were supposed to be doing the hanging-as-a-band shit tonight, but I really want to get out of here." Not just to get this twisted stench of misery off me, but also to stop me from having to watch Angie score. Both primed to push me over the edge.

"Do not call her." Troy grabbed my arm as I got up to leave.

"I won't, trust me. I promise you, I'm not stupid enough to make that same mistake twice." I'd rather cut my own dick off than see or speak to her again.

"Then go do whatever it is you need to do to get your head right. I'll handle the Q and A if anyone sticks their nose in." Troy gave a slow nod, giving me my out.

"Thanks." I met his eyes and nodded. I wasn't just thanking him for this. It was more. Much, much more.

"All good, brother."

"See ya."

No one noticed me leaving; they didn't even look up. The conversations had balled together to become a big amount of white noise.

It wasn't just about Em, although she was the springboard. I needed out, in a big way.

Troy was right about one thing; I needed my head right. That shit getting revisited wouldn't help anyone, least of all me. It was done and buried. *Move on, asshole.* Which is exactly what I intended to do.

Waiting outside was our driver—not TJ the guy who usually ferried us around—Jake, the dude we took on tour with us. The ex-seal also doubled as security. It was a pain in the ass but that was our life now, so rather than pissing and moaning about it, I just accepted it.

"G'evening, Sir." Jake stood to attention as soon as my boots hit the outside sidewalk. Though I doubted he'd been chilling even before I'd appeared. Old habits died hard, and despite this guy leaving the Navy a long time ago, he was still rocking *the service before self* mentality.

"Dude, it's just us. You can lose the sir."

"Sorry, s—" He caught himself for finishing. "I'm working on it."

He held the door open of the blacked-out SUV and waited for me to get inside before swinging around to the driver's side and climbing in himself. "Where do you want to go?"

"Drive around a little. Maybe find some company."

Yeah, 'cause sex is always the answer. Great. I really was a motherfucking asshole. Well, I might as well not fight the tide; it's probably the reason why I was in this damn mess in the first place, trying to be something that I wasn't. I wasn't boyfriend material. I fucked and I left, that is what I had told Angie so why I was trying to pretend that's not what I was going to continue to do was beyond me. Best I set things back to the way they needed to be and the sooner, the better.

RILEY WAS SWEET, AS WAS ASH'S BROTHER LIAM, BUT THERE WAS NO way I would be hooking up with either of them. How could I even go there? Nope, I need more degrees of separation than that. Pity, because Riley was good looking. My future self will thank me when I'm not doing the walk of shame tomorrow and having to look Ash in the eye. It would be too weird, even for me.

"Crap, my phone is completely dead." Stupidly I shook it like it would suddenly spring back to life. Predictably the red flashing battery icon didn't change, with the last gasp of juice evaporating and the screen shutting down. Awesome.

"You need a phone, Angie? Here use mine." Riley pulled his iPhone from his pocket and placed it on the table. His smile telling me he was offering me more than just the use of his minutes.

"Thanks, but I was actually looking to email my dad." It had been less than twenty-four hours since I'd left New York, and while my brain told me he was a grown man capable of looking after himself, I still worried. It was the good Catholic, Italian upbringing unfortunately. Here, have a side of guilt with your lasagna.

"Hey, Angie. You need something?" Troy lifted his head from the other end of the table, his concern working overtime between keeping tabs on me and fussing over his knocked-up wife. Megs looked thankful that he found a new target, the smile she directed at me hinting we were both in for a long haul.

"Yeah, I just wanted to email my dad, but my phone died. The battery life is a joke." I shoved the phone back onto the table; it's not like it was any use to me anyway in its current state. "It's just this nightly thing. Keeping an eye on him. I haven't left him alone before; I just like to check he hasn't burnt the house down or forgotten how to program the DVR. It's lame."

"It's not lame, I'm sure he appreciates knowing you are okay. Can't be easy for him, you being so far from home." Megs gently rubbed her small but growing bump. Troy followed up with a nod.

"Yeah, well it's going to take a while for this stupid thing to charge. I should probably head back to the hotel." I started gathering my things and wondering if it would be cool if I snagged the use of one of their drivers. They had two after all, and it's not like I'd keep him occupied for long. The idea of getting into another cab and playing Russian roulette wasn't ranking high on the way I wanted to spend my evening.

"We have a computer in the office you can use?" Ash offered, her chair shifting back as she moved to get up.

"It's cool, I should be getting back anyway." The attention everyone was suddenly paying me, making me uncomfortable. No need to get excited people, just let me slink off and send the email. "Besides, I want to go over a song. It's new."

"I chose it," Rusty unhelpfully added, his fork waving in the air as he finished his second serving of dessert. The man could eat anything he wanted and still not get fat. He really did have such a charmed life.

"You want to use my laptop? It's hooked up to the Wi-Fi in my room. Just get Brad to take you back and send your email from there. Saves you waiting for your phone to charge. Megs wants to hang with Ash a little longer before we head back. Let me just grab my key." Troy reached into his pocket and pulled out the small credit card-sized plastic keycard.

"It's okay, I don't want to put you out. Besides, as soon as I plug in, it will power up enough to use." Seriously, could everyone go back to their pie and not worry about me?

"Yeah, but didn't you want to go over a song as well? Just let the freaking thing charge properly. It's a computer, Angie, no big deal. Here's my room key. Jase, Dan and I are on the top floor. Just use the keycard to get access to our floor and in the shared living area is the desk. It's sitting right on top." Troy extended his hand, the plastic keycard in it waiting for me to take it.

"Are you sure? Won't someone be up there?"

It hadn't escaped my attention that he had listed the occupants of that particular floor. Himself and Megs, Dan and Ash, annnnnnd Jason. Who at some point before we'd even eaten dinner had slipped out and was currently MIA. Not that I was worried, I mean it was none of my business, he could be doing anything he wanted, and I so would not care.

Not at all.

Not in the slightest.

Just as long as he wasn't there.

I could still not care and not want to be alone in a room with him. That still counted. Well it did in my book, and my book was the only one that mattered.

"Jase is off somewhere, and the rest of us are here, so you're good. Trust me, no one is up there. Do what you need to do and then leave the key on the desk. We'll use Dan's when we want access."

He had been very non-committal about Jason's whereabouts. *Somewhere* was not a place. In fact it was the absence of a place and not where you'd want a member of your band to be, especially if they were famous. Surely their record label had them all micro-chipped or tagged or whatever. So either Troy knew, and didn't want to say, which was completely plausible—we'd already established it was none of my business—or he genuinely didn't know, which you had to wonder why he wasn't more worried.

Not my problem. Well, that's what I told myself as I grabbed the key from Troy and got ready to leave.

"Thanks, Troy. I owe you."

"Let's say you coming on tour with us made us even." He gave me a smile and went back to the conversation at the table, his arm slung back around Megs.

I gave everyone a wave and "see ya" as I made my way to the door, Riley offering to "walk me out," I guess in case I got lost. It was a complicated journey, the ten-foot straight shot to the door.

"So you're going?" Riley asked, making an exaggerated puppy dog expression in what I can only assume was a show of disappointment.

"Yeah, I have stuff to do." *Email my dad, learn a song and not have sex with you.* "It was cool meeting you though; if you are ever in New York you should look me up." *Oh please don't look me up, why did I say that?* "Um … So …"

I wasn't sure whether I should wave, offer him a handshake or a hug. High five? Did I mention how bad I was at small talk? I literally sucked.

"It was good meeting you, too." He pulled me in for a hug, solving the what-do-we-do problem. I still wasn't sold. Too much touching and I'd already established how I felt about strangers touching me.

"Alrighty. See ya." Clutching Troy's keycard and my dead phone as I gave Riley a friendly tap on the back and made my way to the waiting SUV. There was only one still parked beside the pub. The other one probably wherever Jase had disappeared to. The magical land of *somewhere*, no doubt. At least I wouldn't be running into him. Definitely a positive.

Brad, the driver who took me back to the hotel, didn't speak. Not unless you counted his nods and grunts as communication. In any case, I was happy to not have to make small talk. Plus he looked liked he ate a side of beef at every meal—there's huge, and then there was the whole fuck-are-you-a-person-or-a-planet mystery—when was the last time anyone saw the Incredible Hulk? Are we sure he isn't moonlighting as Power Station's security? I'd say it would be foolish to completely discount the theory.

As the elevator doors opened on the floor the trio's rooms were situated on, it was clear how different their suites were from ours. Our hotel rooms were lush, stunning even, but this was something else. It was like our rooms, only on steroids.

A huge shared space stretched out in front of me. The three large wooden doors to the penthouse rooms decorated the periphery, past all the expensive furniture and obscenely large flat screen television.

In addition to the television—or time traveling portal, it really could be either—were two huge leather couches, a massive mahogany desk and an office chair. Thankfully the laptop was where Troy had promised, sitting on the desk. That meant I didn't have to snoop around in bedrooms. Because that would have been bad, right? I had no interest in seeing where Jason slept, or what his personal space looked like. Being in his apartment had been bad enough; I mean his bedroom, even if it were just a temporary one would be bad news, right?

No.

I'm not looking. No reason to. I'm sending my email, downloading my song notes, and getting the hell out of here. Focus. This wasn't a reconnaissance mission.

I fired up the notebook, the screen illuminating as it came to life. Thankfully I was able to log in as a guest without the password, seeing I hadn't bothered to ask what it was. The flashy *Dell* was so much fancier than the archaic piece of shit I used at home.

As I sat at the desk in front of the computer, I felt like I was somehow breaking and entering. Out of place. I knew I had Troy's permission, but I couldn't shake the feeling that I didn't belong. Maybe it was the excessive luxury of the room, or perhaps the state of the art computer, but it reminded me that this was not in fact my life. It was an altered reality, a ride at an amusement park. As awesome as it felt, it would inevitably end and we'd have to get off the Ferris wheel and go back home.

My fingers clicked away at the keys as I quickly logged into my email account and accessed my inbox. The message I composed was short and to the point. After all, I had mapped it out in my head on the ride over. Get in, reassure my dad all was fine, ask him how he was doing, send the thing, and get the hell out of their room. Simple. Or so was my plan.

However, nothing in my life is ever simple. I powered down the computer not even bothering to download my music notes, deciding to work off my phone once it was charged. And with my email happily sailing away in cyber space, I became suddenly curious what the bedrooms looked like. I mean, if this was the shared space, I imagined the bedrooms would be pretty spectacular. It wouldn't hurt to look; I would definitely not touch anything. I didn't even have to go all the way in, just poke my head through the door. What's the harm?

Holy shit.

The room was impressive. Well as much of it as I could see from the door. I wasn't tempting fate and going all the way in. That would be taking it too far right? I mean, I didn't even know whose room it was.

It was while I was justifying my argument that I heard the elevator ping, announcing the arrival of a guest. Who the hell was that? Housekeeping? Staff? Security? Was there some hidden security cameras and they'd seen me going where I shouldn't? I'd barely stepped into the room. Crap. I should have just left.

And for no good reason, I panicked.

I could have just quickly shut the bedroom door, sat at the desk like I had been five minutes earlier. But no, I had to act like I had been robbing the place, disregarding that I had a key *and* a reason to be there as I crawled under the desk and hid.

It was a stupid instinct, that instead of just waiting to see who it was, I was now crouching low like an idiot, in the tiny space.

Carefully my hands circled my knees and clutched them closer to my body, my effort to hide myself being taken very seriously.

Not that I'd have an excuse for being under the desk if I ended up being caught. Other than me being an idiot. Which would be the truth in this instance.

Footsteps.

My ears strained against the wooden panel of the desk. It was hard to hear anything, with the thing not being some MDF wannabe from Ikea; it was solid. Possibly antique. I had no idea why I was surprised.

The door opened. Then shut really quickly. The sound of heels and men's shoes clicked on the floorboards. There were definitely two people in the room.

"Jason," a female voice giggled, "I'm so turned on right now."

Great. Not only was it the person I least wanted to see, but he also had company. The giggling annoying variety.

"Yeah? I haven't even done anything yet." His voice was low, dark—a rumble.

Whether or not he'd touched her, I could see where giggling, annoying groupie—I didn't know she was a groupie, I'm assuming—was going with *that*. He had that sexy shit locked down.

Not that he held that power over me anymore. No, of course not.

"Don't you believe me?" More giggling. "Why don't you let me show you how wet I am."

Excuse me while I puke. Seriously, why do girls talk like that? Like he doesn't know what a wet pussy feels like? I'm sure, honey, he knows exactly what it feels like; he doesn't need a guided tour. And another thing, dressing it up like a treasure hunt doesn't make you sound sultry, it makes you sound like a fucking pirate. *Argh, follow me trail to where X marks the wet spot.* I will never understand how guys got turned on by that. Obviously now was probably *not* a good time to ask.

"Hmm, you are wet."

Hold the phone people, the man was a genius. He was also an asshole and I hated him even more. You know, in case I needed more of a reason, listening to him be with a girl would do it. Ignore the fact I didn't want to sleep him and the man obviously wasn't going to stop having sex. *Shut up logic, you have no place here.*

"Oh, yeah. Touch me like that."

There wasn't a need for me to actually see what was going on, the moaning and the rustling of clothes was enough of a tip-off. My earlier idea of hiding was even dumber than I first thought. I might be hunkered down for a while. This was so going to suck.

"Like this?" he asked, clearly needing the treasure map that I had stupidly said men didn't need. Oh look, it was a fucking expedition. I was literally shaking my head and rolling my eyes at the same time. It was a talent.

"Yes. Yes. Oh, yes." The giggles had stopped, however the annoying hadn't. It was just breathier now. Elongating every syllable. My hand clapped around my mouth as I forced myself not to yell, "Oh please."

"Or is this better?"

Was he fingering her or was it an experiment? It still wasn't clear.

"Holy fuck. Yes. Yes, like that."

She obviously liked it, whatever it was he was doing.

"Are you sure? Maybe you'd prefer this."

Seriously? Just fucking *do* whatever it was you were doing before and move things along. I'm getting a cramp in my thigh. Oh and P.S. I hope she has crabs.

"Oh God, you are going to make me come."

Thank God. Let's wrap it up, lady.

"No, you aren't. Not yet."

What do you mean no she isn't? Why the hell not? Just give her the fucking orgasm.

"Jason, oh God. I'm going to come."

Lady, I'm thinking you might have to take care of it yourself. Just reach down there and give him a hand. And I'm talking literally.

"But I haven't done this yet."

No one likes a show off, Jason. I hope she has crabs and herpes.

"Ah, ah, ah. I'm going to come."

I'm yet to be convinced, you said you were before and you let me down. Let's not get too excited.

"So do you want me to stop?"

YES! For fuck's sake just either make her come or give her a vibrator. I can't stand it any longer. Oh, and in addition to the crabs and herpes I hoped she had originally, could we add a yeast infection? I mean, if I'm allowed to have a list, why not.

"No, no. Don't stop. I want to come. I want to come."

Trust me, we all want the same thing, lady.

"Like this?"

Jesus, I hated him. Like hate of epic proportions. Her too,

whomever she was.

So. Much. Hate.

"Yes, I want to come, please."

Honestly, I don't blame her for begging. At this point I was too. For what? Well, who the hell knew? A pair of noise-cancelling headphones would be a good start, followed by some chiropractic care for this crick in my neck I was developing. Oh, and the last twenty minutes or so of my life back.

"What about if I do this?"

Please make it stop. Please make it stop. Was he a sadist? Why won't it stop?

"Oh. Oh. Oh."

"Oh for fuck's sake, make her come already!"

It was supposed to be a thought, I'd had a lot of those through the course of this craptastic experience and yet, somewhere between my mind and my mouth something must have gone wrong. Because, instead of it being harmless internal dialogue, of which I'd had plenty, those words leapt out of my mouth and had announced themselves.

It was quiet.

Really, really quiet.

No annoying giggling, no moaning, no threats of *coming*.

Nothing.

Crap.

"Angie?" Jason's sexy voice was gone and in its place was his what-the-fuck voice. I'd heard it a few times in the last few days so I knew it was him, even without looking, or the fact that his fuck-buddy had said his name fifteen times. Okay, maybe it was only ten. Whatever, she'd said it a lot.

"Heeeeyyyyy." I slowly rose to my feet, brushing myself off as I stood. Pins and needles shot up my leg, the lack of circulation from being curled underneath my body making them feel tingly. "Sorry, didn't mean to interrupt." My lips spread into a forced and probably freaky looking smile.

Really, it's not like there was an etiquette guide for it. I was totally winging it.

Jason's hand shifted from the front of *I'm-coming's* jeans. The look on her face, priceless. That elusive orgasm probably was going to be a while. It's okay though, because given the way things were going, it hadn't been a sure thing anyway.

"Who is she?" The eye daggers she shot me enough of a clue I wasn't going to be winning any fans here. It was only fair though seeing as I had wished the crabs, herpes and yeast infection on her. Although her disliking me wasn't going to have me losing any sleep.

"A friend." Jason answered before I'd gotten the chance. His face, unreadable.

"Actually, I'm not really."

We were so far from *friends* it was laughable he'd even call me that. We were the opposite of friends, we were frenemies. Who'd had sex once and now hated each other. And wished evil fungal infections … oh wait, that was probably just me who wished that.

"Okay, well. I'm not really into girls. So. Um. Can she leave already?"

She didn't bother to address me, my existence meaningless to her, as she turned her attention back to Jason. Her hands scrunched tight around his t-shirt.

She could hold onto him all she wanted, that orgasm I'd robbed from her wasn't coming back. At least not in the short term.

His eyes stayed locked on mine, ignoring her clawing hands.

"Did you need something, Angie?"

He said the words slowly, letting each one settle.

"No, no I'll let you two get back to it. Seems like you have your hands full."

Or at least he had, and there was no way I'd be sitting through another round of *that.* No, no, no. *Get your shit, get out the door and go scrub your ears with bleach.* And, I was going to need about five gallons of ice cream as well to deal with the truckload of emotions I had going on.

"Jason." Ms. I'm-going-to-come-or-maybe-I-wont pulled at his shirt again. In case he forget she was hanging there, or maybe it was a prompt to remind him he had unfinished business.

"Why are you here?" He completely ignored her, his eyes following me as I moved further away from the desk and closer toward the door.

"Did you hear me? Hello?" She was getting impatient, I think she actually stomped her foot.

"No one was supposed to be up here." Why the hell was I justifying myself? Troy had given me his key; I hadn't broken in. And, I was not the one who was trying to satisfy my screwed up need for a casual hook up. Oh, that's right, because I don't do that. I actually have to *know* the person before I let them into my vagina.

"Are you just going to ignore me? I'm right here." She sounded mad, she was probably mad.

"I'm sorry, Kristen. Why don't I give you a call later?" *What do you know, he knew her name.* Jase turned to face her for the first time since he removed his hands from down her pants.

"But. But. I thought—" She tried to argue, and what she was going to pick as her selling point I had no idea. *I thought you were going to make me come? Have sex with me? Love me, and stick around?* No, I was the only idiot who'd have thought the last one. Even *Kristen* wasn't that stupid.

"Yep, great. Talk soon." He didn't give her chance for any further discussion. In fact he didn't give her the chance for anything, and all but pushed her out the door.

"Call me." The words were cut short by the slamming door in her face.

It was a stand off.

The two of us on opposite sides of the room. Neither of us saying a word.

And I knew I shouldn't have looked down, but my eyes had a mind of their own as they followed the lines of his body down. To his crotch, and where his very hard cock was still straining against his jeans.

"See something you like?"

I'd been busted. Not only had it been mortifying enough to have to been caught hiding under a freaking desk while he *dated* some girl, he'd now caught me staring at his pants. And not in a way that was anywhere near innocent.

"No. Been there, done that and got the t-shirt. Thanks for the offer though."

Well at least I could count on my mouth to get with the program. For better or worse, if I was thinking it, I was probably going to be saying it and in this instance I totally approved of my verbal spillage.

"I know you hate me." He was back to the measured words, and the low rumbly sexy voice.

"Wow, you really are smart. Here I was thinking that college education was nothing more than a fancy paper." I folded my arms tightly across my chest, my mood confused.

"But I also know how good it was when we were together." He moved closer.

"And now you're back to dumb again. That night was nothing. I faked it the whole time." Of course that wasn't even close to being true but I wouldn't give him the satisfaction. Even if it meant tarnishing the memory. It's not like it had meant anything to him and for me, it was just a reminder of heartache. Who cared if I tore it to shreds.

"Lie if it makes you feel better, the way you came—on my mouth, on my hand, on my cock—you couldn't have faked that." He was right. None of those times had I faked it, and he knew that.

"Maybe I'm that good of an actress? I was still nice back then, and didn't want to hurt your feelings." I *had* been nice back then. It was before he'd ripped out my heart. Before I knew people did that, before I'd opened my freaking eyes.

He had moved. His feet had progressively walked him to directly in front of me, where he now stood. Still. There.

"I'm pretty sure it was you I was having sex with, and not Meryl Streep." His voice was sharp. Like a ruler slapping a desk and he wasn't letting me off the hook.

"I was easily impressed, and my inexperience worked in your favor." As much as I wanted to, I did not move back. I didn't filch and I didn't run. I stood my ground, playing our stupid game of verbal ping-pong.

"Bullshit, I bet I could make you come just as hard now." *Whoa! What?*

"Dumb and delusional. Sadly, it doesn't make you more

appealing." I'd snapped back so fast, I'd almost not heard the words.

Silence.

He didn't respond which annoyed me. It was his turn to say something, why didn't he say it? He always had a comeback, there would be no way he'd let me have the last word.

And I waited. Nothing.

Instead his mouth stayed tight, his jaw clenched, as his dark brown eyes studied me. Their path travelled over every inch of my body so that I felt naked. Exposed.

"What? Why are you looking at me like that?" I demanded, my voice not as confident as I would have liked.

"How am I looking at you?" He tilted his head to the side, a slow smile working at the edges of his lips.

"Like—Like you want to eat me."

"I'd love to *eat* you." His smile got wider.

"That's not what I meant."

"No, but it's what *I* meant."

The oxygen from the room seemed to have evaporated. Poof! Gone. It was like being in a big black hole, a vacuum. There had to be a plausible explanation as to why I could no longer breathe. It wasn't just my lungs that were having difficulty trying to function, it was my brain too. Sound had also gone to wherever the air had disappeared to as the silence deafened me.

I tried to remind myself how much I hated the man in front of me as my body had kicked into autopilot. Those words he said were making me respond in a way I was not comfortable with. A way I knew he wanted. A way he would enjoy.

And I couldn't stop it because despite what I told myself, my feelings for this guy were so freaking twisted he still turned me on.

Fuck biology and its chemical reactions.

"That is not happening." Oh, thank God I didn't just strip down and offer myself to him. Ain't going to lie, it could have gone either way.

"You don't sound so sure."

"I'm positive. Like I would go there anyway. You were just

about to have sexy time with someone else."

"But I didn't, and now here we are."

"I'm not the alternate, Jason."

"You *never* were the alternate, Angie."

"Stop. Stop talking." My body shook all over.

What did he mean; I was never the alternate? I was never his first choice either.

"Ask me why I was with that girl." He lowered his head so his face was inches from mine. Too close. Way too close.

"No, I don't give a fuck."

"I was with her because I haven't had sex since the first night I saw you again. I can't function, Angie. It is way beyond fucked up. I want you, and I know I can't have you. And I have had a raging hard-on I can't seem to get rid of." His nose skated against the length of mine. I'd never heard the pain before. The underlying ache in his words, not that it could change what he did. Or where we were now.

"Am I supposed to be flattered?"

"No, you should be disgusted and you should leave." His mouth moved to beside my ear, his voice lowering to a whisper. "Why aren't you leaving, Angie?"

"I am." I nodded, knowing I needed to leave.

"Your feet haven't moved."

"They will."

"They better."

There was a snap. Like a band inside of me breaking and flicking me back, my body recovering before I lost my footing. And by some miracle in what I can only think confirms the existence of God, my feet moved toward the door and took me out of that room, my hands also worked as part of the team and shut the door behind me.

My head pounded in time with my accelerated heartbeat. I was confused, turned on and disgusted, and I had no idea which emotion would end up dominating. How could I want him after hearing that? There was something wrong with me. There had to be. Only some sick, twisted or deranged pervert would want that. And yet if I hadn't walked out that door I know I would have gone there. Why? Because all the messed up feelings swirling around were driving me insane and I just wanted to feel good, even for a while. Even if it was the wrong kind of good. Which is why I left. Which is why I needed to go far away from him. Which is why I was standing outside his door wanting to go back in.

Leave, Angie. Put your damn feet one in front of the other and walk away.

So I did.

And then I was gone.

ANGIE SEEING THAT WAS NOT PART OF THE PLAN. NOT THAT IT should've mattered, she could screw whoever she wanted and so could I, but I was better than that. More careful. More discreet. And usually I was. This time, I hadn't given a shit. It wasn't like me. I wasn't Dan, even though I'd probably slept with twice the number of women he had.

She should never have been there.

The reasons of how it came to pass were still a mystery. I stared at my reflection in the bathroom mirror while the water ran over my hands. The temperature so hot I wasn't sure I wasn't going to be rocking third degree burns. The messed up situation echoed in my head as I cut the water, toweled off and went back to the living room. Why the hell did she have to be in the fucking room? I would have assumed she'd been tied up with one of the douchebags. It looked like that's where it was heading.

Yeah, I was going to need a drink. And not a beer.

The bar fridge offered a bunch of options, all of them tiny. Still a drink was a drink, so I opted for the scotch. I opened the bottle and threw it back, the need for a glass non-existent; the damn thing was barely bigger than a swallow.

The burn down my throat felt nice but didn't last long; it also wasn't even close to making a dent in what I needed. There was always the gym, running it out had always been my go-to solution. Well, *that* or sex, and seeing as sex was not going to happen, a run was probably the best option.

Not that my dick understood. No, I was still rock solid. And it hadn't been from Kristen, not even fucking close.

As I toed-off my boots and stripped off my shirt, I figured the run probably wasn't the best idea. Drinking and exercising, not a good mix. Not unless you were on *The Jersey Shore.* Of which I wasn't. So I guess that was out for the night too.

The next bottle I snagged was bourbon, because that was smart. I figured might as well mix it up, it's not like I gave a shit as long as I could continue drinking. Which I was going to have to stop the minute I exhausted my supply of tiny bottles.

This was so fucked up. Downing liquor like I was Ozzy Osborne. Any minute the assholes from *VH1's Behind the Music* were going to bust through the door to interview me about my fall from grace. Might as well make the fall epic, go hard or go fucking home.

My ass sunk into the leather couch, the one near the desk Angie had jack-in-a-boxed out from, and I picked up the phone. My fingers hit the call button, the one that would connect me to room service.

"Good evening. This is Claire, how can I help you?" A sweet, bright voice answered.

My fingers squeezed against the bridge of my nose, the pressure building in my head. I didn't want sweet, *sweet* had just walked out the damn door, so the reminder was just an irritation I didn't want.

"Yeah, I want a real bottle of bourbon. Not this shit in the mini bar." My voice was harder than it needed to be. And yet I couldn't make myself give a shit, such was the intensity of my jacked-up mood. *Fuck you, Em.* I flipped off the air as I apparently started to lose my mind. 'Cause that's what sane people do, tell a memory to go fuck itself. Seriously losing my grip.

"Sir?" Sweet-voice Claire called me to attention. Her tone hinting that she'd asked something. She'd probably asked if I wanted a pair of forceps to pull my head out of my ass. Valid question.

"Sorry, what was that?" I asked, trying to keep the bite on the sidelines. It wasn't her fault she'd drawn the short straw and been on the other end of the phone.

"I asked if *Maker's Mark* would be acceptable."

Of course that's what she'd ask, because it would make sense that she would want to clarify my order. What any normal person would assume. Pity no one in the room was currently flying the normal flag.

"Yes, send it up." I resisted the urge to ask for a bottle of Grey Goose as a chaser. Probably over kill, I wasn't an alcoholic despite my fucked-up behavior.

"Sir, might I suggest something from our extensive menu."

Nice. She hadn't apparently got the memo about me not needing a voice of reason. Or a burger and fries. Both which I hadn't ordered.

"No food, just the bourbon, and I'll take it without the side judgment as well." I really was an asshole. Not sure how anyone thought otherwise.

"Sir, I wasn't implying … I'm sorry. Of course, right away."

The call ended and I tossed the phone onto the desk, not bothering to hang it back on the base. It's one of the things I had marked on my list of don't-give-a-fuck.

The knock at the door came pretty quick, which was just as well because I was all geared to drink myself into oblivion. Putting it off was more an inconvenience than anything; so the sooner I got started, the better.

I yanked the door open, ready to get my party for one started.

Motherfucker.

"Angie, what are you doing here? You need to go."

She could not be here, especially not now.

"No." She didn't even flinch, her hands on her hips, the same fuck-you she usually gave to me.

"What the hell did you say to me?"

"I said *no*, Jason. I'm sure it's been a while since you've heard it but I don't give a fuck it's not what you want to hear."

Well then, she had my attention.

She moved forward and I hoped she didn't trip on my jaw as she passed through the doorway and walked into the suite.

"Do you still want to have sex with me?" She moved closer, her breath hot on my face as she leaned into me. No booze that I could smell. At least one of us was sober.

Wait a minute, how many of those little bottles did I drink?

"Yes." The word was out of my mouth before I had a chance to stop it. Me being honorable tonight wasn't going to happen.

"Why?" Her eyes nailed me, and I had to concentrate to stay upright.

"Because you're beautiful, and I can't seem to stop myself from wanting you."

"Okay." She nodded once, her hands still planted on her hips.

"What exactly are you saying okay to?" The instructions would be good right about now. I'd already said I wasn't a chick-whisperer.

"To have sex." No blushing, no blinking, no flick of the hair. Her eyes on me and she was dead serious.

"Woooahhhhhh. Did you not tell me how much you couldn't stand me?"

"I think I also mentioned hate."

"So why the hell are you agreeing to sex?" This had to be a trap. Any minute she was going to whip out a machete and slice my balls off. Or my dick. Maybe both. I'm sure she already had the plaque picked to have them mounted.

"Because I want to, and this time at least I know that all I am getting is a fuck. There is something freeing about knowing where you stand." She moved closer, the familiar smell of her shampoo invading my nose. Any chance I had of saying no to her was slipping away.

"Angie, trust me. You do not want this."

Translation, we are both going to regret this in the morning and this time around I can't get in my fucking car and drive away.

"How about you don't tell *me* what I do or do not want, and take off your damn jeans and do what we both are so desperate to do."

Well I guess some things had changed. Her mouth, for one. Not that I was complaining. It was completely fucking hot.

"This is a bad idea." Actually, in the history of bad ideas, right here was numero uno.

"I know, and I don't care."

She slammed her mouth on mine, her tits pushing against me. Her hands, they were on a downward trip as they slid down my back and grabbed my ass. She was angry and aggressive, and I was so turned on my balls ached.

"Angie." My hand fisted her hair as my tongue explored her mouth. She tasted so fucking amazing, I wasn't sure I'd ever be able to stop.

"Shut up." Her teeth bit down on my lower lip as she pushed me back. The sting of pain smacked my mouth, followed by the slight coppery taste of blood.

"You fucking bit me?" My hand grabbed a handful of her hair and pulled her lips from mine, her eyes jacked-up on lust and rage.

"You deserved it. You were talking too much and if we're just fucking, there doesn't need to be any small-talk." She smirked, licking her lips with freaking satisfaction.

"You want to be fucked? Is that why you're here?" I kept her hair wrapped around my hand as I pulled her head further back, giving me access to her neck. Her pulse hammered away underneath the olive skin.

"Uh-uh." She struggled to nod, my grip on her hair keeping her head from moving.

"You better know what you are signing up for, Angie, because I'm beyond the point of stopping."

"Then stop being a pussy, and give me your cock."

Control went out the window. My hands, my mouth, they were clawing at her like I was a savage. I *was* a savage, my fucking need for her so off the chain that I wasn't sure I wasn't going to stroke out.

That bullshit top she'd been wearing, the one that curved around her tits within an inch of their life was in my hand and torn from her body. I didn't even give a shit I'd literally ripped her clothes off. It was in my way and I needed her naked. Her beautiful tits heaved up and down in her lacey black bra as I reached down to her ass and yanked at the zip of her tight black skirt. My concern for its welfare also did not rank highly.

She was so hot I couldn't think straight, her skirt dropped down to her ankles and gave me a better look at all her marked skin. She hadn't been afraid of the pain. The color stretched not only up and down her arms, but also across her ribs and down her hips. It was beyond stunning; it was the most beautiful thing I'd ever seen.

The ice bucket moment came just as I'd snapped her bra from her chest. The shredded material still in my hand as the knock at the door happened.

Fuck.

She stopped and grabbed my face. "That better not be a fucking booty call, Jason."

That thing I'd discussed earlier, about her cutting off my balls, she had a look that spelled out the desire to do just that.

"It's room service, I ordered bourbon before you got here."

My brilliant idea, not so fucking awesome now. Who needed a drink anyway, I'd take my high in the form of the smoking, hot woman in front of me.

"Give me a second." My hand reluctantly dropped her damaged bra and I made for the door. It was more than just an interruption. It was a wake-up call. One that I had no doubt she would take. Which was going to be a problem, because letting her walk out of my door tonight was not going to be easy.

"Hey." I cracked open the door, my body blocking the view of the interior of the room.

"Hi, just delivering your drink, sir." Some glorified bell-hop stood beside a silver cart, the *Maker's Mark* sitting on top with a bucket of ice and a couple of tumblers.

"Just leave it there." I reached into my back pocket and pulled out a tip. "I'll grab it in a minute.

"Of course, sir." Was what he said, but his face read differently. More like the man was questioning my sanity for leaving a bottle of booze out in the hall and why I wasn't giving him access to my room.

All valid.

He took his suspicions and wisely didn't ask questions, turning around and heading toward the elevator. The cart being pulled into the room with one hand while I held the door ajar with the other.

Angie was probably getting her clothes back on and getting ready to bail at that very moment but there wasn't a chance anyone was getting the opportunity to look at her while she did it.

Nope, not a chance in hell.

"*Maker's*, nice choice." She wandered over to the cart and picked up a couple cubes of ice and tossed them into a glass. "I hate *Jack Daniel's*."

Not only was she *not* dressed, her tits still on display, but she'd lost her panties as well. Her body, naked, except for the obscene pair of black heels she'd walked in with.

"You're naked." My hands cracked the red wax as I twisted the cap off the bottle.

Her hand tilted her ice filled glass toward me. "Yep."

"So, that last minute time out didn't change your mind?" The amber liquid poured out of the bottle, filling her glass.

"Nope." Her mouth popped off the P before she raised the glass to her lips and took a drink.

My fingers wrapped around the glass and stole it from her hand, not bothering to pour my own. "I like you like this." I took a mouthful, as my eyes steamrolled over the curves of her body. My dick punched out against the zip of my jeans in a show of unanimous appreciation.

"Well, unless you expect me to fuck myself." She didn't even bother covering her tits, her tight pink nipples waiting for me to lick them as she pulled the glass from my hand. "You're going to have to get naked too." She took another mouthful before putting the glass down on the cart. "And unlike your last little *friend,* I'm going to need something more than just your hand to get me off."

My mouth slammed against hers, the taste of bourbon and possibly regret, feeding me as I grabbed her ass and hauled her against my erection.

"That feel like enough of a *something* for you?"

I didn't give her a chance to answer, instead lifting her off the ground and wrapping her legs around my waist. The resistance she offered, non-existent.

As much as I wanted to unzip my jeans and plunge my cock into her right there, the fact we hadn't made it to my room yet was a problem. The shared space of our penthouse apartment, not a suitable location for it to all go down.

"Jase." Her lips sucked at my throat as I opened the door to my bedroom, kicking it shut after we'd walked through the doorway.

"I didn't think you wanted an audience and they're going to be back soon." There was no need to clarify the *they*. I'd been surprised *they* hadn't arrived already. Saying hi to Troy, Dan and their ladies while my cock was buried inside Angie wouldn't have gone down too well. Especially not with Troy. Best the big guy didn't know, because me not having her tonight wasn't an option.

"These need to be off." Angie grabbed at my jeans as I tossed her onto the mattress, my body joining hers on the bed.

She wasn't gentle, her fingers clawing at the denim in a bid to get them down. Her short fingernails my saving grace, with the abrasions on my thighs being nothing more than a few red scratches. The sting of it juicing me up more.

My boxers were the next thing to go, her hands giving me an assist while mine were otherwise occupied. I couldn't get enough, my fingers on her skin setting me on fire. It was a deep fucked-up need to touch every single inch and I felt completely out of control. My hand snaked down between her legs as I sunk two fingers into her hot, wet core.

She moaned against my mouth, which I'd been keeping busy kissing her lips before migrating south to her tits, my teeth gently biting her nipples. The noises she made threatening to make me blow my load before we'd even got to the actual sex.

It was too much.

Wishing there was another way to get a rubber without needing to stop touching her, I cursed out a breath as I reached into my nightstand and pulled out a condom. My intention of making her come with my hand or my mouth first, no longer working for me. I'd do it later, and I would make it worth her while but if I didn't fuck her right now, I was going to lose my damn mind. And probably the use of my cock, which had gotten so hard, it was actually starting to hurt.

I sheathed my dick in the condom, my hand smoothing the latex down the length of my shaft. Her body jacked up off the mattress in protest, her legs kicking open to reveal the slickness between them. It was beautiful, seeing her so wet and ready for what I was about to give her, I needed a second just to look. She took advantage of my distraction by reaching her hand down between us, palming my cock and giving me a stroke. I needed to fuck her. Like, yesterday.

"This is probably going to be faster than I want." I smacked her ass as I gained control of her legs. "But we can do slow later."

"Fuck. Me." The words jutted out through her gritted teeth.

And I'll be damned if that isn't exactly what I intended to do.

While one of my hands peeled hers from my cock, the other one held my dick steady while I drove into her in one swift movement. Smothering her body so completely I wasn't sure I wasn't crushing her.

"Agh!" Her hands griped my shoulders as her body tensed, her pussy gripping me tight like a vice. Her tits pressed hard against my chest.

"I thought you said you wanted to be fucked?" I drove into her again, this time her body easing up on the resistance, the slide of my dick getting easier with each thrust.

Her head thrashed back against the pillow as I slowly picked up momentum. "Yes." She screamed biting against my shoulder. "Harder."

That sweet eighteen-year-old I'd had in the back of my car was not the same girl I was currently screwing. She was different, and it wasn't just her body that had changed, it was her whole attitude.

She grabbed my ass, pulling me deeper into her. Her hips lifting to meet each thrust, pushing me right where I needed to be. I couldn't have talked even if I'd wanted to, our verbal exchange limited to primal noises. The need to be with her was so intense I thought I might actually blackout.

"Oh God," she screamed as her body finally gave in, her pussy milking me as she came hard underneath me. Her body shook as she took all of me, the pulsing against my shaft undoing any hope I had of trying to make it last.

"Fuck." It felt like every single nerve ending simultaneously exploded as my body tensed, my load filling her as I panted against her throat.

Fuck.

Both literally and figuratively, we were fucked.

And it had been so, so good.

"Angie?" My tongue traced the length of her jaw, more hungry for her than before. There was no way I wasn't going to do that again. "Are you okay?"

"Just give me a minute." Her eyelids slowly cracked open as I eased off her, another tremble shaking her body. "It's just been a while." Her satisfied smile enough validation that it had been just as good for her.

"Since you've had sex, or since you came like that?" I wasn't sure which answer I was hoping to hear, either one making me feel fucking awesome. I slowly eased my semi-hard dick out of her—the bastard already limbering up for round two. The discarding of the used condom was a necessary evil but I took care of it quickly so I could climb back into bed and continue the conversation. Her body curled up against mine the minute my back had hit the mattress.

"Oh I can come like that anytime I want, it just usually takes a lot of work and a man isn't involved." Her fingers traced the grooves of my chest, slithering down to my abs.

I bucked out a laugh. "Well then you've been sleeping with the wrong kind of men."

"Yeah, it seems to be a habit for me."

She didn't smile; the lighthearted tone of the conversation taking a dive. That satisfied glow she'd had plastered on her face was also MIA with my stupid attempt at a joke, sounding like a personal taunt.

"I didn't mean it like that." Could we rewind ten seconds so I could pull my foot out of my mouth?

"Actually, that's exactly how you meant it." Her eyes nailed me in a way that was not going to let me off the hook. "But it's okay, the *wrong guy* usually gives the better orgasms."

Bravo. Another backhanded compliment courtesy of Angie Morelli. It was really impressive how good she was at it. Almost made me want to beg for more.

"Is that why you're here, using me so you don't have to masturbate?" *Because straight up, that would not be a problem for me.*

"Yes, that's why I'm here."

If she was on the level with me or not, I had no idea. The let's-just-fuck routine, a complete one-eighty from where we'd both been twenty-four hours ago. Surely no one does that. She hated me; she'd even said so. Who has sex with someone they didn't like? It made zero fucking sense.

"What are you thinking about?" She moved closer against me, her lips kissing my neck. And as much as this didn't make sense, I would rather die than ask her to stop.

"That I generally don't have sex with people who hate me. I'd like to avoid the whole being-smothered-in-my-sleep thing. Call me sensitive."

In all honesty, I couldn't say that if she did give my face some pillow action while I was catching some z's that I wouldn't have gone happy. That alone should have been enough of a warning to prove how bad of an idea this whole *scenario* was. But my dick, it seemed, had a death wish.

Her face broke into an amused grin as she commenced laughing her ass off. "You think this was some sneaky diversionary tactic to try to kill you? Oh my god, that's hysterical. I'm a musician not a CIA operative. And how conceited are you? No man would ever be worth jail time."

"Good." My hand slowly slid down between her legs. "Now, get on your knees and let me do that again."

Angie

THIS TIME, I WAS THE ONE WHO LEFT.

It was two in the morning, or so said the obnoxious clock beside Jase's bed. Its stupid illuminated face taunted me, singing out with judgment, "Well done dumbass, you just slept with the enemy."

I'd never intended to stay. Sleeping over had never been part of the plan. Hell, fucking him had never been part of the plan, but that's exactly what happened. My big plan went right out the window when I saw him and before I knew it, I had convinced myself that this was the right thing to do. It wasn't beautiful or romantic, there were no whispered *I love yous* and there sure as hell wasn't any slow seduction. It was erotic and rough; both of us primed for explosion, which is exactly what we got. Sex. We weren't making love. It was pure unrestrained sex.

What the hell had I been thinking?

Anger.

That was the only explanation as to why I would sleep with a guy who was just about to sleep with someone else. Who does that? Who decides that they are happy to be the next one in line? That had never been me. I should be disgusted. I should be sitting in a shower so hot it peels the top layer of skin from my body.

Because that's the way I'd felt the first time I'd slept with Jason. Or at least, how I'd felt the next day.

Rage. Which was like anger but amplified, so at least I was consistent. That is why my dumbass self decided that the only hope I had of getting over Jason was doing exactly what he'd done to me. Use him for sex, but this time, on my terms. Taking back the control.

It made more sense in my head.

Mind blowing sex—which is what we'd had the last time, so I was hoping that hadn't been a one-time deal—then out the door. Only this time, I would be the one walking.

But all the good intentions in the world couldn't fight the all-consuming fatigue I'd felt after. Screwing him *one time* and bailing hadn't played out quite like I planned, oh no, with neither of us satisfied after just a taste. And the sex, was indescribable.

Maybe it was because we had been avoiding each other for so long, maybe it was because I was so angry, but that great sex we'd had all those years ago was like a watered down *Kool-Aid* version of what we'd just had. I'd never been fucked like that. My body actually ached. At least I could skip the gym tomorrow, lord knows riding Jason Irwin burnt more calories than the elliptical.

So when my eyes couldn't stay open a minute longer, I rested my head on the pillow allowing myself a twenty to thirty minute nap. No harm in that. And then I would wake up refreshed from my power nap and walk my ass out the door. All in-your-face, just as I had planned.

I wasn't supposed to stay the night.

Panic woke me. Or maybe it had been the fact I was dying from an obscenely high core temperature. Probably the latter given that Jason's arms and legs tangled around mine were making me feel like I was in a hot dude cocoon. It might have been pleasant if there hadn't been a history. One where I had fantasized about systematically removing all his internal organs starting with his heart. More to see if he had one. Which I assumed he did because I could feel it sarcastically beating against my back. Ugh.

Being awake presented new problems, ones I hadn't had to face while I had been blissfully ignorant in dreamland. My escape was the most pressing issue and how the hell I was going to unravel myself from Mr. Big Cock.

Of course that wasn't his real name, but honestly I'd forgotten how impressive it was. Not that I had actually looked at it the first time, I had been too excited that he was finally going to sleep with me, nervous too and the vodka I'd had hadn't helped either. Then, in between then and now was the flood of *average dick* I had been subjected to. Nothing noteworthy, that's for sure. All of which contributed to diluting the memory of *it*. Which was such a shame because it really was spectacular in all its pink perfect glory. Which is why I thought up that little term of endearment.

While he impaled me.

With his h-u-g-e cock.

Repeatedly.

Expertly.

Amazingly.

It had not been a problem for me at all.

The problem *was*, getting out and getting gone.

It started off slow. More like a little shimmy of my shoulder to see if my moving would wake him.

It didn't.

Which meant I was able to graduate to wriggle, freeing the upper part of my body from his huge arms. Seriously, the man was tall, he had the wingspan of an albatross; this was not an easy feat.

Still sleeping. Thank you, Jesus.

Next were the legs, this carried a nine-point-eight difficulty rating because his leg was actually hooked around mine. Oh and his cock was hard and pressing into my hip, which meant I had to focus on the task at hand instead of leaning down and giving him a blowjob. Because that would be helpful—not.

Success. I had wiggled, duked and jived my way out of the spoon-of-death, and had gently been able to lower my feet to the floor. My prayers to the gods of good times continued to allow me my walk of shame uninterrupted. *Please do not wake up.*

Thankfully, he didn't.

Other problems, which presented themselves later, were the

state of my clothes. Or should I say, the lack of my clothes. The cute top I had been wearing—torn in half. My pretty black Victoria Secret's bra—toast. My black skirt—a busted out zipper, and a split down the center seam. Oh look, my panties were still in one piece. And I found both my shoes. Wow, there was a silver lining after all. Unfortunately I was not a showgirl in Vegas, which meant my useable items did not an outfit make. Shit!

As quiet as I was able—which was difficult being I was uttering the word *fuck* under my breath repeatedly—I cracked open one of the closets and prayed the man had something I could wear. Like a damn designer dress, worth a few hundred dollars to make up for the clothes he just destroyed. Asshole.

Sadly his closet was not lined with anything other than jeans, shirts, T-shirts and other *man* apparel, so I settled for a T-shirt that was about ten sizes to big that very elegantly said "I Don't Give a Fuck." The irony. Ha. Ha. Ha. I was so freaking funny. The bottoms were a problem. Maybe I could pretend the T-shirt was a dress? It was long enough. Except my room was situated ten floors below the one I was on. Which meant walking out of here, getting into an elevator and—yeah not going to work.

I begrudgingly threw on a pair of his sweatpants as well. Fucking ridiculous. Even with the drawstring pulled as tight as I could, they'd barely stayed up. Sure, that wasn't obvious that I had no clothes. Well at least I wasn't naked. See that's twice with the silver lining. So much optimism I thought I might choke. Which is exactly what I needed to do to myself as soon as I left this room.

With my heels in my hand, and hoping I hadn't pushed my luck with my *Fashion Police* critique, I crept out of Jason's room and into the living area. He slept right through it. Didn't even move a muscle. His sleeping like a stone really was an occupational hazard, and should be addressed however. I could have robbed him blind. The clothes I had taken didn't count as stealing though; they were restitution.

Yes! Home free, baby. With Jase's door shut securely behind me all I needed to do was walk across the large, dimly lit living room and I was in the clear. Thank you Jesus, it was easier than I thought. Oh, apart from having to pull a Houdini to escape his bed, and the improv on the wardrobe. Who was I kidding? Just get the hell out while the getting was good.

"Angie?"

Crap. So much for a clean getaway.

"Hey, I thought it was you." Megs lifted herself off the couch and strode closer toward me, obviously needing a front row seat to my mortification.

"Hi." One of my hands did a lame wave while the other, still holding my shoes, also held up my pants. I mean Jason's pants. Ha. I had literally gotten into his pants. More irony. My lips spread into a smile before I could stop them.

"Um. So, interesting shirt." Her eyes dipped down and gave me an all-over inspection, the edges of her lips twitching with amusement.

"I had an accident and needed to borrow something of Jason's." Lame. I didn't know why I even tried.

"Did your accident involve a penis?" Megs bit her lip as her grin widened.

"Huh? What?" I scoffed, trying to sound surprised and indignant. No one was fooled.

"There's a condom wrapper in your hair." Her fingers gently reached into my hair and pulled the foil *Trojan* packet that had seen fit to lodge itself there. I officially hated the universe. Fuck you very much, Jason Irwin.

"Oh. That. Well. We had sex."

She really didn't need the confirmation. No one was that stupid. Except for Jason, who should have had a better system for trash disposal. Another reason why I should hate him.

"Cool. So, you want some ice cream?" She didn't miss a beat, just lifted the tub in her hands, completely cool and unaffected. "I couldn't sleep. Heartburn is a bitch. The stupid book I'm reading said ice cream is supposed to help but I think it's just some bullshit old wives tale. I'm totally going to have an ass the size of Texas. I don't even care." She laughed flipping open the lid and waved her spoon.

Where the hell was I? Was I hallucinating this? Who has these kinds of conversations? Did I miss the part where she gave me judgey eyes, which usually complemented the you-are-such-a-whore scowl? And ice cream? This was just too crazy.

"I'm sorry, what?" Yeah, because all of that conversation couldn't have just happened like it did. I must have knocked my head one too many times on the headboard. It's not like it couldn't be a possibility.

"Ice cream." She said the words slowly and looked around for a spare spoon. "It's vanilla, so not that exciting but we can call and get—"

"No, I got that. About the ice cream. I mean, I just told you I slept with Jase. We had sex." It didn't sound any less shady the second time, not sure why I was pushing the issue.

"Oh, sorry. Did you want to talk about it? Was he an asshole? Do you want me to wake Troy? He can yell at him if you like."

"No. God, No." Wasn't sure exactly what I was saying no to, probably to all of it. Especially the part where she told Troy, that part deserved a big N to the Oh. "I'm not used to people being so—" What was the word? "Nice to me."

"Why wouldn't I be nice? Troy's told me all about you, and if you are important to him, you're important to me. Besides, don't let this normal exterior fool you, I am completely crazy underneath so I'm in no position to judge anyone. Unless they are wearing bad shoes. Then they are kind of opening themselves up for it. People who wear nice clothes and then skimp on the shoes can't be trusted. I guarantee you, they're hiding something." She had barely taken a breath.

"Wow, you are crazy, and I really like that." And best of all, it had taken some of the weirdness out of the situation. The one where I was standing in the shared living space of Troy, Dan and Jason, wearing clothes I had *borrowed* from the man I'd just slept with. And then left.

"Aw, thanks. Do you want to borrow some clothes? All my stuff is maternity but I'm sure we can ask Ash for something." She moved toward her cell, which was lying on an end table. Her offer to *ask Ash* probably involved waking her, which wasn't ideal. There was no need for anyone else to get drawn into the circus of crazy.

"No it's fine. I'm just going to go down to my room. I'm sure he won't miss them." My hands gripped the sweatpants tight, hoping I could just get to my room without having to make any more post-sex confessionals *or* flashing my ass. Hopefully achieving both was not out of the realm of possibility.

"Alrighty then. Have a good night." Megs waved her spoon in lieu of her hand. Her quest for ice cream more important than my undignified slink to the door.

My hand hesitated on the doorknob, looking over my shoulder before I left. "Thanks, Megs. It was really nice talking to you. Oh and please don't tell Troy. I'm a big girl, I can handle myself."

The one heart-to-heart Troy and I had shared about Jason was more than enough. Me, telling him I'd slept with Jase again, would not be happening. Ever.

"Sure, sure. No problem. And if you ever need anything, you can talk to me if you want. It doesn't have to go any further." She gave me a warm smile. Maybe I could actually have some female friends and it be okay. Ash and Megs both seemed so genuine.

"Thanks. Bye." I gave her a smile on account my hands were occupied, the door, my shoes and the saga of Jase's pants—a wave wasn't happening.

"Bye," she mumbled, her mouth full of vanilla. The door closed behind me to the view of another spoon wave.

Bed. I need a bed. This time, it had better be my own.

"'Promiscuous' by *Nelly Furtado* does not sound like a fuck you song, Angie." Rusty had walked into my hotel room all guns blazing. The text message with our new song suggestion that I'd sent in the early hours of the morning had obviously been received.

"I like the song," I yawned, my mind and body still tired from last night. No amount of sleep was going to change that. "I think it would be a good addition to the set." And give a clear message, which is exactly why I wanted to sing it.

"Firstly, it's a two person song." He sat himself on the small sofa opposite the queen size bed. Our allocated rooms were tiny compared to the Power Station suite I had the pleasure of seeing. "So unless you're planning on doing the half-half thing and flipping around on stage like a flapjack, I'm assuming you're going to need me to do *Timbaland's* part. Secondly, I thought we agreed we were doing the *Beastie Boy's* "Hey, Fuck You." I mean, it doesn't get more prefect than that, it actually says fuck you in the title."

We had agreed to do the Beastie Boy's song, both of us laughing hysterically at how perfect it would be. And it had been, even some of the lines were appropriate. Except then things changed and it wasn't what I wanted to say anymore.

"Rus, I did something bad."

Rusty blew out a long, slow breath and then stood up. "Give me a second to grab a shovel, and change my kicks. I just got these and I don't want to get them dirty." He pointed to his new boots, no doubt purchased with the sizeable advance we had all received.

"You don't need a shovel. I haven't killed anyone." Not unless you counted my common sense in which case, that was most definitely in need of a burial.

"The shovel is to beat you over the head." He rolled his eyes. "The song. You've either gone *there* or are going *there*. And in case there is any doubt as to where *there* is, it's the fucking keyboard player for the band who is paying our ticket right now. And, he's already broken your heart once before." He shoved his hand through his hair for good measure. "So much *bad* in the situation, even I'm washing my hands of it.

"You are such a drama queen, you know that? I went there, but it's different now. I know what I'm getting into." I could totally handle Jason this time around. No feelings involved at all. Unless you counted the sexual ones that still tingled in morning at the mention of his name, but they did not count at all.

"Same thing is going to happen." He gave me a hard stare. "I don't even need a magic eight ball. It's going to end the same way it started. Badly."

His feelings were clear. And I probably wasn't going to get his support, but I had already made the decision. Good or bad, it was my mistake to make. Again.

"I slept with him, and you know what, I am not in love with him anymore. It was like hitting the release valve. Maybe I had only thought I was in love with him back then, I was young. It's not like people end up with the same person they were in love with when they were eighteen. Maybe it was just a crush, and him leaving had hurt me so bad because I was confused and he made me feel used. And that's the hurt I was feeling. Not love. I don't know. I just know that I don't feel that way anymore. I don't love him. I don't need him to love me back. And I got that by being with him and seeing that it was just sex between us. Which is okay, if both parties are aware of it."

As crazy as it or I sounded, everything I said to Rusty was the truth. I didn't feel that way anymore. The love that I may have felt, that had been over a long time ago. This was different. I was different. This time around, I was okay with just having his body. And what a fine body it was.

"Sounds to me like you plan on doing it more than once." Rusty's question was one I had already asked myself. Did it still count as walking away if I requested a repeat performance? He hadn't called me this morning. There was no banging on my door demanding to know why I had left. Not even a note delivered by one of his *people* demanding his clothes back. FYI he wasn't getting the T-shirt back, I'd pretty much decided it was my new sleep shirt.

"Would it be so bad? We actually had fun and look, I'm fine." I twirled in an effort to demonstrate how fine I was, in case my big cheesy grin wasn't enough. "I bit him." The memory made the grin even wider.

"Ew. I don't want to hear your kinky vampire fantasies." Rusty held up his hands, our show-and-tell over already.

"Are you worried I'll turn?" Not that I was in any danger of me going all *Jolie* and wearing a vial of blood around my neck, unless the vampires looked like those dudes from *True Blood*.

"Nah, you're Italian. You guys eat too much garlic to worry about that," he said seriously, like vampires existed and if they did, there was a danger of me becoming one.

"You're so weird. It's a good thing I love you." I threw my arms around him and pulled him in for a hug. He was the one person who I could get touchy- feely with and it not feel weird. Although if I was going to continue this Jase thing, that was probably going to have to change.

"And I love you too. Even if you are going to make the most epic mistake of all mankind." He hugged me back.

"Thanks, Rusty." For always being there, I finished off in my head. See, I had the perfect relationship, we just didn't have sex and if I could fill that void with Jase, then it might just be the perfect solution.

"Alright, now let's learn your fucking song."

PROMISCUOUS.

The song, I meant. Angie and Rusty had duo-ed tonight, the crowd once again loving their take on the *Nelly Furtado* tune. And damn if it didn't send a shiver down to my balls hearing her tease me with every lyric. The roll of her hips enough to make me blow my load. Hell, there wasn't a man in the audience that wouldn't have gone home with her tonight, including yours truly.

That sweet girl I'd first met—the one who had been all shy about touching my cock—gone. In her place was a straight up sex bomb that blew my mind. If her body hadn't been lethal enough, the fucking attitude on her tipped it into a hazard level that there was no coming back from. I wasn't sure if I should be thankful she hadn't left more claw marks on my back or praying I'd get another chance. Intense didn't even come close. It was like waving a lit match in a barrel of gunpowder, unstable with the blast capacity guaranteed to level a city block. And fuck me if I didn't want to be there for that fucking detonation.

The whole-bad-idea shit my brain had been preaching since the first minute I laid eyes on her was null and void. I didn't care if I ended up in a freaking ditch—no doubt at her doing—it would be fucking worth it. There was zero chance of me heeding those alarm bells as I put myself once again on a crash course with fucking disaster.

Angie had ghosted at some point through the night. I'd woken up to a neat pile of her torn clothes on the side of my bed where *she* had previously been. She would have no doubt been pissed; cussing me out for ruining her clothes, and the smile automatically crept across my face. Missing it had been the only part of *that* situation which had sucked. Just her calling me an asshole was enough to get me hard, and fuck me if that wasn't messed up. Maybe all those years of screwing around had made me depraved? As long as I didn't start needing to start jamming electrodes to my balls just to get off I guess it wasn't too bad. Besides, normal was relative and there wasn't a lot of run-of-the-mill hanging around where I was currently kicking it.

"Hi Jason, I'm a massive fan." Some random girl flung her arms around me, her hands getting cozy with my back. It was the usual backstage routine, meeting people after the show. Usually I had no problem with it—I loved meeting the fans—tonight, not so much. Her body pressed tight against mine spelling out exactly what kind of *fan* she was. "Wow, you are like really fit," she mumbled as her head rested on my chest.

"Thanks. I like to run." I smiled back, already sick of this dog and pony show we had to do. I gave her arms a subtle yank as I peeled her off me, her brown hair flicking down across her hazel eyes. She was pretty, I'll give her that, but I had no interest in getting any more *appreciation* other than the hug she seemed hell bent on making linger. "What did you say your name was?"

"Shelley." She pushed out her tits proudly, probably hoping that would get her more attention. Not likely, considering my head was with a dark haired, dark eyed singer who I hadn't seen since she'd left the stage.

"Awesome, Shelley. Glad you enjoyed the show. Have you met the rest of the band?" My eyes darted to the others, each of them engaged in some other conversation or posing for a photo. Great.

Not sure why I was trying to palm her off, it's not like any of the others were going to give poor Shelley what she was after. Of course I was speculating that the kind of autograph she wanted was one where my cock signed her pussy, but given that her hand was now squeezing my ass, I'd say it was a fairly safe assessment.

"I have." She grinned. "You're my favorite." Her nose scrunched up in what I'm assuming was supposed to be adorable but mainly just looked like she was about to sneeze.

"Well thanks," I said with as much enthusiasm as I could without adding sarcasm, hoping I didn't roll my eyes. "Did you want a photo?"

"Actually ..." She bit her lip as her sentence was left trailing.

Here we go, the initiation of the conversation that would end with *do you want to fuck?* Surprising how many variations there were ranging from hey-let's-go-get-a-drink or I've-never-done-this-before-but ... and yet the end result was always the same.

"Hey, man, you cool to do a group photo?" Alex's hand tapped me on the shoulder.

I could have kissed the man, which was saying something seeing I didn't share lip action with dudes. His well-timed interruption saved me from having to listen to Shelley's bumbling attempt at trying to get me in the sack.

"Yeah, sure. Sorry, Shelley. You want me to sign anything?"

"Um. No. That's okay." Her face pinked with embarrassment, perhaps having second thoughts about what she was about to ask. "Maybe some other time."

"No problem. Thanks for coming out and seeing us. It was great meeting you." The standard goodbye fell out of my mouth with very little effort. I threw in a smile at the end to soften the blow.

"Bye." She reached up and gave me a kiss in what seemed like a last ditch surge of courage. Her lips off mine almost as quickly as they'd been on. She was definitely the I've-never-done-this-before girl, her smile almost splitting off her face as she scrambled back to a group of girls I assumed were her friends.

"Nice girl." Alex lifted his brow, the group giggling as they looked back at us, getting his attention. I'm sure the kiss was the topic of conversation, all one point five seconds of it.

"Yeah, thanks for that. I wasn't feeling it." My hand reached up to my neck and rubbed out a knot.

The gig tonight had been great. The energy was easy to feed off, and I had been a little more enthusiastic with my playing, hoping Angie had hung back and watched. Not sure if that made me pathetic or perverted—neither of them favorable.

"No problem. We've got a few more photos then we can bail." Alex tipped his chin to James who rounded up the rest of the guys. Troy and Dan joined us as we lined up ready for the happy snaps.

"So do you think Rusty is doing Angie?" Dan muttered under his breath as flashes from both professional cameras and smartphones started rapidly firing at us.

"Dan, seriously man," Troy managed to hiss out through his forced grin, the crowd in front of us having no idea what conversation was taking place.

The photographers took turns in calling to us to face their direction.

"Over here, guys."

Smile.

"Look this way please."

Smile.

"Did you see them on stage tonight?" Dan briefly broke formation, turning to Troy and smirking. "He is strumming more than just his fret board, I guarantee it."

"Can you just shut up and smile already?" I gritted out through my clenched jaw, hoping I was still maintaining a stupid grin.

Rusty was *not* doing Angie, that much I knew. But whether or not she was doing someone else was always a possibility. We sure as hell weren't dating, and I doubted a girl like that would be single for long. Not that I thought she would mess around on a dude if she was with someone. Still the prospect didn't make me feel warm and tingly thinking about it, that was for sure.

"Fine, but you know I'm right." He faced the group, big grin on his mug.

"Whatever, Dan." Troy elbowed him in the ribs as we took the last few shots.

"Thanks everyone." Lexi motioned everyone to the door, giving them a gentle that's-all-folks and directed them out of the room. Shelley gave me one last lingering wave before disappearing with the rest of the crowd.

"Daddy!" Grace ran into the room and launched herself at Alex, the big guy scooping her up into his arms. Not sure which of them more pleased to see each other, both of them wearing matching grins.

The room that had been emptied of fans, filled up with significant others. The guys gave their girls all kinds of attention while the kids ran around—their late afternoon naps meaning they were still up and pumped. It didn't bother me, I was happy they had all carved out their little slice of happiness, it just wasn't what I wanted for myself.

"Hey, Jase. You have a sore neck?" Megs nodded to my hand that unconsciously found its way back to the base of my skull. The tension build up not all entirely physical.

"Yeah, just a little tight." I flexed my head from left to right for good measure. Nope, none of it did any good.

"Was it the way you slept?" Megs gave me an overly enthusiastic smirk with a raised eyebrow for good measure. Maybe we'd been louder than I thought; noise control wasn't really where my mind had been. Not after I'd seen Angie naked. All the inked skin, and her perfect tits and ass. Yeah, you could have set fire to the bed and I probably still wouldn't have noticed.

"Yeah. Possible."

Definitely felt liked she knew more. Megs was a great girl, super sweet, but as far as being able to keep a poker face, she sucked. I mean seriously bad.

"Something you want to ask me, Megs?" No point in stringing it along.

"No, not really." The smile she was rocking told me otherwise.

"Hey." Troy wrapped his arms around her, his usual routine whenever she was close by.

"Troy Harris, I was trying to have a conversation." She pouted, nowhere near as annoyed as she was pretending to be. "Jason must have slept funny last night. He has a sore neck." The smile was back, as was my belief that she knew something.

"Oh yeah? Troy asked, kissing his wife, showing no interest in my nocturnal habits. "Poor Jase," he said with zero sympathy, shooting me a wink.

"Must have been that girl he brought home. What was with that? Not usually your thing." Dan weighed in, Ash smiling by his side. Whatever Megs knew, she'd shared it with her best friend. That much was clear.

"What is with everyone today? When did you all get so interested in me?" I deflected, thinking everyone needed to find another pet project other than my love life.

"Does Uncle Jase have a girlfriend?" Noah asked, obviously the kid picking up parts of the conversation. Awesome. Even the kids were against me. Fucking perfect.

"On that note, we might get the kidos to bed." James hauled his son up onto his shoulders ending the conversation. Hannah cradled a sleeping Jesse in her arms and was already heading toward the door.

"See you everyone." Lexi waved as she made for the exit, her interest more on getting her family back to the hotel rather than finding out who had been my bed partner. Alex and Grace followed close behind.

"Okay, so they're gone. Who was she?" Dan was back on the attack. I swear he was worse than an old woman. His interest nothing new, but somewhat irritating.

"None of your business." Was as much as he was going to get. At least for now.

"Screw who you want, just don't marry her yet. I've got ten G's riding on you waiting six months. And while I'm all for your happiness, Troy doesn't need any more of my money." The bastard grinned, his true motivation shining though.

"Dan, you can shove your ten grand. There is no way in hell I'm getting married in the next six years, let alone the next six months."

Or ever, which was more to the point. No fucking way. I'd rather pull my fingernails out one by one than get hitched.

"Famous last words," Dan laughed. "Just make sure whatever tail you're screwing doesn't get her claws in for the time being. That's all I'm asking. Be a team player."

"For fuck's sake. This is why I don't bring girls home." I ran my hands through my hair, wondering if the asshole was baiting me intentionally. Probably not. Dan wasn't that smart.

"You cool, brother?" Troy laughed, noticing my game was off. Not so long ago it had been his inability to get his act together that had been the talking point. He too was enjoying this shit a little too much.

"Yep. Laugh all you want, but you aren't getting dick out of me."

Megs laughed, as did Ashlyn. And I don't think it was over my use of the word *dick*. They'd both had seen plenty considering their husbands could barely keep their hands off them. The fact one of them was knocked up, evidence enough.

"Spill it, Megs Harris. And don't pretend like you don't have something to say." I eyeballed her, knowing she was close to breaking.

Out of the two of them—Ash and Megs—she was the weakest link, and the sooner we got it over with, the better. I assumed this was where she said she heard something last night. Those moans on both sides had been well and truly earned. Whatever. If they were looking to embarrass me then they were going to be waiting a while.

"I saw her. This morning. Coming out of your room. I'm sorry." She shot me a pained look of apology. Seems it wasn't speculation she'd been hiding after all. More like insider knowledge.

Fuck.

Yep, did not want to have this conversation.

"Who did you see, Megs?" Troy asked, his eyes looking between us for an answer.

"She saw Angie," I volunteered, knowing one way or another they were bound to find out. It's not like shit stayed under wraps in this band for long anyway. Worst group of people ever to try and keep a secret from. Their track record, fucking horrible.

"Ha, very funny asswipe. She hates you, there's a better chance of me sleeping with her than you." Dan folded his arms across his chest smugly.

"Dan!" Ashlyn shot back, not impressed by her husband's analysis. No one dug a hole like Dan. He really had a talent for that shit.

"No I didn't mean I would, I just mean probabilities." He tried to justify himself and reassure Ash. "Which would be zero. So her sleeping with Jase would be less than zero."

A few days ago, I might have agreed with him. Now. Well weren't we just a fucking example of never say never.

"Well then there must be some crazy quantum mechanics at work because that negative probability happened, asshole."

And there it was. The admission—for everyone to see. Whether or not Angie or I had wanted anyone to know was no longer relevant, because guess what? They fucking knew now. And I wasn't ashamed of it either. She and I had wanted the same thing, which is exactly what we got.

"What. The. Fuck." Dan paused between each word, with a look of complete disbelief. The are-you-serious vibe also coming from Troy.

"Don't start." My head shook as I went on the offensive. "And Troy before you go all losing your shit, no one took advantage of anyone. It was completely consensual."

"As long as you both know what you're doing, I'll keep out of it." The eyeball that came with it warning that his keeping-out was contingent on shit not going bad. Predictable.

"We're good. Trust me."

My words were solid but I wasn't sold, in fact I had no freaking idea what the hell I was doing. And as for us being *good*, another assumption that was made without evidence. Who knew where Angie would land on the whole situation. One thing was for sure, I was going to find out.

"Okay, new bet." Dan rubbed his hands together, shit eating grin back on his face. "Double or nothing says Angie kills him in his sleep."

Well that was fun.

Still, not as bad as I'd assumed it would have gone down. Even

Troy had kept the warnings to a minimal, well for now at least.

Ash and Megs—those two were going to be trouble. I could already see how freaking pleased they were. They'd been hell bent on hooking me up with someone for god knows how long. My solo routine the reason for most of the grief they threw my way. Of course they were probably reading more into it than there was, i.e. Angie and I weren't looking to buy matching bath towels anytime soon. But if it got them off my ass and quelled the why-don't-you-have-a-girlfriend discussion, then that was just a bonus. Who knew if Angie was even interested in a repeat. Let alone an extended performance.

"You lost, asshole?" The devil herself stepped out from the shadows. She was alone and looking more incredible than the last time I saw her. Her dark hair loose but pinned away from her face, her body barely covered by a tight, black dress.

"I could say the same for you. Your set finished hours ago."

The rest of the band had left, grabbing a ride back to the hotel, but I liked to hang back at the venue after the show a little sometimes. Like the running, it gave me a reality check of sorts, and if ever I needed one, it was tonight.

"I was watching you." She moved closer, her body showing a dangerous amount of exposed skin.

The area we were in was secluded, filled with road cases that would soon be loaded onto a truck for our next gig. The roadies were too preoccupied with tearing down the stage to be worried about shit they'd already packed away.

"Really. You channeling your inner stalker?" My smile was automatic as was my feet moving closer toward her.

"Yeah. Figured you watched me, it's only fair." She shrugged, the smile tugging at her lips. And God help me if that smile didn't make me want to take her right here.

"So you left this morning without saying goodbye." I tilted her chin toward me, my eyes locked onto hers.

"I didn't realize we did goodbyes, sorry. Was just following your lead." She squared off her shoulders without even a hint of apology. It was so fucking hot.

"Well, in the future I think you should say goodbye." I moved my mouth inches away from hers.

"Who said there was going to be a future?" She smiled, like she knew exactly what she was doing.

My lips crushed down on hers answering her question. My tongue invading her mouth as my hands hauled her body onto mine. I had no desire to be gentle; with the need to feel her more desperate than the last time I'd been with her. My cock was already straining against the seam of my jeans, begging to get out.

"Just so we're clear, just because I'm having sex with you doesn't mean I like you." Angie's hand moved down my back and grabbed at my ass, her body rubbing against me as I continued to kiss her.

"Good, I'm glad you don't like me. You shouldn't. I'm not a nice person." I pulled my lips away from her mouth long enough to answer. Her beautiful eyes giving me the all clear as I moved one of my hands up her thigh. My fingers teased the edges of her panties, while my lips sucked hard at her neck.

"I like that." She arched her neck back, giving me better access.

"Just as well. Because I like doing it to you," I mumbled against her throat as my fingers got bored playing with her panties and sunk into her pussy.

"Fuck," She gritted out, her eyes flying open as I stretched her out with another finger. The fabric of her underwear strained against my hand.

"Is that what you want? Me to fuck you?" My thumb joined my fingers, circling her clit while I pumped into her. She was so wet and ready.

"No, this time I'm fucking you." She pushed me back, my body hitting a wall of road cases as she attacked me with her lips.

Her hands pulled at my T-shirt as her tongue plunged into my mouth. Whatever she was doing, she wasn't playing as she shoved me harder against the metal boxes.

"Get it off," She ordered, my T-shirt obviously offending her as she moved her attention to undoing my jeans.

"You know, this isn't exactly private?" My mouth shot out, our location far from ideal. "Anyone could walk in here at any time. There are over a hundred people roaming these halls." The sound of footsteps echoed not more than a hundred feet away, as did the voices of rowdy men who'd kill to be where I was. Not that I'd ever give them a chance.

"Are you shy, Jason? Because I'm not." She stepped back and slid off the tight black dress she'd been wearing, her body completely exposed except for that pair of lace panties I'd been playing with. No bra, her tits standing proudly. And so they should, they were absolutely spectacular.

"No, I'm not shy." My eyes didn't leave hers as I pulled off my shirt, and I kicked off my boots. My dick screamed for attention as I stepped out of my jeans and stripped off my boxer shorts.

"Nice." She glanced down at my hard-on, her lips spreading into a grin.

"If you want *nice*, sweetheart, then you're with the wrong person."

I wasn't sure if it was her or me who moved first, both of our bodies crashing into one another as our mouths got busy. My hands pulled at her panties, determined to strip the last barrier between us.

"Don't rip them, asshole, you still owe me for the rest of my stuff you ruined," she warned as her fingers gripped tight against my skin.

I couldn't help it.

The shredded panties were tossed aside the minute I'd torn them from her body. It was her fault, her telling me not to just made me want to even more. Sure it was twisted logic but that's the way we operated, and there was no way I was backing down from a dare. Her threats and venom just served to turn me on more.

If she was genuinely mad, she didn't show it, her hands stroking my shaft as I once again attacked her mouth. The need to be in her had me so crazy I could no longer think straight.

Her promise to be the one doing the fucking wasn't an idle threat, taking control, her hands wrapping around my cock as she ordered me to "lay down."

Every single time I'd had sex, it had been me calling the shots. Not because I was a sexist asshole, but because that's just the way

I liked it. I liked the control to watch a woman unravel underneath me, knowing it was me who put that satisfied look on her face. And I liked sex. The feeling of freedom after just having blown your load was addictive. In that moment, nothing else existed. No problems, just two people making themselves feel good.

Giving up the control—even if it was just for now—was not something I was comfortable with. I'd rather walk my naked ass out in front of all those roadies and ask one of them to jerk me off, that's how much I wasn't down with it. But with Angie, there was something about her that I just couldn't say no to. If she wanted me to lie on the floor and call me an asshole then I'd probably thank her for the privilege. Sure, that wasn't messed up at all.

And that's exactly what I did. Metal cut into my back as I laid on the rolling cases, her hands tight around my wrists as she climbed on top and straddled me. I had no idea what she was going to do. Her hands were probably going to need to let mine go if she was hoping to move this past just rubbing my junk against her pussy, but I didn't ask. I was mesmerized by her.

"Don't move," she warned as she let go, her fingers tracing the lines of my torso as they moved down my body. Her lips followed where her hands had been, kissing and licking their path. My body rose to meet her lips half way in a show of appreciation. "Don't move." She nipped at my abs, her teeth grazing my skin, my punishment for not following her instructions.

"You're not making it easy for me." My neck craned off the case just in time to see her beautiful lips take my cock into her mouth. "Fuck."

I didn't care how loud I'd yelled it. In fact, there wasn't a lot that could have been more important other than what she was doing. She could have asked me for my bank account details and the deed to my apartment and I would've asked her where I needed to sign. As long as she kept doing exactly what she was doing, her tongue expertly working every inch of me.

"Jason." She hissed as I pulled my cock from her mouth, my hand around her hair. I'd taken as many orders as I was going to, and I'd done the lay still bullshit long enough.

"You wanna punish me, Angie, go right ahead. But I need to be in you."

"You want me, Jason?" She shuffled back up to her knees—which would no doubt be sporting road rash after we were done—and placed each one of her legs on either side of my thighs. "You want this?" she asked again, her hand snaking around her tits then down in between her legs.

"Yes. I want you."

"Then take me."

In a moment of freaking clarity my brain finally kicked it. No way was I doing this without protection. Not even if it meant my balls were going to explode because I was so turned on.

"Angie, I need a rubber."

"Well look what I happened to have?" She reached into her hair and pulled out one of the pins, the condom that had been tucked away up there, now visible. "I'm like a regular girl scout." Her satisfied grin lit up her beautiful eyes as she fished out the foil packet and held it proudly.

"Well thank fuck you aren't selling me cookies."

I snatched the condom from her hand, tearing the wrapper open with my teeth before rolling it down along my length. We could commend her brilliant prior planning later; right now I didn't think either of us was interested in anything that didn't involve us getting busy. And I needed her more than I needed my next breath.

She barely let me get the thing on when she sunk down on me, my cock sliding into her and stretching her out. She wasn't full ready, the fit tight, not that it seemed to stop her.

"Angie." Her name was like a fucking curse. I said it over and over again as any control I'd had went out the window as freaking want took over. I grabbed her ass and pistoned hard against her, unable to stop.

"Yes," she screamed, her teeth sinking into my shoulder as I felt her come hard against me. That sensation alone was enough to finish me as I exploded into her, my breathing like an out of control freight train about to derail.

"You're crazy." I panted against her neck, her body still shaking slightly on mine.

My good mood immediately flipped to pissed off after seeing her beautiful skin marked by the red scratches our little exercise had caused. "Shit, did I hurt you?"

"Don't flatter yourself," she laughed. "It's going to take a lot more than that to hurt me."

God I hoped she was right, because hurting her was the last thing I wanted to do and selfishly I knew I wasn't going to be able to stop.

"Just promise me you'll tell me if I do." And I wasn't talking about the grazes on her knees.

"Fine, Jason." I didn't need to see her to know she was rolling her eyes. "I promise."

'16

Angie

Last night had been insane. My behavior crazy, and yet I regretted nothing. It had been out of character, but not in the way that most people would think.

I wasn't a whore, but meaningless sex was pretty much the only sex I had. No, it wasn't as horrible as it sounded; it was actually better that way. Considering the few times I had done it for the "right" reasons the guy left, I'd say my way was healthier. At least there were no surprises. That didn't mean I slept with just anyone, and of course I had boyfriends, it just wasn't lovey-dovey. I wasn't looking for that beautiful love. Because don't they always leave? Even if it's perfect, someone always has to go. My dad had loved my mom like no other love I'd seen, and she'd been taken too. I knew it wasn't the same thing, but he'd never found anyone else.

Two people. That perfect love. Someone was going to have to go, one way or another.

That's why meaningless sex was best, except meaningless should be emotionless too. And with Jason, it wasn't.

Anger—emotion

Hurt—emotion

Revenge—emotion

Lust—emotion

Did I need to go on? It didn't matter they weren't good emotions; they were there nonetheless.

As long as I kept them in check, it would be okay. Well at least that's what my vagina was telling my head because she didn't want happy time to end. And no one made *her* happy like Jason did.

I knew he watched me perform, I felt his eyes on me as I sang and I liked it. The thrill that he was there in the wings was almost as big a rush as being on stage. He hadn't worked it out yet—my game of musical clues still being unappreciated for its full genius—but every time I sang that final last song, I loved it just a little bit more.

"Hey." I poked him, not quite believing he'd spent the night. "It's morning, you should probably leave."

"Screw that, it's early." He rolled onto his side, taking me with him. My body tucked next to his. He had a habit of doing that as I'd come to find out. Holding me throughout the night. Funny, I'd never have pegged him for much of a cuddler. Wonders will never cease.

"Well, you should be in your bed, not mine."

We'd been careless. Part of the thrill was the dancing with danger, the prospect of getting caught. The sex backstage, I have no explanation for. Perhaps some sex fiend had momentarily possessed my body? While I wasn't the poster woman for missionary sex, I'd never been so reckless and brazen. But I'd been inspired to let go and jump. So I did.

"They know, Angie. Don't worry about it." He yawned without opening his eyes. His lips kissed my neck as he tried to go back to sleep.

Unlike our previous nights together, no one had left this time.

By some freak of fortune, our wild sex on the road cases had gone undetected, which was reason to celebrate. Our choice of celebration was easy—more sex. This time with less metal gouging into my skin, and less chance of giving some random roadie free material for his spank bank. So we moved our party of two to my room, where there was less chance of running into pregnant wives of other band mates. Speaking of which.

"Megs?"

"She hinted. I confirmed. No one cares. It's not like we're dating." Jason's hand travelled up my body, resting on my breast. I felt his smile against my skin.

I liked it. His smile, and his touch.

"True. I wouldn't be stupid enough to date you." I tried unsuccessfully to wiggle out of his hold. God, he was strong. He must lift weights in addition to the running. I silently praised his dedication to fitness, not willing to give him the satisfaction of actually praising him.

"Well seeing as you woke me." With a twist of his arm he'd effortlessly flipped me onto my back so I was facing him. Yep, definitely lifted weights. "We should probably talk about something."

"I thought we didn't have to talk. The whole not dating thing we had going for us."

Besides now I was facing him, I really didn't want to talk. Unless by talking he meant kissing me, which I was totally on board with. And that wasn't as sappy as it sounded, because I didn't mean I wanted him to kiss me on my mouth.

"Are you seeing anyone?"

Not what I thought he was going to ask me. I'd assumed it would be more something along the lines of *so what's your stance on anal* and not *do you currently have a boyfriend.*

I should've been offended by the question and what it implied. That he thought I could possibly cheat on someone I was dating, but really what kind of girl was I? Having sex with a guy I repeatedly said I couldn't stand, sometimes in public places. Not the kind that you'd expect to be sitting in church on Sunday. Maybe someone who fucked around?

Something in his voice also stopped me from calling him an offensive asshole. Like maybe there wasn't more to the question than what he was actually asking.

"Don't you think you should have asked me that *before* you had sex with me?"

"You didn't mention a boyfriend, but I wanted to be sure." His fingers moved my hair out of my eyes.

Well, he had asked me. Sort of. When he wanted to know about Rusty. Which made no sense then, because ... well who cared. Now, it just made me curious as to why.

"Was that something you were worried about?"

"No. I mean I wouldn't have gone there if I thought you were with someone. That's not something I'd be part of."

We all know that when it came to insulting Jason Irwin, I wasn't shy. Remember I had all those lovely names for him, tucked away just waiting for me to blow off the dust. But this conversation was not one of an asshole.

His voice lacked the sarcasm for that. There was no fake smile, or flirty eyes. Nothing even remotely asshole-ish. What we had instead was the makings of a serious conversation where two adult people spoke and didn't dissolve into name-calling or obscenities.

While one part of my brain figured this was going to add some serious complications to the meaningless sex rule, the other part wanted to go a little deeper.

"Infidelity?"

It was a word I was familiar with. I'd been on the receiving end and felt its hurt.

"Yes. I want no part of that." He answered with no hesitation.

While I admired his respect for the institution of relationships, it was kind of at odds with the rest of his philosophies. The ones that had him sleeping with people i.e. me, and then leaving without a second thought, or the ones that let him have sex with numerous people he didn't really care about.

I guess I sort of fell into both of those categories.

"But you said it yourself, you don't date. So what does it matter?"

It was supposed to be another thought. Like the others I'd had while trying to figure him out, but stupidly, my mouth opened and the words just fell out. Just like that. There they were. Me asking things I wanted to know but really had no business asking.

"It matters to me." His brown eyes locked on mine, and for a tiny second I remembered exactly how easy it was to fall in love with him. That flicker of vulnerability. Kindness. It was there, but very well hidden.

Thankfully, it was in the very next second that I remembered why I shouldn't, and no longer loved him.

"Do you ask all those other girls? Make sure they weren't cheating?"

"Every single one. Some try and lie, but there is usually a tell, not many people can do it convincingly. If I have any doubts, I don't."

"A whore with a conscience."

It sounded so insensitive, but I hadn't meant it like that. Once again, my big mouth just spilled the thought with zero filter. But I was caught off guard, not only by the conversation, but his honesty. This was a new place we found ourselves in.

"Yes, a whore with a conscience." He laughed, not offended. He probably should have been. I really wasn't in any position to call anyone a whore; there was no way I was going to be able to wear white on my wedding day convincingly.

"So, while you aren't dating people *but* sleeping with them ... Do you sleep with other people?" My mouth spewed out a jumble of words that didn't constitute a sentence by anyone's standards. "I mean, is it one night stands generally or are there times where you continue to sleep with the same person?"

Better, but I hated how vulnerable it made me sound. Because what I really was asking was, so what exactly are *we* doing and do you plan on having sex with *me* only to go have sex with someone else?

The more I thought about it, the more I didn't feel good about myself. I was breaking my own rules. Those damn emotions poking their head around where they didn't belong.

"Are you asking me if I plan on sleeping with other people while I'm sleeping with you?" He waded through my stumbling mess of words and knew exactly what I was asking. He was so smart. I hated how all together he seemed to have it. It just shone a mirror on my shortcomings.

"Yes, I know you think I'm a freak." Which given what I'd displayed recently wasn't too far from the truth. "But I'm not great with sharing."

If he was being honest, then I would be too. I wanted to have sex with him again. I loved that while I was with him I wasn't thinking too deeply, that my body just let go. Maybe it's because I didn't need to impress him, maybe it's 'cause he'd seen it all before. But there was a freedom that came with the sex, and the things he did to my body. And that's what I wanted.

"You know," Jason laughed. "You and Dan are a lot more alike than you think."

"Please don't compare me to him." I recoiled in horror. "He's a social moron with a constant boner. I'm nothing like him."

"I meant your inability to share." He stopped laughing, his finger tracing the line of my jaw. God, he was smooth. "I take it by your question you might like to do this again?"

"Well I'd hoped that wasn't the last time I was ever going to have sex." This time it was my turn to laugh. Nervously, I might add. "It was good but certainly not good enough for me to slap an eviction notice on my vagina."

I was flat out lying. It had been *that* good.

"With me. Did you want to have sex again with me?"

There was that smooth, hot combination that he seemed to throw at me like a one, two punch. Not even taking into account the sex—which was out-freaking-standing—I knew I'd want more.

"Sure, I guess. I mean, if there was nothing better to do." I lied again. Not willing to admit that I was that easy. Gah. I hated him.

"No, Angie. Without the attitude." I guess he didn't find my off-the-cuff answer as amusing as it had been intended. "If this isn't something you're into then I'll stay away."

Was I into it? Yes, and probably more than I should be. But all that rationality that existed in the world wasn't around at present. It was probably dealing with other people, who it probably would have stood a better chance with. Crazy is who we were in bed with. Both of us. Because only crazy people sleep with someone they had a past with.

"Yes, it's what I want."

Jason Irwin was a lot of things—sexy, smart, and intense. He was *not* romantic, sensitive boyfriend material, in other words, he was not *Ryan Gosling*. Girls were not lining up with their boxes of Kleenex ready to declare their undying love, no matter how badass his abs were. Which they were—he could totally give RyGos a run for his money. And the tattoos. Ryan was too clean cut for my liking, but that was just my personal preference. But seeing as I wasn't going to be declaring my undying love for anyone, I was okay with that.

And I wasn't delusional. No relationship. He'd been clear about that from the start.

Eyes wide open.

It was a *Hey I like sex and you like sex, so lets have sex together. Yippee.* But without the messy *feelings* that could make the sex less pleasurable. And when I was sick of him—which eventually I would be—I could just walk away, vindicated.

And I *could* walk away.

"Hey, where did you go? What are you thinking about?"

He waved his hand in front of my face, pulling me back to the present. I didn't even blink, my mouth doing what it usually did, flicking on autopilot.

"Plotting your demise. I just need to figure out a way to keep your penis viable."

"This is a long ass list, Angie." Max scanned the length of the page in front of him. "You want us to learn all these songs?"

"Yep. Let's have some fun with them. Who knows when else we'll get the chance to play stadiums."

I had amused myself greatly choosing the next few musical clues in the game of *fuck you Jason Irwin.* Except it wasn't so much fuck you any more, it was like an aural treasure hunt. The songs reflecting the many moods he seemed to evoke: angry, sexy, and I'm-going-to-fuck-your-shit up. I really was a ray of sunshine.

"This list looks like it's drunk." Joey twirled his stick, while randomly hitting the base drum. It was a drummer thing, I didn't question. "Are we a rock band or auditioning for a fucking Vegas lounge show?"

"I can already smell the fourteen-ninety-nine buffet." Max laughed.

"Gentlemen, where is your sense of adventure?" Rusty clapped his hands dramatically. He was late but no one had seemed to mind. "Let Angie stretch her pipes on the musical diversity, poor girl is trying to impress her new boyfriend."

"Rusty." I threw a guitar pick at him, hoping none of the crew walking around were paying us any attention. If they'd heard what was being talked about no one seemed to care. I'm sure shadier stuff went down on tour. Like public sex displays ... oh wait. Yeah.

"What new boyfriend?" Max stopped scanning the list.

"Angie, has a boyfriend?" Joey chimed in just as interested.

My hopes of keeping my *arrangement* under wraps vanished before my eyes with both the guys looking to Rusty for answers. He had already displayed his inability to keep his mouth shut. I needed a more discreet best friend.

"Oops. I've said too much." Rusty clutched his chest, screwing his face up in mock horror. The smirk he was struggling to hide a dead giveaway it wasn't just a slip of the tongue. "Sorry. We were not talking about *it*." The "it" whispered for effect. Killing him wasn't completely off the table.

"He's not my *boyfriend*," I started to explain, knowing Rusty would just make it worse if I left it up to him. "But I'm sorta *seeing* Jason."

I wasn't sure of what word to use. *Dating* was out. *Fucking* sounded way too crude. *Sleeping with*—yeah still not much better. So *seeing* it was. FYI the English language sucked, we needed more words to describe people we were involved with that we weren't emotionally attached with. Something like, funfriend or pleasurepal, right 'cause that didn't sound like a cheesy blow up sex doll or a bad porno.

"She means she's seeing him *naked*," Rusty clarified, as his stupid ass grin got wider. He was enjoying this way too much; we needed to find Rusty a girl. Someone to distract him so he didn't have to be so interested in my life. Hopefully a fan girl who'd tie him to a bed and gag him.

My best eye daggers were fired in his direction as I folded my arms across my chest. Oh, he was history the moment *he* started dating, as I mentally tucked away this memory for future revenge. H-i-s-t-o-r-y. I was Italian; the whole vendetta thing was hard-wired to my DNA. Horsehead in your bed anyone? "I hate you, Rusty."

"Is that like you *hate* Jason?" Rusty continued to laugh, oblivious to my plots for my revenge. "Does that mean you're going to want to see me naked too?" He wrapped his arms around me, his guitar hitting me in the ass as he gave me an awkward backward hug. "I'll strip for you, babe, no problem, but we don't want Max and Joey feeling inadequate."

"Does he mean inadequate in that he thinks his dick is bigger than mine, because I'm positive microscopic is *smaller* than ridiculously huge." Joey completely disregarded the issue of Jason, his attention diverted by a stab at his manhood. Boys. Every single one of them was packing a twelve inch penis in their own minds.

"Tell yourself whatever you need to, Joey—"

"Can we stop talking about dicks for a second here and focus?" I interrupted Rusty before the conversation degenerated into a need to *contrast and compare.* Sometimes I was convinced they forgot I was a girl.

"We can talk about tits if you prefer, that's more my area of expertise." Joey laughed, Max and Rusty joining him. The whole I'm-sleeping-with-the-guy-in-the-other-band glossed over in favor of anatomy.

"So are you guys okay with me *seeing* Jason? I mean, nothing is going to change with the band. I'm not leaving or anything and it doesn't affect the tour."

The band was my family, and while other people's opinions didn't matter to me, theirs did. It was important. Next to my dad, Rusty and the guys were all I had.

"Angie, see, date, fuck or whatever it is you want to call it, whoever you want. We know you're with us." Max's warm smile said more than his words. There was no judgment here.

"Yeah, there is no breaking up this band." Joey tossed a stick before catching it midair, his goofy grin putting me at ease.

"Rus?" I knew he had his reservations, knowing better than anyone how bad this could potentially end up, but his endorsement was the one I craved the most.

"Whatever makes you happy, babe." His eyes meeting mine as he shot me a wink. "But I'm not calling him dad."

His wisecrack earned him enthusiastic laughter from the others. They were so easily amused.

"You're all assholes." More guitar picks were thrown at them. The endless supply of picks and strings was a very cool perk of playing with the big boys. Thanks Power Station.

"Yeah, but you love us." Rusty deflected the plastic shrapnel with very little effort. He was right—I loved them.

"Yeah I do. Now let's do this sound check before the audio guy gets any angrier. He's been giving us a stare down for the last ten minutes."

THERE WAS A DEFINITE THEME WITH THE SONGS. THE ONES ANGIE would chose for her colorful finales. Last night's effort had been "Black Widow" By *Iggy Azeala*. Not very subtle.

It was so obvious I wasn't sure how I'd missed it. Each song, a new hidden message. It was kind of adorable but mostly sexy. Impressive too. That her band was able to churn out a new tune every night. Sure, occasionally they messed up, a dropped note that hardly anyone would even pick up, but for the most part they nailed it. And Angie—was flawless.

If her renditions were supposed to piss me off or offend me, she'd failed. It just made me want her more. If that could even be possible, considering I'd pretty much wanted her all the fucking time.

Not sure what kind of death wish I was rocking by making Angie and me a regular thing, but it was one I didn't have any intention in changing. The fact she didn't kiss my ass just made it better. Safer almost. Less chance of it ending in tears. Which is exactly what I needed to avoid.

Our time in Boston was over, with a new show—and no doubt new song—awaiting us at our next destination.

New Haven was next.

My fingers mindlessly ran across the keys, playing some tune that had been stuck in my head for days. The messed up bed served as an impromptu stand. It wasn't even a song I'd been working on, just noise, but I kept playing it anyway.

"Is that Chopin?" Angie walked in from the bathroom, towel wrapped tightly around her body, another twirled around her head.

"Nope, just noise." I stopped playing, flexing my fingers as I lifted them off the keys.

"Well it was good. I liked it." She sat in my lap, her hands moving my fingers back to the keys. "Play for me."

"Maybe later." My fingers found a better place to be as they wrapped around Angie's waist.

"Fine, be a spoilsport." Her hands went down to the keyboard as she tried unsuccessful to make something sound musical. "I'm pretty sure I remember it."

"I know what you're doing each night." I figured having the conversation while she was half-naked on my lap meant less chance she'd be able to pull a dodge and run.

"Blowing your mind with my amazing sex moves? I didn't think I was trying to hide it." She didn't look up from her fingers, bung notes flying left, right and center.

"*Sex moves* isn't a thing, Angie."

"Sure it is, and if its not then I'm copyrighting that tomorrow. Because it should be. It's okay Jase, you've got them too, just not as impressive as mine."

"That's not what I meant, but your diversion tactics are also impressive." My hands moved on top of hers, no longer able to suffer the torture of her rendition. My assist meant at least her fingers were hitting the right keys even if the timing was jacked-up.

"So what *did* you mean?" She ditched the playing altogether, her body twisting toward me. Those eyes I loved so much sent a shiver right down to my cock as they gave me their full attention.

"I know what you are doing with the songs. It's cute." My fingers picked up where hers had bailed, the notes ringing out despite the distraction.

"Cute? Cute?" she scoffed. "Take it back before I start playing again and prove how uncute I am." Her hands T-rex'd in front of her ready to assault my keyboard.

"Fine, it's not cute," I conceded, not wanting the ebonies and ivories to be subjected to her wrath. Or my ears for that matter. As a keyboard player, she made an excellent guitarist. "Clever then. Inventive." My offered replacements.

"Those adjectives are much better. Your instrument is safe." She lowered her hands and settled back into my lap, appeased.

"*And* sexy as hell," I added, no longer interested in the bullshit I was playing.

"Really?" She didn't even try and hide how pleased she was. "Tell me more about how sexy it is." The smile it earned me worth every second.

"Very sexy." I leaned in closer. "You need visual demonstration?" My hand moved to her thigh, sliding under her towel.

"Nope. Not right now." She sprung up out of my lap, grabbing the phone off the nightstand. "I'm ordering room service. I'm hungry."

"Yeah, I don't think you're going to find what you want on the menu." I leaned back into my chair and watched her bite her lip as she waited to order.

"Fine," She tossed the phone to the side as she settled again in my lap. "Just wait until my encore tonight, buddy. We'll see who wants what from the menu." Her mouth fusing to mine as my hands got busy.

We eventually did order food, but only after we'd both had our fill of each other. Which didn't leave much time for anything else. Not a problem as far as I was concerned.

So when I found myself a few hours later in my usual spot stage side while she sang, I couldn't help but grin at her song choice.

"Buttons." By *Pussy Cat Dolls.* And *loosening up her buttons* was not a fucking problem at all.

East Rutherford, New Jersey.

"So, why the Army?" Angie leaned over the front of my treadmill; the only part of her body currently getting a workout was her mouth.

"Give me two miles and I'll tell you." My head tilted to the treadmill beside me that could use some feet on the belt.

"How about you run them for me and I'll give you a blowjob." She smirked.

"Jesus, Angie."

"Is that a yes? Talk and run, you'll be rewarded later." She leaned over the display and cranked up the speed slightly. "And feel free to take your shit off at any time"

Had to hand it to her. She made an excellent case.

My past wasn't something that was publicized. Lawyers, NDA's and a lot of coin kept the shit buried. That, coupled with the fact most people who knew anything about it weren't the most reliable sources, meant People magazine would be running another feature on Kim Kardashian's ass before they'd get anything on me. Plus—for the cheap seats—I was the keyboard player. Fucks given, total of none.

"I got into trouble as a teenager, more so than most because I was running with a bunch of morons whose future looked set to include orange jumpsuits. And my moving in the wrong circles saw me making some choices that weren't the best for my personal growth. So it was either serve jail time or enlist."

My chest burned from having to talk while my feet kept moving, my neck starting to prickle with sweat.

"You were a criminal?"

Cue the wide-eyes and open jaw that I was one hundred percent expecting.

"I had a juvie record, it's sealed. Breaking and entering, petty larceny, destruction of property, getting into fights. Nothing huge but enough to get me on the wrong side of the law. But I got a DUI when I was seventeen, almost killed myself by wrapping my car around a tree. So I made the change."

"Wow. Jason. Um."

"Not what you thought I was going to say, right?"

"No."

"See, not so honorable am I?"

She didn't answer, her hand reaching over and pulling the emergency stop key, the belt underneath my feet grinding to a sudden stop.

"Fuck me." Her eyes spelling out exactly what those words meant, her lips parted in invitation.

"We're in a hotel gym, Angie. Security cameras. People." Not to mention I was slick with sweat and smelled like yesterday's gym socks. "You don't need to prove a point."

"I'm not trying to prove a point. Fuck me anyway."

I didn't bother trying to talk her out of it. Partly because as I said, I wasn't honorable, and partly because talking about my backstory made me edgy. And sex is one hell of an equalizer.

We settled on a compromise. Taking the *fucking* back up to my hotel room, where I pushed her up against a wall and fucked her so hard she had small bruises on her ass where my hands had been.

That night's song was "Bad Romance." By *Lady GaGa.* Never had a song been more fucking appropriate.

Philadelphia, PA

The traveling schedule was brutal. Usually it was only a couple of days in one place and then packing up and rolling into the next town. Nights on stage, mornings sleeping late. And as for free time, there wasn't a lot, but what we had I usually spent with Angie.

We weren't always naked either, spending a large chunk of the daylight hours actually just hanging out. We were even able to talk without her hurling insults at me. Wonders would never cease. There was definitely more to her that met the eye and damn if I didn't want to know more about her.

"So, why not go to college? It can't be that you didn't have the grades?" I dipped a fry in ketchup before shoving it in my mouth.

"Money." She picked at her salad, looking at my plate with envy. She'd convinced herself her ass was getting bigger which was utter shit. And I should know considering I stared at every inch of it, every single night.

"When my mom died, things got tight at home. Small business. Medical bills. Funeral expenses." She shook her head as I inched my plate closer, offering her a reprieve from her miserable dinner. "Besides, my dad needed me."

"He's lucky to have you." I took a bite of my burger, the size of my ass not being a concern, and enjoyed the mouthful. Then chased it down with another bite.

She caved, snagging a fry off my plate and popping it into her mouth, the smile that spread across her lips validation enough it was better than the rabbit food she'd been chowing down on.

"Can I ask you a question?" She stole another fry before taking a sip of her soda, and I had to stop from staring at her mouth so I could concentrate on what she was saying.

"What is that?" I pushed my plate toward her, more than happy to give her the other half of my dinner. Hers was just too sad to even be called a meal.

She didn't take much convincing, picking up half the burger that was on the plate and taking a small bite. "So you've fed me the line about the no girlfriends, but I know it hasn't always been like that, right?"

"Angie."

"C'mon Jase, we're just talking, right? Just talk to me."

"No, it wasn't always like that."

"There was one girl in particular. In your past, who messed you up."

If she had meant to ask a question, she didn't. Instead she nailed exactly why I was happy to keep doing my solo routine.

"You want to have sex?" I pushed away from the table, wiping my mouth with a napkin. "Let's go do that."

Pulling at her hand I yanked her out of her chair, my mission to get her naked sooner than later. She squeaked as her body hit mine, fries still in her hand as I went to scoop her up. To bed. That's where I wanted her and the conversation.

"No. I want to talk." She wiggled out of my hold, escaping just as I was about to throw her over my shoulder.

"Yes, fine. There was one girl in particular in my past." My hand raked through my hair in frustration.

"She cheated on you, right? That's why you are so against it. Because she hurt you and you don't want to do that to someone else."

"Fuck. Yes, she cheated on me. I thought I was in love with her and she slept with my best friend. It's over. I'm not going to be part of that again, in any capacity." My voice bounced off the walls and I was fucking thankful we were in my hotel room and not having this conversation somewhere else.

"Don't yell." She stood her ground. "Look at me." She pulled my face into her hands. "I'm sorry she was a bitch and did that, but don't yell at *me*."

Now it was my turn to give the goldfish impression.

The apology I was working on got stuck between I'm-sorry-I'm-an-asshole and I'm-sorry-where-would-you-like-my-balls?

"What was her name?" She ignored me and took another bite of our shared burger.

"Why, you going to look her up? Swap recipes?" I laughed, but at myself not at the questions themselves. Because I'd been delusional in thinking I had any control over anything when it came to Angie. Including the topic of conversation.

"No. I just need to rename my voodoo doll." She gave me a smile that just about knocked me on my ass. "The old name isn't working for me anymore seeing as it's the same name I'm scream-ing most nights. Besides, I think I've punished you enough."

She pulled me from rage to amazement with a flash of a grin. It was more than just seduction that those dark-brown eyes were packing.

"Em."

It burnt my lips saying it, but I volunteered it anyway. The additional information about how she stole my car, my money and most of all, my fucking sanity was conveniently left out.

"Em." Angie's lips moved as they pushed out the sound. The chill jacked-up my spine hearing her say that name, knowing I'd do whatever I had to so she wouldn't ever say it again.

"Don't say her name, Angie." It was halfway between a plea and a warning. "I don't want something so ugly ever coming out of your mouth."

"You've heard the way I talk and you think the ugliest thing I could say is her name?" Angie's eyes widened in disbelief as the blast of leave-it-alone I was throwing hopefully hit its mark.

"Trust me on this, even when you are swearing like a sailor it's still more beautiful than those two fucking letters." And I meant every word.

"Even when I call you an asshole?" her voice moving from serious to playful. That was the place I wanted her to be, and where I wanted to keep her.

"Especially when you call me an asshole."

My smile was back, as was my absolute awe of the woman in front of me. The memories of the evil got shoved back where they belonged as I focused on the only thing that mattered right now—her.

"Thanks." She moved closer, her head rested on my shoulder, my hands finding their mark on her body. "For telling me. About her."

The song that night had to be a coincidence because there is no way she could have predicted the conversation. "You know I'm no good." By *Amy Winehouse.*

And later, when we had our own private encore, she had screamed my name so loud I wasn't sure we were going to have the cops knocking at my hotel door.

I started waking up early, my internal clock jerking me awake without the need for an alarm. My prize for my early bird ritual was watching her sleep beside me. It was addictive; me living for those quiet moments where I could just look at her, and be awed by her perfection. It never got old.

The other thing I hadn't been able to shake was my inability to sleep until I knew she was safely inside dream world. The need for my own Z's taking a back seat until I'd felt her breathing even out and her body relax beside mine.

"Ugh."

The moan coming from Angie's lips wasn't the good kind, not like the ones she'd been giving me earlier. Her head was tilted away from me, the room still pitch black thanks to the early hour of the morning.

"Angie?" I lifted my head off the pillow as my hand reached for the bedside lamp.

"No," she all but screamed, the light flicking on for only a second before I killed it again. "Don't turn on the light." Her body scrunched into a ball, rolling to the far side of the bed.

"What the fuck?" I moved closer to her, my hands finding her in the dark. "You want to tell me what's going on?"

"Head. Bad," she stuttered. "Headache. It hurts." Her body rocked in the dark as I massaged her back. More moans following after.

"Do I need to call someone?" I fumbled in the dark for my phone while trying to keep my hands on her. Calling 9-1-1 for a headache was overkill, right? Still, this didn't seem like the run of the mill kind that was going to be killed by a couple of Tylenols.

"No, it's okay. I get them from time to time. Stress. Fatigue. My dad gets them too. It's nothing major; trust me, I even had my head scanned a couple of years back ... you know ... just to make sure," she mumbled while she kept her back to me, her body still tightly coiled as the pain griped her.

There was no need to elaborate on what the scan might have been for, and I was surprised by how relieved I felt that there wasn't more to it. Just the thought of something serious being wrong making me swallow, hard.

Uh-hum. Yeah.

So maybe instead of sitting there like an emotional dumbass with no clue, I should actually do something to help her.

"Okay, give me a second." I moved off the bed and went to the bathroom, doing my walk in the dark so not to make the shit any worse for her than it already was. My hands managed to locate the ibuprofen while I rummaged through my toiletry bag before I made my way to the mini bar, grabbing a couple cans of Coke.

"Here." I crouched down beside her side of the bed, the hiss of the can making her wince as I opened it. "Take some pills and drink the Coke."

"What? That's crazy. It will make it worse," she argued, her hands holding her head like it was going to explode.

"Trust me. It works. I can Google the science behind it later, but trust me, it works." My hand moved to her back and gently lifted her. "Take them." My fingers brought the pills to her mouth, her lips reluctantly opening for me.

"That's it, good girl." I snagged the opened Coke from the nightstand and lifted it to her mouth, easing the can slightly so she could take a drink. "Drink." I repeated the action, giving her a little.

When she had a few more sips that I was satisfied with, I lowered her back on the bed. Leaving the open can sitting on the nightstand beside her.

"I'll be right back." I gave her a kiss on the forehead and grabbed the other can of Coke and went back into the bathroom. This time I shut the door so I could hit the lights, my vision needed for the next part of playing doctor Jase.

My eyes blinked as they tried to adjust to the bright overhead light, the attack brutal, making me glad I'd shut the door. I placed the can on the sink before sinking to my knees in front of the tub, reaching out and turning on the faucet. I adjusted the water so it was running a little on the hot side; the water level in the tub rose as the bathroom started to steam.

While I waited I grabbed a couple of towels and stuck them on the edge, wanting to make it as comfortable as possible.

Didn't need a full tub, so was able to cut the water pretty soon after, hitting the light before opening the door. My eyes once again had a minute or two of black and white dots before being operational. The door back to the bedroom was pulled open as my vision started to return.

"Ugh," Angie moaned again, her body rocking slowly in the bed.

"Angie." My arms moved under her, lifting her body off the mattress. "Come with me, sweetheart."

She didn't fight me. There was no backchat or asking what-are-we-doing, with her willingly flinging her arms around my neck as I carried her into the bathroom. I kept it dark even though it meant making the journey harder. If anyone was stubbing their toe, it was only going to be me so my care factor was low.

Her breath heaved against my neck, her whimpering not as loud as I moved her feet into the tub. Her ass gently lowered onto the towel-covered tub edge as I eased her further down.

"Ah, it's hot." She pulled her feet out of the water, the splashes hitting both of us.

"It feels hotter than it is. Just give it a minute." I felt her body ease as she lowered her feet back in. The telltale splash told me her toes had hit the water. "That's it. Doing awesome." My hand rubbed small circles on her back as I sunk down to my knees beside her.

My fingers fumbled around in the dark and snared the other can of Coke. I cradled it against the base of her neck, the cold metal hitting her skin making her jump.

"Easy," I laughed. "Just relax. I've got you." My hand kept contact with her skin while I balanced the can against her neck. The contrast in temperature between her feet and the base of her head supposed to help.

We didn't talk, just sat there in the dark. My knees were not doing so hot on the tile but I didn't dare move. My comfort not a priority right now as I made sure she had what she needed.

It took a while but finally her body eased a little, her shoulders relaxing with her breathing a little less rapid. Either the ibuprofen with the Coke chaser had kicked in or the temperature remedy was responsible, but I was glad she was no longer sounding like she was wounded.

"Better?" I lifted the Coke can that wasn't so cold anymore away from her neck and put back on the sink.

"Yes, it's still there but not as bad. How did you know all that?" Her head stayed tilted forward as my fingers moved to massaging her neck.

"Just stuff I've picked up here and there, you'd be surprised what other skills I have." My hands worked the base of her skull.

"Oh yeah, was the massage the next step? Like after the other two?"

"Nope, step three my fingers do a different kind of rubbing. Orgasm, if the blood is rushing to other parts of your body, it can't be giving you headache."

She laughed, her body gently shaking as the noise escaped her lips.

"Whatever. Who wants sex when they have a headache? I'm calling bullshit."

"You know, I'm going to prove you wrong." I pushed up off my knees, my body coming to full height. "Let's go." I didn't give her much of a chance to protest as I lifted her off the edge of the tub, her feet wet and dripping on the floor as we made our back to the bed.

Lucky for me—and her as the case may be—she was already naked. It's not that I hadn't noticed earlier, it had just been other shit that had my attention i.e. doing whatever I had to do to make her feel better. But now, as I laid her down on the mattress, her legs spread out in front of me, it was hard not to notice.

"Jason—"

"Relax, we're not having sex."

My hands travelled up her thighs, my fingers going to where they needed to be as I lowered myself down on the bed in between her legs. And what a beautiful sight it was. So much so, that I gave up on letting my hands have all the fun. My mouth lowered onto her pussy, my tongue giving her clit all the attention while my finger gently slid inside of her. Which she seemed to enjoy. My tongue and my hands working together like a team as her breathing, which had been all settled a few minutes ago, kicking back up in tempo. This time for the right reasons.

"Jason."

Unlike the first time she had said my name, there wasn't any hesitation. Her hands finding themselves in my hair as I stayed where I needed to be—in between her legs, my mouth alternating between licking and sucking. Of course now my face was getting most of the action, so I upped the ante with my hand, adding another finger to the one I already had buried inside of her. Both of them got busy finding a good rhythm.

It didn't take long. A lot less time than I would have liked to be honest. My hands and tongue happy to continue on this prescribed course of therapy a little longer, but it seems Angie's body had other plans.

"Yes." Her body bowed off the bed, moving closer to my mouth as I picked up the pace and made sure every single inch of her pussy was getting that lovin' feeling.

"Yes." She grabbed my hair, her legs moving restlessly while I worked to bring her undone. One last flick of my tongue was all it took.

Watching her come never got old. Her eyes were tightly shut as her body stilled, even though everything I was doing didn't stop. The crest coming like a wave before she finally exploded on my mouth and hand. Both happy to have been of service as they teased every last inch of pleasure out of her.

"I liked your third solution the best." Her breath rushed out between her lips.

"Yeah, I bet you did." I lifted my mouth away from her but not before one last pass with my tongue, her body shaking in appreciation.

"Now, go to sleep." I pulled up the covers over her beautiful skin.

"But what about you?"

"Don't worry about me. This was about you."

I didn't bother to mention the hard-on that had developed the minute I'd lowered her onto the bed and spread her legs. Best that piece of information stayed on the backburner, my dick cursing me out for the hell I'd condemned it to.

"No, I can ..." Her hands reached for me on the mattress.

"You can do whatever you want to me in the morning if you still feel inclined. How's that for a deal?"

"Okay. Her voice and her hands settled, my body not sharing the same sentiment. So juiced up, just the brush of the covers probably enough to set me off.

"Awesome." I watched her body relax on the bed, her eyes closing. "We'll play in the morning."

It was going to be a hell of a long night.

Angie

FATIGUE. ROAD WEARY WAS AN ACTUAL THING, MY EYES DROOPING slowly as the plane came into land. It was midmorning, though unlike the cheery airline staff, I hadn't the five liters of coffee that would get me to their shared state of happy. It wasn't just lack of sleep, it had been physical fatigue too with my body more sore from the after show performances than my bouncing on stage.

"Hey, guys, over here."

Security pushed and pulled us in different directions, moving us through the arrivals section at Chicago's O'Hare. My feet trudged slow down the walkway as I hit a wall of bodies, a few die-hard Power Station fans slowing up the process by trying to get the band's attention. They went first—Power Station. Their band with their significant others more alert than us in what I can only assume was an acquired tolerance.

"Hey are you, Angie Morelli?" A short, dark-haired girl who was wearing more eye makeup than clothes stopped in front of us.

My eyes dipped down to the front of my shirt to check if I was wearing some kind of nametag. Nope, nothing there. Unless my name had been changed over night to The Ramones.

"Ummm, yeah," I answered, not wanting to be rude.

"Oh. My. God. I love you. Your band is amazing." She grabbed a hold of my arm and started to shake uncontrollably. "I love you so much."

"Err, thanks?"

Doing something—anything—would have been the smart thing to do. But I was kind of frozen. The surprise of someone I didn't know knowing me, had my feet glued to the floor. No one had ever stopped me before, not outside my neighborhood. And even then, it was usually someone I had already met.

The girl attached to my arm had a friend, who grabbed my other arm and between the two of them roughly played a tug of war with my body. Not hard, but enough that I was starting to feel a little freaked out. More hands touched me and I had to remember to breathe. The overwhelming urge to run burned through my body yet my feet wouldn't respond.

I watched in slow motion as the rest of my group moved further away, everyone too consumed with conversations to notice I was stuck. The faces I recognized blurring in the distance as my pulse started to race.

"You need to keep moving." Jason's hand circled my waist, having appeared miraculously by my side and pulled me forward. The girls attached to my arms, still holding on. Neither of them doing much more than babbling—I heard *I love you* a few times too.

"Thanks, see you at the show." Jason peeled the girls from my body in what seemed to be very little effort. "One foot in front of the other," he whispered in my ear, his hands on my hips encouraging me to perform the simply function, which apparently was too hard for me to do on my own.

"Is that what it's like for you?" His body slipped into step beside mine, his hands directing me forward to where everyone was filing into cars.

"Yeah, most of the time they just want to say hello. Are you okay?" He stopped, his face on me despite others waiting for him.

"I'm fine, you should go."

The impatient security guard held the door open for the one Power Station member not currently sitting in one of their assigned idling SUV's, his jaw tightening more by each second. Me, not necessarily being at the top of his list of concerns given a crowd was starting to gather.

"I'm riding with, Angie." Jase waved off Mr. tight-jaw and pulled me into one of the not so flashy vans that had been designated for us. The topic of conversation not open for discussion as he pulled closed the door.

"I'm fine." I pulled across my seat belt, my body settling into the cloth seat. My racing pulse disagreed with my assessment of me being *fine*.

"Yeah, I know you are." Jase fastened his seatbelt, my other band members giving me the why-is-Jason-in-our-car look. "Your windows aren't tinted." He knocked on the glass. "I'll be able to see more of the city going in."

That excuse was bullshit if ever I heard one, but I didn't argue because having him in the car with me actually made me feel better. And right now I wasn't going to stop something that made me feel good.

The car ride was filled with the usual chatter—talking and laughing, and my pulse finally returning to normal. Jase reached over, his hand brushing over mine. His eyes stayed on me despite him saying he wanted to see the view, the landscape whizzing past.

The hotel was the same as they all were, big and impersonal. Jase's hands didn't move from my body as we traveled through the lobby and then up to his room. The discussion on where were going, not had, at least not verbally.

It was huge.

The room, the bed and the window. All of it, big and fancy, which by now shouldn't be surprising, but it was.

Jason and the view distracted me from my mild freak out, and with his hands shoved into his pockets, he joined me at the glass.

What had been happening with us, with him—there was no denying things had changed. He was being kind, sensitive, caring ... he was acting like—yeah, that word neither of us would say.

Boyfriend.

Even my subconscious whispered it.

So instead of bringing it up, I focused on the landscape in front of me. My eyes unable to be peeled away from the view.

"Wow, the city looks great from here." I leaned my body against the floor-to-ceiling window, the sunlight hitting the tops of each of the buildings, making the skyline sparkle.

"I don't really look anymore." He moved beside me, mimicking me by pressing his nose to the glass. "You're right, the view is impressive. Not sure why I don't take the time anymore to appreciate it when we travel. I guess it's all become second hand now, more of the same."

"You're so fucking jaded." I laughed stepping away from the window. "If I start talking like that, I'm going to kick my own ass."

"Is that what you want to do? Kick my ass?" He grinned; the prospect of me doing just that seeming to excite him.

"Ah, if only there was time." I wrapped my arms around his neck, knowing that while today my schedule was wide open, the keyboard player who I was canoodling with had places to be. In bed, with me, not at the top of the list.

"Yeah, well I have a surprise for you."

"Is it a vibrator to keep me busy while you're gone? If not, that's cool. I bet the shower head in this place is five-star."

Staying with Jason hadn't been discussed. But seeing as my bags usually found their way into his room, and I spent most nights in his bed it was a fairly safe bet this is going to be my room too. Besides, there was that view, and having him screw me up against the window was quickly added to my list of requests.

"It's not a vibrator." He pulled me from the window and I hit the wall of flesh that was his body. Well hello, pectoral muscles. It's nice to see you again.

"I'll take care of anything that needs to be taken care of when I get back." His hand floated down to my ass which he then squeezed. Fair, seeing as my hands were doing the same to him. "But until then, you've got company. I figured it might be a good distraction. At least until I get back to give you a better one."

The company, I found out about five minutes later, was in the form of Ash and Megs. Apparently he'd texted them on the car ride over assuming I'd need the comfort. Not that he said as much, selling it like it was them who wanted to spend time with me. But I guessed he was worried about leaving me alone after the airport. His busy day meant it couldn't be him.

And as the bubbly duo bounced into the room, the sexy considerate guy who promised to wow me with plentiful orgasms left.

As much as I hate to admit it, I was really going to miss those two. They were so friendly and while our time had been limited over the past two weeks, their company on the tour had been one of the highlights. Other than playing on proper stages, and the mind-blowing sex.

Lexi and Hannah were great. Both had earned their commendations of greatness and my hero worship. Juggling jobs, husbands and kids all the while looking flawless. Unlike me, who looked like hot mess on a nine a.m. flight with no excuse except an active libido and willing partner. But they just didn't have the same dynamic the other two did.

Ash and Megs were different. Smashing through uninvited and welcoming me into their group, my usual feelings of inadequacy not getting a second thought. And they probably should have because these girls were perfect, and imperfect in the most amazing way. They might have been the first *real* girlfriends I'd had. Ones I didn't worry about stabbing me in the back, or judging me. And in a complete flip in my usual character, I trusted them. Blindly, even though I had no reason to.

It was while Megs was giving me a manicure—trust me, arguing was futile with that girl, red flag and bulls being what they were and all—that the I casually steered the conversation in the direction I wanted.

"So ... did you ever meet any of Jason's *girlfriends*?" My contribution to our *girlie chat* was thrown into the ring.

Casually.

Like a grenade.

I was going to need more practice.

"No, not really. He doesn't really date," Ash volunteered, my lack of finesse either overlooked or politely ignored. I *really* liked these girls.

"Other than you, we mean," Megs added, twisting the lid off the fire engine red nail polish that apparently I *needed* to be wearing.

"It's okay." I nodded, my fingers spread out, ready for the assault. "I know we're not *really* dating."

Not in the real sense of the word. At least not on his side of the equation, my side had been pretty blurry lately. Hence the sudden curiosity into Jason's past, and the jealousy that seemed to accompany it.

"Of course you are." Megs threw me a look of utter disbelief. "He's crazy about you." Her voice rose with enthusiasm.

"No, we're both crazy but not about each other, which is great because it works out." My mouth did that thing where it spat out words without properly processing them. It was right about one thing, both of us were certifiably crazy. Me, tipping the scales a little higher in my effort to be an overachiever.

"Well you're wrong." Megs held down my hands, red brush in between her fingers ready to do her worst. "Whatever you *want* to call it. It's most definitely dating."

"I'll let it slide 'cause you're knocked up." And because very few people lost an argument when it came to Megs. "But I don't want you to be disappointed by the lack of save the date cards we'll be mailing. Jase made it pretty clear he doesn't do commitment."

For the first time I heard the disappointment in my own voice. Well look at that. I think I may have developed feelings.

Well. Fuck.

"Plleeeeeaaassseeee," Megs almost screamed. "That man is head over heels for you. I don't know why he's saying that bullshit, but I can tell you that he's never looked at a girl the way he's looked at you. And there have been plenty around."

"Did you guys ever meet Em?"

There I went, another grenade. Because the first one hadn't exploded in my face, I needed to tempt fate and throw another. My need to know obviously worth the risk of a possible messy fall out.

Of course neither of them had. The bitch-face troll—my new name for her—was well before their time with the guys.

"I think she was a big bitch anyway." Megs continued with my nails, the shiny red beacons shimmering like a stop sign, or the light out front of a whorehouse. "Broke his heart. Why anyone would want to do that to Jase? I just don't understand. He's a sweetheart."

"He totally is," Ash agreed. "Such a nice guy."

"And he's really good looking." Megs nodded, the shopping list of how wonderful Jason Irwin was growing.

"Super good looking." Ash nodded, her smile not even close to being discreet.

"And have you seen him with his shirt off?" Megs took to fanning herself dramatically. "Wow. Muscles for days."

"You can stop now."

The virtues coming thick and fast weren't actually needed. I was already falling in love with him. Yeah. There was that *word*. Not one I would be repeating, even to myself.

"Why, we're just talking about Jase." Ash shrugged naïvely.

"Yes, telling me how awesome he is."

"Megs, I don't think either of us used the word *awesome,* did we?" Ash looked to Megs, blowing across her freshly painted nails.

"No, Ash." Megs smiled with satisfaction. "I don't recall saying awesome at all."

"You are both so transparent. We are not a couple." I waved my hands in the air to prove my point.

"But you like him right, you called him awesome." Ash didn't give me a chance to retract.

"Yes, I like him. He is awesome, but—" I tried in vain to stop all talk of Jason and I all kissing-up-a-tree.

"No, you can't put a *but* on there. You like him. He's awesome. That's all." Megs gave me no chance to take back my Freudian slip.

"Just don't get your hopes up. I'm not expecting anything." And by anything I meant reciprocation. Because what I was definitely expecting was disappointment; that was a bona fide certainty.

So in one afternoon I had discovered that I was capable of two things I didn't think were possible. Number one, develop two beautiful friendships with these amazing women. And number two, fall in love with the same guy twice.

Both had been surprising, with only the second scaring the ever living hell out of me.

That night I sang "Supermassive Black Hole" by *Muse*. No explanation was needed.

"GOOD TO SEE YOU DIVERSIFYING YOUR INSULTS, ANGIE. I ESPECIALLY liked tonight's efforts." I held her hands above her head, with my lips at her throat, driving her crazy. And crazy was what she was making me so it was only fair to share.

"That's me, so versatile." She laughed as she tried to kiss me back. I didn't let her, she could do what she wanted on stage but in bed, she was mine.

Tonight's effort had been "So What" by *P!nk* with her enthusiasm higher than usual while singing the word *tool* in the lyrics. She sang that line directly at me with a smirk on her face.

"Call me whatever you want on stage, sweetheart, but you have no problem remembering my name when I make you come." My mouth moved lower, this time her nipples getting my attention. Her body bowed off the bed in appreciation. And didn't that make me just want to do it more.

"Fame has made you so conceited, Jason. I think my next song should be You're so Vain." She closed her eyes as I continued the assault on her body with my mouth. The words she was trying to say barely coming out of her mouth convincingly.

Her list of songs had been extensive. As were her list of insults. And to the outside spectator were nothing more than a random collection of eclectic tunes. Different bands, different genres—all of them given her personal brand of flair as she showcased them on stage.

"Vanity isn't my problem." My mouth kissed the base of her stomach, my hands parting her thighs.

"What's your problem?" She all but begged as my mouth moved further south. Her hand that pulled at my hair to direct where she wanted me, not needed.

"My addiction to making you come apart." My tongue lapped at her thigh, getting close with every pass. "Watching you come, knowing it's because of me."

"That's ...   that's ... " she stuttered, unable to finish her sentence as my lips gently closed around her clit, sucking it.

"That's exactly what you are going to get, Angie. When you're with me. I'm going to make you come each and every time." I slid in a finger to go along with the tongue attention I was giving her.

"Jason," she moaned as her fingers gripped at my hair. Her need to hold me in place unnecessary because there wasn't anything that would have stopped me.

"Yes." My mouth vibrated against her hot, wet pussy. My lips and tongue taking turns in making her feel good. Jury was still out as to which one was giving her the most pleasure.

"Don't stop." Her eyes flew open as she nailed me with a look, hovering somewhere between euphoria and desperation.

"Wasn't planning on it." I added an extra finger, pumping in and out of her as my mouth went back to being busy.

"Yes, Yes." Her body writhed underneath me as I felt her explode on my mouth, my fingers getting a treat as her pussy pulsed around them.

Unfortunately my dick wasn't so pleased, thinking my hand didn't deserve the praise Angie was giving it and demanding a chance to even the score.

"I'm going to need you to do that again." I shifted from my position between her thighs and moved higher up the bed.

The rip of the condom packet prompted her to open her eyes, her change in view coming just in time to see me smooth the latex down my shaft.

"Every time I see it, it gets no less impressive." She licked her lips, her eyes fixated on what I had in my hand.

"My cock impresses you? Or what I do with it?" I asked, regaining my lost position, her legs widening to accommodate me.

"Both." She sighed as I rubbed the head of dick at her opening, the bastard desperate to get inside.

"I told you." I pushed inside of her quickly, the sharp breath she drew hinting she hadn't been expecting it. "I'm not here to impress you, sweetheart. I'm here to make you come."

"Jase." She moved her lips to mine, her mouth begging for everything I had to give her. "I need you."

"And I need you." The words were automatic, my brain obviously suffering a loss of oxygen on account my dick was taking it all. Bad idea, and yet in that moment, I wasn't about to take it back.

I did *need* her. In every sense of the word, and the thought of losing her wreaked havoc on my nervous system. The fear of not being with her every day was only superseded by the fear of hurting her.

"Please," she begged, thankfully not hearing what I'd said. Or showing me how smart she was by ignoring it. "Please, don't stop." Her fingers dug so deep into my shoulders I could feel the skin bruise underneath. Did I care I'd be rocking bruises for the next few days? Not a fucking chance.

The kick of pain only served to juice me up higher as I slid in and out of her. The slow and controlled pace I'd been keeping not anywhere close to what I was desperate to give her.

"Fuck, Angie." I grabbed her legs as she pushed up against me, her hips thrusting against mine in a rebellious attempt to control the tempo. She should have known better. She could have her turn later, but right now, it was me who was doing the *fucking.*

"I want—"

I slapped her ass, not giving her a chance to finish as every inch I had filled her; her pussy fisting me as she came on my hard-on. Her thighs pressed against me as her body shook.

"That's it." I kept moving, teasing every last shudder of pleasure from her. Mine. Every single tremble, every whimper, every ounce of pleasure had been all mine.

"That's it," I repeated, trying to slow down as a battle of wills between my mind and my balls went all out warfare in my body. "I know what you need, Angie. And I'll always give it you." Each drag of my hips made it harder and harder to maintain control.

Her lips crushed mine as she pulled me down onto her. My body smothering her while my hips kept pumping.

Need.

There was that word again. My mind giving up its fight as my body took over.

There was no holding back.

I couldn't stop even if I had wanted to, and I sure as hell didn't want to. My cock pounded in and out of her at an alarming pace. Over and over again, my body invaded hers. Harder and faster each time, as I struggled to get deep enough into her. Her tight pussy gripped me as I filled her with each thrust. Her breath labored as it pushed past my ear, my own bordering on hyperventilation.

"Stop," she almost screamed. The single word enough to make me put on my brakes and for my mind to kick back in.

I was hurting her, crushing her under my weight as I hammered into her. Any common sense I'd had, left as the desperation kicked in, controlling my body in a way that was bordering on possession.

We'd been rough before, but not like this. With my movements no longer being dictated by want, but by that sick and sadistic *need* I had been trying to suppress, taking me over.

It had been dominating my thoughts the whole time since I'd said it, but I'd pushed it down, thinking it was something I could control. But I was delusional if I thought I had a chance, and that stupid word had no business rattling around in my head.

I was a fucking animal. The lowest form of life, and I sure as hell didn't deserve her, let alone the fucking honor of being inside of her.

"No." She held me, preventing me from pulling out, her arms wrapping around me like a chain weighing me down. "No," she said again, more forceful this time and showing no signs of letting go.

"Angie, we need to stop. I was hurting you." Hearing the words made me want to throw up. That I had gone there, treated her like that. Never again.

"You weren't hurting me, you just scared me a little." Her arms remained locked around my body, her eyes trained on me despite mine refusing to meet hers.

"That doesn't make it fucking better." I buried my head into the curve of her neck, the scent of her skin and her shampoo making my insides twist.

"Just look at me, please." One of her arms released its death grip from around my torso, her hand tugging at my hair hard enough to lift my head. I welcomed the pain. I deserved it.

"I can't do that to you again." As hard as it was to own what I'd done, I manned up. My eyes locked on hers. "I won't do that to you again." I'd sooner die.

"And I trust you." Her hand moved from my hair and touched my face, giving me affection I knew I didn't deserve. Her other arm had refused to relinquish its hold, her tiny frame holding on with everything it had. "But I also need you and you promised me you would always give that to me."

The same words I had spoken to her minutes ago smacked me in the face. The stupid, arrogant promise I'd made before my brain checked out and my body had gone rogue.

"Angie, it's not the time to be cute." My head shook, not in the mood for the word games we used to play. Not in the mood for *any* games any more.

"I'm not being cute, Jason." There was no laugh, no smile, no sarcasm—her voice demanding my attention. "Look at me. *Really* look at me."

I couldn't have looked away if I'd tried. Not after that. She owned every single cell in my fucking body, and there wasn't anything I wouldn't have done if she'd asked. Jump of a cliff? Thanks, it's been nice knowing you.

"God you're fucking beautiful." My eyes committed to memory every single curve of her face. I could've gone blind tomorrow and I'd have every line and every dip burned into my mind. She was more than beautiful; she was perfection. And I was so freaking undeserving, it fucking hurt. "What the hell are you doing here with me?"

"It's where I want to be." Her answer simple and uncomplicated, with zero doubt. "Be with me. Slow. With me." She paused between each word, adding more weight to what she was asking me to do.

"I can't believe you still want to after that." My lips fell to her forehead, her skin on my mouth more precious than the air in my fucking lungs.

"What, and give up that impressive cock?" She smiled, every inch of her face lighting up with amused delight. "Not a freaking chance."

While my cock was on board with giving her whatever she wanted—we'd already established she owned me—the rest of me wasn't sold this was a smart decision. Check that. Probably motherfucking dumb if I was honest.

"Are you sure?" This was no longer about the sex, and everything to do with her. "You can say no at any time."

"I know, but I'm not saying no." She lifted her head and pressed her lips on mine, not wanting to take the out I was giving her. "Just go slow."

"Slow," I repeated, my mouth kissing her neck while my hands got reacquainted with her body.

Her hand moved down my back as she pulled me closer to her body. "Slow."

20

Angie

THAT NIGHT CHANGED EVERYTHING.

Something had happened in that room. A shift where he'd morphed into something else, *someone* else and I'd lost him. The level of anger and aggression wasn't something I'd seen before. He'd always had it all together. Cool, calm, collected. I'd never seen him lose control. Especially during sex. He had such a tight handle on it, that now, I wasn't sure if he had been holding back this whole time.

Something inside of him had become unhinged, and he was no longer Jason. His eyes dark, void, soulless. Like his spirit just got up and left. Gone. Done.

It scared me.

Not because I thought he would hurt me, but because I no longer knew the man I was in bed with. He was a stranger. He was uninvited and cold, his body mechanical, aggressive and being used for punishment. And I wasn't sure which one of us the punishment was intended for. Honestly, I didn't think it had been directed at me—and that scared me even more.

It would have been easy to walk out. To leave, but I just couldn't go.

And he came back.

Slowly, at first. It had been almost impossible to get him to touch me again but he did. But it wasn't like it had been. I wondered if that was part of the reason he'd kept his distance, why his relationship ban was in play. He'd been holding back. It was something just below the surface, and I wasn't sure if I should scratch just a little bit further. Or if either of us was ready to face it.

It didn't happen again.

Every night Jason was not only gentle but incredibly considerate. That control was back, but it was different. He was slower, more deliberate and less aggressive. The edges had softened as we'd moved somewhere else.

We didn't talk about the R word, because it wasn't important. The label on what we were, unnecessary. This was more than what I had with anyone else, but I knew he was still holding back. Rocking the boat wouldn't work.

"Hey, Pops." My hand gripped the phone tighter, missing him like crazy. "I'm in Atlanta."

"Hey, sweetheart. You having a good time?" His voice sounded weary and I knew it wasn't fatigue. The date that so blatantly displayed itself on the calendar marked the anniversary of my mom's death and it was the first time ever that I hadn't been home for it.

Talking with him, thinking about my mom, being away from home, fatigue and all the other emotions of the past few weeks washed over me in a huge rush. And while I tried to keep it together, I knew if I didn't get off the phone soon, it was going to be more than just a few stray tears I was going to have to deal with. I didn't often cry but sometimes your eyes didn't give you the choice. Stupid leaky eyes.

I ended the call, shoving my phone into the pocket of my jeans. My head lifted high and my shoulders pushed back as I prepared to deal with the world. Today that wasn't going to be easy.

Jase and his band were going to be doing press all day. My morning and afternoon free and clear to do whatever I wanted, and while Rusty and the guys weren't too far away, I didn't want anyone to be dragged down with my mood.

The elevator was my new destination. Where I was going to be headed hadn't been decided yet but it at least it got me out of my room—the room I never slept in anymore. Besides, its not like the day could get any worse.

"Hey, are you crying?"

The metal elevator doors opened to reveal something that *could* make it worse.

"Why are you crying?"

Dan fucking Evans.

"I'm fine. It's not a big deal." My hands quickly wiped my eyes as I cursed the freaking universe. Really? You sent me Dan? Sometimes there really weren't enough variations of the word fuck.

"Bullshit. Girls don't cry for no reason. Especially you." He stepped out of the elevator and moved closer toward me.

"Don't be an ass, Dan. I'm allowed to be sad sometimes." My traitorous eyes letting go another fucking tear as if on cue. Goddamn it. Now I didn't know who I was more pissed off with, him or me.

"No. No you're not. There's no crying on tour." His head shook, affirming his stance.

Really, the man was begging to die.

"Dan, please. Just leave me."

"No. Not until you tell me what's wrong." He disregarded my telepathic urging that he shut-the-fuck-up and continued. "I can't have you crying on tour, it messes up my mojo. Like for real, epic bad shit could happen so you need to stop."

He was officially public enemy number one.

"Look at the fucking date, asshole."

Dan stopped as his eyes widened in recognition.

"Oh. Fuck. I'm sorry."

The penny finally dropped.

He, like Troy, had been with me the day my mother had died. Cynthia Morelli had been battling cancer for years, and when all the chemo and surgery hadn't worked she did what she always did. Held her head high and left on her own terms. I'd held her hand until the last moment before they took her away. The Harris family and their "adopted" son, Dan, had stayed with me while Pops went and did whatever adults needed to do when they lost the love of the life.

"Okay, you need to come with me." Dan reached into his pocket and pulled out his cell, his fingers furiously texting.

"What?" My feet unconsciously took a step back. "No, I don't want to go anywhere with you."

"Yeah, well put *want* in one hand and *shit* in the other and see which one fills up faster. You're still coming."

With his texting session apparently over and his phone shoved back into his pocket, his hand was free to grab me and pull me into the elevator, which at the touch of the button opened on command. Of course it did. That elevator was an instrument of the devil that clearly had a personal vendetta against me.

"You know kidnapping is a crime, right?" I tried to pull my arm out of his grasp with no success. Wow, he was stronger than he looked. "Even you can't smooth talk yourself out of unlawful detainment."

"Blah, Blah. Big fancy words blah." Dan mocked me, his free hand pressing the button for the top floor while the other stayed clamped around my arm.

"I hate you, Dan." I pouted and short of head butting or kicking him in the nuts I was going wherever he had designated.

"Nah, you love me." He smiled. Arrogant asshole. "All that shit we did to each other in the past was classic brother and sister stuff. You didn't have one, so I had to pick up the slack."

"Um, I'm pretty sure my *brother* wouldn't have tried to sleep with me when I was sixteen, Dan."

"Yeah, that was a moment of weakness. You got hot. Couldn't be helped." He shrugged like it had been no big deal.

The metal box from hell finally pinged, opening its doors and freeing us from its demonic clutches. Dan didn't give me a chance to hesitate, dragging me out with him into the foyer that lead to the penthouse apartments.

"Got the message, what's the emergency?" Jason appeared from another door, his phone still in his hand. "Hey." Jason stepped closer, his eyes on me and the arm that was being held ransom by Douchebag Evans. "Let her go."

"Relax, asswipe. I didn't hurt her, but your girl needs attention." Dan all but pushed me at Jason. "Oh, and I'm telling the guys we're cancelling all our shit today. We're all taking a day off."

He walked off, cell at his ear, planning our scheduled day off without any further argument.

"We can't just take a day off, we're in the middle of a tour." My eyes turned to Jason.

"We can do whatever we want, Angie." His thumbs gently wiping away any remaining tears. "We're not cancelling shows, and that is all anyone is going to care about. Now, talk to me."

My mouth opened ready to spill. And I do mean spill, as everything washed through me. It wasn't one thing, it was all of them heaped together and I needed someone. But like always, I just couldn't ask. My mouth closed just as quickly as it had opened with no words coming out. It was stuck. And so was I.

Jase didn't wait for the answer as he pulled me out of the foyer and into his room. His arms moved around my body, pulling me close to his chest and whispering, "Hey, I'm sorry I didn't notice the date. I'm an asshole, remember?"

I didn't want to smile but my mouth had its own ideas, spreading into a grin at the sound of Jason calling himself an asshole, and that he'd remember something about me that happened so long ago.

"Yeah you are." My head nodded against his shirt, wondering if it was bad karma that something sad had facilitated this moment.

I was completely in love with him.

Again.

With his asshole status decided, we didn't talk anymore, which was okay because his mouth found something better to do. Which was great because my mouth was right there with his, not talking and doing other things ... with each other.

It would have been easy for it to dissolve into sex. It seemed to be a pattern where we used it to deal with the other emotions—both of us guilty of it. But for some strange reason it didn't go that way with the action staying pretty tame and our lips being the only things that got busy. It was kind of nice.

But just because there was no sex on the horizon, it didn't mean we didn't make it to the bed. Jason pulled me down with him onto the pillowy mattress as he continued to kiss me. My mind completely scrambled like the eggs I hadn't been able to eat for breakfast.

And then it hit me. The words Dan had used when he not so subtly threw me at Jase. *His Girl,* and Jason hadn't set him straight and I had no idea what that meant. I needed to know. Because if he didn't feel the same way then this had already gone too far—I had already gone to far.

"Jase?" My head pulled away from his mouth, my brain and my mouth having an internal war.

"Yes," he said tipping my chin up toward his face, his lips not stopping despite mine now doing less kissing and more talking.

"Douchebags." The knock at the door stopped any further conversation. "Whatever you're doing in there, wrap it up in thirty. I hired helicopters and we're going to Disneyworld. Oh and I'm a motherfucking genius 'cause the idea about going to the happiest place on earth was totally mine. Yeah, I'm that badass. Go back to fucking." His voice trailing as he walked away.

"You want to kill him, or should I?" Jase kissed my neck.

"It should be a collaboration." I tried to smile, the interruption totally killing my nerve.

It could wait until tomorrow. Maybe the day after. It didn't have to be today. The words just needed to be said, and I would say them. I totally would. Just not now. Not here, and not now.

I nuzzled back against Jason's chest, the heart that I so desperately wanted to be mine thumped strong and steady against my cheek as his hands played with my hair. Thump, Thump. Thump, Thump. And just being able to breathe proved difficult.

"You good?" Jason asked, his lips giving me another kiss on my forehead as he pulled away to look at me.

"Yeah," I lied, the word almost getting stuck in my throat. "I'm going to Disneyworld with freaking Power Station. What could be wrong?"

THE SEPARATE HOTEL ROOMS WERE REDUNDANT.

We ended up together every night anyway, unable to keep our hands off each other and needing the release. So in my bed was where she had to be. And if she ended tucked up by my side when she fell asleep, well that was a fucking bonus.

Shit had changed between us. There was no denying that. The fact she was still here was something I marveled at every single day.

I'd fucked up.

Lost control, with my handle on things no longer steady.

The rage wasn't a new thing; me and my inner demon had been kicking it together for a while. It was at least part of the reason why I kept the sex casual, and the girlfriends, non-existent. It was better for everyone concerned. Case in point, me losing my motherfucking mind.

Those lines I had worked so hard to keep neat and tidy were no longer straight. I knew it, and yet, I couldn't make myself stop. I didn't want to stop. Craving every little bit of whatever it was we were doing, to continue.

"Why are you awake?" The dark-brown eyes that should have been closed stared back at me. Her tired smile giving me the best good morning a man could ever ask for.

"I was watching you," she confessed, hijacking my daily habit.

"Creepy. I like it." I pulled her closer toward me, wanting to feel more of her skin on mine. "Go back to sleep, it's early."

"Okay." Her voice pushed out a breath but her eyes didn't close.

"Do you need me to help you get back to sleep?" My hand slid up her side, finding its mark as it palmed one of her breasts. My cock stirred at the prospect of getting some morning attention.

"Okay," she said, but her body didn't give the usual reaction despite what my hands were doing.

"Angie, what's wrong?"

Last night I had comforted her in the only way I knew how. Having her underneath me, screaming my name never got old but lately going slow was becoming a new favorite. I still made her scream—that was not negotiable.

"You thinking about your mom?"

"No," she answered with zero hesitation.

"Then what's on your mind?" I scooted up on to my elbow to get a better look at her. God she was beautiful, the view never got old.

"The tour ending, things going back to normal."

"The tour? Sure it will eventually end, but the band has done well. The crowds love you. I would be surprised if there isn't a recording contract waiting for you in New York when you get back."

"I wasn't talking about the band," she said slowly.

"You were talking about us."

"Is there an *us*? I mean we're here, in this bubble and it feels like a relationship but it's not really, is it?"

There was that word. The one I had been fighting so hard to avoid. Anytime I had attached a fucking label to it, the fucking thing went down the tubes. This wasn't a relationship; it was something else.

"What do you want me to tell you?"

There was no way I could explain to her what was going on in my head when it didn't even make sense to me.

She sighed slowly, like she'd been holding a breath for too long and then closed her eyes, the conversation shutting down with them.

I swallowed, refusing to move the hand that was glued to her side, keeping her close even if I wasn't sure it's what she wanted. "What do you *want* to happen?"

"I want us to be together." She said it slow, letting each word fully ring out before she said the next.

"Aren't we together now?" My hand around her tightening, bringing her even closer so her face was inches from mine.

"I'm serious, Jase." She pushed away from me, her hands straining against my chest. "This all ends tomorrow. We both go home. What happens?"

"I don't know." She was asking me questions I had no answers for. "Let's not worry about it for now."

"Then *when* do we worry about it?" She shuffled up against the headboard, pulling up the sheets to cover her body.

"Jesus, did you want to fight? Is that what you want?" I sat up, flicking on the lamp on the nightstand.

"No, I don't want to fight but I also need to know that when we go back home there is going to be a place for me." Her voice louder than it'd been before.

"There's a place for you, we'll work something out."

"What's there to work out?" She laughed, and not in a funny cute way. Condescending was more the vibe she was rocking. "Are you going to work me into a rotation? Do I get you on weekends or when I can come visit you in the city? Or am I like the alternate for when you feel like slumming?"

"That was a cheap shot, even for you."

"No, it's reality. It's my reality and I need to know what I mean to you."

"Angie, this is the closest I've come to anything real in a long time. Just please don't push it."

That handle on things I was struggling to keep, wasn't doing so hot under the current conditions. My need for control also extended to this conversation. The one where the good stuff we had going on between us, distanced itself like Angie had, moving herself as far away from me on the mattress as possible.

"Would it be so terrible to be in a relationship? It's not so different to what we are doing now. It doesn't have to be a big deal." She pushed her hair back from her face in frustration.

"Why are you worrying about hypotheticals when we don't have to? Like I said, it's months away. We'll work it out." My voice had more edge to it than I would have liked.

She didn't back down, her tone matching mine. "You're not sleeping with anyone else, neither am I. We don't use words like girlfriend or boyfriend, but what are we?"

"We're here, in the moment. So let's enjoy that." My hand slammed down on the mattress in frustration.

She flinched as her eyes nailed me from the other side of the bed as I pushed back the covers and grabbed my boxers from the floor. The conversation had entered into fucking territory I no longer wanted to be in.

Things had been fine. Why couldn't we just leave things the way they were? I wasn't sure who I was madder at—her for pushing, or me for being unable to give her what she obviously wanted from me. Like she'd said from the beginning, I was an asshole. And we'd rehashed that so many fucking times, it had its own soundtrack. No shit, and I had to listen to it every fucking night.

Her voice had stayed level despite me ejecting from the bed. "Do you remember what you said to me the first time you left?" She reached out and touched my arm trying to pull me back onto the mattress.

"Of course, I said we'd made a mistake." I answered without turning around to look at her. My body giving the wall some face time even with her hand on me. My feelings jacked up.

My not turning around didn't help the situation, with the thud of her feet hitting the floor soon after. The rustling that followed I assumed was her getting dressed. But it didn't change anything. My heart beating so fast I wasn't sure it wasn't going to explode.

Stopping her and talking about it probably should have happened, but I didn't think anything was going to be solved tonight. And the last thing I wanted to do was say shit I didn't mean, because I felt backed into a corner.

She stepped in front of me, mostly dressed; the hurt on her face evident. Her eyes on me demanded that I look at her and I wasn't surprised she was ready to leave. The bed beside us wasn't going to be getting any more attention tonight.

"But you didn't ask me, you just told me you made a mistake and you left. I didn't get a say. No right of reply, nothing. I had barely got my clothes back on."

"How many times can I say sorry?" My fist punched against the headboard in frustration, my hand hitting the wood hard. It hurt but I didn't care. Hating myself was an understatement, I hated *everything* about this situation. "I'm sorry. It was a mistake."

"I was in love with you." The first tear fell.

It all stopped. Noise. Movement. I couldn't feel or hear anything. The words she had said hanging there, between us.

"What?" I asked like a dumbass, not because I hadn't heard her but because it didn't seem real.

"I was in love with you," she repeated, her eyes wide. "I was young, but it didn't make it less real. I hung on your every word. Every single time you showed me the slightest bit of interest it would make my world turn. And then you slept with me and left. I felt like a whore, Jason. Used. I was *in love* with the guy who treated me like that. I would have given up everything for you. Just to be with you, and you didn't even care."

There was lots I knew about that girl she'd been back then. She was beautiful, she was smart and she was full of attitude. Same as she was now, and for some unknown reason would give me all kinds of time. Loving me was not one of the things I knew.

"Angie, I didn't know. I thought it was a crush, I wouldn't have done that if I had known."

Never. I would have been stronger, put my dick in a fucking blender before I would have used her like that.

"You mean you wouldn't have slept with me or you wouldn't have used me?" The pain in her eyes floored me as she waited for my answer. "Actually." She raised her hand as she looked away. "Don't answer that."

"I'm no good at this. I've tried to tell you from the start, but you didn't want to listen."

Every single muscle in my body screamed to touch her and yet my fists stayed white-knuckled at my side, neither my hands nor my feet able to move.

"You're wrong." Her voice shook, unsteady. "I listened, but not to *you*. I listened to my fucking heart instead." Another tear fell. "And I'm in love with you again."

I couldn't breathe. It felt like a hundred pound weight was sitting on my chest as I tried to suck in air.

"Angie."

"I know, I know." She wiped her eyes as she gave me a weak smile. "Dumb, right? Who makes the same mistake twice?"

The pain in her eyes was real. Like someone had just punched her in the face. And it was there because of yours truly. Me. Well done, asshole, take a motherfucking bow. Those fucking tears she was crying had my name all over them. I had done that.

"Then this has to stop." My mouth said the words as I wanted to rip out my own fucking heart. "I don't want to hurt you again."

"Too late for that, dumbass. You already have."

"Which is why it has to stop." I fished around for my T-shirt, pulling it over my head in an effort to move away from her.

"So you're just going to dump me? You're not even going to try?" Her face contorted, horrified.

I was the last thing she needed. She needed someone who was going to be there in every capacity, not some asshole with commitment issues. I couldn't change who I was. I couldn't be what she needed me to be.

"I can't *do* what you are asking me to *do*," I fired back, wondering why the hell she wasn't listening to me.

"Are you fucking serious?" She coughed in disbelief. Like actual bewilderment flashed across her face. "You can say whatever you want to fucking say but we have *been* in a relationship. I wasn't your whore. We shared other things besides bodily fluids. Nothing bad happened." Her rage kicked up a notch as she continued. "I understand some *bitch* from your past fucked you up, but for fuck's sake, get over it!"

The mention of Em wasn't a slap in the face, it was an

explosion. That control I thought I'd lost a few minutes ago not even close to what was happening now as I struggled not to put my fist through the fucking drywall. *Get over it?* Like I hadn't been trying for the last ten years?

"Get out." I didn't recognize the voice that flew out of my mouth. The words distorted I'd screamed them so loud.

Angie flinched, her voice not as confident as when we started. "No. I deserve an explanation. I'm not Em—"

"Don't fucking bring her into this. Don't you fucking dare do it." I cut her off, my nerves juiced up at the mention of that motherfucking whore's name.

"You don't get to walk out on me twice," she screamed, her fists flying at my chest. "You don't get to break my fucking heart twice. That's not fair."

"Life isn't fucking fair, Angie." I took every hit in the chest she gave me as I watched the tears bleeding out of her eyes. "And I'm all out of explanations. I warned you. I told you what I was like." I stepped forward, the edge in my tone making her slowly back away. "You didn't fucking listen because you know everything." Her back hit the wall, her effort to get away from me running out of room. There was a moment of panic that flashed through her eyes when she realized she had nowhere else to go as I got real close to her and sneered. "Why don't you take your own advice and *get over it.*"

Evil. Pure evil was pouring out of me and I couldn't stop it. This is why I couldn't be with her; right fucking there was the evidence. She wanted to see it; she wanted to know how much I could hurt her. Well, there you fucking go. Rinkside seats, right on the motherfucking ice.

"Why are you so cruel?" She wrapped her hands around her chest, looking like a wounded animal. "God, I hate you so much right now." Her voice was barely a hum.

"Good." I got closer to her, no doubt scaring the hell out of her as I measured each word. "Remember that, and walk the hell away. We're done. Now leave."

22

Angie

THE HARSH REALITY WAS WORSE THAN A SCREAMING MATCH. HIS words had felt like barbed-wire, stinging just as much when he hurled them at me as when he ripped them out.

The unrelenting pain consumed me. Swallowing me whole. My heart, my mind and soul completely shredded. My body empty, like something inside me had just gotten up and left.

And the depth of how cruel he was chilled me to my very core. He had cut me so deep I wasn't sure I'd ever stop bleeding. I was so fucking raw I didn't even want to go on stage. Rusty and the band the reasons for me getting in front of that mic.

I still cried myself to sleep though.

Every. Single. Night.

It was over.

Really, finally and truly over.

The one thing I hadn't been able to do was the finale. What was usually the highlight of my evening made me want to dry heave. I wasn't strong enough, not even to give him the *fuck you* he deserved.

Did he deserve it though? Maybe he was right, and I just liked playing the role of the doormat. He had warned me. He had spelled it out in the beginning that he did not want my love nor would he be giving me any in return.

I was the one who had changed the rules.

So instead of bouncing around on stage, tricking up some pop song and laughing at the irony of the lyrics, I walked off. Rusty and Max took over and sang the old *Beastie Boy's* song "Hey, Fuck You." And wasn't that appropriate. Yep. Fuck you. It wasn't just directed at Jason. There were plenty of *fucks* that were directed squarely at me. Not in the song, but in my own head. Which just made me cry harder.

Avoiding Jason was surprisingly easier than I thought. It seemed that all our past interaction had been intentional, with there being no need for the bands to even cross over. We did sound check at different times, our rooms were on different floors, traveled in separate vehicles and when we flew we were in coach. It was better that way; it's where we belonged.

Show after show I sang. My body and my voice gave the audience a hundred and ten percent, even though my heart wasn't in it. And the performances were amazing despite my soul being crushed. The accolades I had dreamed of finally getting thrown at my feet, and yet I couldn't enjoy the ride.

At least my career was on the incline—rave reviews coming in after each performance—even though my love life was in the toilet.

The set list changed as well. The colorful finales—done. We kept it simple and wrapped with one of our more upbeat originals, took a group bow and walked off stage. Then left the stadium before Power Station even hit their first note. Better to be safe than sorry.

"Where are we?" I laughed as I finished my sixth beer for the night. I knew the laugh was alcohol-induced and yet, even though it was manufactured I didn't care. It still felt good and it had been a while since I'd laughed.

"Phoenix." The bartender took the empty bottle from in front of me and wiped down the condensation on the bar. His hand movement so efficient and I couldn't help staring. Whoa. Look at that. Fascinating.

"Awesome, I like the desert," I responded, not peeling my eyes from his hand and the bar.

"Hey." His voice snapped me from my daze and called me to attention. "I'm going to have to cut you off."

"But why?" I whined, annoyed that I was just starting to feel the buzz and Mr. No Fun wanted to cut-me-off. It was a total power play, making the big man feel good by telling me no. I bet he probably hadn't gotten laid in a while either. There was no way I was that drunk.

"I know I sound drunk, but I'm just happy." I tried to stand up but had to hold onto the bar to steady myself. "See." By some miracle I was able to stop swaying and lifted my hands triumphantly. Look, barman, no hands. "Just happy and I'm staying in the hotel so it's not like I have to drive."

"Even still, you've had enough for one night." He folded his arms across his chest, the international sign for we're-done-discussing. Was poking my tongue out an acceptable response?

"Fine." I sunk back onto the bar stool, my need to show my sobriety no longer valid. "Ruin my life even more." My dramatic flair usually increased the drunker I got, and while I wasn't going to be winning any *Oscars*, I would have definitely been a shoe-in for a daytime soap.

It was late. We'd—by we, I meant the band—come off stage sometime around eight and I'd—by I, I meant me, solo, lone wolf—come straight to the bar. It's not that I'd turned into an alcoholic, but I was spending more downtime with a synthetic high than not. It beat facing reality, which was that I was a dumbass. *Give me a D, give me a U, give me a M and B, give me an A, give me a S, give me another S—what does it spell? Dumbass. Hurray.* All I needed was the pom poms and the fucking ability to do a backflip. I'd have to work on my cheer though, not smooth at all.

"Rough night?" A tall athletic guy in a nice suit sat down beside me. He smelled nice. And he had nice eyes. All four of them.

"Pfft. When did everyone get so fucking sensitive about public intoxication?" I slurred at the four-eyed-man. "I mean it's not like I took my top off and flashed my tits." My eyes rolled so hard I almost saw my brain. Not really. I meant, mentally. Because I was being sarcastic. Oh, never mind.

"Maybe that would improve the bartenders disposition. Who can say no to a beautiful, topless woman?" My suited companion laughed beside me.

Wow, look at that. Boom. He grew another head. Two heads. At least he's good looking. Not that I really was in any condition to judge.

"I bet *he* would still say no." I pointed to the bartender who was doing his best to ignore me. "Besides, I'm not beautiful." I scoffed as I stood up to illustrate my point. "I'm too short and my ass is too big. Plus I have these fucking childbearing hips." My hand moved around my body like a game show model. "Look at this. It's like the trunk of a Cadillac."

Newsflash. I was not my biggest fan.

"I think you're beautiful," the two headed, four-eyed and obviously delusional man responded.

"Then you my friend, must be drunker than I am."

I'd meant to think it but it came out of my mouth anyway. Meh. I'm not sober enough to care and hopefully drunk enough not to remember.

"Actually this is my first beer, so maybe *you're* the one who is wrong." He lifted his mostly full beer as he stared at me amused.

Great, now I was the sideshow.

"Didn't your momma tell you to never tell a woman she's wrong?" I laughed not having a more coherent or intelligent argument.

"My mother's been gone for a long time, so I must have missed out on all those words of wisdom." He took a sip of his beer before placing it on the bar.

Awesome. Hey foot, meet mouth. Get acquainted, it's going to be a long night I feel.

"I'm sorry. I don't have a mom either." I fumbled my apology, the over share of me having lost my mom not intentional.

"Well I guess we have something in common then." He moved his hand to where my fingers were and gently rubbed them. It felt wrong but I didn't move my hand.

"Yeah, I guess." I'd stopped laughing, my eyes following his thumb moving over my knuckles.

Crap. He was hitting on me. Well, that was just great.

"So seeing as I don't think you are going to get anymore service here, you want to come up to my room?" He edged in closer, that nice cologne he was wearing tickling my nose. "I have a full stocked mini bar and a credit card that is begging to get maxed out."

The last time I'd had sex, was with Jason. Actually, that wasn't sex; we'd made love. Because I'd loved him. The fact he didn't love me back didn't change what it had been. But that was over. Done. Finished. Kaput. And I was single, and free to have sex with whomever I pleased. But no one pleased me enough to want to. I mean, I wasn't pleased enough to try. I mean, I wasn't having sex because I still wanted Jason and was in love with him. Ah. Fuck. I hope I wasn't saying any of this out loud.

My eyes glanced up; the two-headed beautiful man with his astonishing four eyes was still waiting patiently for my response. The one that wasn't about a drink, but about whether or not I was willing to get naked and have sex. Because that's what he was asking me, right?

"Sure." The word left my mouth before I'd even really decided. "Why the hell not." My backup statement concurred with my first. It's not like I needed to be holding out for anyone. Besides, casual hook-ups are the *thing* right now. Sex and no commitment, why not. Surely that's what Jason has been doing, returning to his old habits.

"But I won't drink bourbon. Anything but that." I shook my head at the thought.

That's what he drank and if I was going to do this then anything that reminded me of him was out. God, I hoped I didn't cry. That wouldn't be cool and not very sexy either. The first time would be the hardest and then I would see that I was okay, so it was better to get it over with.

"No bourbon. I think we can work with that." The man I was about to have a drink with, aka have sex with, stood up and threw some money on the bar.

"Hey Angie, I was about ready to send out a search party."

Rusty circled his arms around my body and pulled me off my barstool. His warm smile almost made me want to cry. It seemed to be my usual response lately. I was so leaky it was pathetic.

"Rusty! Oh I missed you." I swayed on my feet as I hugged him back fiercely. "Hey, meet my friend." Ummm what did he say his name was? Did I even ask him his name? Shit, was I about to sleep with some guy whose name I didn't even know?

"Sorry, what was your name?" I asked my *friend* the question I probably should have opened with.

"Jason." He nodded, adding a wink and a smile.

I'm sorry, excuse me? Jason? There's like five billion—okay, maybe not that many—names in the world and he has to have *that* one. Fuck you! I'm not sure to who that fuck you was directed at, but someone sure as hell deserved it.

"Wow, really?" I tried not to cringe, his nod confirming his name. "Well that's unfortunate. Anyway, Jason, this is my bestest friend in the whole wide world, Rusty." I wasn't sure if that came out exactly right. I didn't mean to say the unfortunate part. I had nothing against the name. Or maybe I did. Not that it was the name's fault. Oh for god's sake. His name was Jason? Who does that?

"Okay baby, let's get you up to bed." Rusty pulled me close to his body, my feet stumbling unsteadily under my weight. Standing up was hard work.

"He your boyfriend?" Jason—not the Power Station one, the bar one—tipped his head to the man who was currently keeping me vertical. Rusty, my knight in shining armor.

"Who Rusty?" I laughed. I didn't mean to but it was just that so many people assumed. Hell even Jason—the Power Station one, not the bar one—had.

"No. We tried to have sex once, it didn't work out." My mouth once again spewed things it hadn't meant to say.

"And on that note, you've had enough." Rusty, wrapped both his arms around me, caging me in. Oh, look. I'm in a Rusty cage. I laughed out loud at my private joke.

"Oh come on, Rusty, don't be such a buzz kill." I wriggled unsuccessfully trying to free myself. "Jason is going to take me to his room where we are going to drink everything in his mini bar. Except the bourbon."

Because *he* likes bourbon and I refuse to even touch anything that *he* likes. I reminded myself, in case I'd forgotten.

"Who is *he*?" Jason asked, my private reminder having not been so private.

"Nobody. I mean literally nobody." I meant to say it confidently but it came out as a whisper. Maybe because I wasn't convinced he was a nobody, maybe because I knew I was lying.

"Hey Jason." Rusty scooped me into his arms and lifted me off the floor. "Thanks for looking after my girl, but I've got it from here."

And before my brain registered what was happening we were out of the bar and into the elevator. I didn't even say goodbye. Goodbyes and Jasons didn't have a good track record it seemed.

"Rus, put me down." My legs kicked in his arms as he held me close to his chest. The elevator had already started to move.

He didn't answer, instead waiting until the door slid open on the floor where our rooms were situated.

"Rusty." I protested again.

Nope, still nothing.

With what I can only describe as an amazing amount of skill, Rusty was able to wiggle his key out of his pocket and pressed it against the lock. The amazing skill did not extend to being able to holding me and open the door, which meant he had to put me down.

"No. I don't want to go to bed. I'm not a fucking child." I stomped my foot exactly like the child that I was not.

"Then stop acting like one." With a flick of the wrist, the door was open and Rusty had pushed me into his hotel room. "What the hell are you doing, Angie, this isn't you."

"What?" I asked naïvely pretending I didn't know what he was talking about. Duh. Like I didn't know.

He tossed his keycard onto the coffee table, leaning against the back of the couch. "You mean to tell me that you weren't about to go to some strange man's room for sex?"

"So what if I was? Maybe I just wanted to have sex. You have sex with lots of girls you don't know. I don't fucking judge you, all high and mighty."

I wasn't sure if I was mad that he was right or mad at myself for actually considering it.

"I'm not judging you." His voice didn't rise, nor did eyes move from mine. "I would never judge you, but don't tell me this is about sex. It's about *him*."

"Not everything is about Jason. The band one, not the bar one. Sometimes it's just about sex." My voice yelled where his hadn't.

I wasn't convincing, tears threatening to spill at any moment at just the mention of his name.

"Fine, then you can wait until you are sober and then you can have sex with as many random guys as you like," he yelled back.

"I'm not that drunk." More yelling, this time, me.

"Yes you are, you can barely stand." Yelling again, Rusty's turn.

"I don't want to wait until I'm sober. I want to have sex now, damn it." My voice was raised, as was my temper. Are you seeing a pattern yet?

"Fine, then have sex with me."

Oh I must be loaded because I could have sworn that Rusty just asked me to have sex with him. And that would be ridiculous.

I burst into hysterical laughter, taking a minute to catch my breath. "Oh my God, Rusty. I'm dying here." Well at least we weren't yelling anymore.

"I'm serious. You want to be on top or the bottom?" He slowly unbuttoned his shirt, the fabric slipping off his shoulders and onto the floor. His toned chest displaying his crazy detailed dragon tattoo that flexed as he went to unbutton his jeans.

Holy shit, he was serious. He was actually, serious.

"Have you lost your fucking mind?"

"Why? It's just sex, right?" He kicked off his boots, cool, calm and collected. "No big deal. You want sex so let's just fuck, take care of that urge for you."

He moved closer pushing aside my hair and looked me in eyes.

"No." I pulled away, my world feeling like it had been turned on its head.

"Why, no, Angie?" He didn't yell this time, pulling me into his arms and kissed my hair. "Didn't you just finish telling me how much you wanted it?"

"We can't have sex because it would be … a mistake," I answered, knowing that everything we had, would change. I'd already lost one man I loved, I couldn't lose a second. Not my best friend.

"Yeah it would." He nodded, his hands holding me still as I started to shake. "It would be a huge mistake, and still not as big as the one you would make if you went and fucked that other guy."

The point.

And there it was. And there I was. Completely unraveled. And the only one who hadn't seen it had been me.

"I'm a mess, Rus."

I tried not to cry. I mean really tried, but I couldn't stop. The pain, the hurt—I'd lost Jason, twice. And this time, it was so much worse.

"Yeah you are." Rusty, slowly rocked me. My fat ugly tears falling over his beautiful ripped chest. And yet, there wasn't one thing that was sexual about it. "Lucky for you I like my friends messy." He laughed. "It makes me feel more normal."

"Thank you." The palms of my hands wiped away my tears. The stain of mascara smudges all over my skin, both under my eyes and on my hands. Lucky I wasn't trying to be seductive because my latest effort would have most definitely failed.

"You know, usually the girl thanks me *after* the sex but sure." He shrugged, giving me a kiss on the cheek.

"We're not having sex." I shook my head. Rusty still standing there with his jeans unbuttoned, wearing no shirt wasn't going to convince me otherwise. As fine as the man was, what we had was better.

"Fine." His arms fell dramatically to his side as he sighed. "Let's be boring and *not* fuck." He flashed his amazing smile, the one that usually sent the panty population into overdrive. Well, all except for the ones I was currently wearing.

"I'm probably going to need some coffee. And an exorcist." My reflection stared back at me from the obnoxious mirror across the room. What I saw—wasn't pretty.

"Coffee I can do." Another hug. Another kiss. "The other part—I think we just get you showered and into bed and see where we land in the morning."

BIGGEST CLUSTERFUCK OF ALL TIME.

Of all the dumbest, most monumentally stupidest shit I'd ever done, this has to take the cake. And what made it even worse was I saw it coming a mile away and still, it didn't stop me.

Angie was right. I was an asshole.

She loved me.

Those words confused me so much I couldn't breathe. I'd heard them before, and the last time, they didn't bring good things.

I couldn't expect her to understand. There were the things she was asking of me that I wasn't able to give. Not because I didn't want, but because I couldn't. And if I pretended, it would have just made it worse—for me and for her.

In the crystal ball department I had come up empty. And who knows what forever even fucking meant. Did she want a promise? Say I'd never leave, that she'd do the same? Like words actually meant something. My actions were stronger than any words I'd ever spoke, and it hadn't been enough. She owned me, I wasn't going anywhere but she had to push.

It was always going to end up the same way. Both of us were delusional if we'd thought there'd be any other outcome. She deserved better. And not because I didn't love her—yeah, there was that word I'd promised I'd never fucking say—but because I was too fucked up to give her what she needed.

Well done, Jason. The minute you meet a girl worth a damn, you fucking run like a pussy. Because that's what I was doing. *I* let her walk out the door. *I* didn't stop her.

Table for miserable asshole, party of one? Yep. I had the standing reservation.

Every time there was a knock at the door I wanted it to be her. I wanted it all—her rage, her fury, her fists flying at my face. Except, the knock—and her rage—didn't come.

Her nightly *dedications* to me had stopped. Finished. No more. Nothing about what a cock I was. No odes to my death. No tributes to my demise. Just nothing. Radio fucking silence. That, ladies and gentleman, was the worst kind of hell. Because I knew—I'd broken her.

I'd done that. Me. Well done, motherfucker, you are a real champion.

I saw her even though she didn't see me. My messed up stalker routine not taking a breather even though we were done. Just hoping to catch a glimpse of her here or there when she didn't know I was watching. That light in her eyes? Gone. The firecracker attitude? Gone. And there wasn't a second out of every fucking day after it that I didn't fucking hate myself more. Dan was right. I was the gift that kept on giving.

"Hey, asswipe." Speak of the devil. "You want to get in on a game? Troy's shuffling the deck."

My zero fucks policy had extended to my door. Which had meant it was open. Which allowed the cocksucker to come in. Mental note, close the fucking door.

"Nope. I have this thing going on where I'm busy being a miserable fuck. It's taking up all of my time." My arms stretched out behind my head. My mind firmly cemented on hanging out in my hotel room, on my couch. Preferably, alone. "Thanks for the offer though."

It was nice to be asked, even if he knew the answer. Same answer as it had been the last night, and the night before that. The whole *sharing is caring* rule didn't apply to me. I wasn't sharing jack.

"Hey look at this way, at least she is no longer telling most of the continental United States what a dick you are." He parked his ass on the sofa beside me, his eyes scooting around looking to see if there was a bottle. There wasn't. The drinking myself into a stupor had already gotten old. Besides, getting on stage with a hangover wasn't giving me a case of the warm and fuzzies. Neither was acting like an obnoxious dick. Other than what I already was. You could only fight nature so much.

"I know you are trying to help." My thanks-but-no-thanks coming thick and fast. "But you're not. So don't."

"Okay, okay." He raised his hands, hopefully throwing in the towel on operation cheer up Jase. "I'm not Troy, and I don't always know the right thing to say. But misunderstandings happen. You fuck up, you say sorry and you move on. That's the way it works. You obviously give a shit about this girl, because I don't notice dick usually and even *I* could see that."

Of all the fucking times for Dan to be perceptive, now was not that time. It just added another layer to the shit that was already piled on there. *Hey, we all noticed you loved her, yet you still let her go. Bravo. Dick.*

"Is there a point somewhere in there, or you just trying to contribute to my misery?"

Not that it mattered. The misery was pretty maxed out, so an extra helping here or there wasn't going to make a difference. Still, I hoped leaving was going to be featuring on his agenda soon. Misery most definitely did *not* love company, and who ever coined that phrase needed to go eat a big bag of dicks.

"What I'm saying is." I prepared myself for the *awesome* that was Dan logic. That was sarcasm in case you didn't know. "If you care about her just go back and get her. You'll work it out."

Sure, because shit is just that easy. *Sorry* wasn't a fucking cure-all and exactly what had changed in the last few days? I had no more to offer her than I did before I ended us. A heart to heart over a box of Kleenex wasn't going to cut it.

"There are some things that can't be worked out, Dan. But

thanks."

I admired his commitment. The bastard had shown real growth of late. A world away from the selfish, arrogant dude he used to be.

"So you're just going to sit here and be fucking miserable?" Dan's session offering pearls of wisdom was obviously not over. "Newsflash, it doesn't work out, asshole. When Ash left me, I tried to convince myself I'd just find someone else. But there wasn't anyone else. She was it. Troy—he came to the same fucking conclusion. His girl didn't even ditch him; he just had his head too far up his ass that he couldn't see what was right in front of him. James and Hannah, they broke up and guess what, they got back together. Alex and Lexi, same fucking thing. Those two were more dramatic about it because let's face it—they are both fucking drama queens, but in the end, there was no keeping them apart."

No words. Which is exactly what you have to say when Dan starts making sense. My silence gave Dan the floor once more, to wow me again with his astounding attempt at being friend of the year.

"I'm not going to put words in your mouth, but it looks to me like you might love this girl and if you don't go after her, you're going to regret it."

"I already regret it." My clipped response shot out of my mouth like a bullet out of a gun. Regret rocked the number two position on my list when it came to Angie. Right after how much I fucking loved her.

Well ... Fuck.

"So why are you sitting here talking to me?" He punched me in the arm, the leather of the couch creaking under his ass as he moved. "She's in the same fucking building and I've seen her, she looks like shit. That's not me being a douchebag about it because it's Angie, I mean she looks sad. She's miserable without you too."

But she'd be more miserable with me. "I can't go get her back."

"Why the fuck not?" The I-don't-understand face came right after the sentence. "I take back what I said about Lexi and Alex, *you're* the fucking drama queen."

"Because I'm the fucking one who ended it, asshole." The voice boomed, making the bastard sit up in his seat. "It was me." I shook my head, the gravity of the situation hitting me, as I owned it. "I'm the one who told her we were done."

"Well why the hell did you do that, loser?" Dan stared in disbelief, finally seeing I wasn't the dude who had his shit all together. "Aren't you supposed to be smart?"

"Because I fucking love her." My head fell into my clenched fists. It was the first time I'd said out loud. The word hung in the air for a second before I was able to continue. "Because I fucking know that if she is with me, I'm going to hurt her."

"What the *fuck* are you talking about?" Dan continued on his trail of disbelief, the big picture not being drawn for him yet. "Are you fucking moonlighting as a serial killer? How the fuck are you going to hurt her? Unless you count dating a jerk-off like you as a personal injury, what the hell could you fucking do? You're the sensible one. The reliable one." He listed all the things I was *supposed* to be, not the things I actually was. Broken, should have topped out the list.

"No. I'm a fucking fraud," I yelled, no longer giving a shit with the pretense. "You see what you want to fucking see. But I'm not a good guy. You've seen the real me, dude. You've seen me so drunk that I couldn't stand up. You've seen me break some guy's nose I didn't know because I was so angry I couldn't take it. And I think even you know how many women I've fucked in the past in an effort just to keep myself from going over the edge. That shit doesn't go away, it's still there just waiting to fucking come out and play. You want to put her on the crash course? And even if by some kind of walk-on-water miracle I can be guaranteed that someday my shit isn't going to be jacked-up, what can I fucking give her? Marriage? Kids? What am I going to tell her if she wants to have that conversation?"

Dan stared at me, his mouth wide open; the outburst not the first he'd seen, but it had been a while since he'd been up close and personal with my crazy.

"Em wasn't just some high school crush who just screwed my best friend. I had my life together. I stopped all that shit, and she dragged me right back to hell. I know Angie is not Em. But the shit that bitch put me through just about ruined me. Straight up, I wanted to kill her. Not pretend kill. Like actually do it. And the thought of being in a relationship again scares the fuck out of me. That someone could make me go that fucking crazy, or that I'd hand over the keys to my sanity again."

So there it was. On the table. All of it, and I hadn't held anything back. Never in a million years did I ever think I would fess up to being afraid of anything, but I'd said it anyway. I was scared. Scared as fuck of breaking Angie's heart. Scared she would break mine. But most of all scared that I was so fucking defective that I didn't have the capacity to be normal. To have a normal relationship where I could be with her. Trust issues. Giving over a power. None of it simmered well with me.

"I can't tell her that *love will conquer all* bullshit when I don't believe it myself."

Fuck knows what I believed anymore, my reality had twisted so much in my head I was convinced that maybe it hadn't been true. That all that shit from the past was a bad dream. Drama queen, like Dan said. And then I realize, it all happened. And I live that hell all over again.

"It's not because I don't want to, it's because I can't."

"Fuck me, Jason." For the first time since he walked in Dan wasn't wearing his shit-is-going-to-be-ok glasses. "This is really fucked up."

"Yes. It is."

My coming clean, now full circle. It wasn't going to change, we could pretend it was different and wrap it up with a freaking bow but it was always going to be the same.

"I am fucked up and I am not going to fucking bring that down on her." The thought of any of it touching her, ripped the rage right back to where I knew I could be dangerous. "Do you get that? I left because I loved her, because I'm in love with her, and *not* because I didn't care enough."

"I don't know what to say." Well, someone call Guinness. Dan was speechless. "Like legit, I have no words right now."

"Yep, so you see a bunch of roses and a *sorry* isn't going to cut it." I laughed. Not because it was funny, because really, what else was there to do? Yep. World of fucking shit—population one.

"Maybe we should get Troy, he's better at this shit than I am." Dan conceded that he was in over his head.

"Nope, we get no one else involved. I will deal with this my way. I'm good, really." First came the nod. "Give me a few more days, let the sting wear off and then I'll move on." Then I moved on to the forced smile. Fake-it-till-you-make-it was going to be featuring heavily in my repertoire for a while. The bullshit about moving on was thrown in for good measure.

"Do you really think you can?" Dan took about a second before he called me on it. "You said you loved her. I don't know many men who can just walk away from a girl they're in love with."

Surely there was some catastrophic event about to take place. Like the end of the world or something. Because there we were, Dan being responsible, and me being the recipient of the advice. It was my time to step up.

"Yeah, well I'm not *many men*." I swallowed, hard. "I'm me, and I can walk away because I know it's the right thing to do." It *was* the right thing to do.

"Stop being so fucking perfect, douchebag." Dan punched me in the arm, his grin unsteady. "You're going to make me look bad."

"Only *you* can hear what I just told you and still think I could make you look bad. Trust me, Dan. I'm far from fucking perfect." I shook my head in disbelief.

"You're a lot more than you think. If it's one thing Ash taught me, it's that perception is subjective." Dan slapped me on the shoulder.

"Wow dude, big words and everything. That beautiful wife of yours use flash cards when she taught you that?" I laughed. No seriously, someone needed to check the date. When did those Mayans say the end of the world was coming?

"Go fuck yourself." He flipped me off, big ass grin of his face.

"Thanks." The *for everything* that I didn't attach to the end of the sentence was unnecessary. The eyeball exchange we had going on said more than that word anyway.

"Anytime. And for the record, my wife *is* fucking beautiful." The smugness was back as was the smile he got when he spoke about his wife. "And if I weren't such an arrogant asshole, I'd admit she's way better than I deserved. But whatever her reason was for giving me a chance, I'll take it. In fact, I applaud her lack of judgment. Maybe give *that* some thought."

"Dan, stop, dude. You are freaking me out with all this maturity." It was my turn to punch him in the arm.

"Ok loser, I'm going to go call my beautiful wife. Hopefully she'll talk dirty to me so I can jerk off. This long distance thing blows, I think my balls might actually explode." Dan stood up, pulling at the crotch of his jeans.

So much for Dan and his maturity, I've got to admit, it was starting to make me more than just a little uncomfortable. "And everything is once again right with the world." I laughed as I watched him walk out the door.

24

Angie

THE NIGHT IN THE HOTEL ROOM WITH RUSTY WAS MY BOTTOM. MY low. There was nowhere further to go. The drinking, the idea of sleeping with some man I didn't even know—punishment, because I was stupid enough to fall in love with the same man twice. Have my heart broken by the same man, twice.

So, I'd been an idiot. Dumb beyond belief. But I needed to start healing and love myself. Not in the narcissistic way Dan Evans loved himself, although he wasn't as conceited as he used to be. But in a way where I accepted that what happened wasn't a personal flaw.

I loved. That's who I was.

I would never be perfect, my ass would always be bigger than I'd want it to be. My hair wasn't going to suddenly be shiny, blonde and perfect. And I was probably always going to be the girl who said the word *fuck* too much and didn't wear the right kind of clothes. It was okay, because I'm me. And rather than try and worry about what I couldn't do or what I didn't have, I would focus on the fact that I had so very much. A band that was more like family than friends, a father who loved me enough for the mom I missed, and friends new and old who accepted me for who I was. Fuck Jason Irwin. He didn't deserve me.

"I hear Megs and Ash are coming in this afternoon. We going to lose you to the *Sisterhood of the Traveling Pants*?" Rusty nudged my shoulder, taking a seat beside me. His grin proved he wasn't anywhere near annoyed.

"You'd never lose me, but I'm glad they are spending the weekend with us. I miss those two so much." My own grin widened. And my smile was totally not faked.

"So is that why you called this band meeting? You're worried about my defection to my own sex?"

Rusty had sent a message early this morning saying we needed to discuss the rest of the tour. While it wasn't completely out of character, it seemed way too structured for him. He was more a let's-get-a-beer-and-discuss, not the-first-point-on-the-agenda-is. Which is why the four of us had gathered in my hotel room, the venue for our makeshift meeting.

"Yeah, about that." Rusty rubbed the back of neck awkwardly. "Just remember how much you love me and how much your life would suck without me." His sentence punctuated by a knock at the door.

"What did you do?" My eyes widened as they darted from the door back to him. Bodily harm hadn't been ruled out.

"I'll get it." Max stood up, apparently bored with Joey and talk of his newfound fame. His face not showing surprise led me to believe he was in on whatever was about to go down. Bastards. Screw them and their unflagging loyalty to each other.

"Rusty, who is on the other side of that door?" I demanded, watching Max move to the door and pull it open. My heart had suddenly started beating so fast I was convinced I was going to have a heart attack.

"Hey." Troy walked in, the rest of Power Station behind him. Jason being that he was part of that band was included in the people who entered the room. "Good to see everyone could make it." He looked around and nodded to Rusty, some secret telepathic exchange taking place.

It was all rather inconvenient. Not the meeting part, whose purpose hadn't been ascertained yet, it was the having to find another guitarist part that concerned me. It wouldn't be easy to replace Rusty, as his death catapulted to the top of my to-do list. Of course I'd make sure he was properly mourned, it would be the least I could do.

"What's all this about?" Jason's eyes flared as they came to rest on me.

The asshole still looked good, wearing the hell out of the jeans and T-shirt that had been lucky enough to grace his body. I had given up hope that was going to change, obviously asking too much of the universe that he suddenly become grotesquely ugly. His body was also a problem. He needed to stop working out so much too. Thank god, he was still wearing a shirt. And why the hell was I even thinking about *him* and any of that? My to-do list was going to need an amendment. Shaking myself had now taken the number one position.

"Relax, brother. Take a seat." James patted him on the back. By him I meant Jason, the guy who was currently staring at me. This I knew because I happened to be staring back. Awesome. It couldn't get more awkward if we tried. At least I wasn't the only one in the dark, the good-looking asshole I was currently eyeballing also seeming to not have received the memo.

"So anyone else chilly?" Rusty shivered, before nodding to Max and Joey. "Yeah, think we should move this meeting to the pool. Boys, follow me."

"What, where are you going?" My stare match with Jason took a backseat to the threat of being deserted. Being alone with him never worked out well and my feelings were still very much off kilter. As much as I was planning Rusty's demise, I needed him to stay. We needed a buffer; the Rocky Mountains would have been good, but at this stage I'd settle for the substitute that was my band.

"Angie, just know we love you. We'll be back later." His hand rubbed my arm in reassurance, his eyes spelling out that he wouldn't be far.

My head nodded that I would be okay even though I didn't believe it, which allowed Rusty to turn his attention to Troy. "Troy, you better know what you are doing. This goes bad, you'll be finding yourself a new support band."

"I've got it from here," Troy reassured him, the *it* that he *had* still very much a mystery to me. The prospect of finding out wasn't automatically filling me with excitement.

"You guys better come with us too." Rusty glanced over at Power Station and jerked his head to the door. I almost fell to my knees in relief that the meeting just would be Troy and me. While not ideal, but just the two of us, I could handle.

"Looks like our cue to leave too, Dan and Alex." James rounded up only two of the three band members who were supposed to leave. "I think the pool sounds like a good idea." My relief short lived.

Great. We were being sandbagged.

"Is this some fucked up intervention?" Jason echoed my very thought. He'd obviously not been informed of the plan either, the two of us apparently the only ones in the dark.

"Jase, just listen to Troy." Dan clapped him over the shoulder. "Sorry brother, but you're both fucking miserable. This shit can't go on."

There was no further discussion, with both my band and Power Station leaving. And then there were three. Three was never a good number unless you were into threesomes, which I wasn't so I could only expect bad things to follow.

"Troy, I know what you are trying to do but it's unnecessary." My voice finally found itself as I tried to reason my way out of it. The *it* still undefined. "There isn't anything that we need to talk about." We'd said it all before. Back to front and sideways. Nothing was going to change.

"Have to agree with Angie, nothing to discuss here." Jase joined the party, his tone clipped and annoyed. Which just annoyed me more. In case anyone forgot, he was an asshole.

"Oh, so *now* you agree with me." I couldn't help the sarcasm as it leaped out of my throat before I had a chance to stop it. Honestly, not sure I would have anyway. "Allow me a minute to bask in the wonder that is Jason Irwin's approval." The eye roll was unnecessary but once again, couldn't be helped.

"I'm not engaging in this, Angie. You want to talk shit, go right ahead." His stare was fierce but not of hate—like mine—but of something else. Resolve? Intent?

"God forbid you engaged in *anything*." I couldn't help myself pushing it further with the hurt subsiding, as anger became my new best friend. "How's life on asshole island?"

"Original. Still not interested." He was so cold.

How could anyone be so unfeeling? We'd had tender moments, it hadn't been just sex, but it was like a switch had been flicked and we were back to where we'd started. The weeks erased, with the Jason standing in front of me being the same one who was with the band when they'd asked me to first join the tour.

"Fuck you and your *not interested*—"

"Okay, both of you. Sit down and stop talking," Troy exploded, the vein on the side of his neck doing the thing it did when he got angry. Which he seemed to be right now. "You are both giving me a headache."

"Troy, thanks but it's obvious neither of us want to talk to each—"

"I said, sit down." Troy repeated, calmer than the first but no less intense. My butt hit the chair without any further encouragement.

Jase stayed standing, defiantly.

"That wasn't a fucking request." Troy paused after each word incase Jase was not reading the scary vibe he was rocking. That vein bulging at the side of his neck, threatening to explode.

"Fine." He conceded and took a seat opposite me, which incidentally was as far as he could get while still satisfying Troy's urge to have us both sit down. I was both offended by his conspicuous distance and relieved by the comfort of the safeness.

"You know what, you are both acting like fucking dumbasses." Troy didn't back down, holding his ground even though Jason didn't look pleased. "And you both need your asses kicked as far as I'm concerned. You don't want to sort this shit out? Well guess what, neither of you have a say in it anymore." He eyed us both hard and I had no doubt that no one would be leaving the room until some sort of resolution was in place. Who needed a negotiator, scary Troy was enough of an incentive.

"There is nothing to be sorted." My throat got tighter as

emotions jostled for position.

"No, you need to hear something first." While Troy's voice was directed at me, his eyes were solely focused on Jase. Whoa. Scary Troy sounded like he had some insider knowledge. Here was the loop, and here I was—completely out of it.

"Troy, don't." Jase gained an understanding in their wordless exchange that clearly I didn't. "This isn't any of your business."

"Is that how you see it? That this is none of my business?" Troy shook his head in disbelief. "You are so fucking wrong. That day you joined us—the band, you became fucking family. Doesn't matter you weren't there from the start, it doesn't mean shit. You're my brother, same as Dan, Alex or James and I don't sit around when I see my *family* doing something I know they will regret. So you are wrong, it is very much *my* business."

The urge to wave my hand and say *umm … hello, I'm still here* was overwhelming. Instead I went with sitting silently. Less attention that way.

"Em—" Troy started.

"Don't. Don't you fucking dare," Jason warned, up out of his chair, almost lunging for Troy. Holy shit. I think he might actually hit him.

"You wanna take a swing?" Troy stretched out his arms, his eyes welcoming it. "Fucking do it. Because the only way this isn't happening is if you lay me out. So you better make that first fucking hit count, because I'm only giving you one shot."

The fists clenched by Jason's sides were white and ready to take a swing. Troy's face absolutely ready to take it to that level if that's where it needed to go.

"Troy." My voice wavered as I stepped in between the two heavyweights. Getting in the middle of a fistfight wasn't smart, but I wasn't going to sit by and watch them duke it out either.

"Angie, you need to know." A ripple of calmness cracked through as Troy flicked his eyes down on me. "There is a lot of shit that you don't know about. Jason's past, before you knew him. Things that will fucking mess a man up."

"He told me." I nodded, hoping the situation had been defused. Not that his reasoning made complete sense to me, and not that it made it hurt any less. In fact it made it hurt more, that I was paying for the sins of someone else. "His girlfriend cheated on him. I get it. He has trust issues."

"That's what you told her?" Troy's head whipped around to Jason.

"That's what happened." Jason's words barely audible through his tight jaw.

"Look, it doesn't matter. He had a girlfriend who betrayed him and—"

"Em was his fucking wife." The words echoed off the walls.

Silence.

No one spoke.

Wife.

I heard it over and over again. It hadn't been a girlfriend. It had been his wife.

"What? You were married?" My mouth dropped open in total disbelief. "You told me she was your girlfriend." I scaled my memory to make sure I hadn't heard incorrectly. Nope. Wife was something I would have remembered. The *Oh, hey I was married* never having been mentioned.

"No, I told you I was with a girl and she cheated. You assumed she was my girlfriend. I didn't correct you." Jase's eyes focused on me, his tone unapologetic.

"Are you fucking with me?" My voice almost choked in disbelief. No seriously, was he fucking kidding?

"I've been divorced for longer than I was married. It is not important."

The man I had known was a complete and utter lie.

"You." Troy pointed to Jase, his gaze enough to level a ten-story building without the use of dynamite. "If you were going to tell her anything, you should have told her the whole fucking story. And you," his attention turned back to me, "you shouldn't just automatically jump to conclusions that it was just *a girl* fucking around that has made him so detached. No one is that much of a fucking pussy."

I was stunned. Troy had never yelled at me like that. In fact, I'd never seen him lose his cool. The words I had planned to say lost their way from my brain to my mouth as I stared, wide-eyed and mute.

With both Jase and I subtly silenced, either from shock or the I-have-no-idea-what to say, Troy took a seat. Jase encouraged by his friend's ass-in-chair position decided to replicate it and also sat down.

"So you know about his past."

I nodded as sorrow and possibly regret flicked through Jase's beautiful brown eyes. If I hadn't been so mad and hurt I may have wanted to hold him.

"Problem was, while he left his delinquent buddies behind, his evil bitch of a girlfriend tracked him down," Troy continued. The mention of the evil bitch enough to make Jase flinch. "Military life didn't suit her by all accounts."

"Why did you marry her if she was a bitch? And why so young? If you were trying to make a change, why keep her?"

"Originally because it was habit. I thought I cared about her and when I tried to break up with her, she got pregnant. As much as I didn't want to be with her, I didn't want my kid growing up without a dad."

The news of his marriage was nothing. It just got a hundred times worse.

"Holy shit. You have a kid too?" My hands moved up to my throat as I struggled to breathe. "Did I know anything about you? Like at all?"

It felt like the walls were closing in on me, as the lies continued to unravel.

"Yes, you did." His eyes refused to leave mine, pleading with me to believe him "You know me *now*. Who I am, now. I didn't want you to know the other stuff. I'm not proud of who I was. My life was a mess; I'd made shitty choices. I put my family through hell and they never deserved any of it, they are good people." He swallowed hard, as if fighting an internal battle as to whether or not to continue. "I was turning it around. I figured I could help her do that too, and we could raise our kid together. I take care of what's mine."

I continued to freak out over the current downloading of

information I was receiving. Asking if it could get any worse would be surely tempting fate. Troy was the one who first broke through the current silence.

"I'm going to let you guys talk it out." He nodded to both of us, seeking permission before leaving. "But I'm going to be outside, so if either of you get out of control expect me to be coming right back in. We clear?"

"Yes." Both Jason and I answered simultaneously. In truth, the horror would be better *without* the audience.

"So where is your kid now? With your ex-wife?" I asked Jason as Troy closed the door behind him.

"I assume so," he answered, very non-committal.

"You assume?" I said louder than I intended. "You don't know where your own kid lives?" The whole I-take-care-of-what's-mine argument still ringing in my ears.

"I don't have any rights anymore." The words seeming to sting as he spoke them. "So *no*, I don't know."

"What do you mean you don't have any rights? You just signed over your kid?"

"He wasn't mine!" he shouted, the sound exploding through the room. His face a mix of pain and anger as his body seemed to struggle with remaining still. "She came clean just before his first birthday. I'd come home from working a twelve-hour day and found her passed out drunk on the floor. Thomas was crying in his crib wearing the same fucking diaper for who knows how long. I threatened to divorce her, told her that if she didn't sober up I would leave and I'd take our son with me. She just laughed and told me he wasn't my kid. Bragged that she didn't know whose he was." His eyes blinked rapidly, as his voice tightened. "I watched him be born, fucking held him for months. Was up late while he cried. *I* was his father."

There was nothing I could say, the pain ripping through him enough to tear out my own heart. My own tears threatening to spill as he continued.

"I thought she was full of shit, that the booze was talking. So we got the tests done. For the first time ever, Em had told the truth. He wasn't mine." He shook his head, as he seemed to struggle to go on. "And even knowing all of that, I stayed. Because I loved Thomas more than I hated Em. I didn't care he didn't have the same blood type, that kid was mine."

"So what happened?" My voice was barely a whisper, not wanting to contribute to more of his pain.

"We tried to make it work but we couldn't. The drinking didn't stop and my enlistment was almost up. Honestly, the thought of signing up again scared the fuck out of me. Knowing I could be shipped away and leaving Thomas with only his mother. So I decided to get out, and just before I separated from the Army, she left. Cleared out my bank account and took my car while I was at work one day. Didn't say goodbye. No note explaining why, and she had taken Thomas with her."

"Did you try and find them?"

"Of course I fucking tried to find them." The hurt visible in his eyes. "I was granted leave and went looking for them. She kept moving and it wasn't until she got into trouble and her mother was awarded temporary custody of Thomas that I tracked them down. She had been doing drugs and sleeping around, not far from our hometown; she didn't even care about him. So consumed with herself, she didn't even give a shit." His jaw tightened with rage, seemingly reliving his hell with the telling of his past. My heart ached for him and the pain I knew he must have endured.

"I fought for him." He shook his head and he rubbed his eyes. "I used every single cent I had left to fight for a kid that wasn't even mine, and I lost. I had no rights, no say. Apparently loving a kid for the first twelve months of his life doesn't mean shit to judges." He coughed out a laugh of disbelief.

"Can you believe she sat in that courtroom and laughed? She thought it was funny that I knew she had slept around, knew that Thomas wasn't my son and that I was still willing to raise him anyway. She laughed her ass off; confessed Thomas was my best friend's kid. Said she never loved me, that she just said the words. Because I was convenient."

"I can't believe someone could do that to another human being. Be so cruel." *I'm so sorry* I finished in my head, overwhelmed by the desire to hold him. My hands, like the rest of me, didn't try, scared that my touch wouldn't be welcomed. The back-off his body was screaming, loud and clear.

"Needless to say, the day of the court case I bought a used car and left town. Canada seemed far enough, so I sat in a bar and got messed up. Lucky for me it was the same bar the guys were playing in. Not sure if it was fate or some higher power that they found me, but they took me in and gave me a reason not to go home. Which was a plus, or I'd probably still be doing jail time right now.

"So yeah, it wasn't *just* that she cheated on me. It's not just something I can just get over. That vile excuse for a woman almost destroyed me. I gave her that power, married her and handed over my fucking heart. She used me so many times I lost count. So, yeah. I have a bunch of issues. Commitment and trust in relationships not a good experience for me."

"Jason, why didn't you tell me?" I struggled not to cry, wanting desperately to make it better, say something to change it.

"Why Angie, so I could have your fucking pity?" He stared at me with emotions I couldn't even define burning through his eyes. "You think it would have made it easier to be around me knowing how fucked up I was? You didn't need all that extra baggage in your life. I saw the way you looked at me. Like I was a decent guy, and I wanted you to believe the lie. I didn't want you to know any of this."

"But you *are* a decent guy." I finally stopped fighting the urge, my hand reaching out and touching his. "You fought for a kid that wasn't even yours."

"I should never have been with her." He pulled his hand out of mine and got up out of his chair. "Do you know how many people warned me about her? I didn't listen. The shit I put my family through, because of my *friends*, because of *her*. That's not a decent person. Open your eyes, Angie; I am *not* a decent person. She fucking destroyed me but I've owned what I've become. And that is not someone you should be around. You are too fucking perfect, and even on my best day I wouldn't deserve you."

It killed me. Jason unable to see what an amazing man he was, for him to feel like his past defined him. For him to think that he was undeserving of love.

"I'm not perfect." My head shook as the tears started to fall. It was too late, my leaky eyes deciding they had waited long enough. "You are all I ever wanted. I just wanted *you*."

"Oh hell, Angie." He kneeled down in front of me and wiped away my tears with his thumbs. "Well that's dumb." He gave me a sad smile. "Why would you want an asshole like me?"

"Because I love you, asshole. I tried not to, but that didn't work out so well." The tears continued to fall, any hope I had of stopping them long gone.

"Angie, all I seem to do is hurt you." He pulled me in close to his chest, his thumping heartbeat pounding just as fast as mine. "What if I can't change? What if I can't be anything other than this? I don't know that I can ever get married again. Kids? I just don't know that I can do that. It killed me to lose him, for me to say goodbye to a child I thought was mine. I can't ask someone I love to hang around on a maybe. I won't do that to you." His hand gently stoked my hair as my tears wet the front of his T-shirt.

"You love me?" My head jerked back in shock, the words almost knocking the wind out of me. My eyes tried desperately to focus despite the tears.

"Yeah, I love you. I always knew you were something special, Angie. Which is why I resisted sleeping with you for so long. I didn't want you to be just another girl for me. There was something so inherently good about you; I could tell that just in the time we spent together. And I just wanted to feel that, just once. I was selfish for wanting that, but I couldn't stop myself."

"But I'm not perfect. I'm not as good as you think I am. And I wanted to be with you."

"You are perfect. In every single way. That fact you can't see that makes me want to punch a hole in a wall. Look at you, you're beautiful. But that isn't even the half of it. You're so fucking talented, it's ridiculous. And so freaking smart. And that mouth of yours ... " He gentled thumbed my lips. "I love every single word that comes out of it."

"Then be with me. Take a chance with me."

I'd never begged a man in my life. In fact, begging for anything wasn't in my nature. It wasn't who I was; the idea frowned upon in my family. It wasn't in my make up to sit and hope something happened, I either made it happen or I moved on. And the only other time I begged for anything was for my mom not to die. For her to stay just a little longer with us. But I knew that my Pops had begged for the exact same thing so that made it okay. But, as Jason held me in his arms, I was begging. Begging that he gave us that chance. That I wouldn't lose the only man I'd ever really loved other than my dad. That he wouldn't walk out on me again.

"You deserve better. You deserve so much better." He kissed the top of my head, his arms tightly wrapped around me.

"No, you do."

It was as if my mouth had a mind of its own—which to be honest, it usually did—and it stopped talking and started kissing him. I knew the kiss wouldn't solve anything. It wouldn't take away his pain or mine. It wouldn't change the wasted years, the misunderstanding. But I needed to anyway. I needed to connect with him, to be closer to him than I already was. And right now, the only way I could do that was with my kiss. And I was going to kiss him for as long as he would let me.

"ANGIE, SWEETHEART." I PULLED AWAY FROM HER MOUTH, MY LIPS cursing me for the distance the minute I'd moved away. "You're making it hard for me to stop."

Sex shouldn't have even been on my radar. Hell, walking out and making sure I never made her cry the way she just did should have been my only priority. But her kissing me like that threw whatever ideas I had out the window. My cock didn't give a shit how inappropriate the timing was; it wanted her and only her.

"Then don't stop." She pulled me back against her. "Be with me and don't stop." She sucked against the skin at my throat as my hard-on kicked at the front of my jeans.

"Sex won't solve anything." By some miracle I was able to say something other than get your clothes off and let me bury myself inside of you. "I can't use you; I can't do it just because it feels good." My hands not listening to my mouth as they palmed her tits.

"Don't be with me because it solves anything; be with me because you want me." She clawed at my shirt, the fucking thing following her every command as she ripped it off my body.

"Angie, Troy is right outside that door. And it's not locked." My eyes flicked to the door the big guy was no doubt still standing behind. His words crystal clear that he wasn't going to be far in case we needed a referee.

"Then lock the door, but I don't care what he sees or hears. I want you, and I want you to be with me, now." Her fingers fumbled with the front of my jeans, my suggestion that we put the brakes on not even getting airtime.

"Look at me." I tipped her chin toward me so I could get a good look into those drop-dead gorgeous eyes. "No one gets to see or hear you like that. And there is nothing I want more than to be with you right now, but I can't do it and hurt you again."

"You aren't going to hurt me. I'm not asking you to give me forever, just be with me now."

Walk away is what my mind screamed. *Kiss her goodbye and leave her the fuck alone.* But I couldn't. It wasn't in me.

"Hell, I can't ever say no to you. I know I should, but I just can't." I grabbed her T-shirt and tore it from her body. "I want you. I've always wanted you." My mouth sucked against her skin, her bra getting in the way of what I wanted.

"Good, then take me because I want you, too." She rubbed her body against the front my jeans, my cock ready to give her whatever the hell she demanded.

The unlocked door got my attention for about a minute, and then I settled myself knowing if anyone came through that door I'd tear them limb from limb. No one would get to see her the way I did, naked and exposed with nothing but that fancy ink to cover her body. That was mine, and even though I had no claim to it, I wanted it tonight.

"Take them off." Her fingers clawed at my jeans, her effort to get them off not getting them further than my hips.

"Not here." I stood up, grabbing her ass and hauling her up with me. "I want you on the bed, so I can lay you out and look at you properly."

She didn't protest, just a quiet little moan as I ground my cock in that sweet spot between her legs before lifting her higher so I could carry her to her bed.

Unlike our hotel rooms, hers was basic. Which was convenient being that I only had to take five steps from the couch where we'd been situated, to her bed, which is where I needed us to be. The sheets were still unmade, the comforter hanging half way off the bed as I tossed her down on the mattress.

"This bra is pretty but it's blocking my view." My fingers got busy releasing the clasp from the back, the lace getting tossed aside the minute I was able.

"I want you naked, too." She pulled me down on the bed, scrambling up onto her knees before I had a chance to have any more play time.

"You wear the fuck out of these jeans, but I need you out of them." She yanked at the denim, encouraging me to lift my ass as she moved them down my legs.

"Now what's your grand plan, beautiful?" I lifted my head off the pillow and studied the bunched up jeans pooled at my feet, their journey off me and onto the floor being stopped by a pair of heavy, black boots.

"You think that's going to stop me from getting what I want?" She smirked, her eyes going straight to the bulge being housed in my boxers. "Mmm, I like to see you hard and know it's because of me."

"Christ, Angie, I just have to look at you and I get hard. You touching me just accelerates the process." My pulse worked overtime as I watched her lean down and lick the front of my boxers. "Fuck me." The words poured out of my mouth as she pulled down the fabric and swirled her tongue around the head of my cock. I had no hope of stringing together anything more coherent than cuss words and heavy breathing.

My hands fisted her hair as she sucked my shaft deeper into her mouth, her tongue tracing around my length before allowing it to pass between her lips. The action of licking and sucking driving me so crazy my lungs were having problems remember-ing how to function.

"Jesus, Angie. Slow down." I yanked on her hair, needing her to ease off the award winning blowjob or I was going to spill my load right into her mouth.

"You having a problem with control, asshole?" She flicked her tongue against the head of my dick one last time. "My mouth tempting you to come already?"

"Yes. I've told you how much I love that dirty fucking mouth."

It was my turn, my back jacking up off the mattress as I grabbed her waist. My mouth claimed hers while I toed off my boots and kicked off my jeans. My hands got busy with her jeans, Angie getting on the same page as she kicked off her heels and wriggled out of her pants. It felt like shit was moving in slow motion as we stripped down to just our underwear.

"You're still wearing too much." My eyes went from her beautiful naked tits to the lace that was still covering her pussy. "So unless you want me to tear them from your body, I suggest you get them off." My plan was for her panties to be off any way possible. Her way or mine, didn't faze me either way.

"You aren't naked either, smartass." Her short fingernails grazed just enough of my skin to sting, her attention not being on the material covering her body, but on the one covering mine.

Any thoughts I had went out the window, with just one remaining.

Her.

And I needed her in every sense of the word.

"That's better." She pushed the boxers far enough down my thighs that my cock was able to spring free, my hard-on hitting my stomach.

"Following instructions isn't a strong point for you, is it?" I finished the job of getting naked, getting rid of the boxers and tossed them to the floor.

"We were getting you naked." I grabbed at the side of those delicate panties and pulled, the fabric easily tearing away from her body. "Don't say I didn't warn you." The shredded panties swung playfully off one of my fingers before she even had a chance to realize she was bare.

"You're paying for those." She grinned and snatched them out of my hands.

"I'm just giving you what you wanted, and I'm not paying for shit." I grinned back, pushing her body down on the mattress so she was stretched out in front of me.

Every single curve of her body was a work of fucking art. The color that covered it just enhanced an already perfect canvas and I wanted to kiss every square inch of it. So rather than stare at her like a creepy asshole, my mouth got busy doing just that. Starting with her neck, then to the swell of her tits and then further down to her flat stomach. She mewled with approval as my mouth got creative, kissing or licking parts of her skin, my hands parting her thighs so I could see just how much she was ready for me.

"Jesus, Angie." My tongue moved along her pussy, her body more than ready to take me. "You get this wet from sucking my dick?"

"Yes," she moaned arching her back and lifting her body closer to my mouth.

"I want to taste you so bad but my cock is getting jealous." My fingers plunged into her as my lips moved to sucking her clit. "Very jealous." My mouth hummed against her skin as I continued to lick in between her legs.

"Yes." Her fingers dug into my shoulders as I watched her come apart, getting her there not taking very long with the finger and tongue combo I was working.

"That feel good, Angie?" I kissed the inside of her thigh while her pussy tightened against my fingers. "That what you needed?" I couldn't bring myself to stop, seeing her writhe underneath me as the orgasm I provided echoed through her body.

"You want more validation, you egomaniac, or you finally going to take me?"

There was no more thinking involved. The game I had been playing, teasing the pleasure out of her, was no longer fun as I moved up her body and sunk my cock into her. It was automatic, our bodies coming together like they belonged. I'd been fighting it for so long that the minute she'd given me permission I couldn't stop. Her lips kissing my throat while I slid into her, dragging my length out before pushing back inside of her. It was heaven.

It felt so good.

Too good.

Which is exactly what made me stop, my body freezing mid stroke as I realized I wasn't wearing a condom.

"Fuck." My elbows dug into the mattress as I scrambled to pull out. "Angie, I'm not wearing anything."

"It's ok. I have that thing in my arm. I can't get pregnant." She locked her legs around me, stopping me from pulling out all the way.

"I don't think it's a good idea." The thought of accidently getting her pregnant enough to make me break out into a cold sweat.

"Look." She stretched out her arm and wriggled her fingers around on it. "You can see it just below my skin. Jason, I'm not going to trap you. I'm not her." Her hand reached up and gently stroked the edge of my jaw.

The fact she felt she had to prove it just about broke my heart. That I had moved her to a place where she thought I questioned her motives. I trusted her completely—big call coming from me—and deep down, I knew that Angie would never do what Em had done. But going bare wasn't just about me; it was about protecting her as well. And that right there was more important to me than anything.

More important than protecting myself—both physically and mentally.

"I know you aren't, I just don't want to do anything you don't want to." My brain not convinced we shouldn't be pulling out and getting suited up before continuing down this road.

"Look at me. I'm clean and you get tested, right?" Her hand moved down my neck and across my shoulder. Her fingertips tingling my skin in their wake.

"Yes of course, I've never had sex without a condom except … well except for her and you." I couldn't bring myself to say her name. She had gotten enough of a mention.

"Let go, Jase." Angie strained her neck to kiss me, her lips only making it as far as my pecs. "I promise nothing bad will happen. Trust me." She kissed my skin trying to coax me back.

"It's me I don't trust." My body took over from my brain as I slowly slid back inside of her. "It's me."

There was no more talking; the fast paced fucking had also stopped. Our bodies found a slower rhythm as I moved against her, feeling every inch of my length fill her before pulling out again. The skin-on-skin contact making it harder to hold out while my body welcomed the delicious torture.

She tilted her hips, joining me in every thrust as I watched myself sliding inside of her bare. It wasn't going to last much longer, her tight pussy fisting me each time I slid inside her wet, hot center. Every second seemed to drag out, and yet not nearly long enough.

Her hand reached down between us, alternating between touching herself and cupping my balls, the sensation sending me so close to the edge I couldn't see straight.

"I'm coming," she breathed as her body convulsed underneath me, my ability to hold back voided as the pulsing sensation traveled against the length of my cock. Her orgasm chasing down mine as she came apart while I watched.

"Angie." My body shook as I erupted, my load spilling into her as my arms gave way and I all but collapsed onto her. My out of control breathing matched hers as I kissed her neck and tried to push myself back onto my elbows.

"No, stay like that." Her arms wrapped around me, holding me against her body. Her arms strained in the effort to stop me from lifting off.

"I'll crush you." I pulled away, worried I was going to hurt or break her, her tiny frame dwarfed by my massive body.

"You already did, and I survived." She blinked, her arms trying to coax me back. "I need to feel you on me. To make sure this is real."

Hearing her say that just made me hate myself even more. Knowing what I put her through, knowing what I continued to put her through, made me want to drive a knife through my own heart.

"I'm sorry." I buried my head against the curve of her neck.

"Don't be sorry, just please don't leave me right now. I promise I won't pressure you, but don't run from me, Jase." Her hands gently strummed my back.

"I can't make promises, Angie. I want to, but I can't." My voice vibrated against her skin and I wished to God I had something better to offer her than that. I wouldn't lie to her though, never again would I do that. Even if the truth wasn't pretty.

I lifted my head, and while my lips were pissed off they were no longer on her skin, my eyes were treated to the most spectacular view of her smile. There was no hesitation in her voice as she looked up at me.

"Then don't. I don't need promises, I just need you."

"WHAT DID HE SAY?" MY BODY AUTOMATICALLY NUZZLED AGAINST Jason's the minute he'd climbed back into my bed. It's where we both wanted to be—my body and I—my brain still wasn't convinced any of what we were doing was a good idea.

"I think the towel around my waist was a tip-off we weren't trying to kill each other. He also mentioned that if he didn't hear my name screamed by you ever again, it would be too soon. But he didn't say much else other than giving me a don't-fuck-this-up look or two. He's probably just glad he doesn't have to jump in between us." His arms wrapped around me as he kissed my forehead. Those kisses I hoped would never stop.

Things had been said. Things that would forever change the way I saw Jason. But not in the way he thought they would. He was worried about how I would have reacted to the news. But all his past did was prove to me what a remarkable man he was, and validated what I had always known. It's why I loved him, and why I knew I would love him forever. He was a fighter. He was exactly the man for me.

The sex hadn't been the plan, but my body took over and it was a connection we both seemed to need. Who was I to argue?

Troy waiting for us had been unfortunate. Some prior planning before we got naked would have been better, to let the poor guy off the hook. Maybe give him a heads up that we were all good now, and were going to have sex so he didn't have to stand outside and wait. That would have been the polite thing to do. Sadly, manners were the furthest thing from our minds.

"I could have gone out and told him, you know." My lips showered his arms with kisses. They were such strong, capable arms. They definitely deserved their own Tumblr.

"If you think there was any chance of me letting you get out of this bed and talk to Troy naked, you're even more delusional than I first thought." He pulled me closer to his body, and I felt his smile against my skin.

"Firstly, you don't get to *let me* do anything." I poked him in the chest for good measure. "If you think you, or anyone else, has any control over me then you are the one who is *delusional.*" My fingers did the little air quotes for delusional just for extra effect. "Secondly, Troy is like a brother to me. He would never look at me that way even if he wasn't happily married with a baby on the way, which he is. So. Yeah. You're wrong." My arms folded across my chest as I smiled.

"So quick to be defensive," Jason laughed. "Firstly, I would never tell you what you can *or* can't do. I'm not feeling suicidal. Well, at least not today. And secondly, I wasn't worried about Troy seeing you that way. I was worried about myself. Seeing you stride to that door naked, no way in hell I wouldn't have my hands all over you. I didn't think Troy would appreciate the show. So my statement was less about *you*, and more about my self-preservation." He pulled me closer, nipping at my shoulder.

I promised I wouldn't push, not when I knew why Jason had been so resistant in the first place. And as far as reasons go, his were pretty good ones. Even though I would never do what *she* had done, I wasn't going to start demanding stuff either.

I was going to let him go.

If he came back to me, then I would know. If he didn't then it's not because he didn't want me but because he couldn't be with anyone.

It would still be the most epic of heartaches but that was old news for me. I'd been through it once or twice before. For me, it was worth the risk.

So I kicked him out of my room, telling him I needed to get ready for Megs and Ash's arrival. Which was the truth. But also gave us that time away too.

Here I was, letting him go.

"Hey you!" Megs grabbed me and pulled me into a hug, her belly noticeably bigger. "In the interest of full disclosure, I know everything. But I'm going to need to hear it again because Troy Harris sucks when it comes to gossip. I love the man, but he isn't great with details. Oh well, it's my reassurance that he is still human." She barely took a breath as she pulled away from me and gave me a look over. "You look thinner. Ash, has she lost weight, or is it just because I'm like gigantacon now?"

"Megs, gigantacon isn't a word and even if it was, you aren't." Ash smiled before taking her turn to hug me. "Hey Angie, ignore her. Megs is getting crazier with each passing month."

"I've missed you both, and all your crazy." My arms wrapped around both of them. Happily accepting the affection. It wasn't even weird that I welcomed it.

"So," Megs smiled, her eyebrow arching in question, "you still having accidents with his penis?" She slowly eased into a chair.

"Yeah, but were taking things slow. I'm not expecting anything. There is a lot that he went through, shit I will never understand and he needs time. Maybe we won't make it anyway, but I'm not walking away and not pressuring him."

"What do you mean you're not expecting anything? Like he's not making a commitment, and you are just going to hang around and wait? Get Jason down here right now so I can kick his ass." Megs tried unsuccessful to leap out of the chair, with her attempt ending up a weird wiggling display. "The minute I get up, I'm going to kick his ass." She pushed against the armrest of the chair and slowly righted herself on her feet.

"You don't need to do that. I'm fine with the way things are." A calm floated over me in a way it hadn't before. Either way, this time I knew I was going to be fine.

"Well that's the most important thing, right, Megs?" Ash tried her best to play peacekeeper, even if she didn't seem to buy it herself.

"I know you don't understand; I don't expect you to. And maybe when this is all said and done, I will totally regret this." I took a deep breath. I'd said it all in my head a million times, and if ever I was going to talk about this with someone other than Jase, these two were who I'd confide in. "But I know that I can't walk away. I've tried unsuccessfully for years to forget him and I keep coming back. It's where I need to be, and hopefully, he'll come to the same conclusion. If not, well at least we tried, right? That has to be better than nothing at all."

"Sounds to me like he doesn't know how lucky he is." Megs slunk back into the chair she had so passionately tried to get out of, hopefully shelving all ideas of confronting Jase and attempting to kick his ass. Pregnant or not, I didn't doubt she would do it.

"We're both lucky."

This wasn't just about Jason. It was about me and my own unhealthy outlook. My idea that loving meant desertion, and that I'd deny myself the chance. It didn't matter if he left. If there were a hundred men that left after him. I wanted to love and I wanted to be loved, and I wasn't going to be scared of it anymore. I would stand out on the edge of the cliff and whatever was going to happen would happen. And it would be enough.

"You know, *all* relationships have their ups and downs." Ash gently touched my hand. "And if it's the right one, it's worth fighting for."

"Thanks. I know this is the right one." In fact I'd never been surer of anything in my life. "I love him and he loves me too. And I'm going to play this out, and if it all ends in tears, I'll still have you two, Rusty and the band."

And most importantly myself.

I am woman, hear me roar, right?

"Hey, we should find Rusty a nice girl." Megs immediately got distracted at the mention of Rusty. "He doesn't have a girlfriend, does he? He's gorgeous too. I can't believe you've never gone there with him."

"Megs, don't." Ash laughed, neither of us holding much hope of convincing Megs no one needed a relationship doctor.

"Fine. You people spoil all my fun."

I was going to wait. And while I waited, I was going to love him beyond measure and let him love me, too. Because I'd rather love him now and have an uncertain forever, than give up now for definite heart break.

The road.

No matter what happened with us, some things didn't stop. The revolving door of cities and stadiums were constant. Planes, buses, cars and hotel rooms, they were also on high rotation. And we continued to exist in the snow globe of the insanity, every day a new shake up yet still things stayed the same.

I watched him from the bathroom. His keyboard splayed on the bed as he played that tune he sometimes did. It was simple and beautiful even though he said it was nothing special. To my ears, there was nothing more perfect.

"I thought the *watching* thing was mine?" His head twisted to see me in the doorway. "You want to come sit in my lap and help me play?" His fingers didn't stop moving even though he wasn't looking at them.

"Ha. Too much going on there for my liking. I'll stick to the guitar, I like an instrument I can get my hand around." The double entendre intentional.

My body moved away from the doorway and found itself in his lap. A place my body often liked to be.

"Really? You're going to say that to me when there is a bed in the vicinity?" His eyes darted to the mussed up sheets, his response completely predictable.

I flipped him off which was also predictable, but I did it with a grin. Service with a smile was in such a decline, I felt it was my duty to do my part. You know, so he knew I cared.

Of course this earned me a flashing smile in return, which I loved. Jason had always had such a great smile, and I was glad we'd seen more of it these days.

"So, you given any more thought to your encores? I miss your little odes to me." One of his hands continued to play while the other tiptoed up my arm, his grin getting bigger.

"Aww. You feeling neglected, Jase? Missing me calling you an asshole?"

Despite our situation going back to sort of normal, my finale songs had stayed sidelined. Firstly, because there was no further need for the fuck you's and secondly, it was really fucking hard learning a different new song every night. Even if they were usually easy, over-played pop songs that didn't usually have more than four chord progressions, it was still a feat. It had been fun while it lasted, but we had both moved on, its purpose well and truly served. We, like the songs, had moved to another place and going back wasn't an option.

"You know." His arm moved causing my body to dip, my mouth spontaneously letting out a squeak as my head flew back. "You could sing songs about all the orgasms I'm giving you. That might be fun. I'll even help you compile the list."

His head bowed down to meet mine, kissing my exposed neck.

"Nope, no one wants to hear about that." I wiggled in his arms. "Besides, why tell the people about all the orgasms *you* won't be giving *them*. Think Jason, that's just plain mean." His laugh matching mine while he continued to kiss me.

I loved him like this. Playful, happy—mine. The edginess was still there but it had evened out, and for the most part he was different. And he was either trying really hard or he'd changed, either way massive progress had been made.

"I love you," he whispered in my ear, both his hands completely given up on the keyboard as they solely focused on me. My body still tilted, the angle making the blood rush to my head.

"I love you, too," I whispered back, my hand tracing the line of his jaw.

And that's where it would usually end, the conversation about us or love.

Most of the time it would go back to playful, a throwback to our earlier days of name calling and mild teasing, the bad intentions completely gone.

Sometime I'd catch him studying me, like he was now. His eyes scanning my entire face, like he was waiting for me to say something. What for, I wasn't sure. So I'd usually just whisper another I love you and it would usually be enough.

And it was enough.

I'D EXPECTED AN ULTIMATUM.

The *we're-either-together-or-I'm-done*, but it never came.

A week.

It had been a whole week since the showdown in Angie's room and I'd told her everything. Told her about Em, told her about Thomas. Told her how fucked up I had been.

She hadn't left.

She hadn't demanded shit.

She hadn't tried to push the issue.

Not even a little, which blew my freaking mind. Buttons and Angie, they were like a done deal. But this one just didn't happen.

Then the next week came, and the week after that. Same thing. Status quo was maintained. We were as together as we ever were going to get. Back to spending our nights together, back to me being unable to be away from her. It was a sickness and one I didn't want a cure from.

Still, not a fucking word.

It had to be killing her. The limbo, wondering if all of a sudden I was going to turn around and bail. Who sticks around on a possibility? No one. Except the one girl who said that's what she was going to do, and regardless of how difficult it was, she was keeping her word. And if she could do that, then I knew whatever fucked up crap I had rolling around in my head wasn't going to land with us.

I loved Angie. I loved her enough to know there was never going to be another girl. And I sure as hell wasn't letting her go and have some other guy take her. Not freaking happening. It wasn't even about marriage; it was knowing that I couldn't be without her.

Forever.

It was the first time I'd been able to think about that word and not need a fifth of vodka chaser. And I wanted the forever with her. I wanted her to be my wife, for that word to mean something for the first time in my life. I'd been running a really long time and I didn't want to run anymore. I wanted to stand still with her. And I wanted to have a million fucking kids, too. But only if she was their mother. I just knew it would be different, and I would take that jump if she was willing to go with me.

She was still too good for me, but like Dan had said not so long ago—if she was willing to give me that chance, then I'd applaud her lack of judgment. I was going to marry her and I was going to spend the rest of my days loving her the way she deserved.

"Hey." I took a seat at the table, everyone already situated and waiting. My message had been ambiguous. The let's-meet-to-discuss-a-new-tune usually came from Alex or James, still they all showed up ready to hear me out.

"Hey." Troy gave me a nod, the bastard losing sleep over the fact his wife was getting close to popping out a baby soon.

The other hey's or hi's came soon after, each of the guys giving me a tip of the chin, ready to get this show on the road.

"I'm going to need a favor."

There was no point dragging it out more than it had to be. Asking for help wasn't something that came easy for me, but this was something that I couldn't do on my own.

"Of course, brother. Whatever you need." James tapped me on the shoulder, his unwavering support not unexpected but still floored me.

"All good here." Alex agreed before even hearing what I was

asking.

"Yep, same goes with me." Troy nodded, throwing his stamp of approval on my ask just like the other two.

"I'm down as well." Dan's smile settled in as he folded his arms across his chest. "Looks like we're all on the same page."

"You've all agreed without even knowing what I need?"

"Doesn't matter what it is, you're asking for it. If it's something you need, that's enough." Troy tapped on the table, affirmative grunts coming from the others.

If there were ever any doubts that my life had been saved that day in the bar, they had very much been put to bed. Total game changer. That I got to work with these men was an honor—that I got to call them friends ... fuck, that was a lottery win. That knowing them led me to Angie, yeah. Some guys just get more than their fair share of luck. And looking around this room, knowing the girl I have waiting on me, I've more than exceeded my share.

"Our last song, I need it to be this." I handed them each a sheet of paper with the title and artist of what I wanted our finale to be. It wasn't one of ours.

"Um, okay," James laughed. "We haven't done a cover in years but yeah, I'm cool."

"Ha. Nice," Alex agreed. "Yep. That isn't a hard ask."

"Your sudden need to do a cover have anything to do with a certain front woman?" Troy smirked cupping the back of my neck. "Guess we're playing a cover."

"What?" Dan looked up from the paper I'd handed him. "No fucking way. Pick something else." The paper dropped from his hands to the table like the thing was carrying a disease. "We're not playing that."

"Dan, it has to be this," I insisted, bending on the song choice not an option. I'd play it and sing it myself if I had to, but it had to be that one song.

"Why the hell would we want to play that?" Dan screwed up his face in disgust. "Did you leave your fucking balls in a purse somewhere? Or did you fucking hit your head on the way over, because there will be a cold day in Hell before I will ever play *that.*" The paper got his attention again as he pointed at it accusingly. Seemed Dan wasn't going to be so down with my plan after all.

"The song isn't that bad, Dan," Alex weighed in, no doubt hoping to try and smooth things over.

"Not that bad of a song?" Dan shot Alex a horrified look like the dude had suddenly grown another head. "Fuck me, sideways. Someone get Lexi on the horn right now and tell her that her husband has dumbass disease."

"Dan, c'mon. It's for Angie."

The full reason of why we'd be rocking a tune that wasn't our own being spotlighted in case everyone hadn't already joined the dots. "She used the covers at the end of her set as a message, and as fucked up as they sometimes used to be, it's the only way I know how to say what I need to say. This is the way I need to say it."

She might have started it, her game of musical clues, but I was most definitely finishing it. There were things I needed to say and this was a way I knew she would understand.

"Well say it with some other fucking song. What about that Bruno Mars, he's a smooth motherfucker. Choose something of his. Better yet, we'll write one for her. James, get a piece of paper and let's knock something out real quick. What can be better than getting her own song? She'll cream her pants for sure." Dan pushed back, the song choice unorthodox because we were a rock band.

The minutes ticked over. Dan glaring at the page like it was going to suddenly spit in his eye while I reinforced there wasn't a back-up plan. This was it.

"It's not about her creaming her pants, and it can't be another song." My finger drummed nervously on the desk. "Just this. Dan, I need to do this."

"You look at me, you fucking tell me you love that girl." Dan reached across the table and got up in my grill, his face fucking fierce. "Then you tell me there will never be another girl for you. Because I can tell you right now, you're only getting a pass like this one fucking time."

"I love her," I said with zero hesitation.

Absolutely none. She was it and I wasn't afraid to fess to it either. Angie was mine and I was hers even without the formalities, but it was about time we took care of them anyway. "There will never be anyone else. It's her. I need her." I took a swallow as I met each of my brothers in the eye. "And I'm going to ask her to marry me and hopefully, if I'm lucky enough, she'll say yes. Because there is no way I can live without her."

Dan blew out a breath as he weighed my words. "Motherfucker."

"Yep." I nodded, meaning every single word I'd said.

No one talked, my intentions for Angie just hanging there in the air. Me ever getting married again was a bet that no one would ever take. They'd assumed I'd eventually settle down with someone and do the living in sin thing. But me putting a ring on someone's finger, again—that was the equivalent to an apocalyptic prediction. Funny that me getting married was once rated on par with the end of the world, and in my eyes—used to be one in the same.

"I love her. I need her to be my wife. And this is the way I need to ask," I repeated. Not because I thought they hadn't heard me but because I couldn't stop saying it. I may have been late to the party but I sure as hell was here now. Going anywhere else wasn't happening any time soon.

"One time." Dan broke the silence first, clocking me with a look I knew meant business. "We do this song, one fucking time, so you better make sure she's watching." He shook his head as he agreed, giving my plan the final green light.

"One time." I met his eyes, my smile finally making an appearance. "I promise it's all I need."

Dan bucked out a laugh, the bastard slamming his fist down onto the table. "Well, hold on to your fucking hats boys because Power Station are about to play Taylor fucking Swift."

I'd never been nervous about a show. Not even close. And yet with every song that we got closer to the end, I felt like I was going to puke. Public displays of affection weren't my thing either; as for putting my ass on the line in front of thousands of people, let's chalk that up to never. But tonight wasn't about me. Thank Christ the audience wouldn't know the whole story, other than Power Station losing their minds and playing a pop song. The headlines it was no doubt going to attract—epic. The care factor on that—nonexistent.

"Yo, you ready to do this thing?" Dan leaned over my keys, his fingers glued to his fret board ready to play.

"As ready as I'll ever be." I looked over to the side of the stage where Angie was standing, her appearance there guaranteed by Rusty. "Let's do it."

"You realize if she says no, we just played Taylor Swift for nothing. I'm pretty sure I'm going to have to insist she says yes just on principle." Dan smirked, his eyes looking over to an amused Angie who had no idea why glances were suddenly being shot in her direction.

"I'm hoping she won't say no, but if she does, you'll shut your mouth and be grateful I'm not making you play Miley Cyrus." I mouthed I love you to Angie as James hit the mic, ready to announce the song.

"We have a special request tonight." His voice barely audible over the noise from the crowd. "But before we play this last song we want to thank you for being on this road with us. We never thought we'd be lucky enough to still be here so many years later, doing what we love and getting to call it a job. We're here because you put us here and it's a fucking honor to play for you. So as we wrap up tonight, know this isn't goodbye but see you later. We love you and you'll always be with us." The thunderous applause reached ear-bleeding proportions.

"So here we go; this song goes out to a special someone. You know who you are." James looked to Troy who counted us in with the sticks.

The opening notes of "Love Story" started and the crowd hushed into a confused calm of silence. Like Angie had done with her renditions, we had put our own spin on it, but there was no denying what the song was. The words James was singing slightly changed so he didn't sound like he was looking to seduce a dude. Dan's insistence, and I didn't disagree.

It was a song, written by a teenage girl comparing her first love to one of the greatest stories of all time.

Romeo and Juliet.

The words were cheesy and not at all my speed. In fact, I hated it. But it told a story of how the young couple tried to keep away and couldn't. And unlike the Shakespearian play, those two lovebirds didn't end up with matching headstones, which is always a plus. Instead Romeo pops the question, down on one knee after asking her daddy's blessing. Just like I had. Only I wasn't on one knee on account I still need to play.

Angie's mouth dropped open as the significance of those lyrics hopefully came to light. Either that or she really hated Taylor Swift, in which case I was SOL. It didn't matter, whether she said yes or no, I needed to say what I needed to say.

We'd been trying to keep away long enough. Fighting a love that had threatened to break us both, but the only real love either of us ever had known. It was where we both belonged; we'd just taken the scenic route to get there.

It got to the part of the song I was waiting for, my chance. And as James screamed out the lyrics, I mouthed, "Marry me, Angie." My eyes nailed directly on hers as she watched, her tears already flowing thick and fast.

There was no indication on how she was going to respond, the rest of the song playing out as she stood on the side of the stage and cried. Rusty held her so she didn't fall, her body seeming to have trouble staying vertical. And I wanted off that stage and her in my arms more than I wanted my next breath.

As the last cord sung through the amp, we took our place on the stage and waved a quick good bye. Usually I'd stay a little longer and bask in the adulation, but there was only one person whose approval I needed and that was the girl who I was heading toward.

"Angie." I ignored Rusty completely and pulled her out of his arms. "I love you, marry me."

She didn't answer, her beautiful eyes flooded with tears as she looked back at me. The fear crept up on me slowly that maybe I'd missed my chance.

"It doesn't have to be right now. Fuck knows you waited long enough for me. I'll wait forever if I have to. And that is a promise that I have no problem making. Forever, Angie. That's what I want. That's what I'm asking you for." My mouth couldn't stop talking, needing to tell her how dumb I had been.

"My baggage still exists, and I'm still fucked up. But I know that if I don't have you then me being destroyed again is a certainty. I'd rather have twelve months of happiness with you and the most epic breakup of all mankind than go the next twelve years without you. And I swear I will never hurt you again, I'll —"

"Shut up, asshole." She covered my mouth with her hands, stopping it from spewing words that it needed to say. "I love you." She slowly moved her hand away and smiled. "Yes. I'll marry you, but on one condition."

"Anything, name it." The words couldn't shoot out of my mouth fast enough. "Whatever it is. You've got it."

"Neither of us ever play another Taylor Swift song again." The smile slowly spread across her lips.

"Halle-fuckin-luiah!" Dan called from behind us, the fact that I'd been doing this with an audience just now coming to light.

I laughed, looking around at the people around us. Their faces an easy read on how happy they were for us. Even Angie's band seemed fucking ecstatic, Rusty shaking my free hand while the other was still around my girl. That was the other thing, my girl. Looking into her eyes I knew I'd been saved all over again. Not because this was a relationship, because it wasn't. She was more than that, just like the band wasn't just a band. Both of them were so much more.

This was my family.

"Yeah, let's stick to originals from here on out." My mouth found its mark on hers. "It's time for a new soundtrack."

EPILOGUE

Angie

"LOOK AT YOU, BARE FOOT AND PREGNANT. I'M STILL REELING FROM the shock." Rusty wrapped his arms around me, my swollen belly stopping him from giving me a proper hug.

"We're sitting beside a pool, dumbass, of course I'm going to be in bare feet." My hand playfully slapped him across the chest. It had only been a couple of weeks since we'd seen each other, but somehow in that time I'd ballooned to waddle size. That there was a tiny human growing in my body was still a sense of wonderment.

"Rusty, you better not be upsetting my wife. I like you, and I don't want to have to rearrange your face." Jase's arms found their way around me; it's where they usually were when he was around. Which he was a lot since our wedding fourteen months ago.

"Easy there, *GI Joe*. I've told you people a million times, I'm a lover not a fighter." Rusty reached out his hand to Jase, the handshake evolving into some manly hug.

"Hey, Rus." James lifted a cold beer from the cooler and handed it to Rusty. "Good of you to make it."

"Well it's not often I'm summoned to the Power Station compound." Rus looked around at the lofty Bowden mansion, kids squealing in the pool beside us. "Besides, I haven't met Briana yet.

Figure two birds, one stone and all of that." The easy smile spread across his face.

"Ha, you think Dan is going to let you anywhere near his daughter? Oh this I've got to see." Troy wandered over, his year-old son, Evan, hanging off his dad's arm like he was a jungle gym. "Hey buddy, how about you let daddy say hi to Uncle Rusty?" He reached down and scooped up the boy who had somehow managed to win the genetic lottery of both his mother's and his father's good looks. "Mama," Evan demanded, missing Megs, who was already back to work and would be joining us for dinner later.

"I've been around kids before. It's not like I'd drop her or anything." Rusty shrugged, not having seen Dan in action since his little girl had come into the world two months ago.

"Drop her?" Alex laughed, adjusting Grace's goggles so she could cannon ball into the pool with Noah and Jesse. "The only way anyone gets to hold that kid is if he is either out of the country or sedated. It's hysterical; I cannot wait until she starts dating." He laughed, kissing the top of his daughter's head as she ran off to join her mother in the pool. Lexi and I were sporting matching bumps, her due date three weeks before mine.

"Yeah, well as long as you keep recording, you can pop out as many kids as you want. Although Jase, I hope you give my front woman a break every now and again, we're going to need her for a tour in six months." Rus took his seat on the poolside chair, Hannah waving to him as she carried out a huge platter of cut fruit.

"Yep, tour still goes ahead." Jason smiled, "I'm going to enjoy being backstage for a change." He took his seat on the huge patio couch, pulling me into his lap as he did so. The fact that I could barely fit obviously escaping his attention.

"So, what's the deal? Other than the reunion, you must have a reason for calling me out here." Rusty eased back into his chair, his smile fixed on Troy who was still wrestling with Evan, and took a slow slip of his beer. "I have to admit, I'm more than a little curious."

"Rus, they have a proposition for us. I know Joey and Max will agree to anything as long as they get to play, but I wanted to talk it over with you before we took it to the band." My nerves had been shot all morning, James and Alex's suggestion still tossing around in my head.

"Angie, last time Power Station had a proposition for us we ended up on a massive tour and you came home with a husband. Seeing as you're already knocked up, not sure how much more they can offer us. I'm not having anyone's baby if that's what's on the table."

"Hey, did I miss anything?" Dan waltzed in, baby sling wrapped tightly around his chest, his arms free to carry a diaper bag in one hand and hold his wife's waist with the other. It was multitasking at its finest.

"Nope, just about to start." James directed him to an empty chair.

"Hey, Angie." Ash gave me a wave. "Hey babe, why don't you give me Briana so you can have your meeting." She turned her attention to Dan who had already taken his seat, the sleeping kid attached to him not seeming to hinder him in anyway.

"Got it, babe. She's fine with me. Go relax, I'll call you if she needs to be fed."

"You know you are going to eventually have to loosen up your grip, right? You can't hold her forever." Ash laughed, her smile hinting it was probably not the first time she'd argued the point.

"Ash, stop saying stuff you know is going to upset me." He waved off his wife, his hand instinctively wrapping around his daughter.

"She's pretty." Rusty peered over the swaddling at a sleeping Briana. "Definitely takes after her mother."

"Yeah she sure does." Dan looked down at her and smiled. "Which is why I'm letting no one near her. I'm actually going to build a bunker. I saw some shit on Doomsday Preppers. They are all batshit crazy, but some of their ideas I can work with."

"Okay, so other than certifying Dan for an institution, why am I here again?" Rusty looked around confused. The circus that was Power Station a lot crazier than our own band.

"They want to sign us," I blurted out, not able to hold back any longer. The fact it had been suggested days ago and I still hadn't said anything was a miracle in itself.

"We got a deal, weren't those fancy papers we signed twelve months ago a record contract? I know I'm not as smart as you, but I seemed to remember reading record label somewhere on them." Rusty rubbed his chin, the sarcasm dripping from his voice.

"Yes, we signed a deal but you said it yourself, the control they had was a pain in the ass. You hate that they choose which singles get released. You even hate the cover they made us shoot." The romantic notion of being signed didn't live up to the hype. As an unknown quantity we had very little control over much. We were able to fight any creative changes but other than that, it was sit down, shut up and let the big boys do what they needed to do. We didn't do so well with the directive, but the paycheck they'd already paid us meant we had to at least pretend to play nice.

"Well yeah, I hated it. Other than getting our shit out to a wider audience. It blows donkey's balls. So what exactly are you suggesting?"

"We're starting our own label," James interrupted, itching to get Rusty on board. "We're all married with kids, and while we aren't ready to hang it all up just yet, we're looking to the future. Music is always going to be our thing and we've learned a thing or two about what to do and what not to do. What better way to help promote emerging talent than to produce it and help get it out there—the right way. Without all the suit and tie bullshit."

"So how are *you* going to be different to the New York heavyweights we're dealing with now? No offense dude, but it's been a while since you were *emerging*." Rusty took another swallow of his beer, in no hurry to sign another deal.

"Because we'll give you creative control. Ash is coming on board as our business manager. Lexi will deal exclusively with our clients. Hannah will work with client relations. This will be a family-run set up, and we know how important family is. We'll buy out your current deal, you sign to us and we work with you, not you working for us."

"Why? It can't be for the money." Rusty asked the exact same questions I asked. The sudden shift from musicians or businessmen not immediately clear.

"The band was never about the money for us, we just wanted to do what we did." Alex nodded to James, taking his opportunity to turn on the charm. "But if it's one thing we learned from the last tour—and having you guys on the road with us—Trust, loyalty, integrity—that is shit you can't buy, and it's missing from our industry in a big way. Thankfully not everyone has sold out. We're going to find those guys and pay it forward."

"This is a good thing, Rusty. Our next album could be our own." The baby in my belly kicked, obviously concurring with my decision. "They are giving us the keys to the car, we drive it how we want."

"Alright," Rusty nodded looking around at the mayhem that was surrounding us. "Yeah, let's drive."

It was a stark difference from the boardroom we'd been in when we signed our first deal. The impersonal handshakes and cookie-cutter secretaries, a world away from five guys who had a dream and made it happen. And that's what it all came down too, having a dream and seeing it through, even if you tripped along the way.

"You okay?" Jase asked, his hand going to the part of my belly where junior was practicing field goals. The tiny kicks making me marvel at how far we'd all come.

"Yeah, it took us a while but I think everything is finally okay."

ACKNOWLEDGEMENTS

This was the series that made me believe that I could write full time and follow my heart into the pages. It wouldn't have been possible without my extremely supportive family. Thanks for everything Gep, Jenna, Liam and Woodley—you let me jump off the cliff and believed that I would fly.

Thanks to my amazing support team of extended family, valued friends and trusted consigliere (Wait! Wrong acknowledgements. Disregard the last part and the Horse head in the bed . . . nothing to see her folks.) Best Cheerleaders around.

Special thanks to my beta team, there were a few who contributed to this series and they were all valued. Amy, Terri, Maz and MK.

Thank you to the authors who have become good friends or are kind enough to not call the cops for my stalking. Lili Saint Germain, JB Hartnett, Monica James, Skyla Madi, CJ Duggan, Lilliana Andersen, Rachael Brookes, JD Nixon, Natasha Preston, Kirsty Mosely, Jane Harvey-Berrick, Ker Dukey, LA Casey, Jill Patten, Kelly Elliot, Tillie Cole, Andie Long, Abbi Glines, Chantal Fernando, Helena Hunting, Christina Hobbs and Lauren Billings, Penelope Louleas, Jay Crownover, Kim Karr, SC Stephens, Joanna Wylde and Kylie Scott—and to anyone I've left out, I'm sorry.

Hang Le—I bow to your greatness.

Thank you to the bloggers and blogs who have and continue to support me. I see your love, shares and shout outs and it honestly just makes my heart full. You make my world go around and your support is appreciated beyond measure. If you were with me from the start of new to the ride, a million thank you.

Thanks to the T Gephart Entourage! I love our little group of awesome.

Thanks to my Fictionally Yours, Melbourne team. Penny Rudge, no words, just hashtags. #Epic #ShutUpAndWrite #WordWizard #GifQueen #DanceOff #GetYourProtection #BurnTheSage.

Thanks to my editor, Marion Archer (High Strung). It was fleeting, but I learned a lot.

Thanks to my editor Nichole Strauss, from Perfectly Publishable. (Crash Ride and Back Stage) Ahhhhhhh what can I even say? Fate has a strange way of making sure the right people meet, it was meant to be. Thank you for everything, you have truly helped me beyond measure.

Thank you to my proofreaders for picking up pesky mistakes.

Thanks to Max Henry from Max Effect. I don't know what I'd ever do without you. Awesome writer, awesome formatter, awesome friend.

And lastly, a MASSIVE thanks to my readers who wanted the stories of Dan, Troy and Jason. This was a journey I'll never forget, it taught me so much about myself and what I am capable of. I am continually humbled and honoured by your support and promise that it will never be taken for granted. You are the real rock stars and I'm here right now giving you a standing ovation.

ABOUT THE AUTHOR

T Gephart is an indie author from Melbourne, Australia.

T's approach to life has been somewhat unconventional. Rather than going to University, she jumped on a plane to Los Angeles, USA in search of adventure. While this first trip left her somewhat underwhelmed and largely depleted of funds it fueled her appetite for travel and life experience.

With a rather eclectic resume, which reads more like the fiction she writes than an actual employment history, T struggled to find her niche in the world.

While on a subsequent trip the United States in 1999, T met and married her husband. Their whirlwind courtship and interesting impromptu convenience store wedding set the tone for their life together, which is anything but ordinary. They have lived in Louisiana, Guam and Australia and have traveled extensively throughout the US. T has two beautiful young children and one four legged child, Woodley, the wonder dog.

An avid reader, T became increasingly frustrated by the lack of strong female characters in the books she was reading. She wanted to read about a woman she could identify with, someone strong, independent and confident and who didn't lack femininity. Out of this need, she decided to pen her first book, A Twist of Fate. T set herself the challenge to write something that was interesting, compelling and yet easy enough to read that was still enjoyable. Pulling from her own past "colorful" experiences and the amazing personalities she has surrounded herself with, she had no shortage of inspiration. With a strong slant on erotic fiction, her core characters are empowered women who don't have to sacrifice their femininity. She enjoyed the process so much that when it was over she couldn't let it go.

T loves to travel, laugh and surround herself with colorful

characters. This inevitably spills into her writing and makes for an interesting journey - she is well and truly enjoying the ride!

Based on her life experiences, T has plenty of material for her books and has a wealth of ideas to keep you all enthralled.

CONNECT WITH T

Webpage
http://tgephart.com

Facebook
www.facebook.com/tgephartauthor

Goodreads
www.goodreads.com/author/show/7243737.T_Gephart

Twitter
@tinagephart

BOOKS BY T GEPHART

THE LEXI SERIES

Lexi

A Twist of Fate

Twisted Views: Fate's Companion

A Leap of Faith

A Time for Hope

THE POWER STATION SERIES

High Strung

Crash Ride

Back Stage

THE BLACK ADDICTION SERIES

Slide

Sticks

Stand